THE CRATER

RICHARD SLOTKIN

THE CRATER

WITH A FOREWORD BY
JAMES M. MCPHERSON

A JOHN MACRAE BOOK

HENRY HOLT AND COMPANY
NEW YORK

Henry Holt and Company, Inc.
Publishers since 1866
115 West 18th Street
New York, New York 10011

Henry Holt® is a registered trademark
of Henry Holt and Company, Inc.

Published in Canada by Fitzhenry & Whiteside Ltd.,
195 Allstate Parkway, Markham, Ontario L3R 4T8.

Library of Congress Cataloging-in-Publication Data
Slotkin, Richard.
The crater/Richard Slotkin; with a foreword by
James M. McPherson.—1st Owl book ed.
p.   cm.
"A John Macrae book."
"An Owl book."
1. United States—History—Civil War, 1861–1865—Fiction.
I. Title.
PS3569.L695C7   1996   96-16512
813'.54—dc20   CIP

ISBN 0-8050-4247-4

First published in hardcover in 1980 by Atheneum.

First Owl Book Edition published in 1996 by
arrangement with the author.

Designed by Harry Ford

Printed in the United States of America
All first editions are printed on acid-free paper.∞

1   3   5   7   9   10   8   6   4   2

For my parents, ROSELYN *and* HERMAN SLOTKIN,
and my son, JOEL

President Jefferson Davis/Secretary of War James A. Seddon

Army of Northern Virginia
General Robert E. Lee
Col. G. W. Brent
Capt. Hugh T. Douglas, Engineer in Charge of Mining

Dept. of Southern Virginia and North Carolina
Gen. P. G. T. Beauregard,
Commanding Petersburg Front

Maj. Gen. Hoke's Division

Lt. Gen. R. S. Ewell,
Commanding Richmond Front

Maj. Gen. Mahone's Division

Br. Gen. Elliott's Brigade

22nd North Carolina Infantry*
Col. Davidson
Lt. Bruce

Capt. Allen   Capt. Hawken   Lt. Penwaring
                                 Cpl. Marriot
                                 Pvt. Dixon
                                 Pvt. Caldwell

III Corps
Lt. Gen.
A. P. Hill

Maj. Gen. B. R. Johnson's Division

Cavalry Corps
Maj. Gen.
Hampton

* See Author's Note

President Abraham Lincoln/Secretary of War Edwin A. Stanton/Major General H. W. Halleck, Chief of Staff

Armies of the United States
Lieutenant General Ulysses S. Grant

Army of the Tennessee
Maj. Gen. William T. Sherman

Army of the Potomac
Maj. Gen. George C. Meade
Maj. Gen. Humphreys
Maj. Duane
Capt. Sanderson

Army of the James
Maj. Gen. Benjamin F. Butler

XVIII Corps
Maj. Gen. E. D. C. Ord
(detailed to Meade)

IX Corps
Maj. Gen. Ambrose Burnside

V Corps
Maj. Gen. G. K. Warren

II Corps
Maj. Gen. W. Hancock

Cavalry Corps
Maj. Gen. P. Sheridan

1st Division
Br. Gen. Ledlie

2nd Division
Br. Gen. Potter

3rd Division
Br. Gen. Willcox

4th Division
Br. Gen. Ferrero

2nd Division
Br. Gen. Turner

Brigades
1. Gen. Bartlett
2. Col. Marshall

1. Col. Bliss
2. Br. Gen. Griffin

1. Gen. Hartranft
2. Col. Humphrey

1. Col. Oliver
2. Col. Thomas
   Lt. Pennington

14th N. Y. Heavy Artillery
Lt. Oostervelt
Sgt. Stanley
Pvt. Neill

48th Pa. Infantry
Lt. Col. Pleasants
Sgt. Rees
Pvt. Doyle
Pvt. Corrigan
Pvt. Dorn

43rd U.S.C.T.
Col. Hall
Maj. Booker
Capt. Shugrue
Sgt. Randolph
Cpl. Brown
Pvt. Tobe Young
Cpl. Matt Colehill

19th U.S.C.T.
Col. Perkins
Maj. Rockwell
Lt. Dobbs
Pvt. Johnson #5
Pvt. Duckworth

CONTENTS

FOREWORD

When The Crater *was first published in 1980, the History Book Club offered it as a main selection. Never before had the History Book Club featured a work of fiction, but there was good reason for doing so in this case: Richard Slotkin's gripping novel is also a splendid work of history. It blends fictional and historical characters and events in an imaginative re-creation of one of the most dramatic and tragic episodes of the American Civil War: the explosion of a huge mine under Confederate trenches at Petersburg on July 30, 1864, followed by a Union assault that promised to end the war but instead resulted in a humiliating repulse. And the war continued. The author employs the novelist's art in a narrative that is true to the facts of history while revealing incidents beyond the ken of a historian tied to the sources.*

The Crater *appeared while I was finishing the writing of my Civil War textbook* Ordeal by Fire *and preparing to write* Battle Cry of Freedom. *I had found other Civil War novels useful in helping me to conceptualize and clarify key aspects of the war. So I ordered* The Crater *from the History Book Club in the hope that it would deepen my understanding. I was not disappointed. From the novel I gained new insight into the ethnic and racial tensions in the Army of the Potomac and the jealous rivalries within its command structure that doomed the Union attack to failure. I also gained a new appreciation for the humanity, even nobility, of junior officers and men in the ranks who became victims of their superiors' bungling and their society's class and racial fissures.*

The story told by The Crater *is the climax of the bloodiest campaign of the Civil War. During seven weeks, from May 5 to June 22, 1864, two Union armies commanded by Generals George Gordon Meade and Benjamin Butler, under the overall command of Lieutenant General Ulysses S. Grant, had converged on the Confederate capital and industrial center of Richmond and its crucial railroad junction at Petersburg. A series of brutal battles between these armies and two Confederate armies commanded by Robert E. Lee and Pierre G. T. Beauregard had left 110,000 soldiers in blue and gray dead, wounded, or missing.*

When the smoke cleared from this carnage, Confederates held a twenty-five-mile network of trenches and fortifications from one flank east of Richmond to the other south of Petersburg. Repeated Union assaults on these earthworks had produced enormous casualties but no breakthroughs. Those Union troops who did not become casualties were fought out. The high hopes of the Northern people at the outset of Grant's campaign for an imminent and victorious end of the war were dashed. President Abraham Lincoln's prospects for reelection in November dimmed. Confederate prospects for victory brightened. But from an unexpected source came renewed hopes for a breakthrough that might lead to the capture of Petersburg, the fall of Richmond, and an end to the war.

At a point southeast of Petersburg, Union lines were less than two hundred yards from the Confederate trenches. The Forty-eighth Pennsylvania Volunteer Infantry happened to occupy that sector of the Union lines. Many of its men were coal miners. They suggested to their colonel, a mining engineer named Henry Pleasants, a daring plan to run a mine shaft some five hundred feet underground to the Confederate lines and blow them up with four tons of gunpowder. Pleasants took it up the chain of command to Ambrose E. Burnside, Commander of the Army of the Potomac's Ninth Corps (and once commander of the whole army). Burnside liked the idea. He pursuaded an initially reluctant and uncooperative Meade to allow the Pennsylvanians to go ahead. They did so, overcoming many technical obstacles and the skepticism of the army's engineer corps to dig the longest military mine shaft in history to that time.

One of the four divisions in Burnside's Ninth Corps was composed of black soldiers, most of them former slaves. Despite successful fighting by black regiments in other theaters and the capture of some Confederate artillery on June 15 by a determined attack of another black division in the Eighteenth Corps, high-ranking officers in the Army of the Potomac, including Meade, distrusted—even scorned—the fighting potential of black soldiers. But Burnside believed in them. His three white divisions had been decimated by constant combat; the black division was fresh and eager. Burnside decided to give them special training to lead an assault after the mine blew a hole in the Confederate defenses.

It probably would have worked. But at the last minute—literally only hours before explosion of the mine—Meade ordered Burnside not to lead off with the black division. The reasons for this decision were complex: racism, petty jealousies in the officer corps, a fear of political repercussions if the black troops suffered heavy casualties and Meade was perceived as having sacrificed them as cannon fodder. The result of this last-minute change was tragic. Burnside's plan collapsed; he abdicated responsibility for effective leadership with a new plan; the commander of the white division selected (by lot!) to lead the assault was an incompetent drunk. The mine exploded at sunrise on July 30 and blew a huge crater in Confederate lines, but the subsequent assault proved a debacle. When the black division finally went forward, after the three white divisions had created a shambles of the affair, they suffered more casualties than they probably would have if they had led the assault. Some of them were shot in the back by white Union troops and many more were deliberately murdered by counterattacking Confederates who had vowed to take no prisoners.

When it was all over, General Grant pronounced an epitaph in his dispatch to Washington: "It was the saddest affair I have witnessed in the war. Such opportunity for carrying fortifications I have never seen and do not expect again to have."

The best account I have ever read of this "saddest affair" is Richard Slotkin's novel. And The Crater *is more than a battle narrative—superb though it is in that respect. It is good social history. Its sensitive yet dramatic explorations of tensions between Irish Americans and other ethnic groups in the Forty-eighth Pennsylvania, of racial tensions and stereotypes in the Army of the Potomac, and of the class structure mirrored in both the Union and Confederate armies offer a window onto the ethnic, racial, and class fissures in American society during the Civil War era. This is truly a "multicultural" historical novel written before that term was even thought of. Its republication offers a new generation of readers more than a vivid story—it will give them new insight into the meaning of America.*

JAMES M. MCPHERSON
Winter, 1996

We Are the Boys of Potomac's Ranks

We are the boys of Potomac's ranks,
    Hurrah! Hurrah!
We are the boys of Potomac's ranks,
We ran with McDowell, retreated with Banks,
And we'll all drink stone blind—
Johnny, fill up the bowl.

We fought with McClellan, the Rebs, shakes, and fever,
    Hurrah! Hurrah!
We fought with McClellan, the Rebs, shakes, and fever,
But Mac joined the navy on reaching James River,
And we'll all drink stone blind—
Johnny, fill up the bowl.

They gave us John Pope, our patience to tax,
    Hurrah! Hurrah!
They gave us John Pope, our patience to tax,
Who said that out West he'd seen naught but gray backs,
And we'll all drink stone blind—
Johnny, fill up the bowl.

He said his headquarters were in the saddle,
    Hurrah! Hurrah!
He said his headquarters were in the saddle,
But Stonewall Jackson made him skedaddle—
And we'll all drink stone blind—
Johnny, fill up the bowl.

Then Mac was recalled, but after Antietam,
    Hurrah! Hurrah!

Then Mac was recalled, but after Antietam,
Abe gave him a rest, he was too slow to beat 'em,
And we'll all drink stone blind—
Johnny, fill up the bowl.

Oh, Burnside, then he tried his luck,
    Hurrah! Hurrah!
Oh, Burnside, then he tried his luck,
But in the mud so fast got stuck,
And we'll all drink stone blind—
Johnny, fill up the bowl.

Then Hooker was taken to fill the bill,
    Hurrah! Hurrah!
Then Hooker was taken to fill the bill,
But he got a black eye at Chancellorsville,
And we'll all drink stone blind—
Johnny, fill up the bowl.

Next came General Meade, a slow old plug,
    Hurrah! Hurrah!
Next came General Meade, a slow old plug,
For he let them get away at Gettysburg,
And we'll all drink stone blind—
Johnny, fill up the bowl.

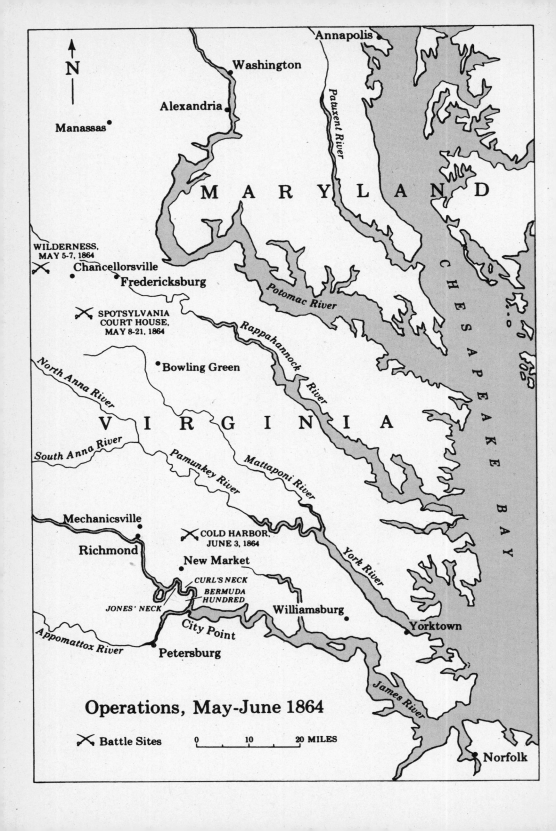

Operations, May-June 1864

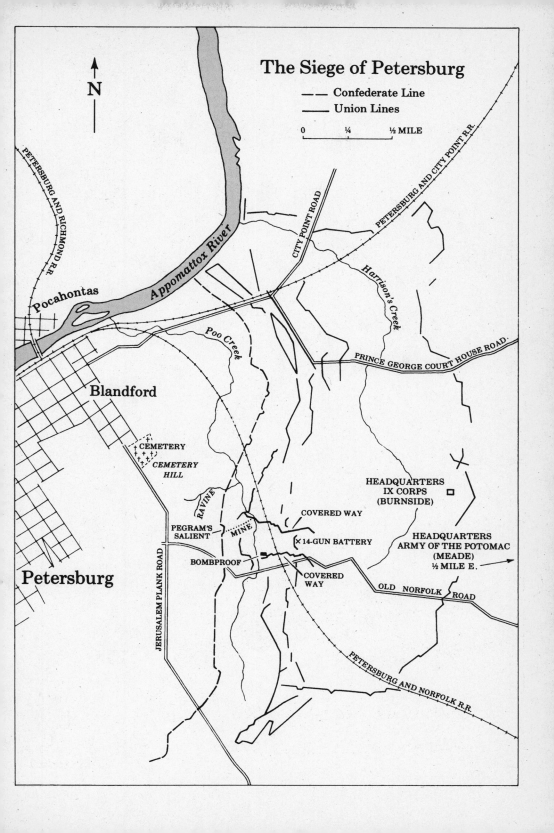

THE CRATER

PROLOGUE

In the fourth year of the Civil War, the Union Army of the Potomac crossed the Rapidan River one last time, to fight the Confederate Army of Northern Virginia.

The soldiers began to kill each other in a dense second-growth forest called the Wilderness, and for the next month moved through days of constant battle, concentrating murderously at crossroads and river crossings and small inequalities in the ground. They were two armies of veterans. They had learned how to kill and stand killing. They had Generals able and willing to force them forward, doggedly, as if they had used up the ingenuity they once had expended on arabesque maneuvers round the flank and on keen, pointed tactical strokes. It was as if the accumulated mass of men and equipment and experience somehow clotted the intellect, preventing all but the most muscle-bound movements, the simplest exercises of the will.

Viewing these movements from a height and distance no people of that time could have achieved, you would have seen two abstract beasts (or perhaps you would have said mechanisms), one muddied blue, the other muddied gray or brown; electric fire or the flash of claws spattering where they touched; and spouts of waste issuing at the rear, an offal of bleeding parts of bodies, arms, legs, hands, dead men, wounded men screaming in springless wagons to jerry-built hospitals; a slag of dead horses, tent-flies, ordure, broken wagons, wrecked gins, gutted barns, eyeless churches.

And you might have said that the two armies, having made contact, fought; and shifted by the left flank, blue leading, gray following, while the intelligence of the beast (or the operators at the levers of the machine) sought an opening for the decisive thrust, the body blow.

Never finding it.

When he reached the James River, General Grant succeeded in a surprise maneuver, crossing the broad river to come up against the fortified city of Petersburg, south of Richmond, the nucleus of the supply roads and railroads that fed the Confederate capital and the armies of General Lee.

On June 15, 1864, the advance elements of the Union Army began to break through the outer defenses that ringed Petersburg, and the veterans sniffed victory, heard it in the depressed volume of the cannon and the riflefire that told them the trenches were half-manned and that Lee was still north of the James. They chanted their willingness to go in and end it, end it now, end it at last, mobbing General Hancock—a General who respected his troops, who would listen—"For God's sake, General, put us in now and end it."

Hancock, unfamiliar with the situation, deferred to General Smith. General Smith wasn't sure and waited for his staff officers to examine and report; he hadn't been with the Potomac Army in two years but he knew better than to trust its Generals, and anyway Meade and Grant would be on hand tomorrow.

Meade arrived. The Generals were weary of unremitting combat. They were wary of the strength of the fortifications. They feared the temper of their regiments, diluted with conscripts and bounty-men. Had they truly sneaked away from Lee, or was Lee preparing his own surprise? They were worried when they were out of touch with him, although they'd worked so hard to lose him. They were ordered to attack, but—

"I do not understand the arrangements for my supports."

"Is it intended for the Ninth Corps to go forward simultaneously?"

"Is the order to attack peremptory, or shall I be allowed some discretion?"

Lee was catching on, shifting men south. More and more Confederates were coming up to man the lines, and the Union men were running into trench lines and fields of fire that winnowed regiments, and Meade finally threw up his hands and wired the commanders of his army corps: "What additional orders to attack you require I cannot imagine. . . . Finding it impossible to effect cooperation by appointing an hour for attack, I have sent an order to each corps commander to attack at all hazards and without reference to each other."

Done. Attacking by divisions, the army rolled up against trench lines now fully manned. The men, who had exhorted their generals to put them in on the fifteenth, on the eighteenth of June pinned pieces of paper with their names to their uniform blouses to permit identification of their bodies. On the night of June 18, they gave up the assault and began digging in.

By June 20, the trench lines had become as strong as regular fortifications, with obstructions set out in front to break the force of an attack, and carefully sited artillery to blow apart an assault wave.

The trench lines sliced across the countryside like parallel knife-slashes in a mangy hide—here a sharp incised zigzag, there a rough haggled cut where the blade had run dull. The men in the opposite lines of trench stared at each other across levels of grass, or through a screen of cornstalks, around a stand of trees, behind a line of fence-rails, or across a peeled swale of earth and litter of bodies and broken boxes. Each trench line became a labyrinth of traverses and covered ways behind the line of the first trench. These were dug so that the men could get from the front line to the rear, where the regimental sinks and field kitchens and reserve ammunition and officers' bombproofs were. The earth thrown out of the trenches had been piled to form a parapet on the side fronting the enemy; elsewhere the land around the trench lines was covered with loose mounds of earth, giving the appearance of a desert or of badlands on the Great Plains. Slotted into the lines at inter-

vals, and sited on elevations of ground, large, square enclosed forts were being dug for the heavy guns.

Snipers' bullets whined overhead, and little coehorn mortars dropped shells over the parapets whenever an observer in the trees back of the lines felt like stirring the pot. The summer heat was thick and breathless, and between the lines the unburied bodies of the dead began to swell. The damp earth piled up from the deep-dug trenches turned from brown-red to pale pink, became friable, began to powder. A fine dust settled on everything, stirred by the movement of feet along the trench lines, the dry heaviness cut only by the clinging odor of the dead, or the stink from latrines back of the lines. Sometimes a soldier would stand up on the parapet, gesture obscenely, and dare his enemy to kill him.

On June 21, President Lincoln arrived at the army's headquarters to confer with his Generals and visit the troops at the front.

PART ONE

THE MINE

President Lincoln Visits the Front
June 21, 1864

Noon. IX Corps front

Sergeant Harry Rees of the Forty-eighth Pennsylvania Veteran Volunteer Infantry shuffled along the line of trench held by what was left of the company he commanded. A half-dozen men stood at the rifle-slits cut in the parapet to return fire. The rest reclined along the wooden fire step that ran along the front wall of the trench. The stunning full glare of noon was on top of them.

The enemy line was only one hundred yards off, across the upward slant of an open field.

Rees moved in a limber half-crouch. He had been a miner, used to digging in the narrow seams of coal that were slotted between the layers of sandstone, shale and hard rock all through the Schuylkill country. He had had the habit of walking stooped over to avoid cross timbers and juts of rock down in the coal seams, and the habit had come back to him. The constant greasy whine and slide of the rebel bullets was like having a roof of lead overhead.

The rebs had started shooting as soon as word came along that the nigger division was up on the Ninth Corps line, and they kept it up. Rees heard a special nastiness in the sound of the bullets overhead. It made him wish the niggers in hell, and the rebels piled in on top of them, and the whole set on blasting powder enough to smithereen the lot of them.

As he moved, Rees held his arms out sideways to steady himself, touching the sides of this narrow front-line trench with alternating swings of his arms. He felt the deep safety of his trench and was proud of its clean line and floor, the well-timbered sides with logs laid straight and properly braced. He had helped dig this trench, and he knew it as well as he knew the old seam he'd leased from the company and worked for years and years, timbering it proper and working it hard and right. No, he knew it better: for he never saw the seam but in the sickly light of his cap-lamp; the trench he knew by day as well, and from its beginnings.

Rees turned a corner of the trench where a covered way slanted back towards the rear, and the stink of someone's shit smacked him across the face like an insult. The sudden rage in him jerked his short body upright, just as a reb bullet squirrelled its way through some chink in the parapet three inches in front of his face and slapped into the rear wall of the trench. Sergeant Rees's rage swelled in him like a gigantic bubble, which blew up, filling the air with a rich profanity of Welsh and

English curses, a rage against trenches in the earth, with a lid of stone-stunning sun and pain; and damned rebel snipers; and most particularly against the goddamned, nest-fouling, potato-eating, egg-stealing Irish Mick sons of bitches that would shit like an animal or a nigger right where they were living rather than walk three feet to the privy like a human being. And as he cursed he could picture in his mind the full development of the Irish character of which leaving your shit on the doorsill was merely the local instance: he felt again like a mine boss, begging the damned Irish who'd come swarming into the mines with their brats (renting seams that good Welsh Christians had worked for a generation) to take the time to timber enough and properly for their own safety and the safety of every other man down in the mine—and the damned Micks laughing at him and his Taffy accent, timbering it up any way at all. And the cave-ins would take them out by single cubs and whole clans, and sometimes good men would suffer for the ones as wouldn't timber—just like good soldiers would. The good ones got shot and the bounty-men went back to boiling coffee.

At the other end of the trench Privates Doyle and Corrigan were doubled over with stifled laughter at Sergeant Taffy's Welsh splutter, which Doyle had just denominated the ":Taffy National Anthem." Doyle and Corrigan were miners also, and from the same pits as Rees, and they had no great love for their ex-boss and present sergeant. It was four years ago, when Doyle'd just started working his own seam, when he was just nineteen and had married a black-haired girl named Kate Roy. After an eighteen-hour shift at the coal face-working in a shaft so narrow he had to swing his pick while lying flat on his stomach, in air so foul he strained for consciousness, Doyle had come up with his trolley to the air and light and found Rees had complained of his not taking time out to timber it up right, and the purser had docked his trolley for 10 percent. And so there was not any supper for him and his wife the last night of that week, and he'd had to borrow of his old man, a bad thing with him still bitter about Doyle's leaving him and the one young lad to bring wages into the house. So far as Doyle was concerned, Mr. Rees or Sergeant Rees was the master's toad, part of the gang who arranged things so that a man could lose his supper by taking time to timber and mining less coal, or lose it by having his pay docked for not timbering, but never could arrange them so a man could earn his bread and eat it in peace. Now, as a sergeant, Rees was less bad—in the war a stick like Rees was better for the boys than an easygoing slob—but wasn't it always the Taffy who'd be straw boss in any outfit he found himself in?

"Now if Taffy was a bomb, we could fire him up the slope at that damned Rebel fort and blow the lot from here to Pottsville," said Corrigan.

"Or if Taffy was a miner," said Doyle, "instead of a timber contractor, we could set him to digging a tunnel over to the fort, plant him at the end of it, send him the word that an Irishman has been made King of England, and stand from under."

Sergeant Rees rounded on them, pushing past other men lounging at the foot of the fire step. Having relieved himself for the moment of the rage and the tension of days of battle and living under the bullets in the trench, he felt himself in control of things again; not least because he was convinced not only that Doyle or Corrigan had done it, but that just as he'd always been able to catch them when they sloughed on timbering, he'd be sure to catch them dropping their load, and his plans for what he'd do after that made him smile. The army had this over coal mining: if a man didn't do his work properly, you had the buck-and-gag to keep his nose to it; and if he decided to go on a bit of a tramp to see if the wages were better in the next patch, you could have him shot for desertion. Doyle and Corrigan faced him with identical expressions of subdued defiance.

"Now, Sergeant," said Doyle, "you've no cause to come down on Corrigan and me. We're that seized up with gripes from eating old hard-tacks that we've not shat since crossing James River. As the boys here will tell you, Sergeant, we've but been sitting here discussing ways of discomoding the enemy."

"Such as by blowing up the Johnny's fort," said Corrigan, by way of supporting Doyle's testimony.

The sniper's bullet and the brief lash of sand across his cheek was in Rees's mind. "And I can tell you how you were proposing to do that. But we've not got the cheap Irish whiskey enough to fill your belly, light your fuse, and drop you in the midst of em; though if a breeze would come along, blowing from here to there, we could hoist you over the parapet and let the stink of you murder them!"

Since Rees had descended to insults, all was well. Once matters came down to man cursing man, there was no fear of sergeants or bosses coming into it, and so Doyle became easier in his mind, and said, taking the joke on himself, "It's not that we'd say no to a drop, you understand, Sergeant; but we'd heard you'd some experience in the mining profession, and were thinking you might dig yourself into the ground up under the rebel fort, and blow yourself and all to the next world—by way of a forlorn hope, and for the glory of the Ninth Army Corpse."

"Yes—and if I let you Irish peat-diggers do the timbering for me, I'd get to daylight as fast by digging forward as I would by trying to come back the way I went in."

Private Corrigan was looking abstractedly into space—at a spot on the rear wall of the trench. "You know," he said, "we might really do it."

Rees looked at him, and so did Doyle.

"We've done naught but dig sidewise and hide in the trenches while they drop cowhorns in on our heads. Dig a tunnel and you go straight over and at em, and all under cover."

Rees's thought ran side by side with Corrigan's. He could see it as a problem in mining, and a way out of his problem as a soldier, which was expressed in this fine hot stinking trench. *Smithereen the lot of them.* And he could see beyond it that there might be promotion for the man with an idea, who made it work and helped the army out of a fix: like the German who invented the system for ventilating deep shafts, and had the big white house in Pottsville. And promotion made him think of officers: "Yes. We'd charge the buggers from underneath; and wouldn't the tunnel do us like one of those bombproofs the officers sleep in? No cowhorns dropping in your can of beans."

Doyle and Corrigan got warm about the subject; Rees too. They began raising objections about the quality of the soil: took so many glimpses through a chink in the parapet (estimating distance) that they drew fire. Rees was so happy at the thought of having a project, one that would get him out of the place he was in and give the world a shake, that he forgot about the pile of shit in the covered way. Doyle and Corrigan forgot their old anger for the moment—it was mining they were talking about, and soldiering, and how to get out of where they had got themselves to.

They were still at it when Lieutenant Colonel Pleasants came down the line in the dead heat of noon, followed by the company cook with the noon ration of salt beef, hardtack, and water. The Colonel was a slender, small man, with smooth black hair and mustache and clear olive skin. He had been a mining engineer before the war, designing and building rail-road tunnels and coal-mine shafts in the Pennsylvania coal patches most of his men came from. A neat man, smart about his business too. But his dark eyes had an odd, pained, nervous look; had seen trouble, expected more. His men generally liked him, worked well for him, and he took pride in the fact without quite understanding it; so he always timed his visits to the line to coincide with the rounds of the company cooks.

Rees, Doyle, and Corrigan wanted urgently to talk with him. The company cook moved down the line to the sound of the usual banter. The three soldiers laid their plan out briefly for the Colonel. He looked intently at Rees, no matter which of the three was talking; and after a while, Doyle and Corrigan fell silent, while Rees spoke.

Pleasants asked a question. His face now wore a businesslike sternness. He was questioning Rees closely, systematically. At one point he knelt and picked up a clod of earth from the floor of the trench, crumbling it slowly between his fingers as if testing its quality. At another point Rees gestured to the front, and Pleasants moved to mount the fire step; but Rees restrained him and Pleasants stepped down, with a nervous glance overhead, where the occasional bullet zipped by. More talk. Then Pleasants shook his head vigorously, pursing his lower lip in such a way as to suggest his seriousness, and moved off down the trench. Rees parted with Doyle and Corrigan to follow him.

The two privates sat there, feeling drained, a bit let down. The great idea had made the morning; but Rees and Pleasants seemed to have walked off with it. And they were somewhat sorry it hadn't stayed with being a joke.

"What did he say?" asked Private Dorn, coming over to sit by them on the fire step.

"Oh, the Colonel will think on it, and talk of it with the General," said Doyle.

"And let the newspapers know, in due time, of the brilliant inspiration of General Whichever, by which the Great War at last was ended," added Corrigan, and they raised their tin cups in a toast.

4:00 P.M., City Point, Virginia

The weathered buildings of the hamlet stood on a small point poking into the James River estuary, the broadening lower reach of the river at its foot and behind it the dishevelled woods. There were two battered steamboat docks sticking out into the slack flow of the river, a broad grassless strip between the docks, and a few houses, sheds, tobacco and cotton warehouses.

Floating on the flat water, burdening the quaysides like driftwood, were dozens of ships—side-wheelers, tugs, sailing ships with masts like bayonet-tipped muskets. The shore was heaped with stores—barrels and boxes, lumber, cannonballs in little pyramids like small black skulls, cotton and tobacco in bales. Staff officers walked about full of brusque purpose. There were horses tied to the hitching rails, the cavalry escorts lounging in whatever shade offered. Behind the screen of trees, in fields and clearings, the Medical Corps was extending its field hospitals into a semipermanent medical encampment. Dust settled on the wounds of men lying on the ground, waiting for tent space. It was two days since the last big fight, and the doctors had about caught up with the waiting wounded. Freshly wounded men in diminished numbers still were being unloaded from ambulances. The dead were laid in rows for burial. All arrangements were being made to turn the area into a fixed base: it had been decided that the army would adopt siege tactics against the Petersburg trenches.

There was a black-hulled side-wheel coasting steamer at one of the docks. Out of its hold wound a column of dark-blue-uniformed men, two and two, 150 of them, shuffling out of the belly of the ship, between two rows of armed soldiers with fixed bayonets who lined the deck space between the hold and the long gangplank. On the dock itself, and extending out onto the open strip of ground, was a similar double line of twenty soldiers, in shabby uniforms weathered to shades of paler blue; and lining the waterfront to right and left of the dock, facing the water, were half-a-dozen pale-blue-clad soldiers with unbayonetted rifles, held at the ready. The column of men in darker blue uniforms shuffled down the gangplank to the dock, the last twenty men in new uniforms had been shackled together at the ankles, and their chains chinked as they marched.

The sergeant in command of the guard detail herded the new men up against the gray wall of a tobacco shed, and spread out half his soldiers facing the men at twenty-paces—space enough for them to shoot if any of the men against the shed tried to run away. Then the shackles were unlocked and returned to the corporal of the coaster's guard detail.

The men so carefully guarded were a delivery of new troops.

In different ways, the men were conscripts. Some had had their names drawn by lot from the big drum in the fire station or post office, and had not been able to run or buy their way out, and here they were. Some others had been hired as "substitutes" by men whose names had been drawn but who could afford to pay $300 plus a finder's fee to buy their way out of the war. The best of the substitutes were those who had taken the dollar when drunk and been unable to escape after sobering up. Some were nominally volunteers who had enlisted for the cash bounty paid by states to encourage poor citizens to enlist, thus filling up their required quota of enlistments and sparing the more respectable members of the community. The bounty-men were the ones who had been in shackles. Their idea was to take the bounty, desert, and take another bounty. If the new men had decided to rush the line of guards, they'd have overwhelmed them easily; but what was the point of running away from the war if you had to charge a line of infantry to do it?

The sergeant commanding the guard detail in front of the warehouse stood in the sun, looking with anger and disgust at the prisoners under the gray wall. Sergeant Daniel Smith of the First Minnesota, Gibbon's division, II Corps, a thin man in a pale blue uniform. The cloth of his uniform was worn to velvet fineness, rubbed out and coarsely patched at the elbows and knees with darker, fresher cloth; the chevrons on his sleeve had also lost all their stiffness and sizing, moved in one piece with the rubbed softness of the shirt. His face was peaked, his eyes set in crow's-feet above dusty cheekbones. Though he was miles from the front he held his head and shoulders slightly down and in, as if he still heard rifle balls clipping leaves and twigs over his head. He was filled with a boundless and hopeless anger that seemed to twist the muscles in his body and keep him erect, while at the same time a mindless weariness seemed to suck downward at the back of his eyes, drawing his mind to sleep, pulling his body down toward the ground. He had just turned twenty-one, and had been a soldier three years.

Sergeant Smith was tired to death because he had been in action nearly every day for the last month and a half and had seen and done too much of what a soldier does. What he had seen and done had made sleeping worse than being awake. Some of his dreams were simply the reliving of the horrors of past battles: the small flames that licked through the dry underbrush in the Wilderness, and the way the wounded men screamed when the fires reached them and their cartridge boxes began to explode; the faces of the dead, who were men he had marched with from St. Paul three years before. Worse than these dreams were those in which sometimes the faces he saw, half-decomposed, were those of men still alive in the regiment, so that when he woke he would look around him and not be sure if he was not waking into a dream of the living from a true vision of the dead. Or he would wake shivering, remembering how he had leaped up on the parapet of the trench in the terrible downpour at Spotsylvania, carried out of himself with the rage of killing, thrown his life away into the rage of fighting, into the dark trench—and woken up at the bottom of a heap of dead men in the bottom of the trench, his face pressed close to the split breast and open mouth of a dead bearded man, his face blue and blackening, covered with his own and everybody else's blood, and swum drowning to the top, choking panic. He even saw, in flashes, the black faces of devils and ghouls who had come in the night to devour the dead, and remembered their hands on him, and their cries.

He had always been the best of soldiers. So now they were using him and his men as jailers; and if he hated the murder of battle, he hated more herding a regiment of bounty-jumping conscripts as "replacements" for troops on the line. The First was one of the fine old regiments of the army—the "Shattered Thunderbolt" they called it when they stopped the rebels twice on Cemetery Ridge above Gettysburg, and lost 180 killed and wounded out of 225 men engaged. Using them to herd up conscripts, using conscripts for replacements of the old volunteers, showed the high command's contempt for the soldiers of the army. To the Generals, the Daniel Smiths and their regiments must be like parts of a machine, to be replaced when broken or worn out: but it wasn't conscripts that Hancock commanded when they countercharged Hood's Texans as they came screaming through the gap in the lines at Gettysburg.

While Smith stood there, swaying slightly on his feet, a battalion of infantry came marching around the warehouse. Smith couldn't believe his eyes. The battalion consisted of about a hundred coal-black niggers, some of them with sergeant's chevrons on their sleeves, and three white officers. The battalion halted smartly. The Major commanding stepped up to Smith, and Smith saluted before he could think.

"Sergeant," said the officer, smiling, "I'm Major Booker. I'm to relieve you of these replacements and escort them to the Ninth Corps."

Smith felt his anger twist in him. The Major was shorter than he, his speech a touch precise. Smith hated him and his troops automatically: they brought back to him the vision of all the dead men with the little paper tags pinned on their shirts, now to be "replaced" by bounty-jumpers, sewer rats, substitutes, and niggers. "Yes, sir. They're all yours, if you think these *boys* here can keep a-hold of them."

The Major looked sharply at Sergeant Smith, sensing the edge in the casual remarks. Realizing, a shade too late, that the sergeant's familiarity was not what a Major ought to expect. But how *does* a white sergeant talk to a Major of Colored Infantry? Everybody knew that Colored regiments were officered by men who were lower ranks, even sergeants and privates, in white regiments. Booker felt that white troops took him as a paper dollar—they had to accept the legal tender, but discounted the specie value more than half.

He had to say something. "Very well, Sergeant." That was weak: did he have to take himself at a discount as well? He looked at the men sitting in front of the warehouse, noting the segregation of the group that had been manacled. "What about these men here?"

Smith's lips twisted slightly. "Bounty-jumpers, sir. They were brought in in handcuffs and leg irons."

One of the bounty-jumpers rose slowly to his feet, standing up in front of one of the guards, who gestured for him to sit back down. The man smiled very slowly, revealing long teeth in a wide mouth, the two front top teeth twisted overlapping. The man was a brilliant redhead, the map of Ireland on his face. He stretched his arms and shook each leg insolently. "Call of nayture, boys. Shall I go to the bushes, or would you rather me piss on yer boots?" His accent was heavy, possibly exaggerated deliberately. He looked intently into the eyes of the sentry, who stared back, dully, then uneasily attentive.

Smith heard the exchange. He wanted suddenly to get his men away from here. It was very important that he not have to provide an escort so that the bounty-jumper could go piss.

"Platoon tenshun!" Smith called. Then to Booker: "Sir, I'll leave these men to you."

Booker returned the salute. He was well aware of what the sergeant was doing and he was, suddenly, angry at the sergeant and at himself. "Thank you very much, Sergeant. And you'll oblige me by escorting that man"—indicating the smiling bounty-jumper—"into those bushes just by the road there before you go. Sergeant Randolph, get your men in position to relieve the guard detail!"

"*Sir!*" Sergeant Randolph's voice came heavily from his deep chest.

Sergeant Smith looked his hatred at Booker and Randolph but ordered his platoon into line, and sent two privates off with the bounty-jumper. He was too good a soldier to go against a direct order, however insulting. *Besides,* he thought, *I'm outnumbered.* The black troops shook out a line to stand in front of the replacements, moving smoothly under the commands of their sergeant. The bayonet-tipped muskets of the guard platoon pointed toward the replacements; the remainder stood at ease, looking at the white troops with yellow eyes and black faces dusted with ash. Smith was aware of liking the rebels better than he liked either the mokes or the bounty-jumpers. He thought, *Maybe I'm in the wrong army,* and had a brief image of the familiar enemies, gray and blue, joining to remove these black intruders from their war. He moved his men off, the piss-escort returned, the bounty-jumper being marched back into the group by two smiling niggers. The Major grinned, and waved to Smith.

From around a bend in the road, where it cornered around a broken-windowed cottage, came the sound of cheering. A staff officer on a lathered horse careened to a stop in front of Smith's platoon, then trotted forward. "You, Sergeant! Get your men in a line, side of the road. Ready to salute when they come by." His eye caught Major Booker, flanked by two white officers, and he trotted up to the Major and saluted. "Sir, President Lincoln and General Grant are just coming back from the front. Will you get your troops in line, ready to present arms as they come by? What's this?" And he gestured to the replacements.

"Replacements, sir. Just off the boat. They haven't been issued weapons yet."

The staff officer grinned sardonically. He knew very well why they had not been issued arms. He was just happy that they weren't still in shackles.

"Well, get them on their feet at least; and if you can, have them salute, or hurrah."

"What was the cheering we just heard?"

"The President was reviewing General Hinks's Colored division. These boys aren't part of that division are they?"

"No. We're Ferrero's division, Ninth Corps. I'm Major Booker, Forty-third U.S. Colored—this is Lieutenant Dobbs and Lieutenant Pennington, from the Nineteenth."

"Yes, I'm Captain Sanderson. There was quite a demonstration of enthusiasm for Massa Linkum, and a speech of course." The officer was smiling, as if at a private joke. He had in mind the image of the gangling giant President, with his too-long legs and too-short horse, and his trousers hiked up to the calves, speaking in crack-voiced dignity to Hinks's Minstrels, who capered enthusiastically around his horse.

At that moment Sergeant Smith called, "Atten-*shun!*" and his faded line snapped to. The cry was echoed, the black troops stepping to flank the road, stiffening, pulling in stomachs and thrusting chests out against knapsack straps. The guard detail stood straight; some of the replacements rose, but most remained sitting. "Get those scum up," called the staff officer. Booker called an order, and the guard detail prodded the replacements to their feet.

Just then the drum of hoofbeats brought the President and the rest of the cavalcade around the corner of the building at a trot. The President, in dark civilian coat and dusty white shirtfront, stood up out of the army blue like the upthrust stack of a steamer; his stovepipe hat completed the image. He was bouncing out of rhythm with his horse, while the army officers glided smoothly around him—the piston engine and the waves. He was the center of the group. Bumping up and down, he turned his face, caught sight of the tableau against the warehouse-side, the black troops prodding the replacements erect with bayonetted muskets—looked steadily at the scene, while behind his turned head the rest of the black troops were cheering and calling his name. The Generals—stubby Grant and hawk-faced Meade were recognizable—were grinning. They trotted past the warehouse, and down the waterfront toward the dock where a gunboat waited for the President.

The dust drifted down the road between the facing columns: the black troops, and the replacements and guards.

Booker stepped into the road. The staff officer, Sanderson, had gone after the President's party. Booker gestured his officers forward. "Lieutenant Pennington, you'll form your troops on the right side of the road; Lieutenant Dobbs, you'll form yours on the left. Get these replacements lined up, column of fours, between your lines. Sergeant Randolph"— Booker turned, looked directly at him—"you'll take your squad and form them across the road as a rear guard; you'll want good shots—in case these fellows want to make a break."

"I'm to shoot them, sir?" Randolph's deep voice was careful and slow. He had brought his voice under a new discipline, a formality. It was flat, said what it said, without inflection.

"Yes, Sergeant."

"*Yes*, sir." Sergeant Randolph began to think of the soldiers he knew who were good shots, and who could be trusted with the responsibility of shooting white men, if needed. *It will be a damn funny thing if the only white men I get to shoot this war is Yankees.*

But it will have to do.

And thank the Lord for small vittles.

Sergeant Randolph smiled as he turned to pick his men. He was a deep-chested man, with the upper body of a giant and powerful legs a shade too short for his build. His rear end jutted out strongly, so that

the cartridge box on his belt jiggled and swung peculiarly when he
walked. His black skin and heavy lips were powdered with the ashy dust
of the road; his eyes were dark in yellow whites, like agates in ivory. He
tapped his men, considering each carefully.

The troops were lined up, the replacements standing grumpily between the hedgerows of bayonets. At an order they moved off toward
the front. In the distance they could hear the dull flatulent rumble of
artillery.

*6:00 P.M. The Road between City Point and the center of
the Union lines*

Major Booker marched his column along the road that flanked the
City Point–Petersburg railway. The men moved but the air did not. A
long plume of dust hung in the air; the men walked out of it, extending
it. Two hours away from the estuary the Major called a halt near an
open field full of shin-high corn plants. The Major let the prisoners—he
couldn't think of them as recruits—sit against the worm-fence that bor-
dered the field, posting his guard detail opposite. Two large oaks and a
pine gave scattered shade. From where they lay at ease the guard detail
could see any prisoner who tried to bolt across the parched cornfield; the
little plants were too sparse for cover.

The Major stayed at the head of the column, and told Pennington
and Dobbs to post themselves at the rear and send Sergeant Randolph
forward. From their position at the rear of the line the two Lieutenants
could see Randolph and the Major talking about something. At one
point, Randolph threw back his head and laughed, and from the movement of his arms it seemed he might have patted the Major on the
shoulder. They appeared to be two friends, talking and laughing about
something while keeping one eye on an unfinished piece of work.

Pennington was struck by the strangeness of it. He hadn't been in
the army long, only five months, nor had he seen many Negroes in his
life. Yet he had been raised among people who took notice of manners,
and he knew and had seen enough to know that the manner of Major
Booker and Sergeant Randolph was not the usual thing between officer
and man, or white man and black. It seemed so normal a gesture; yet
nothing about the army, in Pennington's experience, had been normal.

He looked at Dobbs in time to catch him taking a quick hard look
at Booker and the black sergeant, as if Dobbs found in the sight something bitter and funny. He wanted to talk with Dobbs about things:
Dobbs wasn't much older than he, but was so obviously a man of experience. His fair skin was shot through with fine lines from continual
sunburn, around the eyes especially. Dobbs stared intently at the men;
at the fields, at the weather. He was eager to go somewhere. His nose
was peeling and raw, and fine fragments of skin framed the wounded
front ridge of it: you had the feeling that he paid no attention to such
things, and Pennington saw him suddenly as a man heedless of his body
or punishing discomfort as he runs a long race, running right through
the weakness of his flesh in some angry exaltation of the spirit.

"Lieutenant Dobbs?" Pennington felt the blush rise in his cheeks as Dobbs shifted his stare to him. He couldn't frame the question he wanted to ask. "What do you think of Major Booker?"

"What do you mean?" As usual, Dobbs seemed reluctant to talk with him—though he seemed friendly in other ways. Another mystery.

"Well, you hear things about him. He was out West in the beginning, wasn't he?"

"That's right. Booker and me used to be with Jim Lane's Jayhawk Army. But that was before he got to be a Major, and got involved in this here respectable kind of war."

"I didn't know you knew each other," Pennington said awkwardly. "It's a shame you're not in the same brigade. . . ." He remembered Dobbs and Booker meeting each other back on the dock where the detail had assembled—not like old friends meeting again, but with an uneasy embarrassed watchfulness—like a couple that had quarreled and parted, then met unexpectedly after a separation of years.

Dobbs looked sharply at Pennington, and his mouth was tight. "No, it ain't such a damned shame at that. He ain't the same man with shoulder straps to hang on to and a whole lot of new friends and all," and he jerked his head toward the front of the line where Booker had sat down next to the black sergeant.

"What was it like?" Pennington had begun to imagine all sorts of piratical adventures, banditti of the Plains, forbidden yet exciting.

"Kill and be killed." Then Dobbs was silent and Pennington groped for a way to keep the talk going.

"But there was the Cause, too: our own people, John Brown, the Border Ruffians. . . ."

Dobbs came to life again, grinned. "Oh yeah, well, the Cause: now that sure was an important thing, and politicians too. But look, people out in Kansas weren't exactly Abolitionists, if you mean folks interested in the nigger—excuse me, Negro. Mostly what they were after was land. Man had a claim, he'd need some friends to help him hang on: friends with guns. Abolition folks had guns, so they were good friends; Missouri Ruffs had guns, they were friends too. Oh yes, Bleeding Kansas.

"I'll tell you one thing about it: in Kansas, when you saw something that had to be done, things worked out so that you could do it. Not like East, around here. This'll let you know something about Booker, too. This was the beginning of Sixty-three, just the end of winter, and we'd been out scouting down into the Indian Territory with the battalion. We'd had a damn long ride; picked up any number of folks from off some of the Cherokee plantations there and hauled em north on wagons. But mostly what we got was range horses and beeves. We were driving a couple hundred head by the time we got back to Kansas. Now this was after Emancipation, but before they'd decided niggers— excuse me, Negroes—could be soldiers. And this Colonel that the army'd appointed, he wanted Booker to send all his folks back where they belonged; he wasn't going to arm any black army, and he didn't cotton much to Indians, while he was at it. And since we'd never been regularly enlisted, it turned out that Mr. Army wasn't going to pay us for the work we'd done, neither. When we'd got all this tucked into our minds, we went back to the battalion and had a meeting. Now, the Jayhawk boys were all right, because they were white, and it could be made out they were in the regular Kansas militia. But they couldn't swallow the idea that the rest of the troops were going to be 'treated like niggers,' as one of em put it. 'Hell,' says one of the bucks, 'we *is* niggers!' And the Jayhawk gets all red in the face, don't know which way to spit, and finally grunts, 'Hell you say,' and sits down.

"So they thought about different ways of handling it. They proposed that the Colonel should have an unfortunate accident. They figured on holding up the paymaster, taking out their due, and going back to work. But it wasn't going to do for all of them, not those as had families around the fort in Kansas, which meant a lot of the niggers—excuse me. Anyway, Booker says, 'Boys, it looks like the army ain't interested in our services; well, so be it. But the question is, how do we get our pay for the work done? Maybe we can't get the specie: but most of you'd probably take the money to buy land anyway. Maybe there's a way we can work a deal. Senator Jim Lane's in town, and he's carrying some interesting papers in his carpetbag.'

"We talked on it: some said they didn't want to settle for anything but the cash, and they'd get land warrants for serving anyway. But Booker reminded them that so far as the army figured they hadn't been soldiering at all, just riding around for exercise. And the Injuns said they had land, what they wanted was some cattle. In the end, we agreed that we'd help the Injuns run off about half the cattle; and for the rest, me and Booker would go see Jim Lane.

"Next day we go in to see Lane. 'Boys,' he says, 'I'd like to help you, but my hand is tied. I'm bound hand and foot. Lincoln is in the hands of evil men, bad counselors, and won't heed my voice. So much hangs in the balance, boys! Y'all come back soon now.'

"Booker smiles, and takes out his Navy pistol. 'Let's talk about what you've got in that carpetbag, Senator,' he says, smiling.

" 'Why, boys,' says the Grim Chieftain, 'these are just a bunch of Homestead warrants I've been carting around till they open the Land Office. I just couldn't let you have any of those. My honor's at stake!'

" 'Well, shit, Jim,' says Booker, 'the Land Office been open for a couple of months now. Talk is you're starting a claim club, just you and some friends. We're your friends, Jim: best you've got!'

" 'How do you figure?'

" 'We saved your life.' And he moves the pistol a little bit.

" 'Take the papers and be damned,' says Jim Lane. 'If you're in Kansas any time this century, expect to be dead by morning.'

"So we gave the boys their warrants that night—it was for prime land too, on the Republican River. And recommended that they hang onto their guns and ammunition, in case Jim Lane or some of Quantrill's men decided to jump their claims. So we all had a drink, cut the Injuns' beef out of the herd and ran it south; then split up and went our ways."

Pennington listened, all rapt attention. "Lord, that's magnificent! Give them the land they'd fought for! That's pure John Brown! It's . . . heroic!"

Dobb's look soured suddenly as if the word griped him. "No," he said, "it was just pure poison. But I tell you, it was a hell of a lot better than this regular *war* we've got here." He jerked his head toward Booker, who was rising from his seat next to the black sergeant and gesturing for the rest of the column to get up. "They took a pretty fair fighting man and made a goddamn soldier out of him. That's what associating with shoulder straps will do. And bossing niggers. Excuse me —*Negroes.*"

Pennington blushed. "But that's what we . . . what we all . . ."

"Aw, never mind the way I talk," said Dobbs as he stood up. "Losing friends is one thing in this war, and seein' 'em spoilt is another."

Pennington checked Dobbs as he started off. "I'm Chris—that's what my friends call me."

"O.K., Chris, 'Lem' does for me."

Up ahead Major Booker was mounting his horse. The guard detail was standing up, some of them moving under Sergeant Randolph to prod the white men to their feet. The lines recomposed themselves, and began to shuffle off once again.

Major Booker rode his horse at the head of the column.

The sun was hot, stupefying, blazing in his face as he led the march south and west. These Southerners would grow their trees so they wouldn't shade a man on the road from the sun. There wasn't anything at all efficient or enterprising about the South, except at a horse swap or a slave market, or maybe a card game. Nobody is sharper than people who deal in people.

The burning sun heated his thighs. Dry heat, that was Virginia. A bake oven. He didn't like Virginia. He had a grudge against Virginia, the dust, the road, the damned trees, the egotistical houses in their selfish shade. Virginia. Why lay it all on Virginia? Enough of it belonged to her, but not all.

Let's think of something good about Virginia.

Sometimes, when they'd pass by a little shaded swamp, there would be the bright sweet smell in the damp, some Virginia plant or other, its odor baking out of it: subtle but sharp, warm and sweet but with a tang. It was like enough to her smell, to Miriam's smell, to remind him. It was easy to think of her, as he rode, the rhythmic movement of the horse's haunches lifting ass and hips, carrying him effortlessly along— yes, easy to think of her.

He felt that sexual tickle in the base of his spine and the root of his belly, and he wanted to let it just grow and build, to relax here as the horse moved under him, and just dream of her.

Wrong, somehow, to do that—wrong. They were so far apart in time and distance, his mind would play tricks, smutch her features. He needed her. Not any woman—her. The strong sun leaned against his chest, and that reminded him also. He could imagine her as a lioness in the sun, the color of sun, her fur heated with the sun. A maned lioness, he smiled at the image. A maned lioness in the sun.

There was the cub: she batted it softly with muffled paws, shoulder muscles shifting under soft hide, her predatory eyes fierce and tender.

*They raised and he looked into them. There was Miriam, and she smiled.
The child next to her, it was Eli, and had his own face.*

He would write her a letter. He dreamed that in this letter he
would be able to say absolutely everything; it would all be in the letter,
as if himself were in the letter meant for her eyes. She would sit in the
parlor and read it to their son. It was the perfect letter, it was for both
of them, perfect for each.

The bright smell twisted through the stagnant air, a living thing.

He turned, to look back over the column, a blue dragon-snake
wrapped in smoke.

Usually he preferred to walk at the head of his troops, mounting his
horse only when he needed to move rapidly along the line. There was
something inherently displeasing to him in the sight of an officer riding
above the dust while his men shuffled along below him. It reminded him
of the slave coffles he'd seen moving along the dusty roads back in Missouri before the war. But after they had passed about half a mile beyond
the buildings at the dock, he'd begun to feel an itch in the small of his
back, and he had motioned his orderly forward and mounted. From his
saddle he could look back over the line. To the white men shuffling along
between the lines of black soldiers he was simply a jailer. And though
Booker wanted to deny that—he was a soldier, an officer in a cause in
which he believed deeply—the fact was that he could not help feeling
like a jailer; acting like a jailer. Mounting his horse, the better to over-
see his column of—prisoners—signified his accepting of the role.

Feeling that way about himself, he couldn't act with the kind of
simple decisive sureness he had shown back in Kansas. That was why he
had handled that sergeant back on the dock so badly. That was why . . .
the blood rushed to his face when he remembered meeting Dobbs again
for the first time since they'd both had to leave Kansas for the east. He
had felt a sharp sense of shame standing before the jayhawker with his
major's insignia and his detail of ex-slaves in army blue. He had been
expecting and dreading the sight of that familiar *damn-you* look of the
eyes that was Dobbs's defiance of all authority and officialdom. In Kansas he had taken pride in that look on his comrade's face. Now, suddenly,
he had become afraid that he would be included in it. And the fear
showed, and touchy Dobbs smelled it quick as a wild animal will, and
that chilled him in an instant. And then he gave Booker the look: Well
damn *you*.

You had to know—without words and right down to the bone—
exactly who you were and what you were doing and why if you wanted
to command men in battle . . . and if you wanted to stay friends with
men like Lemuel Dobbs. So many things had changed for Booker. Had
they changed what he was?

He had been born in Germany: Judah Bookser, the name so often
misspelled that he'd let it stand as Booker when his commission came
through from Washington, and he'd left Kansas and Missouri and come
East. What did his name matter? He would be whatever his deeds might
make of him!

He'd been a lot of things: an apprentice iron-molder, working with
his father in the Sinclair Factory and going with him Fridays to the

Union Hall for drill and singing, beer and stories of '48, till the accident, when molten iron nearly cost him a leg, and after, a wanderer, trading on his skill with languages to find work on the wagons carrying goods to Santa Fe, and later trading for hides and horses with the Crow Indians. He'd gotten lonely, and gone home to St. Louis round by California and the Isthmus, and up the river. He'd seen the gangs working the big plantations with the drivers watching them, and he remembered Sinclair's Factory; and when he returned he worked for the Molder's Union and he worked for Abolition. Then came the War and Kansas, and though he'd taken some whippings and some losses, as he thought back on it Kansas had been the first time and place in his life—and maybe in the lives of generations of his people—when he'd taken a good deep drink of victory, and got the taste of it and let the fumes of it raise and lighten his mind. It was as good in its way as it had been when Miriam had said she loved him, as good almost as when Eli was born and his eyes took the light—every bit the same color as Booker's own. He had used his strength, he'd given everything of himself he'd had to give, and by God if he hadn't managed to wrench something real and something good out of all the waste and oppressive evil around him.

Somehow it had started going bad when he'd taken this commission and come East to command freed blacks along the Carolina coast. It had been different in Missouri and Kansas, somehow: you chased off Ole Massa and the people came to you by themselves and that was all there was to it. Down in Carolina they were conscripting the blacks, those that they didn't need for working on the forts or on the old plantations they were leasing out to Northern businessmen—taking advantage of the booming prices on cotton. Things got complicated; it appeared there was so much more at issue in the East. On the other hand, there was a lot more talk in Carolina about uplifting the Negro, plenty of missionaries and teachers, folks in the army and out who'd fight the civil and military government to get schools for the freedmen. Nobody thought much of schools on the Border these days. Booker liked the idea: he would be a teacher, too. He'd love that, teaching them to be soldiers, to fight for themselves.

But what kind of people needed to be dragged out and taught to fight for themselves? How can you trust people when they depend on you, strive with you by borrowing your strength? Or maybe—maybe I don't see it clear myself, and they do: hanging back from conscription somehow being as right for them, who and where they were, as jumping hotfoot into the soldier business was right for him.

Miriam would tell him: "It is always one way or the other with you, Books. Either it all has to hang on you, or it's beyond you, out of your hands. You either take a thing; or you walk away from it. What about sharing, Books? What about staying? I want you, Books. And I don't need you at all. . . ."

Randolph had said something similar once, when Booker had first offered to help his people buy their plantation: "Nobody here *need* help, Major. If you knows that, you kin help."

Randolph's eyes had been intently focussed on his own, the contact close and lively, brightened suddenly by the irony of his turning about the roles of teacher and pupil in which Booker and he first knew each other. There was a little electric shock in that reversal—of surprise, of unsuspected understanding. Unsuspected affection. And a little touch of fear as well at how much one hadn't suspected: the bright agate eyes took in the lessons, *This is how you march and fight,* listening; but then the lesson took a twist somewhere under the wooly skull and came different, got shifted to a black man's hidden direction. He felt as close to Randolph, almost, as he did to his wife and son, but the drift of the black man's mind was as obscure and difficult for a man to read as the mind of a woman or a child. We fear what we don't understand and can't control.

So what was the result? You felt close to the men, but apart. You didn't know who you were or where you stood, with white soldiers or black, and let a white sergeant show you up for not knowing your rights or your men's. You had this tendency: to betray your men's trust in you, maybe because you tried so hard to hold it. Why did they need to trust him anyway? Weren't they fit for the weapons and work of free men? Pah! He turned with a sudden jerk and glared back at the column that followed him.

Angry at the twists and turns of his doubts and fears.

Ashamed to be an officer leading these helpless white men as prisoners to die in war they did not consent to join. And most of the blacks too, for that matter. What was freedom if another man could withhold your bread, or require your life of you, or the murderous works of your hands, without your saying yes to it?

Through the trees he could see the conical white shapes—like Indan tipis, almost—that were the headquarters tents of the Ninth Army Corps.

HEADQUARTERS NINTH ARMY CORPS,
June 21, 1864—7 P.M.

General MEADE:
    Do you care to consider a proposition for an assault on the enemy in front of our lines?

A. E. BURNSIDE,
Major-General.

Major-General BURNSIDE,
Commanding Ninth Corps:
    The major-general commanding directs me to say that it was intended to act on the defensive, but he is quite ready to hear whatever you may have to propose.

A. A. HUMPHREYS
Major-General and Chief of Staff.

Major-General MEADE,
Commanding Army of the Potomac:
    GENERAL: The colored division forms the second line on our front. From an inspection of the ground (in front of Gen-

eral Potter) I am pretty well satisfied that General Ferrero can mass his troops along our picket-line on this front, and at a given hour in the morning make a charge which will result in breaking the enemy's line, and if the movement can be followed up by other parts of the line of the army we would have a fair chance of driving the enemy across the river. General Potter has built a covered way to our main line. Three o'clock would be a proper hour to charge.

> Very respectfully,
>
> A. E. BURNSIDE
> *Major-General, Commanding.*

HEADQUARTERS ARMY OF THE POTOMAC
June 21, 1864—11:30 P.M. *(Sent 11:40* P.M.*)*

Maj. Gen. A. E. BURNSIDE,
Commanding Ninth Army Corps:
> Your dispatch received and will be considered. The time proposed does not admit of simultaneous attacks from other parts of the line.

> GEO. G. MEADE
> *Major-General.*

The commander of the Ninth Army Corps looked up from reading the dispatch and handed it to his aide-de-camp, Lieutenant-Colonel Richmond. They were in the large headquarters-tent Burnside had been given by the Illinois Central Railroad—of which he was (despite his commission) a director—high white canvas with a center pole like a ship's mast. The air was hot, breathless, and sweat streamed over the round, rosy face of the general and darkened his magnificent frieze of mustache—the swooping scallops of beard that men everywhere now were calling Burnsides in honor of the commander of the Ninth Army Corps.

Richmond was angry. "Well, I suppose that ends it. Meade will never take up any suggestion you offer, sir. When I think how generous you've been, setting aside your seniority to serve under that man, I have to admit my blood boils!"

Burnside was pleased with Richmond's loyalty, but it wasn't right to give countenance to criticism of the Army Commander. Loyalty to one's colleagues was essential to an army—was the keystone of his own command system in the Ninth Corps—and he felt he could say, without vanity, that most of his men felt as loyal to him as Richmond here. A band of brothers, in fact, comrades tried and true. Yes! Meade didn't understand loyalty, that was his defect as a commander, despite his technical competence. However much Burnside might humble and abnegate himself, Meade would always suspect him of scheming to usurp larger shares of command. *Judges others by himself; he'd never have consented to serve under me, if positions had been reversed—wouldn't now if I should be restored to command of the Army of the Potomac (though I*

*have no thought, truly, of that)—even though I commanded this army
first, and am his senior in the rank.*

He shook his magnificent head slowly, sadly. He had no wish to offend Richmond for his loyal remarks: he smiled a trifle, modulating it
exactly so as to suggest, *You mustn't, really, say such things, not to me.
Yet I'm not angry with you.* He imagined that Richmond understood
all that he meant.

To Richmond, he seemed to be saying, *Ah, well, our day may come.*

"Did you see the President at headquarters?"

"Yes, I did," said the General. "He's a fine, good man, Mr. Lincoln.
Too good. [*Like another I could name.*] His treatment of me when I
first received command of the army, and . . . after"—he flushed
slightly—"was full of the utmost sympathetic regard and respect. I
could not have hoped for more from my own father, if the truth were
told. A wonderful, good man."

Burnside thought a moment.

"In a way, it was the President who suggested the idea of the attack. When he rode by Hinks's division, and they cheered him to the
sky, you should have seen his face! He told them something . . . Ethi-
opia carrying the colors, something like that, the great meaning of their
charge for their people and for the nation. Well, it actually wasn't that
much of a charge—one of Baldy Smith's Brigadiers told me that there
were only some clerks and Richmond militia in the forts, and Baldy
Smith laid siege to every picket post and had half his troops watching
for A. P. Hill to pop in on his flank. So he sent in the black boys, and
they captured some guns."

He mused.

"Still," he said, looking dreamily toward the ceiling, "you can
see why, so much is at stake—it's important that the Negro does well in
the army. It makes everything that's been done—the emancipation, en-
listing the slaves—makes it appear *right*. I thought the President looked
at me, particularly—remembering, perhaps, how I had been involved in
setting up the first contraband camps and schools in New Bern—that
was before you came on, I think. Remembering my advice to him, at that
time, yes. Well, I'd like to do something for Old Abe, I guess; and for
the nigger too, since that's in the cards. This charge by Ferrero—if
they'd let us do it, it would put Hinks and Battery Wagner in the
shade."

Colonel Richmond nodded. He thought, *Yes, Hinks, and Battery
Wagner—or Fort Pillow.*

Burnside lit a cigar. "And another thing: they'd have to let us
keep Ferrero's division permanently, instead of sending it off to guard
trains or Warren's flank, or to Ben Butler. It's not enough I have to
make way for Meade (which I don't really mind, I can see the necessity); they've got to keep whittling away at my Ninth Corps in the bargain. Butler's been trying to have all the colored troops consolidated in
his army. Butler!" An expression very like fear came and went on his
hearty cheeks.

Colonel Richmond closed his orderly book, and left. "Goodnight,

Sir." Burnside puffed on his cigar. The smoke rose and hung in motionless, fragrant wreaths around his beautiful whiskers and smooth bald head.

HEADQUARTERS U.S. ARMIES,
June 21, 1864

Hon. E. M. STANTON,
Secretary of War:

All has been quiet at Petersburg during the day, except that the enemy threw a good many shells at the right of our lines this morning, doing no damage. The President arrived here about noon and has just returned from visiting the lines before Petersburg. As he came back, he passed through the division of colored troops commanded by General Hinks, which so greatly distinguished itself on Wednesday last. They were drawn up in double lines on each side of the road and welcomed him with hearty shouts. It was a memorable thing to behold the President, whose fortune it is to represent the principle of emancipation, passing bareheaded through the enthusiastic ranks of those negroes armed to defend the integrity of the American nation.

C. A. DANA.

11:00 P.M. *Main cabin of a gunboat lying off City Point*

Mr. Lincoln has had a long day, *he thought*. But then, everything about Mr. Lincoln is long: his legs, his arms, his patience—yes—his memory; his face: that long lugubrious phiz hung with a beard of crepe —I look like an undertaker. I guess I have buried enough folks to join the lodge. No, maybe an undertaker would look cheerfuller in these circumstances, it being a flush year and me being situated to hold a corner on the market. Undertaker would hang out some side-chops for politeness, to keep the grin from getting the start of his manners. May be I look like an undertaker who has a suspicion that the Resurrection is going to happen right during the best of chills-and-fever season.

He sees Willy lying in bed, his small body withering into the mattress and his eyes burned out with fever, his two feet making small peaks a third of the way down the bed.

My son, my son, would I had died instead of thee.

I must not think of this.

It comes of the talk about wanting to rest in Abraham's bosom. As if I was a graveyard, and people buried in my chest.

It was Jess Platt of Sangamon first put the phrase to me: he meant he wanted a good safe job with the administration.

I probably gave it to him.

I hope I didn't make him a General.

Abraham Lincoln blows out the lamp and stretches out in bed. The

*air in the cabin is stifling, despite the open portholes through which the
thump of the sentry's boots is heard. He is running over in his mind
the day's business in its minutiae; occasionally he smiles. Thinking
about Generals: handsome Hancock, with his sleek face drawing itself
thin because of the pain of his unhealed wound from Gettysburg last
July; Burnside with his beautiful and luxuriant mustache-and-side-
whiskers framing his well-fed face; narrow Meade with his vinegar-cruet
mouth, vibrating with suppressed temper. Grant, the last and only choice
for commander, staring at his stubby fingers while the palaver goes on
around him—the conference with the President is not central to his
business; he is not even engaged enough in it for one to say, "He suf-
fers it."* Butcher Grant. Supplies the candidates for Abraham's Bosom.
He could block out what was going on around him, brooding on his real
concerns, while his body continued to function doing courtesies—the
art of the virtuoso drinker who can drown his sorrows and still ride his
horse. Pa had that skill: he could carry his jug right into meeting, no
one the wiser. What makes Grant so good at what he does? Forget that
joke about what kind of whiskey he drinks. He's a man who has seen
the bottom of his life, and sunk down to it, and hauled himself up again;
and knows that if he lets go and falls back one time, he'll drown: and
so he must fight to win, or lose everything. Now, Little Mac could go
back to his railroad or even be President, but if Grant isn't the all-
victorious General he'll be back clerking store.

I can trust Grant, because he needs to win—for himself.

Generals. Tomorrow I must view the Cyclops—Butler. I will come
away grateful if he hasn't gotten me to name him the heir of my worldly
fortunes. Butler, Hancock, Meade, Burnside . . .

Burnside's the man with the true undertaker's face: well-fleshed,
well-pleased, accommodating: shares your sadness out of sheer politeness,
has none himself. He'd sell you a new model coffin too, just the thing:
likes his gadgets.

These Generals here all give me the peculiar feeling that I'm interrupting their vital business—like when I'd walk in on Tad and Willy
playing with their blocks back in Springfield, and they'd startle some;
want me to burst with wonderment at the city they'd built—and then
linger about, but let them get back down into it. Boys, I made you, and
I bought you those blocks. Have fun, boys, and be sure to wash for supper. (Willy! Dead.)

*He feels the sadness stir and swell in his chest like a shapeless be-
ing—a live creature swallowed and stuck in the throat behind the breastbone.*

He will think of business, of the work of the day: the Generals. I
raised them up from pups, and set them after coon. Boys, you'd best
learn to heel. Oh, yes, I raised them, and called them up their armies.
"I can call armies from the vasty deep" / "But will they come when
you do call?"

They have come.

Now the thing is, after you've called them, how do you get them to
do the work and go home? And stop killing. And stop dying.

Sees in memory the lines of black soldiers in Hinks's division, cheering, waving wildly, black faces white teeth blue uniforms, as he rides by Massa Linkum, Massa Linkum ("As I would not be a slave so I would not be a master of slaves") *and making his speech to Hinks's boys with all the usual and expected words* the whole war passing through my mind, the war I have had to make. Don't you see that if I hadn't, they'd have ended by putting us all under the yoke? That the only way to throw it off was to call up the armies, to call up the slave out of bondage, and bring him to the war for the killing? Massa Linkum: who wanted to free the white man by freeing the black man and ended up conscripting the white man and the black man so as to free them both.

The tableau before the warehouse as the cheering fades behind him: the black soldiers with their bayonetted rifles hedging in the drove of white conscripts rooted anyhow out of their lives by Massa Linkum's damned conscription that any man with $300 cash money could buy his way out of—and any man poor as Lincoln was back in New Salem or Pigeon Creek would have to go to kill or die.

It was an image out of a dream, when things get turned around so black is white and right is left and good is wrong.

An image out of memory: my first trip all the way from Pigeon Creek to New Orleans in '28. It was like all the folks of a big city had suddenly turned black. Like all the people you'd see in a real town like Cincinnati, say: carpenters. workmen, loafers, whatever, had all just been turned black. Like they'd caught a smallpox; an epidemic of nigger had broke out. New Orleans you'd see women the color of coal and earth and deer, with clothes that whispered things about the shape of their bodies and the way they might smell. Big mouths, heavy lips—tongues too pink and wet, teeth too big and white—you thought too much about the big teeth in those big smooth wet lips. Ain't a man till you've had one. New Orleans.

Boys, did I ever tell you about the time I flatboated down from Indiana to New Orleans? *It was like this lately: when his mind threatened to racket itself to pieces with contradictions like the off-coupled grinding of mismatched cogs, he would stop the flow of words; and imagine himself in the boys' bedroom back in Springfield, lying in bed with Willy leaning against his right side and Tad his left, his arms looping round each of them—always that way, by ritual, Willy right Tad left, they'd not stand for any change—telling them stories while the light faded, and Mary sat downstairs, waiting impatiently for him. He would tell them a story; in the telling, as in a parable, things would be worked out. It used to be he'd tell over the troubles of their own day's playing; now it was his troubles he storied to their wraiths. Since Willy died two years ago, he is only alive for his father in these reveries.*

Allen Gentry and me built a flat on the Ohio bank. It took us most of the fall and into the winter; then, when it was done, we had to wait for Allen's wife to give birth. When the baby came, we went off. Now, I'd been on the river before. This was in 1828—I'd just be nineteen when we got to New Orleans; two years before I'd got as far as Memphis when we sold off all our stuff—corn and barrel staves and tobacco. That time we didn't make much: in fact, I had to work for wages at a lumber mill over on the Arkansas side. There was a Negro man there, about thirty-five years old, name of Pomp, and we worked top and bottom sawyers in the pit there. He was the experienced man, so he'd be atop, pulling up the saw, and me below, pulling down, and every pull it snowed sawdust in my face. After a morning's work down there, what with my face running sweat all the while and the wood dust coming down, I looked like a man had stuck his face in the honey and then in the cornmeal bag. Whew! And while I'm breathing sawdust, and choking sawdust, and spitting sawdust, and picking sawdust out of my eyes, Pomp is up atop singing like Easter Sunday. Came the end of the week, and the job was done: I drew my pay, not much. Mr. Ferguson says to the nigger, "Pomp, you tell your Masr to come round any time for your pay." Well, now, there you see the difference between free labor and the slave: I get to take my pay, and Pomp has to let his master take his. Well, let him have top-sawyer: I've got what *I* need.

Go home, and walk into the cabin. Pap looks up, with his one good eye shining. "Howdy, Abe. Good you're back. Let's see what you have for wages." Runs through the silver, hands me two bits, and pockets the rest. Those days: a boy owed his Pappy whatever wages he made till he turned twenty-one. Well, I still had it over Pomp: if he lived forever, he was never going to be twenty-one.

He no longer really imagines himself talking to the children; but has cuddled their wraiths against his sides, absorbing them, speaking to them as to his other selves.

I remember: how cold the mist was in Pigeon Creek in December. (Jackson had just been elected President.) It rose out of the ground and filled the air, filled the air in the houses through the cracks, sifted into the clothes so you could feel them hanging to you, wet. Cutting logs and sawing timber, you'd suck the fog in deep and blow it out. Ma would always worry about us breathing in the chills; but I had got my growth then, and could breathe fire or ice and show no ill effect. What it felt like, then: to feel yourself lengthening out, your muscles toughening like whipcords when you swing the axe or the top maul. Work all day and feel stronger when you finish. Got your growth: and know you'll not only be a man-size, but giant-size.

I am the biggest man in Pigeon Creek and adjacent counties. When a man wants to wrestle me, I can't help but smile: when I fight, I whip. (And I'm still paying my wages to my daddy.)

I am also the ugliest man in Pigeon Creek. Even Pa with his one eye looks handsomer. Had to get Pa's permission to go South, of course; but he never cared, because of the wages. Ma Sarah worried, and Sally would have. But Sally died before I left. Tall sister Sal, who they said had my mother's face. I wept in her lap when Ma died, the only time I cried for her; and Sally took care of us all, young as she was, till Pa married Ma Sarah—same name as Sally, Sarah. Abraham and Sarah, like in the Bible. The first time I went down river, to Memphis that time, I knew I couldn't be going all the way South, for Sally was to be married to Aaron Grigsby, and I had to be there to see her married.

All the way back from Memphis walking through the woods, I knew she shouldn't marry, and the feeling grew on me. A year later, when her time was coming, I had a strong feeling I should go to be with her, the way Ma did when she nursed folks during the milk-sick (and caught it herself; and died). They say Sally cried, and the Grigsbys let her lay too long. Let her lay. Her spirit seemed to go, and her strength, when the baby came; and she died. And those Grigsbys, standing about, wondering if maybe they might should do something. They never called me till she was gone. I saw Ma die, and spoke with her just before; but I saw Sally big with her child, and then the next time she was emptied out, and lying in her bed: I walked across the farmyard, knowing she was already gone; Aaron standing there with his mourning face on, and his father, Old Reuben with his blue-white eyes looking a little stary in his head. I thought, Wonder if he's prayed for my sister yet? because Old Reuben had been taken by Injuns as a boy, and raised like one, and always was sneaking off to the wood and dancing like a turkey, silently, every time the leaves begun to fall. He was Pa's best friend, Reuben. I thought, He looks like a loony. And his son Matt began to howl like a mourning bitch one night, and hasn't stopped since: they tied him to a tree in the yard, and had to feed him like a hound. And I thought, I will not cry now. I look real ugly when I cry. I'd sour milk.

But went back down to the landing to work on the flatboat with Allen. We'd be working on planing deck-boards, and someone would come running down: "Oh Lord, Allen, she's going to have it *now!*" And Allen'd give me one wild look, drop the plane, and light for home. Come back three hours later, the board's planed, "Sorry, Abe; it was just something she ate." After the third time I said, "Allen, if I were a doctor, I'd conclude your wife hasn't really got a child; she just swallowed a watermelon."

A lump below the breastbone. A grief. A child. Dead child.

Then the baby came. Sally had been under the ground for about nine months. No women to hold us back now. So we loaded the boat, trimmed her real careful, and in the morning fog before New Year's day we poled off, and set her into the current. Pigeon Creek dissolved behind me.

When the fog lifted we were well down the Ohio and toward evening another boat come down, full of boys from Vincennes that we knew real well; so we tied up together and had us a sociable for the next two weeks. We'd let the current move the boats, poling or sweeping just to stay in the current and off the snags and bars. And we'd sing while we did it:

> *Hard* upon the beech oar!
> She moves too *slow*—
> *All* the way to Shawnee*town*
> Long time *ago!*

Nights we'd gather in the cabin, tip a jug of Monongahela that Allen'd brought along to remind him of his wedding night. Tell yarns we'd heard. I'd tell some things I knew from books I'd read; even call up speeches from the plays of Shakespeare I'd memorized when I was in blab school, reciting. I'd troubled to learn some of the stories, and told them about the death of Julius Caesar, and the villainies of Richard III. They preferred the villainies: I remember relishing the speech about his hating "these piping times of peace," and the "glorious Sun of York." Allen said he was plenty discontent with winter himself, but would settle for the sun of New Orleans, and let New York go hang. Then one of the Vincennes boys told us about the Harpes, that robbed keelboats along by the Cave-in-Rock. I believe it was when we first heard about a man named Marle or Murrell, who they told us was worse than Harpes. He was a nigger-stealer: he'd take free coloreds from up North, put them in a sack, and take them south to sell.

But Murrell didn't stop there: he didn't do it keelboat style: down full and back by steamboat or shanks' mare, with an empty carpetbag. No, he'd talk some nigger into running off for the Free States; then either sell the coon in another county, or return him for the reward. This besides the usual robbery, and murder.

"Oh yes. He dresses like a gentleman; like a real macaroni. Talks to you ever so nice by the road; then cuts your throat, and splits you open to let out the guts; stuff you with rocks and drop you in the nearest swamp."

"They say he runs all the gangs up and down the river."

"Oh yes," I said, "and owns the *Lightning Packet*"—which was a big fast boat that worked the Ohio.

Later they found out that Murrell did have henchmen all through the Valley, and planned to have the niggers rise and burn out the plantations, and become the King of Mississippi, like Prester John in Africa.

"Right," says Allen. "There were some niggers stole right nearby us. Pretty nigger wench named Carline. Whew! I *don't* think they'll set her to picking cotton—not right away they won't."

"Well, you know what the Kentucky boys say. That you ain't really a man yet, till you've had one."

Pass the jug.

"That's true! That's true!"

"Oh Lord, when we get to New Orlins!" Allen's dream, him and fifteen of every possible shade of nigger wench or woman, Mahomet's Heaven.

And I turned it over slow in my mind, like a kid with his first tobaccer cud. Thought about it good, as I recall it, and spent the nights thinkin about it too, and the long days with the sun heating up my belly and hips, till by God—just like the boy with his first chaw! Didn't know whether he should spit the cud, or where, or how, but he can really taste it and his insides is all swelled up with it, and by God—he's got to fire that wad any how! Well, well. I was going to learn a lot in New Orleans. Little salmon going down, big salmon coming back. Closer we got to town, I could have used my pecker to pole us through the fudgiest bayou Mississippi ever made.

Down onto the big brown level of the Mississippi. Father of Waters. That's what the Injuns called it. We'd pole some, sweep some, keep off bars and snags; but mostly moved with the heavy current, gliding miles at the river's own speed, same water around us all day, river always moving like the flow of blood, the sweep of time. The air got softer. As you went South, you saw where the spring was coming from. Nights we'd lie up on deck with the air moving over us: clog-dance when we felt like it, stomping the deck and kicking for the moon; maybe somebody from another boat with a fiddle. Or me with the Jew's-harp, twanging away on "Old Dan Tucker," or "Jump Jim Crow": *"Boy-dada-boydada be-dobow!* Wheel about, turn about, Step jess so. Eb'y time I wheel about, I Jump Jim Crow."

Learned clog dancing from a bunch of niggers that belonged to Old Man Bates, who owned the store and landing at Troy, where we built the boat. Now slavery was outlawed in Indiana, but Bates never worried about it. Just held those niggers as if they were in South Carolina. One evening with the chill in the air, I came down and saw them gathered in a ring, clapping on while a big buck kicked his feet and moved his head around, little bit like Reuben and his turkey dance, whopping all together in time, slapping their legs in rhythm. It seemed to me that their hands struck their dark skin with a soft, popping sound, as if their skin was thicker, a kind of padding; where a white man would slap hard and flat, if he slapped himself at all, like his skin was a shirt spread on a rock—no real sound to it. And I jumped into the circle, and kicked high and jumped, and did my head the real turkey way Old Reuben did in the woods. The niggers laughed and clapped on. Their clothes were flapping like feathers, they were wearing rags that were heavy and soft as velvet with use, and smelled nigger. After that I was the best clog-dancer in Pigeon Creek. And later that year, when we got back, I fair spoiled the marriage party for Grigsby's two brothers; all the men watched me clog-dance, and paid no attention to the women and gals.

(Men admired the dance, it was so like jumping—never see how ugly the face was, watching him jump. How long, how ugly and twisted up.)

Well, we drifted down the river. Days got hotter. We'd lie on our backs and feel the weight of the sun along the tops of our bodies; and through the deck boards you could feel the vibration that was the big current moving us downstream: feel the big weight of the sun all over, and the big force of the moving river down below, a brown heavy current wide as a sea pouring down out of Minnesota and the Ohio and down from the Rocky Mountains that I've never seen, like the backbone of the world. Thinking about New Orleans, like a city in some fable, full of strange women: Spanish eyes and hair, black clothes, their skin just that much softer, the lines of the face just that much rounder so you wonder, *Is she? Is it so?* Blood moving in you like the river, a force you can't stop, you grow bigger and bigger till your head brushes roof beams and your arms and fists are top mauls swinging.

> *I went down de river,*
> *I didn't mean to stay*
> *But dere I see so many gals*
> *I couldn't get away*
>
> *Wheel about, turn about*
> *Step jess so!*
> *Eb'y time I wheel about*
> *I jump Jim Crow.*

Pa went to New Orleans, and came back looking like the man who saw the elephant. I'd never talked to him about it. But watched him talking to a bunch of his friends, backslapping and guffawing; and walked off, not hearing what he told. Standing there in the mud, and all the cash money they had just then had been invested in the jug they were passing.

We started to work the plantations along the shore as soon as we'd got below Memphis. We drifted down along the Cotton Coast, toward the Sugar Coast—the real Congo. We'd lay off heaving on the sweeps, and lean our weight on them against the shove of the current, and see the gangs working the flat country either side, like black ants in a patch of grass. If we got closer, we'd hear the calls of the drivers, or a muttering sound like water chuckling under ice, only just enough repeat in it so you knew it was the slaves singing to themselves as they worked.

Watching at night—Arkansas, I think it was. They were loading cotton onto a steamboat at night, big torches flaring, the steamboat lit up, and the smoke foaming up out of the double chimney-stacks. Niggers working on the cotton bales: so many of them, all aglisten with sweat. Looked like a big pile of ants, tumbling sugar cubes; priests parading sheep to an altar of blood; or like the ship was a big factory, and they were millhands piling in. I'd never seen so many niggers in my life; it was almost like a dream. Thought it was: next morning the landing was empty, except for an old uncle fishing off the end of the dock.

Sometimes we'd tie up at a landing, sell off a prime hog, or some Kentucky twists, seed corn, barrel staves. Allen'd trade off a little Monongahela on the side—applejack from Grigsby's still. The niggers would gather round, and offer stuff in trade. Traded a cup of jack for a better Jew's-harp than the one I had, then traded my old harp for more whiskey that I'd had before. Sometimes they'd call up a gang of the niggers to load some cotton, or barrels of the sugar they'd boiled. Sweet burnt-sugar smell of burning cane made you think of a world made of sugar cake. Once, when we were walking around, we saw a whole gang going up to work in the cane mill, and they were all women with infants slung in scarves over their shoulders and behind their backs: "Suckers' gang," the man told us. "Easy work chopping cane stalks while their cubs need the tit." Sell 'em off when they grow up. It was strange: I'd never seen so many women in one place, kids all about the same age; walking in a line down the road. Suckers' gang.

We got down to a plantation below Natchez. We'd avoided Natchez because of its cutthroat reputation. We thought of Murrell, suave and well-dressed; he would have a gold-head cane, and ask us politely about our boat and cargo. So we tied up at Duchesne plantation, Madame Duchesne, some miles below. Went to a *coonjai* dance that night: the niggers all in a circle, singing in this high voice through the nose, you couldn't ever catch the words; dancing real slow, then faster, fiercer. This time it wasn't like at Troy; I wasn't called to clog-dance.

That night, we're lying on the boat, just off a swamp. I dream I can still hear the drumming sound of the feet; then I think, in the mid-

dle of a dream, *Someone on deck!* Allen give a yell, and I was awake!
Feet thudding, and a humped big shadow jumping across the deck toward me, he's got a club or something that looks like the whole tree. I
thought, *We're gone,* and then my body just began to move, and I rolled
away as the shadow came up, got my legs under me and came up at him.
Saw his face, *Nigger,* he was already around on me again, and swung
the club and socked me hard in the forehead. I heard the sock, felt it,
but it never stopped me: and I knew, as I just moved right through the
blow like it wasn't there, that I was too strong and was never going to
die. I came up with a little hand gaff-hook, and swung it into him, and
thought I felt it crack and him fold over around it, gave him a knee and
pushed him over the side. Allen was yelling, "Shoot, Abe, for Christ's
sake shoot!" And I come around swinging an axe, and he took off:.so I
turned the axe, cut us loose and we began drifting off.

Allen and I were laying there, sick as with fever.

"Oh Jesus, Abe. Do you think it was that devil Murrell?"

"Surely, Allen. I saw him myself. Knocked him into the river."

"Shit, Abe! How'd you recognize him?"

"He was just like the Vincennes boys told us: dressed like a gent;
talked like a gent; dove-gray coat and shiny boots. Only . . ."

"Only what, Abe?"

"Only they never told us he smelt like a nigger. Well, I guess down
here that's how gentlemen smell."

Things got real good after that. It was as if we'd passed through a
guarded door to a treasure. The sun came out brighter, birds sang songs
when we'd tie up at night, flutes playing under clear water—mocking
birds; the air warmed and smelled of growing things; we traded off the
rest of our stuff at the next two plantations, and even sold the boat.
The South opened its golden air and we helped ourselves to chests-ful and
rode into New Orleans in style, deck passage on a steamboat, lying and
smoking on top of a mountain of cotton bales, singing, "Get out the way,
old Dan Tucker," around the last horn of land, till we could see the city
lying low to the smooth water behind a wall of masts and stacks that
looked like a burnt-over pine forest.

We came down the gangplank, and the air was like some of the
lighter river-mud had floated to the surface and silted up the parts that
would usually be air. We walked through canyons of cotton. There were
piles of tobacco, and barrels of stuff off-loaded from the ocean ships:
some of the barrels were open, and they'd sell stuff out of them. One
little man who spoke a kind of French, and looked more than half nigger,
was selling *crevettes* out of his barrel: little white things, shrimps, like
crayfish, only from the ocean, and cooked in brine, so you tasted the
sharp, weird, salty taste that was like nothing I'd ever imagined: the
deep cold of a deep salt sea, not the flat water out of ponds, or the icy
iron taste of well water.

In a big warehouse, white men (and some I'd not have thought
white) all packed in together, like the crowd at a brawl or a stump
speech. There's a white man speaking. Allen and me walk in, but somehow we don't get it yet: it's just, you don't pass a stump speech by, no

matter what the party. There's usually somewhat to refresh the weary
and aid in the deliberations of the citizenry; and I always left a stump
speech more full of . . . wisdom . . . than I had when I came. But it's
all *coonjai* to me. Then, the man is just pointing around, and chanting
something—"Seize sont wheat, seize sont wheat,"—and Allen catches
on first: "Jesus, Abe: it's an auction." And then you could see that the
man was making the auctioneer's movements, chanting the bids probably in French.

There was a woman standing just below him on the platform. I
thought she was assisting him somehow. When I first looked, she looked
like all these French folks to me, oiled-walnut face and a white turban.
Then a man stepped up to her and tapped her lips with his leather
crop; she moved her lips, and he took her chin, and tipped her head
sharp so her mouth came open, and held her so. He studied her open
mouth deeply with his eyes. Dropped his eyes and stepped back, nodding abruptly. Then the auctioneer rapped the gavel, and the woman
stepped down. A man stepped up, who looked like he had had tar poured
all over him, and I finally got it. The man looked up, toward the door.
His eyes were like brown stones set in yellow amber. He had a metal
collar around his neck, so that his head seemed to be resting on a plate.
His muscles bulged like a horse's muscles under a horse's dark hide. His
eyes stared out over the crowd. He held his head tilted back, as if the
collar were too high. He never looked at the mob of buyers at all. He
looked at a place in the door over our heads. Without thinking, I turned
around to see what he was looking at. There was just the wharf, the
man with the barrel hawking shrimp, and a small fishing boat behind
him with one yard cocked across the mast. What does he see? It must be
he sees the mast and yard, like a cross in the sky. I felt sick, and began
to walk, without thinking, back out toward the dockside; thinking of the
woman in the white turban, I thought she was his sister or his servant
girl, just sold off. The Suckers' gang. I remembered Sally, and coming
back from Memphis to her being married, back from the farm to find
her dead.

"Seize wheat." I wonder how much that is in money? I thought, we
must buy as many as possible, and take them out of this.

We were walking along an alley leading up from the dockside, Allen
and me, looking around at everything: the plaster-covered houses, pale
colors, all with their wrought-iron balconies hung out like pots of black
ferns and ivy. Women leaned down from some of these, their faces
shaded with black hoods. There were a lot of women in each balcony. It
seemed you could smell their smell: strange, powdery smell like sugar
and the smell of those velvet rags the niggers wore in Troy. This is New
Orleans, I kept thinking. This is the place. This is where we've been
coming to all this time. This is what I killed the nigger so I could get to.
The big cut over my eye where he'd clubbed me began to jump with
blood working in it. I could feel the big man as I hit him, heard the crack
—it was his ribs, I never broke the hand-gaff—felt him fold over and
go slack.

"Jesus, Abe, let's buy ourselves one of these. *Abraham!* My oh
my. And they say you ain't a man till you've had one! Maybe we'll

come back here tonight and get ourselves *weaned!* Buy one, or anyways take out a lease and rent a spell. My oh my! My oh my!''

We could buy one. She would belong to us and do whatever we wanted: whatever work, cooking, cleaning, chores. Never a word. Ask whatever, curse her whatever. Never a word. Do whatever you will. Do whatever you will. She can never refuse, or laugh, or walk away, or go with anyone else, or do anything for anyone else. Do whatever. Let you be never so ugly, face of a sick hound, face of a raw-head, face of a looney harnessed up in the yard. Bear your child like the Spartan boy with the fox in his belly, and die of it without a word. A girl in a white turban, her skin gets darker as you look: milky mud of the Ohio, darker mud of the Mississippi where the Missouri comes in. Feel it moving under you, carrying you off, carrying you down. What is *it* like, at last I'd like to know what *it* is really like. Going down to New Orleans, and getting to New Orleans, and being in New Orleans. It doesn't make sense, but that's how it seems: if I had had a woman before I left, in Pigeon Creek, a white woman, maybe I could slip inside a dark one here, and take no harm. I thought of myself as a bar of silver, taking a mint stamp —a white stamp shaped like a star, or a dark one shaped like a deep hole. The first stamp would be with me forever, woven in my metal even if melted down and stamped again. Allen was married; he had that magic to protect him, that knowledge.

So I got off the raft and the brown river, and let it slide past the bank. I kept my money, and spent for no luxuries in the City of New Orleans: I hardly saw the marketplaces that I had dreamed of as places where wishes are granted. I had refused to buy the one thing, the magic thing; so all business was closed to me.

But I couldn't go out when Allen slipped out, on the sly. There are things about yourself it's better not to know. If I bought one, if I owned one, and *took* her here, I'd have to stay here till I die.

Came back on the steamer, against the brown river. Pigeon Creek was just as it had been when I left. The mound on Sally's grave had sunk flat with the ground, and a new year's grass had sprouted on it, over her face. Pa looked up from his planing a cherry log. ''Well, Abe! Howdy son. Good you're back. You're looking real fit.'' And held his hand out: took my wages, the profits of the voyage; hefted them, and counted them out, twenty-four dollars and odd silver. ''Well! This is good, Abe. This'll clear us with Squire Bates, and leave something besides.'' I never said anything, but let him take the money. It was his right to do so. He never did anything to me that he did not have a right to do, as the laws were written then. It was as if I had never left, and had brought nothing back from a voyage I never took.

I never knew what had happened to me, how I'd changed, till later that spring, when I went over to the Kentucky side to work for wages moving hogsheads of tobacco around in the big warehouse at Fifth and Main. Niggers and white men working together; we'd haul on the same barrels, then go off and talk by ourselves. After a while, I had to go over and talk with them. I looked at their faces closely while we talked. It seemed to me that perhaps we'd been to the same place, different times; that we knew something the same. But their faces were black, their eyes glazed like a dog's, and their noses oddly shaped, and it didn't seem there was any way to ask them, or talk about it.

The pay was bad there, and they treated everybody like dogs: we ate sitting on the dirt floor of one of the sheds, and slept in the same; and found out they were taking the cost of any meat we ate out of our wages. Then one day the son of the warehouse owner comes in and starts to abuse one of the niggers about stealing spoons or some trash, and pushes the nigger into the water jug, and knocks it down, *crash*. The white man starts cursing the nigger and walks out. It's dead quiet, and dust is floating like spangles where a beam of sun hits through to the floor. The nigger hasn't moved, he's sitting in the middle of the cracked pottery and the spill. I'm looking at his face, and he sees my eyes and looks at them. "Well," his eyes say, "it's going to happen."

The white man comes in, and he's got a blacksnake whip. It is not like anything real: long, shiny, black. He lashes it round, and cracks it into the nigger's shoulder.

I feel my strength rising so suddenly that I can't help but grin, because I can feel that all that heaving on the bow oar has made my arms as full of power as the Big River is with water and moving mud, and this son of a bitch is going to collect all of his wages right now.

Spin him round by the wrist, and whip my fist around and into his gut so that he folds around it like the man on the flatboat did.

And I straighten him (though he'd *like* to bend) and swing my fists hard, left front-and-right back across his face, and can feel the bones and teeth behind his skin.

"Oh man, you better get out of here before he calls up the boys on you!" The nigger boy pushes me out the back door by the woodshed, and I run through it to the street. People are walking by as if nothing has happened. Nothing has happened. Then there are shouts, and I'm off running down the street for the water. I am the strongest man, and the fastest runner, and the best clog-dancer, and the sharpest joker, and the biggest man in Pigeon Creek and five adjacent counties.

They can never catch me.

I will live forever, and grow stronger every minute.

I will leave home next year. I will never look back (to see Pa looking slant-faced out of his one eye and holding out his hand).

I may never strike slavery dead; but I believe I can stunt its growth.

> *I whip my weight in wildcats*
> *I eat an alligator*
> *I drink de Mississippi up*
> *Oh, I'm de very cra'ter*
> *I set upon a hornet nest*
> *I dance upon my head*
> *I tie a snake around my neck*
> *An den I go to bed*
> *I kneel to de buzzard*
> *I bow to de crow*
> *An ebry time I wheel about*
> *I jump Jim Crow.*

I am Abraham Lincoln, fresh from the backwoods, half-horse, half-alligator; I have seen New Orleans. I have seen the elephant.

"Shit, boy," says a voice. "You that big, you must *be* the elephant."

Mr. Lincoln is suddenly awake. His body is bathed in liquid. He realizes he has been dreaming. The boys have vanished: he fell asleep telling them stories.

No, Tad is in Washington. Bob is with Mary—I expect.

Willy is dead.

I'm down at the army, tomorrow I go to see Ben Butler, only man in the army uglier than myself, maybe that's why he thinks he ought to be President—uglier.

Uglier.

His mouth has a vile taste. He has been wrestling the demon of sleep again, and losing, he thinks. Tries to remember his dream, it's important: dreams always have your answer, if you can read them right. Always dream before a great battle: a dark ship sailing to a dark shore. Power, I was the strongest, most powerful, I was running for the river, the brown current of the river carrying it all away in a sweep down to Orleans, yes: I remember. The elephant. I thought I was so strong. I rise on the bones of small children, I bury people. Suckers' gang. White turban. What was I thinking of?

It is a claim on him, somehow: those blacks with their pleading eyes, their eyes that suck at your soul, and remind you of your deep sins. To be free of that, free to leave them and go home (as he had left New Orleans a virgin still, in 1828). To not have to own them, or to *rescue* them to keep from owning them, to put away the sin of owning and wanting to own, the ambition that sends the children to death (Willy!) and the mothers to the madness of insatiable grief, insatiable grief!

If they would only do it themselves, and take it out of his hands! Hadn't he done enough already? How much more guilt did he have to bear? How many more sons and fathers and husbands buried in Abraham's bosom? If the woman with the turban would strike her master dead and run, the boy in the warehouse strike the black-snake man for himself, and let me be and let me be, and let me never find out about my strength. He must get the generals to let the blacks fight, to put them where they can win a victory for Father Abraham: to set him free.

HEADQUARTERS SECOND DIVISION, NINTH ARMY CORPS,
June 24, 1864

Maj. Gen. John G. PARKE,
Chief of Staff, Ninth Army Corps:

GENERAL: Lieutenant-Colonel Pleasants, of the Forty-eighth Pennsylvania Veteran Volunteers, has called upon me to express his opinion of the feasibility of mining the enemy's work in my front. Colonel Pleasants is a mining engineer and has charge of some of the principal mining works of Schuylkill County, Pa. He has in his command upwards of

eighty-five enlisted men and fourteen noncommissioned officers, who are professional miners, besides four officers. The
distance from inside our work, where the mine would have to
be started, to inside of the enemy's work, does not exceed 100
yards. He is of the opinion that they could run a mine forward
at the rate of from twenty-five to fifty feet per day, including
supports, ventilation, and so on. It would be a double mine,
for as we cannot ventilate the shafts from the top, we would
have to run parallel tunnels and connect them every short distance by lateral ones, to secure a circulation of the air, absolutely essential here, as these soils are full of mephitic vapors.
A few miner's picks, which I am informed could be made by
any blacksmith from the ordinary ones; a few hand-barrows,
easily constructed; one or two mathematical instruments, which
could be supplied by the engineer department, and our ordinary intrenching tools, are all that are required. The men themselves have been talking about it for some days, and are quite
desirous, seemingly, of trying it. If there is a prospect of our
remaining here a few days longer I would like to undertake it.
If you desire to see Colonel Pleasants I will ride over with him
or send him up to you. I think, perhaps, we might do something,
and in no event would we lose more men than we do every time
we feel the enemy.

Yours, very truly,

ROBERT B. POTTER,
Brigadier-General.

HEADQUARTERS NINTH ARMY CORPS,
June 25, 1864—2:45 P.M.

Major-General HUMPHREYS, Chief of Staff:

We have commenced a mine that will reach the batteries of
the enemy in our front by a reach of 115 yards. I have given
orders for all the necessary changes of the line to make the work
ordinarily secure. We want about 7,000 sandbags or more. I
think we can break the line of the enemy in due time if we can
have the necessary facilities. We want heavy guns very much.
Can we have the sandbags?

A. E. BURNSIDE,
Major-General

HEADQUARTERS ARMY OF THE POTOMAC
June 25, 1864—3 P.M.

Major-General BURNSIDE, Ninth Corps:

I have directed Duane to send you an engineer officer and a
company of sappers, and Hunt to send you sandbags and siege
guns. I am delighted to hear you can do anything against the
enemy's line, and will furnish you anything you want, and
earnest wishes for your success besides. I would have been over

to-day, but certain movements of the enemy on the left have kept me here.

GEO. G. MEADE,
Major-General.

GENERAL WEITZEL'S HEADQUARTERS
June 25, 1864

General BURNSIDE:

I have just ordered 8,000 sandbags to be sent to you from my depot at Bermuda Hundred with all possible haste. I imagine they will reach you about 1 o'clock.

G. WEITZEL,
Brigadier-General and Chief Engineer.

General Burnside looked up from the last dispatch and stared out the window. Weitzel was chief engineer for Butler's Army of the James: so right away Butler knew about his plan, and was being helpful—a small gift of sandbags Meade had neglected to bring up conveniently to the front. He now had Meade's good wishes for "his success," and a present from Ben Butler. *A man with less spirit and more superstition,* he thought, *would take those as a pair of bad omens.*

General Burnside's Poker Game
June 22–July 4, 1864

June 26, 10:00 A.M. The Mine

The Mine had been begun, starting in the sheltered face of a fold in the undulating ground. The point was opposite and slightly north of the rebel fort. A hundred feet forward was the new main advanced line of rifle pits, which were still being improved. Looking at the raw earth, Colonel Pleasants felt reasonably confident. Already they were twenty good feet underground, in a hole that measured five by four feet. Soon they would need to commence digging the parallel tunnel that Pleasants had designed to permit ventilation of the long shaft. And they'd need to be a bit more scientific about their direction. That would have to be done soon, too—but not immediately. Probably in a day or so: he'd best write it down.

Colonel Pleasants kept a small memorandum book. Always there were so many factors to balance; he felt uncertain of his ability to hold it all in his head. Worries: Have the men been getting enough vegetables? Has the reserve ammunition been properly sheltered and placed conveniently? What point of the line should he go to in case of attack? At first, the mining operation seemed to simplify things, his attention centered on the one, familiar task. Then concerns began to multiply: he worried over the plan, modifications and objections kept coming to mind (*jot them down*), there was need of all sorts of supplies and equipment, and the routine of the regiment on the line had still to be preserved.

He had been taken with Rees's idea right at the start; had talked it over with the sergeant and some other of the miners in the regiment, and finally sent the note to Potter. He was so full of the plan he'd talked Potter into an active enthusiasm in about half an hour. He'd gone back to get something down on paper to show to General Burnside. It was then that the nervousness started. Talking with Rees and Lieutenant Douty, it had been all a kind of free give-and-take. Putting the thoughts into a report, signing his name to it, made him wonder whether there wasn't something radically wrong with it all, something that would embarrass him terribly. Only by plunging ahead into the work, driving himself and others to do it before doubts could overtake him, could he carry things through.

Yet it had been pleasant, planning the Mine. He, Rees, and Douty had met in his bombproof in the evening. During the day they had looked all along the line, checking the earth and figuring angles of sight to find a place where they could dig a solid tunnel and still be out of

sight of reb observers. Now they plotted on the map the way the tunnel
ought to go: a slight upward slant, not too much, just enough for drainage, the ground sloped up toward the rebel fort. Five hundred–odd feet,
if the map scale was right. A long tunnel with no shaft ventilation.

He'd thought of an answer for that problem, and relished the admiration of Rees and Douty when he'd laid it out. Side by side with the
main tunnel they'd dig a narrower shaft, connected to the main tunnel
by lateral holes at intervals. Then dig a fire pit in the sideshaft, with a
chimney piercing the ground vertically right above it, and block off the
original opening to the firepit, venting smoke up the chimney; that
would create suction through the only other opening, the entrance to the
main tunnel.

Douty whistled. Rees shook his head up and down. "We'd have to
be sure the chimney vented behind a bush or sidehill so they'd not suspect tricks."

"There's a small clump of bushes between the Mine entrance and
the picket line. That should do for a screen."

"I've given some thought to the timbering," said Rees. "We'll
need God's own quantity of strong timbers for the size tunnel we're digging. Not saying anything about what kind of soils we'll come to—what
we've got is pretty sandy, though there is clay. Also there's plenty of
springs and small marshes all along here: I'd not be surprised to strike
a spring or quicksand bed in there." Pleasants made a note in his book.

Douty said, "Maybe they'd let us put the Colored to work. They
should be able to handle that all right. They've been hewers of wood
and drawers of water for the rebels, and for every damn other corps in
the army. Might be they'd let us use them a while."

That was a notion: but there were always problems about the Negroes. Best let them alone. Pleasants had gotten so anxious about Burnside's scrutiny that he had stayed up all night preparing tables and
charts, projecting answers to objections that might be made. He found
himself composing a spirited defense of the business of engineering
mining-tunnels, beating down hydra-headed military objections and offering as important evidence on his behalf the entire weight of the theory of competitive economics: if such tunnels could not profitably be
dug, then businessmen wouldn't hire the digging.

He'd ridden up to Burnside's with his head full of worry and his
mapcase overloaded with papers; and Burnside had been so affable, was
already so convinced, that he'd ridden home again without once opening
his portfolio.

As Pleasants watched, the shift changed in the hole, and the new
diggers leaped in. The last shift, for their part, went out slowly, maybe
tired, but also reluctant to give up what they thought of as a kind of
privilege. Quite a change from having to bully men into the coalpit in
the Schuylkill country. The men had a kind of proprietary interest in
the Mine, and they were working with gusto. Well, maybe that wouldn't
last. He'd have to watch their morale. Just then he remembered: he'd
told Potter and Burnside the idea had come from the men, but had forgotten to mention their names. He made a note to do that.

Near the Mine entrance Sergeant Rees was checking his shift roster. Six of the men who'd volunteered for mining had come down with dysentery that morning, and that meant he'd have to work fewer men longer or shorten the digging day. The problem had a couple of aspects. He didn't want to work the men too hard right away; they'd far to go and would be needing patience. On the other hand, the present enthusiasm for digging might not last, and it might be well to use the energy while it was freely offered. But there was also the matter of calculating the direction of the shaft. Pleasants hadn't been able to get his surveyor's thing yet, and so they might be wasting effort, digging by dead reckoning. Best to go slow then: he cut off the last shift and moved its members into two earlier shifts for next day: Private Dorn was handy, and he told him to hunt up the men and give them the word.

It had been almost like a holiday at the start. Pleasants had had him tap all the miners in the regiments and bring them down to a spot in the railroad cut where they could talk. Then he'd laid out the plan for them, and they'd whooped and volunteered in a rush. "All right men, thank you," Pleasants had said, and appointed him and Douty foremen. They'd all gone tearing back to the spot they'd picked, and the men went right to it, chopping away with their bayonets and cups where they didn't have picks or shovels. They believed in the Mine, Rees thought. It was the first thing on which the big Generals had ever listened to them. They felt good because they knew they were right; and they even felt that the generals might not be quite so stupid as they had thought.

That evening, when they'd worn themselves out and chopped out a hole about five feet down and haggled around the edges, Rees stepped in to organize things. First there were the shifts to get set: he went over the list with Douty. Then he had to get men working on altering their picks for deep digging—shorter shafts and blades. He'd need the off-shifts to carry the dirt out, and others to cut brush. They'd figured that the best way to hide the raw earth would be under brush, since the army was so slow sending up sandbags. They'd have to pick some spots along the trench line to dump the stuff; couldn't be all in one place. Rees would tell Pleasants about it, see what he thought.

The next day they were at work on shifts, and he had realized they would need something to dolly the dirt out of the hole and down the trench. There weren't going to be enough sandbags; and anyway he didn't want his diggers worn out toting sacks of dirt. Doyle came up with the "muck-pram": a wheelbarrow knocked together out of some hardtack boxes, small timbers for handles, and wooden wheels cut from log-rounds.

Timbering: I'll have to send somebody back to get us more timber for when we get deeper down. We can't do the whole thing with cracker-box boards. Rees smiled. *I'll send Doyle after the timbers. For the old time's sake. I might make a miner of the bhoy at that!*

Sergeant Rees walked off down the trench. Private Corrigan, his sweaty face covered with the dirty brown-red sand, called after him: "For the love of God, Mr. Rees, bring us some shovels and picks. Isn't it

the *army* of it, to dig a mine without a bloody pick or shovel between
three men?'' The other men laughed, and Rees was smiling himself as
he ducked round the corner of the traverse trench and into Pleasants'
bombproof. At first he could see nothing; then, as the brightness cleared
from his vision, he saw the Colonel fidgeting with his papers, and writing
in a notebook. Rees paused, thought better of interrupting him, and went
out. *I'll check the dump spots myself,* he thought, and started to walk
away down the line.

At that moment he saw brass coming toward him, out of the covered way, and ducked his head quickly back in the bombproof—''General
officer, Colonel''—and out again to see that it was General Burnside
himself. Rees threw a salute and tried to look military without standing
up straight at attention. Nobody had ever been shot along this stretch
of trench, but maybe there was a reb sniper saving the spot for a special
occasion, like brass visiting the front. Generals were like battle flags:
you had to have them to follow, they were symbols of undying glory,
and they drew fire like a hound draws fleas.

Pleasants was out beside him, straightening his coat and looking
nervous.

''Ah, Pleasants! Good morning, good to see you, we've come to see
how things are going.'' The General was bluff and hearty; he looked a
man who dined well.

''Certainly, sir. We're honored. Um, Sergeant Rees, won't you lead
the way?''

He did. They arrived in front of the Mine. Burnside pursed up his
face into a serious expression, and walked up to look at the hole. The
working shift climbed out and stood at a duck-shouldered attention while
he inspected the hole. The hole was now about sixty feet deep into the
side of the cut. Around its mouth was torn-up red clay and sand, with
some larger rocks piled in a heap. These caught the General's eye.

''What are you saving these for, Colonel? Build fireplaces?''

''Well, sir; yes, sir. The one fireplace I told you about, in the ventilator. Also, we'll use them to fill in under the floor and around the
timbers.''

''Ah yes, that's right.'' He turned and gazed in the direction of the
rebel trench. His line of sight was blocked by the bulge of ground between the Mine ravine and the advance line. ''Yes, angled just right, I
should judge. But we'd best check it anyway, hadn't we? I've ordered
your theodolite, Colonel. There's some problem about it; those old bid-
dies at Army Headquarters don't seem to have one with them.'' He
winked conspiratorially. ''Maybe a short delay. But you'll have it, I
promise. In the meantime, I should judge you're heading right.'' He
turned and looked again. Rees thought, *If he can see anything five feet
past his nose with that hill in the way, he's a bloody clairvoyant.* ''Keep
on then, Sergeant. You're doing splendidly. Your name is? . . .''

''Rees, sir. Sergeant Harry Rees.''

''Well yes, thank you, Sergeant.''

Followed by his staff officers, who had not said a word, the General
vanished down the covered way. And after a pause, in which he said

nothing, but stared into the space Burnside had vacated, Pleasants left. Rees shrugged, and started again to look for spots where he could dump the dirt.

HEADQUARTERS, NINTH ARMY CORPS
June 26, 1864—11:30 A.M.

General MEADE, Commanding Army of the Potomac

We succeeded in moving our main advanced line out to the skirmish line beyond the railroad cut and within 100 yards of the battery to which we are running the mine, so that the mining party is now pretty well protected. If we are not disturbed today I think we can make it so strong to-night that they cannot attack us with much chance of success. We have fine positions for heavy guns. The attack on us last night was feeble, and our loss small.

A. E. BURNSIDE,
Major-General.

June 26, Noon. General Burnside's Headquarters

By noon General Burnside had reason to suspect that his forebodings of the day before were not idle pessimism. He prided himself on his card-sense, his ability to intuit the falling-out of chances. He had a knack for sensing the drift of affairs, he felt—something like having a direction-bump. It stood him in good stead at the regular poker games he played with his staff and his fellow corps commanders. Not that he was infallible: he made mistakes. But afterwards, it always seemed that his *sense* of the matter had been sound; only, he had somehow failed to read or respond properly to his intuition. Even back in New Mexico, in that horrible time when he'd nearly had to resign his commission over gambling debts, regimental funds he had almost been unable to restore —the worst time in his life, almost as bad as Fredericksburg had been, the stares of his brother officers, the sense of having made a horrid messy failure—even *then,* he was going to say, he had known deep down that his play was wrong. But he'd paid everything back in the end, hadn't he, and gone on to make a reputation for probity and trustworthiness after. And he'd learned his lesson, his card-sense itself had sharpened because he didn't press it too hard or, on the other hand, trust it too little (which could be just as bad!). No, now he knew how to gamble moderately, and to risk more then he could afford to lose only when the drift of chance was substantially in his favor.

Now, with so much at stake, his chance to play at last the heroic role for which he had patiently waited, preparing himself—now he must play his hand well, and cautiously.

Meade had wished him well: a bluff. Because (a peep at the possible hole card) Burnside had requisitioned a theodolite, the instrument needed for triangulating the position of the rebel fort and guiding the direction of the tunnel. Now here was a note from some understrapper saying that the Engineer Department had no theodolite to spare! Incredible! A major operation in progress, and no technical assistance from the engineers! By itself, the denial might mean a temporary delay, till an instrument could be made available. Worse, there were rumors, rumors that Meade and his engineers had no intention of cooperating at all. Then the delay would stretch on, the impetus of the work would halt; the opportunity would fade and pass. Thank God Meade had so many disloyal subordinates who kept Burnside informed! There was *his* hole card: the loyalty of his officers, their ingenuity and *esprit de corps*. They had thought of this wonderful idea, brought it to him, confident that he (unlike Meade) had no jealousy, would both aid the project and see they got credit for it. He must back them too, to the hilt!

"Richmond!"

"Yes, sir?"

"Lew, there you are. I'd like you to ride down to the telegraph at City Point and have a private telegram sent for me, to James Harkins, Ninety-three D Street North West, in Washington. We'll make the message brief. 'Jamie—Can you oblige an old friend by sending down a theodolite? Important. Can't explain in detail. Best to you and all, Burny.' Jamie is sure to come through, and there's our theodolite."

Richmond strode out of the tent and across the flat parade. General Burnside sat in the yellow shade of the tent. Its flies had been raised to admit whatever air was moving; but there was no breeze. He looked at his watch. In half an hour he would have to review General Ferrero's black division. Ferrero had been taken away from him again, to guard trains or picket the left flank of the army. Burnside scowled. Somebody was always trying to winkle Ferrero's division away from him.

This was turning out to be a depressing day. It had started so well, too! He had gone down to visit Potter's front early in the morning and had been so pleased by what he had seen that he had praised everybody to the skies. He'd even asked the names of some of the enlisted men— just being asked your name by a Major General seemed a compliment to them, as Burnside had learned from his old friend, General McClellan. (*Though I don't have Mac's facility with names. I can't remember a blessed one.*)

Potter had acted quickly once Burnside had given him the go-ahead. He'd had brush cut for abatis, stacked sandbags; then used the nighttime to push more troops out to his picket line in front of the main trench, had them dig in deeper, stuck the abatis up in front. By morning they had a new line dug, sandbagged, and manned, and though they drew fire there weren't many casualties. So already the Mine project had resulted in his corps taking up another twenty-odd yards into the main line! Everything was so well organized, well thought out, being done with thoroughness. Burnside felt he could take a justifiable pride in his organization, in the example of thoroughness and efficiency he set for his men.

Every time he thought of his conference with Potter and Pleasants he felt that glow of honest pride. He'd invited them up in the evening, after dinner: had cigars and some special brandy set out for them. *Greets them in a friendly way, lets them lay out their scheme—Potter very cool; Pleasants, nice young man, a bit tense meeting the Old Man.* "*Are you aware, gentlemen, that the longest mine ever run in siege op-*

erations ran more than two hundred feet shorter than the mine you pro-
pose?" Then leans forward, looks each one in the eye: wink: "Let's do
it. By God, let us just do it!" Sits back, beaming. Pleasants so relieved
he takes a quick glance over at Potter, rolls an eye. Potter, the cucumber,
even he grins a little with one corner of his mouth. Of course, I'd in-
tended to let them do it from the beginning; but holding back a little
was important—let them know I consider things carefully, don't com-
mit myself rashly. Then I spring my own idea on them: we pack the mine
with twelve thousand pounds of gunpowder, arranged so and so—gun-
powder's something I know about, and this arrangement will give us
maximum compression and force. "Gentlemen, it will be the biggest bang
ever. A shot heard round the world. And we will be able to walk right
through that hole and into Petersburg." Even Potter was impressed by
that!

He'd see to it that they got their share of the glory, as sure as his
name was Burnside! And the name of Burnside would be worth something too: because it would be under Burnside's aegis that the plan was
begun, Burnside would organize it, Burnside's troops would do the fighting, it would be Burnside's Bomb that opened the door to Petersburg,
Richmond and Victory! By heaven, it was a good day after all!

He rose crisply. Pulled down his long blue dress-uniform coat, set
the epauleted shoulders at the right angle; then the big crowned hat with
the gold cord, his trademark, like the whiskers. White gloves. General
Burnside strode from his tent to review the black troops of General
Ferrero's division.

The division marched across the field toward the spot where General Burnside loomed, a burly giant among his staff. At a signal, its
officers drew their swords and swept them to the shoulder in salute. As
Ferrero and the staff came abreast of Burnside, they dipped their
swords in salute and turned to wait beside him while the long column
marched by, black faces looking so odd above the dark blue jackets, almost like a clash of colors. At the head of the brigade were brigade
color-bearers, carrying the flaring national colors, and the green-and-
white swallowtail of the brigade's own guidon. At the head of each regiment, the regimental flags were unfurled. These, too, looked odd: the
colors so bright and unfaded.

The division marched very smartly, in perfect alignment. Evident
care had been taken with drill. They stopped on orders and faced right,
standing in rigid rows for inspection. General Burnside dismounted, and
motioning Ferrero to accompany him, began to walk down the first row,
inspecting a rifle here, an item of kit there.

"What's your name, soldier?" Burnside had stopped in front of a
young private in the Nineteenth Colored Infantry, Thomas's brigade.

"Private James Johnson numbuh Five, *suh!*" came the answer. The
soldier was tall and skinny, but his voice was surprisingly rich, textured,
and deep.

"How's that, son?"

"Sergeant says, suh."

General Ferrero touched Burnside's sleeve. "I can explain that,
sir. A lot of these men, before they enlisted, they hadn't any last names,

so they had to pick names when they signed up. Most tried to pick names that sounded 'just plain.' Johnson sounded regular enough, so we have about five or six James Johnsons in every regiment.''

Burnside smiled at the idea, and turned to a sergeant. "Sergeant, how do you call this private when you want him to do something?"

"Sir," said the sergeant, "I just calls, 'Johnson Five, front-center fo' *de*-tail,' sir."

Burnside seemed to find this very funny. He threw back his head and laughed while the sergeant stared impassively ahead, braced at attention.

Burnside and Ferrero continued down the row. Burnside was thinking what a good story he'd have to tell tonight when he went over to Warren's for poker. He chuckled again at the prospect.

June 26, 4:30 P.M. *Bivouac of the Fourth Division, IX Corps*

General Edward Ferrero had established his temporary headquarters in the shade of a pine grove. Around him in the open fields and meadows his two brigades were bivouacked. Their conical white tents might have seemed like some Indian village on the Great Plains, except that they were too close together. It was the last time the division would be intact for the next few weeks. One brigade—Thomas's—was going out to the flank under orders of General Warren of V Corps. The other brigade—Oliver's—might go back to fatigue details and guarding the trains, or even back into the trenches. Another man might be bitter about that, but General Ferrero had schooled himself in patience. He commanded a division, at least—even if the division was never kept in one unit for him to command.

The hubbub and movement in the camp had subsided, and a hum or buzzing sound, regular and rhythmic, told the officers in the grove that the Negroes' services had begun. It was Sunday, after all. Some of the regiments and battalions were worshipping as units. Others of the Negroes preferred meeting with particular denominational ministers; these had crossed the camp to join Methodist or Baptist meetings. The shifting around of the individuals and groups had vaguely disturbed Ferrero, with its suggestion of organizations within his organization, patterns of allegiance and fellowship that had no reference to his command. He was, however, quite glad that his men were religious; he found that fact reassuring.

Ferrero held in his hand a white handkerchief, with which he occasionally mopped his brow and cheeks. Another handkerchief lined the collar of his blue-serge uniform coat, where the rough heavy cloth chafed his neck. His olive skin and black hair and beard (shot with gray) glistened with sweat: a handsome, impressive-looking man, with an impeccable manner. He had kept a hotel and fashionable ballroom near West Point before the war, and had been moderately active in politics. He enjoyed the company of military men, and had been an avid promoter and participant in amateur drill and rifle companies. He was an excellent, graceful, and athletic dancer, and his companies usually excelled in dress, drill, and gymnastics. He had treated his West Point guests with a wistful deference, making them feel privileged in his rooms and at his table. He flattered himself on their regard. When the war had broken out, it had been the inevitable thing for him to raise a regiment—the Fifty-first New York Volunteer Infantry—and obtain an appointment as its Colonel, with Robert Potter—the Regular Army soldier who now commanded the Second Division—as his Lieutenant Colonel.

When Potter had been jumped over his head to command first a brigade, then a division, Ferrero had not been at all piqued: he liked Potter, and knew him to be the better soldier. Still, it irked him to discover that the Regular Army officers regarded him with something bordering on amusement or disdain. They did as much for all volunteer officers, yet there seemed a special amusement in their condescension towards him, as if they sniffed something ridiculous in making a man an officer ''because he kept a hotel near West Point and taught the cadets to dance.'' For all that, Ferrero bore things rather well and had learned enough to be counted a good brigade commander, and assigned the difficult task of organizing the Ninth Corps Colored troops. That, of course, had added to the amusement: for weeks the division had been spoken of as Ferrero's Minstrels and Dixie Cut-ups. But Ferrero believed in the work, and that he and the division would yet be given a chance to show what they could do. General Burnside had promised him his chance, and he believed in Old Burny. He also could take comfort in this: whatever regulars might think of his professional skill, he was known to be a man of personal courage, who had led his troops across the cannon-swept stone bridge at Antietam.

He was chatting now with his two brigade commanders, Oliver and Thomas. The latter had brought with him a young Lieutenant of his staff, Pennington, whom he evidently favored and wanted to introduce.

Colonel Henry G. Thomas had been in the Regular Army Medical Corps before the war. He was about forty, a vigorous man, with a clear and lovely fair complexion, smooth cheeks above a rich brown beard. His pale blue eyes gave him a slightly wide-eyed, naive look. Small, neat white teeth gleamed amid the brown beard when he smiled, which was often. He was the one officer in the command of whom Ferrero was fond in a personal way: it was impossible not to like Thomas. Oliver was another matter. Colonel Charles Henry Oliver—the descendant of several distinguished generations in Boston, ministers and magistrates, governors before the Revolution, Judges of the state and federal courts, Ambassadors. (Even at St. James's an Oliver could maintain his dignity.) In the maternal line, there were Presidents as well—the Adamses. He was a short man, with a pudgy, unathletic appearance that belied the fact that he was physically robust and a good horseman. His skin was pale and his close-shaven cheeks made his face seem as bald as his head.

Thomas, introducing young Pennington to Oliver, seemed to think that Oliver ought to be acquainted with the Lieutenant's people. Pennington's blush and Oliver's stiffer-than-usual face suggested this was not the case. Thomas himself felt a shadow of doubt flicker, though he continued to smile as he spoke. ''I thought you might be acquainted

with the Penningtons, Colonel. They are fine people. From Boston.''
This did not seem to resolve matters, and Thomas's uneasiness increased.
''I'm greatly in Reverend Pennington's debt, for the good counsel he
gave me when I was stationed at Fort Adams. My son had just died of
pneumonia. I've not been much of a Christian, and was never of his
church; but his words to me, as one man to another, gave me great
comfort then. His son is a fine officer—don't blush, Chris, it's so—he's
got genuine talent for handling the men, and he's learned the rest of
the trade faster than I would have believed possible.''

Oliver stared at Thomas's face as he spoke, in a cool pose of courtesy. When Thomas stopped, he shifted his gaze to Pennington and
waited with a mild expectancy for something he should say. Pennington,
after a pause, said, ''Colonel Oliver, I'm honored to meet you, sir.''

''Yes,'' said Colonel Oliver. Then: ''I don't believe I do know your
family, Lieutenant. Christ Methodist is your father's church, isn't it?
Yes, I've heard of his work, but not had the pleasure of meeting him.
I am glad to meet you, Lieutenant.''

Ferrero was an old hand at smoothing over this sort of thing. ''I'm
pleased to hear Colonel Thomas speak so highly of you, Lieutenant.
And you needn't be embarrassed at the praise, either. It's important
for us to know which officers we can rely on, when we need to call on
them suddenly in the heat of action.''

''Thank you, sir.''

''You say he handles the men well, Henry?'' he asked the Colonel.
He turned back to Pennington. ''What do you think of them? You've
seen them in the trenches and on the march. How do they seem to you?''

''Well, sir,'' Pennington swallowed, the flush deepening on his
cheeks, ''I have to say, sir, I find them truly . . . admirable, sir. They
do what they're ordered to, and without complaining a bit. I've never
seen such patience, digging trenches with the heat, and these flies all
about. They seem to do everything so . . . *earnestly,* I guess is the
word. And I have to say, sir, I think it's a shame that they've not been
given their chance, sir; a chance at the enemy. I'm sure they'd do as
well . . .''

''Yes? You were going to say?''

''Well, yes: as well as those white conscripts we brought in last
week. I hope I don't give offense, sir; but those men didn't look like
they would be much use in battle, sir, even if they *were* white.'' Pennington's blush was furious. Colonel Thomas beamed proudly.

''I'll second that,'' he said. ''If we could get a chance to train these
troops properly, they'd be as good as any we've had for the last year.
They're volunteers, most of them, like the older regiments that enlisted
before Sixty-three and the draft. Regulars cuss volunteers plenty, but
there's no material for soldiers like men who signed up because they
wanted to fight.''

Colonel Oliver seemed to be debating with himself whether to
speak or not, then evidently decided to. ''I agree with you about the
early volunteers, Colonel. And I don't like conscripts and bounty-men
either. But I have to say I think you may be mistaken about these
troops of ours.'' There was a curious lack of feeling in Oliver's voice, as

if he expected that his listeners would automatically disagree with anything he said. ''Of course, the experiment will have to be tried. But I
think we can predict the outcome with some safety. I've had some experience in raising and organizing these troops that may differ from
your own. In North Carolina I found them patient and docile enough,
as the Lieutenant here correctly observes. But patience and docility
aren't the chief virtues of a soldierly race, I'm afraid.''

From the nearest of the meetings came the sound of a hymn, sung
in unison and so emerging clearly above the background buzz and hum
of the other meetings. To Pennington's ears the song had the swing and
cadence of a march of wild men, spirited and unrestrained in feeling.
The thought that such stirring, exotic music was also Christian shot
tears of pride into his eyes, and he felt himself sway.

> *''Rock-o ma soul in de bosom of Abraham,*
> *Rock-o ma soul in de bosom of Abraham,*
> *Rock-o ma soul in de bosom of Abraham,*
> *Lord, rock-o ma soul.''*

Under the unison he could hear, flickeringly at moments, other times
clearly, one unmistakable deep voice. It seemed an undefinable essence,
a clue—to the power of the music.

The music in the near meeting was hushed. A single voice, its words
unintelligible, chanted high and low, without music, punctuated by gutteral thrusts of sound from the congregation. ''Wenananna, *uuh,* uh.
Wenananna, *huh,* uh.'' A descent from music to . . . stupidity. Nearby,
a locust cracked its wings in the heat.

The shift broke the spell for Pennington; he blushed, embarrassed.
He forced his own voice forward, covering the repellent gutteral of the
congregation. ''I don't have your experience, sir, so I can't presume
to judge. Still . . . I can't help but feel . . . our troops will do at
least as well as those conscripts. They brought them off the ship in
chains, some of them; and Major Booker had to post a squad at the rear
with orders to shoot them if they bolted before we got to the depot. I
can't imagine that men who have to be bribed or coerced into joining
the army, and driven to the front at the point of a bayonet, will do any
very smart fighting.'' Pennington was speaking out of love of his Cause
now, hot for it and perhaps a bit stung by Oliver's haughtiness. ''Major
Booker says—do you know Major Booker? He fought in *Kansas*—Major
Booker says he thought any war you couldn't get volunteers to fight in
wasn't worth fighting. At least our men are volunteers!''

Thomas and Ferrero now looked uneasy at Pennington's outburst,
but Oliver, surprisingly, seemed to like the boy's response. In fact, he
liked argument, and was gladly surprised to find anyone able and willing
to argue with him—there were so few who could. He too began to warm
to his subject. ''That's an interesting notion of Major Booker's—quite
what I'd expect of him, too—but a trifle impractical. The fact is, at
least half of these men are either conscripts or have joined because of
some explicit or implicit form of coercion. You didn't know that; few
people do. I remember Major Booker from North Carolina—he had an
idea of allowing the Negroes to elect their own officers, as many of the

volunteer regiments used to do at the beginning of the war. My God! What a spectacle: an army run by men elected from the ranks the way we elect our Congressmen or Aldermen—popularity and what-can-you-do-for-me! Colonel Thomas, you remember in Sixty-one how impossible it was sometimes to get anything at all done, any order obeyed.''

"That's true enough.''

"Yes. You know, the war has made a great transformation in this country: not just in its physical power and wealth, but in the minds of people, a moral change. We've outgrown some of our more primitive conceptions of liberty as an end in itself. We've begun to conceive grand enterprises—vast armies, railroads to the Pacific, canals—and to achieve them we'll have to make over our relations with each other as well. Soldiers don't want a friendly man to lead them; they want a man who knows his job. They don't like slackers either; they know that if one man malingers, the whole organization will be diminished. It's a new principle for us: men putting their individual wills under the guidance of the man who knows how to organize and direct their work. A few years ago they'd have called that slavery, and beneath their dignity as Americans. The army's the school for a new kind of society.''

"I'd judge from the success of our conscription that some are less-apt pupils than others.'' Pennington was standing his ground.

"Inevitably.'' Oliver took Pennington's response as agreement. "But you know—''

"Listen.'' Pennington held up his hand.

From the nearer meeting they could again hear the voice, an unmistakable, ringing bass, rising out of a meeting grown suddenly quiet.

> *"No mo peck o' cone fo me,*
> *No mo, no mo,*
> *No mo peck o' cone fo me,*
> *Many thousan' go.*
> *No mo pint a salt fo me,*
> *No mo, no mo,*
> *No mo pint a salt fo me,*
> *Many thousan' go.''*

The voice was slow and careful in its singing. A deep unison joined its refrain. Pennington found himself drawn down toward it.

> *"No mo driva lash fo me,*
> *No mo, no mo,*
> *No mo driva lash fo me,*
> *Many thousan' go.''*

Even from a distance Pennington could see that the singer was the tall, thin soldier whom Burnside had talked to that noon: Johnson Number Five.

Oliver was saying something: "Conscription isn't a simple matter. Certainly you draft a man into the army, under threat of jail or fine, you coerce him directly. But when you offer a hungry man, a jobless man, a bounty to enlist, there is a kind of circumstantial coercion there as well. Certainly there is when you drive the poor Negroes off their plantations with promises of an unimaginable freedom, then leave them to rot in contraband camps; and the only way out is marching in ranks. It would have been infinitely better to have begun by making the law clear: if you would be free, you must serve; if you serve, you must obey.''

A hundred yards away, Major Booker squatted cross-legged in respectful silence in the shade of a bush on the edge of the meeting of the men of his battalion of the Forty-third United States Colored Troops. They had been recruited from the same county on the Neuse River in North Carolina, and preferred worshipping together to meeting with their denominations. There were men among them who could preach, that they were used to. Booker sat attentive, not pretending to be a part of something that he felt to be strange, particular to a culture not his own. It was a Christian ceremony. Though he thought he had left old beliefs and narrowness behind him, something of his family's deepest knowledge remained: the Christian world, of all worlds, was the one from which he must feel excluded, where he must see in the believing Christian a potential enemy. Well, he didn't believe it: Randolph was certainly no enemy, and if they had differences it was not on religious ground. But there it was.

He listened drifting with rhythm of music and strangely inflected speech, thinking of some great underlying theme or rhythm that bound this singing and speech to all other worship he knew: the sobbing arabesques of the synagogues he knew as a child; the dances of the Crow Indians he'd seen, joined in, with their nasal falsetto playing against gutteral base over the reiteration of the drum and footstamp and the *skree* of bone whistles. He had been a wanderer, a stranger in different countries, and he had the fugitive's gift of learning foreign speech. Yiddish and Hebrew and German and Polish he knew from his childhood. It hadn't taken him long to acquire English. In his wandering in the West he'd also learned Spanish, and in three months enough Crow to get along, plus the sign-talk. But it was more than the fugitive's need to translate in order to survive. In making over to his own inner speech the meanings of the words and the resonances of meaning, in feeling the rhythms of different speech, he felt he touched the core of some reality, a universal reality, a sense of kind that linked him to others. Words spoken, songs sung in that universal language were instantly intelligible; and all mankind was one.

Although he knew this for fantasy, and organized his actions on more rational principles—men were different, alien to each other, often in conflict—this belief remained at the heart of his actions. When he heard the music, listening to its rhythm in reverie, he believed he could hear the rhythm of that fictive language.

What were they singing now? The sounds were soothing, so apt to the soft, slow melody, yet mysterious, in some way untranslatable.

> "*Titadolla light de lamp*
> *En de lamp light de road,*
> *En ah wish I ben dere*
> *Fo to yedde Jo-dann roll.*

Oh de city light de lamp,
En de what-man he will sold,
En ah wish ah ben dere
Fo to yedde Jo-dann roll."

Ki Randolph's voice sounded strangely nasal, different from his speaking voice, as if in singing he used another tongue:

"Oh de what mahble stone
En de what mahble stone
En ah wish I ben dere
Fo to yedde Jo-dann roll."

"White marble stone," that's what he was singing. To hear the Jordan roll. But what was it about the city and the white man?

Booker thought back to his first meeting with Randolph; in the spring of 1863, when he'd come East from the Border and had been put in command of a small district on the Neuse River up in North Carolina. He had been a Captain then. His command consisted of a corporal's guard of white infantrymen, mounted on plowhorses, and all the blacks he could recruit or dragoon into the service. Ostensibly, his function was to maintain a workable military police in the district, and a force to resist secesh raiding parties. In reality, as he soon discovered, he was supposed to recruit, organize, and police a laboring force to keep the district's cotton plantations running. This was the regime of liberty and enlightenment, bringing schoolteachers and Christian missionaries to uplift the slave, teaching him useful skills, teaching him the advantages of wage-labor over slavery. Of course, the wages were generally lower than would be paid to white men; but then, slaves could not be expected to be as efficient as white workers, and in any case what could they know of wage scales elsewhere? Booker found this part of the enterprise, and his role in it, to be utterly detestable, a kind of treason to whatever he had fought for and to his own life. Not a liberator at all—just a slave driver in army boots, an American Cossack. And the worst of it was, he could see no way out of that role without leaving the army altogether.

Until he met Ki Randolph.

In May a black boy on a lathered horse rode into the yard of the farmhouse he was quartered in. "Massa Brickhill" was having trouble with "some bad nigguhs." Brickhill leased three plantations in the area, a brisk, efficient little Yankee, with strong convictions about how to make the South "a paying proposition" again.

The boy guided him to a field on the Colehill Plantation. At the end of the field Mr. Brickhill stood, with his white assistant near him, and half a dozen blacks around them. A gang of about thirty black men and boys sat or sprawled on the ground, at the edge of a line of newly turned earth—a half-dug drainage ditch—into which they had thrown their picks and shovels.

"Good morning, gentlemen," Booker said. "What is the trouble?"

"Captain! These men here—this field has to be ditched or we'll get no cotton at all from it. These men are simply refusing to do the work. In fact, sir, it must be done. I hope you will make them see that."

Booker had looked at the tallest black man, expecting some answer. Instead it came from a shorter man, with deep black skin and heavy features: Ki Randolph.

"We free men now, Capn. Dis ain't our plantation: we is from Hewson place. Maz Brick'l order us out here this morning, en when we don't come he send buckra wit his rifle and march us out. Tole him, sah, we don't work off de land dat's ours, widout mo' pay. He say it's all the same, Colehill an' Hewson both his. That not our concern, sah. Take more than usual wages to git us off the lan' dis time the year. We not workin for five dollahs. Ten or none. Buckra tap his gun. We got to do the work. Den buckra don't pay close mind to us, and den he ain't got de gun. So now we'll talk about de wages." The man talked looking directly into his face, without either fear or bravado. He didn't care what Booker said. He was not afraid to die or go to jail. His men were not moving an inch.

Booker was surprised, but he could identify his own side with the greatest ease. "Mr. Brickhill, it appears that you've got a strike on your hands. Free labor, Mr. Brickhill, involves a free bargain between employer and worker. You've got free labor here sir, as you've said you wanted. I suggest you make your best deal, and pay up prompt."

He'd gone off laughing. Even the rebuke that came down from Oliver's headquarters hadn't soured his mood. If anything, it had sweetened it. Although a stranger in a strange land, he felt he now knew where there were people who might be friends; and he was back in a game that he knew how to play.

But he played it too openly. Oliver removed him from command of Brickhill's district and put him in charge of drilling recruits and digging fortifications around New Bern city. He heard rumors of trouble upriver. Blacks on Hewson's plantation, it was said, had planted corn instead of cotton. When Brickhill had brought in soldiers to force them to put in cotton, they'd slipped out at night and planted corn between the cotton rows. Someone had got into the gin with a sledgehammer and smashed the works into scrap. Someone else bushwhacked three of Brickhill's overseers on their way back from a tavern. Booker thought of the short black man.

He saw him again, dressed in a blue uniform, in a gang of conscripts that came to him in August. He knew something of what had been going on. Brickhill had got Oliver to send his press gang out to the plantation and draft the worst of the malcontents, as he saw them. Once in the army, they could be disciplined, or better yet kept away from the land, sent to work where they would have neither their old ties to the land nor the support of their own communities.

The men were supposed to be drilling, carrying brooms and shovels in place of muskets. A black drill sergeant was shouting orders. The men were stumbling around, following him incompetently, if at all. Some of them stared at the sergeant with frank hostility. The sergeant, baffled as a bee-stung bear, suddenly shot one fist out and punched a soldier on the chest, then followed in with both arms stiff and jammed him hard right back into the ranks. The disjointed line of contrabands gave slightly and held the man up with a surprising tensility. Eyes that had been glazed, stupid, absent-minded, swung around and focussed sharply.

There was a word from the ranks, and the eyes relaxed, the bodies slackened. Booker recognized the short black man from the drainage ditch. Instinctively he marked him in his mind: he would make him a sergeant.

And that brought him up short again. He could no more make the short man a sergeant than he could unmake him. The way the other blacks had followed his lead, first at the drainage ditch and now with this drill sergeant, was a suffrage as clear and as universal as the caucus of volunteers that had given him his own rank as Lieutenant, back out in Missouri in '61 while they were making their way out of the bust-up of General Lyon's army at Wilson's Creek. That was the way it should be, in an army that was really just an armed people fighting in their own cause. Not like a professional army with a lot of *junkers* on top and the riffraff on the bottom. It should run like the Crow war parties he had ridden with out West, where you follow the man who's got the best sense for the business and the best medicine for it, and call him down if he proves out bad. Once you learn your business, you don't make many wrong judgments, either.

Booker grinned. Hell, he thought, it looks like I voted for the short man too.

The next step was to teach them something about war, so they could know what to expect from the man they'd chosen to lead them, and judge him accordingly. Booker had sent the first sergeant off and taken the company of recruits directly. Then they were issued uncapped muskets and lined up on the parade. For half an hour he drilled a platoon of white troops in front of them, demonstrating the basic maneuvers: line into column, column into line; forward, about-face; right turn, march; right oblique march. Then he put the men through as much of the drill as they could take. After, they sat down under the shade of some oaks, and he sketched in the dirt with a stick and gave the reasons why soldiers had to move that way.

The next day he put one white man through the drill while the rest of the white platoon stood at ease alongside the blacks. The man ended the drill facing the blacks, and on orders brought his rifle to point straight at the line (there was a ripple of surprise); then stood at order arms. Next the white platoon went through the evolution, wheeled and came towards the blacks, and on an order snapped their muskets up in a rippling line to aim at the blacks. The black line surged back a step in an uncontrollable panic. "No!" called a voice—Cato Randolph's, of course.

Two things had been accomplished. He had shown the troops how much more potent was the threat and power of a line of armed men than a single man with a gun; and he had let them see how Ki Randolph responded to that kind of threat.

Two weeks later he ordered an election held. Ki Randolph was elected sergeant.

In September they finally got a chance to get into action. A reconnaissance in force by the rebel division defending Wilmington forced the commander of the Federal army in New Bern to send every available troop northward. Booker's battalion found itself lined out among the fallen logs and heaped leaves of an oak forest. Booker placed his men carefully, showing them by word and gesture how to use the available cover. He motioned to Sergeant Randolph to follow him as he went. When they reached the end of the line he indicated that the sergeant should take cover with him behind a large tree trunk.

From off to the right they could hear the *spat-spat* of skirmish fire. Booker could see Randolph's hands clenched tight on the grip of the musket stock, and smell his acrid sweat. When he rested his hand on Randolph's shoulder he could feel the man's tension, then feel it suddenly take a tighter twist. He realized the man's feelings in a flash of intuition, and made the movement a way of gaining Randolph's attention. "Listen." The *spat-spat* continued. "That's just skirmish fire. Means nothing much is happening, nobody's moving. People shooting at whatever they can see, but nobody's out in the open."

Randolph nodded.

"Where would you say it's coming from?"

Randolph pointed out to the right. "That way, maybe half-mile."

"Yes—but maybe less. Woods will cut the sound down, make it sound farther off. There's another line off to our right, if you look careful you can see their flag." Randolph looked. "All right. The first thing is to know where you are, and where everyone else is. Our folks are over that way. We're in the second line, a little back of the left of the front line. Anybody comes through those trees up front here, they'll have to be our own folks, right?"

Randolph nodded. "Then . . . I'll pass the word, don't fire if you see folks coming through."

"Right. Unless we tell em fire."

Randolph walked down the line speaking to the men. Booker could hear grunted speech, a burst of laughter, but no words. After a while Randolph came back. The sound of firing from the right and in front became more rapid and louder: first like rain-spats on a tin roof; then louder, a downpour, until there was a roaring of undifferentiated noise coming back through the trees. Then, behind the noise, a long-drawn throaty shriek sounded.

Booker had his hand on Randolph's shoulder, neither aware of it now as they stared intently at the woods in front of them, Booker speaking rapidly what Randolph had to know. "The yells are the rebels; rifles are our boys shooting back. Union boys don't yell, they cheer or hurrah. Rebs are charging. If they whip, you'll hear the yell get louder, rifles will get quiet when our troops retreat. If we whip, you'll hear more shooting than yelling."

The roaring of the rifles touched a maddening, unbelievable pitch of intensity then seemed to slough off towards quiet. They could no longer hear the shrieking of the rebel yell. They relaxed. Nobody at all would be coming out of the trees.

After a while Booker asked him, "Sergeant, why wouldn't you all take orders from that black sergeant back in August?"

Randolph grinned: "Any nigger that takes pay to order other

niggers around, he's got one name: Driver. Free man don't need *no* driver.''

But who was Ki Randolph, and what was it that gave him the quality that riveted the eyes of the men on him, that gave Booker the sense that his own power of rank was somehow offset by the strength of the short black man? His face and eyes spoke a language that was barely intelligible to Booker, that repelled understanding as much as it invited it. To translate him into Booker's own terms was to lose something even while you gained something: he was an ex-slave, illiterate till Booker began teaching him—who had somehow very clearly grasped the essentials of his position, and understood quite well how to respond to his circumstances and even how to begin bending things to his own purposes. He had a sense of the gulf between the laborer and the owner that was at least as clear as that which it had taken his own iron molders generations of mill labor to achieve. Randolph was, to be sure, in other ways a . . . *peasant,* if the word could be voided of its contemptuous connotations. His work was agricultural, he was a man of a people tied by life and tradition and skill and inclination to the land. To own the land, that was what Randolph aimed at. But to gain that land, he had gone beyond the selfish grasping of the ambitious peasant—he had his people acting together to establish control of a whole plantation, committed to act together. To put him in charge of a platoon of soldiers simply militarized his situation. If he had been on the land, he'd have learned to read out of agricultural journals. In the army he'd learn out of Hardee's *Tactics,* the ''School of the Soldier,'' the ''School of the Company.''

Booker wanted to help. The land of Hewson's plantation had been confiscated, and some day it would come up for auction. Congress was working on a law that might give them the right, as laborers on that land, to buy it at Homestead prices. They'd need cash to bid for it against Brickhill and other leaseholders. All right: Booker took the company fund that paid for comforts from the sutler's store, and took a tithe of the men's pay—officers included, if you please—and put it in an account against the day of auction.

And tasted with Randolph the bitter sense that while they deprived themselves of the tobacco and fresh meat and sweets that eased the salt-pork and hardtack regimen of the army, putting dimes and dollars up against the Day, out of their pay that was two dollars less than the thirteen dollars a month they paid white troops—that all the time Brickhill was making cotton on their land, using their home folks, building up his accounts out of cotton selling at two or three times the prewar price.

Booker and Randolph drew towards each other, testing, feeling each other out. Booker's understanding reached to the dollars and cents of it, to Randolph's need to get the land and the poverty of failing to get it. But that wasn't all of it. He would look at the black face and think, *The man has been a slave. Once we were slaves unto Pharaoh in the Land of Egypt, yes. But he has lived the real thing.*

It was in his role of translator, as he thought of it, that he got the clearest look into what his sergeant had been. It was in December,

Christmastime. Randolph came into his tent to ask if it might be possible for him to send a letter to someone in deep Secesh—Mississippi, somewhere below Natchez. Booker told him it could be done now that the army had cleared the river. He could send the letter down to New Orleans by the military post. Who was the letter for?

"For my wife." There was a silence. Rain dripped on the outside of the tent.

"I thought you had a wife down at Hewson's."

Randolph's eyes seemed sunken below a layer of thick glaze. His drawn face showed no emotion and he would not look at Booker's face. "Captain, my first wife, Cassy, was sold south in Fifty-eight, with the son of old man Hewson. Captain, I need to ask something of you, ain't easy thing to ask. Got to have the letter written out the right way. Got to be clear, no mistakes."

"I'll write it for you if you want. Gladly. Is that what you want?"

Booker sat on the opposite side of the camp table, pen and paper ready. Sergeant Randolph stared at his hands folded before him on the camp table and spoke. Booker took it down as he spoke, correcting—translating—nothing.

"My wife Cassy,
I call you by that name still, for you feels and seems to me as much to be my wife as you ever did, Cassy. I must tell you that I am married too, to a woman name of Coffee. She is a good mother to Siah and wife to me, and we expects to have another child in spring. I had much rather you get married as I have done. Cassy, I could not stand to think of you and the children alone with none to protect you. Long as I am married, I am glad you be married too. It never was my wish to be separated from you, and never was our faults. I can see you plain, whenever I close my eyes. As I am, I cannot say do I love you or my wife Coffee the best; because I could never live with a woman the mother of my children not loving her with my heart. I do pray that this man Barnbas treat you fine, and is smart and can take care of you and the children; and that he loves you too, because it will keep him good in his heart to you.
Cassy, I have got a wife, and truly am sorry things have happened this way. I am glad you alive and well; though it better if we never meets any more in this life. If I was to die, now or tomorrow, I would not be satisfied till I had seen you. But if we are to live we'd best not meet, or our families might be dissatisfied.
Please to remember me to my children. You feels this day to me like myself. Please send me something of the childrens' to have them, a bit of hair in a paper with their name on it; and tell me if they well, and if they remember their Daddy's face.
Your loving husband,
Cato Ezekiel Randolph, Hewson's Plantation."

Booker could remember every word of the letter even now as he sat in the sun, feeling the music flow over and around him.

For Death he is a simple ting,
An he go from door to door,
An he knock down some an he cripple up some
An he leave some here to pray.

O do, Lord, remember me!
O do, Lord, remember me!
My old fader's gone tell de year roll round,
Do, Lord, remember me!

SERGEANT CATO EZEKIEL RANDOLPH

He shall feed them on Judgment.

Named Cato by his master (a disciple and distant relation of John Randolph and Thomas Jefferson), from the hero of Addison's play about the last exemplar of the virtues of Republican Rome, before the Empire; and Ezekiel by his mother and father, who sealed him to the covenant of the church in the small spring back in the woods where Uncle Josiah preached when the moon was dark, and again when it came full.

Ki is four years old. He's going out to the field today with Daddy. Mama wraps the batter cakes and a slice of cold bacon, and a slice of dried apple dipped in molasses, a special treat. Mama's belly swells out big in front—goin' to have a baby soon. Daddy comes in and says, "Let's go." Goodbye Mama, and they're outside walking to the fields; everybody else is coming out of the cabins. Daddy rests his hand on top of Ki's head as they walk, bounces it a little to feel his hair spring. The hand is big, it covers his head like a hat. Daddy is real big: his chest is like a big rock-face. In the chilly air Ki feels a glow of heat coming from his Daddy.

The sun warms as they pick down the cotton row. Daddy tells Ki what to do, and he tugs at the soft springy bolls—they spring like his hair, and he imagines they are his little children and his big hand covers their heads. Or he holds the sack open; or watches his father's hands move swiftly among the branching stems, in and out, like small dogs worrying a hidden coon.

Daddy stands up and stretches to his full height, his back to Ki. His shadow darkens the air around Ki. "Hoo! Ki-boy! we—" something swift-dark swoops in from back of Ki's head, snaps, and Daddy's head whips around and there's a lick of blood across his forehead, and Overseer yelling, "Down *to* it now, dammit, and none a your damn slackin." Daddy stoops over quickly to his task; he bends over double, face towards the ground. Ki has gone rigid with a bolt of terror so fast he can't feel it till it's begun to go. And he's shamed because his Daddy did something wrong; and he'd like to destroy Overseer; and he's shamed cause Daddy did something wrong, and Ki did wrong, and now Daddy's face been cut. Ki's sorry, Daddy. Ki's shamed of you, Daddy. Ki's sorry.

I won't eat my 'lasses apple.

Ki is twelve. He's been picking cotton for five years. He's gotten strong arms like his Daddy, and his hands are clever. Uncle Josiah takes him into his carpenter place and shows him how to use some of the tools; been training him to fix things—plow handles, wagons now, maybe cabinets and fine things from the House later. Ki is proud of his skill. Going to get him up out of the fields.

One day Colonel himself rides by the field and hollers, "Cay-*tow!* Y'come here now, boy!"

He drops the sack and comes over.

"How'd you like to earn some money for store-candy, Cato?"

"Sho, Masr."

"Well, you go along with Mister Hewson here, now. He's hiring you to do some work for him. He'll pay you a good wage, and you'll have enough to keep for that candy. Go 'long now boy."

"Got to get my dinner-bag, Masr, and my clothes."

Colonel's face gets hot, but he isn't angry, which Ki can't figure. "Grab your dinner, then, but you needn't worry about the rest. We'll send it along."

He runs back down the row, and he's full of his news. He's going to work for Mr. Hewson. Not plantation work, because he doesn't know Hewson as a planter; he figures carpenter-work. He looks at the three of them standing there, Mama pressing hands into the small of her back, Sis-Jane looking like she'd just like a nap; Daddy with his clouded-over eyes, not saying anything.

Mr. Hewson is sitting on a buckboard wagon. There's a big cracker sitting on the seat with him, pistol in his belt, chawing. Ki jumps up in back, and they rattle down the road.

"Things going to be good on my place, Cato. You be real good and do what Mr. Lat'more here tells you, and things be just fine."

They stop at another field. Six boys, and his friend Tyre's big sister, Dorcas, who has small hard points of breasts just poking out of her smooth chest. Everybody is quiet as the wagon loads up.

When the wagon moves again he knows he's been sold and that he'll never see Mama and Sis-Jane again in all his life long; never see Daddy and show him his wage-money.

Hadn't said goodbye.

The deep horror of it swells up over him right then. He'd never said goodbye: it seems that because of that the three of them must always be poised, frozen so as he's left them, waiting for the word that would complete things, tell them that he was gone.

Ki Randolph is twenty, and he's top boy on Mr. Hewson's big plantation on the Neuse River. He works hard in the field, he's tireless, his muscles are wired with a special nervous energy other folks don't have. He's not mean, exactly, but not all that friendly either: he's suspicious of people. Trusts the folks came with him from Virginia, but few others besides. He's smart too: can fix things like broken plow-handles, barrels; once when the gin got stuck, he figured how to mend it. Mr. Hewson brags on him every now and then. (Mr. Hewson sees Cato Randolph as vindication of his methods of slave management; he's written an article on it for *DeBow's*.) When Cato marries Dorcas he's real pleased Cato's strong and smart, and Dorcas a big strong girl with wide shoulders and long legs, healthy as a good horse.

In the numbness of the first days after they'd been sold, and later on Hewson's place, they'd watched out for each other. She'd sometimes bake something special for him. Once she gave him a dried apple dipped in molasses. He didn't eat it. Couldn't bear to throw it away; couldn't keep in the cabin he slept in with twelve other boys. So he took it to the woods, risking being took for a runaway, and buried it under a clump of moss. Till he got it under the ground, he felt like his head was swollen tight as a drum, tight as a blood-poisoned leg bloated up with corruption. When he buried it, it was like lancing the swelled part. His face melted and dissolved in the dark and he sobbed into the ground.

After that he was courting Dorcas. When she saw that he knew himself now, she laughed, and looked right in his eyes. Over maybe a year's time they moved slowly towards a time when they would be ready to slip out of the circle of the cabins some warm night, and be together. The night they finally did it was June, warm and mild. They wrapped themselves around each other and in each other, and he felt first seized and carried by her strong arms and legs and body and back, and then his own power sweeping from the loins and back and into his arms lifting and carrying her too, strength in strength, power in power.

Made the furniture for their cabin himself—bed, split-log chairs, table. Learned from Uncle Tobe how to make a good chimney. When he was working in the carpenter shed he'd see her through the window frame coming with a pail of field pease and some bacon for his dinner, and his heart would lift. The front of her dress swelled out, there was a baby inside her; but she walked straight as ever, her big shoulders and long legs helping her carry the burden easy.

Night his son Josiah was born, the women helping, he stayed in the room, and saw the boy's eyes catch the light for the first time. The flash of light frightened him for that second; he had felt himself changed, suddenly, into the body of his father—smelled of his father's smell on his own skin and felt how his shape was his father's—and fear touched some bottom inside himself so that he almost wept. He took the child, almost too fiercely—he hadn't dreamed how like a weak small rabbit it would feel under its loose-soft skin of blanket. He looked down at Dorcas's face, feeling they were all haunts, they'd all been changed to strange things in that minute. Dorcas was his mother, and he was his father.

She looked at him then, and smiled. Her lips were big and strong, and her teeth white as the meat of an apple, and she looked just the same as before. And it was all right.

But he remembered his fear. And he swore in his heart he'd never let Josiah see him whipped, never let them take Josiah as Daddy'd let

him be taken. And after, when a girl-child was born, they named her
Jane.

Ki Randolph is thirty. He's the best carpenter in the county, and
Mr. Hewson sends him out often to work for wages on other plantations
and in town. Sometimes he takes Siah with him. Usually Mr. Hewson lets
Ki keep a quarter of his wages; lately he's been taking all but what Ki
can squirrel away, or spend before he gets back—and that can't be much,
no more than Mr. Hewson expects Ki to steal (as he puts it), or there'll
be a whipping.

(They'll never whip me in front of my boy. Kill me first.)

When he's leaving the plantation even for a day, Ki always says
goodbye to Dorcas and little Jane, and baby Eliza—two years old now—
and he makes sure Siah does too, though the boy is so eager to be off
with his Daddy he's running half down the road already.

He goes downriver for a week to work in town on Mr. Ladd's new
store-building: Ladd says he wants walls that will stay up and look
square, and shelves that will *hold*, this time, and has asked for Ki spe-
cially.

A week later Mr. Hewson comes by for him. As they ride back Siah
naps a little, leaning against his father's back, feeling the deep vibration as Ki hums quietly, a tune without words.

When they round into the long alley of oaks that leads into the
plantation, Siah is off and running through the trees, shortcutting to
home; the wagon stops at the head of the quarters road a bit after.

Looking down the road he feels there is something bad. He waits
to let himself know it. Just the same, he gets down and walks to meet
it. The road goes between the cabins, and the people come out to watch
him walk. The air is filled with a keening that sometimes comes from
the cabins, sometimes from inside his head. The people pressing around
him, mourning, are haunts. When he gets to his cabin, Siah is standing
in the middle of the floor looking at him with the great question swelling
his eyes to the size of deep holes.

The open door of the cabin is like the open belly of a gutted deer:
dead face, big hollow cave where the innards should be, wide open to the
air.

Siah is standing there in the middle of the floor. His small hands are
relaxed and open. The doubt that strains the skin of his face hasn't
grabbed onto the muscles of his chest and arms yet.

*His Daddy's words are going to make him feel that. He won't know
it till his Daddy tells him. His Daddy is going to have to tell him.*

Siah's eyes are like glow-haunts that suck the spirit out of a man
when he walks late by a swamp. He can't look at them. Behind the boy's
head is the table he'd made, and on it the jar where Dorcas kept the
money he'd sometimes bring. Ki hopes she's taken it all.

Then he realizes that all his wages are still in his pocket. Mr.
Hewson has let him keep all of it, this time.

He can't weep or mourn or pray. His body is locked and his soul is
sealed. When Aunt Jen takes Siah out crying for his Mama, he hasn't
moved a muscle. He hasn't told the boy either.

Let Tobe tell him. Then he'll curse Tobe.

He runs that night and when morning comes the paterolls catch him. He's run so hard and long his nerves are numb and their blows fall on dead flesh, it seems. This isn't anything. When he gets back to the plantation, Hewson is going to whip him. That will be right. He will pay out his debt that way. Siah will see him punished, so he will forgive him. Siah will say he'd paid off for losing his Ma and sisters.

Hewson trices him up and has Driver whip him in front of the quarters. The first lash wakes him, and makes him feel his blunted, bruised muscles straining around the fiery cut where the lash rips at him. The pain of it begins to bang through his body and into his head; his back is a pulsing sun radiating precise shots of pain to the rest of him. He feels the rigid muscles of his face breaking up, and cries and tears breaking out of him, *O Jesus O Lord,* and he hears quite clearly Siah saying, "Don't let em whip my Daddy!" and he breaks through into a kind of dream where the lash can be felt but it doesn't matter. A voice says, "Why did you wait so long to call on me?" very soft, and there is Jesus standing in front of him. He almost laughs because Jesus is a black man. Black as the dark of the moon, with a cut on his forehead that leaks blood that is bright as light. He had never thought that Jesus was a black man, but it seems so simple now he is ashamed to confess that he hadn't known. But Jesus knows that, and they share suddenly a secret knowledge of why the truth has been hidden for so long. Jesus points a black finger to the blood-red sun. A bridge of fire, flaring with each lash of the whip, leaps from his speaking tongue to touch it.

He is a field hand again, after that. He works in the cotton fields in the day, and he picks real good, so that Hewson beams and begins to meditate writing another article for *DeBow's.* He works deliberately, deftly, but also with a kind of detachment: in some way the whipping has given him the power to draw his soul in from his body, so he can let his mind run on important things while his body does its work. For a while he keeps the secret to himself, about Jesus. Then he tells Uncle Tobe, who is something of a preacher. When he tells it at meeting it is dark night—not the regular meeting that Hewson sometimes would come to, but the special one in dark of the moon where new sisters and brothers come to Jesus. Ki feels himself break and open as the story comes out of him; and when the people sing around him he feels himself lifted on their voices and the broken parts begin to heal.

Felt like it must have felt to Siah when I held him against my chest and let him weep it all clear, weep the misery out. Hand on his back you could feel it working through him, and feel when the change come and the crying begun to empty out and end.

He is patient because he knows that a Day has been promised to the poor, when the oppressor will be cast down and the righteous rise in glory. Prophet Ezekiel—his own name—Uncle Tobe told him—"I will seek that which was lost, and bring again that which was driven away, and will bind up that which was broken, and strengthen that which was sick: but I will destroy the fat and the strong; I will feed them with judgment."

He watches Mr. Hewson and smiles to see him prosperous, seeing there a sign that the prophecy is true.

He can't write to Dorcas, but tries to send word. Nothing comes back. She's gone to wherever it is his parents have gone; nobody ever comes back. If he's not going to die, he must live. He's lonely in the cabin, listening to Siah's breathing. His manhood is alive, and he feels he wants to live, but can't see how. When he meets a woman named Coffee who lives on a nearby plantation where he goes to work, he remembers how things can be. She's tall too, but more brown-black than black like Dorcas, and she favors red headkerchiefs. She's got a baby who plays around in the chips when she stops by the workshed. He's half himself without a woman and babies around. When this woman laughs he feels a burden ease off.

It's three years later when he gets word from Dorcas. Coffee's with him in the cabin when Cujo, who's come back on visit with Masr Hewson's son, brings the note. She puts her shawl on and goes out, taking her children. Tobe, who learned his letters, reads it for him.

"My dear own Kie,
This the third time I have wrote to you by hand of Uncle Aleck who can read and lives nearby hear, but never heard, so supposed you had not got them. Kie, I have to tell you I am marry now to a man name Barnbas. Kie you know I wood not love no man more than you; but it is hard for a woman that is young and has chirren to keep from harm. And young Masr Hewson would insist too. Barnbas is a good man, and love our chirren as his own, Kie, and is kind to me respecting my feelings which remain for you. Even so, I wisht my marrying day would be the day of my death; but it didn't happen so.
Kie I hope you is willing to be married too. I yearn for my little Siah, and pray you will find good Mamy for him. Take care yourself, and do remember me as I can remember you.
With good respects and love,
Cassy Randolph now being Danilson."

1862.   Mr. Hewson is sitting on his horse listening to the guns booming off down the river, where the Yankees are coming ashore, attacking the Southern troops near New Bern. Ki Randolph, Siah, and a bunch of men are ditching a field to help the water run off it better. It's February and there's a little bite to the damp air. Mr. Driver Lat'more is right by Masr's side, leaning on his hunting rifle.

"That's the Yankees all right. We'll whip, though."

Hewson doesn't answer the Driver. "Now you boys," he says, "you boys want to remember this. If you see any bluebellies, get under cover fast. Don't you trust that Abolition talk you've heard: Lincoln don't like niggers any better than he likes Injuns; all he catches are getting sold down to Cuba. Work you to death growing sugar for the Spanish." The words have a rote-sound: they've been spoken often.

A bunch of horsemen wearing gray uniforms comes down the road, one of them stops to whisper a little with Hewson, and he blenches and rides off towards the house.

"Yankees comin," goes the whisper.

"They got gunboats that Ladd's Kiley seen big as reg'lar steamers. Cannons on em to blow up the whole bilin'."

Lat'more turns around on them, punches Uncle Tobe in the back with his rifle butt. It is all very clear and very slow. Ki is standing to one side of Lat'more, and he just grabs out and gets the rifle barrel in one hand and pulls it back hard, then gathers his legs and drives forward and Lat'more goes ass-flat into the mud. Lat'more grabs once for Ki's leg and looks up. Tobe steps up with his shovel and drives it spade-point into Driver's neck and Lat'more yells and they all swing on.

They move down through the quarters and by a field where hands are working. Overseer there sees them coming, sits his horse just calm, then turns and rides off. When he gets to the road, he turns and heads after the long-gone cavalrymen.

Mr. Hewson is just having a bite of something in the kitchen, with Aunt Jen mixing something in a bowl behind him. Cornbread. Hewson is lost in thought: *Should he run, or stay; maybe go talk to the Yankee General and see what could be arranged?* His son is in Confederate service, but that's in Mississippi. Maybe he would be able to—

There is Cato standing in front of him with the rifle. Some problem with the Overseer. "Yes, Cato, what—"

Pulls the trigger, and the bullet socks Hewson in the gut and knocks him back on his tail into his chair and back over. He lies there with a quizzical look on his face and his feet up in the air. The half-chewed ball of bread is in his open mouth: *Fed him on judgment.*

HEADQUARTERS ARMY OF THE POTOMAC
June 27, 1864—7 A.M.

Lieutenant-General GRANT:

Nothing important occurred yesterday in the lines of this army. A working party of the Ninth Corps were annoyed during the night by frequent discharges of artillery and infantry. No casualties reported.

GEO. G. MEADE,
Major-General.

HEADQUARTERS ARMY OF THE POTOMAC
June 27, 1864—2:15 P.M.

Major-General BURNSIDE,
Commanding Ninth Corps:

The major-general commanding directs me to say that if you desire to relieve any brigade now in the trenches on your front by the colored brigade on the left you can do so, sending the relieved brigade to the trenches commanded by General White, in lieu of the black brigade.

A. A. HUMPHREYS,
Major-General and Chief of Staff.

June 27, 7:00 P.M. IX Corps Front

The First Brigade, Fourth Division, marched from its bivouac to the head of the covered way leading forward to the lines, with the Forty-third Regiment in front. As they marched up they saw Colonel Oliver conferring with a group of officers, and he motioned the commander of the Forty-third to form his men in single file. Two files of soldiers would move through the covered way in opposite directions, till the relief was accomplished: a line of black soldiers and a line of white, moving side by side in opposite directions.

The covered way was a narrow trench, cut deeply into the undulating ground, zigzagging to take advantage of every angle that could provide concealment from the enemy. At vulnerable points it had been shielded by heavy sandbagging, and sometimes had been roofed over and bombproofed. But it was "covered" not in the sense of roofed-over, but in its promise of absolute shelter from enemy observation and fire.

Major Booker walking at the head of his file was dreading the meeting in that narrow canyon. At best there would be words passed that as an officer he ought not tolerate, but that as a practical man he could do absolutely nothing about. His men might be hurt in their feelings or pride, and also in their trust of him. Still, he would just have to face it through. If an exchange of words could alter their trust in him, he must not be very trustworthy, or they must be unconscionable fickle and stupid in their understanding of him. He hoped neither was the case. Still, the dread was there, as the first white face emerged around a corner of the trench.

"Well, well," said a wry-faced sergeant. "What's this? Looks like new blood, new blood. Well, good hunting to you, *sir!*"

"O Jesus, boys, look at the uniforms! Fresh fish for sure, fresh fish!" (It was the veterans' term for new troops).

"Phew!" called another, holding his nose. "Damn me if it isn't smoked herring. And pretty damn high at that."

"Excuse me there, General, but your division is a mighty dirty looking bunch."

"Move along there."

"Didn't know better I'd say they's niggers, but they don't let niggers in the Army of the Potomac."

"Oh no, boys it's them famous coal miners you've heard tell of."

"Move along there."

Booker, half turned, saw a white soldier "slip" and throw a hard shoulder-block into his color-bearer, Corporal Colehill, knocking the thin black man back against the trench. The white man grabbed the flagstaff.

"Hey, Jesus, Privit Boyd captures flag! Notify the"—when suddenly Randolph grabbed the man's collar, jerking him back and down, and everyone in that angle of the trench stepped back sudden, and there was a swinging of rifles that nobody could get up or around in that narrow space, and there were Booker and Randolph with their Colt pistols out.

There was a white Captain too, sputtering, "Dammit, can't you keep these savages of yours in line? Your corporal struck my man!"

Booker rounded on the man. "Your man struck mine first. I saw it myself. If you can't keep this gutter trash you command in line, I'll have you before a court-martial—*Captain!*"

From around a corner of the trench came the call of "Nigger lover." It was the necessary, the obligatory element. *Everything is fine*, thought Booker, *everything is as it should be. Nobody gets killed just yet.*

"Yes, Major," said the Captain. He wouldn't apologize. Booker wouldn't risk a brawl by pressing it. He stared at the man till he saluted.

"Move out, Captain," said Booker. The lines shuffled along once more.

When they got up to the front line, Booker sent his men down into the forward trench. He stopped Randolph. "Sergeant, you'll take your squad out on picket for the first watch as soon as the pickets we are relieving come in. Do it quickly, keep everyone low down. The approach trenches might be pretty shallow, and you can't tell if the rebels can see us. Staff officer says the rebel trenches are higher up than ours, over by the left. They can see down our backs. If they spot anything moving we'll have artillery down here."

"Yes, sir." Sergeant Randolph looked around, stepped up onto the firing step, and turned towards the front. The firing slit was a good six inches above his head. He looked around, and motioned to Corporal Brown, tallest man in the company. Brown stepped up. The firing slit was barely level with his eyes. There was no chance of firing a rifle out of it, unless you were seven feet tall, or stood on a stool, or sat piggyback on someone's shoulders. Randolph walked a ways down the trench: the firing slits were all at the same height. He turned and looked at Booker, and shook his head, grinning.

"Damn tall outfit, was here before."

The white pickets came into the trench in a tumbling rush, looked around surprised at the black faces, then, led by their sergeant, pushed past and down towards the covered way. Booker held the sergeant a moment. "What regiment is this, Sergeant?"

"Sir, Fourteenth New York Heavy Artillery."

"Thank you, Sergeant." The white pickets continued on towards the covered way. Before they were out of earshot Randolph said, "Damn gun-shy outfit if you ask me."

The laughter exploded all along the line of the regiment like a train of powder going off, and the white pickets moved through it towards their retreating comrades.

June 27, Evening. Bivouac of the 14th New York Heavy Artillery.
  First (Ledlie's) Division, IX Corps

Sergeant Stanley did not like the look of the replacements that the Dutch Major (or whatever he was) and his company of mokes had delivered last week. There was in particular one redheaded customer with

Erin go bragh swashed across his mug and that sock-me-jaw look these gutter Irish liked to put on. Nearly four days of trench duty and fatigue, and still it sat there. Sergeant was Irish himself; but he wasn't gutter trash.

He'd have run the man out of the regiment if he had had him back in the good days, when the Fourteenth Heavies were still part of the Washington garrison, tending the big guns in the forts there and seeing to the readiness and fine appearance of their accoutrements. A buffing wheel they'd had, for their buckles, boots, and gun stocks! And here not a set of clean linen in the whole regiment. The crossed cannons of the regimental insignia were a mockery. Cannon fodder they were, not cannoneers, and no wonder they were being shipped the scourings and the scraps. In a pinch the field artillery would fire a keg of nails or old tin, and were they any different now? He must make any garbage at all serve his turn.

"Attention!" The line of men fidgeted to no purpose, except for two men who snapped into exaggerated Prussian friezes: old soldiers caught in the toils. The sergeant gestured, and two corporals moved in to push the men into proper formation. The Irish mug was grinning at him. "Happy are you, boyo? Ready for the dancing ball? We do a step here called the buck-and-gag, do you know it? Stand to attention, and wipe that smile, or I'll teach you myself."

The Irish private, whose name was Robert Emmett Neill, allowed his grin to fade. For the first time since he'd signed his papers, he felt comfortable in his situation, knew where he was and how to handle himself. He'd been dealing with types like this Sergeant Stanley all his life: his older brother Mike, for one, and the straw bosses in the pits back in Pottsville, and the cop O'Malley who'd leaned all over him back in New York, and finally got him landed here. You were gutter Irish, a no-good tramping drunkard, shame to the house; they were always the sons of the Old Sod, descendants of the Kings of Tyrone, keeping the Island green in memory, and the days when they owned their land in Kerry. And grew the wee small praties, till the praties got so small even an Irish cotter couldn't live on em.

He'd never been in the army before; but if all the army could throw at him was Sergeant Stanley, he'd mostly get by.

ROBERT EMMETT NEIL

A red-faced, long-headed man, with thin red hair lying close along the skull, and big, beat-up looking hands: twenty-year-old face, forty-year-old hands, heavy, with heavy wrinkles of flesh at the knuckles.

His old man worked down in the coal pits at Pottsville, and took his older brothers down there with him. They'd work, sometimes in ice-cold water that would fill up in their end of the shaft, day by day, till they'd have to stop working and pump it out, losing the wages while the pump sucked up the black water and when they could work the rock-face standing there till their legs felt like stumps; and their pants, when they hit the cold air, felt like they were made of iron plate, frozen. And would stop for a warm-me-up at the saloon on the way home. Weary old black-faced man, with the smell of coal and sick-sweet whiskey.

Dig yourself a grave, old man, just leave me out of it.

"You'll come down into the pits with us when it's your time, boy. You'll do your part, or so help me you'll not eat."

Or: "If I'll get my hands on you, boy, by God you'll feel it. By Jesus, you will! I'll have your hide, you redhaired bastard."

Mother: "Now Michael. Now Michael." Wringing her hands. The house smells of coal and cabbage, and small potatoes.

At fourteen he goes into the pits, hauling out the coal his father and brothers hack out. "Watch what our brothers do. Be like them. Learn how to do what they do. Soon as one dies or gets married, you'll have to step in."

Will you have another little bugger on the way to take my place, Dad?

The straw boss looks down his face. "You, Neill. How many times have you been told to do the timbering right before you undercut the bank? You'll be docked for it next week, I promise you, if it's not done."

Unless the roof falls on your head first, you dirty Mick.

Smile at him, Dad. Or why don't you tell him that you'll have his hide, the black-haired Scotch bastard. You're a hard man for sure, Dad.

It's better drinking at Kerrigan's with the boys, planning ways to get out, talking politics.

"Well boys, there's an end of Stevie Douglas by the look of things, and it's Honest Abe for sure."

"Yes, and freedom for the naygurs."

"Well, it's serious stuff, you know." Everybody listens to McCarthy: the rumor says he's a Molly Maguire, and beat up the mine super at Mauch Chunk. "I've heard some say that there's devil a naygur will be freed while the Irishman can vote. But you know and I know that money talks, and not with the brogue neither. Ever think what would happen if they could get naygurs to do coal mining?"

"Yah, Mac—but they'd be losing them in the pits unless they could paint em white, or keep em laughing."

"Well, laugh about it, sure. But the only one on God's earth will take less pay for work than an Irishman is a black naygur and you see if that don't mean something when it's time to talk about the cost of bread and the price of coal with Mister Himself."

He broods about it. It's true. Every Irishman knows it, though he talks about being in the line of Kings: Mr. Naygurlips Naygur is worth two thousand, cash, any time, and his keep and the keep of all his little pickaninnies and coons; but when the day came and the wee small praties wouldn't grow, the Irish weren't even worth the slaving. It was cheaper to let them all die.

McCarthy knew that. McCarthy was worth some respect, he was a man that could look ahead. When the war came, the recruiters came into the fields; and some of the boys went, but McCarthy says, "Let the fools fight to free the naygur so he can take their work. Meanwhile, boys, there's a war on I hear; and there may be some money, at last, to be made in coal."

But the government needed cash and needed coal, and the mine owners got a ruling: no strikes for pay while there's a war on. No work unless you sign the contract, boys; and the contract sets the wage low, while the price of bread goes up whenever the rebs win a skirmish (and they always win!) and cotton cloth is not to be had (mend and fend). And then the government ran out of soldiers, too, and sent the press gang, the conscription into the coal fields.

"Boys," says McCarthy, "it's the hour to strike and be damned. They've had our sweat; they've took our wage, and bumped the price of coal so high we can't buy any; and now they've come for our blood itself."

The conscription office in Pottsville burned; and two officials were assassinated one dark night in December 1862.

Robert Emmett Neill came home in the dark morning, threw some extra clothes into a blanket, rolled the blanket. The Old Man was up already by the pump, wheezing where the cold air was hurting the lungs that were all raw from black coal dust. He hawked and spit black onto the ground. Robert Emmett pushed right past him, without a word, as if the man was invisible, a ghost. He was.

He came into New York on a hay scow from the Jersey shore, and went to the saloon in Five Points McCarthy had told him of. It was in the cellar of a three-story brick tenement, damp and dark and fusty with sawdust, lathered over with the smell of thin beer and sharp whiskey. He gave the owners a token from McCarthy, and was introduced to the "bhoys," as they liked to call themselves. It was all right. In the evening the place filled up with the men from the fire brigade station, and then there were lively times: stories told of great blazes in merchants' warehouses, and the pickings a smart man might find; of fine ladies rushing in night-dress or Eve's garment from burning homes into the arms of the stalwart boys of the brigade for rescue. It would be fine to be on the brigade; but you'd need a pull with the ward boss. *See what I can do for you, Emmett; after what you did for the cause.*

There was no work to be had. The Irish were not well liked: they were disaffected, cheered rebel victories and cursed Black Republicans, supported the disloyalist Democratic mayor of the city, and needed to be taught a lesson. "No Irish Need Apply" was the word on all signposts: let them enlist in the army if they lacked for bread. Robert Emmett Neill walked the streets, finding no work. Even hod-carrying was hard to find. On Second Avenue the new sewer line was being dug by a gang of niggers under a German straw boss.

O'Malley the cop would come into the saloon, where Neill slept and paid his way by sweeping up. He was the little king of Five Points, O'Malley, with his big clubstick and brass buttons. He knew all the rackets that were going, and for consideration—in money, in kind, and in respect—he allowed them franchise to operate. Sometimes he would collar somebody, or break up a fencing ring, or run a gambler out—sometimes because he had orders, sometimes because he had a whim and was feeling his strength. Robert Emmett Neill hated him by definition. O'Malley recognized the look, and would smile coolly at Emmett. *I see you boy, I've got my eye on you boy. Do something. Please. Don't let me get impatient, laddy.*

There was a man named Fino Reilley—he favored a Spanish brandy of that name, served to him special at his table in the saloon. And Fino Reilley was a coming man, often working on special projects for a group of the ward leaders that met in the firehouse. He "had a pull" that went pretty high in the city. O'Malley the cop had it in for him, because his "pull" covered O'Malley's graft, and the cop couldn't touch him but O'Malley waited and watched his chance. The Republicans were the boys, and maybe they'd be needing some help among the Irish; maybe they'd like O'Malley if he landed them a big fish. And Reilley had his weaknesses: small, quick-moving men would come to him with small parcels, pick up cash money and deposit the parcels in a back room, leave by the rear door.

Robert Emmett came in from the wet cold one day in late October, and looked at Mr. Fino Reilley, and came to a decision, and went up to him and asked if he could use a good man. Fino looked him up and down. "Some of the boys are thinking of attending the Republican rally in front of the Union next Tuesday. Why not make one with us, and we'll see how you do."

On Tuesday Robert Emmett egged a Protestant preacher who talked through his nose like a Yankee about freeing the niggers. And when some Republican Wide-awakes came after the bhoys with their bats there was a quick scuffle, Robert Emmett got to whack a few heads before they pushed off down an alley. Next day he walked up to Fino, who put him on to something good for that night: Robert Emmett stood in the cold, shaking with the wet and with wrung-up nerves while four men were peeling Sullivan's jewelry emporium on Broadway. (*Sullivan's probably an Orangeman.*)

Fino paid him ten dollars in greenbacks, and introduced him to the firehouse gang when they came by. They all knew Robert Emmett from his sweeping-up days; but Fino was introducing a new man to them. He was to be one of the bhoys now.

That night a bunch went up to niggertown to stick some black pig. Robert Emmett went along. His nerves were strung tight as fiddlestrings; he felt his flesh shake like a dog's coming out of cold water. At the house a black moon-face opened the door, his smiling mouth had more teeth than a shark's and they seemed to gleam. There were cribs off a central room with whiskey bottles and a piano in it. Behind one of those doors was a woman with skin like an animal's and big square teeth like the moon-face man. He was supposed to stick her; she would muffle him all up to her in her arms and down under her belly.

He knew, very suddenly, that his cash wouldn't carry him into that room and out again as he'd gone in.

He thought he might wait till he tried that. But the men were laughing and joking, and he'd his new life to make with them: so he bought a round of whiskey, and another. Then said to Barney, who was the man drove the horse team on the big boiler engine, "I'll drink with you glass for glass: a man from Sligo beats the Dublin drayman every time."

He got drunk: too drunk to notice whether he'd gotten laid or not (he hadn't) ; not so drunk he couldn't stagger home with the bhoys. And he still had three dollars rolled up with string around his ankle.

Things went on like that. He slept warmer through this winter than the one before, wrapped in a shoddy-blanket on his cot. There was still no work to be had, so he stayed on with Fino. Every so often O'Malley would come in, and notice Robert Emmett drinking with the bhoys and looking all right if not exactly well set up. And he'd tip him a wink to say, *My eye on you, laddy.*

Robert Emmett was still waiting his chance for a job with the fire company. He'd hang about Fino listening to talk of Ireland, and the English, and the Famine, and '48, and '98 (For the French are on the sea, says the Shan Van Voght) ; talk of the next election, and of the war.

"I read in the papers that the Irish Brigade came within the devil's own chance of taking the middle of the whole rebel line at Fredericksburg. And would have done, if they'd been supported as they should. Oh yes, it's the Irish every time, if you want the downright fighters."

"It was a Yankee brigade that was supposed to move up to the support you know. And the Colonel of the brigade, brave Tom Meagher, comes up to the Protestant commandant, saying 'For the love of Christ come on ; they're murthering my boys, but we'll take all hell if you'll come on !' And what do ye think the Yankee tells him ?"

In chorus : "NO IRISH NEED APPLY." Laughter all around.

"Well, here's confusion to the damnyankees, however."

Fino looked about him, mock-angry—maybe not altogether mock: "Now isn't that the Irishman in politics every time. First he hurrahs for the Irish Brigade ; takes a drink ; and the next breath he's cursing the damnyankees and cheering every time the rebels beat. You know, there was an Irishman once in the Roman Empire, that was in the Emperor's guards when they were throwing the Christian disciples to the lions. And this Irishman enjoyed the show so much he'd sit there yelling, 'Go lions.' Then, when the lions would get the upper hand, 'Go Christians.' And here you sit crying, 'The Irish Brigade for ever, and hurrah for Robert E. Lee !' "

One day in July the head of the fire company called to Robert Emmett as he was coming down the street to the saloon. The boys were all moving out together : "They're starting the conscription today, over in Jones Street. The bhoys are going to serve some papers on them ; the mayor says it's not legal."

"Then the police'll not be in it ?"

"Well, lad, they say not. But what's that anyway, even if they are ?"

Right.

He follows the fire brigade. The street outside the hall is full of people, but they part to let the fire-bhoys through, and give them a rouse.

"They've drafted my Billy," yells an old woman. "For the love of God, boys, don't let em !"

"Burn em out, boys. Run em uptown and let em draft the niggers."

"Burn em out, and let's us go draft some niggers."

There are men in work clothes, and some in old army blue in the crowd; and one man has a green flag and an empty sleeve, and hurrahs for the New York militia and the Irish Brigade.

Fire axes splinter the door. Inside he sees the big drum full of names, white-faced bluebellies looking up from it as the door splinters; turning for the rear as he is swept in on a wave of people that presses his arms to his side so he can't move. Then the room is full of men ripping down hangings and smashing furniture, using the drum to kindle fires. The bluebellies are gone, pulverised to invisibility by the crowd. People are pouring out of the dusty brick house-fronts, shinning down the vertical posts of the three-tiered ramshackle porches. They just keep pouring and pouring out. He had never imagined so many people had been living in the houses all at once. They pulse out like blood from an artery, water from a squeezed sponge, ants from a hill, bees from a hive. They shift and surge uptown like a river. A man comes bursting out of the door so hard and fast the top hinges spring out of the wood and the door hangs cockeyed.

"Be damned to the thing anyway," yells the man, and he rips the rest of it down, lays it on his step and stamps it into boards. Men watch him wreck his door and seize the pieces to brandish as clubs. It is the most shocking thing yet: the door doesn't matter because the man is never going back inside. They are all leaving. They are going to die, or live, or they are going far away.

Through the sea the fire company comes moving like a tugboat through the flood, and Robert Emmett attaches himself to it. Suddenly there are shouts, a twitch or eddy in the crowd, and the company jumps forward. They are facing a brick wall, at the foot of which there is a nigger crouching. His eyes are wide-staring, and he is babbling something, pleading. Begging. It is the most ugly, insulting thing to see the nigger whining for his life in the midst of that powerful crowd.

Robert Emmett looks in the man's face, and feels the blood twist in him as it had the night in nigger-town.

His body galvanizes, he shouts something, throws something at the nigger groveling on the ground there. It seems as if he has thrown the whole crowd on him, because they suddenly surge down and in on the man, and Robert Emmett is pushed back and the nigger vanishes behind a wall of bodies, screaming.

The crowd moves down the street like any army. Windows begin to go smash.

There are shots in the next street. Were the cops coming on? The militia? He thinks of the nigger's face.

Someone says, *They've burnt the nigger Orphan Asylum.*

Good thing. Nits make lice.

"If it's the cops shooting, then it'll be militia next. Let's get ourselves some guns, boys, and give em the old Irish Brigade for good and all!"

There is a tall man, a stranger, standing with the Captain of the fire company. "The lad's right, Dougherty," he said—speaking like an educated man, not Irish, or New York, either—"Why not try for the Arsenal?"

They move out, purposeful now, quieter, heading for the Arsenal. "Who's the tall buck with Dougherty?"

Wink: "Ah, him. That's Mr. Smith, a traveling man for the firm of Davis and Lee—the cotton business, Richmond, Virginia—Secret Service, lad. I tell you, there's big things to happen here today."

Wink's as good as a nod: here's the rebel army in New York, and the French are on the sea for a truth.

Two days later Robert Emmett is looking down the barrel of his musket at a street littered with broken wagons and a sleet of broken glass, with paper trash blowing through it like dirty snow. A barricade of broken wagons and crates straggles across the street, and behind it Robert Emmett and some of the boys are lying about on sentry duty. There's yelling from the next block, but everybody stays put. They're all dead tired. Up the street a man is staggering, carrying a barrel of something. He's weaving with the weight of it on his shoulder. Emmett thinks, *If he gets here, and if it's whiskey, we'll charge him toll for that freight, and lighten the burden.* From a lamppost halfway down the street the body of a nigger shoemaker is hanging by the neck. Some boys are swinging from his feet. The neck is stretched out too long. *Like taffy.* A bunch of women stand around on the other side of the street, jabbering, looking up when the gunfire rattles. One of them yells at the boys.

A man comes running around the corner, and then there's a mob of them, and they spin toward the barricade, running hard, and come pushing and bulling through it. The man with the keg is spun round, drops it; it bursts like a bomb: flour.

"Jesus Christ, it's the army!" Emmett, rising up from the lee of the barricade, sees the blue coats coming round the corner, trotting in line with bayonets out. Mr. Smith is right by him: "We'll cover the retreat from here. Wait till the people clear and—"

Before he finishes the line halts, snaps to, and a riffle of fire shoots down from end to end, and there's that whining overhead and bits of wood jumping like bedbugs out of the barricade. Before he runs he sees the nigger swinging, and a couple of small bodies lying around below it.

The police were combing out the city, looking for reb agents, looters. They'd take whatever they could catch, they had reputations to remake. The Irish cops had to redeem their standing with the Protestants. The air stank of wet charring wood and brick dust, and every now and then the metallic reek of blood, or the rotten stink of a corpse left lying about. The fire companies were back on the job.

Fino Reilley was not in evidence. O'Malley the cop had been to the saloon looking for Robert Emmett. He kept on the dodge for the rest of the summer, into the fall. There was still no work. He was not to come round the firehouse till things cooled down: "Someone's informed on you, Bobby, that you robbed Sullivan's store, and murdered Mrs. Riordan, the pawnbroker's wife."

There was one good way out of town, and one only for Robert Emmett Neill, because he had to get out ahead of O'Malley. There was a substitute broker working out of a saloon a few blocks north: he needed to get into the army fast, and without having to account for himself or give his name. As he shifted over the back fences he caught a glimpse of the fire company: Dougherty was giving the orders, and they were pulling down a tottering tenement building frame with long hooks, the hose standing by in case of live embers. O'Malley the cop stood by, watching.

He enlisted on April 15, 1864, as Emmett Roberts, substituting for a Mr. Edward Tate, a businessman from Brooklyn, who paid the broker $1,000 for his finder's fee. Robert Emmett got small change, and orders to join the Fourteenth N.Y. Heavy Artillery, serving as infantry with IX Corps in Virginia. There was a wait in a jail near the docks; then another wait on the steamboat. All the while the bounty-jumpers in the crowd were watching their chances; and meanwhile, they laughed at Neill for missing the bounties. When the ship touched at land on the Jersey coast to pick up another consignment of cannon fodder, he tried to desert to redeem his manhood; this time he'd find himself a bounty regiment, now he was out of the city. But the corporal of the Invalid Corps guard was too smart, and he had the drop on them when they came up to the rail to jump. So he spent the rest of the trip down in the wet, stinking hold, chained up; but even so was luckier than the three men the corporal had his men shoot in the water, calling the shots as he hung by his one arm from a ratline.

So now he was in platoon with Sergeant Stanley of the Fighting Fourteenth New York Heavyweights. Stanley didn't like him, but that was to be expected. He could handle himself. He could watch out for number one. He'd not put himself where Stanley could come down on him. In fact, he was thinking of being the model soldier-boy for the while, the steadfast tin soldier indeed.

Though he'd not get killed doing it.

There were work details in plenty off the line. And back of the army were the piney woods.

"Yes sir, Sergeant Stanley, sir."

> HEADQUARTERS NINTH ARMY CORPS
> *June 28, 1864.*

Major-General HUMPHREYS, Chief of Staff:
> It was unusually quiet during the night. The enemy opened upon us with a mortar battery early this morning. Shells have dropped in our line, but as yet without damage. The mining operations are progressing well—140 feet of gallery has been made.

> A. E. BURNSIDE,
> *Major-General.*

9:00 A.M. *48th Pennsylvania*

Doyle and Corrigan began their shifts in the Mine at nine o'clock. Working with them this morning was Private Dorn—a nonminer who'd just be passing the dirt back from the front of the mine to the men who'd cart it off. Lieutenant Douty, his face still puffy from a bad night's sleep—interrupted by rebel shelling—was tending the fire that kept the air circulating. Doyle looked at him somewhat sourly as he stripped his shirt—he didn't want the Lieutenant falling asleep on them, but didn't know whether he ought to say something. Lieutenants were a touchy lot of bastards. The Lieutenant stretched and strained his flesh, and blew a large fart.

"There's the bell, bucko," said Doyle. "Our shift, and down you go."

They went into the hole at the crouch. There was a five-foot clearance, floor to ceiling, and the tunnel was four feet wide at the bottom, tapering slightly to three feet at the top. Ample space, compared with some of the seams they'd worked for coal; but still close enough. Even without the burning up of the air that would come as they worked, the sense of the earth made the air feel close, breathing constricted, movement constricted: you swung your pick or moved your shovel in short arcs, there were walls all around you at every hand.

The timbering was good enough, and that was reassuring in this sand-clay soil they were working—damn brittle, crumbly stuff. *The fact is,* Doyle thought, *if we run out of timber this boy isn't going to be working down here. I'm not trusting packing crates and crackerboxes down here—not for these wages, when I get paid the same standing in the open air and picking my nose.*

Corrigan liked the Mine. He felt the idea had, partly anyway, been his own. Doyle had really come in after he'd spoken up, and usually it was the other way round. Doyle was two years older than Corrigan, and married. Corrigan had tagged along after Doyle, admiring the way he handled himself, first in the mines, then later in the army. He expected that Doyle, the married man, could give him good advice about women too, though he'd never actually brought himself to ask any of the questions that sometimes burdened his consciousness, never quite voiced. Still, he would ask Doyle all about things someday, and stayed close to him, waiting. He was following Doyle's lead now, too: Doyle would pick and he'd shovel, then they'd switch. But still and all, it had been his idea first: maybe Doyle would begin admiring him a little bit now.

The shaft now ran 130 feet into the embankment. Above their heads they could hear the muffled stamping of the pickets when the guard changed or a large party came down the trench. They could hear the men overhead digging the trench-line deeper where the picket was being strengthened. That was strange too, for men used to deep mining, being so close to the surface. Somehow it made one more conscious of the earth overhead, the distance to sunlight, although that distance was less here than where they dug for coal.

Corrigan tapped Doyle on the right buttock, and whispered hoarsely, "We'll have to remember, when we get close to the rebs: if we can hear what's going on up there, they may be able to hear us."

"What are you whispering for? We haven't got any part of the way there yet."

Doyle lit the stump of a tallow candle that had been stuck onto the peak of his forage cap. Its fitful light made the blackness dance about the walls of the pit as he began to work in short, chopping strokes, his back hunched just slightly, because of the low clearance. *It was a damnable height for a ceiling*, Doyle thought, *just high enough to make you think you can stand like a man, and low enough to make you twist and hunch that little much that breaks your fucking back.* He dropped to one knee and began to pick at the section of wall in front of him. Behind him, Corrigan scraped the loose dirt onto his short-handled shovel, and dumped it in a crackerbox. Dorn, on the other end of the rope, hauled the full box out. Back in the trench behind them the dirt would be transferred to the wheeled-crackerbox dollies Doyle had rigged up, and hauled down the winding trench to a place out of the rebel view where it could be dumped. Taffy Rees had been worrying about the dumping. If the rebs noticed the loose dirt, they'd get suspicious and break hell loose. But the sandbags they'd been sent from City Point were nine-tenths of them rotten. So they'd been dumping the dirt and covering it with cut brush.

Doyle worked steadily, without speaking. As he worked the close air of the tunnel heated up, till he felt he was baking in a clay oven, and the air was filled with particles of sand and dust he and Corrigan stirred up. The dry dust settled in his nostrils, and rasped his eyes raw. His sweaty skin took a coating of dust out of the air. At first, he'd try to wait for the dust to settle; but no position was comfortable, the air was getting foul, it all made him impatient to do the work and be done—so he would start to work again, quickly, and the air filled with dust, and he grew warmer. There was some kind of stink or gas that came out of the ground, made him feel slightly dizzy and nauseated. Gradually he felt the muscles in his arms and shoulders knot and congeal. When he felt their spring was gone entirely he grunted, "Time!" and passed the pick to Corrigan, and Corrigan picked while Doyle shoveled, and Dorn hauled the boxes of dirt back to the trench, and the other men trundled their barrows to the back of the traverse, where Rees had said to dump it.

Corrigan had worked himself nearly to the point of his muscles giving out, and had stopped for a minute, leaning his weight against one hand held to the rough cross-timber that held the roof of earth off them, when he felt the timber jar.

His heart bumped and the sound—*Ump!*—came to them through the earth and Corrigan felt the panic shoot through him. He and Doyle stumbled back through drifting dust and the *ump! ump!* sound, till they broke strangling out of the hole into the light, the trench.

They could hear the whistle and *wham!* of rebel shells hitting and that flat bang of their own artillery replying. Their eyes were blind, streaming with tears from dust and fear.

Rees was there, suddenly. "You men all right? You all right there?" Then: "How's the tunnel? Did the timbers hold?"

"You goddamn Welsh Taffy bastard," yelled Doyle, "you and your fucking timbers! We're nearly buried alive and all you care about is your fucking timbers! Jesus!"

Rees sat back for a minute. Then he grinned. "Well, you're all right I guess, from the sound of you."

"Yeah," said Doyle, calmer now, wiping his eyes. "And your precious timbering held up beautiful. I'll always have a due and reverent appreciation for good timbering as long as I live."

"What happened?" asked Corrigan.

"A little artillery is all," said Rees. "The rebels noticed the work on the picket line, I think, and decided to stir up the ants and see what came out."

The shelling had stopped. At a distance they could hear someone yelling, a thin reiterative call. The words were unintelligible. Wounded? Just cussing?

"Well," said Doyle, "let's go back in and finish the shift."

Rees looked at his watch. "Never mind. You'd have been off in a quarter-hour anyway."

The two looked at Rees in amazement. War was certainly different from mining, even when you were mining; and a good sergeant wasn't necessarily the same thing as a good straw boss.

"Well bless my soul," said Doyle, "I never noticed."

"Ah yes," said Corrigan, "time does pass when you're enjoying yourself."

HEADQUARTERS NINTH ARMY CORPS,
June 28, 1864, 11:15 A.M.

General HUMPHREYS, Chief of Staff:

The firing commenced on our left, and was evidently brought about by the noise of our working parties attracting the enemy's attention. No ground has been lost. All is now comparatively quiet, and the work will go on. The object of the work is to so strengthen the skirmish line as to really become the main line. The telegraph has been out of order; otherwise we should have reported earlier.

A. E. BURNSIDE,
Major-General.

HEADQUARTERS NINTH ARMY CORPS,
June 28, 1864—7:45 P.M.

General POTTER:

The general commanding understood from you and Colonel Pleasants this morning that the gallery was extended 140 feet, and so reported it to headquarters. Major Cutting understood this afternoon that it was 130 feet at the time he was there. Will you be good enough to send word to the general how the matter now stands.

Very respectfully, your obedient servant,
J. L. VAN BUREN,
Major and Aide-de-Camp.

HEADQUARTERS SECOND DIVISION, NINTH ARMY CORPS,
June 28, 1864—8:00 P.M.

Maj. J. L. VAN BUREN, Aide-de-Camp:

Sir: Colonel Pleasants reports that the gallery was 130 feet at 12 M. to-day by measurement. It was reported to me to be 130 feet about 9:30 A.M. this morning. That was, however, only estimated. The gallery was run fifty feet the first day, and forty feet each day since, which rate of progress Colonel Pleasants thinks he will be able to maintain.

Very respectfully, your obedient servant,
ROBERT B. POTTER,
Brigadier General.

HEADQUARTERS ARMY OF THE POTOMAC
June 30, 1864

General BURNSIDE:

Five tons of blasting powder and 1,000 yards of safety fuse ordered last night.

HENRY J. HUNT,
Brigadier-General and Chief of Artillery.

July 1, 8:30 A.M. *The Mine*

Colonel Pleasants was having breakfast in the bombproof shelter just off the covered way. The earth- and log-covered shelter was still cool from the night air, slightly damp and smelling of earth and mildew; but behind the screen of moisture he could sense the heat building. Another scorcher. Captain Brooks came in, looking beat-tired, slumped onto the stool opposite Pleasants, and poured himself a mug of coffee from the battered pot. "Morning. Colonel."

"Anything doing?"

"Nothing much. They were shelling over on the right this morning. Rebels saw something over by Butler's and tried to shoot it up a little."

"Um." Colonel Pleasants had no real interest in routine shelling on a front not his own. Through three years of fighting he had developed the soldier's knack of hearing only what it was useful for him to hear. He could sleep soundly through the biggest bombardment the rebels could muster, so long as the shells were not coming in on his own front; but the dropping of a single shell in the sacred circle covered by his secret attentiveness, or a rattle of musketry, however faint, would bring him stark awake in an instant. Such sounds were meant for him.

Brooks reached into the pocket of his infantryman's shirt and extracted a crumpled note. "This came for you, sir, just as I was coming off duty."

A note from Burnside: the theodolite and transit were waiting for him at headquarters. It was about time. The tunnel was already two hundred feet long and he hadn't been able to take a single good bearing.

Dead reckoning was no way to run a mine shaft. *Dead.* If the engineer planned it wrong, he might be dooming a hundred men to death under the crushing burden of earth.

He'd inspect the Mine, then go on up to headquarters for the instruments.

At the minehead was Rees, standing with the shift just coming off. The diggers held out tin cups, and Rees was pouring their drams of whiskey from a black commissary bottle; it was Pleasants' idea, a fillip for keeping the men happy with the hard work. Rees didn't approve. He came over to sit on an overturned crackerbox next to Pleasants. With a somewhat sour look he proffered the bottle. Pleasants grinned, borrowed a cup, and poured himself a dram. The hot whiskey went through him like a bolt, and he shivered involuntarily. "How are things going, Sergeant?"

"We're two hundred forty, two hundred fifty feet down. Soil is still the same, sand and clay. Little bit moister these last few feet. Sir, we're starving for timber. The soil here is rotten, and if we hit near a spring she'll just dissolve on us. I've used up all the stuff that was cut, all the big pieces from the packing boxes. We're out of lumber as of noon today."

Another problem. Pleasants had ordered more lumber to be brought up from the rear. It should have been at headquarters yesterday. It hadn't been. "All right, Sergeant, I'll look into it when I go up to headquarters today."

"Yes, sir."

Pleasants stared into his cup, and swirled the brown liquid about. He thought of asking Rees's advice on how he might get out in front for his sighting without getting shot. Then he thought better of it. His business. You don't let the hands think they have a say in what is none of their concern.

The hot heavy air was like a blanket, muffling everything. There was no sound of bird or insect. In the quiet the whispering of the fire-keeper and the dirt haulers at the minehead sounded clear. Then a garble of sound came from the shaft, and they all shut still. Rees and Pleasants glanced in each other's eyes.

Then they were up, Rees ducking ahead of the Colonel down into the shaft with a swooping, graceful motion. They could hear a gargled yell, hollow-echoing in the dark close tunnel, then Pleasants cannonned into Rees's back, and Rees was backpedalling, hauling something with his hands as he stooped over, weight dragging on the floor. Pleasants scrunched himself over to the side, then bent and helped Rees haul on one of the diggers' arms. He heard the heavy breathing of the other digger, stumbled when the man pushed against him in haste to get out.

In the sunlight of the trench the wet mud on the diggers told the story before they spoke. "We hit some water, a spring of some kind, or maybe quicksand. I couldn't see it at first, but the shovel felt funny and I look down and there's water seeping up slowly, then like it sprang a leak. Walls just started to melt." The man shivered. "Jesus."

Rees could picture it; staring as he himself had stared at sandy rock when suddenly the wall that looked so solid seems to go all loose, and you know it's all going to slough down at once.

Pleasants grabbed a candle and went quickly into the tunnel. After a minute, making sure the men were all right, Rees went in after the Colonel.

They could smell the wet before they could see it. At the end of the tunnel the walls were all caved, and the ceiling too, the timbers loosened and uprooted for twenty feet till they collapsed in a heap of mud and wreckage. They must have struck a good-sized spring. The two men looked silently, then backed out of the tunnel.

The men outside were waiting silently. They looked at Pleasants when he came out.

"Sergeant Rees, the mining will be suspended until we can bring in some heavy timbers to retain the wall till we get past the spring. I'll want someone that knows what kind of timber we need to go to headquarters with me; and a detail to get the wood, right away."

"Yes, sir."

"Are your men all right?"

"Yes, sir."

"Well then. Sergeant, have your men at my headquarters in twenty minutes."

When they reached Corps headquarters, General Burnside was out, but Parke let them have the box of instruments.

He didn't know anything about the timber Pleasants had requested. Apparently none had been sent.

Pleasants met Sergeant Rees and his detail just outside the headquarters area, and motioned the sergeant aside.

"The timbers haven't come."

Rees said nothing, but his face set.

"Leave two men with me to carry the instruments back to the bomb-proof. Take the rest of your men, and get us the timber. I don't care how you do it, and I don't want to know any more than is good for me. You understand?"

"Yes." Rees was grinning.

"I'll write you a pass," Pleasants dropped to one knee, and began scribbling with his pencil in his notebook, "that will give you roaming commission for three days. Don't take that long unless you have to." Rees took the pass. The Colonel's script was fastidious, and the lines clear and sharp. Colonel Pleasants always had sharpened pencils with him.

Rees was back at nightfall, with good news. They had had what Rees thought of as Sunday School luck, virtue rewarded as the sermon and tract held it should be but as it almost never was. They'd scouted around headquarters, asking around about where the lumber was being stockpiled. A sergeant just in with dispatches from Ferrero's division, out on the flank, said he'd heard something about picketing men in a sawmill. Rees got his men together and went down to investigate. He formed his detail in single file, rifles held in good marching form, and marched them *hup-two* down the road punctiliously saluting everything in shoulder-straps that they passed. In this way he avoided all inquiries, and marched seven miles down the packed white earth of the Old Norfolk Road. The division pickets passed them into the lines, and Rees reported to General Ferrero. The General seemed inordinately pleased to see them, almost as if Rees had been sent as a token of personal affection from the corps commander. He'd sent an officer to show them the mill.

They'd walked through the encampment of the First Brigade, staring about them at niggers in blue uniforms, marching about and imitating soldiers almost to the life.

The sawmill was set in a clearing full of stumps no one had even bothered to remove. Its unpainted boards were weathered silver-gray. An obviously crank steam engine drove the saw; its boiler and pipes were rust-pitted, and the gauges grimed to unreadability. But Rees didn't spend more than a second looking at the engine, because stacked in cords around the millyard were great blocks of cut lumber, sawn into planks and boards of varying lengths and thicknesses still smelling of raw wood. The yellow piles shone in the sun. Golconda. El Dorado. Rees was wealthy beyond his wildest dreams, a Croesus of lumber. And all of it cut for him, and wanting only to be carried off.

And then the Sunday School luck came to him. Out from behind a pile of boards came a detail of black soldiers under a corporal, lugging a stack of cut boards—probably to floor some officer's tent.

Here was Rees looking at God's own quantity of already cut and sized lumber, with an entire brigade of niggers sitting around, waiting to haul it off for him.

HEADQUARTERS SECOND DIVISION, NINTH ARMY CORPS,
Before Petersburg, Va., July 2, 1864

Maj. Gen. JOHN G. PARKE,
Chief of Staff, Ninth Army Corps:
General: Nothing new to report on my front. The miners struck some quicksand yesterday; all the props thereabouts sank through the bottom of the tunnel and a good deal of the top fell in. This will require a more complicated system of propping, but will be remedied to-day. We are in about two hundred and fifty feet.

> Very respectfully, your obedient servant,
> ROBERT B. POTTER,
> *Brigadier-General.*

July 3, 7:00 A.M. *IX Corps front: picket line of the 2nd Division*

The theodolite sent by General Burnside's friend was an old-fashioned one, larger and heavier than the modern equipment Pleasants had been used to as an engineer in private industry. It had the look of a "contraption," with all of the extraneous complexity and cumbersomeness the word implied: a small telescope set into a heavy frame of steel and brass, with wheels to raise and lower the sights, arcs of scored brass to measure angles, three stubby legs to hitch to the tripod that would uphold and anchor it. Colonel Pleasants would never have thought of it as a contraption in the mining business, even allowing for its old-fangled appearance and extra weight. It was an instrument or tool of precision his assistants would carry about and set up for use; he'd stand behind it, sighting carefully on the marking staff and the relevant landmarks, taking careful notes in his precise handwriting, with his sharp pencil. Here and now it was different. He'd have to use it lying down or crouching in a half-trench or picket hole, the tripod legs left off, the thing anchored anyhow on the ground in front of him; and he'd have to hide his head under a burlap sack, too, or run the risk of being potted by a sniper in the trees over behind the rebel lines. He'd chosen the predawn and earliest-morning hours for just that reason: he could take his sighting while the light was still burning into the eyes of the rebs west of him, before it got so high it could glint off the glass lens, the steel, or the brass, and betray him.

Captain Betts from Potter's staff was waiting for him at the head of the communication trench; he'd evidently been there some minutes before the appointed time, and stood bouncing impatiently on his toes. In the gray air of the morning, he looked pale and tense. He grinned at Pleasants, and elegantly bowed him into the communication trench, "After you."

They scuffled, bent over, into the advanced picket post, and two of its three occupants crouched waiting and ready to exchange places with them and return to the main line. In his haste, one of the pickets bumped Pleasants, upsetting his balance so that he nearly dropped the theodolite. The third picket shifted over into one corner. Pleasants moved towards the front of the post, where a natural bulge of the ground had been improved with earth-filled wicker baskets. In the mounded earth atop one of these he set the tripod. Its shadow appeared, spiderlike, as he set it into the little bay that had been scraped for it. The sun was up.

"Ah," said Betts. "Going to be a nice day. Nice day."

Cheerful, fidgety Captain Betts was going to be a damned nuisance and distraction. Pleasants wished he had one of his own assistants here with him.

He worked himself up under the burlap sack, letting it cover his whole upper body and head, as well as the bulky theodolite. Still in the dark of the cloth, he set the instrument firmly into the earth. Then with the fingers of his right hand he eased the cloth slowly back till light peeped under the front; then more slowly still, until he had a clear view. The burlap was stiff enough to keep a projecting curve out beyond the end of the telescope's short barrel. Pleasants would take no chances with stray glints of light. The telescope eye stared at the rebel fort out of a tunnel of burlap. He took his observations, made his notes, quickly and deftly: bearing of the rebel fort from this position; gauged elevation above this position; distance from this position. Later he'd take a second bearing from the other side. Then by triangulating he could compute the actual elevation of the fort above the plane of the tunnel, and fix the bearing of the tunnel so it would end up directly beneath the rebel work.

He stopped looking, wiped his eye with a clean finger. Took a pencil from his pocket and jotted some additional notes: distinctive landmarks, colors of vegetation and ground, so that when he made his second observation his reference points would be—

"How is it coming?" said Betts, stepping up close and speaking just outside the burlap cover.

Pleasants' tongue seemed to catch in a muscular contortion, wrung among annoyance at the interruption, courtesy, and the pure surprise at this abrupt invasion of his intense absorption and concentration . . . bah! What could he say? Betts had been chattering like a damned magpie all morning. Although the sound of it had been blocked somehow while he stared through the glass, now that he was aware of it it seemed that the man's nattering had been going on the whole time, registering and accumulating in his mind. And now, now that he was aware of it he couldn't shut it out.

"I'd make it a hundred yards even, wouldn't you say?"

Pleasants felt like a fool, sitting there with a damned burlap bag over his head while this chatterbox stood outside making small talk.

"Yes, Captain. You'd best stay back, now."

"What?" said Betts. "Oh yes. Quite!" Just as Betts finished and seemed to step back, Pleasants heard a loud complex *crack,* like the sudden kicking-in of a wooden door, and felt a burst of splatter, heavy liquid on the burlap. Clumping sound, something fallen, and Pleasants sensed the scurry-scrabble of the picket across the floor of the trench behind him. "Jesus! He's shot!" Sounds of fumbling. "Right in the side of the head."

Pleasants, still under the burlap, asked, "Is he dead, soldier?"

After a pause, the man answered, "Yup. Goner."

"Stay here," said Pleasants, "till I've finished." He put his eye back to the telescope. It had taken planning and effort to bring himself and his theodolite here, to make these vital calculations. It was important to finish the observation while the light was right. Methodically, Pleasants continued taking his sights, and making his notes. So long as he remained covered by the burlap sacking, he need not consider the death of Captain Betts; it had no importance or even reality.

He completed the work, without further distraction. Still covered by the burlap, he slid the theodolite off its perch and brought it carefully down to the ground. Crouching, he lifted the sacking off his head, and blinked in the hard new light.

Betts was laid out on the floor of the picket post; the soldier had covered his face with a yellow handkerchief and set the man's kepi on top of that. Except for the white hands, the nails with their half-moons of gray dirt, the dead man was anonymous, not even human—a rag doll with a head of cloth.

Pleasants looked at the burlap. It was spotted with drying splotches of black and dabs of mottled moist gray stuff.

It hit Pleasants in a jolt: the loud crack and splatter—it was Captain Betts's blood turning black, and small gobs of his thinking brain. Small electric shocks shot up from the base of Pleasants' spine, shivering him hard and hurtful and uncontrollably, and he gripped himself against it; he had more observations to make, work to do. *That damned chattering magpie,* he thought. His rage returned, and calmed him. It overlaid the strong shivers, oil on troubled waters. *Well, that's shut him up properly.* Pleasants was two people, part of him wondering—hardly daring to wonder—at the anger of the other part, which willed his hands to pick up carefully theodolite, notebook, and burlap; to check the ground to be sure nothing was left; and to leave the picket post with a nod at the soldier, going alone back to the main line, remembering to remind himself to have someone go pick up Captain Betts and return him to headquarters. There was a second observation to be made; he'd do it right now.

While the sun was still in the eyes of the rebel snipers.

GENERAL GRANT'S HEADQUARTERS,
City Point, July 3, 1864—10:30 A.M.

Maj. Gen. George G. MEADE:

Do you think it possible, by a bold and decisive attack, to break through the enemy's center, say in General Warren's front somewhere? If this is determined we would want full preparations made in advance so there should be no balk. Roads would have to be made to bring the troops up rapidly; batteries constructed so as to bring the greatest amount of artillery to bear possible on the points of attack; and all to the right of the attack strengthened to be held by the smallest number of men. I have felt unwilling to give the troops any violent exercise until we get rain to settle the dust, and now, even if we should get rain, all operations except preparations will have to be deferred until the cavalry is again fit for service. I send this to get your views on the subject. If it is not attempted we will have to give you an army sufficient to meet most of Lee's forces and march around Petersburg and come in from above. This probably could not be done before the arrival of the Nineteenth Corps.

U. S. GRANT,
Lieutenant-General.

HEADQUARTERS, ARMY OF THE POTOMAC
July 3, 1864

Lieutenant-General GRANT:

Your dispatch received. Before replying it will be necessary I should see both Warren and Burnside to obtain information. I am now under the impression that the former does not consider an attack in his front practicable, but the latter some days ago was of the opinion that he could, in his front, break through the enemy's line. I will advise you as soon as possible of my views fully.

GEO. G. MEADE,
Major-General, Commanding.

CONFIDENTIAL.   HEADQUARTERS, ARMY OF THE POTOMAC,
July 3, 1864—12 M.

Major-General BURNSIDE:
The lieutenant-general commanding has inquired of me
whether an assault on the enemy's works is practicable and
feasible at any part of the line held by this army. In order to
enable me to reply to this inquiry, I desire at your earliest
convenience your views as to the practicability of an assault
at any point in your front, to be made by the Second and Sixth
Corps in conjunction with yours.
Respectfully,

GEO. G. MEADE,
Major-General.

July 3, noon. Picket line of the 19th U.S.C.T., along Blackwater Creek

Lieutenant Dobbs was resting in the shade of a pine tree. The men
of his company were posted at intervals through the woods along the
creekside, in groups of two and three, one man in each group keeping
his eyes peeled for any movement in the fields and open woods across
the creek. His men were well-posted, noncoms spotted to keep them
alert, but Dobbs was convinced there would be no action today. Dobbs
was convinced that the very fact that his Negro troops had been assigned to picket this empty stretch of woods was a guarantee that no
rebel forces were expected this century. Where others might express
bewildered resignation at the seemingly arbitrary and illogical shifts of
position the brigade had been forced to make—on the line and off, left
to Prince George Courthouse, right to Blackwater Bridge, left again out
on the Norfolk road—Dobbs understood perfectly that the commanders
of the army were straining every nerve and brain fiber to find places
where the Fourth Division would never see the enemy. This perception
made Dobbs grin sardonically, in lieu of gnashing his teeth. He was a
man with a grudge, and his commanders seemed bound to frustrate his
settling that grudge, and so became included in it.
Not that Dobbs liked war: he hated it, and hated the army. He was
a man who wanted to kill something, and had made the mistake of
thinking that war was the right way to go about it.
He heard hoofbeats behind him and turned to see Pennington. Chris
was a good kid, but the fact was he liked the idea of the war, and the
army way of going about it—"Onward Christian soldiers, marching as
to war/With the Cross of Jesus, going on before." Dobbs had no truck
with Jesus either—no Jesus and no army. Jesus was the spirit his
mother had called on, in her weakness, when the Old Man had come
swinging round on her to shut her blethering while he walloped little
Lem. He didn't see any use in Jesus.
"Hi-dy, Chris. Set."
"Anything stirring?"
Dobbs grinned at the never-failing eagerness in Chris's perennial
question. "Boy, don't you ever learn? Rebels are so scared of nigger

soldiers they avoid us like leprosy. They're afraid to use us too close to the front for fear we'll scare off all the Johnnies, and it'll take months till we catch em again.''

Chris scowled. ''There's a lot they're afraid of. Afraid they'll find they're no more than even Christian with God's own creatures, instead of the lords of creation.''

''Now Chris, I judge you've been to dinner with Old Doc Oliver. He's the only thing could sour *your* milk.''

It was true: Oliver filled Pennington with a peculiar kind of rage that disturbed his moral direction. He sucked in his lower lip and gnawed it tenderly. Every time he thought of Oliver's patronizing attitude towards his father he felt this rage, and the troubling mixture of dismay that went with it. The fact was that in the Pennington household it was not at all impermissible to contemplate the idea that the Reverend Pennington had not achieved highly or greatly in his calling. His mother's hopes, he knew, had been disappointed. There was his father, a small, round-shouldered man distributing tracts and words of Gospel comfort to the mill-girls at his brother-in-law's Lowell factory, and receiving as often as not some fishwife slanging in return— his dignity was no proof against that. And for Christopher Pennington, his father could never be a match for the high ideal he had chosen. As a boy and as a student at Harvard, he had worshipped the austere Emerson, and the noble and heroic Doctor Howe, who had not only fought by Lord Byron's side for the independence of Greece, but who had been physician, healer, philanthropist—everything that a man should be. And above them all was Colonel Robert Gould Shaw, riding erect with viligant and forward gaze at the head of his regiment of freed Negroes through streets ablaze with bunting and the lavender dresses of girls and women flowering amid the frock coats, singing the song that Dr. Howe's wife had written, ''Mine eyes have seen the glory of the coming of the Lord.'' In his passionate reverie, Pennington had imagined that the climactic words of the hymn were for Shaw himself: ''As He died to make men holy, let us die to make them free. . . .''

Against the mighty shades of Emerson, Howe, and Shaw, what was the Reverend Samuel Pennington?

And that question, evoked most sharply by Oliver, appeared to Pennington now like a kind of treason, a false thread in the noble fabric of his idealism, his worship of the heroic and good.

He preferred to shift the talk away from this feeling. After all, he had disagreements with Oliver that had to do with matters of principle rather than with personal vanity. ''Oliver says they won't fight their old masters. That they follow us just because we're white and their old masters have run off. As if they were sheep. . . .''

Dobbs looked at the younger man mildly, speculatively. ''What do you think, Chris?''

''I think . . . you know what I think. But Oliver has known them a lot longer than I have. What if we're wrong and he's right? I know what I'd like to think.''

''But you figure Oliver 'understands the nigger,' as they say. Listen: nobody understands the nigger. Some times I think there ain't

anything to understand.'' Dobbs looked around, as if his words were
scattering and running away from him. "I don't know how to say it.
Maybe ain't any such thing as a nigger. Listen, I can tell you a story
about it.

"We had a fellow in Kansas somewhat like the Colonel, there. Me
and Booker were captains under him. Kind of a rough-mannered sort of
chap, good friend of Jim Lane's who maybe'd been in the army once,
but then again maybe not. He got command of the battalion, and we
were ordered to take a sweep out along the flank of the army as it was
heading back to camp over on the Kansas side. Now this Major, name
of Harrison, was an orator of sorts, and he had some strong opinions
on 'the nigger.' He had maybe fifty-sixty of them in the battalion, but
he had this way of talking like there wasn't but the one: 'the nigger.'
Seemed like 'the nigger' couldn't be expected to fight, cause he had no
gumption; couldn't be expected to vote, cause wasn't no way to educate
him; couldn't have no farm, cause he wouldn't know asshole from
eyeball on a mule without a white man to tell him all about it. Mostly,
couldn't make a soldier out of him cause everbody knew that the nigger's eyes wasn't up to a white man's for pot-shooting. 'Hey,' I'd tell him,
'you may be right about the nigger, but keep your voice down or he'll
hear you.' 'Oh, no fear of that,' he'd say. 'The nigger is constitutionally
unable to take offense at anything a white man would want to say about
him, and anyway couldn't hardly understand much English.'

"Well, we were out foraging around, on one of these scrubby backwoods plantations they have there, and we're reconnoitering around
in the front yard when all of a sudden, *blam blam blam*, there's bush-
whackers shooting at us from the woods. Well, we all grabbed hats and
guns and what-all, and looked around for a better situation. And after
we'd all found that, we looked around to see where everyone else was.

"I'm lying behind this old wagonbed with this big buck sergeant
named John Coal who'd been with us quite a while, best shot in the
battalion and knew a hell of a lot more about fighting than Harrison. In
fact, if ever there was 'the nigger,' this Johnny Coal was *the* nigger. I
look at him and he's smiling like a gator. I look over the wagon bed and
I see what's so cute: Harrison's lying out there in the middle of the
yard, between us and the woods, hiding behind a broken horse-trough.
'Hey, you men,' he raises up and yells. 'You-all give me some cover
now. Lay it down good.' 'Yassuh, Mist' Harrison!' sings out Johnny
Coal. Harrison waves his hand, and Johnny ducks out around the
wagon-side and gives them a shot. We watch for the smoke, thinking to
shoot when the rebs give their positions away, but Johnny says, 'You lay
quiet, let me handle this.' Harrison waves his hand, Johnny shoots again,
and then Harrison is up and dodging towards us, zig and zag, bobbing
and weaving like a calf trying to shake off a rope, quicker and crazier
than a water skate with a trout after him. And Johnny stands up,
firing and pumping this big Spencer repeater he used, and we're all
watching Harrison coming on: *spang!* and there's dust spitting up
around his ankles and he jumps away; *spang!* and something snatches
his hat; *spang!* and you see something tug him by the coat sleeve; *spang!*
and you see him slap his ear where he's got stung; and then he takes a

flying leap over the wagonbed and lands in a heap. "Goddamn," he yells, "what's the matter with you men? You call that giving cover? Every time you shot at those goddamn rebels you damn near killed *me!*" "Shit, Mist' Harrison," says Johnny, "you lucky the nigger can't shoot, or he'd have gelded you first shot like I had in mind."

Dobbs laughed at his own story. Alone.

Pennington blushed and shook his head, his lips pursed up—a good boy hearing smutty talk; a serious student taking in his tutor's correction, taking it to heart. "I see what you're saying. I shouldn't jump to conclusions. There's a lot more to them than I could know, right *now*. Maybe Oliver's experience, even, hasn't been enuogh, or the right kind. You *have* seen them fight, he hasn't."

Dobbs shook his head. "You don't get it. He *has* seen them fight, only he never knew it. And even if he saw them fight right out on some big battlefield, flags and all, he still wouldn't see it. He couldn't see it. He'd figure out some way that it wasn't so."

Pennington seemed doubtful. "I don't know. Oliver's a smart man, even if he is . . . the way he is." He fell silent, studying it every which way. "You're saying, they will fight. They do fight. You're saying they fight just like white men."

Dobbs threw back his head and laughed. "Jesus, Chris. You're a good kid, you really are. It's just that when you get onto a thing, you can't get off it. Now, just because Johnny Coal didn't like Harrison talking low about him, doesn't mean he's just like me. Hell, he just shot to scare Harrison up some, so he could laugh at him and run him out of the battalion. I'd have shot the son of a bitch stone dead, first crack I got."

"Why didn't you?"

"Because he never insulted me."

"Why didn't Johnny Coal?"

Dobbs looked serious. "Because niggers got a funny sense of humor."

Pennington blushed beet red and he said huskily, "Don't make fun of me, Lem."

Dobbs leaned forward and punched him lightly on the arm. "Ease up, boy. I do it cause I like you." Now Dobbs looked embarrassed. "I'm not making fun of you. There's some things that are just too hard to put in words, explaining like. You've got to see it happen. Best way is not to worry about the nigger at all. Fight your war and let the nigger take care of himself."

The road behind Dobbs's position angled back through the woods towards the rear of the army. Down this road they heard the distinctive thud of hooves and jingle of bits and spurs.

"Cav'ry comin'," called the sentry, and all around Dobbs and Pennington the men rolled off their backs to lie prone looking over their rifles, or scrambled to their feet and dashed at a half-crouch behind their sergeants and corporals to take assigned positions. Dobbs continued to sit under his tree, apparently unconcerned. Pennington noted his coolness, his confidence. He had obviously trained his men well. Everyone seemed to know the right place to be. The entire company was con-

cealed in bushes and behind fallen logs, or in rifle pits dug and placed
with care, and shielded with cut branches. It was, he thought, like seeing
how things were in Kansas, when Old Brown was leading the fight for
the Cause, and Dobbs was an Abolitionist guerilla—"bushwhacker,"
Dobbs would have said, determined to speak as low as he could of the
high and heroic things he had done.

Down the road came a cavalry squad under a sergeant. Blue uniforms. Probably a patrol scouting for rebel vedettes or guerillas—some
of them had ripped up a bridge just the other day.

A black sentry stepped out into the road, his rifle pointed forward
towards the cavalrymen, who came jog-trotting steadily on to the tinny
music of their accoutrements.

"Halt, an' give the countersign."

The sergeant heading the dusty blue-coated file seemed not to
notice, and jogged on.

Dobbs suddenly leaped to his feet. "Hey! . . ."

Pennington saw the cavalry sergeant draw saber and pivot his
upper body, slowly, as his horse clopped steadily on. Everything happened slowly, as if in a tableau or animated frieze. The sergeant's
saber made a curvetted flash as he swept it out and slashed it back-
handed—*thwuck!*—down on the sentry, as the horse's forequarters
blocked the black man from Pennington's sight.

Suddenly everything rushed towards the center of the scene like
water down a whirlpool, Dobbs running up to the sergeant on horseback
yelling, "Nineteenth Niggers! Stand up, goddamn it! Stand up!" The
men rose up out of the bushes and from their rifle pits. The cavalrymen
were reining back suddenly. Their horses whinnied. The sergeant's
horse shied at something near his feet while the sergeant jerked at the
reins, and Dobbs, still running towards the roadway, yelled "Aim!"

"Don't shoot, for Christ's sake!" yelled one of the cavalrymen.

Dobbs stood in the road, holding his pistol at arm's length, like
some strange magic mechanical hand with an exaggerated index finger,
steadily pointing it at the sergeant, who was holding his horse steady
with his left hand wrung back and in. The saber was held in his right
hand. Fear shimmered through the horse's hide.

"If you move, sergeant, I will shoot you dead."

The sergeant's lips moved.

"Give the wrong order, Sergeant. My men will shoot you down
like the dogs you are."

The sergeant didn't move. He held his horse in with his left hand,
his saber gleaming in his right. A red glaze covered the tip, slid down
toward the hilt and froze.

As Pennington ran up, he could see that Dobbs was grinning wolfishly.

"Go ahead," said Dobbs to the sergeant. "Do it. Come on. I'd like
you to try."

Next to the sergeant's horse was a bundle of black clothes, which
rested in a puddle of mud.

In the silence you could hear the harsh sound of the horses' breath whoofing through their nostrils. The strong smell of the horses was cut by a sharp smell, metallic.

Dobbs spoke, quietly. "Drop the saber, Sergeant." It fell clattering. "Private Johnson. Step out, nice and careful, and take the sergeant's pistol." The tall thin black man stepped out of the bushes at the roadside; reached up and opened the sergeant's holster, lifting the pistol gingerly out. He seemed to be taking care not to touch the sergeant. The sergeant seemed peculiarly rigid while he did this. The sergeant was a small man, long-bodied with short legs; sandy hair peeked from under his slouch hat; his face was fair, covered with freckles; under a red drinker's nose he had a small, immature mustache—a slick of blond hair across the top of the upper lip.

"You'll have your men dismount, Sergeant, and drop their arms in a pile, over *there*."

While this was going on, Pennington walked slowly up to the bundle of clothes. One of the black soldiers was already bending over it. Out of the glare of the sun, you could see the bundle of clothes was a man, and that the puddle was a shiny pool of blood, already thickening in the air. Flies dipped and buzzed, touching and taking off.

Somehow it was not surprising the see the dead man. His black face was a weird mask, the staring eyes like dull glass, the open mouth not like the mouth of a man, but of a puppet, an extraordinarily lifelike puppet. It was normal, somehow, that the puppet's head should loll crazily to the side, where the neck was cut nearly through from the chop of the heavy saber, a gleam of white showing in the red.

What was so shocking then was the quantity of blood spilled out on the road. Who could have imagined that a man might have so much blood inside him, or that it would be so dark, and have so strong a smell?

Pennington felt dizzy. Dobbs's hand fell on his shoulder.

"Chris? You all right, boy?" Pennington nodded. "I need you to do something, Chris. You saw everything?"

Pennington nodded again. It seemed impossible to speak. His throat felt sore, as if he had been punched in the larynx.

"I've put this whole bunch under arrest, but it's the sergeant who's got to be charged. I'll give you a squad. You'll march them back to provost guard—Fourth Division provost guards, back near headquarters. I don't want these boys going to anybody else's provosts."

"Yes," said Pennington.

"Charge the sergeant with murdering a sentry, without cause, and while the sentry was in exercise of official duties. There must be some law covers that."

"Yes," said Chris hoarsely, "I'm sure there is."

"Don't let the sons of bitches ride. They walk; one of your boys can lead their horses. Keep up close to them." Dobbs turned to the cavalry sergeant. The man had dismounted. "I want to be sure they *swing* this bandy-legged son of a bitch." The sergeant looked sullen, defiant. Dobbs grinned. His hand with the pistol in it whipped right to left swiftly, a snake striking, and the sergeant went down hard almost before Pennington was aware of the cracking sound the pistol made against the sergeant's skull.

The man lay in the dust. The side of his face was marked with a red cut where the blood welled out along the cheekbone. Already the skin was turning blue-black.

"Pick him up," ordered Dobbs, and the cavalrymen raised the sergeant.

As Pennington marched his squad back down the road, his head seemed to clear, as if he were awakening from a dream. The shock and horror seemed to bubble up in him. Odd disjointed thoughts foisted themselves in his mind like bubbles rising in the eddy of a stream. He was surprised to remember that he had understood, without explanation, why it was that Dobbs insisted that only the Fourth Division's provosts handle the arrest.

All of the other divisions were white. That meant that even Christopher Pennington, who was as white as any of them, couldn't trust them to do their duty by the murdered Fourth Division sentry.

Because the Fourth Division was black.

July 3, 10:00 P.M. *IX Corps Line: 43rd U.S.C.T.*

Major Booker, Sergeant Randolph, Corporal Matt Colehill and Privates to be Young and Jethro Cousins crouched behind the wicker basket full of rocks that buttressed the picket station.

"You got everything?" asked Booker. "Check it now."

"Knife. I got my sidearm. Jeth' got the cord."

"You got our buttons, Major?" asked Colehill. There was a low, muffled laugh. They were all nerved up. Although the night was sultry, little riffles of chill ran through their stomach muscles, like cold shallow water running quick over a rocky bed.

Sergeant Randolph, fretted to distraction with days spent in the trench, doing nothing but listening to the bullets whine, had come to Booker asking permission to go out and get a prisoner.

"What for? Nobody needs a prisoner. There are enough deserters to satisfy the staff officers."

"I need a prisoner." He grinned. "Maybe just to keep for a pet. There's another thing, too. The secesh, they pushed their pickets right up close, way out from their line. Them gunshys here before us probably couldn't see that close to the ground, for looking up through those damn high fire slits. Can't let Johnny get too sassy with us."

Hell, why not? "What's your plan?"

"There's a gully goes down towards the secesh from the number three picket. It kind of sidles off away from one their posts. I go round by that way, I come in behind em. Snake em out before they know what. Going to take some good men with me. That Jethro the best man for snaking hens out the roost."

"All right. But I guess you'd say he needed the chicken. We're not going to eat any prisoner."

"They say black folks partial to the white meat."

"All right. Let's do it. Pick your men."

What good was it sitting around in the bombproofs and trenches, taking orders and getting stale? Anything was better than doing nothing, feeling the days pound you down. The pointlessness of it appealed to him: war for the hell of it, to show what you could do. It reminded him of how it had felt going out after horses with Wolf's Brother and his other friends among the Crows. You went because that was what you felt like doing. The medicine was right, it felt like a good day to go out and take chances and see what could happen to you, see where you stood with the Powers.

It was going to be Sergeant Randolph's show. Booker was going along as one of the older warriors often did, not necessarily to fight, but to watch how the young ones did.

"All right," said Booker, "one more thing." He broke a piece of charcoal in his hand, spat on it. Then he rubbed it over his cheeks. The men watched him, their faces inscrutable. "When I spent time out West," he said, "I stayed with the Indians awhile. Whenever they went out to fight, they blacked up their faces some. Good spirits, they figured; and your face don't shine in the moonlight. You all have your warpaint on already." That got grins all around.

They slipped over the parapet and into the gully. Their black faces, dark blue uniforms with the buttons removed, reflected no light. They went down the gully silently, Randolph leading, Booker bringing up the rear. There were a hundred yards to the end of the gully, and they measured it with their bodies. For the last thirty feet they could hear the muffled voices of the rebels on picket. Careless.

They inched forward. The sound of the voices approached them, passed back to their left. They were behind the rebel picket line. Following Randolph's lead they turned so that they lay parallel, facing the trench. Booker could smell Jethro's sweat. He could feel the tension crackle in the man's arm. He sensed, rather than saw, Randolph make his rush, Tobe after, silently, a thud and sounds of struggle, and Booker was glaring into the face of a terrified white man, pale in the moon, his lower face swallowed up in a black hand that held his mouth. The white man's eyes rolled as he saw Booker. Booker took out his knife, motioned for silence, jammed a rag into the man's mouth and bound it in with his neckerchief. Randolph rolled the man and tied his wrists. They looked up. Jethro had pinned the other man against a crackerbox. "No!" the man said, then like a snake striking, Jethro punched his knife into the man's neck, so the point *thunked* in the wood. Then he grabbed the face: "Shut, you!"

"He dead," said Colehill, "leave him."

"Hell you say."

"Leave him," whispered Randolph. "Let's git," Booker grabbed the tied-up soldier and faced him towards the dead man. "No noise," he said. Then they began to crawl back up the gully.

They came in through the picket, back to the lines, and took the prisoner into the regimental headquarters. The man's face looked like the belly of a fish. He couldn't stop shaking. It was as if all the nervous shivering the five men had had before they started had been passed on to the reb prisoner.

Colonel Hall, roused from sleep, tried to question the prisoner. What regiment? What division? "I'm in the Thirty-third Virginia. Listen, just please keep them away from me now. Just cut the man throat like he weren't no more'n a hog. Just cut the man throat. Jesus Lord."

Major Booker turned and left the bombproof. A little light spilled out of the door. In it he could see Jethro looking at his right hand, which looked like it had been dipped in bright red paint. The sleeve of his blouse was stiff with blood, had stuck a little bit to his skin. He plucked at it with his left hand. His right hand hung limp. "Jesus God," he said, "what was it made me do a thing like that?"

"Don't take it to heart, Jeth," said Colehill. "Remember how they done ours at Fort Pillow. They do worse to you they ever snatch you out of a picket."

"You men," said Booker. "Jeth, Tobe, Ki, Cole—you did good work. We'll learn a lot from this prisoner." He was quiet a moment. Then he said, "This is just how it is."

HEADQUARTERS NINTH ARMY CORPS,
July 3, 1864.

Major-General MEADE,
Commanding Army of the Potomac:
I have delayed answering your dispatch until I could get the opinion of my division commanders and have another reconnaissance of the lines made by one of my staff. If my opinion is required as to whether now is the best time to make an assault (it being understood that if not made the siege is to continue) I should unhesitatingly say wait until the mine is finished. If the question is between making the assault now and a change of plan looking to operations in other quarters I should unhesitatingly say assault now. If the assault be delayed until the completion of the mine I think we should have a more than even chance of success. If the assault be made now I think we have a fair chance of success, provided my corps can make the attack and it is left to me to say when and how the other two corps shall come in to my support.

I have the honor to be, general, very respectfully, your obedient servant.
A. E. BURNSIDE,
Major-General, Commanding Ninth Army Corps.

HEADQUARTERS ARMY OF THE POTOMAC
July 3, 1864.

Major-General BURNSIDE,
Commanding Ninth Corps:
GENERAL: Your note by Major Lydig has been received. As you are of the opinion there is a reasonable degree of proba-

bility of success from an assault in your front I shall so report to the lieutenant general commanding and await his instructions. The recent operations in your front, as you are aware, though sanctioned by me, did not originate in any orders from these headquarters. Should, however, it be determined to employ the army under my command in offensive operations on your front I shall exercise the prerogative of my position to control and direct the same, receiving gladly at all times such suggestions as you may think proper to make. I consider these remarks necessary in consequence of certain conditions which you have thought proper to attach to your opinion, acceding to which in advance would not in my judgment be consistent with my position as commanding general of this army. I have accordingly directed Major Duane, chief engineer, and Brigadier-General Hunt, chief of artillery, to make an examination of your lines, and to confer with you as to the operations to be carried on—the running of the mine now in progress and the posting of artillery. It is desirable as many guns as possible bearing on the point to be assaulted should be placed in position. I agree with you in opinion the assault should be deferred till the mine is completed, provided that can be done in a reasonably short period—say a week. Roads should be opened to the rear to facilitate the movements of the other corps sent to take part in the action and all the preliminary arrangements possible should be made. Upon the reports of my engineer and artillery officers the necessary orders will be given.

Respectfully, yours,

GEO. G. MEADE,
Major-General, Commanding.

July 3, Midnight. Burnside's headquarters

Despite the sudden pulse of angry despair that had gone through him when he received Meade's letter, Burnside had determined not to cancel the scheduled poker game with his staff and division commanders. Now, late at night, well into the game, assured that it would be one of those glorious, comradely sessions that would last till dawn with no one wearying and dropping out, he was glad he had done so. He had sat right down, with Richmond and Parke, and composed a reply; though really, "composed" wasn't the word. It was a sincere letter coming direct from the heart, and so carried its conviction. He had never dreamed of usurping his commander's authority (as if his abnegation of seniority weren't sufficient proof!). Meade was certainly his superior in technical skill, he'd never deny that. (Though there was more to commanding an army of men, winning their loyalty, than Meade understood!) "My desire is to support you, and in doing that I am serving the country." That was Richmond's phrase, and a good one. One could read the difference in the character of two men, contrasting Meade's waspish preoccupation with the protocols and powers of command to his own generosity, which placed duty before personal gain, or even dignity. (The people would appreciate that difference, if word should somehow, some way reach the papers!)

He felt fine. He had held Meade at bay with his reply. As he'd been holding the line here at cards. But, Lord, how he yearned for some appreciation of his efforts. He really did not deserve Meade's suspicion.

He tipped up his hole cards to look at them again. His attention had drifted. He was betting into—probably—two pairs, and holding three cards to a straight, with two cards . . . he should have folded sooner! He turned over his cards and smiled ruefully, as if the last card had foiled some combination. (There was no point in letting them think he wasn't paying attention. They'd skin him!)

He looked round the table. Parke was playing his cards with mournful seriousness, his yellow complexion emphasized by the glow of the oil lamp. Parke didn't look well—malaria acting up. Burnside was afraid he'd be applying for sick leave, and he didn't want to lose him just now. But Parke had denied any illness when Burnside had expressed concern; and Burnside had quickly invited him to the game, as if to fix that reply and forestall any qualifications or changes. Richmond had on his poker-face, but his eyes couldn't help looking crafty. He fancied his cunning as a cardplayer. *Lew! Read you like a book.* Willcox is another matter. Old Army man, cool as an iceberg. He plays his cards like an engineer: got 'em, he bets; hasn't got 'em, he folds. No bluff, no flair; no win, not likely lose. Ed Ferrero has more the swashbuckler style, plays cards like the pirate he looks, with his dago skin and eyes. Still, he's a good man, he's deserved well—better than he's received.

Ferrero had worked hard, he'd really got those niggers of his to where they were some use to the corps. But everything the man touched seemed to get spoiled somehow. Burnside had recommended him for promotion to a full Brigadier-Generalship, replacing his temporary brevet commission with an official promotion that would preserve his entitlement to command a division. Now you would think that that was luck enough for any man. But what had happened? No sooner had Burnside recommended him for promotion than the whole political hive came swarming after him. Congress's Committee on the Conduct of the War had to check to find out if he was a McClellan sympathizer; the McClellan party in Congress wanted to know the same thing, but of course expected a different result. And there were plenty of sneaks afraid to show their faces who were Burnside's own enemies, and would do anything at all to frustrate him.

Burnside stole a look at Ferrero, and shamefacedly looked away. The fact was, it was beginning to appear that Burnside's recommendation of promotion had so aroused the various political partisans that Ed Ferrero's promotion was going to be denied. And worse, they might even fail to confirm the brevet promotion under which he could serve as an acting division commander. That would make Ferrero revert to his previous rank as Colonel of the Fifty-first New York—a rebuff no gentleman could bear, that would unquestionably lead to his resignation. Now how was that for luck?

The deal passed to Ferrero, who flashed his smile, riffled the deck thoroughly, and dealt with practiced elegance. Involuntarily, Burnside found himself watching extra closely when Ferrero dealt. Burnside caught himself and looked up in some self-annoyance, and caught Richmond in the same action. They grinned at each other: a touch of intuition, like a bond. Burnside nearly laughed. Comrades! What a lovely evening.

The cards weren't lovely. Two down, one up: nothing matches anything else. The luck was turning sour tonight, he was down now . . . $250. Already? Oh, Lord.

Still, luck was bound to turn. He had an overpowering intuition it would. Such shifts operated according to laws, rhythms. Two hundred and fifty—a dollar for every foot of mine we've dug. Something in *that* coincidence, surely! A subtle mathematics, not to be thought about though. After years of calculation, he told himself, he'd trained his instincts to respond to the shifts and turns of probability, to sense when the turn back to restore balance would come. Same instinct a soldier has for picking the best ground, the *coup d'oeil*. What was it Napoleon had said about it?

There was a mathematics of compensation involved. When he thought about it, a saying of his mother's came back: "You must deserve your luck, son. If you deserve it, it will come to you." He'd lived by that rule, so far as it was in his power. It was, for him, the deepest utterance of moral law, the form of God's operation in the universe, for good, always tending for good.

Well, how did the balance run? A hard calculation. He ran it through his mind, examining each relic in turn. Had worked himself up from poverty of the family farm in Ohio, gone to West Point, an officer and a gentleman, did his duty; married well, made many friends around Fort Adams, good solid businessmen of Newport and Providence. How had he earned that? Simply by doing his duty, and cultivating a good character. It was so easy to be honest, and frank, and friendly (why couldn't Meade see it?), it came naturally as God in His wisdom meant it should. The reward would come, never fear.

On the other hand, when he'd sinned badly, as in New Mexico—gambling debts, good Lord!—that was awful.

Another hand had gone by. He'd bet himself into it before realizing the cards were hopeless. Fold again.

Sometimes you can deserve good luck and not get it. The thought made him sweat. His carbine business was the proof. He'd done everything right, worked hard, been honest, then been robbed of his just return by the malice and treachery of that rebel sympathizer Floyd in Buchanan's War Department. A crooked deal can defeat even the best-deserved good luck.

But not forever. Certainly hope it's not forever,

A new deal, his own. Perhaps this hand things would turn. His own hand on the cards. He tipped up the hole cards: nothing.

He'd had the "deal" at Fredericksburg, too. Much good it had done him! Commander of the Army of the Potomac, replacing General McClellan—and not by any crooked backstairs politicking either, be it remembered!—and he'd made such a good plan, had outmarched Lee to the river crossing, and the idiots or traitors in Washington had lost or neglected to order out the pontoon train he'd asked for, and he had to sit there while the surprise was wasted, and Lee came up and started digging in on those big hills in back of the town overlooking the whole crossing.

Fifth card out. A good one! *Now I'm four to a straight. Inside straight, but still. . . . What am I looking at? Pair of threes, maybe a pair of kings.* The betting went round, no raises; that looked good. Burnside raised. Richmond and Willcox called. The next card was no help; they'd wonder if he didn't bet, though. If he was going to carry through the bluff, he'd have to bet. If he wasn't, fold now and save the money. Hell. He'd worked the cards all night, it was his best position yet. Go for it. He bet, Willcox raised—to test him, probably. Just call.

The seventh card. He thought, *I won't look at it.* But the urge was too strong. *No, that's bravado,* he thought, and tipped up the seventh card.

His heart leaped into his throat. He'd made the straight. Oh Lord! Richmond's bet, with his pair of deuces showing. Deuces! He'll pass, then fold.

"Fifty," said Richmond, dropping a stack of chips onto the pile.

Burnside's heart sank down again, suddenly. He felt the vacuum left by its passing suck the wind from him. Why was Lew raising? He looked again. Pair of . . . but three of the cards were hearts! *Maybe Lew had pulled a flush! And I'm watching his pair of deuces. . . .*

For a moment the card game and his earlier reverie merged, and Burnside stood on the frigid north shore looking across to the heights beyond Fredericksburg where Lee was dug in and waiting, and himself thinking, *Such a good plan, it deserves to work; everything is right for it. How much can have gone wrong? I'll go through with the attack. Even if I get half of what I deserve, I'll whip Lee out of his boots.*

Willcox called. *With what, can't have more than two pair? . . . Up to me. Dammit!*

They'd talked of having him up on charges after Fredericksburg. The viciousness! They blamed him for a butchery. They demoted him from Army to Corps commander. If they'd done *their* jobs, obeyed the plan . . . and he'd almost bought their view; he'd even tried to ride out to charge some guns and end it all. Well, maybe he should have . . . thrown in his cards. Cashed in his chips. No! No defeatism! He had been right. He had deserved success.

Now now now . . . all right. A straight is easier to get than a flush, that's why a flush is worth more. Whatever he's got showing, the odds still favor me. And God knows, God *knows* the luck is due to take its turn.

"Call."

Richmond flipped his cards over, grinned. Two pair! Willcox . . . three threes! Well, *now!* Well, *now!* Here was something *like!* But where in hell had that third trey of Willcox's come from? For a minute there was that thrill again: Willcox had been that close to the full house that would have scooped the lot of them . . . he'd never even noticed . . .

But here was Ferrero looking grim. Poor man. He'd no luck at cards or war. A problem there: he deserved advancement for his work, did Ferrero. He never seemed to hold the cards.

There was the necessary qualification of Burnside's Law. You had to have the cards. There was a tendency for cards to fall in certain patterns: you had to know when the pattern was coming your way. Coincidences but not coincidences, combinations working for you in a pattern. You can't go out and seek it. Overeagerness, obvious ambition, is offensive; it is as if the cards sense it, and avoid the grasping player. He himself had never sought position ambitiously, selfishly. When command of the army had been offered to him after McClellan's dismissal, he had been, genuinely, surprised. Had expressed his own sense of unfitness for so great a responsibility. He was an honest man! (Too honest by half). Yet there were those who believed he had schemed for the position, simply because he had, modesty and all, taken it in the end. They had no understanding. A man might believe sincerely in his own limitations; yet it would be almost an impiety to turn aside from the gift of a great command, coming unsought (as it had!) as if from on high. As if one were to draw a straight flush, and fold the hand without betthing: unnatural. Surely his mother would have thought so (though she didn't hold with cardplaying). "A God-given opportunity" was how she described such things, talking in her small insistent voice to her husband reluctant to make some decision, to her son hesitating about the appointment to the Military Academy. It was sinful to let such things go, and surely God would decline to repeat such offers: "Opportunity knocks but once." Well, it had led him to defeat in '62, almost to disgrace and ruin. But here he was, sitting now with a stack of chips before him and (he looked) very, very good cards in the hole for the next hand.

In the hole. The Mine was his ace in the hole. Meade didn't like the idea, was doing all he could to delay and sabotage, and divorce himself and his engineers from it. That was fine. When the coup came off, it would be by Burnside's plan, conceived and executed by Burnside and his men, using instruments Burnside had had to obtain outside the army, against the shortsighted objections of headquarters. His letter to Meade, which he would post this morning, was a masterpiece of self-effacement, if he said so himself. He knew how to play his cards close! Meade was no poker player.

He would smile at Meade, rake in the chips, and then go home to Rhode Island with a light heart and a smile on his lips!

A fortunate combination of circumstances made a man successful at cards, and at other things too. Look at Grant's luck: the coincidence of the "U.S." initials, chiming with United States, Uncle Sam, and Unconditional Surrender. Those initials: probably the difference between being commander of a small force out on the Border, and Lieutenant General! And look at his good fortune in taking Vicksburg, on July 4, same day that Meade stopped Lee at Gettysburg.

He looked at his watch. Twelve-thirty. Here it was July 4 again. Too bad the Mine wasn't ready.

He looked round the table, and his eye lit on Ferrero. Then the idea came to him, and even as it went through his head he thought in an undercurrent how Burnside's Law *did* work, because if Ferrero had missed this poker game he might have missed this Opportunity, but now he wouldn't. . . .

He called Ferrero aside as the game was breaking up. It was four in the morning, and the sky was going gray. "General, I have an important task for you. I'm assuming that your division will remain with my command; in fact, this plan of mine will help insure it. Our Mine should be done in a week, perhaps ten days. General"—he paused for effect—"I want the Fourth Division to lead the assault. The Fourth Division will lead the Ninth Corps right through the line and into Petersburg."

Ferrero, weary to stupidity and stunned with surprise, could only stammer his gratitude.

Burnside beamed. "Now, I'll want you and your officers to examine the ground as carefully as you can. Oliver's brigade is on the line, but they're to be relieved this morning. I'll want a plan of attack from you as soon as possible. And I'll try and see to it that your troops are given a chance to prepare for the attack with any special drills you may require."

In his mind's eye, the beaming Burnside could see it all: the explosion of Burnside's Mine, Burnside's assault, and Burnside's black brigades leading Burnside's Ninth Corps into the breach and through it to victory. What an image was there, of himself towering above the infatuated, cheering columns of the emancipated race as he entered the rebel capital. It repeated the image he had of Lincoln being cheered by Hinks's division, but how much more significant and noble was this scene, symbolic of Victory, and with a central figure somewhat more prepossessing (even modesty admitted) than the lanky, awkward President.

He had no presidential ambitions, himself—of course.

He patted Ferrero on the shoulder as the man went off to his tent. Yes, this certainly was Ferrero's lucky day.

CONFIDENTIAL.   HEADQUARTERS NINTH ARMY CORPS,
July 4, 1864.

Major-General MEADE,
Commanding Army of the Potomac:
   GENERAL: I have the honor to acknowledge the receipt of your letter of last evening. I am very sorry that I should have been so unfortunate in expressing myself in my letter. It was written in haste, just after receiving the necessary data upon which to strengthen an opinion already pretty well formed. I assure you in all candor that I never dreamed of implying any lack of confidence in your ability to do all that is necessary in any grand movement which may be undertaken by your army. Were you to personally direct an attack from my front I would feel the utmost confidence, and were I called upon to support an attack from the front of the Second or Sixth Corps, directed by yourself or by either of the commanders of those corps, I would do it with confidence and cheerfulness. It

is hardly necessary for me to say that I have had the utmost faith in your ability to handle troops ever since my acquaintance with you in the Army of the Potomac, and certainly accord to you a much higher position in the art of war than I possess, and I at the same time entertain the greatest respect for the skill of the two gentlemen commanding the Second and Sixth Corps; so that my duty to the country, to you, and to myself, forbids that I should for a moment assume to embarrass you or them by an assumption of position or authority. I simply desired to ask the privilege of calling upon them for support, at such times and at such points as I thought advisable. I would gladly accord to either of them the same support, and would be glad to have either of them lead the attack; but it would have been obviously improper for me to have suggested that any other corps than my own should make the attack in my front. What I asked in reference to calling upon the other corps for support is only what I have been called upon to do and have cheerfully done myself in regard to other corps commanders. If a copy of my letter has been forwarded to the General-in-Chief, which I take for granted has been done, that he may be possessed of my full opinion, it may make the same impression upon him as upon yourself, and I beg that you will correct it; in fact I beg that such impression may be as far as possible removed wherever it has made a lodgment. My desire is to support you, and in doing that I am serving the country. With ordinary good fortune we can pretty safely promise to finish the mine in a week—I hope in less time.

I have the honor to be, General, very respectfully, your obedient servant.

A. E. Burnside,
Major-General, Commanding Ninth Army Corps.

CONFIDENTIAL.   HEADQUARTERS ARMY OF THE POTOMAC,
July 4, 1864.

Maj. Gen. A. E. Burnside:

General: Your letter of this date is received. I am glad to find that there was no intention on your part to ask for any more authority or command than you have a perfect right to expect under existing circumstances. I did not infer from your letter that you had any want of confidence in me. I rather thought you were anticipating interference from others, and thought it best to reply as I did. Your letter has not been shown to any one nor forwarded to the General-in-Chief, and my answer has only been seen by the confidential clerk who copied it. I am very grateful to you for your good opinion as expressed, and shall earnestly try to merit its continuance. In the trying position I am placed in, hardly to be appreciated by any one not in my place, it is my great desire to be on terms of harmony and good feeling with all, superiors and subordinates, and try to adjust the little jars that will always exist in large bodies to the satisfaction of each one. I have no doubt by frankness and full explanations such as have now taken place between us all misapprehensions will be removed. You may rest assured all the respect due to your rank and position will be paid you while under my command.

Truly, yours,

GEO. G. MEADE,
Major-General.

Trading with the Enemy
July 4–12, 1864

Just before the battle the General hears a row,
He says, "The Yanks are coming, I hear their rifles now,"
He turns around in wonder, and what do you think he sees?
The Georgia militia eating goober peas!

HEADQUARTERS NINTH ARMY CORPS,
July 4, 1864.

Brig. Gen. EDW. FERRERO,
Commanding Fourth Division:

GENERAL: On being relieved by Gen. Hancock's troops, you will march your command to these headquarters, and establish your bivouac in its former location.

As soon as possible to-morrow morning, you will detail one company from each of your brigades to escort the officers drawing rations for the Division at City Point, and the wagons on their return to the Division.

By order of Major-General Burnside,

LEWIS RICHMOND,
Assistant Adjutant-General.

July 4, 10:00 A.M. Near City Point

The two companies, drawn from the Forty-third and Nineteenth regiments, U.S.C.T. reached the supply depot near City Point at ten in the morning. Coming out of the forests along the dirt road, they felt like country people approaching the verge of a large city. After the soft dark light and muffled sounds, the physical isolation of picket duty in the woods; after inhabiting a landscape in which the occasional clearing showed only the small group of tents and the blue-coated soldiers in bivouac—now they approached the hub of the army. Trees had been cleared left and right of the road, the fields were crowded with wagons and massed artillery, the wheels hub to hub. In enclosed fields draft horses and mules were kept, stirring fitfully. The smell of horse manure became thicker as they went along. There were crowds of soldiers, work parties and men lounging off-duty—teamsters and artillerymen, ambulance drivers; stations of the provost guard; armed men standing at parade rest; a small group around a corporal and a Lieutenant, examining the papers of two soldiers and an officer who stood by, fidgeting.

Staff officers tailed by escorts jingled up the road at a trot heading out towards the front. Off through the trees a floating flag marked the location of the big army hospital, a city of white tents.

The detail halted in front of a large gray warehouse. Off to the side were wagons, some marked with the IX Corps insignia. Captain Shugrue and Major Rockwood, followed by Sergeant Randolph, walked together into the warehouse. Standing outside in the heat and dust, the men could hear them talking, then arguing with the quartermasters.

"Your divisional returns say you're drawing for four thousand officers and men."

"That's the last month's return, Captain. We've had a lot of sick come back to the ranks, and other troops coming back from detail to other divisions. It's all here. . . . Sergeant, give me those papers you're holding."

Silence. The dust in the courtyard settled on blue coats and black faces, powdering them ashy. All around them they heard the cries of teamsters, drillmasters, orders for other soldiers.

"These are official returns?"

"They are."

Silence.

"Well, Major . . . I haven't authorization to let you draw for that many. The other corps must have drawn rations for the units detailed to them. We can't issue two rations for one soldier."

"Captain, if the other units have drawn our rations, you've already given out more than they were supposed to get. Our troops have had *no* rations at all. You can appreciate that, can't you?"

"I see your problem, Major. But I'll have to . . ."

"All right. You issue what you're authorized for. I'll write out a protest and a requisition, and you'll endorse it for me. You can do *that*, can't you?"

Another silence. Flies buzzed in the heated air.

"All right, Major. Does that satisfy you?"

"No. But it will have to do, won't it?"

Captain Shugrue came hustling down the steps of the warehouse. He motioned to the Lieutenants heading the two companies. "Bring them round back. Stack arms, and stand ready to load the wagons."

Behind the warehouse were mounds of boxed crackers, pickled beef and pork in barrels, burlap sacks of vegetables. Fresh meat was wrapped in cloth in a shed, out of the sun. Rockwood, Randolph, and the quartermaster Captain stood on the loading dock behind the warehouse, ticking off the inventory.

"You've got pork, fresh and salt, five thousand, two hundred pounds; beef, fresh and salt, eight thousand, seven hundred and fifty pounds. The stuff marked with a red X is yours. Hard bread . . ."

"Wait a minute," said Rockwood. "How much fresh, how much salt?"

The quartermaster shrugged. "What's the difference? Ration entitlement is the same whether it's salt or fresh."

"It makes a difference to us, Captain. We've been getting nearly everything salt. It ruins the men's digestion, Captain, and it lowers morale. But that doesn't concern you.''

"I have my orders, Major.'' He turned to his list. "Hard bread, twenty-eight thousand pounds. Over *there.*'' He gestured to a pyramid of boxes. "Now you've got pease coming, one peck dried per hundred rations, and a special issuance of cabbages, thirty pounds per hundred —that's in lieu of half your pease; hominy, ten pounds per hundred; coffee eight, sugar fifteen per hundred. No molasses, no potatoes—I've set out some desiccated vegetables there, which is the appropriate replacement.'' He waited for Rockwood to disagree or protest, then continued. "Vinegar, at four quarts per hundred rations, salt two quarts, soap a pound and a half per hundred, four ounces pepper . . . sorry, no pepper. I make that forty pecks dried pease, twelve hundred pounds cabbage, four hundred pounds hominy, three hundred twenty pounds roasted coffee, six hundred of sugar, fifty pounds soap, eighty quarts of salt, one hundred sixty of vinegar. Desiccated vegetables to replace twenty bushels potatoes. Will you sign, Major?''

Major Rockwood took the list. "Not just yet. I'll want a chit for the cash equivalent of the molasses and pepper. Also, there's the matter of the money for the rations we didn't draw while we were on the march down from the Rapidan.''

"I'm sorry, Major, I have no power to . . .''

"That's not true, Captain. You are required, as I believe you well know, to pay cash equivalents for rations not drawn while the troops are on the march and away from their camps.''

"I believe, Major, that that allowance applies only to *combat* troops. Negro soldiers are officially listed as laborers and paid according.''

Rockwood grinned wolfishly. "Captain, you are a damned liar. The regulations make no distinction between troops on campaign as to rations. If they did, why is it that quartermasters never go hungry, and never die poor?''

The quartermaster Captain blushed angrily. "You have your accounts? . . .''

"Sergeant!'' snapped Rockwood. Randolph stepped forward and handed him a sheaf of papers.

"Very well, very well,'' said the Captain as he riffled them. "These seem to be in order. I'll just be a minute writing you a draft.''

Rockwood grinned at Shugrue as the quartermaster vanished. "All right, Captain. Let's get these wagons loaded!'' The men turned to, and began to lug the heavy boxes and barrels over to the wagons, and heave them inside. Single men picked up the big sacks of pease and cabbage and slung them over the freeboards.

Rockwood watched the sergeant as he hustled the men along, bouncing tensely on his toes with held-in nervous energy, looking impatiently up at the sun. He smiled, and said, "When you've got that stuff all loaded, you can take a detail and see what mail has come in. Won't mind an early delivery, will you, boys?''

"No, sir!'' they cried out together.

"All right, all right,'' yelped Randolph, "let's stir it up there, lambs. I been waitin on the word too long already!'' Every mail delivery now was important, because Randolph was waiting for word of when and how the Hewson plantation was coming up for auction. Every week, it seemed, news or rumor had it different. But he trusted Uncle Tobe and his wife, Coffee, to use some sense and tell him only what was true. He read their letters more carefully, and awaited them more tensely, than the generals of the army studied and waited on the reports of reconnaissance of the enemy.

While the wagons were being loaded, Shugrue and Rockwood took a detail of men to the commissary. They had orders from their fellow officers in the division to pick up certain articles at the store : soft bread and fresh beef, small consignments of whiskey or brandy, cakes, and what-not. There were also bundles to be picked up—packages from wives and sweethearts, from mothers and aunts. There was one large package, addressed to Colonel Thomas, that drew a laugh—a large padded box that sloshed audibly, and bore the legend ''CAREFUL PICKLES.''

''I've heard of dill pickles, cucumber pickles, sweet pickles and pickled relish—but I'm hanged if I've ever heard of careful pickles before.''

The commissary men served the two officers a glass of whiskey each—Rockwood buying. Then they went out into the heat again. Randolph and his detail had loaded the wagon and were ready to go. The officers swung aboard, and the wagoneer clucked the team up.

To get back to where the other troops and wagons waited by the warehouse, they had to swing around a corner. This took them round by the Provost Marshal's headquarters. Shugrue had just tipped his hat forward over his eyes when he was jolted upright and wide awake, the teamster hauling back the reins and yelling *whoa!* while Randolph grabbed the brake, making it screel against the axle.

''Sergeant, what in *hell!* . . .'' and then he saw it.

There was a gang of blue men, provost troops and some obviously just hanging around. They were spread across the face of the Provost Marshal's building. Against the front wall, set up on the small uncovered porch that ran around the building, was a coffin set on end—a coffin with the separate door opened over the part where the corpse's bust and shoulders would be seen. They could see the face of the dead man, and Shugrue sucked in his breath—nightmare, no face at all, just a mass of crusts and boils, a horrible pasty gray color, and flies going at it.

I must be drunk or going nuts, he thought. *Provost guards and coffee boilers standing around looking at a corpse that must have been rotting for a week. Oh God! Laughing at it?*

Then the corpse lolled its head, and Shugrue's stomach heaved, *The damn thing's gonna just fall off,* and the corpse rolled its head back and stuck out a tongue that looked red as a dog's penis against the horrible gray crust.

''Wadduh. G' in whadduh.''

Randolph was leaping down off the wagon seat, and Rockwood suddenly jerked Shugrue's shoulder back sharply, poking his head out of the wagon, ''Sergeant! You stand right there!'' Rockwood dropped to the ground. ''You just *stand* there, Sergeant, and I'll find out about this.''

Shugrue squinted closer at the figure in the coffin. Wits must be addled with sun, he thought. That's just some nigger they've got in there, having some fun with him. But what'd they do to his face?

Rockwood, his face drawn and angry, was talking with one of the officers in front of the coffin. The officer he was speaking to snorted and turned away, and Rockwood came back to the wagon.

"This fellow here stabbed a couple of the provost guards. According to that *officer* over there, the provosts were 'making polite conversation' with the man's wife when he went crazy and started swinging a butcher knife. He's from over in the contraband camp; his wife's been doing odd jobs around the depot here and he come up to visit her. Polite conversation!"

Shugrue was sweating. "What'd they do to him?"

"Gave him the morning bucked-and-gagged, to teach him manners the *officer* says. Then they stood him up in the coffin at about noon, tied up—to straighten him out, the man says—and stuck honey and flour all over his face."

The flies—Jesus. Shugrue smiled thinly. "What's that supposed to teach him?"

Sergeant Randolph spoke: "What happen to a nigger who think he good as white man." His voice was absolutely without inflection.

Shugrue looked back at the man in the coffin. His tongue gleamed redly, and you could see his black lips against the gray-white stucco that covered his face, and his eyes like bubbles of oil. *Like some minstrel show all backwards, nigger painted up like a white man.*

He looked down at Randolph. The sergeant had stood rigid. Now he put one hand on the flap of his pistol holster. Behind him in the wagon someone cocked a rifle. *Oh God!* thought Shugrue. *Oh God!* "Sergeant!" his voice sounded strangled. It cracked. "Sergeant, you just hold it right there. You hop right on back up onto this seat here, or by God I'll have *you* in one of those coffins before night."

The provost soldiers and hangers-on had turned to watch. There was a loud laugh from the rear rank.

"Uncock that piece, soldier," Rockwood said quietly.

Randolph came up on the right side of the wagon, Rockwood on the left. The teamster clucked to the horses, and the wagon pulled out.

"How'd you like that, nigger?" someone called after them. "Plenty more cornmeal where this came from."

"Coffins too, nigger!"

Shugrue heaved a sigh of relief. Randolph sat behind him on the food boxes. They rode back to the command in absolute silence, except for a soft thudding sound: Randolph pounding his thigh with his balled up fist.

City Point, Va. July 4, 1864.

Hon EDWIN M. STANTON,
Secretary of War.

No new developments at the front. Burnside's mine is hindered by springs and quicksands. . . .

General Barnard has laid before General Grant a memoran-

dum explaining various plans for immediate operations, and
concluded with an elaborate recommendation of an assault upon
the key of Petersburg, which is a strong earth-work in front
of Warren. . . . Barnard proposes to make very careful preparations to concentrate the fire of at least 100 cannon upon the
point, and to attack with heavy masses of men. I do not think
that General Grant is much inclined to this idea, but he has
sent to ask Meade's opinion about it. All our experience shows
that with the mass of Lee's army to defend the works assailed
they cannot be carried, and that the attempt, if made with
vigor, would cost us at least 15,000 men. . . .

A good deal of sickness from the extreme heat is reported
from both Smith's and Meade's commands, in front of Petersburg. . . .

C. A. DANA

July 4, Noon. General Ferrero's Headquarters

There were a dozen men in the big headquarters tent: Ferrero,
Oliver and Thomas, the commanders of the eight regiments that made
up the division's two brigades, and the division's chief of staff. They sat
around a camp table, made of planks laid across empty cartridge boxes,
on which was spread a sketch of the opposing lines and the terrain in
front of the IX Corps.

Ferrero was still looking worn out from last night's poker game,
although he had washed in cold water and spruced up his uniform. He
had told them his great news, and now waited for some response from his
commanders. He kept telling himself that here at last was his great opportunity; but whether he was too worn with a night of losing money to
General Burnside, or could not believe in any promise of good fortune in
the army, he could not seem to appreciate the quality of his new assignment. Today he thought of Burnside's smiling rubicund face almost with
loathing, for which he inwardly reproached himself. He hoped to see
enthusiasm in his subordinates' faces, from which he could take confidence.

But here Oliver looked grim, and everybody else looked just tired
or bewildered, except for Thomas, whose fair skin began to flush red.

"Well, gentlemen, what do you think?"

Thomas cleared his throat. "Why, General, it is too much to take in.
I had thought they would have us on endless fatigue, till Judgment. Now
they want to put us in front of the grand assault. It's a lot to take in all
at once."

Oliver said. "I agree, General. We have not led these troops in any
significant action since that skirmish after Spotsylvania. We have never
gone into action as a division. We have no idea, really, how the troops
will behave. Has all this been carefully thought through?"

It hadn't, of course! What did the man want? He'd just gotten the
word that morning. Before Ferrero could speak, Thomas interrupted.

"Excuse me, Colonel, but it wasn't my intention to disparage our troops or suggest that we're not able to carry the thing off. We'll need to prepare the men carefully, we've had no time to drill them even in the ordinary way. We'll need special exercises for this and . . .''

"Yes," said Ferrero. "Yes, thank you, Colonel Thomas. I told General Burnside that I had confidence in you all, and in our troops. I believe we ought to do this."

"By God," said Colonel Hall of the Forty-third, "it's about time. We've been digging ditches so long we've lost confidence."

Colonel Bates, commander of the Thirtieth Regiment, gestured slightly with his hand, almost like a schoolboy seeking recognition (he had been a schoolmaster, and reverted easily to the usages and patterns of the schoolroom). Ferrero nodded, and Bates cleared his throat. "Sir, I must say that when you first spoke, I thought to myself, 'My God, it's impossible.' But I've thought again. I think we can do it, and I think we must. I could think of no more fitting end for this great struggle than one of the character General Burnside has proposed to us. It is *right*. It is just. If I were a better Christian, I might even call it providential!''

"Hear, hear," the voices mumbled around the table.

Ferrero, feeling better, looked at Oliver with a feeling of triumph, as if in the mustering of these voices against Oliver's objections his own doubts had been routed.

"Very well, gentlemen. Now, what shall our next step be? We'll have to study the ground to be gone over. General Burnside will give us facilities for using the observation posts in the Ninth Corps area, and will instruct the other division commanders to allow us to move freely along their lines and pickets. Staff officers can make a general inspection first; but I'd hope we could all reconnoiter or overlook the ground in person before the attack."

Thomas spoke: "General, we'll also need to know some other things before we can plan properly. When is the Mine to be exploded? I mean, what time of day? How big a crater do they expect to make, and where in the line will it be? We'll have to know that before we can plan our assault and begin training the men." Ferrero busily took notes in his orderly book. Thomas, the professional soldier (*he knew his business*), waited for Ferrero's pen to stop scratching, then continued. "Also, we'll need some sort of commitment from Army Headquarters to give us time to train the men for the assault, and put them through drill by regiment, brigade, and division. They've not done that for us *yet*. But if they mean business now, that's what must be done." There was a rumble of agreement.

Except from Oliver. "Do you think, Colonel, that troops as raw as these ought to be sent against fortifications that have stopped the best veteran troops we could throw at them? Suppose something goes wrong with the Mine? Suppose we meet heavy opposition?"

Thomas looked directly at Oliver. "Frankly, Colonel, it is a risk. But there always is in fighting. Green troops"—there was a snicker— "yes, or green black troops, can do impossible things, if they're enthusiastic and properly led. Veteran troops get smart, they react quickly to shifts and changes; but they get too smart, too cagey to fight or go up against something that they know is impossible. They get as bad as army engineers sometimes: they take a look at the mathematics of the thing, and say, no, can't be done. But good troops, green troops, if their blood is up, don't know what they can and can't do. I've seen troops like that take positions that Napoleon's Guard would have hung back from.''

''And you've seen them break and run at a rumor, too, Colonel.'' Oliver's eyes flashed now, alive to controversy.

''Not troops that I've led, Colonel.''

Oliver grinned ruefully, and nodded. *Your point.*

''Gentlemen,'' said Ferrero, ''thank you for your support. I'll be making my observations from the Ninth Corps signal tower, this afternoon and again tomorrow morning. Colonel Thomas, perhaps you'll accompany me? Good. The rest of you can make arrangements to do so at your convenience. I'll speak to General Burnside about the training time. We will work out a plan of assault after we've made our observations. Any questions?''

''Yes sir,'' said Colonel Bates. ''Shall we tell the men?''

Ferrero thought for a moment. ''You can tell the men that we have been designated to lead a grand assault. You won't speak of the Mine, or the specific place—''

Colonel Thomas was nodding vigorously. ''I approve, sir. It will lift the men's spirit enormously. They will feel part of the army at last.''

Lord, Thomas was thinking, *won't Chris be pleased!*

HEADQUARTERS ARMY OF THE POTOMAC
July 4, 1864—12 M.

Lieutenant-General GRANT :

After examination and conference with corps commanders, I am satisfied an immediate assault on the enemy's line in my front is impracticable. The enemy now occupies the line held by him on the 18th ultimo, which I vainly endeavored to dislodge him from. Not having succeeded then, when he had only occupied this line some twelve hours, I cannot expect to do it now that he has been two weeks strengthening and adding to it. The only plan to dislodge the enemy from this line is by a regular approach. Major-General Burnside is now running a gallery to a mine to be constructed under a battery on this line, which General B. thinks when exploded will enable him by a formidable assault to carry the line of works. I have directed the chiefs of artillery and of engineers to examine into this point and to make all the necessary preliminary arrangements for the establishment of batteries bearing on the point of attack, opening roads, and preparing places of arms for the assembling of the supporting columns. Should this attack be made, which, under existing circumstances, I deem the most practicable, it will be necessary to withdraw the Second and Sixth Corps to take part in it, and the left of the Fifth Corps will have to be thrown back for self-protection. A line for this purpose will be prepared in advance, but this will require the giving up the Jerusalem Plank Road. With our present numbers and existing condition of affairs, I am of the opinion active operations against the enemy in his present position the most advisable, as it leaves our communications open and intact. The movement on the enemy's right flank as suggested is liable to the objection of separating your forces with the enemy between the two parts, with having to abandon the communications of this army, and the danger after crossing the Appomattox that the enemy may be found strongly posted behind Swift Run, requiring further flank movements, more time, further separation from a base, and more hazard in reopening communications, our experience since crossing the Rapidan having proved the facility with which the enemy can interpose to check an onward movement. If we had the force to extend around the south side of the Appomattox I should prefer doing so and employing the cavalry to destroy the enemy's communications. It will take General Burnside over a week to complete his mine and General Sheridan two weeks to get his animals into a serviceable condition.

GEO G. MEADE,
Major-General.

2:30 P.M. Bivouac of Thomas's Brigade, near Prince George Courthouse

Christopher Pennington was holding his afternoon class in reading and spelling in the shade of a large oak tree. The stunning heat of the day hadn't permitted much drill, and he had his colonel's permission to hold these classes whenever opportunity offered. It was one of the things he loved best about the army, this teaching. He had always been a student before, the good little scholar in town primary school, at the academy, and later in his two years at Harvard. He had thought of learning as sitting in his seat or his pew, listening to the lecture drone: his father preaching in church or chapel, his teachers. To teach others was as much proof of his new manhood as the uniform he wore, the unused sword he carried, the unloaded pistol in its holster on his hip.

He hadn't known what to expect of these men either, many of them older than he. There were the stories of how ignorant and brutal the negroes had become, under the harsh regime of slavery; and there were stories returning missionaries from the Sea Islands told, of how tractable they were, how childlike, how eager to learn.

Well, he had found them altogether a puzzle. You could see how those opposite stories could both be true. Here they were, sitting or sprawling around him where he sat on a nail keg, when they might be loafing or singing or doing anything else. That spoke of the desire to learn, surely. Yet they wouldn't (or was it *couldn't*) keep their minds on the subject, but kept straying into every bypath that offered. It was . . . interesting, he admonished himself. The stories they told were fascinating. Yet it was frustrating to hear someone go maundering off into some story that the text reminded him of, just when Pennington felt he had gotten them into the subject. Then it was all he could do to

preserve his patience; and in fact, he knew he was too quick to chuckle or
applaud the conclusion of the story, to end it as fast as possible and get
back to business. And the chastened, earnest looks of the men as they
turned again to their spellers somehow was a rebuke to him. He couldn't
quite say how: after all, he was giving them the knowledge they wanted.

Today he had them at work on the alphabet, out of the *Primer*. At
first, things seemed to go straightforwardly, and he felt that his father
would have been proud of his mastery in guiding the lesson.

> *A: Adam. In Adam's Fall*
> *We sinned all.*

They had gone through it once, from "Adam's Fall" down to
"Zacceus he / Did climb a tree / His Lord to see." Now the drill, and
they'd go over it from the start, each one taking a letter and a verse.

"*A*," said Private Stebbins. "In. Adam. Fall. We. Sin. All." And
so on down to *D*.

It was the turn of Private Johnson Number Five to recite. "Dee,"
he said, and with his left hand reached up to draw closed the V of his
open shirt. The hand rested there, against his chest, holding the shirt
closed. "That my letter," he said solemnly, and he looked around at his
comrades, who nodded and mumbled as if there was some special signifi-
cance to the statement. Then Johnson smiled, and said, "Dee."

> *"Jeff Davis he,*
> *Done climb a tree,*
> *And there he be!"*

The class whooped as one man, with slap-thigh and elbows in ribs,
and Pennington felt his control shake. But he wanted to laugh himself.

"Now that's *it*," said Private Duckworth, "take it back from
the *A*."

Johnson Five shook his head. The deep mellow voice rumbled: "It's
Uncle Abe, have free the slave."

"That's right now! Sure! Go on!"

"Bee. The buckra go to ketch the wolf, / But he get caught he owen
self."

"Cee is for Coon, man. Bro' Coon, / Gettin home soon."

"Dee—we done that:"

"Eee." It was Johnson again. "The Elephant was big in size /
Untell the Rabbit burnt his eyes."

Suddenly they all looked solemn. "Hoo Lord," said Duckworth,
and there was a rumble of agreement. Then silence. Pennington couldn't
repress the curiosity. "Private . . . Johnson? What does that mean
about the elephant and the rabbit?"

"Oh, well now," said Johnson, and he grinned his alligator grin.
The rest looked sly, and eased back. "One time Buh Rabbit had a corn
patch, and Elephant come trompin through with his big feets like tree
stumps, snortin and bellowin. Rabbit lay low till Elephant go by. En he
track em through the woods till he come to the Elephant cabin. Big
cabin, all paint white. Elephant yawn a little bit, so Rabbit start singin

to him the quietest way. He have a sweet voice, Rabbit do, real soft and sleepy. You never can keep awake when you hear the song Rabbit sing. And Elephant go sound asleep. When he see that, Rabbit rip up some dry grass and some old pitchpine branches, and he tun up and jam em quick in Elephant's eyes, and in his ears and in his mouth, and then, quick as a flash, he light them with sulphur match. Whoosh! The pitchpine and grass go up like that, and Elephant come awake, roarin around to kill the whole world. But he blind with the fire, so he can't see; and he deaf with the fire roarin in his ears, and the fire so hot in his throat he can't breathe. And after while he burn down to death. En the Rabbit take the meat and bring it home to his family.''

''That's right,'' came the chorus of assents.

''Well,'' said Pennington. ''That's really an interesting story.'' He was thinking how crude it was, how simple, how improbable. Obviously these Africans knew the elephant only from books; there was no hint of practical knowledge in the tale. He knew more about elephants himself! ''Shall we continue now?''

''Yassuh.''

They got as far as *L* this time. ''El,'' said Private James. ''Only thing el for is *Lincoln*. 'Lincoln say what Pharaoh know, / Driver, let my People go!' ''

''Amen to that.''

Oh no, thought Pennington, *they're gone again*.

''Lieutenant,'' asked Private Duckworth, ''you ever see Mr. Lincoln?''

''Not really, no I haven't. I just saw him as he rode by once.'' There was nothing to be gained by impatience.

''You know,'' Duckworth continued, ''Lincoln come by the place one time. Was before the war. He come dress like a peddler-man, carrying big old pack on his shoulder. Stop by Maum Sairy cabin, and ask for hoe cake, field pease, anything we could give im to eat. Maum don't say anything, but she look over at me, and I could see it was something special about the man. She say, after, she see a light coming round his head. I didn't see that, but it was something there, and she had the sight. After he eat little cake, he take some water. And he say to Maum, 'You people been kind to me. It ain't right how you been treated, and I'll do you good turn some day.' Then he goes off.''

Pennington was bewildered. ''What . . . are you sure? I mean, I don't believe it could have been Mr. Lincoln. I don't believe he ever was in North Carolina before the war. He was out west, Illinois, campaigning against Senator Douglas.''

''No, now Lieutenant, I know you means well, but this is the truth.''

''I testify to it too,'' said Private James. ''He come by our place about the same time, with the peddler sack. I didn't see him myself, but heard from the people up to the House. He come by, real humble like, and stop round the kitchen. Ole Mistiss in there, laying about with her tongue that was bad as any lash, and peddler says, 'It ain't right to 'buse people that way. The Lord will take notice of it.' Ole Mistiss took the words to heart: she died that winter of the ager, and fore she went she said how sorry she was to all the folks she abused.''

"Everybody talk like that fore they die, brother. Can't tell me the peddler made her say that."

"Well, you may be right on that. But you don't forget : she *did* die. Now that's the truth."

Private James was humming slightly under his breath :

> *For death he am a simple thing,*
> *He go from do to do,*
> *En he kill up some and he cripple up some,*
> *An leave some here to pray.*

Someone now interrupted from the back : "What color of man was this peddler you-all says was Lincoln ?"

"He was a white man. Tall, and he wore black ; and sallow-complected."

"Now that's what you know about it. I heard that Lincoln was a colored man."

"Oh now ! Where you hear that ?"

"White folk at our place all say so. And it make sense, too."

"No colored man get to be President, fool."

"No buckra man . . ."

Sound froze. Their faces turned slowly to Pennington. Pennington came to with a start : he had been so absorbed in the discussion that he had forgotten himself.

They are looking to me for information, he thought. "No," he said, "I know Lincoln is a white man." Strange how the words almost caught in his throat. Mentioning his color in front of them was as embarrassing as letting them stare at his skinny naked body.

"Sallow-complected," said a voice from the rear, which was shushed sharply.

Private Johnson seemed to rouse from a reverie. "Lincoln a white man. But that John Brown was black."

Pennington felt he must speak, but didn't know what to say. These men were parroting the slaveholders' propaganda about Lincoln and Brown, the old accusation of Negro blood that was the last resort of scoundrels seeking to discredit Abolitionists.

"Oh man !," came the doubting voice again from the rear. "You seeing black everywhere. Next you tell me Jesus a nigger too."

Johnson turned round, and spoke slowly. "John Brown my one good friend, brother. So you don't talk about what you don't know about. I bury him with these hands."

There was silence. Pennington could not imagine what Johnson was talking about. These men were either prodigious liars, or were talking a language he could not comprehend.

"Say, brother," said Private Duckworth, "all this talk about the skin. There's plenty folks don't know the first thing about it. Now you mind my friend, name of John ?"

At this there was a wave of laughter, and loud agreement. Oh yes. Everybody knew about John.

"Well, this story John tell me hisself. Seem John got scripted into the army. And he go and get himself shot in the side. Some folks say it was the secesh done it; and some say he done it himself; and others say, that it was one of the own Yank soldiers shot him for fun.''

"Never mind the others, what John say?''

"Some time one thing, some time the other.'' Laughter and groans. Duckworth shot one look toward Pennington, then continued. "Now let me tell this. Anyway, the Captain send John back to the hospital, and he the only nigger in the place. This true now! Now everybody knows that in this army, they haven't let no niggers get where they can kill them some secesh buckra. So there ain't been any wounded ones comin by there. Well, the first doctor come by, and he check down the cot-rows, and he look in this man's face and say, 'Take him out, he gonna die,' and in the next man face and say, 'Give him the quinine medicine, he gonna live,' and so on till he come to John. There he stop.

"He glare a minute.

"Then he look round on the orderly: 'God blast your bones, you damn skulkin hound,' he say, 'didn't I tell you to wash the men up before you put em in here?'

"So the orderly take the bucket and soap, and start washing John's hand and feet, like the hard-shell Baptist. But he's not gettin any black off, so he rub like he was skinning with a file. So after while in come another doctor and says to the orderly, 'Man, what the devil are you doing to this man here? Can't you see he's powder burnt from head to foot, and his hair's all singed up? Don't wash him! Get some greaze and greaze him up slick!'

"So orderly go after the greaze bucket, and come on back. And he's laying it on John with a brush, when down the row come the Missioner Man. Sanity Commission. He's got the Book in his one hand, and fistful of tracks in the tother. And he stop by each bed and ask the man, 'Is you a Christian?' And if the man say no, he say, 'Well then you going to Hell sure.' And the next man he ask, 'Want a drink o whiskey, brother?'' The man say yes, he say: 'Then you's a damned drunken man, and Satan's child.' Then he come down where John was.

" 'Well bless my soul,' he says, 'What have we got here?'

" 'Sir,' says John, 'you a minister of the Gospel. Can you please tell these folks here that I ain't burnt up with powder, and I ain't all over dirty, I'm just a nigger private in the Potomac Army that has got shot by Johnny Reb.'

" 'Lying speech!' say Sanitary Man, 'lying speech. Get thee behind me Satan! Any fool knows they ain't no niggers in the Army of Potomac. You a damn skulking Irishman, paint hisself black to get out the fighting. An if I hate one thing lower than a nigger it's a low skulking Irishman.'

"So they grab ole John, and frog-march him out the hospital, side shot up and all. And that goes to prove that there's folks don't know a black man when they see one.''

"All right,'' said James, "but what happen to John later?''

"Oh, nothin. They put him in the Irish Brigade, and I heard he a sergeant now.''

Just then the roll of the drum sounded across the field by the white tents of the bivouac. The men started out of their reverie, and began to hustle across the field. Pennington, gathering his books, followed them, too lost in his lost lesson to wonder what was happening. The regiment was assembling. Here was Colonel Perkins, and Colonel Thomas with him. Thomas motioned Pennington to stand beside him.

"It's good news, Chris," he whispered, then gestured for silence.

Pennington looked out over the regiment. His scholars stood in decorous ranks before him. Faceless somehow. He could never look at men in ranks and pick up the faces of men he knew. They all blurred. He felt it was a weakness, and that he must correct it to be a good soldier.

"Men," said Colonel Thomas in a ringing voice. "Men of the Nineteenth United States Colored Regiment. I have proud news for you. The men of this division have been chosen to lead an attack on the lines of the enemy. I cannot tell you when the attack will be made, because such plans must be kept secret from any who might inform the enemy. But I can tell you that the plan is intended to break the rebel line once and for all, and brings us finally to the victory we have sought so long. This is the plan, and I believe it will succeed. I believe you will make it succeed. I believe that I shall lead the soldiers of this brigade and this regiment into the capital of Richmond, and strike slavery dead!"

Thomas stopped, as if expecting a cheer. But there was only a silence. From it broke a single voice: "God be praised." Then nothing.

Colonel Perkins stepped forward. The troops seemed not to have understood, they seemed to need prompting. It was important that things go as they should. "Let's have a cheer, boys," he cried. "Hip hip."

"Hurrah!" cried the officers.

"Hip hip!"

"Hurrah!" they cried, many of the men joining the officers now.

Colonel Thomas nodded to Colonel Perkins. "Troops dismiss!" shouted Perkins. Thomas turned to go off to the next camp. As he came up to him. Pennington saw that the Colonel looked puzzled, even a bit hurt. A pang went through him. For a moment his own frustration with the blacks found an outlet in sympathy for the Colonel. How dare they wound the feelings of this good man who loved them?

A half hour later they returned through the camp of the Nineteenth Regiment and saw the troops still milling around, talking quietly in small groups. Only then did Pennington notice the peculiar hush of the camp, the absence of the usual sounds of song and banter and argument. They had taken in the meaning of the words, in their own way, in silence.

Then a voice began to sing:

> *"My army cross over,*
> *My army cross over,*
> *O Pharaoh's army done drownded,*
> *My army cross over."*

But no voices joined it, and the song died. There was silence again. Then the deep voice came again. the voice Pennington had heard above the camp meeting, and at the spelling lesson : a song never heard before.

> "*We-e looks like men a-a-marching on,*
> *We looks like men a war!*"

And again, the voice tentative, trying the melody, varying it:

> "*We looks like men a marching on,*
> *We looks like men a war!*"

And there were more and more voices now joining, building a harmony on the deep bass of the singer's voice:

> "*We looks like men a marching on*
> *We looks like men a war!*"

And the sound of feet as men drifted through the camp to assemble, as if at the call of the drum, in ranks on the parade, where no officers had bidden them and no officers were. Except for Thomas and Pennington, watching from the edge of the woods. A soldier drifted by, heading toward the parade, and Thomas held him. "Who is the man singing, with the deep voice? The man who started singing?"

"Oh him? Dat mus be Johnson, sir. Number Five Johnson."

> "*We looks like men a-marching on,*
> *We looks like men a war!*"

HEADQUARTERS OF THE ARMY
Washington, D.C., June 28, 1864

Lieutenant-General GRANT,
City Point:

GENERAL: I am informed that the delay in paying the Army of the Potomac has resulted from the failure of the Treasury Department to furnish the money. Not only are the requisitions for May and June unfilled, but some $18,000,000 for April is behind. The Paymaster General has made a special requisition of $2,000,000 to pay officers in the Army of the Potomac, who require it for their current expenses, and that the moment the money is received paymasters will be sent to the army with it.

Very respectfully, your obedient servant,
H. S. HALLECK,
Major-General and Chief of Staff.

CIRCULAR
July 4, 1864.

3:00 P.M. Bivouac of Oliver's Brigade, 4th Division

In the First Brigade the news of the planned assault arrived at nearly the same time as the appearance of Rockwood's wagon train, filled to the freeboards with food and mail from home. It was too much like Providence to be taken calmly, and the men broke from their tents to mob the wagons and march them into the bivouac in parade. Shugrue, his face numb with the whiskey he had drunk, watched the riot uneasily. Rockwood's round face blushed: he was torn by embarrassment for the tribute he imagined he was receiving and by the image of the black man he had had to leave behind remained sharp in his mind. A brief look of vivid intensity from Sergeant Randolph struck him like a chill.

The orderly riding the second wagon shifted attention his way with a cry for sergeants to come get the mail sacks for their companies, and the soldiers surged that way like a wave sliding off a rock. Shouted names sang like lookouts' cries above the roar of laughter, outcries, and jabbering talk. Here and there beyond the commotion, knots of men gathered around the readers, waiting patiently for their turn to hear words from home.

Clutching his own letter in his fist, Randolph walked stiff-legged through the camp for Booker's tent, paying no mind to the yelling and the foolish palaver about an attack. He forced his legs to swing him forward simply and directly, but something made him doubt his purpose and his way: the image of the black man in the coffin, telling him that it was all for nothing, his life was useless, his prayers were jokes, his body a thing for white mocking devils to play with. *Nigger in a soldier unit, getting set to buy hisself a plantation. Tie you hand and foot, nigger, and do you like that.*

He pushed aside the tent flap, and Booker raised his head from where he was writing, and smiled. The white face: *damn my soul, how that face is white.* Why had he come to this man? Just some damn habit, like his feet took a mind on their own, just because of something in the letter that he always talked about with this white man. The white man had said something in greeting, but Randolph was locked in the grip of his feelings like a rod clutched by two fists: wanting to preserve his connection to Booker and the hope of finally owning the Hewson place; and wanting to put space between him and this white face. "Is it from home?" asked Booker, and at the word Randolph thrust the letter forward.

"Tobe say there, they gone hold sale of the Hewson place soon— maybe two or three weeks."

Booker glanced over to a black ledger on his camp desk. "As I calculate it, we've sent back maybe fifteen hundred dollars. If they sell it at homestead prices that will be enough."

"*Enough!*" said Randolph, so sharply that Booker looked up. "How you be sure they do that? Tobe say, word goin' round that they sell it at auction, with reg'lar bids, top dollar take the farm."

Booker looked at Randolph, the awareness of something wrong making his pale eyes narrow the least little bit. "Well," he said, "we know that Brickhill is working to have it go at auction. But I thought General Palmer and the Commission people were supposed to get the government to confiscate it and sell it cheap. I thought it was set. . . ."

"Well it ain't," said Randolph, looking intently at Booker's face. "You can't skin the fox till you catch im, and that Brick'l is plenty fox."

Randolph's eyes were brilliant with some feeling whose source Booker did not know. The sight made him uneasy. He was not aware of having done anything that should have made Randolph angry with him. He had in fact been sitting here waiting for him, basking in the glow of the good news he would have to tell Ki, anticipating the look of triumph in the black man's eye. He thought of saying something, asking . . . but something, some tension in his throat prevented him, and he found himself turning again to the ledger, to some matter that might neutralize the tension of the moment, redirect it to that part of their relationship in which they had always been able to think rationally and work together. "Well . . . so it would be best if we could send more money back to Tobe, just in case. . . ."

"And no pay yet this month," said Randolph.

"Not yet, no," said Booker, looking up, thinking this perhaps was it. Now he met the black man's heavy glare. "No enlisted pay has come through as yet. Officers have been paid, though."

"Well, that's fine." Randolph's face became impassive, the eyes thick and impenetrable. *Now ain't that something too. First they draft the nigger, cause the war need him so bad. Then they pay him two dollars less than they pay buckra, cause he just a nigger. Then they don't bother to pay him the eleven dollars anyway, cause what a nigger do with all that money?*

"There's no way we can get the usual draft back to Hewson's. I'll get the officers to pool some of their money and advance it to the men, but it won't amount to much."

"No, sir."

"Maybe the paymaster will come before the sale."

"Yes, sir."

It was back, whatever it was, in the slight emphasis Randolph put on *sir*. Randolph was angry at him and he had no idea why. "Can't you raise any money among the other companies?"

"No, sir. There ain't a lot of money in this brigade. We don't get paid much, or regular, it seem. And the men has fam'lies of their own. Sir." He was angry now, feeling it for Booker as much as for anyone: Booker who more than anyone had sold him the idea that being in the war was going to come to good for Randolph and Randolph's folks.

Booker saw the face of his friend for the first time as the face of a stranger and an enemy, and it stung him. He must not let that look of hatred and of closure remain or where was he? What was he? Just another damned *junker* driving peasants into the slaughterhouse. "Ki, I . . Ki, haven't you heard the news today? Don't you know what it could mean? Haven't you heard about the attack?" Randolph grunted, *Huh!*, as if in contempt, and Booker began to explain it, to set it out for Randolph so that he could see it. Listening to himself, he was aware of a false note—this was not how he had planned to tell it. It was as if he had to sell the attack to Randolph, cajole him into accepting more than its face value—as if that value were not enough to buy back a friend's love or buy off a comrade's anger.

He saw Randolph take it in, saw the tension melt, the angry contraction of the eyes give way to a look of weariness and puzzlement. Booker felt relieved as the tension went slack between them, but some misery remained threaded through the mood of relief, like a wailing note heard in a fog that might be a human cry, or a bird's. He had evaded Randolph's strange incomprehensible anger, and something in his success now seemed false and filled him with a mood of loss and absence.

Randolph now looked at him questioningly—without rage, but as if he too sensed the difference between them and the cancelling of the understandings that had made them friends. "I want you to tell me, Major. Why you care anyway, whether we get the Place or not? I never ask you that before," he said as if thinking aloud. It embarrassed him, suddenly: why had he never asked? It seemed weak in him, as if he had been in awe of this white man, and of other white men before this one; as if even after the pain and the anger and the killing, he hadn't managed to get the habit of being free even yet.

The Major looked tired too. His pale eyes were full of blood. "It's hard to explain it. I *believe* in doing this." He stopped, and his vision seemed to turn inward. "I believe the way someone might believe in God. My family . . . my people have suffered from this way of living we're all getting into—this way of rich men owning the land and the money and holding the power, and using it to take even the small part that's left. I believe . . . people ought to be their own boss of their own work, or their land, their lives—nobody but themselves tell them how to live. Sharing what they've got so that everyone can live decently. I see . . . forces, classes of men gathering all the wealth and power to themselves, and I feel that what they will do with it will take life and health and happiness from all the rest that have nothing, or only a little. I believe that. And I believe that ending slavery and seeing your people get the land they work on is one way to stop that."

Randolph looked hard at Booker. What the white man had said was clear enough. You could understand what he said, it was not unlike what Jesus himself might have said, *but there was something not complete about it—what?* "I don't see . . . I can't see what you mean about *believing* on this, what you say. For me"—he tapped his chest, and his eyes held the white man's—"I *believe* in Jesus, and the Words of promise: that the meek should inherit, I believe that, and that there is forgiveness and meeting hereafter"—his voice thickened, his neck-cords were full of grief Cassy lost, and the children—"and that a man should divide his cloak, and the rich man that spurned the poor man be cast into hell and will feed him on Judgment."

"A Day of Judgment," said Booker. "Yes, only I would say, men will make that judgment, and bring the new world into being by their will to do right."

Randolph shook his head. "I can't believe on that, as I believe of Jesus word. A day shall come which shall burn like a fire, and the fountains of the deeps broken up. It is written. And the Lord come down, saving his chirren." Randolph looked at Booker's face, and saw that the words did not touch the man, not in deep where the soul is. He felt a great gentleness, pity for the man, the man wanted to do good but had not got the spirit of belief in him, and Randolph said, softly, "Well, now, but I guess I knows that Jesus is not for you."

Booker thought, *It is because I am a Jew—how does he know it?"*

But Randolph thought, *It is because he is a white man, and Jesus's face is black as my own.*

JUDAH BOOKER, BORN JUDAH BEN-LEVI BOOKSER

The Bookser house was on the edge of the ghetto. From its rear windows they could look beyond the gray confines of the ghetto and the looming bulk of the city to the fat green fields of Prussia. Wheat fields and alfalfa, blue in springtime deepening to green, then going yellow to be harvested in shocks of gold, molten in the varnished light of the low evening sun. The shocks of wheat in that light were lions, glowing with sleeping strength on a burning plain. Beyond the wheat field was a cherry orchard, black branches covered alternately in its two snows, of crystal and of blossom—a white touched pink at the base.

Once they walked into the field, Judah and his father, to buy cherries from the farmer. The farmer, suspicious, bit the coin three times. It was a good coin; but still he wouldn't take it. The cherries were his; he wouldn't sell. "One day, Daddy, will we have cherry trees of our own?"

The Law says you must have nothing, from the day you are born until you die. The Law says: on pain of punishment, withdrawal of the protecting Hand, you must live in the style of your death, empty, so that when you die you will not be missed.

They are not from this place, but from somewhere else. From Poland—and before that, from someplace else. Poland was an empty land, endless black woods and a vacant sky in which there was no god nor good light. Home was a circle of huts in the great vacancy, a huddle of furred and thatched warmth about a fleck of fire. The warmth drew wolves out of the darkness. Back in an impossible time before that they had lived in Jerusalem, under a vine and a fig tree. The telling of this story is part of the sacred duties of a man, the retelling of the story of the Exodus at Passover: "This year men are slaves, next year may all men be free. This year we are here; next year may we all be in Jerusalem." His mother, or her mother's mother's mother, had been a woman of valor, her price above the price of rubies; and his father's father's father and mother's mother's mother were praised in the gates. One is always from some other place.

Over the mantlepiece is an engraving of a Russian troika in the snow, its people bearlike in furred coats. A pack of wolves, slavering whitely with white eyes that glare in the black scoring of the fur, surrounds the troika; two men stand and face them grimly, with pistols aimed; a woman with a child twists upward from her furred robe, her mouth stretched to screaming, her child held up and away. . . . In the foreground snow, a small crater of darkness, its edges broken by tossed fragments of bone, a broken collar, speaks of the fate of a faithful hound, and prophesies the end of the family in the troika. A wolf hangs from the ear of a writhing horse, the second horse rears in panic and threatens to overturn the troika, the third horse lies with outstretched neck, blood running from his nostrils into the snow—the wolves are doing something unimaginable behind the bulk of his barrel. There are lights and moods in which it seems that the woman is holding the child aloft to preserve him for a last second from the jaws. And there are times when it seems the infant will be thrown far out into the pack, to appease the Teeth and the Belly.

His father is Levi Bookser, an iron molder. The ironworkers of Berlin are progressive, forward-looking. A group meets regularly for *lieder und lager*. In their meeting hall they play chess, and their newspaper—published irregularly because of the interference of a fearful government—discusses the most enlightened philosophy of the day, *Kultur* along with matters of more immediate concern : wages, the conditions of life in the factories. There are a good many socialists among them : they dream of a liberal republic replacing the rule of king and *junker*. In that Republic there will be no aristocrat and peasant, no landlord and tenant, no taskmaster and worker : all will labor, all will enjoy.

Of course, in such a Republic, there will no longer be a Jewish question. The order that made the Jew a Jew will have disappeared; Jews being unnecessary, they would imperceptibly merge somehow with the mass. And in that withering away, all antipathies would vanish.

In the meantime Levi Bookser was all right, a good worker and a comrade, even if he was a Jew. (A Jew, even if he was a good worker; and a comrade, of course.)

In his home, at his table, Levi Bookser spoke and dreamed of the Republic that would come. His voice was loud, overriding the mumble of grandfather's prayers; yet with his anger, his eyes were windows on a sadness reaching to despair. He felt he must silence the old man's prayers and stories. The Jewish past was a deep pit, the burnt-out crater of a volcano, a snare, a nightmare from which the living Jew must somehow awake, to make a new place for himself in daylight. Beyond it were fields and orchards of shocked gold and flowering snow.

In 1848 the Revolution came sweeping out of the West like a tide, and his father and his comrades appeared in the streets of the city with weapons in their hands. There was a time of triumph, when the wolves groveled, and the Republic began to appear, premonition of Messiah, Berlin would be Jerusalem. Then the army came, and the Uhlans in their black coats out of Poland, chaos and the night of wolves.

The day they fled Berlin was, strangely, a day of liberation. They had decided to go. Though the Revolution was dying here, they had seen it, they had tasted its reality. They would go to America, where it was already real. They would do that, because they had beaten the wolf once, however briefly. They took ship from Hamburg to New Orleans, and the river steamer from New Orleans to St. Louis. On the journey grandfather died, and was buried at sea. Because of this his ghost was unquiet.

The steamer from New Orleans shuddered against the muscular brown current. It slid out of the main stream to hide from the current in safe side-channels, where the jungle came down to dip its feet and hair in the flow. From the deck Judah could smell the jungle smell, huge acres of rot and ferment, fish and reptiles sliding above the muck, snakes and wildcats in the trees. The eyes of the people in the waterside shacks were sharp and furtive, like the eyes of the snakes; but their children laughed and called, and waved to the steamboat. When the jungle laid back the plantations were there. The gangs and gangs of the Black People took the fields in swarms, chanting.

His father shook his head. "People bought and sold like cattle. As in the Pharaoh's day. It is a *crime*."

Pharaoh. Let my people go. This year we are here, next year in Jerusalem; this year men are in slavery, next year may they all be free.

Including these with the skin of animals and the eyes of cows, and the huge red mouths of beasts?

The steamboat leaves that coast in its wake, the riddle unsolved. But Judah is glad to leave it: *here* the Pharaoh is not for his people, only for these others. He decides he will pray for them, according to the form of the prayer, each year at Passover. Next year in Jerusalem. Next year all men to be free.

St. Louis was "the most foreign city in America," the German émigrés of '48 intruding into a town with roots in the French and Spanish past of pre-Revolutionary days, over which were laid the Anglo-American settlers from North and South: the Irish who labored on canals, riverboats, railroads, and construction gangs; Negroes and masters out of the slaveholding hinterland of the state. Queen City of the crossroads, where the Missouri River traffic to and from the great distant West met the great north-south sweep of the Mississippi River trade that bound the Great Lakes to the tropical Gulf, and tied the Alleghenies to New Orleans.

In some ways it was like Berlin. The Germans had their clubs where they organized lectures and *lieder,* did their Turner exercises, read German papers, and talked of *Kultur* and of the Revolution. All around them, it seemed, the Revolution they had fought for was rising, succeeding, here in a New World. What could not be accomplished with the combination of their German philosophy and experience, and the practical know-how of these Americans! They read *The New Rome,* and dreamed of the United States of Europe. There was slavery still: it was all around them, *schwarzes*—strange people with faces like those of animals, monkeys. But the Republic would deal with such anomalies. Slavery, like the Jewish question: one of those matters the new system would cause to disappear.

Levi Bookser got a job as an iron molder in a factory north of the city. Skilled workers with his kind of experience were few. Mr. Sinclair valued him, listened solemnly to his advice on reforming procedures, buying new equipment. At the same time, the Germans—he called them that—in the Society began to alienate him. He was, frankly, a little tired of their eagerness to "have the Jewish question go away."
"I'm the Jewish question. It's me they wish to send away!" Passover became a memory of Poland, and a vision of America. In this New World, there were opportunities to succeed that one never dreamed of in Germany: there was another way to resolve the Jewish question—make a life for yourself here, in American terms. Jew, Gentile, it doesn't matter—as long as you aren't *schwarz*.

Judah went to the factory with his father early in the morning. He was a privileged man, an apprentice to a skilled molder. Such positions were few, and jealously guarded by the molders for their children. Mr. Sinclair did treat his father's opinions with a certain deference. Solemnly the two would consult about the affairs of the factory as a whole, not just about the molding. Father knew a thing or two, gave good advice. The boss respected him. "I'm the next thing to a partner there," Levi Bookser would sometimes say. "There have been hints, even, that something formal will be done. I say no more." It was a wonderful country.

Judah attended meetings of the Land Reform Association. There was to be land for all, settled and developed on a cooperative basis. While he poured flaring iron down trenches of gray stone, to cool in the ingot molds, he dreamed of exploring western valleys for the Cooperative Commonwealth.

He met Miriam at one of these meetings. She was just a girl, listening to Judah and his friends talk about how to organize their imaginery western enterprises. She had large black eyes, and walked with a vigorous stride, swining her arms like a boy; she had long arms that looked strong, and big hands. One day she said, "But you know, there isn't really enough land for everybody to have some. Unless you stop having children, eventually you run out of homesteads. It's plain arithmetic."

On April 25, 1853, he was pouring molten iron from a stone ladle when the stone crumbled and he watched the slow lava drip out of the cracked crater in stop-time movement, and he had already been screaming for an eternity when the full power of the agony from his leg shot all through his body and blew his consciousness out like a candle.

He rose on waves of torture pulsing out of his burnt leg and sank into fevered blackness. Days on days. Once he heard his father speaking with Mr. Sinclair, "Levi, Levi, you must understand. You must see this as a reasonable man. If I pay you anything here in the way of an indemnity for the boy, I establish a precedent that I can't live with. You know it. How often we've discussed it ourselves. The business can't survive if we're liable for the full cost of any injury. I know the payment is a token, it's not equal to the suffering, yes. But I will make it up to you, later, in other ways. It's just that, we must not have the precedent. I feel that the business is in a sense in your hands at this moment. For the sake of our friendship, Levi, don't disappoint me."

There was a scene of rage. The pain that rose in his leg and from his heart twisted an almost speechless anger out of him. His father wept. His broad heavy back bent sideways at a painful angle and shook.

When Judah healed they would sit in the parlor, unable really to speak to each other. Judah's mother fluttered nervously; she felt that her family had already been broken before she had had time to see it wearing out. How terrible it felt for him to be sitting there, feeling still that tenderness for his father, yet having to see in him that *failure*. There was nothing to say. Levi Bookser had not gone through with Sinclair's deal. His son's rage and grief had turned him back the way— even Judah knew—his heart had told him to go. He had demanded compensation, quit when it wasn't granted, and gone to court. Lost the case.

A Dutchman now had his job. When the leg healed, Judah was to go West, to join an uncle in the Nevada mines. There was some thought of starting a factory to make miner's tools. When he left, riding with a freight wagon, Miriam came to say goodbye.

On May 1, 1854, the freight-wagon crossed the Missouri-Kansas line, and Judah smelled the different air of the plains, the heavy scent of green grass. The wind moved toward him from a limitless horizon. A few clouds moved across the space, trailing shadows beneath them over the long grass, and he sensed the depth and solitude of western space, the distances between things. There were huge absences and losses: the empty sky, no people, the clear fields, the dry and sparse-grass prairies that burned brown before they had crossed over. There were sudden unbelievable revelations of a colossal opulence: sudden valleys full of brilliant green-leaved cottonwoods in the brown prairie; random patches of wild flowers erupting in the grass; a sea of buffalo, brown-humped and earth-smelling, like an ocean of living muscle and blood, through which they moved carefully for days till they saw the other side. The taste of the meat was strange and rich, with a tang of wild herbs. The heavy blood and melted fat ran out of the corners of his mouth, and he wiped his hands on his shirt. When they crossed South Pass the mountains hovered like ghosts against the sky. His life—Poland, Berlin, St. Louis, Judah Bookser, Iron Molders Union, Land-Reform League— vanished into insignificance. He threw it all away.

He left the train in Salt Lake City to head north with some rough-looking types that wanted to trade for furs and horses up in the Crow Indian country. They had an Indian guide with them, an old poor-devil. Judah had an ear for languages: by the time they got to the Crow country he was their interpreter. He thought his family might grieve for him; yet this bothered him only distantly. As if out of habit, he somehow kept track of the Sabbath, and went aside to pray as he had at home. Once the old trapper with the party, a hardcase named Moutry, surprised him at it, and backed away; spent the next few days looking at him suspiciously. In Judah's mind the images of Poland surged. It was all so familiar, an eternal and inescapable story. Finally Moutry spoke: "A man's religion's his own business, but something about what you was doing, some strange language and all . . ."

Judah decided to meet it straight on. "I'm a Jew, Moutry. A Hebrew. You understand?"

Moutry stared at him a moment. "Hebrew. All right. Well, I don't know much about that. Don't care neither. Dammit to hell, boy, if you didn't have me thinkin you was a Mormon! I can't abide a Mormon."

When the traders headed back for the settlements, he stayed behind with Moutry, who had a wife among the Crows, riding to meet the Indians over a high pass where tiny flowers spreckled a mat of intricately intertwined springy green, in air that was thin to starvation and smelled of snow—and down to a valley full of the odor of people and horses living closely.

He spent a year there. They followed the buffalo and gathered wild berries and roots, caught, herded, broke, and bred their fine Appaloosa horses. They made war with the Sioux and Shoshones, stole horses. In the winter they holed up and lived off what they'd been able to save up, and what they could hunt. In the wintertime the healthy ones got gaunt, and the weak ones died. They shared what they had, but the weak ones died.

There were dances and ceremonies. Sometimes these were totally strange, alien. At other times the floating, dipping sound of the keening chant reminded him of the rhythms of the synagogue, and he felt that the village of conical tents was a strange dream. He had a woman to warm him in the lodge at night: Moutry's sister-in-law. She was the first woman he'd ever had. She smelled of sweet-grass and sweat, and after they'd made love, of strong female juices. Her smells enveloped him. When they made love he felt like a man riding a galloping horse, he felt himself plunge into her belly and explode there, and expire.

She was bought and paid for in the Indian way, with horses and blankets and a bolt of cloth. What that meant for the woman and her people was one thing; for himself, another. The woman of valor and wisdom has a price above that of rubies: this one was bought with horse-flesh and store goods. *For the lips of the strange woman drop as a honey-comb, and her mouth is smoother than oil, but her end is bitter as worm-wood, her feet lead down to death, her ways are changeable that thou canst not know them.* What does the bought woman think, moving beneath him in the dark or smiling across a steaming bowl of meat or chewing skins for clothing? The goods are between them, even a higher price would not make this different: for him, she is a woman bought with money, her responses purchased, never the free response of desire to desire.

He has a friend there, too—Wolf's Brother. The Indian is his own age, a warrior, Moutry's relative by some connection; he wants to learn the white man's language. All right, a bargain is struck—Bookser would teach him English and learn from him to hunt and go to war as the Crows did. He wants something too, Bookser thinks: wisdom or knowledge, where the other is content to exchange the use of her body for goods. But the principle is the same.

Or is it? Trading word for word leads to speech, talk of actions, states of mind: "I feel good when the wind blows from the south." "Why do you?" A shrug, the question makes no sense. Wolf's Brother says, "From the *south*"—as if that answered.

Hunting, or scouting the Shoshone horse herds, the two of them together are alive in their eyes and senses, seeking out, listening for ambush. But what can this savage teach beyond his simple skills, any more than his sister can teach of love?

Once they go to steal horses from the Shoshone, to fill out the string Wolf's Brother is building to buy his bride. Everything is done carefully and well, they black their faces and bodies and run the horses off in the dark. They dodge and obscure their trail, misleading the pursuers by all kinds of devices, taxing all forethought and calling up all they had of instinct for treachery to preserve themselves and their horses. Finally, on the border of that territory in which they might hope to meet friends, a party of four Shoshone appears across a small creek and a sloping meadow. They are far enough off to escape, if they ride moderately fast, shooing the horses through a narrow defile to safety on the other side. Wolf's Brother looks at Bookser and grins. He shifts the weight of his torso from hip to hip, and his horse moves with the rhythm, beginning to jitter and snort with excitement, and Wolf's Brother says, "I am going."

"What? Why? We can run the horses through that canyon and have them safe."

Wolf's Brother nods up at the Shoshones, who sit calmly watching. "They are waiting for me," he says. "It feels like a good day." He is smiling and nodding, he looks up at the sun and grins, and he begins to sing:

> *Let us see*
> *is it real*
> *this life I am living?*
> *Let us see*
> *is it real*
> *this life I am living?*
> *Let us see.*

and winds his snorting pony in tighter circles, then lets him go, and the horse takes him spattering through the stream and up toward the Shoshones, who come swooping to meet him, and Bookser spanks the rear of the nearest horse to start them down the defile, and dismounts, dropping the reins, and takes his rest with his rifle across his saddle, the horse between him and the Indians; and he sees Wolf's Brother pass through, and the Shoshones wheel and charge back again in mirror image, and Wolf's Brother charge his horse straight back across the stream. Wolf's Brother is grinning. His body radiates heat; it shines with sweat. Maybe a man does not know what it is to hold his life unless he has once in his life thrown it away, can't feel it unless he throws it to the wolves again, and again, "Let us see / is it real . . ."

Once a blizzard struck when he was hunting away from the camp. The air froze, turned white, and rushed in his face, a wall of blankness. Tree sap exploded in the trunk. In the frozen rush of air he could hear wolves howling, near at hand or far off there was no telling. The rush of white wind and sound blinded and deafened him. He moved in cotton wool. A blackness loomed in the blank white and he moved toward it. In the lee of the black bulk there was a lessening of the white rush, and he could see that it was a small group of buffalo brought to bay by the storm as he had seen them bayed by wolves, a humped-up brown circle, bull-horns and heavy heads outward, pig-eyes glinting toward the howling jaws. He stumbled toward them as if toward shelter, expecting them to run. He hoped, somehow, he might get a shot at one, kill and gut it, and shelter in the cavity. But the bulls didn't move as he approached, stirred only slightly as he wriggled among them and pressed into the shaggy coarse wool. Out of the white storm other animals stumbled toward the huddle. He made out deer, perhaps a pronghorn; a gang of coyotes drifted in, wolves. Predator and prey were held in truce by the terrible white power of the storm.

When the storm lightened he felt the heavy body next to him heave up and move off. He wondered if he should shoot for meat; or if in shooting he might violate some law of the place that he had kept that night, as had his brother wolves; and in the breaking bring on some kind of doom.

When the round began again in the spring, he knew he had to leave. There was a story to life, a parable, one had to go on toward an answer. Here there were no answers, only traps: sloth and sensual pleasure, followed by danger and death. He was a stranger here, his place bought, his love bought, friendship bought. He did not understand the Indians any more than he could speak the language of the buffalo. Perhaps there was nothing to understand.

Yet when he left, the woman hid herself in the lodge and would not come out.

And when he raised his hand in farewell to Wolf's Brother, the Indian grabbed his two forearms in a grip of iron, held tight, and looked hard at him with his black eyes, and Judah remembered, *Let us see / Is it real / This life we are living?* And he seemed to catch, but questioned his hearing, a sound in the earth like keening or lamentation moving in a vibration from their feet to the rigid muscular grip of their hands on each other's arms. He broke the grip, and moved on.

California and the gold fields, El Dorado: valleys that were virgin in May were crawling like a tenement by July; and there were sagebrush and wolves in the streets by September. But he made enough money in a poker game to buy passage home around by the Isthmus.

Coming back up the river, he saw again, as a man, the scenes he had passed when a boy coming from Germany: the jungle, death and life tangled and trampling each other; the plantations, and the black gangs swarming in the fields.

Looked more closely now. A circle of them shackled together on the deck: the men sat around the outer edge, fifteen of them, with three women with sucking infants, and a teenaged girl-child, sitting in the middle. The passing white men who stopped to make the customary lewd proposals to the girls had to speak to them over the shaggy wool of the men's heads. The men's eyes never lifted from the deck. Their arms and legs were shackled to bolts in the deck. Yet from their heads an emanation of some . . . presence, no more palpable than their smell, rose as barrier between their women and the white men, that no white man's hand could cross—until they arrived at their destination, and their master unshackled them and took them off to sell.

And again they seemed like animals, but different this time. Their heads reminded him of the wooly heads of the buffalo, circled at bay sheltering him against the storm.

When they reached Vicksburg, the master of the slaves released the shackle binding them to the deck. The slaves filed toward the gangplank. Judah stood by the railing and watched.

As one woman in a red turban stepped off she stumbled. The man behind her reached with his left hand and grabbed her round. "Kierful, ol ooman," he said, and it seemed that the two looked at the brown rush of river as if it tempted them.

Judah remembered what he had heard, the stories of slaves killing themselves and their children to escape slavery. Judah felt he was in some dream or fantasy. Nothing was real, here. Perhaps he had made it all up, about the shambling *schwarzes* preferring death to slavery. On impulse, he ran down the gangplank after the coffle.

He took a pair of cigars out of his vest, stepped up to the man. The man stood, seemingly as indifferent as an ox at auction. "Here," said Judah. "Take these."

The man's eyes, all brown pupil set in a rim of clear yellow glaze, looked at Judah.

"Thank kinely, bose," said the man. "Thank kinely," and he tucked them quickly inside his shirt. Judah wanted to feel an accomplice in something against the master. What was there to say or do?

"Next year in Jerusalem," he said.

The black man's round ball-like eyes seemed to fill and swell, like black coal heated in a fire.

"Ay-men, sah. Ay-men."

"Ay-men. Amen.

The man had understood after all.

His parents were still there, but diminished, two old people named Bookser, time eating into their substance the way fire brittles wood into charcoal, then eats it away in tiny licks. His father's face had withered and become strange: Judah's anger now could burst it into nothingness, a smear of ashes.

He had no money, and there was a Panic on. He took a job in a factory—not molding, unskilled work. When the boss cut wages they struck, and the boss brought in Negroes from his plantation, and bullied one of the older men into bossing them and showing them the work. Judah, looking through the window, saw the black shapes hauling against the fire, like devils in some Christian hell, their white teeth flashing.

He thought of the black man, the woman and the child on the steamboat. *Not like machines at all,* he thought, *not like animals either. Children of Israel, like myself, and born to the covenant. Next year in Jerusalem.*

There must be some way out of the trap, some escape. There always has been before—from Poland, from Berlin, from St. Louis after the iron wounded him, from the eternal round of the Crow camp. Something to break the chain that binds a man to his place, binding which is death, the snare that holds you for the wolves. He remembered, "Let us see / Is it real / This life, . . ." and looked for something to do. Joined the National Labor Union, organized by the Iron Molders Union to organize against the oppression of capital, the enslavement of the wage-earner to the wage and the machine.

Not enough.

There was a war in Kansas. By the end of 1857 he was running guns to Free Soil settlers past the watchful eyes of Border Ruffians along the Missouri line. Disguised as a peddler, disguised as a salesman of Bibles: bravado and defiance hidden under a cloak of meekness. He was tempted, often, to throw it aside, to charge the way his friend had charged the Shoshones : to throw his carefulness away, and find out what is real. Something held him from the test.

Instead of death and the guns of the Border Ruffians, he found Miriam. She spoke at a meeting, for the women of the National Union : her words were absolutely clear, passion and wisdom linked. Her eyes caught the light like a cat's eyes in the dark, her hair hovered around her face in loops and curves that held by their own strength, her hands and arms made curvetting shapes in the air as she spoke. Her body rode her hips like an athletic girl a strong-haunched horse. When he went up to her after the meeting she said, "Well, it seems you are back," and took his hand. Her breasts looked heavy under her cotton dress. Her lips moved in a smile, showing strong white teeth, and her black eyes seemed to him soft and affectionate, holding his image. She had remembered him.

He spent evenings telling her his adventures, or some of them. But these were approximations of a truth, parables. What was most real to him of those evenings was that fact : she had remembered him. An image of him in the mind and heart, held like his minute reflection in her dark and gentle eyes, dark and fierce eyes : real, ineradicable.

At first he did not consciously court her, but pursuing his needs found himself seeking her out, putting himself in her path for chance meetings. A strange game, what was he doing? A test : each time, she remembered him. Speaking to her, his words struck responses, sometimes calling up more power in her than had been in him.

"You haven't forgiven the Old Man, Books! You're just afraid that your anger will finish killing him, finish what Sinclair started. And he can't forgive himself any more than you can."

And of Wolf's Brother : she bit her lip. "He was saying that he loved you, Books. Didn't you even sense that? And did you just ride off saying nothing?"—and he knew that she could guess the presence of the woman, silent in the lodge. Should he tell her?

He must—only if she could know everything of him, holding it all clear in mind and heart and eye, would he be safe with her. A woman of valor, who can find? Her price is far above rubies. Strength and honor are her clothing. She openeth her mouth with wisdom, and in her tongue is the law of kindness. Let her be as the loving hind and the pleasant roe, let her breasts satisfy three forever, and be thou ravished always with her love. . . .

You are my wife, my love, my teacher. Whatever I know of my body and heart I know from you.

Wrapped in each other, one in one, twisted round and over in bindings of corded muscles, interpierced and penetrated by tongues, fingers, cock, and cunt, wrapped in an atmosphere of sharp and mellow odors. And in her he touches it : that dark place, that place of un-self.

> *Let us see*
> *   is it real*
> *   this life we are living.*
> *Let us see.*

He had thrown himself into Miriam as Wolf's Brother had thrown himself at the Shoshones. It was the same: he had bound himself to life, he had bound himself to death—touching one touched both. What intelligence could read the parable of that, the parable of Judah and Miriam, and say what was life and what death, what right and what wrong? There was no control, no logic. With her I know nothing, can anticipate nothing. Her eyes hold and preserve me, her body holds me close—

—and hurls me into space.

Their child was born in spring—*Like the buffalo calves,* he thought —and smelled again the smell of the camp, sweetgrass, smoke, sweat. The midwife's kettles filled the room with steam, like a sweatlodge of the Crows. Miriam lay on the bed, clamped to her huge pulsing belly, writhing as its anger shook her. He looked deep into her face, seeing the answer, anger at him, some deep anger coming from the same irrational well as the love, the sexual hunger, the burgeoning substance of the child itself, devouring her like the fox the wolf under the coat of the Spartan boy. But when he looked closely he could see nothing like that; no anger for the pain, but between the assaults of the hidden wolf a deep satisfaction, as if each surge of pain were the accomplishment of some difficult craft.

The birth surged in her, and her body arched and rose, head thrown back, neck cords standing sharp against the curve as thick vines snake on the limb of a jungle tree. She screamed and he thought of Death, and the midwife reached into her crotch, gripped and twisted, and he saw its face break out into the light—but it was life, after all, and not death. The child, the Eli, not the wolf.

He had been so sure that it would be death.

The life was strange and rich, taste of imagined cherries in a foreign orchard, forbidden and withheld, dear with a double meaning. Elijah ben-Yehudah Bookser, the small soft body still held the eggshape of the enclosing womb. The baby's deep eyes, shape of face, might be his own face, his own eyes. *Mine.* But the smell was of Miriam, smell of sun on lake water, smell of milk.

But when the child cried out, its small intricate frame shaken with grief, he remembered the troika in the snow, and the wolves. A man who works for his bread must go abroad, and in a society where all men are predators he must snatch his bread from the jaws of wolves—his fellow wolves. And for a man who has seen that it is injustice in society that makes wolves of men, there is not only the snarling over bread, there is the harder longer hunting for a new Law, a new basis for the pack. How was he to do battle with the wolves, and among the wolves and for the wolves, and not become a wolf himself?

When the war came he was ready to go, ready to leave the circle of peace as he had left the buffalo-circle in the blizzard, to go again where anger and strength were law; where his strength directed violence toward an end that would be good for all, peace in heart and home, mother and child safe, next year in Jerusalem and all men free. He went with the army against the Confederates in Missouri, and with the Jayhawkers against the rebel guerrillas in Kansas, and he turned some of the wolves into comrades who howled with him on his scent, and they tasted the blood of enemies.

When he came to St. Louis again, on his way east, her eyes were strange as if she no longer saw in him the remembered Judah Bookser. He'd been away for months Jayhawking Kansas and Missouri into freedom, but it wasn't a matter of the time. Their language seemed stilted, as if their words were translated from another tongue. They clung tightly, wrapped each nakedness in the other again and again. Deep in the fierce craving of their bodies was an exhaustion like peace, in which their understanding must lie.

Is it that you don't want me to go, Miriam? You know that it isn't for myself, but for you and Eli, for everyone who . . .

You say you love me, love us. But when you look at us, at Eli even, I see . . . it is as if you hate us, as if you were filled with rage at us. You look at us the way you looked at your father all the while he was dying, hating him but saying nothing. . . .

I forgave him for what he . . . what he failed to do . . . long ago.

Not that. It was the being weak. It was the dying you couldn't forgive.

Everyone dies. . . .

Not you. You will not stay still for it. You will go away. . . .

It is that you don't want me to go.

You have already left. When you are with us, we make you feel . . . how weak we all are. How easily broken or destroyed we may be. You say you hate the strength of evil—and you do hate it—but you envy it too. And weakness makes you afraid, and you hate what you fear . . .

You are my love, my wife, my teacher.

And you never learn what I have to teach. And you are going away.

I will come back. Don't say that you think I won't.

Why ?

If you were not there . . . if there was no one who remembered me, or held my face . . . no one and he saw an image of the child with his face, perfectly weak and helpless, looking hungrily and trustingly at the lion-maned head bending over him.

Yes, she said, *then there would be nothing to keep you from turning wolf yourself.*

3:30 P.M. The Mine

The sentry by the bombproof door ducked his head in and called, "Brass coming!" and Pleasants arose quickly and went outside. Three officers were coming along the trench, one of them a General—Hunt, chief of artillery—and Major Duane, the chief engineer under Meade. The third man was a staff captain, Sanderson : a natty man with a neat mustache and sardonic expression. Pleasants buttoned the top of his soldier's blouse, stepped forward, and saluted.

"Colonel," said Hunt.

"Your servant, gentlemen. Can I assist you in some way?"

"These are our orders," said Duane, a sharp little man buttoned up to the collar in his uniform coat. He reminded Pleasants of a shorter, younger Meade, and he dizzily wondered for a moment if high Generals surrounded themselves with staff who resembled them in some way. He'd always felt that Richmond might have been Burnside's son and . . . he didn't really read the orders, but imagined they were to inspect his proceedings. He swallowed, tensely.

"Would you care to see what we've done?"

"That can wait until later," said Duane. "Just now I'd like a look at your drawings. You'll be responding to our questions in writing, of course, but a preliminary look will do no harm."

Pleasants stood to one side while they went through his plans. He tried to think through replies to the questions they would be most likely to ask. But they asked no questions, until the very end, when Duane looked up and said, "Colonel, these plans are well laid out. You've done some tunneling in the mines, I've heard. Let me ask you: do you know the length of the longest shaft for a military mine?"

"No, sir."

"It was dug by the English, at Sebastopol in the Crimea, by professional military engineers. It was less than three hundred and fifty feet in length, took months to dig and ultimately failed of its intended effect."

"I was not aware of that, sir. However, I can assure you that longer mineshafts have been dug than the one we project. . . ."

"In these soils? And with men unused to military mining? And in the face of a hostile enemy, with every capability of countermining? I would not question your professional skill, Colonel Pleasants. But if you'll forgive me for saying it—though really it can't be taken as a criticism of you—you are not a military engineer. There are differences."

"Still, Colonel," said General Hunt, "I must say these drawings look quite promising. I wish you well."

"Thank you, sir." There was a pause. "Will you want to look at the Mine now?"

"No," said Hunt, with a small smile, "that won't really be necessary. We'd best continue with our inspection of the line."

The officers saluted and left. Pleasants looked at the drawings on the table. He took out his pencil and tapped it on the margin of his master diagram. Then he threw the pencil down on the table. He had been patronized within an inch of his life, and had stood for it! Military mining indeed! A shaft was a shaft, and if it was well dug it stayed and if it wasn't it fell in, and if you dug it straight it took you down to the coal or under an enemy fort or wherever. It would be a pleasure showing them up. And he was grateful for one piece of information: knowing that if they finished the tunnel, it would be the world-beater! He could tell from their manner with him that they never expected he would do it. They'd know it when he blew the fort sky-high and dropped it right in their laps!

Feeling better than he had for days, since the quicksand had undermined his props, Pleasants trotted down the trench toward the minehead. He wanted to be with the men working on the Mine, to get in touch with its reality once more.

Only a military engineer, he thought, would have looked at the drawings and never even stuck his head down in the hole.

5:30 P.M. *Burnside's Headquarters*

"I still can't comprehend why they would not have reported to these headquarters. It would seem a simple courtesy to the commander of the corps!" General Burnside's face was flushed with rage, and his deep voice had a slight quaver.

"Sir, I'm sure they had no wish to be discourteous. It is possible that their orders, or circumstances, may have required them to return early," said Richmond. Burnside's anger was dangerous. His General must do nothing, but above all say nothing, in haste. It was obvious that the utmost diplomacy was required with Meade. Even the man's own officers declared he was impossible to get along with.

" 'Their orders,' " said Burnside. "I'll vow they had orders from Meade to say devil a word to me!"

"Sir, I'll make some inquiries at headquarters. I really don't believe there's cause for alarm here. We know Meade's attitude."

Burnside's rage abated with its utterance. He was ready to be reassured. "All right, Lew." Then his full lips drew in grimly, and he had to ask, "Is General Ledlie here yet?"

"He's waiting outside."

"All right. You'd best send him in. And leave us alone."

This was a really regrettable thing, this meeting with the commander of his First Division. But there had been rumors. . . . He wouldn't countenance gossip, malice in his command. The IX Corps organization was built on mutual trust. Still, there were some rumors one had to look into, they were too serious to ignore. If they were true . . . well, but if they were untrue, and that was most likely, they had to be scotched. Immediately.

Ledlie came in. He was a handsome man, with a shock of white hair above a red, sunburnt-looking face, with iron-gray heavy brows, small blue eyes and a strong firm jaw. Burnside liked the man's face—frank and manly, anyone with an eye for physiognomy could easily read it. "General," he said, with heartiness that was only partly feigned, "it's good to see you!" It *was* good to see him! The reality was so much better than the rumors. How to approach the subject?

"I've been wanting to confer with you, General—you know I have great respect for your abilities, from what I've seen of your work in this corps so far. General . . . how is your division? Have you everything you need?"

Ledlie smiled, showing strong square teeth. "Well, General, there was never a man in uniform that could answer that question affirmatively. We need more men, better food, a little female companionship now and again." The two Generals nodded and chuckled. "But by and large sir, yes, except for something more in the way of sandbags, we're in good shape.''

''The morale of the men is good?''

''Certainly. That is, as good as can be expected. We have been on the line for some days now, and the men show signs of wear. A week's relief would not hurt them.''

''Certainly, although you know how difficult it is to arrange.''

Burnside made a mental note. Perhaps some relief was all the division needed. Overworked and overwrought men imagined all kinds of things about their commanders. The thought of that made Burnside flush slightly; then he thought, *I mustn't let him see my embarrassment, or he'll guess that the purpose of this conversation is not strictly social.* A clever notion occurred to him. He glanced craftily at Ledlie, then reached into his field desk and brought up a brown bottle and two glasses.

''General, will you join me?'' He looked intently at Ledlie, aware for the first time of the small broken lines of capillaries in the man's nose and cheeks.

Ledlie stared blandly into Burnside's face. ''No, General, thank you. I don't believe I will. I don't care much for whiskey just before dining. It doesn't agree with me.''

Burnside looked at the bottle. Thought of continuing the play and pouring himself a glass; but there was no point. Ledlie had passed that test, with flying colors. Burnside was feeling better about things already. He determined to make a frontal move on the question—without, however, being so brusque as to offend the man.

''General,'' he said, ''I wonder how your subordinate officers are bearing up under the strain of this campaign. Do you have entire confidence in them? Do they seem . . . *responsive* to your orders? Or is there . . . hesitancy, reluctance?''

''Sir, I believe I understand your question. I can assure you that I have the utmost faith in and admiration for my officers, especially the regulars under me, and I rely on them implicitly. I am not, as you know, a military man by profession, and I see no shame in admitting my limitations.'' Burnside nodded his head—he liked that way of thinking. ''I hope I may say,'' continued Ledlie, ''that they have the same confidence in me.''

Burnside was taken aback. It would be terribly cutting to answer that question in any other than a reassuring way. Yet the fact was that it was the regular officers who were the source of the rumors about Ledlie. Stories of drinking, and worse. What to say?

Seeing Burnside at sea, Ledlie came to his rescue. ''I think, sir, that some of my officers may have supposed that my indisposition was such that continuance in command posed a danger to my health. Some such rumors reached me, and I fear may have done me some injury in the opinion of the division, and perhaps with you, sir. I must say, I am troubled with recurrent bouts of malaria. Still, I am quite fit, I assure you. The indispositions are temporary, and the heat of the trenches is occasionally cause of an attack.''

There was no doubting the man's sincerity. And it was a plausible explanation as well. A man subject to bouts of malarial fever might well acquire the reputation of being a drunkard, in an atmosphere as charged with tension as the trenches. And mark that Ledlie had never denied he did take a drink; but he had shown he could turn one down. Perhaps the best thing would be to relieve the First Division and give it a day or so of rest. That would restore morale, and Ledlie's health as well. It wouldn't be necessary to ruffle IX Corps' peace or embarrass the corps by firing a General of Division for unfitness in command.

"Thank you, General," said Burnside, rising. "I have enjoyed this frank discussion with you. I can assure you of my concern and support, and I'll do my best to give your division some relief. We must all be ready for the great days that are ahead."

"Thank *you*, sir," said Ledlie, and saluted. Burnside was pleased to note that the man's face did not show the slightest symptoms of relief, but still held the modest and businesslike and unemotional expression it had worn when he had first sat down.

When he had left, Burnside poured himself a glass of whiskey, raised it in jaunty salute to the closed tent-flap, tossed it back. Then he corked the bottle, and primly tucked it away in his desk.

11 P.M. Headquarters, Army of the Potomac

General Hunt, Major Duane, and Captain Sanderson had returned late from their inspection of Burnside's line. They had spent a full day going from observation post to observation post, climbing the wooden ladders into the trees, where Signal Lieutenants with long-distance glasses overlooked the rebel lines to the west. They inspected the siting of the major batteries, spending a good deal of time at the fourteen-gun battery Burnside was constructing on a small rise in the center of his line. From here, slightly above ground level, they could see the rebel lines. To verify their impressions, they had gone down to Warren's headquarters. Warren was a congenial man, an engineer like themselves. They found his views on Burnside's project thoroughly professional. Cautious: he reserved his judgment on the technical side of the project. Perhaps they'd succeed in digging the Mine; perhaps they wouldn't. Did he think the rebels had constructed a second line behind their first? It had been impossible to be sure they had one, viewing from any of the available observation posts. Well, Warren had said, if he commanded the rebel army or that part of it, he would certainly construct a second line; and he would not want to assert that his opponents were less professional than himself. Courtesy aside, one must never underrate the enemy.

But the real difficulty was the salient in the rebel line that projected out toward Warren's line, extending beyond the front of that smaller salient that Burnside proposed blowing up. Drafting their report now by candlelight, amid yawns, the men agreed that this was a crucial matter. Even if Burnside should explode his Mine successfully, his assault columns would be enfiladed by fire from the salient in front of Warren.

Of course, there could be a prior attack on Warren's front; but this seemed precluded for the very reasons that made Burnside resort to his Mine: it was impossible to take trench lines by frontal assault.

Hunt stared at their sketch-maps. "It might be done," he mused, "if Warren made a diversionary attack."

"I don't agree," said Duane. "The troops in the salient could keep off a diversionary attack; and as soon as they realized Burnside's was the main blow, they'd turn their guns on him. It must be a real attack by Warren, and a successful one, or we lose. That's all."

"Perhaps Warren could wait for Burnside to explode his Mine. Then, assuming we have the rebels surprised, Burnside could take his line; attacking together with Warren, they could pinch off the salient."

"If the guns in the salient don't stop Burnside's attack. If Burnside's Mine does go off. If the rebels are surprised, which they won't be if they hear the men digging."

"And can you imagine," said Captain Sanderson, "General Burnside surprising anyone?"

Hunt stared at the map. "Why did they begin the Mine there? Perhaps if Warren had pushed his line closer. . . ."

"General," said Duane, "they started the Mine there because that's where the miners happened to be. There wasn't the least military thought about the project at all. And there's no question of pushing Warren any closer. It would require a major effort and cost thousands of men. The position's too strong in that salient, they've got good cover, elevation, and a field of fire every way they look."

"Perhaps the best thing," said Sanderson, "is if they never do finish their Mine." They looked up at him. "If they do bring it home," said Sanderson, serious now, "we'll be attacking through the breach as sure as Grant's in command and there's an election in November."

There was silence. Hunt said, "Then I take it we're agreed that the headquarters of the Army should not give support to this project."

They nodded.

"All right," said Duane, "I'll have my aide write up the report as we dictate it and then we can go to bed."

While waiting for the aide, their minds ran on Sanderson's grim speculation: Grant's determination to take the offensive and bull his way by Bobby Lee; and Lincoln's prospective defeat if the war dragged on to no conclusion. Who would be the Democratic candidate, the man who might make an arrangement with the South and put the damned Radicals in their place? Hunt voiced the thought they all shared when he muttered, "I wonder what McClellan would have done in this situation?"

"Have you seen Barnard's little pamphlet?" asked Duane. He reached into the drawer of the camp desk and came up with a whiskey bottle and three glasses.

"And who has not?" replied Sanderson. He lounged nonchalantly in the camp chair, but his eyes looked sharp and he watched Duane's face. There were no such things as casual conversations about Little Mac, not in Little Mac's own army. The General had been gone more than a year and a half, and in his place had passed Burnside, Hooker, Meade, and now Grant. But Sanderson, and the other officers who had come up with McClellan in '61, still thought of the army as McClellan's by primitive right, the General as a kind of King in exile, Bonnie Prince Georgie, and as legitimists they held him chief in their hearts. Duane filled the glasses with whiskey, and Sanderson knocked his back with a silent toast. *If not as General, then as President, Mac will be back, amen!*

Duane, having tossed his own drink down, now reached into an inner pocket, and came out with a small packet, from which he spilled a brown powder into the dregs of the whiskey, added a small dip of water and stirred it round. "Quinine," he said, and drank it off.

"Barnard was never any damn good as an engineer," said Duane, his face flushing hot, then paling as he felt the quinine. "What makes him think he's a judge of the General's military decisions? Wait, I've got it here, listen to this." Duane took out a small red-covered booklet and laid it on the desk. "Listen to this : 'Of all General McClellan's faults and incapacities'—faults and incapacities!—'nothing'—now listen—'not even his *irresolution and mismanagement* in the face of the enemy, nor his *inability* ever, in any case, to *act* when the time came—furnishes a clearer proof of the lack of those qualities which make a great general or a great statesman, than his failure to do this.' "

"My favorite part," said Sanderson dryly, "is where he finds that the nation's forces were 'paralyzed' in Sixty-two because McClellan's officers were all complaining that if only Mac were in charge and the incompetent government put aside, all would be well." Duane and Hunt could take that anyway they liked. He would watch and see how they did take it. He knew they would remember quite clearly the time he was alluding to. There wasn't an officer in the army who had been with Mac on that night in November when Lincoln relieved him and put Burnside in his place, who didn't have ready a clear and plausible account of where he was and what he had said while McClellan's junior staff officers stamped about the headquarters urging the General to take the army and march on Washington.

Hunt looked hard at Duane, with his lips pursed. "There's merit in what the man says about the fight on the Chickahominy. The General was just fooled. There wasn't a day of the Seven Days when he couldn't have pushed Lee over and moved into Richmond."

Duane flushed again. "Mac thought he was outnumbered. The Intelligence Corps served him badly. And I'd think, after what we've seen of attacking fortifications frontally, that you'd know better than to think he could have waltzed through Lee's line even if it was held by half the numbers."

"Anyway," said Sanderson, softly, moderatingly, "it's clearly a Republican pamphlet General Barnard has lent himself to writing. I wonder if all of it is his own writing?"

Duane snorted, and Hunt shrugged. Whatever they thought of McClellan or of Barnard, what Barnard had written was politics. Bad thing for an army man to get involved in. Sanderson, who had counted on this reaction, felt relieved as they shied from the subject. You couldn't talk about Mac in this army without making enemies. If you criticized the man, or praised him faintly, his friends would mark you down a traitor; if you praised him, the Republican crowd would use you as a whipping boy. That was the way with these Republican radicals. Embodying the mediocrity of the mob, envious of true merit and worth. They'd driven the South out of the Union, and the cream of the army and the Congress with it. They'd driven McClellan out, and with him the only chance for victory or for peace.

Sanderson remembered how it had been, starting out to build the army, with Mac at the helm. To the young officers he was the *beau idéal,* the model of the soldier they might become. He'd been brilliant at the Point, fought well in Mexico, explored in the West, gone to Europe to observe in the Crimea. Then he'd resigned, and run a big railroad for years; then dropped that and picked up right where he'd left off, and in six months was in command of the whole thing. Talent, brains, beauty, style—he had vision, too. Sanderson remembered the long hours working over those memoranda to Lincoln; he'd warned Lincoln against touching the slavery thing: how could you expect the South to make peace and accept reunion with slavery abolished and nigger equality put in its place? He remembered the phrase, he'd helped Mac write it: ''Military power should not be allowed to interfere with the relations of servitude, either by supporting or impairing the authority of the master except for repressing disorder, and in other cases.'' The Southern aristocracy— they had to be convinced that they must return to the Union—how do that if slavery were abolished? And for their own people, ''A declaration of radical views, especially upon slavery, will rapidly disintegrate our present armies.''

Well, it would perhaps have been stronger coming from him if he'd beaten Lee at Richmond. But it was no disgrace to lose to *that* man: a soldier. And hadn't Mac fought him to a standoff at Antietam? Who could say if the General wouldn't have taken the rubber match in the end?

And there was this to consider, too: that Gorilla Lincoln and Butcher Grant were no match for Lee, together or separately. The Gorilla's blundering about the niggers and Grant's colossal casualty lists would waken memories of the days when Mac swept from Washington to the James without loss of a man. Yes, and stood up for the nation as it was, too, and never truckled to the Radicals! Who could say but what, in the end, Mac would take Washington easier and sooner than he'd take Richmond?

HEADQUARTERS ARMY OF THE POTOMAC
July 5, 1864—2 A.M.

General BURNSIDE,
Commanding Ninth Corps:
  What is the firing that seems to be in your front?
GEO. G. MEADE,
Major-General.

(same to General Warren)

2:30 A.M. IX Corps front: 14th New York Heavy Artillery

The last shell of the night did the damage. Sergeant Stanley's platoon was under arms in a section of the main trench. The men were huddled against the front wall. *We should have dug it narrower,* thought Robert Emmett Neill, *the fucking thing is wide enough for them to just bounce one of them cowhorns in here.* To Neill the trench seemed like a cup or gutter. He could picture a mortar shell hitting anywhere along the raised lip of the trench, sticking a moment, then rolling down the slope to his feet. In his vision he saw himself rooted to the spot with fear, watching the thing sputter its fuse, bewitched like a bird by a snake.

From the darkness in front he could hear the popping of skirmisher fire, punctuated by the bang of the big guns and the muffled *whump* of exploding shells. He listened fox-eared to each rise and fall in the pitch of the firing, and for the sound of yelling that would mean the rebs coming over. Whenever the pitch accelerated, his heart began to pound harder with it, and he clutched his rifle tighter. The sky was black above him, and there were stars, and at intervals flashes of light from bursting shells, and then occasional drifts of dirt from the eruptions. Over on the reb side there was a son of a bitch with a coehorn mortar who had been feeling for this trench all night in the dark. You could distinguish the sound of the small mortar shells, a sharp *pop* followed by the *whizz* of shrapnel. Damned vicious little man-killing bombs. The things were no damn good except to kill people, cut them up. Couldn't drive troops out of a trench. or bust the line with em. Just kill and cut up. What the hell use were they in an army anyway? Like the snipers. He'd like to kill a damn sniper. Bastards are supposed to be picking off officers, and that's all right, but these fucking Johnny snipers shoot anything that moves. Like they could snipe the whole fucking army to death. Bastards.

A line of fire traced itself across the trench, and from behind the rear wall came the *pop-whizz,* and Neill thought, "Oh God, if they hit the privy."

Then he heard the screaming. "Oh Jesus, Oh Jesus. Oh help me! Oh I'm hurt bad. I'm hurt bad. I'm hurt bad. Oh please come on and help me! Help me!"

They got sombeody.

"Oh Jesus God look what they did to me. Oh Jesus, can't somebody help me here. Now help me, oh, please. Oh Jesus."

He's going to stop directly, when they get to him.

"Oh Jesus, please help me. Somebody please come here help me. I'm all cut up here. I'm cut up real bad. Hey believe me, please, hey somebody. Oh Jesus God, please help me."

Somebody's going over there to help him. Must be hit real bad. He's gonna die soon. Neill wanted somebody to help the man, or for the man to die. He didn't hear the bombardment any more, or the bullets, or the coehorns. All he could hear was the guy yelling. He saw the coehorn shell lighting with its fiery tongue right in front of a man with his pants dropped in the privy, the shrapnel ripping the guy's balls off, right up his belly, and Neill curled around his rifle tight in a ball hearing the guy yelling like a woman now, "Oh Jesus, oh help me, I'm all cut up here, oh God somebody help me," and Neill began to shake in sharp cold shudders, without sound, without tears, hard shakes that knotted his muscles with cramps.

Not me! Oh sweet Christ let it not be me! Holy Mary Mother of God, don't let it be me. Oh my God I am heartily sorry for his balls *my sin, my sin, my great sin,* never again I promise it.

He felt a sharp kick in his rear end, and looked up to see Sergeant Stanley.

"What the fuck are you doing with that musket, boy? Jumping it or sucking it or what? Get on your feet. We're going out to relieve pickets."

The bombardment was over.

Neill felt weak, as if he'd brawled with a strong man all night; drained, bruised.

"Yes, Sergeant." *Damn filthy-minded brute. One day I'll blow the back of your head off.*

HEADQUARTERS NINTH ARMY CORPS
July 5, 1864—2:50 A.M.

General MEADE:
The firing was only sharp skirmishing and a little more than the usual artillery firing. The enemy in our front are very nervous, I think, and do three-fourths of the firing. Our lines are being shelled by mortars, but our losses are not large, amounting to 480 in the last ten days.

A. E. BURNSIDE,
Major-General.

8:00 A.M. *Confederate Lines: 22nd North Carolina, Elliott's Brigade*

Private T. W. Dixon, Jr., was up a tree with his sharpshooter rifle, braced with his back against the trunk and his feet against two big branches. "What a position," he thought. "If I was a woman I'd say I was making a pretty fair target, and come on and get it. Whoo! I could use some. I *could* use some." All he could think about lately was women. He thought of how they looked when they walked, and how their cunts smelled when you were prodding them. Oh man. Oh man. This damn tree smells just like it. If I don't get some I'll go crazy.

"Hey Billy," he husky-whispered down, "you ever laid a nigger wench? Oh man!" He grinned down between his legs, to the bottom of the tree, where Private Billy Caldwell and Sam Marriot were stretched out with their slouch hats over their faces, trying to nap. He spat, and ticked the edge of Billy's hat. Billy tipped his hat, showing a pale freckled chin with a slick of immature reddish whiskers.

"Cut it out, Dix. We been up all night making noise to scare off those damn Yankees, I ain't slept for a week."

"Meaning you ain't had one. Boy let me tell you, you ain't a man till you have had one, and that's a fact. Oh man, what I wouldn't give right now . . .''

Billy dropped his hat and pretended not to listen.

"My Daddy and me, one time, we were riding pateroll down between New Bern and Davidson's place. We're coming through some woods, and my hound sniffs a nigger, and gives this howl, and who should come walking out the bushes but that nigger driver of Penwaring's that come on so high and mighty. Daddy grins on him, and says, 'Boy, don't you know there's curfew for niggers? Let's see you pass. This here don't say nothing about your wandering around the woods by night.' And the nigger starts to shake real bad, 'cause he knew we're gonna whip him.''

"You want to shut the jaw-works down so's a man can sleep?'' yelled Marriot without tipping up his hat.

"Anyways, I suddenly remember that this nigger's got a wife at the Davidson place he's been visiting, and she is prime yellow. Oh my! Walk on her to raise the dead. Yes indeed.''

Billy knew the woman—Geneva was her name. He could picture her. In the darkness under his hat, smelling the stale-sweat damp-felt smell, he thought about the woman Geneva walking down a white dusty road in Carolina.

"So I say, 'Hole on there, Dad, this boy just going to see his wife, let's just give him an escort.' So we ride along, him walking in front, till we get to her cabin. She hear something, come out, take one look at us and she turn white—almost, that is—and start to shake. Oh, and when she start to shake! 'What you gemmen wants,'' he mimicked. 'Gone whup this boy, mam.' 'Oh white gemmens, don't do dat, please. I give you mose anything not to whup him, white gemmens.' And Daddy say, 'All right, we ain't hard men, but then again maybe we is.' Well, we tied that nigger to a tree, and we got down to it. And when Daddy give out it was T. W. Dixon Junior, and when Dixon Junior had his full, Dixon senior was ready again. Oh man! All night. Oh man, oh man.''

"Will you shut up!'' yelled Billy.

Dixon went on musing. "Nigger never said a word the whole time we were working on her. Ain't that something?''

Billy had squinched his eyes up under his hat. The sun was already hot across his belly and loins, and he felt his old devil stirring up. *Dixon is a bad 'un. He ain't no Christian.* Always working away on his one old song—women, women, and women—because he knew it got Billy all . . . *riled* somehow.

"No sir,'' said Dixon, "you are *not* a man until you've had yourself some of that poon tang.''

He didn't like to think bad of Dixon. Dixon was a soldier, his comrade. But Dixon was like Billy's Pappy and older brothers had been, before the Old Man died and the others run off: always thinking dirt and doing it too. Badmouthing everything that come across their path. Dixon was a soldier, but when he wasn't talking unChristian about women he was talking low about officers, and always behind their backs, too: face to face with them, wasn't he just pie? And better 'n pie?

"Hey Billy, you ever had any of that poon tang?''

No, he hadn't, as Dixon well knew. He hadn't ever done but one true sin in his life, knowing it beforehand, and that one even his Ma would have praised over : and that was when he lied about his age to the recruiter, saying he was eighteen when he was only sixteen, so that he could do his duty and be a soldier. That was two years ago : so the Lord had made over his lie into truth. That was a satisfaction to him. And that he was a good soldier too, and had always done his duty and more. Hadn't Jesus praised the centurion, who was a man under orders, and did what he was told with a good will, and not badmouthing it like Dixon was always ?

"Hey, Billy, you asleep down there ? I said, ain't you ever had any of that poon tang. You ain't man till you've . . ."

Billy's old devil warmed and stirred, and he couldn't help but think about the woman, the heat, the loose dress, the road, and thought anxiously, *Maybe I ain't no more of a Christian at heart than Dixon. Maybe I ain't either a Christian or a man if I can't stop thinkin about it but I never done—*

"You know," Dixon said, "there sure as *hell* is something funny going on over there. Yankees is moving around like worms in a carcass."

Marriot tipped his hat back, scratched, and got up to piss against a tree. "Well for God's sake don't tell anybody about it, will you ? That bastard Davidson will have us out skirmishing all night again."

Pam! "Ah, shit! Missed the bastard!"

"Hey Dixon," yelled Marriot, "don't just go shooting that thing off like you was potting rats in the barn! They'll start the damn artillery going again!"

"Don't you know this is war ?" asked Dixon. "If you don't like the way me and Marse Robert runs it, come on up here and run it yourself."

Anything is better than lying here with the hot sun in my lap like a strong woman. Billy heaved himself up. Dixon dropped out of the tree, leaving the rifle slung to a cut-off branch. Billy grabbed the handholds and climbed up. The tree was back in a grove screened from the Yankee lines by some scattering shrubs. There was enough screen to hide the smoke of the rifle, but not enough to hide the Yankee lines.

He took the field telescope out of its case. This early in the morning the sun looked directly toward them from the southeast. But slightly north, up to where the Yankee lines bulged toward their own, there was no glare; and morning was fair hunting time. The Yankees sometimes got careless, thinking only about the sun being at their backs, thinking only about the men just opposite them, never thinking about them off to one side.

The three men had used the tree fairly regularly, whenever they didn't have to be on the line, and when they couldn't get some fatigue that would keep them out of the zone of firing. They were the three best shots in the regiment.

Billy swept the glass northward. Over on the Yankee side there was a bulgy little hillock humping up behind their main line. He'd potted somebody right between two small bushes on that hillock. It was his reference point: he always began looking there, a ritual for good luck, like licking top-lip-bottom-lip all around before you shot a deer.

He couldn't find the bushes at first. *Damn Yanks must have cut em down.* Then he saw them. But they looked different. One of them was a little bit thicker, like another tree had grown next to it since the last time he'd seen it. He said nothing, but screwed his eye to the glass.

After ten minutes he thought, *All right. If somebody kicks a rock out of line over there, I'll know it now.*

"Hey Billy," called Dixon. "Know what happened after that? Time come around, she threw a calf that had blue eyes. 'Shit,' says Daddy, 'after we go to the trouble making that calf, and Davidson get the meat. Now is that justice?' "

Billy didn't answer. Dixon, lying on his back with his hat over his face, felt his lips go all tight. It hadn't been near funny when Old Man Davidson had come riding up to the cabin with that big driver, and some of his men overseers with pistols and a big shotgun. Sitting there like the King of England on his big horse, looking at Daddy like he was spit, saying real cold, "You got a big mouth, Dixon, and something else too. If I find you meddling my property I'll shorten it up for you. You hear me?" Then he doesn't wait for answer, just flicks the reins and they go off, and Daddy standing there, just shaking like.

"What Davidson do with it, Dix?" asked Marriot.

"How the hell I know. Sold it West most like."

"Oh?" Marriot munched on a hardtack. "Well I guess that explains why you don't like the Colonel so much."

"Yeah?" said Dixon, suspicious.

"Seeing he sold your half-brother West."

Dixon rolled over fast, and started to get up, but Marriot was ready, and dodged behind a tree. "Or was it your son? I mean, how could you . . ."

"Hey, you men," yelled Billy, "stop all that. One of you come on up here and take a look at something."

The second bush had just sprouted another section as thick as the first two.

ARMY OF NORTHERN VIRGINIA,
HEADQUARTERS JOHNSON'S DIVISION,
July 5, 1864.

Colonel GOODE,
Commanding Wise's Brigade:

COLONEL: There is a little ravine running parallel to the general direction of your line, on your left. This ravine is just in front of your pickets and between them and the pickets of the enemy : it is necessary that you should send some intelligent men to crawl out two or three times every night from your picket line to the edge of this ravine, to listen there and see if the enemy might run an underground gallery to that ravine and then open a trench in it, or they might move quietly into the ravine and open a trench out of sight.

Very respectfully, your obedient servant,

B. R. JOHNSON,
Major-General.

P.S. Please report to me whether you think you have enough men for your line, and if not, how many more you want.

B. R. J.

Morning shift, The Mine

They were changing shifts at the minehead. The two men just up, covered with sweat and grime, were sipping water from a dipper passed back and forth. One of them held a small ball of gray earth in his hand, which he rolled and kneaded with his fingers. Small flakes of drying earth dropped from his fingers. Doyle, getting ready to go down in the Mine with Corrigan, noticed. Then looked again.

"What's that stuff?"

The digger flipped it over to Doyle. It was a ball of grayish doughy earth, malleable and moist on the inside, flaking to white rockiness where the air hit it. *Some new damn kind of clay,* he thought. He hated working with the stuff. It gummed up the pick, and slicked you over so that you picked up sand and pebbles like a tarball.

Corrigan and Doyle went down the tunnel, a tube of wood in which they walked bent nearly double, smell of cut wood masking the smell of earth. The whisper of air at their backs, just stirring the air of the tunnel (perceptible only to the heightened air-sense of men used to working deep under earth), eased them down.

The earth wall at the deep end of the tunnel felt different to Doyle's hand as he braced himself against it before kneeling to begin his pick-work. It felt rock-hard, all along the face as he explored it with his hand. He held his pick short, and jabbed at the wall experimentally. The pick rebounded. Doyle knelt in his regular position and swung hard. The pick cracked on through the hard outer face into a gummy earth. *What in the name of*—? Doyle swung again, a downward arc, intending to chip off a hunk of the stuff, but the pick glanced off the surprising hard surface, and Doyle lurched off balance. His second swing was in, but the gummy earth held the clod in the rockface, and Doyle had to swing again before a piece the size of his fist chipped off and fell. He picked it up. Already the gummy side of the clod was turning rock-hard where the air touched. Doyle flipped it to Corrigan who looked down at it, his features unreadable in the shifting dull lights of Doyle's candle.

Doyle turned to the wall and began working. The wall was bad stuff to work with. You had to learn the different weight to throw in the swing of the pick—too soft, like for sand, and you'd glance off; too hard and the pick went in and stuck. His muscles took the new strain

differently, he tired sooner, his head began to ache with attention. It
was like mining in rock, like mining in dough.

After an hour Doyle was exhausted, and the wall had been worn
back, but not near enough for the time and strain. Corrigan came
forward and Doyle shifted back to loading the trolley. Sweat ran over
his brows and into his eyes and the corners of his lips, bringing the irritating odd taste of the gray soil into his mouth. He looked at the
side wall, felt it in the dark with his hand. Back behind him where the
tunnel slanted towards the light, the wall was sandy. The dough-rock
began in a rough line that ran from the floor forward and upward at a
low angle till it began to approach the level of the roof. *Will we be
working this seam all the way to Richmond?*

The hour passed in hot, slow-stirring air, the continual thud, scuffle, and grunt of Corrigan working on the tunnel face. Load the crumbling dough-rock in the box and hear it scrape bumble back towards
the daylight.

Blinking in the hard sun, Doyle came up almost too tired to curse.
"That damned stuff! That damned fucking useless rock-pudding!"

"Here now, Private. Don't be calling the Lord's work useless."
The man flipped something at Doyle, who dropped his pick and caught
it. It was a little bowl, pierced for a reed at the side, finger-molded out
of the gray dough.

"Makes a damn good clay pipe."

1:00 P.M. *22nd North Carolina, behind the Confederate trench line*

The regiment had pitched lean-tos against the side of the ravine. The
ravine was a natural trench, deep enough for protection but not too deep
to fire over, and bushes fringed it like natural abatis. The ravine ran
parallel to the main trench line that cut the dry earth five hundred
yards to the east. At the bottom the sandy soil was marked where
rain runoff had slanted down towards the stream that cut east-west
through the Confederate and Union lines. There had been no water in
it for a long time.

"Billy, why'd ye have to tell him?" complained Dixon.

"We had to."

"Don't answer him, Billy. He'll just keep after you." Marriot's
voice sifted out from under his hat. His body was utterly immobile. He
believed that if he didn't move at all he wouldn't feel the heat.

"Besides, the next boys would've noticed."

"You made sure of that, good boy that you are. You'll make
corporal. And no doubt you'll forget your friends."

A shadow fell across them, and Dixon and Caldwell looked up at
Lieutenant Bruce. Marriot stayed under his hat. *I am asleep,* he told
himself. *If I lie here like I'm really asleep, I couldn't never notice
whoever that is anyway, and he'll just go off not noticing me.*

Bruce stood there, looking down. After the slightest hesitation,
Dixon and Caldwell rose to stand before him. They stood slouchily, and
of course wouldn't deign to salute. Lieutenant Bruce fought back a grin:
it was so predictable, that little bit of holding back on a formula of

deference. *They are so satisfied with their little defiances,* he thought, *but they always do stand up.*

"I want you men to take me up there and show me what's going on."

"Yes, sir." Dixon kicked his foot backwards. "Let's go, Samuel."

Sam Marriot came out from under his hat with a start, then slowly, miming a man just roused from deep sleep. But his eyes were clear, as Bruce noted. The three soldiers gathered their gear and followed Bruce. The land rose gradually from the back of the ravine till it formed the long roll of the ridge along which the Jerusalem Plank Road ran north to Petersburg and Richmond. The clump of trees was on the side of the incline, half way up. Bruce whistled down the sniper on watch. He stepped aside, making a tight smile as he motioned Billy to go up before him. The private vaulted to a low branch and stepped up a level. Crouching, he reached down to hand the Lieutenant up. Up in the green leaves, Bruce sat in the sniper's cradle, Caldwell clinging with arms wrapped among the branches so that he hovered behind and over the Lieutenant. "Sight on the yellowish forked kind of branch there. You see the hill with the brushline on top?"

"I see it."

"Yesterday there was one, maybe two bushes over there. This morning it was a lot bigger."

The hillside quivered like jelly in the glass as Bruce tried to focus on it. There was a hillside and a line of brush on top, a line of black against yellow. *Probably nothing,* he thought. *Hot air distorts every damn thing.* He took the glass down and wiped his eye.

"Yanks doing something, sir."

"They always are, Private. They're noted for their industriousness."

Could you believe the kid really saw something? What would the Yanks be stacking brush for?

"All right, Private, we can go down now."

The men looked expectantly at him when he came down. *Let them stay curious,* he told himself. *Half the thing of being a leader is having some mystery about yourself. I'll get more out of these men if they don't know what I'm doing. If there is anything there at all, which to be honest I don't know, I'll figure what it might be if I think on it long enough.*

"Keep a sharp eye, you lookouts." He turned to the three soldiers and jerked his head. They followed him back down to the ravine.

HEADQUARTERS, ARMIES OF THE UNITED STATES,
City Point, Va., July 5, 1864.

Maj. Gen. A. E. BURNSIDE:

Dear GENERAL: The accompanying list of questions was drawn up, by my directions, by my Prussian engineer, Captain Munther. They are unnecessarily minute. All I want is to get the main facts, so as to judge of probable results and form data for any future work of the kind. If you will put Lieutenant

Oberteuffer in communication with the officer in charge of the mining gallery he will work out the answers.

I sent you yesterday the only copy I have of my review of McClellan's report. Anyone who reads it must read the preface and there find my justification and motive.

I am, respectfully and truly,

J. G. BARNARD,
Brevet Major-General, &c.

HEADQUARTERS, ARMIES OF THE UNITED STATES,
City Point, Va., July 3, 1864.

(Lieut. Col. HENRY PLEASANTS :)

In order to be enabled to have a clear judgment of the progress of the mining work in front of Major-General Burnside's rifle pits, I would like to be furnished with—

I. A rough longitudinal section made after a certain scale and laid through our works neighboring the mine, through the mine gallery, and through the enemy's works to be attacked by the mine. This section, with all important numbers inscribed, will show, besides the profile of our and the enemy's works, the location of the mine-gallery entrance with reference to our own defense line; the arrangement of the entrance, whether by a shaft or by an inclined gallery, &c.; the height of the gallery in both the places not framed and such as are supplied with frames; the length of the intended gallery; its depth under the natural horizon near the entrance and near the powder chamber, and finally the location, length, and height of the latter.

II. A profile of the gallery showing its width in framed and unframed places and the width of the powder chamber.

III. (a) When was the mining work begun? (State day and hour.) (b) Has it been continued night and day without any interruption, and how many men were and are engaged on it at the same time? (c) When will the gallery be finished?

IV. What kind of soil is probably to be expected around the powder chamber?

V. What is the intended weight of the charge, and what is the expected diameter of the crater measured on its surface?

VI. By what means shall the mine be fired, supposed that it shall be fired as soon as possible and with the least loss of time?

VII. What means shall be used for tamping the mine, and at what length shall this be done?

VIII. Where shall be the stand-point of the miner firing the charge? (Distance from the latter, &c.)

IX. At what time in the day shall the mine be fired?

X. What measures are premeditated by the engineer department in accordance with the commanding general to secure the possession of the crater effected by the mine and to facilitate its defense?

The questions above should be answered without delay and as shortly as possible only with reference to its numbers, i.e., answer to III, a, b, c, e, &c., IV, &c.

> J. G. BARNARD,
> *Brigadier-General, Chief Engineer:*
> *U.S. Armies in the Field.*

2:00 P.M. *The Mine*

Rees sat with Doyle, Corrigan, and a circle of miners around the box of dirt at the minehead. "How does the belt lie?"

"It's no belt," said Doyle. "It's ahead of us wherever we go. There's not much of it above the line of the roof, or below the floor. All of it is straight ahead."

"We've been at it all day. We only made ten feet this morning, and it's all through the stuff," said Sergeant Bradley. Bradley was a mine foreman now too, but he deferred to Rees. He'd been a donkey-man, not a miner, and was boss now only because of his stripes.

"Here's the Colonel," said someone, and the circle parted to let Pleasants in. The Colonel picked up the rock, sniffed it, cracked off the hard outer layer and crushed the interior in his hands. He had to slap his hand on his thigh to shake the stuff off. Rees handed him one of the pipe bowls the men had been molding.

"Smokes rale sweet, Colonel," said a voice from the rear, and the the Colonel half-grinned. The bowl was hard as baked pottery.

"This is marl, Sergeant."

"Yes, sir."

"How does the stuff lie?"

Doyle spoke up. "I'd say it's a ledge, tilted up a little towards the rebs. We hit it endways."

"Let's take a look." He and Rees grabbed candles from the box at the minehead, and went down into the tube of wood.

In the flickering light Pleasants explored the border of the seam, the line between sand and marl that slanted up towards the head of the mine at a low angle. At the end wall he saw the careful gouging a foot above and a foot below the usual top-bottom lines of the tunnel, where Doyle or somebody else had tried to find the top and bottom edges of the seam.

"What do you think, Rees?"

"Unless it's a bubble on top of something deeper, I'd say Doyle has the right of it."

"Yes." Pleasants let his candles shine along the side wall. "All the rock here lies the same way. It's flat, ledge on ledge."

"We could take an auger hole into the side wall and see if we might go around."

"All right. I don't know if the carpenter augers will be any good. Maybe if you pick the hole and start boring fast before the stuff dries." But he had the feel of the underground here, and he'd bet the borings

would show marl as far left and right as you might go. He'd best think
of going above it. That would put them much closer to the surface.
Perhaps he'd better recalculate the height of land over the tunnel. And
remember to warn Rees to keep the men quiet so the rebel pickets would
never hear.

HDQRS. FORTY-EIGHTH PENNSYLVANIA VET. VOL. INFTY.,
Near Petersburg, Va., July 6, 1864.

Answer to question 2: The gallery or tunnel is supported
by props along its whole course at a distance from each other
ranging from three to thirty feet, according to the nature of the
roof. When the tunnel reaches a point immediately underneath
the enemy's breast-works it is proposed to drive two galleries
each about 100 feet in length, whose position will be immediately underneath the enemy's fort and breast-work.

Answer to question 3: (a) At 12 M. on the 25th of June,
1864. (b) The mining has been carried on without interruption
since it was begun. There are 210 men employed every twenty-
four hours, but only two can mine at a time at the extremity of
the work. (c) The tunnel will reach the enemy's work in about
seven or eight days.

Answer to questions 5, 6, 7, 8, 9, and 10 still under consideration. The mine is ventilated by means of an air-shaft, with
a furnace to rarify the air and boxes to convey the gases from
the interior of the gallery to the shaft.

HENRY PLEASANTS,
Lieutenant-Colonel Forty-eighth Pennsylvania Regiment.

HEADQUARTERS ARMY OF THE POTOMAC,
July 7, 1864.

Major-General BURNSIDE,
Commanding Ninth Corps:

GENERAL: I am instructed by the major-general commanding to say, that upon an examination of the enemy's intrenched
position by the chief engineer and the chief of artillery, it has
been concluded that the operations upon your front cannot be
carried to a successful conclusion until the salients on the front
of the Fifth Corps are in our possession or under our control.
Accordingly it has been determined to conduct regular approaches upon the two fronts of your corps and that of General
Warren simultaneously, and in order to give unity and harmony
to these operations the siege works will be constructed under the
direction of the chief engineer of the army, and the disposition
and use of siege artillery will be under the direction of the chief
of artillery of the army. An order to that effect, prescribing in
general terms the manner in which the siege operations will be
conducted, will be issued, and in the meantime the commanding

general prefers that no additional batteries of siege guns should
be established.

Very respectfully, your obedient servant,

A. A. HUMPHREYS,

Major-General and Chief of Staff.

Humphreys' dispatch made General Burnside choleric. Richmond
was hard put to calm him down, pointing out patiently that Meade
had in no way overstepped his legitimate authority. But these orders
confirmed what Burnside had been hearing from headquarters gossip
for two days. His Mine was a dubious thing. An attack on Burnside's
front could not be contemplated before something had been done on
Warren's; or perhaps Butler's front was best of all! And now he was
being told (it amounted to that) to back off and let Major Duane and
Henry Hunt direct all the operations—and of course stop everything
until those two gentlemen can have the time to take hold!

"Nothing is really changed, General. We can proceed with the
mining, at least—there's no hint of our having to stop that. They won't
help, but they can't hinder. There are all kinds of shifts at headquarters."

"Oh yes. Barnard's a coming man again, I suppose. That will do
me no good at all. I may not have agreed with General McClellan in
all things—you can witness, Lew, that's true—but I'd not be so disloyal
as to kick a man when he's down."

"Well, perhaps he's not down permanently. But Barnard's got
no great love for Meade either, and there's talk of a big change."

"Is there?" said Burnside. "Well, I'm not surprised." His mood
suddenly improved. He was, after the impossible Ben Butler, the senior
Major General in the army.

CITY POINT, VA., *July 7, 1864—8* A.M.
(*Received 6* P.M.)

Hon. E. M. STANTON:

A change in the commander of the Army of the Potomac
now seems probable. Grant has great confidence in Meade, and
is much attached to him personally, but the almost universal
dislike of Meade which prevails among officers of every rank
who come in contact with him, and the difficulty of doing business with him felt by every one except Grant himself, so greatly
impair his capacities for usefulness and render success under
his command so doubtful that Grant seems to be coming to the
conviction that he must be relieved. The facts in the matter
have come very slowly to my knowledge, and it was not until
yesterday that I became certain of some of the most important.
I have long known Meade to be a man of the worst possible
temper, especially toward his subordinates. I do not think he
has a friend in the whole army. No man, no matter what his
business or his service, approaches him without being insulted

in one way or another, and his own staff officers do not dare to speak to him, unless spoken to, for fear of either sneers or curses. The latter, however, I have never heard him indulge in very violently, but he is said to apply them often without occasion and without reason. At the same time—as far as I am able to ascertain—his generals have lost their confidence in him as a commander. His order for the last series of assaults upon Petersburg, in which he lost 10,000 men without gaining any decisive advantage, was to the effect that he had found it impracticable to secure the co-operation of corps commanders, and therefore each one was to attack on his own account and do the best he could by himself. Consequently each gained some advantage of position, but each exhausted his own strength in so doing, while for the want of a general purpose and a general commander to direct and concentrate the whole, it all amounted to nothing but heavy loss to ourselves. Of course there are matters about which I cannot make inquiries, but what I have above reported is the general sense of what seems to be the opinion of fair-minded and zealous officers. For instance, I know that General Wright has said to a confidential friend that all of Meade's attacks have been made without brains and without generalship. The subject came to pretty full discussion at Grant's headquarters last night on occasion of a correspondence between Meade and Wilson. The Richmond Examiner charges Wilson with stealing not only negroes and horses, but silver plate and clothing on his raid, and Meade, taking the statement of the Examiner for truth, reads Wilson a lecture and calls on him for explanations. Wilson denies the charges of robbing women and churches, and hopes Meade will not be ready to condemn his command because its operations have excited the ire of the public enemy. This started the conversation in which Grant expressed himself quite frankly as to the general trouble with Meade and his fear that it would become necessary to relieve him. In such event he said it would be necessary to put Hancock in command.

C. A. DANA.

HEADQUARTERS IN THE FIELD
City Point, Va., July 8, 1864—9:30 A.M.

Hon. EDWIN M. STANTON,
Secretary of War.

Nothing of much importance this morning. Firing pretty active in the trenches yesterday, but without consequence. Directions have been given to make regular siege approaches to the rebel lines. General Meade reports that Burnside's mine will be of no value. He thinks the best place to work is at the salient angle on the Jerusalem Plank Road in Warren's front. This is the point which Barnard proposed to assault, as I reported several days since. We had a trifling shower yesterday, without effect on the drought.

C. A. DANA.

July 8, 10:00 A.M. 22nd North Carolina Infantry

The officers of the Twenty-second North Carolina were having their breakfast in Colonel Davidson's big bombproof shelter. The bombproof had been set into the reverse of a small hillock, its entrance invulnerable to all but providentially directed mortar shells. Lieutenant Bruce had laid it out himself, and took pride in it. Inside was a table flanked by half-a-dozen officers, the Colonel presiding at the head. The Colonel's manservant, George, stood at the Colonel's left and reached over his shoulder to pour burnt-bread coffee from a battered pot. The Colonel went on speaking, not leaning even the slightest fraction of an inch away from his servant, as if the man were impalpable. The Colonel's heavy cheeks shook ever so slightly as he spoke, and his magnificent eyebrows rose and fell with the rhythm of his speech.

"Have I sent you the *Examiner* on what Early did to Hunter at Lynchburg, Captain Allen? For once the facts seem to outstrip the hyperbole of our popular journalists, hard though that is to conceive." There was a rumble of assent.

"I've seen it, sir, thank you," said Allen—a small neat man with an extraordinarily quiet, smooth voice. "It appears General Early has the Jackson touch."

"Why do you say that?" asked Bruce. He'd been preoccupied lately, and hadn't seen the papers, although like everyone else he'd heard the story of Early's defeat of Hunter.

Allen turned his mild earnest eyes on Bruce. "It appears that General Early more or less bluffed General Hunter into believing himself outnumbered before all of Early's force had even come up. When Early attacked, the man simply fled the scene, abandoning wounded, wagons, equipment—everything."

"The man must have been a damned fool or a poltroon!" exclaimed Davidson. "Another one of these Abolitionist political officers, with stomach to burn farms and steal negroes and none at all for fighting!"

"I don't know, Colonel," said Bruce. "Some of the Abolitionists have done fairly well. And we have our own share of political officers in high places."

"Not the same thing," said Davidson, and he drained his coffee. "There's a military tradition among our people that has no counterpart in the North. It's why we've done as much as we have, though we've been outnumbered and outgunned at every turn. In a war between a race of soldiers and a race of merchants, it won't be Shylock who comes out on top."

"Though there's a chance he might make some money out of it," said someone down the table, and they all laughed.

"It's certain they've no one like Lee among them," said Allen. "I imagine I see in that man George Washington reborn."

"Amen to that!"

Bruce looked narrowly at the table. He liked a good argument, and after days of speculating about and inspecting the Yankee activities, he felt his mind had gone stiff and stale. Still, one had to be careful arguing with these colleagues of his. *Amour propre* was an explosive substance with them.

"There's no one like Lee," he said. "Certainly neither Grant nor Meade has shown the same technical skill or tactical brilliance, setting moral qualities aside as we have to. I'll go further also: take the next level of command—Jackson, Stuart, Johnston, Early, now this man Forrest—there aren't their equals on the other side."

"Or look at our soldiers," said Davidson. "God knows they're a bad enough lot, and have to be kept up to the mark harder than my servants do. But man for man, and even at odds, they'll stand off any number of New York counter-jumpers and bounty-men."

"Yes, sir," said Bruce, "but what I was going to say is this. Granted we're the quality: there aren't enough of us. You don't replace a Jackson or a Stuart that easily. You don't replace good private soldiers that easily, either. Every time we fight we trade good men for worse, like changing hard money for soft: the specie goes, and the shin-plasters keep on coming."

Colonel Davidson began to blush. He was angry, though it wouldn't be proper to show it. "I'll answer you this way, Lieutenant. Before secession it was the South that provided the leadership of the nation in peace and war. I once heard the situation likened to the gamecock crowing on the dunghill: the South was the gamecock, and I don't have to tell you who the dunghill was. Now, your dunghill is fine for manuring the ground and producing lots of beans and potatoes and corn; but when the gamecock flies off, all you've got is a pile of shit. For fighting, I'll take the gamecock, thank you. What do you reckon would be the outcome of a war between the gamecock and the dunghill?"

Again there was laughter. "The gamecock would pitch right in!" said a Major down at the end of the table.

"And soil his plumage somewhat in the process," said Allen with a small smile.

And leave the dunghill pretty much as he found it, thought Bruce, *if he didn't end up burying himself in it.*

"It's a thought, though," said Lieutenant Penwaring, a young man who sat across from Bruce. "There's just so much water in the well. We can't keep trading life for life indefinitely. We haven't enough to spend."

"It's not simply a matter of mathematics," said Allen. "There is a rapport between General Lee and the men of this army that gives the man special power. He'll call that spirit forth one more time, and then there will be nothing to withstand him. I believe that." Allen looked into the distance with blank eyes, his soft modulated voice never rising above conversational tone.

"Perhaps if Early can get into Washington, or stir up enough trouble? . . ." Penwaring let the sentence hang, and the others began chiming in with suggestion after suggestion for what Lee might do.

It was a familiar conversation—no, to Bruce's ears not even a conversation any longer, but a kind of choral recitative in which they joined their voices, one echoing the other, spinning out beautiful dream-like lines of possibility, and always the same ones. A dodge at the flank, a bodyblow, one of Lee's patented lightning strokes like those of the Seven Days, Second Manassas, Chancellorsville. Then an uprising of patriotic and conservative elements in the North, victory, peace . . .

"Wouldn't it be perfect?" said Allen. "Grant besieges Petersburg, and while he digs away busy as a beaver, Early flashes up the Valley and captures Washington! Ha! The perfect ending. The engineer hoist on his own petard!"

Bruce's mind wandered restlessly away from the palaver. His colleagues were excellent men in the field, but in council they tended to compose fables rather than consider facts. Allen with his flourishes of poetry was the most literary of the lot, but the rest were just as out of touch with reality. *Hoist on his own petard.* As if things ever worked out that way by themselves! You'd have to get up pretty early to work that trick on any engineer worth his hire.

Hoist on his own petard . . . the phrase wouldn't go away, buzzed in his ear like a persistent fly. Hadn't there been something in General Johnson's orders to the brigade about listening for enemy miners along this front? Yes, and a suggestion last week that we construct some "subterraneous torpedoes" as he called them. Johnson was a clever man; he had genuine intelligence, unlike present company. A professor, wasn't he, from some little school in Tennessee? *Subterraneous torpedoes. Petard.* He was due to go up to Brigade Headquarters as soon as Davidson gave him the packet of reports and requisitions. He could talk to his friend Phillips, who was staff engineer for General Elliott. Phillips ought to know if such a thing was likely: if the Yankees could be digging a mine out from behind that little rise, and hiding the dirt under that new-cut brush. Now if only Davidson would let them finish breakfast. . . .

He gulped his coffee quickly and without relish. Before he could push his cup away and rise, George refilled it.

Leisurely breakfast and the Colonel's slow, labored writing notwithstanding, Bruce was at Brigade Headquarters by noon. As luck would have it, it was Phillips himself who took the packet of dispatches. And after a brief sketch of the position and the signs, and a series of sharp questions, Phillips was absolutely certain that this was something that General Johnson would want to know. General Elliott was off inspecting the lines, and in his absence Phillips commanded. "You've never met Johnson, have you?" he grinned. "You'll like him." He scribbled a note, and handed it to Bruce. "This will get you into the Presence. Take it up to him yourself." The smile widened. "I hear he's looking for another aide."

Bruce smiled and rolled his eyes. Phillips's opinion of Davidson was about the same as his own. "Thanks, Phil."

And so Lieutenant Bruce found himself, at three in the afternoon, standing in front of Major General Bushrod R. Johnson. Johnson was about sixty years old, and partial baldness enlarged the already imposing height of his forehead. His wide mouth and heavy lips made a strong line under the overhang of an iron-colored mustache. Lieutenant Bruce liked the man immediately. He was reminded of Captain Hastings, his mathematics instructor during his first and only year at West Point, a man whose intelligence he had fairly worshipped. He had imagined Hastings emerging as a hero on the field as well as in the classroom: but he had heard that the man was mired in some rear-area staff appointment in Washington. He thought of Allen and Davidson, gamecocks and *noblesse oblige,* and the poetry of war—none of your mathematics, please! Why did the Yankees have the brains and the South the horse's-ass heroes? But they said Johnson was different.

The man didn't stand on ceremony. His uniform coat was open in deference to the heat, and he gestured for Bruce to sit in a manner that suggested that he thought standing before a superior was a kind of impertinence. Very much the backwoods college professor. "Lieutenant Bruce: it's good to meet you, sir. I'm familiar with your reports on the observation of the Yankee lines. You seem to have a good eye. What has General Elliott sent you to tell me?"

Bruce took a folded sketch-map out of his breast pocket and spread it on the table in front of Johnson. "We have an observation post and sniper station in the trees, here." He indicated the spot with his finger. "The post overlooks a good bit of the Yankee lines, although it isn't very high and it's difficult to see over the inequalities in the ground." Johnson nodded. "Our snipers noticed, and I've verified, that there is some kind of work going on in this sector—here. It's difficult to say how much, or what kind."

"What have you actually seen?"

"The Yanks have been piling their fresh dirt behind this hill on the opposite side of where this depression is marked on the map. They carry it out at night, or maybe by some trench we can't see, and cover it with brush. One of the snipers noticed that the brush was growing like fungus on a rotten log."

Johnson smiled, briefly. "That's a good eye your sniper has. Pity he can't see through the hillside. Well. Let's see if we can't puzzle it out." Johnson unrolled a larger printed map that lay conveniently on his desk. The lines of the opposing forces had been inked in, in lines of red and blue. Johnson studied the map, then looked up at Bruce, and turned it towards him. "Let me hear what you think, Lieutenant," he said, the ghost of a smile appearing.

Bruce grinned. Johnson *had* been a schoolmaster, and here was examination day. He looked at the map, the shape of the terrain back of the Yankee lines appearing in sharper relief than it could to his observing eye, peering down the jiggling tube of the telescope through waves of rising heat. He took time to examine the map carefully.

"The depression is too deep for anything but a mortar battery to fire out of. But it looks too close up for mortars. They could just be improving it as a reserve trench, or digging a big bombproof."

Johnson interrupted. "But you don't think either of those is likely."

Bruce looked up. "No, sir, I don't. It's not the right place for a reserve trench—too close to their first line, and anyway they've already got a second line, very nicely located in back of that second rise. Also, you'd expect to see some kind of parapet, sandbags, something along the front lip of the depression, but you don't.''

"That's correct," said Johnson. "And as we've said, it's not ideal for mortars." He stopped, waiting for Bruce to continue.

"General, I wanted to be more certain before suggesting this, but frankly I have no idea how to proceed. My thought is, they might be mining."

Johnson's mouth tightened, and he nodded vigorously. "It's not an illogical conclusion." He looked hard at the map, and tapped it rapidly with the back of a pencil. "There are some things against it, though. First, it's a bit far for mining. It must be five hundred feet in an air-line from that point to our lines. Your military studies are more recent than mine: what do the engineers think of as possible nowadays?"

Bruce was ready for the question. "We have a copy of McClellan's reports from the Crimea. The British mined there up to a point short of four hundred feet—unsuccessfully."

"There's the soil quality to be considered. Sandy soil like this can't be good for mining in. Still—we'd best not reach any conclusion till we have more evidence." Johnson took his watch out of a vestpocket and glanced at it. "There's to be a general firing up and down the line this afternoon at five—just to shake the crackerbox a little, so as to see what scurries out. I'd like you to take me to your forward observation post, and we'll see what happens when the firing starts. If they fire mortars out of there, we'll have our answer. It not, we'll think what to do next."

5:00 P.M. *Front-line trenches, Twenty-second North Carolina*

Colonel Davidson, wearing his dress-uniform coat, stood in a small bay roughly in the center of the regiment. He wore this coat only for reviews and battles, and kept it wrapped in burlap in his camp trunk, folded with care by his nigger servant so the braid didn't crimp, the cloth sponged lightly to keep the nap. That was the nigger's care; maybe it was also that with all the shooting, there weren't all that many real fights, and there could never be enough parades for the Colonel.

Next to Davidson was Lieutenant Bruce, and next to him Marriot recognized General Johnson. General or not, and even with the slather of braid up the sleeve, Johnson's coat was no match for the Colonel's for color or for cleanness. He poked Billy in the ribs and pointed. Generals up on the line were scarcer than fresh meat and clean socks.

"Must be something doing," said Billy seriously.

The sergeants came down the line checking ammunition, calling attention to the stations where they'd be holding extra cartridges. There were about two hundred men in the line, mostly from towns around Kinston and New Bern, where the regiment had enlisted. When they first took the train north there had been one thousand of them.

Davidson looked at his watch. "Boys! Here's your orders. At five o'clock, in about ten minutes, the guns are going to start blasting hell out of the Yankees. Five minutes after they start, when the Yanks've got their heads well down, we're going to stand up and give em a volley. Then down, reload, and give em another.''

"Then we give em the rebel yell, and charge with the bayonet. Eee-hah!'' yelled Dixon. *Always sucking up,* thought Marriot.

"Not this time, boys,'' said Davidson. "These Yanks been so quiet that General Lee's begun to wonder if they haven't all gone home. We're just going to find out, that's all.''

They waited for the guns to begin. Nobody spoke. As Billy perceived it, there were two layers of air here in the trench. Down in the trench itself the air was still, close and hot, a solid thing held in the solid earth walls. Above the trench the invisible air rushed with an incredible intensity, to stand with one's head in it was to risk having your brains sucked out and blown away in the wind. When the signal came, they were all going to step up on the fire step and point rifles out through the slots in the parapet through and over which the rushing loose air blew. His face would be naked in that deadly wind all the time he pointed, took his rest, aimed, and fired.

I won't aim. There's no need. Yanks'll all have their heads down. We're just supposed to be making noise anyway. No damn fool sense in taking my rest and aiming. Just up, bang! down, and reload. Maybe I'm afraid to stand up there and shoot like a soldier. A general himself up here in the lines, too. By God, I'd better do it. You've got to be right with all things, you can't start letting down.

There was a ripping burst of detonations as the artillery went off with a rush all down the line from north to south, and the air was full of explosions, the sound of their own shells bursting on the Yankee lines one hundred yards away, and now the *whump!* of Yankee shells coming over and the swish and rattle of shrapnel like hail blown in the wind.

He never heard Davidson give the order, but he felt the others rising, and he rose, too, though the explosions of the shells seemed to fill the air with a sound so thick it was a kind of fog, deafening and blinding at once, and thrust his musket through the fire slit (*pull trigger and down!*). Stuck his face in front of the hole, cheek against the butt of his rifle, lining his sights on the black dot in the raw earth of the Yankee parapet that might be a fire slit like the one he was sighting through, while the wind of that world above the air of the trench blew in his face. Set himself with a quick breath. Rest. Squeeze the trigger, smoke jumps kick in the shoulder-socket, and *down!* He looked down the line. The others were all down before him, and Sam was looking at him. His body shook, as with a chill and he felt dizzy, as if he had run so hard his lungs could never hold enough oxygen to keep him on his feet.

He was aware of the explosions and the whine of shrapnel again. Nothing seemed to be landing near the trench, but the air was full of sound.

"Billy, you're a damn fool,'' said Marriot.

Billy said nothing.

Colonel Davidson was standing in his little bay, looking at his watch. The General and Lieutenant Bruce had their faces hidden behind field glasses. There was no telling if they had even watched the volley being fired. The Colonel's hand raised a trifle as he watched the clock face, getting ready to signal the next volley. Soon he would raise his hand all the way, and shout the order. Then they would all have to raise up and fire again.

The Mine: 5:00 P.M.

Harry Rees had gone down for his shift promptly at five. Stooped forward, he shuffled down the tunnel, through the wooden-tube section where continuous timbering held back the dissolving sandstone that was eaten away by the continual seep of the underground spring; the planks along here were slimy. On past that section the timbering was spaced out where the tunnel drove through stiffer clay and the rock-like marl; then it rose at a fairly steep angle to get above the layer of marl. Here the tunnel ended. Rees stuck his candle to the wall, and watched the flame leaning backwards with the gentle draft of the ventilator. Then he set to work, picking, chopping, crumbling the wall, then pushing the crumbled rock and dirt back to his helper, Dorn, who heaped the stuff in the crackerbox. When the box was full, Dorn jerked on the pull-rope, and it was hauled slithering down the incline, then on the long low slant back to the surface. *More than halfway across now,* thought Rees.

There would be no more talking in the tunnels. They were closer to the rebel lines, and closer to the surface than they had planned. Sound carried a surprising way in the earth. Back in the tunnel they could hear their own pickets tramping overhead, and the muffled garble of voices.

Rees felt a queer vibration in the air. He stopped swinging his pick. From overhead he heard a formless rumble. There was a louder, still-muffled *bump,* and a fine silt drifted down from the roof of his cave.

They were shooting artillery up above there.

His first thought was to get out. A big shell would land on the tunnel and collapse the roof on him. A mortar shell would loop in and seal the end of the tunnel. Breathed-out air would fill their tunnel, bad as a fall of earth. In the candle-flicker he could see Dorn watching him, the whites of his eyes glaring in his dirty face.

Rees grinned. "Bombproof," he whispered, and Dorn ducked his head, nervous. Above their head the thunder continued, its rhythm becoming quicker and more intense. They were as safe in the tunnel as anywhere. There was earth enough to keep the shells off, and the tunnel was built and timbered as solid as any bombproof. He wasn't going to be driven off his shift by shelling.

Rees continued to pick and shovel in the flickering blackness of his cave. Above his head the war went dimly on, as if in another world. *It's no more to me than fishermen's brawling is to the fish.* He was insulated in earth, and in the good numbness that came with hard working. A man who works hard and well, who gives his mind and body to the work as he should, is a man without fear, and without regret, and without vanity. It was his father's lesson, and a good one, though much good it did the Old Man when they locked him out of the mine, and he'd nought to do but chew his insides hollow and think on wasted years and wasted coin.

It was the sight of the Old Man sitting in the white-walled kitchen, with his lips wrung hard round the stem of the pipe clenched in his teeth, the sight of that as much as the hard times that drove Rees out of Rhondda and to the States, looking for a miner's work.

Whenever he thought of his father, and of his mother's kitchen in Wales, he felt again that restlessness, the itch to move and change and get out. There was the white kitchen, his mother kept it so; and the slow drift of the coal dust in, sooting it over, seeping into small invisible cracks in the plastered walls as it did into the small cracks in the skin of his father's face and hands: his father's shocking-white naked back in the bath, and his black hands and wrists and face, scouring and scouring and the black always growing by tiny increments. The heaps of coal-slag on the mine tip spilled down over the valley, a cold lava from a dead volcano, a black vomit. When his Dad hawked phlegm and spat the green was shot with black, then later and it was altogether black. In the night he'd hear his father coming home from the tavern, retching in the alleyway (it was after he'd been locked out), and he imagined the blackness of the vomit. In winter your breath erupted like white smoke from your mouth; but when the cold breeze lifted the dust from the tipple, the mine's mouth smoked black.

In America the valleys were still new to coaling, and the black covered less. The Welshmen came, men from different valleys, they'd have been strangers at home; but here they found each other finding work, and they discovered the songs they knew and could sing. There was work. There were wages that could leave a man something to put by. A man could vote his choices and speak at meetings; there could be chapel but no dominee standing by the mine owner's side to threaten them with the Book. And the mines were growing. They needed more hands, raw hands. A few years hard work, and Taffy could be bossing a gang, less of the black dust in his lungs, gathering his property, engaged to be married to a fine Welsh girl, there will be a wooden house, whitewashed, and the woman in the kitchen there.

In Wales a man who bossed his gang in the pit was townsman to the men with him, a wise head the men would look to anyway; a man to stand between the townsmen and the owner, as much the man for them as the man over them. In America it was different. In that country, all men are strangers, even the Welsh to the Welsh. And when the Irish came through, it was all strangers below, and half-strangers around him. As well be boss of wild niggers as of wild Irish. He liked the bosses no better than before, but the Irish were none of his kind. They lived all huddled up in unpainted leaning-together shanties, rabbits in a hutch. Rees's white cottage sat on grass at the end of the village street. They had no skill in their work, they did it with no quality. Rees was a good workman, a solid man, an orderly and thorough man: a moral man, who'd drink his one beer on Friday and call it good, while the Irish yelled and drowned their wits in rotgut whiskey. In Wales, when his father was chief over his section of the mine, he could drink beer with his mates in the evenings at the Four Chimneys.

But the Irish called him Taffy, and he'd be damned if he'd spend his time sitting by the hour in one of their low shebeens. He'd take his ale with his friends at the hotel tap, or better, in his home, sitting in his chair with his feet on the stool

Restlessness, dissatisfaction, a sense of trouble. The blackness of the pit that he wanted to escape. Rees had joined the army in '61, goodbye to coal mining. If boss was what he was, then let him be Boss pure and simple, and not pretend that coal mining was what it had been (for all coal miners born and bred in the trade are brothers, and the man who truly becomes a Boss betrays his brotherhood).

He became a sergeant almost immediately—that was a matter of course. But these last few months, when the regiment had seen its heaviest and longest action of the war, and they'd begun this mining, he'd come to see that soldiers were brothers the way miners were, and that the sergeant and the boss of it wasn't the thing that mattered, and the Taffy and the Mick of it wasn't the whole story. That Doyle had been playing the part of a man these last weeks, and his bunky Corrigan with him. Maybe it took a war to make Welsh miners out of Irish bog-trotters. They'd come along fine, and done a good job of timbering, too. Taking pride in the work, like members of a family working their same seam of coal down all the generations.

Overhead the thundering went on. Rees's shift was over, but he didn't want to leave the hot darkness of the mine that wrapped him close around, or the soft fingers of dust that sifted down to him from the ceiling while the vibration of the shelling went through it.

HEADQUARTERS NINTH ARMY CORPS
July 8, 1864—5:35 P.M.

Major-General HUMPHREYS, *Chief of Staff:*
    An artillery duel seems to have commenced on Smith's front and extended to mine. There was some little musketry, but nothing of moment apparently. Will have more definite news presently.

A. E. BURNSIDE,
Major-General.

(copy to General Warren)

When Rees came up from the Mine the firing was over. There was no one around the minehead, and that was odd. Blinking a little in the light, Rees looked down the trench. There was a knot of men where the connecting trench cut forward to join the front line to the mining trench. Rees hurried over. The set of the men's backs spoke of death. He had seen that huddle at the pithead before, the men about the body broken on the stones or under the timbers or blown up with coal gas or stifled and blue in the face, their shoulders drooping or held in tight as if by tensing their muscles hard as they could, they might hold life in their bones against the terrible magnetic pull of the dead one in the middle of them. *And it was his own brother Hugh that time.*

"It's Corrigan," said someone. He might have known. Fool kid had been looking out a fire slit when a rifleball came in. The bullet took him on the point of the nose, and it had been bulging and expanding as it came, and it had blown out the center of Corrigan's face. There was a blue-red hole in the middle of his face. One eye hung loose from the socket like an odd ornament. Rees heard himself wondering what had happened to the other one.

The head was resting in Doyle's lap. Doyle's face was the ceremonial stone face of all grief Rees had ever seen, the face of Rees's mother the day Hugh was crushed when the timbers gave way. They'd seen his light still burning somehow in the tunnel, but when they reached him he was dead, crushed, his tongue jabbing out of his open mouth and his face blue.

Someone tapped Rees's shoulder—one of the cook's boys.
"Rations," he said.

> HEADQUARTERS NINTH ARMY CORPS,
> *July 8, 1864—9* P.M.

Major-General HUMPHREYS, *Chief of Staff:*

I have the honor to report that everything has been quiet on my lines to-day up to 5 P.M., when artillery and infantry firing from the rebel lines, commencing on General Smith's front, swept down my lines. The enemy did not leave their works. It lasted about half an hour. No damage done.

> A. E. BURNSIDE,
> *Major-General.*

ORDERS.   HEADQUARTERS ARMY OF THE POTOMAC,
July 9, 1864.

1. The operations of this army against the intrenched position of the enemy defending Petersburg will be by regular approaches on the fronts opposed to General Burnside's and General Warren's corps.

2. The siege works will be constructed under the direction of the acting chief engineer of the army, Maj. J. C. Duane, Corps of Engineers, upon plans prepared by him and approved by the commanding general. Those plans that relate to the employment of the artillery will be prepared jointly by the acting chief engineer and the chief of artillery of the army, Brig. Gen. H. J. Hunt, U.S. Volunteers. Duplicates of the plan of siege will be furnished the commanders of the Ninth and Fifth Corps.

3. The engineer officers and troops of the army will receive their orders from the chief engineer, who will regulate the hours at which they will go on duty.

4. The siege artillery will be served under the direction

of the chief of artillery of the army, who will prescribe the hours at which artillery officers and troops go on duty. . . . By command of Major-General Meade:

S. WILLIAMS,
Assistant Adjutant-General.

CITY POINT, VA., *July 9, 1864.*

Hon. EDWIN M. STANTON,
Secretary of War.

About 5 P.M. yesterday, after a heavy cannonade upon Smith and Burnside, a line of rebel infantry suddenly appeared along the crest of their parapets as if to advance upon our works. They fired a single volley, and received one from the men in our trenches, after which they fell back behind their breast-works. Our troops were all under cover, and we had no losses. The movement seems to have been for the purpose of ascertaining whether we were still there. The Richmond papers have of late abounded in reports that Grant was withdrawing his army. Weather hot; no rain.

C. A. DANA.

HEADQUARTERS NINTH ARMY CORPS,
July 9, 1864. (Rec'd 1:40 P.M.)

General HUMPHREYS:

We are very much in need of sand-bags; where shall I apply for them? It is of the utmost importance that we have more heavy artillery if we remain in our present line.

A. E. BURNSIDE,
Major-General.

HEADQUARTERS ARMY OF THE POTOMAC,
July 9, 1864—2:15 P.M.

Major-General BURNSIDE,
Commanding Ninth Corps:

GENERAL: The major-general commanding directs me to reply to your dispatch that sand-bags are furnished upon requisition of the engineer officer on Brigadier-General Benham, at City Point, approved by the acting chief engineer of the army, and that siege artillery is supplied upon the recommendation of the chief of artillery, approved by the commanding general of the army; that at present the additional heavy artillery you have asked for cannot be furnished.

A. A. HUMPHREYS,
Major-General and Chief of Staff.

HEADQUARTERS ARMY OF THE POTOMAC,
July 9, 1864—2:45 P.M.

Major-General BURNSIDE,
Commanding Ninth Army Corps:
GENERAL: My dispatch of 2:15 P.M. should have explained further that since it is intended that operations against the enemy's intrenchments shall be by regular approaches, the batteries and other works of the adjoining fronts must be determined by the wants of both, and that under the existing circumstances is considered best by the commanding general that no more siege batteries should be established unless in conformity to the approved plans for the whole siege works.
A. A. HUMPHREYS,
Major-General and Chief of Staff.

HEADQUARTERS NINTH ARMY CORPS,
July 9, 1864—2:45 P.M.

Major-General HUMPHREYS,
Chief of Staff:
Your dispatch received. I have no engineer officer. The one I had, Captain Harwood, has been relieved upon my own request, because of his indisposition to personally superintend his work upon my line, intrusting it to enlisted men. Will the sand-bags be furnished upon my personal requisition? My men are being killed and wounded hourly for the want of them.
A. E. BURNSIDE,
Major-General.

HEADQUARTERS ARMY OF THE POTOMAC,
July 9, 1864—3:30 P.M.

Major-General BURNSIDE,
Commanding Ninth Corps:
Please have the requisition for sand-bags made through Lieutenant Benyaurd engineer, who is on duty with the engineer company on your front. The commanding general considered it better to have the requisition go through the regular channel. An engineer officer will be at once ordered to your staff in place of the officer relieved.
A. A. HUMPHREYS.
Major-General and Chief of Staff.

HEADQUARTERS ARMY OF THE POTOMAC,
July 9, 1864—3:50 P.M.

Brigadier-General INGALLS,
Chief Quartermaster, Army of the Potomac, City Point:
The major-general commanding directs that the grain-sacks

of the army be collected for use in the siege operations. If you have any on hand please send them to Major-General Burnside, commanding Ninth Corps.

A. A. HUMPHREYS,
Major-General and Chief of Staff.

CITY POINT, *July 9, 1864.*
(*rec'd. 5:20* P.M.)

Major-General A. A. HUMPHREYS:
There are 8,000 empty grain-sacks here which will be sent to General Burnside, in accordance with your orders. The Corps commanders might obtain a great number by saving those issued to them daily.

RUFUS INGALLS,
Brigadier-General and Chief Quartermaster.

July 9, 5:30 A.M. *Ferrero's headquarters*

Ferrero's headquarters tent was set where the pine trees screened it from the afternoon sun, and open to whatever breeze there might be. Even so it was hot, and the faces to the officers glowed with the heat, and shone with sweat. Every so often a drop of sweat would race down Ferrero's nose and pat on the papers spread out in front of him.

There were maps and diagrams of the front, sketches in pencil and ink and crayon, the result of three days of observation. A printed map in front of Ferrero had been more sparely and precisely marked up, as the officers came to agreement on translating the details of their observation into the picture of their planned assault.

Ferrero sat at the head of the table, flanked by his chief of staff, Captain Hicks, and his brigade commanders, Thomas and Oliver. Next to Thomas was Major Rockwood of the Nineteenth U.S.C.T., a soldier who had had some experience in laying out and assaulting fortifications —a round-faced man with a red complexion and laugh-lines at the corners of his eyes and mouth. The regimental commanders were there as well, except for Hall of the Forty-third, who was in hospital with dysentery; Booker, as the senior Major, sat in his place.

Booker had gone with Oliver, Thomas, Rockwood, and Ferrero over the entire section of trenches facing the rebel fort, checking the facilities there for massing their troops for the assault. They had conferred continually and taken notes: the trench was wide enough for a brigade to muster in closely packed, but not big enough to have the whole division on the line. They would need to have the brigades lined up back into the two covered ways—only one of them built; clearly the second one would have to be done soon—or they could have the second brigade mustered in the dark behind the trench line, out on the ground: dangerous if the rebs got windy and started a barrage, but a good idea if they went up in two lines, brigade following brigade.

The trench is rather deep, what with the rebs only one hundred yards away: have to arrange for ladders or staircases to be built for the men to get over the top. Stairs if we're in the trenches any time before the assault, they're more certain to hold up. Otherwise remember to have the engineer make up ladders beforehand, and we'll bring them with us when we move up.

What about the obstructions, abatis and such—ours and theirs? The engineers are supposed to clear that before the assault. A hundred yards away from the rebel lines? Yes: check that. Will the mine blow up the rebel abatis as well? Find out.

From the hillock where the fourteen-gun battery was being constructed, they had overlooked their own lines, and got a broader view of the front. To the left, southward, the rebel lines bulged forward; there was a smaller bulge on the right, out of sight behind some trees. *What about flanking fire from those batteries? Can artillery cover them? Perhaps a diversionary assault?*

Take it up with the General: the southward salient is on Warren's front, and the northward one belongs to Smith and Butler. We can't write orders or make plans for them, only advise General Burnside.

They had moved back into the trees, where the Signal Corps had established overlooks, and climbed wooden ladders to platforms in the branches of a large oak at the northern end of the IX Corps sector. Then down, and over to where a tower of raw-cut pine boards had been constructed behind a screen of pines, to look over the lines near Warren's front. Here the slits and tunnels of the trenches, the coves and hollows of the batteries, could be seen as an articulated line. With strong telescopes you could see somewhat behind the rebel first line, although there would be dips and hollows you could never guess at from this angle—some of them deep enough to hide a brigade in, no doubt. Still, there was the rebel trench line, with the battery in the center marked by the thickening of the parapet for the embrasures, a bead on a string. The ground seemed to dip slightly behind the rebel line, then it rose to the ridge that ran north-south, shielding the plank road. There were two houses on the ridge, flanked by shade trees—spots of white outlined in black. The glare of turned earth marked where two batteries had been constructed on the ridge: connected trench line for infantry, or just batteries? No way to tell. *If it is a line, and if it is full of infantry, we will all die in this assault, whether the Mine works or not.*

Up at the northern end of the long ridge was the higher bulge of the Cemetery Hill, obscured in heat haze, there was no telling what, if anything, the rebels had up there. But that was where the division had to go: from that small bulge in the ridge line they would overlook the rear of the rebel lines and the city of Petersburg. Whichever way they shot, they would be shooting rebels in the back. If they got there it would be final victory. They had imagined a large Stars and Stripes—so large it would be visible from the distant tower on which they stood—floating over the Cemetery Hill, wreathed in smoke as the hill was now wreathed in heat haze, like the flag Hooker's troops had raised on Lookout Mountain in the Battle above the Clouds.

And if we reach the top, a counterattack: we'll need to entrench, rapidly. Engineers and equipment—they'll have to follow right after us. Make a note. (They are gathered in their hastily dug emplacements when the gray wave begins to come on, shrieking, waving their red flags, front of the line toothed with bayonets; shells burst among them, the flag is flying in the smoke, *Steady men, take your aim, shoot low, steady, hold your fire, steady, steady, NOW!* a thin line of heroes carved in ebony, Ethopia salutes the colors, "The Union forever / Hurrah boys, hurrah," or maybe, "We have buried him with his niggers.")

To get there they would have to go through the first rebel trench line; oblique to the right, exposing their flank to the long ridge with its guns, perhaps infantry; then go up through whatever entrenchments the rebels might have between the rear of their first line and the Hill, and on the Hill. *What can you see? "Almost nothing." "I've been out between the lines on a scout: there's a ravine runs down from our lines to the rebels, over there to the right. My guess is it goes right through to the stream that's marked here. They might have lines, traverses or covered ways, established in the ravine there, and over the stream. The way the land gullies here, there are probably more ravines cutting into the stream every which way." "We don't know they've improved any of them." "No; but they could throw any reserves they've got into there and hold us up. Best to figure we'll have to fight our way up the hill."*

Ferrero cleared his throat, asking for attention. "I've raised the matter of supports with the General, and he assures me that those matters will be arranged by him. We have only to concern ourselves with our part of the assault, and with support from the rest of the corps. We can assume that the salients flanking the point of assault will be taken care of in some way."

"Have the rebels a second line?" asked Colonel Bates.

"The latest reports give no positive confirmation. Still, it seems safest to assume that some supporting line has been drawn, either on the crest of the ridge, or between the ridge and the front line. The General believes that the factor of surprise will negate the effect of any such reserve line, providing we can move forward, deploy, and assault with speed."

"It will take time to train the men," said Oliver. "Will we be given that time?"

"I am assured that we will," said Ferrero. Oliver leaned back in his chair, saying nothing. His studied ease implied skepticism.

"I have asked Major Rockwood, in consultation with Colonel Thomas and some of the other officers of experience among us, to draw up a tentative proposal for the assault. I'd like him to lay his plan out for you, and we can go over it thoroughly. I think speed is important now as well as in the assault. While we have the time to train the division, we have to make use of it. Major?"

Rockwood stood up. He was, surprisingly, much shorter standing than one would have supposed: a long-bodied man with a big head, and short legs. He unrolled a large sketch map and tacked it to a board, then tilted the board so that all could see. The lines had been drawn in dark ink, and troop movements indicated by dots and arrows in red: the movements were clear and easy to follow.

"Gentlemen, can you all see? Very well: here is the section of line stretching from the salient opposite Fifth Corps to the salient opposite the right of our line. I am assuming that both of these points will be taken or smothered by artillery fire. Here in the center of the line"—he pointed with a blunt red finger—"is the fort our troops are mining. The Mine is planned to be some hundred feet wide, following the line of the rebel trench. I'm assuming, therefore, that there will be a gap of some hundred-fifty-odd feet in the line. There may be more or less: mines are tricky things, and the results can't be precisely predicted. I understand also that the General has some special plans for making the explosive force of the Mine greater than anything hitherto attempted— so we are really out of the realm of exact science here. To either side and in front and rear of the gap will be a field of debris from the explosion— earth, rocks, equipment, casualties, guns—this increases the actual gap, perhaps doubles it. Beyond the radius of the debris there should also be further emptying of the trenches—an explosion of that size will panic any troops not made of iron, or stun them so that they will be no use for some time."

Yes, thought Oliver, *a lovely structure of concentric circles: the primary center of explosive force, creative fire decomposing in an instant into the Gap, the vacancy; the radius of the physical debris, created by the fire is laid down around it; and around this the radius of the human, the circle of morale. The manmade antitype of Genesis. Let there be light; let there be dry land; let there be man and woman, and creatures after their kind. Let there be fire; let there be destruction; let there be fear.*

"We have to slip through a fairly narrow hole in the wall here— at least, it's safest to assume so. That dictates an approach in column, rather than in line—you can see why. The usual objections against an assault in column won't apply here—there will be no fire from the front because the Mine will have blown up the rebel guns; and our flanks should be covered by supporting attacks by the other corps. In any case, we have only a hundred yards to cover until we're in the rebel lines."

Ferrero spoke: "What about obstructions, Major?"

"Our own will have to be removed: that's standard procedure for the engineers before an assault, and can be done the night before the attack. I would guess that the rebel obstructions will be all or partly covered by the debris of the explosion; but we'd best have an engineer company with the leading regiments to be sure. Other questions?"

There were none.

"Very well. After we pierce the line, we'll need to deploy. This is really the crux of the attack. This is what we'll need to prepare for most thoroughly. A body of troops deploying can be easily thrown into confusion by enemy fire, counterattack, or simply their own faulty understanding. Veteran troops are hard to confuse because they have been so often under fire that nothing really surprises them; their reactions are instinctive. We must remedy our troops' lack of that experience and that instinct by careful training.''

Oliver was growing more and more interested in the drift of Rockwood's analysis: not so much its specifics, which he felt he grasped easily enough, but its larger implications. Rockwood was voicing ideas he had met and ruminated in other contexts. In a sense, he had expressed in pragmatic terms the deeper character of the whole race problem. Rockwood, the soldier, was showing him another side of the problem, serving his inquiry the way the entrepreneur Brickhill had done back in Carolina, with his interesting talk about reorganizing Southern agriculture. Instinct and experience, the thing that set the veteran white soldier apart from the black; perhaps in other things the analogy held—civilization itself was the offspring of instinct and experience, innate capacity and historical action. In that respect, as in soldiering, the black was a latecomer. To catch up with his own fellow-soldier, he'd need rigorous training, education. But of what sort. Rigid, task-centered, limited— and perhaps limiting? The white soldier could be trusted to guide himself in battle or in affairs—guide himself in accordance with his instinct and experience, his moral sense, or whatever one wished to call it. Trust the white man; guide the black man. How long? And could any amount of such guidance ever bring about a change sufficient so that no guidance would be required? And would not the white man himself have gone on from the place he had been when the black man began his attempt to catch him up? The battle will be an experiment in social and moral philosophy as much as a military exercise, he thought—with a wry inner grin at his own cold-bloodedness, and, as he called it, pedantry.

''There are certain special problems that must be faced by particular regiments in the assault. We'll be attacking in column, so the two leading regiments of each brigade will have to act as guides going into the breach. They will then peel off to left and right to clear the trenches. The second regiments in the column must be prepared for this. In whatever smoke, confusion, debris we find there, they must not follow the leaders heads down, which will be their tendency. When the leaders turn off, the second regiments will become the guides for the deployment and assault; they have to know their evolutions and directions perfectly, so that they could find their places and take their lines of movement in the dark—the confusion of battle, as you gentlemen know, often makes it seem that one is moving in darkness or fog of war. The two leading regiments in each brigade must therefore receive special training; so the order of assault will have to be determined quite early. Are there questions, gentlemen?''

That evening, by candlelight, Ferrero drew up his draft plan for the assault; he would take it to Burnside for approval in the morning.

Thomas and Oliver conferred with their staffs, trying to determine which of their regiments could best handle the different roles to be assigned. Which had the best men? Which the best officers?

Thomas's mind was easily made up: his old regiment, the Nineteenth, would have to lead. He knew the men and officers well, and he'd bank on them behaving like veterans. They'd be able to handle the confused fighting down the trench line; and the officers would have sense enough to hold out enough of a reserve so that they could support the rest of the brigade as required. The First Brigade would make the main attack on the Hill. The Second Brigade was assigned to the protection of the flank: Thomas was a trifle disappointed at that, and Chris would be more so. Yet experience told Thomas that his holding action would inevitably become an attack on that long ridge. Then, with the rest of the corps coming up, he'd pull the Nineteenth out of the trenches, mass the brigade, and take it up the hill himself, right for the white house on the ridge line. Who could say which blow, the one on the Hill or the one on the Ridge, would be the finisher?

Oliver at first dismissed each of his regiments in turn. He was aware of the absurdity of the process. He had to decide in utter ignorance of the most basic facts. Since his regiments had never been under fire—or not for very long or under especially trying conditions—he had no real evidence to go on. Was precision in drill an indication of soldierly competence? Were high spirits the evidence of good soldierly morale, or of a careless, heedless temperament? The training would be crucial: training, not instinctive virtue in the troops, nor experience in battle. Since Bates was the best man for training troops, let the Thirtieth Regiment lead. After it, it would have to be Hall and the Forty-third Regiment, despite the presence of that Jew Booker, whom Oliver had grown more and more to detest. The Forty-third had seen some fighting in the trenches, according to Hall's last report; and they had been in action, however briefly, in the fight on the right flank after Spotsylvania. The other two regiments—settle it by drawing straws, there was no more scientific way to choose.

There ought to be a science that would answer the kinds of question that he had to deal with. He put his orders aside, and began to think about this larger problem, jotting ideas in his notebook as he mused. A science of human character-types would not merely answer such practical questions as he now posed, but would also allow the intelligent mind to grasp the larger meanings of historical development. One was used to descriptions of battles such as those in Prescott, Parkman, or Carlyle, in which rival commanders appear as heroic emblems of opposed peoples and historical forces. But how could one describe the working of those colossal forces whose human embodiments were not individuals, but races and classes of men taken in the mass? And whose field of battle was the whole field of human history, both grander and less easy to conceive and portray than Valmy or the *Noche Triste* of Cortez?

Perhaps he had approached the problem the wrong way around. Perhaps the scientific way to begin would lie not in theory but in experiment. Perhaps this coming battle would give him the evidence that he most needed, the categories most vital to interpreting the grand strife of races which was the ground theme of history.

Take the idea of the Mine, for instance. Here were two societies, North and South, the one embodying all the principles of nineteenth-century civilization—progress, liberty, education, practical philanthropy, industry—and the other embodying the last vestiges of a dying feudalism. And here they had reached an impasse in their struggle, in which neither the technical resources of the one nor the military traditions of the other could produce a victory. What then? The nineteenth century applies its greatest power: its technical mastery of the forces of Nature, its ability to organize and efficiently direct the energies latent in the natural world. The explosion of physical force beneath the dense inertia of the soil infuses it with human will and power, lifts it to the heavens . . . and carries down the inert and useless feudalism with it.

"Hah!" he said, grinning as his pen began to race over the page, hopelessly lagging behind his thoughts (mental against physical power again!), because here was a way of looking at it that offered some insight. What was human progress about but the infusion of intelligent direction into the inanimate or semianimate orders of the natural world? And by analogy, wasn't it the same in the strife of the races for mastery, with the torpid and inert races falling behind while the dynamic and progressive ones surged ahead?

He paused. How then account for the ability of the torpid feudalism to withstand the massively organized force of the nineteenth century? He tapped his teeth with the stub of his pencil, then grinned. The question, posed out of the terms he had been thinking in, answered itself. The principle of progress was racial, a dynamism of character. The Southerner had it as well as his Northern brother. But the situations were different. Here was the Southerner, bound to a system in which his own energetic race could control the levers of power without hindrance from the lower orders; but who therefore could not bring to the field the same *mass* of inert resources—equipment, human material as inert as their own Northern underclasses, the Irish, and *especially* not the niggers that the South had possessed in such abundance. Now for the North: the mass was there, but the democratic structure of the North made it impossible for the best minds to dominate, as they did in the South. There would always be some moon-eyed philanthropist or passionate reformer to insist that the human slag of the state be given the power to rule and direct. That Jew Booker, for a local case in point.

So the war had become a stalemate: energy without mass balances mass without energy.

But if the mass could somehow be infused with energy, that would not only alter the present, it would point the way towards the future. If it could be done with the blacks it could be done with anyone. Oliver's mind ran back to his first acquaintance with "the Question," during the months when he had commanded the occupation forces in a district near New Bern. He remembered vividly the dispiriting sight of the contraband camps, the odor so strong that one could almost taste it. It had reminded him of the stories he had heard of Indian tribes in the West, deprived of their old hunting life, sinking into inanition and despair beside some trader's fort. How much worse was it for this race, which has never known the wild free life from which the Indian had fallen; which had known only the brutish and brutalizing submissions of slavery, and before that the horrors of the benighted African hinterland. Freedom, he feared, would be as fatal to the black man as civilization had been to the Indian. Without political power and protection, the nigger would soon return to some form of bondage, some new abjection before the superior talents of the competing race. But given power, what could the nigger do but . . . let all slide, fall into decay, into *inertia.*

If they could not somehow acquire the capacity to compete with the whites, under the new system of organization they would soon cease to be useful even as instruments. Then their fate would be like that of the outmoded cotton gins and oldfangled steam engines that cumbered the earth all through Oliver's district: their freedom would be the freedom of useless machinery, which is the freedom to rust. Eventually, like the Indian, the black race would begin to wither and disappear before the expansion of the more vigorous and manly race.

Only if some measure of the Anglo-Saxon's conquering spirit could be forcibly infused in the torpid mass could they have any prospects for the future. That was what it had taken at New Bern to get them to do their work and earn their bread on Brickhill's confiscated plantations —military force and discipline from start to finish. The army would be the nigger's great hope, his refuge and his teacher. If ever he could emerge from his characteristic torpor, it would only be through the stern tutelage of organized power. And only under some such regime could the nigger retain a semblance of usefulness. The free-born white man was a hard character to discipline, whether in the army or in the mill. But the black man could take orders, if nothing else. Perhaps even if the race never emerged from its military tutelage, it might still find a useful place as the instrument of intelligence for enforcing a rational discipline on the unruly elements of nineteenth-century society.

Well, well. All that would have to wait on the results of the experiment. It remained to be proven whether or not the nigger was capable of learning enough of the soldier's trade to perform the task he had been assigned.

Special Orders,
No. 152

HEADQUARTERS OF THE ARMY OF THE POTOMAC,
OFFICE OF PROVOST MARSHAL GENERAL,
July 9, 1864

3. Sergeant Madison Stoddard, 5th U.S. Cavalry, having struck and killed a sentry near Prince George Courthouse on the 3rd instant, a Board of Inquiry was appointed by the Provost-Marshal General to ascertain the facts. This Board has determined that the incident arose from a confusion about countersigns and procedures for passing out of the lines of the army. In view of these circumstances, and the distinguished record of Sgt. Stoddard, no Court-martial will be asked for. Administrative action directing the sergeant's reduction in rank, deprivation of leave and privileges for himself and members of

his command, and two weeks punishment duty is hereby ordered.

*   *   *

7. Lieutenant Lemuel D. Dobbs, 19th Regiment United States Colored Troops, is reprimanded for abusing a prisoner in the course of making an arrest; and for improperly instructing his command in the procedures for giving countersigns, etc.

MARSENA L. PATRICK,
Provost-Marshal General.

5:30 P.M. IX Corps front: 14th N.Y. Heavy Artillery

Beeler and Neill were on picket duty, about fifty yards in advance of their front line. The trenches here, just south of the point where the rebel and Union trenches bulged towards one another, were some two to three hundred yards apart. Even that much difference in distance made the place seem more comfortable.

The picket post was at the head of a small brush-filled ravine that slanted northwest towards the rebel lines. It was dug three feet into the sandy soil, and a parapet had been built in front of it, reinforced by wicker baskets filled with rocks and earth. A communication trench, shallow but adequate, led from the post back towards the main line. At 5:30 the sun was still high enough to pour its heat into the hole. Neill licked his lips. They felt dry, almost burned. He felt his face was red with the heat—sunburn. He had finished the water in his canteen an hour ago. Beeler was standing in a half-crouch, peering through the peepholes bored in the parapet. They didn't use the rifle slits at all. They were wide enough to get shot through, and they had no intention of defending the post if the rebels came hollering out of the ravine; they'd duck or run, as the situation suggested.

From the ravine there came a piercing whistle. Neill felt the blood shoot in one bolt from heart into head, and for the second he froze.

"Hey Yank!"

"Take a look," whispered Beeler. Neill rose to the half-crouch and looked through a peeper. From behind a bush down in the ravine, a piece of gray cloth waggled on the end of a slender ramrod. The hand that held it was invisible.

"Flag of truce, Yank! How about we do some trading?"

Neill looked at Beeler. Beeler shrugged one shoulder. Without thinking, the two men had clutched their rifles in their hands.

"What are we talking about, Johnny? What you-alls got to trade? Mule meat ain't to our liking over here."

"Got the latest Richmond papers, Yank! All about how Ginral Early has took Washington and captured Abe."

"We got plenty ass-wipes here too, Johnny." Beeler and Neill were grinning.

"All right then, Yank. What about some prime nigger-head chawing? I done had my man-servant bring it from the old plantation. It is *truly* prime. Let's see : Havana see-gars, might be, from General Lee's private reserve. And something in a jug."

Neill licked his lips.

"How big of a jug?" asked Beeler.

"Holds more 'n a gallon, anyway. Was full when I started, but talkin's thirsty work. Time you Yanks come to business, I might have drunk up my capital."

"What'll you take, Johnny?"

"Now some coffee would be mighty prime. I got a craving for some coffee; papers will do, or greenbacks, Yank—we-uns is a mite short of ass-wipe since the supply of Abolition pamphlets was cut off."

Beeler looked at Neill, and nodded sharply. "Hold right where you are, Johnny. My pal here is gone to tell the boys not to plug you, and see what we got to trade."

"Right, Yank. But don't let him take too long—I'm powerful thirsty."

Neill scurried back down the communication trench, bent nearly to all fours. He heard Beeler calling, "You ain't gonna like our papers, Johnny. Says all about how Ginral Early got up late, and Ginral Wallace bagged him."

"Hell, Yank," returned the reb, "all them folks is liars anyway. I just like to see em lying side by side."

"Richmond!" yelled Neill, as he scrambled into the trench—it was the password.

"Hey! . . . ." Private Dongan started to yell.

"Shut up!" said Neill. "Keep quiet or the officers or Sergeant Stanley will hear. There's a couple Johnnies out there want to trade tobacco and some white mule for coffee, papers, and shinplasters. What have we got?"

"Maxwell has the coffee for the company. How much does he want?"

"I don't know. Let's get what we can, and deal with him. What papers we got? *Heralds?* Anybody here read the goddamn nigger-loving *Tribune?* I love to watch Johnnies reading Greeley."

Dongan and Neill were shuffling rapidly down the trench. The other men who had heard were digging in haversacks for papers, coffee, whatever they thought might buy them into a share of the jug. Army orders made liquor hard to get on the lines, unless you had the right kind of officers. The Fourteenth had the two worst kinds: some who ordered liquor for themselves and sold it to the men at vulture's prices, and others who tried to compensate for the crookedness of their colleagues and the regiment's low discipline by coming down hard on anyone caught boozing.

If Johnny was trading, that meant some strong raw stuff, and the price was going to be better than what the officers were charging. Neill was calculating while Dongan roused Maxwell and had him bring out the platoon's share of coffee. "Listen," said Dongan. "You're in for a full share with us, and you can drink it or trade it as you like."

"Yeah, sure. But you know this coffee is all the men's. They'd kill me if I just traded it off."

"Hell, man," Neill interrupted, "what do you think we are? Every man in the platoon gets his cupful for his share of the coffee. Ain't a glass of whiskey worth ten cups of that muck you boil any day? What we keep over above that is ours. Didn't we find this damn Johnny in the first place? Come *on!*"

The three men brushed down the trench again. "Pass the word: no firing, it's a truce."

"Hey Neill, here's my *Herald*. Cut me in, for Chrissake."

"Fuck you and your *Herald*. The Johnnies only want the *Tribune*." There was laughter at this.

The three men bent over and scuffled down the communication trench. Neill looked back. Heads were peeping tentatively over the top of the trench to watch them. There was no shooting: Johnny had told his boys to keep still. But the damn fools! Those heads would draw officers sure as anything.

"All right, Johnny!" called Beeler. "Come on, and come slow."

"And don't drop anything!"

"All right, Yank. We're comin. Two of us, Yank! Take it easy now!" Two men in slouch hats, brownish shirts, and blue pants rose from the brush and stepped forward, an older man and a kid. The older man carried a big gray stone jug. It had evidently been kept until a short time before in a cool place: in the heat, bubbles of condensation spangled its surface. The kid was carrying several bundles, probably the tobacco and papers. The older man was Sam Marriot, the younger Billy Caldwell. T. W. Dixon was lying in the bushes, out of sight but in earshot.

The two rebs came around the side of the raised parapet. "Nice little fort you boys got here: Who stole your Columbiad?"

"How about a taste of what you're trading, Johnny?"

"Now that's a right neighborly notion. Any you men got cups?" He was speaking slowly; before he had finished the four soldiers had thrust their tin cups towards him. He drew the cork with his teeth and poured four shots; then set the jug down, got his own out, and poured himself one. His companion sat on the edge of the hole without moving. "Billy here ain't being unsociable, just Methodist." Marriot raised his glass, and knocked it back. The Yanks did the same. He saw their eyes bulge in unison as the stuff hit them. That was the best white mule in the C.S.A. As that stick, Lieutenant Bruce, damn well knew.

"Let's do some trading," said Neill.

"Hell, man," sad Marriot, "you can't tell if whiskey is good after but the one taste. And you ain't inspected my nigger-head yet. How do you know it ain't wool?"

They began opening packages. Neill handed Marriot a package of coffee beans (Dongan held the other, in case it was demanded). He decided to say nothing about the greenbacks unless the bargaining got stiff. Dongan handed over the papers: *Herald*s for about a week, and a copy of the *Tribune* Sergeant Stanley subscribed to and Neill took and used for ass-wipes whenever he could.

Marriot poured another round, while Billy opened one of the packages of tobacco. He bit off a chaw, and passed it to Beeler, who did the same. Neill knocked back his second whiskey, and took the plug. He reached round for his jackknife, opened it with his teeth, and cut a chunk off the end; closed the knife, and took out his pipe, crumbling the tobacco slightly so it would fit in. He passed the twist, then scratched a match on his boot sole and lit up.

"Waste of good chawing, burning it up like that, Yank," said Marriot.

The six men were now lounging easily in the picket hole. They could hear loud whispers from the trench, but could not make out the words. Probably telling us to hurry. *Screw em.*

"How you Yankees like the sunny South?"

"Don't it ever rain here? If I didn't know better I'd swear this was the Great American Desert."

"Genral Lee has ordered the rain to withhold its support until you-uns go away. Says right in that paper there: Nature itself done turn its face away from you criminal Yankee host. Why don't you boys all just go on home?"

"Shit, Johnny, if we wasn't here, who would feed all these poor deserters been coming into our lines. Can't live on mule jerky and green corn all your life, Johnny."

"This stuff helps you digest it," said Marriot, and he poured another round.

"What outfit is this-un?"

"Fourteenth New York Heavies. The Bowery B'hoys!"

"Oh," said Marriot, "this is an Abolition outfit then! You Yanks gone to vote for Old Abe this time around?"

Billy was beginning to sweat. Sam was taking big chances. If these Yanks got angry the whole thing might go bad, and they'd wind up freezing in some Yankee prison. But the Yanks laughed at the idea they'd be Abolitionists, so it seemed to be all right.

"Little Mac's our man," said Beeler. "We don't like Abolitionists much, and he don't neither. Mac's the man to put things right."

Neill became very earnest. "You listen this, reb. Important. You tell your officers, tell em to tell General Lee: Mac is a man you can talk to. I used to know plenty of politicians back in the New Yourk, see, so I know what I'm talkin about. We don't like niggers any better 'n you do. Mac's the man. He'll set things right. Tell General Lee he can *talk* to McClellan."

"I'll convey him your communication, sir," said Marriot seriously, "next time he invites me to dinner," and they all laughed. Neill started to, then stopped: was there a joke on him? This Johnny might not have appreciated the importance of what he said.

"You boys having an election too?"

"Hell, Yank. We're too busy fighting a war to elect a new President. Ain't you heard about that war?"

"If we was to vote," said Billy, "Lee would win sure. Be funny if Lee and McClellan ended the war, when they was first leading in the fighting."

"I'll drink to that: end of the war." They drank.

"Only voting we got to do is for the State Legislature, and we got a Governor up this summer too," said Marriot.

"What have you got instead of Republicans?" asked Beeler.

"Now that was a right puzzling thing," said Marriot. "First thing after secession, you know, Jeff Davis looked around, whacks himself in the forehead: 'We done forgot the most important thing! We didn't make no provision for no Republicans in the Constitution! Now we can get along fine without Yankee gold, and Yankee machinery, and Yankee women; but if we don't have anybody to run against down here, political democracy will be dead. Who ever heard of Democrats running for office without any Whigs or Republicans to call names at? Mean the wreckage of our whole civilization!'"

"What's he gonna do about it?" asked Beeler.

"Oh, he's got some Tories on consignment from England. They be running them through the blockade any time now, and then things will be just dandy."

"Listen, Johnny," said Beeler. "Why don't you two just stay on here. You're a couple nice fellers, wouldn't want to see such nice fellers get hurt. We treat you real good, Johnny. No prisons, just some nice easy fatigue behind the lines; some of em even get sent North to work."

"Hell," said Neill, "if I'd known that I'd-of enlisted in the reb army, and deserted to this lot."

Billy's eyes narrowed, but Marriot remained casual. "Not just yet, Yank. We got some pretty comfortable diggings over to our side. Fact, I was just going to invite some of you-all to step on over to our side." Marriot looked away. "Yes, we got real comfortable digs. Running water right in the trench, bombproofs like you never seen—and the place where this stuff came from," and he patted the jug. "I reckon you-uns will be coming over to see it one way or the other. Hope you don't try to do it the hard way: you're a bunch of nice fellers." He beamed all round, his face red.

"Maybe you better enjoy them nice bombproofs while you can, Reb. We got some tricks you haven't heard of yet. Might be you'll wake up one morning and find your nice little fort's all blowed up."

"Long as I don't find my nice little still all blowed up, I'm satisfied. I ain't got no money invested in no fort."

"Hey!" came a call from the trench. "Hurry up, goddamn it!"

The trading was done quickly. Marriot took the bag of coffee and the papers. Billy passed the package of tobacco to Dongan. "This ain't coffee enough for all that good whiskey. You trying to jew me, Yank? How about some green?"

Neill, red in the face, reached into his pocket and unfolded the wad of greenbacks, and peeled off five notes. Marriot didn't take the money, but looked genially into Neill's face. Neill peeled off two more bills; added a third; added the rest. "Thank you, Yank," said Marriot, "that's mighty white of you."

The two rebs rose, and shook hands all around. Then they turned, and moved off at a crouch, swiftly back down the ravine. The bushes waved behind them where they went through the screen.

Beeler and Maxwell were passing empty canteens to Neill, who was swiftly but carefully pouring the white whiskey into them. It was the best way to keep the stuff hidden from the officers and Sergeant Stanley;

they'd heave the jug out into the ravine later. Dongan had unwrapped the tobacco and was counting the twists.

"Officer!" yelled someone. The four men looked quickly at each other. Neill said, "Wait, last drop," filled the last canteen; Maxwell covered it, and Neill heaved the jug into the brush. Weighed down with the sloshing canteens, Neill, Maxwell, and Dongan scurried back towards the trench.

"What the hell is going on here?" yelled Sergeant Stanley. "Nobody authorized any truce."

The men crowded to the parapet near the communication trench. "It's some rebs, sir, wanting to trade for papers."

"Hey, you men," yelled Stanley to the pickets. "No trading with the enemy. Tell em it's no damn truce!"

"Right you are, Sergeant," called Neill gaily. "Sorry now Johnny! No truce! Sergeant says!" He chuckled: that was one on Stanley. And those dumb rebs hadn't even asked for the second bag of coffee.

Back in the Confederate lines, Marriot, Dixon, and Caldwell came running out of the ravine and through the gap in the parapet. Lieutenant Bruce was waiting for them and Marriot handed over the newspapers.

"All right," said Bruce, "I'll look these over later. Were you able to find out anything about their plans?"

"They plan to stay awhile, Lieutenant."

Bruce waited. After a time, Marriot had to speak again. "They didn't say nothing about troop movements, far as I could tell these boys is just sitting still. One of them did say something about blowing up one of our forts, but I figure it's just Yankee bullshit—scuse me. Can't no cannon blow up one of these bombproofs. Got a look at their lines."

"Anything else?"

"No sir."

"What did you swap for that whiskey, Marriot?"

"Got some papers, Lieutenant, like you asked. Couple of Yankee greenbacks, little old cupful of coffee beans. Those boys ain't been paid any more 'n what we have."

Bruce smiled a little, but his eyes stayed cold. "That's mighty poor trading for a man clever as you, Marriot."

"My wits is fuddled with the sun, Lieutenant. And I had all I could do to keep my mind on business, trying to find out what they's up to, just like you asked me, Lieutenant sir."

"By rights, Marriot, I should confiscate whatever you got, and have you court-martialed. It's against army orders, explicit from General Lee, to purvey or distribute whiskey in the camps."

"Didn't say nothing about making it."

"Don't play the lawyer with me, Marriot. And don't play the fool. I'll let you keep whatever you traded for. I've busted up your still, and sent the parts over to the hospital for making alcohol there. Just keep yourself out of trouble, Marriot. You could even go someplace in this army, if you'd show more sense."

Bruce walked off. Marriot stared after him. "He shouldn't talked to you like that, Sam," said Billy.

"Ole Sam'll take it," said Dixon. "He wants to amount to something someday. Wants Bruce to make him corporal, or get him a job drivin niggers."

"Shut up, Dix," said Marriot. "I got to take it from him, this time; but I don't have to take a thing from you."

"Yassuh, corporal," said Dixon.

Lieutenant Bruce hurried off to Johnson's headquarters. He had one more bit of evidence about what the Yankees were up to. It was time for some specific countermeasures to be taken.

Sitting on the roadside on a summer day,
Chatting with my messmates, passing time away,
Lying in the shadow underneath the trees,
Goodness, how delicious, eating goober peas!

Chorus: *Peas! Peas! Peas! Peas! eating goober peas!*
            Goodness, how delicious, eating goober peas!

When a horseman passes, the soldiers have a rule,
To cry out at their loudest, "Mister, here's your mule,"
But another pleasure enchantinger than these,
Is wearing out your grinders, eating goober peas!

Chorus

Mine/Countermine
July 12–24, 1864

HEADQUARTERS JOHNSON'S DIVISION,
July 12, 1864—12 M.

Lieut. Col. E. F. MOSELEY, *Commanding Artillery:*
The enemy's mortar batteries are seriously damaging the left of my line, occupied by Wise's brigade; you will, if possible, divert the enemy's fire from that part of the line or endeavor to silence it; also communicate with the officers in command of our mortar batteries, which may be brought to bear on this part of our line, and see if they cannot afford us some relief.

B. R. JOHNSON,
Major-General.

HEADQUARTERS JOHNSON'S DIVISION,
July 12, 1864—12 M.

Colonel GOODE, *Commanding Wise's Brigade:*
COLONEL: Please report promptly everything of importance on your line. Are the enemy damaging you with shell this morning? How are the spirits of your men? What progress are you making with bombproofs? You will see that your men only construct strong and secure bombproofs. Let the roof be supported by heavy timbers and strong uprights. Let the men be thoroughly in hand, and prepare them to be prompt in coming out of bombproof and manning the parapets when required. Should the woods in your rear be set on fire by shells or otherwise you will have the fire promptly extinguished. Should your line be attacked you will bear in mind that it must be held at all hazards. Of this every officer and man of your brigade should be duly advised. They should be all duly prepared and fully resolved, and success cannot fail to crown their courageous efforts.
Very respectfully, your obedient servant.

B. R. JOHNSON,
Major-General.

July 12. 1864. Noon. Pegram's Salient

The first crash of the barrage had brought the men of the Twenty-second North Carolina stark awake out of their blankets that morning, and they had rushed up to man the trenches near their incomplete battery, fearing an attack. But the rumble of the guns never built to crescendo, continuing unabated hour after hour at a slow pace, a concussion that sounded after a while, to ears dulled by habitude, like the incessant rumble of a train over tracks, mile after mile. Things got livelier when the Yankees shifted their aim, bringing shells raining around the battery. The shells struck all around, ripping up huge gouts of earth and stones, and raining them with metal fragments in the open trenches. The men huddled in bombproofs and traverses, mostly safe.

"That goddamned stupid engineer," said Dixon. "That horse's ass comes down here big as the elephant, with his damn surveyor tools and his pick-and-shovel boys, and starts people throwing up entrenchments like we was digging to China. What the hell they expect but the Yanks is gonna start shelling?"

They gripped their rifles hard, and felt the ground shudder around them. A huge ripping explosion sounded far behind their line.

"Got a magazine, I guess," said Marriot.

The engineer Captain came down the line, Lieutenant Bruce with him. They spoke with Lieutenant Penwaring, the company commander. Penwaring stepped slightly away from the trench wall against which he was huddled, and called out, "Company A will fall out with me, for duty with Captain Douglas's engineer party. You'll stack arms in the Colonel's bombproof, bring shovels, picks, your canteens and rations. Quickly now!" The company, twenty-five men, followed Penwaring and the engineer, Douglas. Bruce smiled sardonically at the three privates as they went by. The shelling had moved off: having hit a magazine back of the lines, the Yankees were concentrating fire there, hoping to find another. The *zip-zippee* of minie balls told that they were also firing to keep work parties down.

Company A was mustered behind a tall bank that formed the rear of the battery.

"Gentlemen," said the engineer Captain, "we're going to be doing some countermining. Scouting reports have suggested that the Yanks may be tunneling under one of the batteries along here, and that they will attempt to blow it up. What we're going to do is dig a listening gallery: dig our own tunnel, and put men in it to listen sharp. You can hear men digging underground pretty far off; you'd be surprised. When we figure out where and how they're coming at us, we can figure some way of stopping them: cut their tunnel with our own, cave theirs in on em—depends on the situation. Reason I'm telling you all this is, what we're doing has to be done quietly. Quiet so you can hear *them;* quiet so they can't hear you, and maybe get cautious, or slant off in a new direction. You men understand that now?"

There was a rumble of assent.

"All right then. My men have marked the head of the shaft. You'll dig into the hillside at an angle, which I've calculated to follow the slope of the ground. You'll pile the earth around the edge of the hole and pack it into a curb: that's to keep rain off." There was laughter, but Douglas went on. "Get started on that, and I'll be checking back later to see how you're doing." He turned to Penwaring. "Lieutenant?"

Penwaring stepped forward. "All right. We'll need two men to pick, two with shovels, and four to remove the dirt each shift for now. Volunteers? Marriot, you, Dixon, Caldwell, Anderson, Woodson, Sylvester, Pickens, and Dwight. You'll take it first."

They began digging in the hot sun. They worked slowly, because the blaze of noon was heavy. Their bodies were greasy with sweat. Soon they were stripped to their underclothes and hats. The dell in which they worked was well sheltered from shells, but they winced involuntarily when explosions sounded close. Their heads seemed to swell with the heat. Water poured out of them. They felt they breathed the air of an oven. The little flags planted as markers by the engineers barely fluttered. *And not a drop of corn to kill the pain. Christ!*

Noon: The Mine

Doyle was working in the darkness. The weariness of his labor and the dull flicker of candlelight wrapped him in a sense of dreaming. He had forgotten the name of the man in the Mine with him. In these reveries he nearly believed that Corrigan was with him still. One part of his mind knew Corrigan was dead, a big red-black hole in the middle where his face should have been; but if the man with him didn't speak, Doyle did not notice that Corrigan was gone, though there was a dull ache in his chest.

Mostly he just dug.

Sometimes when his pick would knock a hole in the wall, he'd think of the hole in Corrigan's face. At first it made him weep when he thought of it. He forced himself to think of it: like looking at Ma's face when she was laid out at the wake; you had to look in the face of death to accept it. She had looked strange, in a frozen waxy sleep, like someone else's mother.

But Corrigan dead had had no face. Where his face should have been was a black-red hole. You could see that he had had a face, from what was left around the hole; but the center was an empty crater.

The image of his father's face, laughing in the saloon, his mouth a red hole in his black face, coal-blacked. "Like some damned nigger minstrel, *haw haw.*"

He labored without thought. The red light of the candles flickered, casting his black shadow before him, into which his pick struck again and again. It was the shadow of his own head.

He felt his partner tap-tap on his back with the flat of his hand. He had forgot the man's name, but he hated him. The man's hand, resting lightly with a pressureless pressure, still was hauling him out of the numbing dark and work in the pit. He followed, drawn by the man's shadow. Light grew at the tunnel's end like a waking into the pain of a hangover.

The two moles were out, blinking in the noon sun.

"How is it, Doyle?" asked a shape out of the light.

"Damned rebels dropping shells on the roof," Doyle said. "Any come in here?"

Sergeant Rees was there, Doyle saw now. Rees said, "Not rebels where you were. Not unless they're shorts."

"What do you mean?"

"Those'll be our shells. We're that far over."

HEADQUARTERS ARMY OF THE POTOMAC,
July 13, 3:45 P.M.

Brigadier-General BENHAM,
Commanding Engineer Brigade, City Point:

Colonel Spaulding reports that a large portion of the sandbags brought up this morning are rotten and otherwise damaged, and probably more than a third are utterly worthless. Will you have what are on hand examined, if practicable, and if the number originally ordered is materially diminished by mildew, or in any other way, will you see to having others procured?

A. A. HUMPHREYS,
Major-General and Chief of Staff.

CITY POINT, *July 13, 1864*
Rec'd. 5:40 P.M.

General A. A. HUMPHREYS,
Chief of Staff:

I have previously directed that no rotten bags should be sent up. I fear that the defective bags are a portion of 30,000 drawn from the engineer department in April when your order was received. The balance of the 100,000 mostly purchased new at that time, I trust are sound and strong as they were then. Orders will go at once to Washington for 30,000 new ones to supply defects.

H. W. BENHAM,
Brigadier General.

HEADQUARTERS NINTH ARMY CORPS
July 14, 1864—9 A.M.

General WILLIAMS,
Assistant Adjutant General:

. . . The work on the mine is progressing favorably, and if nothing unforeseen occurs the gallery will be 450 ft. long at 12 o'clock today. . . .

A. E. BURNSIDE,
Major-General.

HEADQUARTERS ARMY OF THE POTOMAC,
July 15, 1864—10 A.M.

Lieutenant-General GRANT :
    Comparative quiet prevailed along the lines yesterday;
some musketry and cannonading on General Burnside's front
by the enemy during the night. Last evening several deserters
came into the Fifth Corps, who stated that if three rockets
were sent up to indicate they had been well received a large
number would come in. After taking necessary precautions to
guard against foul play, the three rockets were sent up, but
without any result. The siege works, batteries, and mine, in
front of the Fifth and Ninth Corps, are making good progress.
Two divisions of the Second Corps are employed at leveling
the enemy's old works in our rear . . .
                  GEO. G. MEADE.
             Major-General, Commanding.

July 15, 7 A.M. *14th N.Y. Heavy Artillery*

    The rebs had been throwing over mortar shells in single shots and
pairs all night. Neill hadn't been able to bring himself to go to the
privy since the morning of the day before. He lay curled in a knot
with his face pressed into the trench. His bowels churned like a liquid
fist wrenching and twisting his muscles into knots. He felt his body
muscles strain around the center where his guts churned and bubbled.
They hurt steadily now, but at set intervals he would feel the pressure
gather and swell inside him, a deep pain like a stab in the gut; like a
stab going right through his gut rigid, right out to his asshole. He'd
feel like a shell about to burst and he held himself hard till the tears
came to his eyes from the effort. The day before he would fart, and for a
while there'd be relief. Now he'd just hold, until the pain would swell
him up; hold until the pressure began to slack, till it slacked off a little,
and he breathed shallow so as not to start it up again. He could feel
that his guts were beginning to rot and putrefy from holding that poison
stuff in.
    When it was at its worst, the pain he felt was the pain the soldier
felt who'd got blown up in the privy. He'd think to himself, *All right
I'm going,* and in fitful sleep he'd dream about going back there and
relieving himself. Only he knew he couldn't go through with it: the
dream would hold there with his straining with his pants down, about to
feel it all flow out and yet he felt it holding: and the pain in his gut
would become the pain of the man ripped apart by the mortar shell, and
he'd look down between his legs and see cock and balls floating whitely
in the shit and blood, and he'd wake up and the pain would twist him
over again.
    For a day and a night he'd watched for a chance to slip off. There

was a place behind the company commander's bombproof, an angle in the trench where they'd dug, and then stopped digging.

When he saw the Captain and the Lieutenant together, walking down the trench towards the regimental headquarters, and heard Sergeant Stanley's voice down the line behind him, he knew the place was empty. Doubled-over, he ducked around the corner of the trench and walked hunched to the bombproof. Empty. His guts stirred insistently and he threw his gear down and tore at his belt in an ecstasy of haste as if the shift of muscle force and attention from belly to belt was sure to release the strain on his guts. Got them down, squatted, he felt the stuff burst and explode out of his asshole and almost cried at the release; he felt himself burst again; burst again. The smell was horrible, like something dead. But the voiding of his pain was like sexual pleasure. He felt his skin glow.

"God*damn* you, soldier! What kind of goddamn pig are you?" Neill grabbed at his clothes, his nakedness, felt the shame coming over him— "Sir, sir! I'm sorry. Oh, God,"—The pain and fear of shame, and the shame.

"You gutter trash will take a crap anyplace at all. What the hell do you think the regimental sinks are for? Half the goddamn division is down with the flux because of swine like you!"

48th Pennsylvania

Pleasants awoke with a splitting headache. Last night he'd gone to dinner back at Burnside's headquarters with a group of the Pennsylvania officers in IX Corps. Potter was there, and himself, and he'd sat next to General Hartranft from the Third Division. The guest of honor was Ben Franklin Gowen (*His friends call him Frank; I'm one of his friends*). Obviously a "coming man," attorney general of the state. He'd met him once before, when the Forty-eighth was recruiting in Pottsville, and Gowen was there investigating the resistance to the conscription among the Irishmen there. Last night they had talked a bit about that earlier time and about the railroad, and its efforts to buy up the local mines. Gowen was very interested in their opinions; it seemed he had some connection with the project. Gowen, Pleasants, and Hartranft. Gowen's manner suggested an existing acquaintance between himself and Pleasants, which the attorney was hospitably opening to Hartranft. It made Pleasants feel comfortable, for Hartranft was an impressive man with an imposing manner.

"The whole district," said Gowen, "is shot through with these damned Irish secret societies—Molly Maguires, Hibernians, what-not— and they've hooked up with whatever Copperhead sentiment there might be around, so that we can't touch em. Not without stirring up a fuss that would make the New York riots look cheap, and take an army corps to put down. If Lee had gone to Pottsville, instead of Gettysburg, Jeff Davis would be President of the United States today." Gowen tipped back a tumbler of whiskey and water.

"It's certain to be the same people that always made trouble in the mines before the war that will be found behind this," Hartranft rumbled.

"Malcontents," said Gowen with a vigorous shake of his head. "Irish mostly, though I say it to my own shame, being from the Old Sod myself." He grinned. He was a pillar of the Presbyterian Church, as he'd carefully mentioned earlier, so no one supposed him a Catholic Irishman.

"I haven't had trouble with any of the Schuylkill County men, even Irish, in the Forty-eighth," said Pleasants.

"That's understandable," said Gowen. "You'd get the volunteers, the cream. Then once they're in the army you've got a lot more behind you to keep them in line than a mine boss." Gowen leaned forward to refill Pleasants' glass. "I've heard a little something about your 'project' —don't worry, mum's the word, I wouldn't spill it. It's a damned Important Thing. Damned important." The saturnine Hartranft was shaking his heavy head slowly, affirmatively. "Sort of a busman's holiday for you, isn't it?" said Gowen with a twinkle.

Pleasants, feeling the whiskey, felt himself blush and grin. "A corollary to Clausewitz: War is mining carried on by other means!" There was an appreciative chuckle.

Gowen seemed to think a minute. "Perhaps you've got something there. What about applying some of this army stuff to the mines after this is all over? Centralize the planning of operations the way they do in the army, organize things at the highest level right down into the pits in a military way, chain of command. Maybe even get some military discipline into the thing, keep the troops in line. What do you think?"

Pleasants had a hard time shifting from appreciation of his pleasure at the response to his witticism to heed Gowen. He felt he was drunk, and tried to take hold.

Hartranft was speaking. "I have often felt that the hostility between labor and capital is potentially as full of the threat of civil war as the slavery issue ever was. I would hope that they might be brought to realize their common dependence and their subjection to the public good, to natural and economic laws." Pleasants thought, *He's making a speech.* Gowen was giving passionate attention to the man. "Force can only be a last resort: you can't keep an army in the field with only the threat of the Provost Marshal to keep the troops in line. Still, the force must be there. You must be willing to use it, yes."

"My thoughts exactly, sir," said Gowen, beaming, his eyes darting from Hartranft to Pleasants. "May I say how much I've learned talking with you gentlemen? I feel reassured by you." He paused. The odd remark fixed their attention. "I say that," he went on in lowered voice, "because you men will be the leaders of society once this war is ended. The army will give us our next generation of leaders in politics"—he looked at Hartranft—"and business and invention"—he turned to Pleasants. I'll be more specific: Pennsylvania is fortunate in expecting the return of you gentlemen. Once this affair is over—I know you haven't thought of it in this way, but I must tell you—you will be men to reckon with in your native state. Men to reckon with! There will be changes, the whole business and politics of the state, of the country, has been revolutionized by this war. We are going to need men like you, who have known what it is to organize and command and order; we're going to need you. If ever I can be of service to you, gentlemen, I beg you to call upon me." The two officers nodded in solemn promise.

After that the conversation had risen around Pleasants' ears like warm water in a tub, soothing and bland, while his mind ran on the possibilities for the future. The Mine now took on an abstract shape beyond its details of wood and nails and mud and tools. Colonel Pleasants' Mine, the world-beater. The man who blew open the door to Richmond. He imagined himself bearing the clamor of his fame with a modest reserve. Gowen had said it. He would not merely design and build, he would Command. Great projects would become possible. He would conceive them, set out the plans; at his command the designs would be executed.

But suppose the Mine failed? He had never really considered failure till now. The project had been so orphaned, he had become accustomed to thinking that nobody except Burnside cared whether it worked or not. Work on the Mine proceeded invisibly to the world, to the army; if it failed, somehow Pleasants had allowed himself to think that it would simply remain invisible. Now he could see that that was not so. If the Mine failed, the army, the public would know. Somehow it was the corollary of the fame he would have if the Mine worked. He had more at risk than he had realized.

He'd gone to sleep tossing and sinking feverishly on images of fame and failure, and woke to his headache and a sharp taste of anxiety. How *were* things going?

Rees came to report.

"I took the liberty, sir, while you were away, of calling off the night shift."

"You . . . why?" Pleasants' head throbbed. Was Rees mad? Was he simply trying to hector him into a stroke? A mad thing to do!

Rees noted the Colonel's anger, and looked surprised. "Sir, I felt I had to when the men reported they'd heard digging off to one . . ."

"Well then, dammit, Sergeant! Why wasn't I called?"

Rees's face froze, showing no expression. It was the mask of his growing anger. Damned if he was going to be tongue-lashed for no reason by shoulder straps! "It was, if you'll remember, your standing order. And you weren't where I could reach you, sir."

Pleasants felt a momentary pang, then decided he couldn't let the sergeant outface him, even if he was wrong to have taken that tone with him. He was going to have to drive these men hard now; it wouldn't do to appear soft. Nothing must stand in the way of completing the Mine quickly. "Very well, Sergeant. In future you'll report such things to me as soon as possible, even if it is three in the morning."

Rees bit back saying, *You weren't back till four, damn you, did you expect me to sit up all night with a candle in the window?*

"We'll go see," said Pleasants.

HEADQUARTERS ARMY OF THE POTOMAC,
July 15, 1864.

Major-General BURNSIDE:
The powder is at City Point, Lieut. Morris Schaff in charge. There are 12,000 pounds. The fuse has not yet arrived. It was shipped from New York on the 5th instant.
Respectfully,
E. R. WARNER.
Lieut. Colonel and Inspector
of artillery

10:00 A.M. *Rear area of the 4th Division*

The Fourth Division was stationed on the army's left flank, picket lines and new trenches strung out through woods and clearings south of the Norfolk Road. The line ran east-west. North of it, running perpendicular to it, the abandoned and only partly completed line of captured Confederate redoubts stretched up towards the Appomattox River. Majors Rockwood and Booker, with Colonel Thomas's assistance, had two days before examined the part of the old rebel line nearest to the division, till they found a section of trench whose layout and terrain approximated that of the rebel fort they were going to attack. The trench line ran just behind the lip of a low rise, with a good field of fire in front of it. The field was littered with half-wrecked abatis and other obstructions: perfect, as Rockwood pointed out, for purposes of practice, since it was not so littered as to forbid their drilling, but littered enough to approximate the conditions they could expect in the attack.

For three days the regiments of the division had dug and improved their trench line on the flank. They had sent details to cut wood and prepare the practice area. Whenever time and labor permitted, their officers drilled them incessantly in the dense heat, till their wool uniforms hung on their greasy bodies as wet as if they had been totally immersed. Column advance, column into line; forward march; left oblique; left wheel. Manual of arms, *click, snap, stamp, stamp*. Fix bayonets. Forward. Left wheel.

"That's left wheel, Private Cousins," called Randolph. "You knows bout dat left wheel, don't you?"

The line stood round-shouldered with weariness, but grinning. Jethro Cousins was too tired for funning. "No, Sergeant. No, I don't."

"Ever handle two-mule team? Wheel em left? The left mule walks so—slow, just shuffling. You understand that shuffling now, don't you, Jeth? Well, you the left side on this line, you the left mule. You walk slow, let these other mules here swing round. Ten*shun.* Forward, march! Right oblique, march!"

More drill than they'd ever had. Drill by company, by regiment, by brigade, over and over again, the same damn things any baby-school of soldiers would know. *What the hell these officers think we is? Thinks we is niggers, shut up and do as you told.*

The officers drove them, and themselves. Nothing could be left to chance now. They were afraid of things their men might have failed to learn. The Day was coming. Get ready.

On the fifteenth they were ready to try it on the practice field.

Rockwood and Booker had worked out the training plan and submitted it to Ferrero. The General was looking more harried than usual, his handsome Latin face creased by a line between his brows. There were rumors that his commission as Brigadier General was in trouble— those powerful Radicals on the Joint Committee on the Conduct of the War were scrutinizing his record, like a grim Jacobin tribunal searching for evidence of aristocratic lineage or leanings. What did they expect of him? He had taken no position on McClellan, one way or the other. Wasn't that good enough? General Burnside had warned all his officers about staying out of politics.

Burnside was encouraging; he'd said there was nothing to the rumors. Good old Burny.

Ferrero had shaken his head sagaciously over the training plans, and approved them. This was how a division should be run. (Why didn't the Committee come look at *that?*) A smoothly functioning machine, the General providing overall guidance and direction. That was Burnside's command scheme, and Ferrero had studied it well: leave the mastery of detail to trained subordinates; the General is the man for larger questions of policy and direction. Such cares went with promotion.

Maybe it was the McClellan party that was hostile to his promotion, and not the Committee at all? Maybe because he commanded black troops? But he had done everybody a favor by taking this command. Surely they owed him something for that?

He stared at the practice field as the division went through its paces absent-mindedly noting as abstract patterns the shifting about of lines and blocks of men, chewing his worry over and over while officers and men went through the drill.

At 10:00 A.M. the companies selected to act as guide battalions were mustered in a freshly-dug trench line one hundred yards away from the abandoned rebel trench. The morning sun at their backs threw their pointed shadows forward. Major Rockwood, flanked by Colonels Oliver and Thomas, stood out in front of them, explaining the movements, ordering the men to follow their officers carefully. He had just remarked that the trenches before them were empty, but . . . when a titter caused him to turn around. A party of men in blue, armed with shovels, lined the ''rebel'' parapet, watching them.

''Go see what it's all about,'' said Thomas, and Pennington ran off across the field.

As he reached the trench an officer and a sergeant stepped forward. Chris recognized Sergeant Smith, the man they'd had the trouble with when they'd picked up the conscripts on the dock. He was disconcerted by the recognition, started to say hello, realized the military necessity of saluting the officer first, halted in confusion. The officer sketched a salute.

"Lieutenant, I'm Captain Farwell, First Minnesota, Gibbon's division."

"Pennington, Nineteenth U.S. Colored, sir. Sir, we're supposed to be using these trenches for practice." He bit off his words. He hadn't thought to ask Thomas what to say. Were others supposed to know about the attack? He feared this veteran Captain's ridicule, for his hesitation, perhaps for his message too.

"Practice for what?" asked the Captain innocently.

"Well, we've been told that there's to be an assault soon. We're being drilled for part of that. We set these trenches up for drilling the men."

The Captain kept a straight face, but the sergeant grinned a little. "Well, I reckon you'll need a lot of drill. Lot of drill. That's right, isn't it?" His men rumbled assent. "We're ordered to tear down these old entrenchments here. These and no others. Still, I expect it's my discretion to let you use em first. We're in no rush. If your General there don't mind, we'll just sit here and wait till you're done."

"Uh, sir, I imagine we won't be done here for some days, anyway."

"That's all right, son," said the Captain, "we've acquired the art of patience. We'll just sit here and wait till you're finished. Don't rush on our account. Drill those boys good now." Somebody whooped in the background, and before Pennington could turn back the company was drifting off to the shade of the trees off to the side of the trench line.

Rockwood stood at the center of the line. "All right, we'll walk it through first," he called. "At the command, *Forward!* the Nineteenth and Thirtieth come up over the top, deploy in line, and advance. I want the next regiments in line—Forty-third and Twenty-third—I want you to wait till the first regiments deploy; then you come out, right here at this same spot—columns of battalions one behind the other. Understood? All right." Rockwood walked backwards several paces. He paused, then put a silver whistle to his lips and blew a piercing shriek. *"Forward!"*

"Eeeyawp!" yelled the first two battalions, as they scrambled out, the men becoming disorganized and disoriented in the confusion of the new movement, the excitement, the officers and sergeants yelling "Get into line, dammit. What the hell are you—where's your place—well, find it." And the guide battalions were raggedly in line and pacing forward.

The whistle shrieked again, and the milling soldiers in the trench responded. Some remembered the orders and rushed down the trench after their officers for the prescribed jump-off point. A dozen men lost their heads and scrambled right out of trench, whooping. One of them was collared by a sergeant and thrown bodily back into the trench, landing on and confusing the next company, which was shuffling down the trench. There was a tangle all along the trench, confusion spreading outward from the center, where the two second-line battalions, half-strength now because of the mix-up, tried to get in formation but started out ragged and uneven to follow the first battalions. The first two battalions, concentrating on alignment, had finally got straightened out, halfway across, oblivious to the mix-up behind them.

Colonel Oliver, watching from the trees, shut his spyglass with a snap. *It's a bloody minstrel show,* he thought.

The whistle cut through again. "All right! As you were! Attention! Just halt everything right there." The first battalions continued marching, although their officers had now turned back to the whistle. "I said *halt!*" yelled Rockwood.

"All right! Let's start it over again. This time, nobody out of the trenches except right here! Right in front of me! Just take it slow, and for Christ's sake pay attention to my signals."

Randolph had Cousins against the trench side. "You listen to the man, and you listen to me, Jeth. Just wake up and don't act the dumb nigger, because I won't have it. You hear?"

They went through it again, this time with fewer mistakes. The first company came out, followed by the others in turn. They paced across the field guided by the colors, the lines parting to get around lumps of brush and broken abatis, reforming again, blue line, black faces, rifles jutting forward. It reminded Randolph of pickers going down the rows, the bushes like the plants of cotton, but these pickers were standing, not stooped, and they poked their guns before them instead of dragging their cotton bags. All *right!* As each company came up to the trench line it involuntarily quickened pace, taking the dirt parapet with a scramble.

Two officers stood at the left and right edges of the two-company front, Pennington and Booker. "Nineteenth Regiment, left wheel." "Thirtieth Regiment, right wheel." And with some hesitation the two lead battalions wheeled left and right, and Randolph's company of the Forty-third saw the lines opening like two doors swinging wide. Ahead of them was an empty field, with a copse of trees on the other side.

"Halt," called Rockwood, and the command stood still.

"All right, this is it, right here. If this was the rebel trench, we'd be right in the middle of their line. Now, the two lead regiments are going to sweep down the trenches to left and right, clear out any rebs you find. Got that now?" There were laughs.

"The other regiments come on through, and listen for orders." He called, "Forward," and the two lead battalions marched away down the flanks, while the others, in two columns of companies, came up over the trench line and into the open ground behind it. When all six battalions were over, Booker called, "First Brigade, right oblique, march!" and the companies following the Thirtieth swung halfway to the right, and marched away from the trench on a long slant. Randolph saw the copse swing away and to his left, and now ahead of him was a small rise of ground, with a shack set in some trees at the top. Booker shook them into line now, the Forty-third Regiment on the right with the Thirty-ninth beside it and the Twenty-seventh in support. Still pacing slow, they advanced toward the shack on the hill, two hundred yards away.

The Second Brigade also shifted into line, and marched in two lines, three battalions abreast toward the copse. Pennington, marching at the left of the line, saw the soldiers of Captain Farwell's company lounging in the shade. Rockwood's command halted his men before they reached it. He could hear their voices, see their faces turned toward the black line, but could make nothing that they said.

"About-face!" came the command. They turned their backs on the copse and marched back to the trench lines. They went back in file, shoulders slumped in the heat, filed into the trench, and prepared to do it again.

11:00 A.M. *22nd North Carolina*

"They working us like we was niggers," said Dixon.

"Feeding us like it too," said Tommy Woodson.

"Naw," said Dixon. "Niggers eats better than this. Back home, niggers is eating greens and okra, fresh pork, whatever they can cook up in the way of spirits. . . . Oh, they're eating fine."

"These hardtacks, now," said Marriot, "you couldn't get a nigger to eat one a these things. It'd bust out his teeth. They save the hardtacks and the soldiering for the white man."

"I bet the Colonel's nigger don't eat this stuff. Colonel's table scraps be better than this stuff," Woodson rapped his biscuit on his canteen, and a black weevil scurried out.

"That there's the best nutriment of it, don't waste it," said Marriot.

"Problem is," said Woodson, "I can't hardly chew these no more, my teeth are that bad." Woodson was pasty-faced, and his lips and gums were pale and puffy-looking.

Billy took the hardtack out of his hand and put it in his mess plate, tipped his canteen and poured a bit of the warm water on it. He pressed the biscuit with his fingers, working a little water into the crackling surface. "I don't know, Tom," he said. "Give this a try."

Woodson took the softened biscuit, broke off a corner with his fingers and tucked it carefully into his mouth, being careful not to touch his teeth. He chewed gingerly, wincing when a tooth struck the cracker, mostly mashing the cracker to his palate with his tongue, working it till the saliva softened it.

"Ought to see the doctor about them teeth," said Billy.

"I did. He tole me to chew soft food—*Soft food, son-of-a-bitch doctor!*—and try to get my hands on some greens or fruits or something like that. Said this salt pork and hardtacks got me sick somehow. Thing is, I can't get back to hospital, Colonel says he needs every man that ain't crippled up. And we ain't had fresh stuff up here on the line for weeks."

"Colonel's nigger goes out picks him some blackberries. Might be he could get you some."

"That's right, Billy," said Marriot, "you want to ask the nigger yourself, or have the Colonel do it for you?"

Marriot was aware of Lieutenant Bruce coming down the trench toward them. As always he felt the aura of dread, which he fought down.

It was his pride to give ground to no man as his better, given equal odds.
Gold braid gave Bruce the gun hand, and that was enough so he could
follow orders. But there was more to what Bruce wanted, and Sam
Marriot wasn't sure he wasn't giving up that bit extra somehow. As
Bruce came on, Marriot rose to meet him. He had to be at eye level with
the man; he couldn't bear for Bruce to look down at him.

"That's all right," said Bruce as he came up, "you can sit there,
Marriot."

Marriot stayed standing. He was confused by the realization that by
rising he had as good as saluted the man. He was baffled. There was no
way this officer could be beaten, nor even stood off.

"Marriot, you and your squad will be working night shift tonight.
Yankees must be working nights; we sure as hell haven't heard anything
during the day. Nighttime gives us a better chance. We want to get
down deep as fast as possible. You'll be issued candles, and someone will
be there to show you what to do."

Dixon spat. "Shit, Lieutenant. They don't even work niggers
nights."

"But you ain't a nigger, are you, Dixon?" Bruce never looked
away from Marriot.

Marriot held his eyes rigidly on Bruce's face. He would not allow
himself to drop his eyes. He was afraid that the slight movement of his
eyes as they shifted focus involuntarily from Bruce's eye to eye, to his
nose, off the side of his face—that Bruce took these as weak waverings.

"You gone to work us like Yankees, Lieutenant, you might feed us
the same. We ain't had fresh meat or vegetables since we been on this
line. Doc says Tom here's starved and sick for fresh, and there's nothing
but salt pork, pease, and hardtack, and damn little of it."

Bruce actually blinked. Marriot couldn't believe it. "You're right,"
he said. "The way this army is fed is a scandal. I'm sorry for it. . . ."

Dixon was on his feet. The whiff of weakness in Bruce worked on
him like blood spoor on a wolf. "That's the goddamn truth, Lieutenant!
The thing is, what you going to do about it? You can't get blood from
stones, and you can't get work from men that's too starved to stand."

Bruce turned to Dixon and smiled his little smile. "Well, at least
you're able to stand, Dixon. Now that's a comfort." He turned back to
Marriot, but his remarks were addressed to all within earshot. "I know
what you men are suffering. I know that there are farmers out there
selling stuff to the Yankees that won't sell a rotten cabbage to their own
soldiers. General Lee has details out over half of Virginia and Carolina
foraging for stuff. Maybe if we had some of them back here we could
settle the thing and go home!"

"Maybe General Lee could send down some of his table scraps,"
said Dixon.

Bruce looked long and hard at Dixon. The man dropped his eyes.
"You know," he said softly, "there's always a damn fool around that
thinks everybody is just as mean as he would be himself, if he had the
power and the goods. Just what in hell do you suppose General Lee
feeds on, man? When did that man ever sleep soft while his army slept
hard?"

"That's a fact, Dix," said Billy. "I saw Marse Robert after Gettysburg. He was sitting at his desk cracking hardtack."

"It was raining," said Tom, "but damn if we didn't give him a yell as we went by. He looks up, and give us that long look while we went by."

There was quiet for a moment.

Then Bruce said, "Well, I'll be calling for you men after evening roll call. In the meantime, I'll see what I can do about getting some fresh vittles up here." He turned and walked off.

Behind Bruce's retreating back, Marriot still stood looking after him. Dixon had slumped back to sit next to Billy.

"Haw," said Tom, "that son of a bitch sure had your number."

"How'd you like me to loosen some more them teeth for you?" said Dixon grumpily. "I didn't see you standing up to the man, and you the suffering child we're all fretting over."

Marriot felt rage rising in him, and he let it out at this first chance. "You stood up real fine, Dix. Let the man call you a nigger and everything, and you just gave it back to him real fine. You're a powerful tough man, Dix."

Dixon turned beet red. "Listen, Marriot. I ain't looking no firing squad in the face, not for that little shite-poke. He ain't worth it."

"Thing I'm wondering, Dix, is, Are *you* worth it?"

"What the hell does that mean?"

Marriot's face softened. "It don't actually mean *nothing,* Dix. I'm sorry I even said it." He sat down. Dixon sat there rigid, not knowing what was really going on. "That little son of a bitch just gets my hair all stood on end somehow."

"Well now," said Dixon thoughtfully. "All right. then. Let's just drop it."

Tom began to whistle. "We are a band of brothers, and native to the soil. . . ."

"Careful you don't blow none of them teeth loose," said Marriot.

Lieut. JOHN POSTELL,
Engineer Corps:

LIEUTENANT: At Colquitt's salient the gallery has been driven in a distance of 5 feet. A day detachment has relieved the night detachment, and the work in this gallery will hereafter go on regularly, the day and night detachments relieving each other alternately. At Pegram's salient gallery at shaft No. 1 has been carried forward a distance of 16 feet; the gallery at shaft No. 2 has been carried forward a distance of 20 feet. Day detachments have relieved the night detachments at shafts Nos. 1 and 2. Hereafter the work will be continued at those galleries without interruption. A force of sixty men from Ransom's and Wise's brigades, ordered by Major-General Johnson to report for the purpose of forming a permanent engineer corps, reported by your orders to me for duty with my company. With this force I hope to be able to form full detachments for mining operations and extend the galleries rapidly forward.

We are in want of three post augurs to be used in boring forward from the heading of the galleries. We will require candles for our night work, one pound per night.

Very respectfully, yours, &c.,
HUGH THOS. DOUGLAS,
Captain, Engineer Troops, in Charge Mining Operations.

Noon: 4th Division training ground

Pennington watched as Dobbs took his company of the Nineteenth through the last run-through of the morning. The heavy air full of sun oppressed all movements. Pennington felt as if he were making the charge with the full weight of soldier's knapsack and rifle on his back. How must the men feel? But perhaps they are used to bearing such heavy burdens. For the moment Pennington allowed himself to admire their stolidity under the heat, and to feel the shame of his weakness, his indoor breeding, his paleness.

Dobbs was all movement in front of the troops, waving his arms like a bandleader, his face flushed purple with heat and exertion and a peculiar rage he had in action that seemed to make him vibrate like heat waves off a stone pavement. He looked almost demonically red to Pennington. His black troops seemed to evoke this strange fire—rage or enthusiasm, it was impossible to say which. He had to think it was enthusiasm—hadn't Dobbs fought for the Cause in Kansas?—but it seemed very much like anger.

The battalion scrambled up the trench face, Dobbs leaping up ten paces ahead and turning to wave them on. Dog-tired, the men shambled, fumbled to the top, their line ragged as they jumped down into the trench; and turned, tired, to climb the opposite face. Dobbs whirled and leaped across the trench to the opposite side.

"Come *on!* You damn black sons of bitches! Move your black butts like the Driver was back there!" The men heaved themselves out the other side of the trench, too heat-winded to answer.

They formed line, mouths hanging open, and stumbled into the leftward wheel. "Oh Jesus," yelled Dobbs, "if you boys picked cotton like you soldier, Ole Marster would whip your ass till the white showed!" There was an indecipherable mumble back in the ranks, and Dobbs said, "And if you think I can't do it too, think again!" He pivoted, marching with his back to them. And shouted again, "Didn't I whip Ole Marster! Didn't I do it! Well, son of a bitch if I can't whip anybody!"

"You de man, Capn" came a voice from the ranks, and the dried throats managed a laugh. The line moved forward quickly, closing the gap till they marched along right at Dobbs's heels.

Afterwards, when the battalions were scattered out in the grass waiting for the cooks to distribute the noon ration, Dobbs stood in front of his company, bouncing a bit on his legs like a cork bobbing on water, giving them the word. "You niggers go into that trench like you was still worth two thousand dollars a head! I never seen any bunch of soldiers so careful of themselves. Climbing down in there like you didn't want to get dirty. Son of a bitch if you aren't black enough so it wouldn't show if you were jumping in a coal pit! You men break my goddamn heart. Next time, you go up over that trench like you was gonna get shot if you didn't, and you goddamn *jump* into that trench and break one of your two-thousand-dollar legs if you have to, or some Johnny reb will blow your brains out. If you got any. You ain't worth but ten dollars greenback the month anyway, as the government figures.''

"Dat's right, boss," said Private Johnson Five, "only a country nigger would care bout dat little bit of cash money." He paused, "which we ain't even got dis month.''

Dobbs grinned. "The way you men drilled this morning, looks to me like Uncle got his money's worth." He turned and walked briskly away from the men, toward where Pennington stood in the shade, watching him. From behind his back someone called, "You's a *hard* man fo sure, Capn" and there were laughs.

Dobbs came walking up to Pennington, briskly. "Chris! Let's walk over and talk to those white folks yonder. Man, I am starved for company that ain't"—he noticed Pennington's disapproving look, that indrawing of the brows that the kid seemed to think was invisible, and he grinned—"that ain't from Ferrero's Fighting Fourth Division.''

"You don't really like Negroes much, do you?" said Pennington as they walked across the open ground toward the lounging company of Minnesotans.

Dobbs grin became a laugh. "Well, I'm partial to one or two of em. That Johnson Number Five now: he's a good soldier." He looked more serious as they walked on. "Ever see that scar he has on his chest?" Chris shook his head. "Looks like a big letter Dee. They brand army deserters with a Dee . . . oh yes, Chris, they *do*. And to white men too. Only not on the chest—it's done on the hips. Both hips." Dobbs shrugged. "Could just be a funny kind of burn or cut, I suppose.''

Pennington now felt he might have been unfair, or hurt Dobbs's feelings. *Why am I always so self-righteous and moralistic with everyone?* He tried to apologize, indirectly. "They follow you well, Lem. I heard Thomas say your company was the smartest one in the Nineteenth. That's why he picked your men for the lead company.''

Dobbs looked sidewise at Chris. "Well, I come by my talents naturally. My Daddy used to drive niggers in Kentucky and Tennessee. Guess I'm as good a driver as he ever was.''

Pennington was speechless as they came up to the company of white troops lounging in the shade of the trees, but Dobbs said howdy.

They sat down, Dobbs and Pennington making a group of four with Captain Farwell and Sergeant Smith. They began chewing the hardtack and salt pork they had brought with them. Dobbs had a bunch of dirt-covered carrots looped by the tops through the leather strap of his pistol belt. He divided these up and passed them around.

"Thanks," said Smith. "Where'd you find these? We've had nothing but those desecrated vegetables for a month.''

"My flag corporal has a good nose for hideaway patches.''

"Get him to work on some watermelon," said Smith.

Pennington stiffened, remembering the scene at the landing, but

Dobbs grinned. "Watermelon'll bloat you right up. I want the man to find me a couple of fat chickens. One for the pot, and one for the eggs."

Farwell groaned in mock agony. Smith's solemn face cracked a smile. "Oh yeah," he said, "I think I do remember what eggs are."

They brushed the dirt off the carrots, and chewed them with the salt pork. The sweetness of the carrots softened the bite of the pork, but did nothing to cut the greasiness.

"Thing I hate about salt horse," said Farwell, "is how it greazes your tongue so slick you can't taste the water."

"Soften it with this," said Smith. He passed Farwell a small black flask. Farwell looked at Smith with something like surprise, then took the bottle and swallowed a bit. "Yes," he said hoarsely, wiped the neck, and passed it over to Pennington. "No thanks." He blushed hot as if he'd drunk the stuff, and passed the bottle to Dobbs, who threw back a strong shot, grinned, and passed it back to Smith.

"That'll dissolve paint," said Dobbs. "Must of traded for it with the rebs. Take a reb to make something like that for drinking."

"Yup," said Smith. "Man told me they use it to get the cork off'n minstrels after the show. Might be you could use some of that." Smith was grinning, but his eyes were steady, lifeless.

"Now, Sergeant," said Dobbs, "let's not get into no political discussion here, after I've drunk your whiskey and all."

"How do you find serving with the Colored?" asked Farwell. He was serious now; Pennington examined his face for signs of the sarcasm he was used to find with such questions, but saw none.

"They're the most *willing*, hardworking soldiers I've ever seen," Pennington said. "They take the training *well*. I don't think the army has given them a chance to show what they can do." He wanted to look to Dobbs for support, but found he wasn't sure of how Dobbs might feel about it.

"From what you say," said Farwell, "you're going to get your chance."

There was a silence. Smith looked intensely into the sky, which was blank, hazed with heat. "You've never gone up against trench lines, I guess." He paused, and seemed to be listening too, as if someone not himself were speaking. "I guess you'll know about it then. When you go against it."

"We've been training the men carefully for the attack. Everything has been worked out. All you have to do is show them what to do, and how to do it. They really want to make the attack. The spirit is there."

Smith abruptly lowered his eyes and stared at Pennington. "You can't train men to face it. There's really nothing you can do. It's worse when you think you know what you're doing. It's worse when you've got spirit to do it. Then you just go walking up there like a damn fool, and everything is yelling 'Get down,' but you go walking right into it"—his voice trailed off.

Farwell was looking at him with real concern now. "Yes," he said very deliberately. "Dan, that's right. There's just so much you can train into a soldier. The rest you learn when it happens to you."

"The test of battle," said Pennington, then he blushed. He had sounded like a schoolboy, parroting the answers in recitation: "The capital of Pennsylvania is *Harrisburg*. The thing which makes a soldier is? *The test of battle*."

Smith was speaking dreamily again. Perhaps it was the whiskey, and the lazy morning, and the heat of the day. "You'd think that's the way it would be. You'd think that after you'd killed somebody, shot somebody down when they were running toward you, you'd think that would be it. Or getting shot yourself. But it's just the most natural thing in the world to find yourself potting away at something moving off down a field. You've shot plenty of deer. It ain't any harder to look in their eyes when the light is going out of them. Ain't any harder for me"— and he tailed off again.

"That's true," said Dobbs quietly. "There's something *customary* about it, even the first time. Like you've done it before."

"The difference for me," said Smith, and stopped. "Difference for me was that time when we were pulling back, in Sixty-two. We got beat in front of Richmond. We were on this farm there, sleeping in a big old barn. It was after our first big fight; or maybe it was later. I remember we'd lost a good many people in that swamp there, and we came out of it up to this farm. It was like coming up out of a bad dream and finding you were just home; like coming back home. There was this big red barn, hay on the floor and a couple cows that the commissary missed somehow. Some chickens around. Big red barn. Not made any-way and left unpainted like you see around here, but like the one I built with my father. Big beams, squared nice. It took us a year to cut and plane the timber, season it up, dig out the cellarage in the hillside. Hauling boulders out with the team. People came from all over the county for the raising. There was plenty of food: hams, chicken; milk, whiskey, good coffee; cakes, pies, cookies, sweet-potato pie."

Farwell interrupted, "That was a good time, Dan. I remember that. Best raising I ever was at." But Smith never noticed.

"Colonel comes by, says, 'Burn it all, we're pulling out.' Couldn't believe he'd do it. Was an old woman standing in the door of the house when he said it: she just bit her lip and went back inside the house. You could hear the artillery and the shooting getting closer. I just couldn't begin doing it. The Colonel says, 'Damn you, dragging your feet there.' And I say to him, 'Don't burn this barn. You can't do it. It ain't right.' And he says, 'Well you damn fool: you been killing white folks all day for the last week and you think it's a goddamn sin to burn some secesh barn!' He got killed, later. We had a thousand men when we left Saint Paul, twelve companies. Now we're one company. And I took the torch and went inside. The place was full of that cowshit smell, that sweet hay-smell. I threw the torch in a pile of hay, and the fire went up. I went outside, and I watched the fire take the barn apart. Paint blistered up the sides, like moles working underground. Like brushes going back where we'd painted it up, and wiping it away. Then the fire came whipsawing through the boards, and peeled the skin off. Then it was down to the beams. Finally it was down to the ground, just the cellarage left, and I thought, Well it pays to dig a good cellar and wall it good with rock. It took us months to make our barn. It was the least I could do to watch it burn all down. When it was over, I knew . . .'' and he thought but did not speak, *that I would never go home again.*

Chris thought, *I don't really see it. The Colonel was right. A barn is just a barn. How could it be easy to kill a man and hard to fire a barn?*

They were silent. Dobbs said, ''I knew a man had some ideas about barnburning. Colonel Jim Montgomery.''

''The Jayhawker?'' asked Farwell.

''The same. Served with him in Kansas, and down on the Carolina coast after. He was as careful of his own folks' stuff as a man can be. I've seen him break ranks to help a boy catch a runaway cow. But in enemy territory, the man was poison. The way he figured was, in enemy territory whatever you see is like a gun aimed at you. You see a gun or a cannon, you kill the man behind it and take the gun. You see a barn full of stuff to feed the man behind the gun, then you wreck that too. Hell, if you look at it right, it's philanthropy. Man won't join the army to shoot at you if they can't feed him or he's got to stay home and build him a new barn; so by burning the barn you're saving one life anyway you look at it—yours or his.''

''That's practical Christianity for sure,'' said Farwell. He kept glancing at Smith, who stared dully at the ground.

''Still, though,'' said Chris, ''the sergeant has a point.'' He spoke somewhat loudly, as if to a deaf man; he wanted Sergeant Smith to be roused, awakened by someone's sympathy. Somehow the man was in pain or trouble over the barn; Chris felt he must try to speak to that pain. ''Property is . . . part of a man too—what keeps him alive, what he works for. You can't just laugh when you burn up somebody's property, as if it all didn't mean anything.''

''Why not?'' said Dobbs. There was an odd note in his voice, which Chris had to ignore: the strange, conflicting feelings he had toward both Dobbs and the sergeant were making it hard for him to think clearly.

''Because we're civilized, Lem! And because we're Christian. We may have to kill men, and burn or run off their property. But we don't have to like it!''

Dobbs grinned. ''That's a strange set of ideas for a man who spends his time running a regiment of run-off niggers.''

''People can't be property!'' he answered, his voice almost cracking.

''They been that for a good many years. Said it right in the law books, all constitutional and everything. Don't make no difference if you run off a man's stock, or pass a law saying that it's illegal to own horses. Either way you robbed a man.''

Farwell shook his head. ''Difference is this: you steal a horse, the man catches up with you and gets you hung. Pass a law, you get away with it.''

''That's so,'' said Dobbs, ''though from what I see of law it cuts about as good one way as tother. Man who lets law make or unmake his property gonna wind up owning a whole lot of paper, and not enough land to get buried in. No,'' he went on, ''what I was thinking was, supposing it wasn't anybody stole the horse, supposing horse just kicked down the barn and run for it. Stood off the trailers, busted the ropes, and just plain made the man comin after him tired of his kind of pie.''

"I'd say the horse had his freedom coming.''

"My way of thinking,'' said Dobbs. "These here niggers of mine know all bout property. They *been* property. Nothing we can teach them about that. Hell, if they had any respect for property, they'd still be pickin cotton for Ole Massah.'' Dobbs reached over and touched Smith's arm.

"Man ain't any use at all till he's burnt his first barn.''

LEMUEL D. DOBBS

A small-built man, wiry, with sandy hair and a pale, fair complexion, freckle-dusted and sunburnt and blue eyes like the points of nails.

His earliest memory is riding in the wagon coming down from the hills, back in Tennessee. His father is on one side of him, but a shape only, hunched, laboring with a balky team, angered.

His mother sits on the other side, and he remembers her singing:

> *Keerless love is like a robber,*
> *That steals my time, that steals my time,*
> *Like a whinin wind, like a burnin fire,*
> *That waste my life, that waste my life.*

Her voice is thin and high, with small cracks in it, dry like her hands. Her mouth moves little; the song comes from her mouth and her small reed-like nose both. Her skin is white, with a dust of freckles. Her lips are small, and pink and moist; like the mouth of a child, like the lips of a baby. And tired blue eyes, and a seldom smile.

And he would puzzle the words of her constant song over and over, and sometimes hear it.

> *Cheerless life is like a robin*
> *That steals my time, that steals my time,*
> *Like a windin wind like a burnin fire,*
> *That way's my life, that way's my life.*

Growing up in small cabins in the woods, not many folks around. Cold mornings, ice in the wash basin. Cornshucks in the mattress made of sewed-up flour bags. Hoe cake and fat hog-meat; deer meat when Pap shot something with his rifle. Mama swelled up one time, and a baby coming. But the child come dead, and Pap put it in a hole in the ground. Lem could hear the shovel chunkin as he stood out of sight round the corner of the house. Mama's voice come thin and bubbling, like a mourning dove call but longer, longer.

The wagon carried them down further into the valley and toward the west, and Pap got a place driving niggers on a big plantation—hemp, tobacco, cotton. Cash money coming in, and he'd go out in the morning in his heavy boots on a big bay horse he was paying off that the master give him. Lem at age eight was still helping his mother in the garden round the house.

"And damn small use he is. You coddle up that boy, spoil him for any use, woman! I got nigger-boys half his age work the whole of the day like a man." He touched the long crop that swung from his saddle horn.

Fierce man, powerful on his big horse. I will be like him some day. I am afraid of him. He wants to whup me like he does niggers. Mama will not let him.

But every day Pap gets bigger, his chest swelling up. And Mama getting smaller. White skin fades behind her freckles. so they show up dark, more than before. And she smiles one side, with her small fine lips now, where the tooth come out, so the space don't show.

> *Time o time, like a keerless lover,*
> *That come no more, that come no more.*
> *You stole my love and you stole my beauty,*
> *That come no more, that come no more.*

Lemuel Dobbs goes down to the fields to bring his father the bucket of lunch. Watches him sit on his horse in the middle of the green rows of tobacco. He rolls a cigarette, licking the paper with a yellow-gray tongue; his teeth are stained yellow in the front, big square teeth. (Mama's are small and fine, like pearls.) His riding crop dangles from his wrist. He is wrapped in power: the niggers can't even look at him, let alone speak. They keep their faces down and backs bowed around him, continual worship of his strength. You could watch them for hours and never know that they had faces.

One day when Lem is thirteen he brings the lunchpail and is sitting on the fence watching. It's a hot day, he feels as if his body is melting and running down his pants-leg into the ground. The niggers keep bobbing their heads up out of the tobacco—squirrels' curious, persistent bobbing out from covert. Pap's horse moves restless up and down the rows. The voices are deep and sullen; Pap's voice hard and loud. You see his arm swing, cutting down. Left. Right. The boy stays on. Mother is home waiting, but he is watching what his father does. The whip rises and falls, but the black heads keep popping up. The boy imagines that the crop is a scythe, and his father is cropping fast-growing weeds. *Pop!* *Pop!* The black heads coming pop, pop, out of the field, and the crop cutting them down. Some of the heads are women, they've got turbans on them. Pap cuts down on a turban—

And a black man rises up behind him and Pap is flying out of the saddle: you can see the thrust of the black arm; the man grabs the foot in the stirrup and heaves with his whole body, and Pap is falling off the other side into the green, and now black shapes are leaping out of the green all around, like dogs coming in on a down buck possum, and Lem is flying hard as his feet can pound down the white road to the house, "Come quick, the niggers is killing Pap!"

Pap is stretched out on the ground, the house nigger giving him water. The Man is sitting up on a black horse, in a gray coat and a white shirt with no collar on, and a white hat. Pap's face is cut up, half of it turning blue. His blood is black all over his lips swole up like a nigger's, and a tooth gapping. His hand on his side. Talk coming hard, whispered, like it hurt breathing.

"Damn niggers bust my ribs in. Kill the fucking bastards."

The Man talking so cold: "You'll do no killing, Dobbs. I ain't killing no two-thousand-dollar hand for whupping some two-bit cracker that can't drive worth a damn. I've told you not to be so damn free with that whip. If you had the touch of managing niggers you wouldn't need to bully them with it. Whip's like candy: too much and you spoil their taste for it."

Pap is panting, his hand holding his side.

"Wrap that side tight, and rest it a week. Then I want you *gone*. You hear? I'll not have you ruining any more hands for me. Take me the best part of a day to get them back here, and this the late part of the season. Damn you, I ought to take it out your pay!" The merest twitch of the wrist takes the black horse away. As he passes the bay horse, standing riderless cropping in the rows, the Man reaches down and takes up the reins, and leads the horse off.

There were other plantations, cabins to live in while Pappy tried driving niggers. But the niggers were like animals: they could see the yellow in his eyes. and they knew they could get away with anything. The man would come by, and send him packing. "Trouble is"—Pap, querulous—"trouble is you never back your drivers. I say 'whip,' and you say 'no,' and these is just plain spoiled niggers."

"Dobbs, you ain't worth the arguing. Just get."

Whiskey. Pap's smell of salt-sweat always sick-sweetened up now. Mama's face gaunting, gaunting. So strange to see her mouth like the mouth of a little girl—thin, delicate lips, pink and moist—little round teeth in her old-woman face of cracks and spotted skin. Close your eyes, hear her sing, and thinking of her mouth you could imagine she was young still, as she used to be, before Pap wasted her life and used her time and stole her life, her love away.

And he still had the riding crop—

"Boy, you ain't plowing worth a goddamn. You put your back in it, or I'll take this to you!".

"You look at me cross-ways, boy. . . ." The whip whistled. "Damn you, don't look sass at *me!*"

"I seen niggers half your age work twice as much."

Till one day—Lem was fifteen—he grabbed the wrist as the crop whistled round, and punched with his right hand hard into the place where he knew the ribs were sore and soft from not healing good, and he saw the power whoosh out of the man with his breath, and the deep sickness come into his face and his eyes.

His mother was sitting on the porch, the garden side, rocking a little in the split-bottom rocker. When he looked into her face, her eyes were dull and far away. Oh, her mouth was still the same, but her face was ruined. He couldn't stay to look any longer.

He left, and the cabin disappeared. But he could always recall the shape and look of her mouth, and hear her voice.

True love has gone, to Cumberland mountain
To come no more, to come no more,
Like a whinin wind, like a burnin fire,
To come no more, to come no more.

Went north of the Ohio River, tramping, looking for work. Worked as a hired man in Vincennes and Pigeon Creek, Cairo, Illinois. Harvest hand. Hand with the plowing. Cut timber, clear brush. Sow sweat, reap whiskey. Hang around the country stores and taverns, waiting for a hireout. Dusty roads of south Illinois, north Kentucky.

One time in Springfield he thought he saw Pap—white hair on his head. Looked to be alone—where was she? Lying in the ground somewhere with dirt in her eyes and her pink mouth full of dust. Never mind: that door's closed. He moved on, kept moving.

My life is born, to walk and wander,
Down many road, down many road.
And there's no home, to-waiting yander.
To which I go, to which I go.

Learn how to survive on the tramp. If you want the hire-on, you wear your hire-on face, sweet smile and mother's milk on your lips. The farmer's got to be looked at like he's a man of worth and standing, though he's a mean-faced man, usually, a man that's already sweated what he could out of his horses, mules, oxen, women, kids. "Yes sir, I'm a good strong boy and hard worker, anyone'll tell you."

Got to hold what you earn against the pull of whores and whiskey— that isn't as easy as it sounds. Got to hold it against the farmer shorting your pay, taking out of it for this and that. Standing there, with maybe his sons or other kin, or the other hands back of him: "I say this here's what I owe you, Dobbs, not penny more." What in hell can you do but walk on down the road?

But you come back at night and burn out the son of a bitch's barn or hayrick. It don't put cash money in your pocket, but it says, Do what you can to me, and I can give back the same: measure for measure, burning for burning, eye for an eye.

She was clerking in her uncle's store when he met her. You'd have said fourteen to look at her, but she was two years more than that: a slim girl, delicate-made about the shoulders and neck. Her hair was blondy-red, and her face powdered with brown freckles. Smooth pale lips, and she smiled and sung as she worked. Small little hips like a boy, which was why you'd have thought fourteen.

"I'd ask to marry you, Nancy, but I ain't fit for marrying."

And she was angry. "Don't speak bad on yourself, Lem! Don't do it! You're good as anyone."

There was talk about land opening up in the center part of the state, railroad coming down that way, Illinois Central. Choice pickings if a man had some go-ahead. He packed his traps, invested what money he had or could borrow in an axe and rifle-gun, and walked north. There was land above a creekbed, just west of where they were laying out the line. That was for him: hackberry and black walnut and oak trees; some good open ground for the cabin and a first crop—he could put his corn in before he had to do any clearing at all. Blazed his trees and set out stones, and walked back to Cairo for marrying.

Nancy was very slim and graceful. He could hardly stand to look on her, naked: so frail to look at, he felt he might break her, do her some harm, soil the fine whiteness of her skin. But she laughed, and he found out from her what it was all about.

Cleared off some timber, built a cabin, settled in to see that first winter through. He put the walls up practically by himself, levering the logs up by main strength and what he could improvise to aid him. Every particle of the place was put together by his hand; it was Nancy filled up the inside with her own things, and gave the wood color and life.

He'd put in his corn that spring, and turned to clearing, when the railroad man came round and told him he'd got to move. This was re-served railroad land here; he was squatting. Pay rent or move on, was the word.

He looked at the railroad man, and fingered the trigger guard of his gun. The man left.

The folks squatting on Hackberry Creek had a meeting—"Let's club up." They went down to the Circuit Court in a bunch next month, carrying into the saloon where the court met their squirrel guns, Army muskets, rifles, shotguns. The judge considered this testimony; the plaintiff, Illinois Central Land Development Company, considered it as well, and the case was thrown out of court, without objection.

The men were standing around outside the courthouse. after, their guns casually cradled under one arm, laughing, joshing. Their women, those that had come down, stood across the dirt road, huddled, whisper-ing. The railroad man stepped down the stairs in his broadcloth suit. Dobbs spat in front of his shoes.

"Well, mister, let that be a lesson to you. These parts the law is how the folks wants it to be, cause these are folks that understand their own business, and their rights. Now I'd suggest you lawyer yourself out of here right quick, or Judge Lynch will likely want to hear your ap-peal." The lawyer did not speak, looked straight ahead, walked to his horse, mounted, and rode off. Rode on out of town and filed his appeal with the District Court in Springfield.

By the fall, when the harvest was coming, and the railroad sur-veyors working down the valley, there was law-paper all over Hackberry Creek thick as an early snow, every farmer standing in his door looking at it this way and that—what in hell does it mean? Scared sick by a piece of paper with their own name written on it, all by itself.

One day a wagon pulls into the yard, a homemade Conestoga-type with canvas rags flapping on the hoops and a sprung axle. Two shirttail kids and a gray-face woman peeking from the wagonbox—the woman pale, fair hair, a lean face and one snagged tooth, young eyes in her old face. The man was embarrassed: man about his own age, maybe a year more. Showed him the paper: "Name's Tolliver. I bought this place of the railroad man down to Cairo. He didn't say nothing about you-all here." Tennessee in the voice.

Dobbs felt the weight come on him. Another piece of paper. Only way to keep things clear is shoot this poor sucker down this time, right now.

Woman and kids in the wagon watching him finger the rifle's trigger-guard, *primed and ready.*

Shoot him right down, and his wife and children looking on. Nancy standing in the cabin door. "Lem, don't shoot nobody. You've got your rights. Fight law with law. Don't go shoot somebody and I'll never see you no more." Her belly swole right out, and her upper body so delicate-boned rising out of the big belly. Scared him right through when he thought of the bit of himself growing big down there inside the dark.

"I'd pass it by, Mr. Dobbs, seeing you're here first, I truly would; except that railroad man has my last dollar, and some more. We'd truly starve."

Dobbs put up the gun. "You do what you have to do. I'll do the same."

The man was embarrassed, shamed. "I'll have to law on you," he said in a whisper.

Dobbs nodded, and motioned for him to move off. He stood in the yard till the wagon-sound rattling down the road had stopped.

And the pains come on Nancy while he was coming back from the court—court finds for Tolliver (*We'll have to appeal, find the cash*) in the drizzling-rain November, and she laid too long in the pain up in the cabin. She held his hand so tight each time the pain took her away that her nails cut the flesh of his hands, and he put the bloody finger in her mouth so it would nourish her, and held onto her so the spirit would not get out of her body. But it did no good, for she began to scream so loud that it filled all the world around, and the child come dead, and the life drained out of her through the wound.

Buried the child in the yard, wrapped in a clean gunny sack. It was all covered with blood like a slaughtered pig; he never even thought about it. But he couldn't bury her, put dirt on her body.

He thought about the Tollivers coming to take possession of the place. Finding a dead woman in their cabin. Their cabin. *Let them take ahold of that. With their damn paper.*

There was a fire in the fireplace, burned almost to coals. He threw the law papers in and they blazed up. The fire was warm, it flickered on the walls and the shape on the bed. He threw on more paper, the tablecloth, sheets, blankets; tore off the curtains. The stuff spilled out of the fireplace and along the floor. Fire blossomed out of the pinewood floor, and bubbled the sap out of the logs. It smelled good, its fierce heat the color of blood.

He stood out in the field and watched it devour the house. He took little wisps of it up on twigs, and strewed it in the field where the dried cornstalks burned like Indians tied to the stake.

> *A man is born to toil and trouble,*
> *As sparks fly up, into the sky.*
> *A woman's born to pain and sorrow,*
> *To weep and cry. to weep and cry.*

Left the territory and went to walking again. Hired hand for harvesting, plowing, clearing timber; teamster, section-hand on the Pacific Railroad over in Missouri. Sow sweat and reap whiskey. A trifling, wasted life.

On a steamboat going up to Davenport he heaved coal with the niggers on the black gang, what in hell was the difference anyway? They'd been sold down the river, he'd been sold up. Once the smoke had dirtied his face, you couldn't tell the difference between them anyway. Hadn't he been whupped? Hadn't he been sold. Hadn't they taken his family, and his hand work, and his wife and child, just the same as any country nigger that couldn't tell hog meat from horseshit?

Only white thing he'd ever done in all his days was whupping his pappy for licking him. Only that: and burning out the place before anybody else with law paper in their hand could take it from him. Well, and hadn't the niggers done as much to pappy as he'd done himself— yes, and done it while he was still a whole man, on a horse and with a gun and a whip too.

Dobbs looked at the furnace light glowing on the black limbs of the other niggers and grinned, because they'd never burnt out their own place to keep it from the Man. Maybe he'd show em, and repay the favor they done him by showing him how things really stood. In Kansas now . . .

> *True love farewell, I'm bound to leave you,*
> *To go to war, to go to war,*
> *For all our love is burned to ashes,*
> *And come no more and come no more.*

1:00 P.M. *4th Division training ground*

The harsh buzz of locusts in the grass and the powerful heat of the sun filled the air. The troops lay sprawled and sitting in whatever shade could be found, or made with shirts and blankets spread on bayonetted muskets stuck in the ground.

Captain Shugrue, company commander, took a quick look around and settled himself behind a tree, shielded from the eyes of his men but in earshot. He didn't spend more time with his men than necessary, yet he was uneasy about what they might do behind his back—he wished he had a drink.

Cato Randolph also sat apart from his platoon, working on a letter. He sat with legs crossed Indian-fashion, hunched over his board and writing paper. He pinched the pencil tightly, so that his index finger bent concave with the strain. His whole attention was concentrated on the letter. The buzz of the locusts, the heat, and the sound of his men talking blended into a single blank tone.

"Dearst Coffee," he wrote. "How does you feel and our children? I am well, though in my feelings I am sad you are not here. I think of you constant, and of our children. Sometime it seem to be a dream, the time of us all being together''—stopped and stared to the west, thinking *Cassy. Long long gone. My Cassy. Tall black skin woman stand at the cabin door smiling with the one baby girl in the crook of her arm and the other standing by. They ain't changed one bit all this time*—"Does you think of me this day?''—*Cassy. Coffee.* Dreaming. Though he held his eyes on the page, he heard the voices of the men talking.

Jethro, lying down with his face shaded by the brim of his forage cap, said, "Look at dem white folks over by the shade there.'' Off across the field Dobbs and Pennington sat with the company of the First Minnesota. "Spect they's playin poker whit the company fund.''

"Think they got paid fore us?''

"Don't you know it?'' said Jethro, heaving himself to a sitting position. "That Corporal Deevis, works fo Colonel, tole me that officers got their pay las week. You think they didn't pay the white soldiers too, before they give us ours?''

"What you do whit all that money anyhow, Jeth? That sutler truck is pure poison, and they give that feller in first company buck-an-gag for buying whiskey on the sly.''

"Yeah,'' said Jeth. "Niggers got no use for money, that's sure. That's why they pay the white folks early and most, and us whenever and not so much.''

"Oh the buckra fight for money,'' sang Private Colehill.

"Hang, boys, hang!'' muttered a few voices.

"An the nigger fight for . . . what was that now?''

"Whiskay!''

"Freedom!''

"Money too, if he can get it!''

"Now there's the question,'' said Colehill. "What's de nigger fight for? It can't be money, cause I don't see that.''

"We fightin for freedom, Cole. For freedom.'' There was a rumble of assent.

Jethro leaned forward. "That don't make sense. We free already. It's in the *law.* Now that's plain. You think the niggers that scaped scription and stays back home—you think they not free as you is? I tell you this. They got the same freedom, only it's more than what we got here.''

"Figure that, Jeth.''

"Cause in slavery time, there was white man telling us do this, do that, and the whip and gun in his hand the whole time. And back home there's Ole Masr run off, and white folks run off. An here we got nothing but white man all over the place, and the whip and the gun. An you dig as you're tole, and you don't get no pay, and you eat salt pork and the pint o' corn—scuse me, *crackers.*''

"That's right.''

"Yeah,'' said Jeth, "maybe those crackers makes it freedom, what we got right here.''

Colehill—a tall man, lounging on one elbow—spoke slowly in response. "I don't call this gun here, whit this pig-sticker on it—I don't call that no *hoe.*''

"That's true."

"And I don't mind the time Ole Masr ever tole me. 'Nigger, get your black ass out there and kill me some these lowdown white folks!' "

"Hoo-ee. No sah!"

"Amen to that!"

Jethro grinned. "How many white folks you kill this week, Coley? If they paid you head bounty, stead of the month wage, you still come up empty!"

"We get our chance, man! We get our chance!"

"Oh yes," said Jethro. "These white folks give us our chance for sure. Afraid as they is we might get to likin it. I tell you what: this war is for white folks to do the killin, and niggers to do the diggin. Now *that's* truth."

"What you think we been doing all day, Jeth? What you think all this charging back and around is for? You think they just want us to stretch our legs a little bit? The niggers that was in the Hinks division got they chance. Now we get ours. This the new day, Jethro. Talkin don't make this slavery time, no way."

"I tell you what the difference is," said Jethro. "The difference is in the slavery time it was quality owned niggers. And here we got nothin but white trash." He glanced toward the tree behind which Captain Shugrue was sitting: eavesdropping or drinking on the sly, one. "White trash, and niggers that puts on airs to boss the gang." He shot a glance at Randolph's back. "Niggers that likes to play the white man."

A clod of earth struck Jethro in the side of his head and he whipped around to see Young Tobe, Randolph's cousin. "Don't put your mouth on him, Jethro. The white man don't come into it with that man, you hear me?"

"You say," Jethro mutttered.

Tobe spoke up sharply. "You figure if Ole Masr and them white trash wins this war, that the free paper gone be good? Lincoln paper count for plain *nothing* if secesh come out on top."

"That's true," said Colehill.

But Jethro hadn't given up. "Why then, Coley, ain't you got your own gun these nice white folks here give you? What you got to worry about win or lose, when you got that gun there?"

"Talk like a *fool!* We lose this war, you think that bad trash let us keep guns? We lose, man, we lose it *all!*"

"And suppose you wins, Coley—you figure these other buckra here gone let you keep they guns, more than the other kind? I see them talk about teaching me how to kill white folks; but they showin me real good how to dig them holes. Now *that's* fact."

Randolph wrote:

Major Booker have sent the draft of $100 that is the company funds. The men all say it all right, we go without vegtibles but can find stuff around here and there. Tell our pay come in, this all the money that can be sent. Do please put it together with what we have from before, and do not miss the arction

when it come up. Major say that the government will sell the
land low price to us, but we must be able to pay when it come
up. So do keep all the People on the scout, as we say in the
army, for when the arction do come up.

He could imagine the shape of the plantation, the ground sloping
back from the river that was best for cotton or tobacco, and the timbered stretch that they'd want to clear.

If we does this all together, everybody sharing in their
money, and then work together after, we can run the Place
good. Each family will have their peace of ground to be their
land for farming. And a good size peace. What does folks think
about keeping out that fine peace to the river for cotton or ter-
backer? Each working, and share on the crop? We could make
cash money that way, and fix the place up as it should be, also
for schooling the children. We'd have our schoolhouse on the
Place, could be, and pay a teacher wages for teaching the children not to be ignorant. It seem to me that I can see how things
will be just so plain as if they was this very day. Now the war
doesn't seem to me going to last long. We are tole, we will do
something Big. This may bring an end to all, our trouble. Coffee, I believe that soon we will come home, just a short time
more, and a thing we have to do.

He saw the blue line of troops before him swing aside, like a door
opening, and beyond it a grove of trees with a cabin in it. *I will go look
for her,* he thought, *and I will find her too, the spirit tells me this is so.
Is so. She will be standing at the cabin door when I come, and we will
weep and cry in all our pain. Then she will talk, and the words she says
will make the crooked path straight, and it will all work out. Then there
will be no confusion, Cassy, Coffee: we will just gather in together, and
it will be all right, all as it should be.*

"I heard that Hink division, they took no prisoners and they give
no quarters," said Colehill.
"Cause they cut up our people so bad at Fort Pillow, was why,"
said Corporal Brown. "They crucify one man to a pineboard door."
"What Hink boys done? That's me, too," said Tobe. "The day
come, I taken no prisoners either. I give em Fort Pillow quarters with
this," and he patted the hilt of his bayonet.
"Yeah," said Jethro, "you kill all you catch, an you probly eat
all you kill, too. Ain't but one man in this company *has* killed any buckra,
and that's me. So don't talk."
"You forget," said Tobe, "two what's done it. You and *him.* Only
the one he killed was what *you* call *quality.* Now ain't that so?"
"A-men, and hallelujah!"
"Aw man," said Jethro, "he just too damn *ugly.*"
Colehill guffawed, and Tobe cracked a smile.

"Sho is," said Corporal Brown.

"He so ugly he kill the fish when he look in the pond to see his face."

That's right.

"He so ugly he most kill his own self he do that."

Sho is.

"He so ugly his cow give butter stead of milk."

That's right.

"He so ugly he black out the moon, once a month."

Sho is.

"He so ugly his Mama shake de raw-head at him to make him smile."

That's right.

"He so ugly," said Tobe, "Massa take one look an fall, down, dead."

That's right.

Sho is.

Mmm, hmmm!

Captain Shugrue, sitting behind a tree, listening, thought, *Hell, they're all ugly. Damned if I can see why they think that black devil of a sergeant is any uglier than the rest.*

Randolph wrote:

> I am sergeant major since I write to you last time. This spose to mean I get more pay, but it true that two nothings is still nothing, and I ain't had my pay more than the others. Some of the men, don't tell nobody this, does not take to this, I mean my being sergeant over them. In my heart I know that I been true always, but some always talk about those that gets favors from the white People. It is Envy, so pay it no mind if you hear such talk.

But he wondered again about it. The face of Major Booker rose in his mind. The face smiled, it had a mild and friendly look. It filled him with a kind of superstitious dread, face of a smiling devil, a swamp spirit tempting a man to step in and find a good thing, and he'd go under out of his depth in muddy water. *The man give me power over these people, and he show me the way with the money. So far he don't call for his own back. Sometime I think I sign his book back then, and don't remember it; and sometime the ledger come due, and I must pay my soul. Jethro think I sucked around the Man to make me overseer. I could show them, I could give Booker sass. But that's a fool thing, thinking you can prove you're good enough to somebody's lights that hankers to think bad on you. I show that Jethro plain nothing. I do what I got to do, and what I want to do, and let him badmouth—unless it's to my face, or turns the men, then I fix him.*

He was about to finish when Captain Shugrue came down the line, clapping his hands together, "All right, boys, up on your feet. Time to get moving. Up on your feet."

"Grab that hoe, nigger," said Jethro, "and plant cotton."

Randolph tucked the unfinished letter in his knapsack, rose, and turned to the men. "Let's get in line now, lambs, stand still an hear the judgment of the Lord."

Obedient to their officers, the black troops formed their ranks and prepared for drill. Again they filled the trenches, climbed out, and marched in lines abreast across the field. *Like a gang going down the cotton rows,* Randolph thought again, *except for the rifles instead of hoes, and the blue jackets all the same. Rifle or hoe, what's the difference? White man still boss the gang, just like Jethro says. Behind him the whip and the gun. Rifle or the hoe, Hewson or Booker or one of these buckra officers that got to boss nigger soldiers cause they not good enough to boss white. White man still call the tune. So maybe that Jethro right, rifle or hoe makes no difference.*

Hell, makes a difference if I say it does, long as I know my own mind. Makes a difference long as I know what I mean to do with it. Man or a gun or cotton hoe: *nothing is worth anything but what you value it in your own mind.*

But before the drill could more than begin, a mounted courier rode up to where Colonel Oliver stood. They saw the Colonel bob his bald head, and sign a paper. Their officers were called over, and spoken to. They stood quietly in the hot buzzing air.

The officers returned. The orders rapped out. The lines of the battalions segmented and reordered, they moved piecemeal away from the drill field.

Back in the trees were wagons full of picks and shovels. They drew these, and stacked their arms in the wagons. *Sold again.*

For the rest of that day, and the following morning, they dug trenches, a covered way, and a battery emplacement for General Warren's Fifth Corps. It was something on Jethro's side of the argument. But Jethro's mouth was wryed up like he didn't relish the taste of it, and Randolph did not speak at all.

HEADQUARTERS JOHNSON'S DIVISION,
July 15, 1864

Col. G. W. BRENT,
Assistant Adjutant-General:
Colonel: General Gracie relieved Wise's brigade at 8 P.M. yesterday. General Gracie reports from his own and the observations of others that the enemy have made no change in their positions, except to connect the rifle-pits on the left of his right regiment. They threw mortar shells into his lines at intervals of ten minutes nearly all night, without inflicting much injury, however. General Elliott and Colonel Faison report nothing of interest. The losses and annoyance which the enemy occasion in my lines are simply due, in my opinion, to a want of proper ammunition: from necessity, no doubt. So far as appliances with this army are concerned, we are husbanding our ammunition—that is, men or ammunition; one or the other—the enemy compel us to sacrifice. This is the simple question with us: Which shall we expend, human life or ammunition? We have

none of the former material to spare, and the supply of it for future purposes is necessarily limited; of material for manufacturing the latter nature affords a bountiful supply. So far as I am informed, human energy and toil is all that is required to furnish us ammunition enough to give us daily immense advantages over the enemy. Surely this energy and toil can be supplied; if the proper officers are duly aroused to the necessity for their action and of the great responsibility which is resting on them. I refer to the officers whose duty it is to see that the ammunition is manufactured in sufficient quantity and that it is properly distributed. As the contest is now daily going on, our success depends as much upon the active operation of our troops and the expenditure of ammunition as it ever does on field of battle. Daily casualties are reducing both armies, and our object should be to cause double, treble, or quadruple the number of casualties in the enemy's lines that they cause in ours. I feel satisfied I can do this on my line if I am supplied with ammunition; at least, if supplied with ammunition, I shall be able to bring to bear a great amount of human energy and activity which now lies idly wasting away under the enemy's fire. I may also be permitted to state the fact that whilst we husband our ammunition and the enemy are thinning our ranks with comparative impunity—our men being compelled simply to suffer and endure—a moral effect is being produced which may prove very detrimental to our future success. I hope and implore that all the human energy in our workshops may be at once brought into successful action, and I think we can confidently and securely answer for the result in the field. I would also suggest that our artillery, guns and mortars, so far as employed, inflict loss and annoyance on the enemy's front line. While we see within our reach their troops resting securely in the rear, or engaged actively in firing or other measures of attack on our lines, we need ammunition to be used freely on all lines within our reach.

The following list of casualties is respectfully submitted: Elliott's brigade, killed, 2; wounded, 3. Ransom's brigade, wounded, 4. Wise's brigade, killed, 1; wounded, 10. Total, 3 killed and 17 wounded.

Respectfully, your obedient servant,

B. R. JOHNSON,
Major-General.

3 P.M. *Headquarters bombproof, Twenty-second North Carolina*

Colonel Davidson sat at the roughboard table that served as his desk. The bombproof was quiet. Sounds from the outside—the voices of the men, the call of the pickets, the occasional bump of a gun—were heard as if through a layer of water. At such times the Colonel liked to sit and daydream about his plantation at Holywood, appreciating plans well laid and executed—his orchard, his "quarters," his ordered rows of cotton, his feat and simple outbuildings, and his great house. It was almost an act of accumulation, this ritual of review. Each time he looked at and appreciated his plantation it felt more ample and substantial, more productive of satisfaction than before. At such times he would re-cast plans of work and improvement, reach decisions about the cutting of timber or irrigating the soil, devise a new scheme for preserving manure and ashes as fertilizer.

He had not been home in more than a year. Although his wife had stayed on the place, and kept it from the worst harm, it was in de-batable ground between the Yankee forces at New Bern and the Confed-erates at Kinston. Rationally, Davidson knew that the place must have suffered damage and diminution. Yet in his imagination he held it whole.

Davidson was a tall, handsome man of sixty, with a long English face and hawk nose. His hair was dark brown, with creamy-gray waves along the temples. His long upper lip was thin and accentuated by a mustache; his cheeks, except for sideburns, were clean-shaven. He sat in his shirt, to preserve the nap of his last remaining uniform coat—he had lost the rest when the Yankees overran their position on June 16, and had not had time or cash to replace it. His shirt was patched at one elbow.

The black slave George entered the bombproof noiselessly and set a bowl of blackberries down next to the Colonel's left elbow. The black-pebbled surface of the berries glistened like the shells of insects. Glisten-ing beads stood out on the top, where George had freshened them in cold water from a well.

"Is there milk or cream, George?" asked the Colonel, without rais-ing his eyes from the paper before him. On it he had drawn a diagram of the kitchen garden; he was thinking about building a grape arbor, and wondered if it would shade the greens too much.

"No sah, Colonel. Someone run off de cow I milk fo you las time. Whut dere was, spoilt."

"That's all right." He popped a berry into his mouth—tart, a little seedy, but good. He'd use a bit of the sugar he'd been saving—there wasn't much, but he felt like it today.

Blackberries! That damned army surgeon had deviled him all morn-ing about getting fresh vegetables and fruits for the men. He didn't know or trust the man—a West Pointer, sent down by Corps Head-quarters. They had gotten on well enough without any more doctor than himself for three years, and no whining about blackberries and greens any of that time either. He had always provided for his men. It was his pride as Colonel, just as it was on his plantation: he was a good provider, and he took care of those entrusted to his power. He knew well enough what kind of food the men needed—no sawbones needed to remind him of it! This talking to the men, carrying messages back and forth, insinuating himself between the Colonel and his men; and like as not between the Colonel and headquarters too! It was preju-dicial to good order.

On his own plantation, Davidson would never have suffered any overseer—however competent—to presume to act as go-between speaking for his people to him. He had written numerous articles on plantation management for *Debow's* and the *Southern Messenger*—"Old Planter" was his sobriquet, and had been since he had started writing the pieces at age twenty-three, just after his marriage. He had laid it down as a rule that the Master should always (whenever possible) preside over a daily distribution of food. "Negroes," he had written, "are improvident when entrusted with any substantial amount of provisions, and will barter, waste, or consume the same without regard to proper diet, so losing efficiency in their work and becoming demoralized. Also, it is a salutary thing for them to be brought into that contact with the Master, receiving their subsistence of him once in the week at least."

It seemed to the Colonel, as he thought about it, that the principles by which a plantation of Negroes and a regiment of poor white trash are governed were not all that dissimilar. He plumped a berry into his mouth, and chewed thoughtfully. The juice burst, acid and biting, against his palate. He had had to build this regiment out of nothing. It had taken as much effort to reduce them to discipline as it must have taken his father to whip his first boatload of reeking Africans into semblance of humanity. More: the white wan was a tougher nut than the Negro—made him a better soldier, but nearly useless for getting work done. "Ignorant minds are ever inclined to imitate their superiors; a Master negligent about his person or his duties begets a like negligence in his slaves." That was sound doctrine. But the secret was in the thoroughness with which the doctrine was applied to cases. No plantation could sustain itself without the subordination of the hands to the Master. He loved to think of the anecdote he had written up for *Debow's,* stressing just this point: how he had made it a point whenever he saw anything in disrepair about the plantation—a fence, say, or a gate off its hinges—to have his boy fix it up immediately; or if no one competent were by, actually to fix it himself. After establishing this image of good work habits, he had made it a punishable offense for any Negro to pass by anything out of repair without immediately putting it to rights, or informing the proper person for the job. So the positive example was reinforced by negative chastisement, measured to the offense: he had laid it down, following the advice of Governor Hammond, that no more than one hundred lashes well laid on be required for the most severe offense; and in general, fifteen to twenty would suffice. He estimated that he had not lost more than a few days work a month in his years of planting, yet had maintained among his neighbors the reputation of a severe, but fair, Master.

He could have wished that his white soldiers would have taken as quickly to the lesson as his Negroes had. Certainly they did not follow the Colonel's example of personal neatness and order. He thought with more pleasures of his inspections of the cabins of his slaves—despite the rank Negro odor—than he did of his inspections of the regiment. The men would rather drink than wash, rather sleep than shave; without their women to mend, their clothes degenerated into rags a Negro would laugh at. Blackberries and greens indeed! Most likely, their own slovenliness was the cause of their sickness. It was enough to make him doubt the superiority of the white race.

The trouble with the South was that it had tried to mix mob rule and aristocracy. Such half-measures always come to grief—sterile as a mule, or flighty as a yellow wench. Better the one thing or the other. The Yankees had made a good thing of mob rule, if one liked to live one's life in continual shuffle for a place at the hog-trough. The South ought to have had the courage of her convictions. Was it any wonder the South was perishing, with men of the likes of his poor trash electing the highest officials, voting on all the most complicated issues? Here it was coming round again. Now: Vance was up for reelection, and Holden's agents were stirring up dissension among the troops to get out the vote. He'd tried to stop it once. The blacksmith didn't ask the hammer or the anvil how to shape the next horseshoe. The South . . .

Thinking of the South made him melancholy. The tragedy of her fate: to have built a social order on the harmonious patriarchal relation of Master and Slave, and to require the demagoguery of Jacobinism to defend it!

What did democracy come to in the end but an orgy of grabbing and grabbing, and using the government to help in the pillage. Agrarianism! That was what came of it. Children raised with no sense at all of what's "Mine" and what's "Not-Mine," any more than nigger thieves and runaways! . . .

When he thought about the South he thought of Tennyson's great poem of Arthur, and the dying King's phrase, "My kingdom reels back into the beast. . . ." Surely that was happening now, the terrific drift toward mob rule and the Terror: a Haitian Terror if the Abolitionists won, perhaps a Jacobin Terror if the South won, and did nothing to suppress the arrogance of the democracy. Ah, the South . . .

The afternoon wore on. Colonel Davidson finished his blackberries, drinking several small glasses of brandy with the last of them. When Lieutenant Bruce came in to talk about the countermining, the Colonel felt mellow enough to try to open some of these ideas to Bruce.

"Perhaps," said Bruce, "we should have beat the Yankees to the experiment of using the blacks as troops. God knows we've more experience managing them. You remember Cleburne's proposal . . ."

"Cleburne," said Davidson testily, "is not one of our own people. A brave man and a good soldier, but a foreigner. He has no sense of our true relations with our Negroes."

Bruce smiled. "I'm told that General Lee and President Davis both favor some such plan."

Davidson flushed. "I'm not surprised to hear that of Davis! As for Lee . . . Well, if it's so, the man is a professional soldier, and his life is the army. I'd not take his word on managing my People any more than he'd take mine on how to get round Grant. But dammit, man. . . ." His voice trailed off.

"It's a simple bargain, sir—as the Yankees calculate such things. So much must be spent—money or lives—to gain the objective. Gold or greenbacks, white men or Negroes—you pay whatever the market will accept. There are precedents for it, of course. The Romans made slaves into legionnaires, and gave them citizenship after their term of service."

"Aye," said Davidson grimly. "And if you've read your Gibbon, you know that the result was that their own Roman people became degenerate, and the barbarians came down out of the North and destroyed that bastard slave-citizen army, and sacked the city."

Bruce had read Gibbon. He thought that Colonel Davidson would have made a fine Severus or Diocletian—one of those hark-backs to the virtues of the Old Republic, who stood for the Old Roman virtues and the new Roman taxes, and whose efforts to revive ancient glory merely hastened the onset of modern degeneracy. If a tribune from the army of such an Emperor had come to the prince with a complaint of bad food, and discovered the prince seated like Davidson, with his jug of wine and his bowl of berries—certain assassination and a new election to follow.

"The men will need more candles or lanterns for their nightwork, sir . . ."—but before Bruce could continue, Davidson interrupted.

"Certainly, Lieutenant. And I'd like you to tell the men I'll be issuing them fresh vegetables within the week; and that they're not to throw them away this time! If they do, I'll do no more for them, but let them die of malnutrition."

Evening. Headquarters, 48th Pennsylvania

Rees carefully chose his moment for going to Pleasants. He had intended waiting till just after dinner; but when he got the report from the late afternoon shift, he decided to go in immediately, and settle the thing.

Pleasants was sitting at his table, the sketches of the Mine laid out before him in candlelight. Rees entered and saluted. "Sergeant?" said Pleasants, returning the salute.

"I've a report to make, sir. The last shift reports hearing the Johnnies digging for us. That's the third report of it today."

Pleasants held his face as steady as he could. His tension showed in the slight tremor of his left eyelid. "There's no surprise in that, Sergeant."

Rees ignored this. "They've been heard to either side of the shaft, maybe straight ahead. We've to go more carefully, Colonel. We've to go more slowly, to be quiet."

Pleasants looked stern. "The men will have to keep at it, Sergeant. Taking the usual precautions. I've told Army Headquarters we'll have finished the shaft tomorrow."

"The men won't stand for it, sir." It was out now. Rees was committed. He watched the Colonel's face carefully. "They were near to a mutiny this afternoon, sir. Over the sandbags, sir, which headquarters promised, but has not sent us."

Pleasants looked as if he had received a blow. "What do you mean, *mutiny?*"

"If it was the mines, sir, I'd of said 'turned out.' They say the lines ain't safe for want of sandbags, nor the shaft for want of good timbering."

"We've done as well as we could, Sergeant! You are well aware that the army engineers have not favored the project . . ."

"And the boys have helped you build the tunnel on the cheap. They'll not put up any more with shoddy and scrape-by. You'll not get the thing done without trouble."

Pleasants's features shifted, as if winds of feeling blew in him one way and another. Now he tried anger. "And where are you in all this, Sergeant?"

Rees almost smiled. He had expected Pleasants to attack him, weakly, like this. They almost always did, when you were in a strong position, had them dead to rights, and the boys were back of you. "I stopped them, sir, didn't I?"

Pleasants stood silent now, and looked intently at the sergeant. Then his look weakened and drooped. He bit his lip. "What can I do, Rees? The army hasn't sent us one thing they've promised. They'd as soon we failed as not."

Rees's face now assumed a more strict immobility. "That's your responsibility, isn't it, sir? To get what we need from the army so we can build your tunnel."

Pleasants's head snapped up. "Yes, Sergeant, it is. I'll see to it. You just keep the men to the work."

"Yes, sir," said Rees. "Slow and carefully, so there won't be too much noise. And I'll tell them you'll take care of the sandbags, won't I?"

"Of course, Sergeant."

Rees saluted and left. Outside, he smiled: pleased that the army hadn't dulled his instincts for dealing with bosses. He knew how to strike a bargain, and play the men's fear of the boss and the boss's fear of the men and the owners off against each other, to make things right for himself—and for the Mine as well, when you looked at the results. And for the men.

Still, he thought, before Pleasants started getting uppish about "his" tunnel, working on the Mine had felt like something different— like boys on a lark, building a thing for the doing of it and not sparing the effort as they would if they were being made to do it. It had been fun, for a while. Like playing soldier had been, after all those years in the pit. Well, there wasn't all that much difference between soldiering and mining, when you got to know them both. There were always bosses to be dealt with, always bargains to make.

Midnight. Confederate countermine

Billy and Tom Woodson were down in the one completed shaft, listening intently. The darkness pooled thickly at the bottom of the hole. Billy had insisted they put out the candle, he could listen better in the dark.

Through the earth around them he could hear a mechanical *tick— tick—tick.*

"Shoot, Billy," said Tom. "My teeth's gettin worse. Let's us . . .''

"Quiet!"

Tick. Tick. Tick.

"You hear it?" said Billy. He felt Tom stiffen.

"No," he said, whispering now, "it ain't them. It's just our own men digging is all."

"I figure it's coming from out front of us."

They waited, silently. *Tick. Tick. Tick.*

Billy gripped Tom's arm. "Go over to the other holes, and tell em stop digging so I can hear." Tom rose, but Billy pulled him down again. "And get Lieutenant Bruce."

"Aw, shit," said Tom. Then he was gone, clambering up the board ladder. Dried mud scuffed from his boot soles drifted down on Billy's back.

Billy sat alone in the hole listening to the steady *tick, tick.* Sometimes the noise seemed to come closer, and the sound went hollow: *tap— tap—tap.*

He imagined the dark finger of the tunnel, probing toward him underground, to where he crouched in his hole in the earth. He looked up to see a lighter blackness at the top of the black shaft. For a moment he felt vertigo, as if the earth had turned to simple blackness in which he sank back forever, drowning. He half-rose, spontaneously, explosively. He needed to burst out of the ground and into the open air.

"Soldier!" he said to himself. He must stay where he was. It was his bounden duty, even unto the pit of hell.

Anyway, what good going up on top? The dark fingers probing through the earth undermined all everything. One day the fingers would rise out of the soil and pull them down. Or would throw off the covering of earth and burst out, overwhelming them in darkness. And hell was always near you anyway, it was in your mind, Ma said—and never so much as since he went away for a soldier.

Little black men with evil ferret faces, he pictured them scratching through the earth toward him. Patiently, mechanically, mindlessly, like niggers working down a row of cotton, singing a monotonous song like the buzz of insects as their black fingers ate up the white bolls, coming down the rows towards where you watched from the road. Coming at him through the earth, under the ground. Crazy damn-Yankee devils, won't anything get them to back off? Can't face a man down in daylight, they'll work him underground and come at him by night. Like the man whose throat they cut.

There was noise at the top of the shaft. Lieutenant Bruce scrambled down. He said nothing. There was quiet. Through the earth they could hear the noise of the digging.

"It could be our own men," said Billy.

"No," said Bruce. "They've stopped. That's the Yankees." He was silent for some minutes. "Where away do you make it, Billy?"

"I make it out front, quartering to the right. Hard to say."

"All right. I'm going to get some more shovels and picks down here, and candles. You'll start digging out toward them—*quietly!* Quiet as if you were stalking deer. Every so often you stop, and listen."

"Yes, sir," said Billy. He thought with a shudder of the dark fingers pushing toward him underground; and about pushing himself deeper into the earth, looking for them.

Tom came back after a bit, with a candle, pick, and shovel. Billy took the pick, and stood there a minute. The wall of the shaft in front of him was blank and bland. Some spell was on it; he felt he could not begin picking at it. Like chunking stone in a scummed-over slough: what would come out of it?

Tom's face looked ghastly.

"All right," said Billy, more to himself than to Tom. "Let's get at it."

"Fuck it all," said Tom. "I popped myself in the jaw coming out, Billy, and . . ."

"What . . ."

"Three my fucking teeth just drop right out. Shit, Billy! They all loose! I'm gonna lose every one for sure! I couldn't chew no fresh stuff anyway anymore. Goddamn! God*damn!*" He began to sob, hunched over himself in the candlelight.

Billy wanted to kneel beside him. But the dark fingers were probing the wall at his back, and he was commanded to face them despite his fear—no, because he was afraid of them. It was the things you feared that you were most commanded and required to do as your duty. God wanted hard things of you. What was the point of asking easy? You had to set your personal feelings aside.

He turned his back to Tom. Set his feet apart. Rocked back and swung the pick across and *chunk!* into the wall of earth.

CAMP ENGINEER TROOPS,
Blandford, July 16, 1864.

Col. W. H. STEVENS,
Engineer Corps:

COLONEL: . . . At Pegram's salient, in mine No. 1 the gallery has been driven forward to a point 24 feet 6 inches from the entrance. The day detachment made a distance of 4 feet 6 inches, and the night detachment of 4 feet, a total 8 feet 6 inches in twenty-four hours. In mine No. 2 a total distance has been made in the gallery of 25 feet 6 inches, a distance of 5 feet 6 inches for the day's work. The detachment at work in this gallery was exchanged on the morning of the 15th and transferred to mine No. 1, the miners and assistants of this detachment having more experience, and the night detachments at work at No. 2 were reduced to increase the strength of the detachment at No. 1, as this last is considered the most important mine. A total distance in mining has been made in the past twenty-four hours of 23½ feet.

Very respectfully, your obedient servant,
HUGH THOS. DOUGLAS,
Captain, Engineer Troops, in Charge Mining Operations.

HEADQUARTERS NINTH ARMY CORPS
July 16, 1864—9 P.M.

General WILLIAMS:
It has been very quiet on my front to-day. The mine will be under the enemy's works during the night.
A. E. BURNSIDE,
Major-General.

July 16, Evening. Headquarters, 4th Division

The tables in Ferrero's big marquee had been laid out for a meeting in the shape of a large T. Ferrero sat at the head, facing down the double row of brigade and regimental commanders, flanked by his secretary and chief of staff, Captain Hicks. Down at the far end, Major Rockwood stood to make his report. From time to time he glanced down at Major Booker, sitting to his left. Rockwood outlined the course of the instruction so far, and the proposals he and Booker had worked out for the next stage of drilling. The plan was to train a new group of battalions as they had the first group, but with at least one trained company from the first day's group to act as guides. It meant that more men would be involved in the drill—more complicated drilling—and fewer men available for the divisional picket line.

"That seems unnecessarily complicated," said Colonel Oliver. "Why not just drill the rest of the men in turn?"

Booker half rose. "I can answer that, Colonel, since it was my suggestion." He noted that Oliver could not suppress an upward twist at the corner of his mouth—but he found he enjoyed getting under the man's skin. "There is more to making an attack than just going through a series of parade-ground movements under the commands of your officers. We wanted to have a substantial number of men, at all ranks, who were as thoroughly versed in the projected movements of the attack as we officers ourselves."

"To what *point,* Major?" said Oliver.

"So that when they've finished picking off all the white officers, there'll still be plenty of men around who know what to do."

There was silence at that.

Booker went on softly. "I don't think I'm surprising any of us when I say that. You know they always shoot for the officers—we do it too. White faces leading black troops makes it easier. And they'll expect that if they kill enough of us, our troops won't go."

"If we're that badly off," said Thomas, "do you really think the troops will keep going?'' He spoke as if in reverie. Booker had tapped a deep reservoir of thought and feeling, a deep preoccupation in all of them. What happened if your troops ran off and left you behind?

"I've seen it happen," said Booker. "I guess we all have." *I remember Wilson's Creek when it all fell apart, and privates who could handle it took over regiments, and Colonels that couldn't ran away, or shouldered a gun and took orders. I remember that.*

"You haven't seen it with black troops," said Oliver. "And please, Major, don't tell me again that they haven't had their chance. We know all about that.''

"What about Battery Wagner? I thought that settled this business once for all.''

"Gentlemen!'' said Ferrero. "I don't think this conversation is taking a profitable direction. We have all heard the various arguments about the capacities of Colored troops.'' He shook his head, as if clearing cobwebs. "It seems to me almost *unseemly* for men in our position to discuss the matter this way. As if these were not *our* men, and we had no stake in the matter.''

Thomas nodded. "Yes, by God! I'd say we were committed to the idea that they'll fight by definition!''

Oliver closed his eyes for a moment, as if mastering some private pain. "This isn't pleasant for me, gentlemen. I hope you'll understand that I am as committed to the success of this command as any man present. I trust I've never shown otherwise. We must address ourselves . . . there *is* a fundamental question here, that *does* relate to the matter of this attack. We will find out, most assuredly, what the fighting qualities of the race are: we will make the experiment. But we are planning the method of our attack to yield the highest possibilities of success. And we *must* consider what evidence is available to us in making our plans. Majors Rockwood and Booker have made the assumption that our troops can be prepared—or the guide companies can be—to act as veteran soldiers might, with tact and thorough knowledge of the character of the military operation. Am I not right?''

Thomas said, "I did not mean to say that only veteran troops have been able to command themselves when their officers were lost. I've seen raw troops in their first fight do the same.''

Oliver smiled, and quickly said, "Agreed! Some individual, many individuals, with the native capacity to respond well in battle, do endure and take command! It must be said: the race of slaves has never thrown forward such characters—certainly not many—despite centuries of oppression and frequent opportunities for insurrection. Now as to Battery Wagner, which is universally cited as putting questions about their capacities to rest: no one has ever questioned the black man's capacity to endure suffering. But soldiers must do more than suffer and die—they must have the capacity to rise beyond mere endurance, to take command of their powers and successfully combat, kill their enemy. The troops at Wagner suffered and died—they didn't take the fort. They marched forward with the sea on one hand, a swamp on the other, and a press of men behind. One might almost imagine them driven like sheep into a pen.''

Thomas looked shocked. "By heaven, sir! I never thought to hear anyone speak so of brave men."

Oliver looked at him. "I'm genuinely sorry to grieve you, Colonel. I spoke with Colonel Shaw before he left on his fatal expedition. Do you know what he proposed doing?" He paused, as if for effect. "He thought he might have a line of provost guards drawn up in the rear, to shoot down his men if they broke and ran. Yes. The way he put it was, 'Did I think it was a good idea to hold the men in line by keeping them between two fires.' "

"And did you?" asked Booker softly.

"I did. Colonel Higginson, who was by me, disagreed; and Shaw didn't arrange for the 'second fire'—but the way the attack was set up, he had no need of the arrangement. The sea and the swamp and the press of the attacking force accomplished the same end. We, on the other hand, move across open ground with our flanks open, and must make complicated maneuvers in the course of the attack, during any of which we are liable to have our troops routed by surprise attacks of infantry or artillery. We can't trust Nature to serve our turn, as Shaw could."

"What do you propose, Colonel?" asked Ferrero.

"I'd propose that instead of wasting time training guide companies, as Major Rockwood suggests, we train our best and most reliable troops to form a strong line in rear of the advance, and severely check any effort of the troops to break. Or better: obtain a white regiment of veterans for the purpose."

There was silence. Booker, glancing down the row of faces, guessed that Oliver spoke for some of the other regimental commanders there—clearly not for Thomas or Bates or Perkins or Hall, the officers who were committed in principle to the advocacy of Colored troops. But surely he voiced secret doubts they all had.

Ferrero now spoke, slowly, reluctantly, as if to himself. "I can't imagine how we would explain their task to those men we'd draw out."

Thomas nodded. "Morale in the rest of the troops would simply vanish."

Oliver spoke quietly. "I can't say I expected any other response. But it seems odd to me that you are prepared to trust their morale to carry them through an assault, and at the same time see that morale as so fragile as to break at the adoption of a measure that is, after all, common enough in this and other armies."

"I'm sure we all respect your motives, as well as your opinions, Colonel Oliver," said Ferrero. *But he's wrong*, thought the General. *It would never do for it to look as if we had to drive them to battle with a gun at their backs.*

The discussion, unresolved, was allowed to die.

Major Rockwood took up the thread of his report. Booker lapsed into reverie, now that the confrontation with Oliver had come and gone. He was, briefly, elated at having staved off the practical effects, at least, of the moral poison disseminated by the priggish, snobbish Brahmin commander of the First Brigade. How typical of the man, in his refined and intellectual manner, to propose marching troops into battle the way they had marched the conscripts from the landing to headquarters—under guard. Why not in shackles?

As the elation passed, Booker became depressed. He had maintained his point against Oliver, but what had he gained? Although there would be no concrete appearance of force driving the men into action, the threat was still there. All he had done was to convince his commanders not to unmask that force, to preserve for the sake of morale the appearance of trust and shared purposes between officers and soldiers, white and black. Were their purposes the same? Both wished to take Richmond and achieve victory. But Booker did not believe that he and Oliver and Cato Randolph—let alone Abraham Lincoln, Ben Butler, and General Grant—shared the same idea of what "victory" might mean. For Randolph? Freedom, and possession of his farm, and reuniting his family—victory without those things would mean nothing to him. For the others? The power to rule, to shape things according to their will and ideas. For himself? For himself?

To fight for his own cause, and values. His freedom. Freedom for his own people. Power too, to shape things—their own lives according to their own will, not according to the will and power of their rulers.

The power to assign and determine the value and meaning of these events—this war, this attack—that was the power of Oliver, Burnside, Grant, and Lincoln. To make the attack mean that the slave deserved liberation, or was by nature entitled only to labor for others. To make it mean the triumph of democracy, or the triumph of a party or class grasping for rule. It seemed to him that he and Randolph had no power to make these events mean what they wished them to mean—that willy-nilly they executed the purposes of others.

Why was everything so impossible now, here in this phase of the war, where the means of action were so abundant; whereas in Kansas, in *his* war, where the means were so impoverished and the actions on so small and petty a scale, he had felt full of power, able to accomplish miracles?

Perhaps it was simply ambition. *Miriam seemed to suspect me of that. I was so hot to get out of Kansas and the little war that I drove myself to the limits of my capacity; and now that I have my commission and rank in the largest and most important of the armies, I have nothing further to strive for.* No, that could not be the whole of it. If ambition were all, why, he could drive himself to be a General now.

Perhaps this army and this war were too large, choking and muscle-bound with an excess of appetite and strength, ends and means. The sheer mass of agglomerated power and purpose thwarting itself, and individual will and power counting for nothing.

In Kansas war was: you kill this man, or that gang of men; you take this, you burn that—this farm, two buildings and a barn. Bushwhacking and Jayhawking. What was the point of all that petty death? It was too close to murder and robbery and arson for his tastes: as if the sheer size and scale on which murder and looting were carried out in the Eastern war somehow transmuted petty death into high heroism!

There was an image of what this war was. Not petty death, this man or that man (you knew his name) shot in the back or swinging on the end of a rope:

But a trench full of dead men, a long slash in the earth filled to brimming with the bodies of the dead. Spotsylvania. The regiment had had to dig the dead out of each other's embrace, and bury them. What a stupidity, now that he reflected on it. Oliver or whoever gave the orders—himself, who'd carried them out—must have been too numb with the shock of it to think. Why bother to disentangle each individual body from the complicated and impasted intertwining of that mass grave? What absurd homage to a myth of individual salvation had been in their minds? When the proof of its absurdity was in their eyes and nostrils? Looking down from the parapet, the parapet itself a parapet of the dead, he had thought, the trench goes down to the center of the earth, the dead rising out of it like tangled vines out of a swamp, mangrove roots. Don't begin to untangle it: God in heaven, who could tell what you might bring into the light, hauling on those pale twisted roots?

But they had, after all, found something. Down in that tangle, a man had survived. They hauled him out like a sack of hardtack, and he opened his eyes and screamed once—shrill as a woman or a child just born into the light—before he passed out again.

Oh, he must have remembered, when the light struck him, what it was like to be among all that death: and in the horror of knowing the intertangling of his life his death cried out, a blast of sheer noise that blew his brains out again.

That was the new kind of Death and the new kind of War he had left the West to find. To join. Across that trench of undifferentiated death, the warfare of Kansas seemed not petty in its individual scale, but heroic in its evocation of humanity, bushwhacking, and Jayhawking a kind of humane epic against the indifferent bulk and inertia of the war. In Kansas one counted for something. In Virginia, even the struggle for freedom implied bondage.

Bah! Would he never be contented? Hadn't he learned yet that it was his nature always to imagine that there, in some other place, that was where true action and perfected life could be found? For once, for once, abandon nothing and no one—don't leave or dream of leaving. Stay. *Stay Books, she had said. This isn't our war.*

He would stay this time, whatever the end might be. He was bound to seek his answers by the shortest way, across a hundred yards of open ground, a rebel trench, to a hill with a white house and a cemetery on top.

Night. Bivouac, 19th U.S.C.T.

Lieutenant Dobbs had had his eye on Private Johnson Number Five for some time, meaning to promote him to corporal, ever since that day when the cavalryman had killed one of his boys right under his nose—and then, of course, got let off with a reprimand by one of those damned military courts. He'd liked the way Johnson had stayed cool, kept the rest of the cavalry covered. So he'd watched him, and liked what he saw, except the man seemed to have something wrong about his chest. With all the heat, you never saw him without his shirt, even when the rest of them were stripped to the waist and shining with sweat like so many black pistons in a steamboat engine. Well, Dobbs had a sharp eye, and he'd spotted the thing after a time: a scar on the breast, roughly in the shape of a letter *D*. The army branded deserters with a *D,* one on each hip, but Dobbs had never heard of them doing it on the chest.

The point was, could you trust a nigger that had deserted once to do a job for you as corporal? Dobbs figured he could. Whatever had made him run before didn't matter. Hell, there were plenty of good reasons for taking a walk in this army; and plenty of good men got caught doing it, too. And he'd come back, hadn't he?

Dobbs sat by his campfire, and Private Johnson stepped out of the shadows into the orange glow. "I'm here, Capn."

"Set," said Dobbs thinking that the son of a bitch always called him and every other white officer "Captain," no matter what. The fire lit the right side of Johnson's face. "I've been thinking that you ought to be a corporal."

"Yes, sir."

"Does that mean 'yes, sir, I want to be a corporal,' or just plain 'yes, sir?' "

Johnson snorted, his lip lifted grudgingly in a smile, "I guess it's just *plain* 'yes, sir.' "

"That mean you don't want to be a corporal?"

"Yes, sir," said Johnson. then caught himself; but Dobbs pointed at him, and said, "Dammit boy, you've got more ways of saying 'yes, sir' and meaning 'no, sir' than any six soldiers I've ever seen or heard of."

"Yes, sir," said Johnson, and then threw back his head and laughed. Dobbs poured a shot of whiskey into a tin cup and handed it across, then poured one for himself.

"All right. Why don't you want to be a corporal?"

Johnson was silent.

What in hell was the matter with the man? "Listen, Private, I *need* for you to be a corporal. I've seen how you do your work, and I've seen how the men listen to what you say, and from where I sit you're the best soldier of the lot. Am I wrong?" No sign. "I'm right then. Well, I need you to go for a corporal. We only have one sergeant in this platoon, and he's gone sick for the last two weeks." Did Johnson's eyes shift? "Hell, if he don't come back, you can have his stripes too."

Johnson went cold again. So it wasn't the stripes he wanted. Dobbs decided to go for him, once and for all, just right out and find out if he was afraid to take the promotion because of some crazy nigger pride or shame about having been caught deserting once. "Look," he said softly, "If it's that thing on your chest . . . I've seen it. It don't make no difference to me about it." Johnson's fire-lit right eye widened suddenly, and he turned his head sharply to face the firelight and stared at it.

"It make a difference," he said. What could he tell this white man about the difference it made? And how could a white man, hungry as the rest for stripes and bars and stars and all that brass, how could a white man know that it was dangerous for a nigger to show up too much from the crowd?

A long time ago, Private Johnson Number Five had been a boy of four, named Chaney, which got changed to "Dayson's Chaney" when his master, Governor Davidson, sold him away from his folks to another planter in the county. Not before branding him with his initial, *D*.

He suspected it was because when he was little, his Mammy made a fuss over him, and so the Governor noticed and had the Driver take him —it didn't change his mind when the folks told him, after he was older, that Davidson did it to everyone on his place. There had to be some special reason. His Mammy's shrieks frightened him so that he couldn't cry himself. The Driver said, "I hold him good, this don't hurt a bit." He smelled the hot iron, felt it sizzle and smelled himself burn before the pain blew through him like a bolt of ice and then fire. He screamed so loud he felt his head burst and his soul fly all away in pieces, but it always came back to him, and he felt the burning. He remembered days of darkness and screaming, and his Mammy's face bright-colored and cold as stone looking down at him, saying, "Poor little nigger, poor little nigger." But her eyes dead cold.

He knew from that that they had burned his soul out of his body, and he came back a changed one, a demon child. His skin was burnt all over, so she called him nigger. His Mammy loved the child that went out and they burned it, but something in her heart shunned the burnt one. He could understand this, and wanted to comfort her and tell her so.

On his breast was a small scar in the shape of a *D*. When he was small it had a precise shape and puckered slightly at the edges. When he grew older, the scar spread and the shape became distorted.

When he was eleven Mr. Davidson sold him, along with three other of his D-branded slaves. "Mammy, I'm sorry to leave you, even if you never did like me much."

The corners of her mouth drew down in a deep bow, and he thought she would cry. "I done my best, Chaney-boy. I just learned, you can't allow yourself to give your feelings to no one, not a nigger or a white man. They not a thing you can do for em, nor they for you. Ain't no use to love nobody, Chaney. They 'stroy what you love before your face, or sell them away. No use to love nobody."

Years later he met a man named Pendar, from Davidson's plantation, who told him she had died just after he left. She caught cold picking cotton on a foggy day, wouldn't eat or help herself, and the folks found her dead in her cabin when they came back from the field. "When Marse sold you, she didn't want to live."

"I never thought she liked me much," said Dayson's Chaney, "she always looked cold on me, and whup me plenty."

"No, son, you the apple of her eye."

"No, she never liked me much. I was a lot blacker than she was."

His new master was mean as sin, and the plantation was hardscrabble start to finish, rag clothes and bad food and hard work. Man put his eye on you, and you get some special hard meanness, some bad work, maybe even the whip. Everything you are, everything of your own, you get and keep and hold by being secret. There's a man goin' round, takin names—only way to get by him is for nobody to know your name. Better if you never had one.

He was only happy, only himself, when singing in the fields or in the cabins, if it was daylight giving the cadence through the nose, lips clenched tight, everybody taking up and carrying the burden too, wordlessly, simple breathing turned to his music. No white man ever understand how it starts, what it says.

When the Yankees came and burned out the plantation and carried them all off to the contraband camp, it was no different. Just Yankee Massa doling out the poor food, exacting hard labor, locking you in trashy filthy hovels at night, letting the low trash abuse the women. There was one woman named Sukey that took a red shawl from some soldiers to let them do to her, and then like a fool wore it through the camp, and the women threw mud at her for it. Damn fool to make a show of herself that way.

Only one time since he was little had he forgotten that lesson, and that was when he met John Brown. In '59 they heard a rumor out of Virginy that a man named John Brown had tried to raise all the niggers in the state, but that he got killed doing it, strung up by white folks. But it didn't say whether he was black or white. Then, in '61, a black man with that name was talked about in the Neuse River swamps. Some said he was a runaway took the name John Brown to scare the white folks, and that his real name was Williams or Willis. But the scare was real, and it was real when the buckra militia that went into the swamp after John Brown came out, mostly, on pine boards. A Massachusetts regiment paraded by the contraband camp singing, "John Brown's body lies a moldrin in the grave," and they said that he was dead. But it wasn't so: maybe he just pretended, lying up between the pine boards while they threw the dirt on, then raising up and throwing the earth from the grave and shouting death and judgment on the white men.

Some of the stories they told about him were stories about that other one named John, that black tricker, underhand, laughing up his sleeve, do em dirty any which way; but the swamp war was true, and it was true as life when John Brown walked into the contraband camp and called the men out, dressed in a Yankee uniform with golden chevrons on his sleeve.

John Brown's platoon was digging privies. They were resting, leaning on their shovels, when two white privates walked by. They stared at Chaney, and he saluted and grinned, as he had seen others salute.

"Hey!" yelled John Brown. "What you doing! You don't salute nobody without chevrons or straps, white, black, or whatever! You a soldier now, not a slave, fool. And you two move along." And John Brown leaned one hand on his pistol and stared until the two men moved.

When they had gone, Brown turned to the platoon. "You see that?

When you see me standing out in front of you, keeping buckra from doing you up, you gather back of me, and you be ready to fight. Or I'm not having anything to do with trashy, scared niggers.''

John Brown said, ''Every day they calling the Yankee troops away from here. More and more the soldiers here is black. Recruiters from north comin in here, they gets so much a head for who they recruit, never mind how. I tell you this: I'm sick to death of getting paid ten dollars a month when they paying white men thirteen dollars, and a bounty on top of it; and the white boys sitting around while we doing all the work. That ain't my notion of free, and it ain't my notion of soldier.''

John Brown went in to his Captain. He said, ''Pay us thirteen dollars a month like you do the white soldiers.''

''No,'' said Captain, ''I won't.''

''Then let me go home. I signed on to be a soldier, and get soldier's pay. If you won't pay me to soldier, let me go back to my own home and grow corn.''

''No,'' said Captain, ''you my best soldier, you must stay.''

''I'm your best soldier, and you pay me three dollars less than your worst white soldier.''

Captain gets mad. ''That's the law, and you'd best obey it.''

Next day John Brown marches his platoon up before Captain's tent. They present arms. John Brown say, ''Pay us our money that is due, or let us go home.''

''This is mutiny,'' says Captain, cold.

''Then we stacking arms, and going home.'' And they stack their arms in front of Captain's tent.

''Provost guard,'' yells Captain, and there's the men with rifles standing around, black men.

Suddenly, Dayson's Chaney felt afraid again. He saw John Brown standing there bareheaded before the Captain. He was a smaller man than the Captain. In the middle of his wool was a round patch of smooth black skin.

They shot John Brown on a cold morning, with a damp sea fog turning everything gray. They had lined up his platoon, with shackles on their wrists and ankles, to watch him be shot. When he saw John Brown leaning on the two men who walked with him, he saw how weak the man was. And anger rose up in him, and he hated John Brown, who should have been strong but was weak, and scared, and should have been smart but had done things all wrong and got them all in jail and was going to die.

They stood John Brown up to the stake, but he wouldn't let them bind his eyes. They heard him say, ''I want to look in the eyes of these niggers that's going to shoot me. I want them to remember doing this.''

And then Dayson's Chaney knew how it was his mother had felt when he'd got branded. Hating him for hurting so bad when there wasn't one thing she could do for him, and needing so badly to do something.

So his voice began to speak, and the words came out of him like this:

> *"Free, dom.*
> *Free-ee, dom.*
> *Freedom over me.*
> *En before I'd be a slave*
> *I be buried in my grave*
> *En go home to my Lord and be free."*

And the shots came, *ratapang, bang.* And John Brown shivered and slumped. And a white officer came with a pistol, and *pang* went a shot into his head.

Then they cut him down and made the platoon bury him, with their ankle chains clanking.

They put the body between two pineboards and lowered it down. And while they did it, Dayson's Chaney sang, "John Brown's body lies a moldrin in the grave, / En we go marchin on," till the body was covered up and he was gone. He felt the burden of the earth on John Brown, as if it was his own faults that had killed him.

Of course, Dayson's Chaney was discharged dishonorably from the army. But recruiting agents were so eager to get anyone they could to fill their state quota with blacks so hometown boys wouldn't have to go, that they'd even take a man with a *D* tattooed on his chest—sign of a deserter, likely.

"Make your mark. What's your name?"

"James Johnson."

"Oh, you and fifteen others."

He wasn't any John Brown. He didn't want to be Dayson's Chaney. Dayson's Chaney was a slave; he was free now.

Name like James Johnson is common as dirt. But a nigger is still a nigger, burnt child, by any name. It still makes sense not to stand out too much from the crowd.

"No, sir," he said to Dobbs. "I don't want to be no corporal."

HEADQUARTERS NINTH ARMY CORPS,
July 17, 1864—9 A.M.

General S. WILLIAMS,
Assistant Adjutant-General.

We had the usual amount of picket and mortar firing on our front last night. Six deserters came in early this morning opposite the right of our line, belonging to Bushrod Johnson's division, and state that they do not know positively of any troops being on this side of the river, except Beauregard. They think there are others. They represent great dissatisfaction existing among them, short rations, &c. . . . They also state it is understood by their officers that we are mining at some place along the line. A member of their company who is a miner, was detailed three or four days ago to assist in countermining for the purpose of discovering where we are mining. I should judge from their statements that the countermining has commenced at about the right place, but I think the great depth of our mine below the surface will probably prevent discovery. But I deem it very important that the mine should be charged and exploded as early as possible. We will probably have the side galleries ready for the charge by to-morrow morning. All necessary precautions have been ordered, and we hope to be able to complete the mine.

A. E. BURNSIDE,
Major-General.

HEADQUARTERS ARMY OF THE POTOMAC,
July 17, 1864—9 A.M.

Lieutenant-General GRANT:

I forward a dispatch received from Major-General Burnside. It appears the enemy have become apprised of the mining operations and are countermining. The report made last night informed you that it would be a week before operations against the salient (on General Warren's front) which takes Burnside's mine in reverse could be commenced. I see no object in exploding this mine before the advantages gained by it can be followed up. Nothing occurred worthy of report on other parts of the line. All the enemy's old works have been levelled.

GEO. G. MEADE,
Major-General.

Afternoon. The Mine

Down at the end of the tunnel Doyle was digging. Above his head he heard the muffled pounding of hammers, the flat sound of boards dropped bang onto a frame. *Butta-bump, butta-ba-bump. Ba-bump.* What are they building?

The sound from above muffled and hid the noise of the rebel counterminers off to the sides of the tunnel end. When Doyle paused, he couldn't hear them. For a moment he felt a surge of anger at the noise from overhead—he wanted to know if they were coming any closer to him. Then he thought, *If I can't hear them, they can't hear me.* He smiled. *Pound away, boys.* He began to pick harder, not worrying about the noise as he had done before. What are they building, the fine rebel lads? Let it be a battery. Let it be a whole bloody fort. Let them pack the guns in hub to hub. We'll blow the lot to the devil, and stroll into Richmond laughing.

Maybe it's a bloody house they're building, a bombproof house for Bobby Lee. Let em pack the Generals in tight as they'll fit, and we'll take care of them as well. Blow the murdering bastards into the sky.

He imagined a colossal explosion, a volcano burst, the rebels who had murdered Corrigan flying head over heels into a pit of fire.

As he swung his pick he thought about the countermine. Wouldn't it be something if the rebels weren't looking for him at all? If some smart reb had got the same idea they had gotten, and even now they were digging their own bloody tunnel down the slope toward our lines. Two tunnels passing each other going opposite ways, totally invisible to each other. He pictured it, pictured two long fuses streaking fire down two tunnels, two volcanoes going up at once. A hell of a joke on us all if the miners on both sides just blow each other up. Then it will be hole against hole, and nobody to charge nobody. What's the point then, the two armies just blowing each other to hell?

Ah, but suppose they go right on past the lines to under the Generals' bombproofs. Suppose when they give the signal, and the fire flashes down and the bomb goes up, suppose it's the Generals watching each other across the lines with their glasses, their staffs all round—suppose while they're watching for the other ones to blow up, they get blown up themselves, both sides at once.

And the soldiers look round in the trenches. They can't figure it out, why nobody tells them to go forward. After a time, somebody stands up and yells, What the hell is going on, where's the fucking Generals anyway? And they can't find a one. They'd wait in the trenches for hours, for one of them to show up. But none would come.

After a time, the soldiers would get tired of waiting and just go home. Some wouldn't want to, they'd be afraid to go. But someone would look over and see, hey, the Johnnies are starting to leave too and soon everybody's going away, drifting off. They keep their uniforms and their guns, and they stop by the wagons for walking rations. There's long waits for trains but nobody minds.

By the time they hear about it in Washington and Richmond, it is too late. There can't be a war any more, the armies have all gone home, and they'll have to think of something else or give it up as a bad business and go home themselves.

The trenches are empty except for some old niggers who are digging around in the trash heaps for whatever they can find.

HDQRS. SECOND BRIGADE, SECOND DIV. NINTH ARMY CORPS, *Before Petersburg, July 18, 1864.*

Lieut. Col. LEWIS RICHMOND,
Assistant Adjutant-General, Ninth Army Corps.
COLONEL: I have the honor to report that the siege works in front of the Ninth Corps are vigorously prosecuted day and night, and are rapidly approaching completion. . . . The mine at the present time has been carried to a horizontal depth of 515 feet, and reached a point directly beneath the enemy's works. The galleries are already commenced.

Very Respectfully, your obedient servant,
S. G. GRIFFIN,
Brigadier-General of Volunteers, General of the Trenches.

9:00 A.M. *The Mine*

On Burnside's order Pleasants called off operations before the first night shift. All the reports of countermining, and hearing the rebels working overhead, had unnerved the General. It had taken Pleasants a while to calm his fears. Now, sitting in the shaft itself, he wondered at his own assurance. The least sound could be heard above them. He was glad he'd come down to check, after all. He had planned in any case to confirm his guess that they were done with digging the shaft. Now he had been warned again, against taking any further chances of giving its position away. The shaft *was* done, but the galleries had still to be completed.

He put the noise overhead out of his mind, and turned to his technical problem. It was a simple matter of calculating the length of the tunnel and figuring its angle of approach to the rebel redoubt. So far as he could tell, working carefully in the tunnel by candlelight, the line of the shaft was true. It bent slightly to the left from the straight line of its initial direction—that carried through the first correction he'd made after taking his bearings on the fort. The angle of descent into the hillside—it really was an ascent; the rebel fort was higher than they were—that was right too. The tunnel was just short of 511 feet long, and it was fifty feet below the rebel lines at the surface. He calculated they were directly below the redoubt. Now he had to extend two galleries out to either side of the shaft, making the shape of a rambling, irregular T. The crosspiece had to be calculated to parallel the rebel line, so as to blow up the whole of the fort, and the lines extending to right and left of it.

Burnside had been clear and certain about the powder charge. Thirty feet of earth along a 150-foot line was a lot to blow off, but Burnside had figured the charge carefully—it was, he had said, going to be the biggest charge of powder, to top off the digging of the longest mine in military annals. If the crater, as anticipated, was a hundred feet across— that was half a million cubic feet of earth! They had toasted their success last night, the General beaming, chuckling to himself with evident satisfaction. "We've stolen a march on them," he chortled, and gestured over his shoulder. Only after they'd left the tent did Pleasants realize that Burnside had gestured toward their own rear area instead of the rebel lines.

He sat in the flickering candlelight at the end of the tunnel shaft. Rees was with him, the light making his face appear masklike, a shifting pattern of lights and shadows. Enigmatic. Above his head Pleasants could distinctly hear the rhythmic tap of booted feet, where a sentry was walking his post. Thirty feet of earth, and the sound traveled in it so distinctly. Even without countermines and listening shafts, couldn't the rebels hear them as easily up there as they could be heard down here? Perhaps not: they made so much noise themselves during the day, and then it was somehow easier to hear things in the dark, when your eyes didn't work, than in daylight.

It was easier in the dark to visualize the Mine, how it would explode, what it might do. In daylight he found himself fiddling with compass and straight-edge over his sketches, to no purpose. He simply had no good information on which to calculate the force of the explosion, the shape of the crater. Twelve thousand pounds of explosive—six tons of gunpowder. The explosion would be concentrated by tamping the tunnel with sandbags. They'd have to leave space for the explosion to develop itself, but also pack in enough tamping so that the full force of it would brim against obstruction, the sandbags and the half-million cubic feet of earth frustrating and penning it up, holding back the building fury till the fireball would burst up out of everything, carrying the half a million cubic feet of earth straight up.

If it worked.

He turned to Rees. "This is the end of the shaft. I want the right and left galleries to angle out forty-five degrees to either side, for the first ten feet. You understand?"

Rees nodded.

"Once you've gotten the galleries started, you can work double shifts down there—four men, two on each gallery. There'll be more space . . . but I don't have to explain that."

"Same amount of air, sir," said Rees, "for twice the men. Twice the number swinging picks as well. That's twice the noise, as I calculate."

Pleasants looked sternly at Rees. The sergeant returned stare for stare, bland and impersonal. "I'm aware of the problems, Sergeant. We can't build the tunnel without taking risks, as I shouldn't have to tell you. I've calculated the risk carefully. You will simply have to trust me on that."

"Yes, sir."

"I'm going up to see the General again. I'll get him to lift his order to suspend digging. By six tonight we will have been off work for twenty-four hours. The rebels may simply conclude that we've given it over. In any case, you'll have your men prepared to recommence work then."

"Yes, sir," said Rees.

They turned and shuffled back together through the tunnel.

CAMP ENGINEER TROOPS,
Blandford, July 18, 1864.

Col. W. H. STEVENS,
Chief Engineer, &c.:

COLONEL: At Pegram's salient mine No. 1 was extended up to 8 P.M. on the 17th, 4 feet, by the night detachment an additional distance of 4 feet, a total distance of 8 feet for the day's work, and a total distance of 39 feet from the entrance. At mine No. 2 extended up to 8 P.M. on the 17th 3 feet 6 inches, and by the night detachment 2 feet, a total distance of 35 feet 8 inches from the entrance. At Colquitt's salient the gallery was extended up to 8 P.M. on the 17th 6 feet 8 inches, and by the night detachment an additional distance of 3 feet, a total of 9 feet 8 inches for the day's work, and a total distance of 35 feet

3 inches from the entrance. The accumulation of material during the day at this mine, which had to be removed at night,
caused the less distance that was made in this gallery by the
night detachment. A total distance for the day's work was made
at all the mines of 23 feet 2 inches.

Very respectfully, your obedient servant,

HUGH THOS. DOUGLAS,
Captain, Engineer Troops, in Charge of Mining &c.

5:00 P.M. *Burnside's Headquarters*

Burnside had invited Ferrero to join him for breakfast after his return from City Point, expecting (as he had every right to) that he would
bring good news. Ferrero had written to him, appealed to him for more
training time, less responsibility for fatigue details and picket work. It
had been a long-lingering drain on his energies, the struggle to hang on
to Ferrero's division—first losing them as train guards on the campaign down from the north, then seeing them detailed to guard the
flank under Hancock or Warren. He had had his showdown with Meade:
if they wanted to take the division and call off the whole project of the
attack, they would have to say so *now!* He had known that they would
not call it off—they couldn't, Meade had nothing else in the fire. That
was all straightened out. He'd sat back, bit the end off a cigar—perhaps
he'd overdone it, looked too smug. There was that malicious twinkle in
Meade's eye when he'd told him that the last word was that Ferrero's
commission had not been reconfirmed by the Senate. Not only had the
man been denied promotion, but they'd allowed his commission as
Brigadier to lapse. He'd have to be sent back.

Poor Ed! A good man. A good officer. A good division commander.
A *loyal* man. He could do nothing for him. (He would have to be careful. Meade would try to foist one of his favorites on him if he wasn't
careful.)

Now Ferrero was sitting across from him, wiping his mouth and
politely waiting for Burnside to speak. Burnside beamed at him, and
decided to let Ferrero speak first. He wanted this to be a social occasion,
he genuinely liked the man, considered him a friend. Whiskey made him
feel slightly dizzy. He had a hard time following the trend of his own
thoughts. Ferrero said nothing. Seemed to have his company manners
on. Like a junior officer waiting for orders. *Loosen him up.*

"Here, Ed," said Burnside, tossing a packet of folded papers across
the table. "I thought you'd enjoy seeing these."

Ferrero unfolded the papers. His original request to Burnside, for
relief of the constant demands on his division for fatigue parties and details for other corps, was on top. Below it was confirmation by Grant
himself that the division would be given the time it needed to complete
its training. Ferrero took a deep breath, and let it out slowly. He had
carried his point, or Burnside had carried it for him. He could hardly
believe it. He looked at Burnside. "This news . . . it's very good.
Thank you, sir."

Burnside made a deprecatory gesture, but beamed with evident pleasure. "You don't know how close things were, Ed. Warren had asked for full control of your division, and for the permanent assignment of your troops to engineer details for the duration of the siege. You'd have been up to your ears in dirt till Christmas." Burnside's face flushed suddenly with acute embarrassment. *What a fool thing, to talk about Ferrero's doing anything till Christmas, when I have to tell him. . . .*

"I'm very grateful to you, sir. The whole division is." Ferrero glanced at the messages. "I assume we're back with the Ninth Corps again?"

"Not yet," said Burnside, glad of the chance to avoid the painful subject a while longer. "But I have it on good authority that you will be, the division will be, soon." *Damn! I did it again!* Burnside's mind ran desperately through several lines of thought, seeking a way to postpone what he had almost too precipitately revealed already. "You know," he said, "it isn't easy keeping up with what goes on at headquarters. Meade doesn't confide in me, as you are aware."

"Then how did you get these dispatches?"

Burnside smiled again, anticipating the awed respect Ferrero's face would show when he told him. He winked at Ferrero. "Between ourselves, Ed, I've been having our telegraph operators copy all messages that come down our wire." He waved his hand placatingly as Ferrero's eyebrows rose in surprise. "Yes, yes, it's against orders, to be sure. But sometimes—a good soldier must know this—sometimes it's needful to disregard orders for the good of the service. Generals can't know everything or be everywhere, and a good subordinate knows when to obey without question, and when to use his judgment. And you can't be a good commander unless you know how to be a good subordinate." Ferrero nodded agreement. His expression did reflect that awe which Burnside had hoped for. He was obviously overwhelmed by his commander's skill and judgment, his willingness to risk everything for principle—setting everything on the turn of a card, as it were.

Now was the time. "Ed"—Burnside's voice became low and serious—"I'm afraid I have other news, not so good. In fact, very bad for you. For all of us." Ferrero's face had gone dead white.

"My wife? . . ."

"No, no," said Burnside hastily, "not that, no. No, it's your commission. The Senate . . ."

Ferrero shook his head as if in a daze. "Yes, I know. I've been expecting it."

"It's not just the promotion, Ed," said Burnside. "They didn't confirm your brevet commission. There's nothing I can do for you here. You'll have to give up the division—leave the service or return to your regiment. I'm not sure which." He leaned forward, his eyes bright with water. "I'm genuinely sorry, Ed, I hate losing you."

"I know, thank you," said Ferrero huskily. "General . . . what had I best do?"

"If I were you . . . damn it, I'd fight. Get your gear together. I'll endorse an application for immediate leave. Go up to Washington yourself. Talk to people—you have friends, and I can give you a letter to some people I know. Maybe something can still be done.''

Ferrero still looked stricken. ''The division will make the assault without me. That's . . .'' His eyes filled. He had worked so hard.

''Ed,'' said Burnside, ''I can't promise you—anything may happen. But I don't believe we'll make the assault very soon. The Mine isn't quite done; when it is, we'll have to load it and the powder hasn't been brought up yet. Meade wants Warren to make more headway against the salient that flanks the line of attack here . . . I just don't believe we'll go up all that soon. Go to Washington, work as quickly as you can. You may get back in time. If you do, I can promise you you'll have your division back. Grant respects your work, he'll overrule Meade if that's needed. Buck up! Nothing's lost yet!''

But Ferrero could not respond to Burnside's optimism. The words came to him as if through a dense muffling wall. Already he felt cut off, exiled from the corps and from his division. Such hard work, organizing the division, finding officers willing to lead black troops, getting them equipped and drilled decently, fighting off the attempts of the rest of the army to reduce them to hewers of wood and drawers of water—to gravediggers and diggers of privy holes. He'd worked so hard, done so much. They'd hardly even let him see his troops all in one place until recently. To lose it all now, just when the work was ready to bear fruit! The humiliation of it. He thought again of the West Point officers, their genial condescension to their former dancing master. How he'd hated that! He'd studied hard to be a good officer. On the bridge at Antietam he'd led the charge into the teeth of that gunfire. Hard work, courage, the risk of life—all of it gone, just a joke again. Ferrero's Minstrels.

Life was simply absurd. A man might plan carefully, labor hard and give all he had to give—then have everything taken away on a whim of fate, the loss of a vital paper in a bureau drawer, the ineffective maunderings of a committee of politicians. Burnside still urged him to do something. What was the point? There was no connection at all between what you did, and what happened to you after.

For the first time in more than a month, it began to rain.

HEADQUARTERS ARMY OF NORTHERN VIRGINIA,
July 19, 1864.

General S. COOPER,
Adjutant and Inspector General, Richmond:
GENERAL: I inclose for the information of the Department a copy of an order which the enemy has endeavored to circulate among our troops with the view of encouraging desertion. I believe that the disposition of his own men to desert is great, and that it is in a measure restrained by the difficulty they experience in getting home. I have thought that something might be done to encourage them by offering them facilities to reach the North, and inclose the draft of an order, the substance of which it might be well to publish and circulate among them if prac-

ticable, should it meet the approval of the Department. It would do no harm in my judgment, and might have a good effect.

Very respectfully, your obedient servant,

R. E. LEE,
General.

10:00 A.M. *Johnson's Headquarters*

General Johnson sat across the table from Lieutenant Bruce. The two officers had grown rather close in the past few weeks. Johnson evidently respected Bruce's intelligence, and had found him a temporary place on his staff. But he had not been eager to report to Johnson this morning. The countermining had so far shown no results at all. They had heard the Yankees digging, and gone after their shaft from three directions—listening posts, auger holes, extending the shafts—nothing had worked. For days now they had not heard any digging. Maybe the Yanks had given it up—the soil here was bad for mining anyway. Maybe their tunnel had collapsed.

"I don't think so," said Johnson. "No, I believe your original guess was correct. Mining's the only thing for them. This campaign has proved one thing beyond any doubt: that no human beings that ever wore uniform can carry a line of entrenchments laid out by modern means and defended by modern weapons. Now here we're down to simple calculations of profit and loss. The Yankees can't let much more of their own blood than they have already—people won't stand for it."

"Ours have stood it," said Bruce. "We've lost more in proportion to our size than they have."

Johnson shook his head. "The two societies are not at all the same. And I'll add this: the military problem's not the same. To take this place, they'd need to outnumber us—four, five to one, would be my guess. They haven't got such numbers; and every time they let blood attacking with less, they're that much further from it."

"I see what you're driving at," said Bruce. "The same principle applies to the Yankees that applies to us—balancing the expenditure of materials and the expenditure of lives."

"Yes. As I wrote to General Lee, we must be willing to spend more of our inert materials—bullets, powder—and save the human materials for the climactic struggle."

"We can't spend what we don't have."

Johnson looked out the window. "I've got details combing every foot of ground that's out of the line of fire for spent balls—bullets, shells, whatever they can dig up. Yankees shoot enough spare lead over here every day to equip a brigade, if we take the care to gather it in."

Bruce sensed that the General was about to grow speculative. and he hastened to change the subject. There were measures he wanted taken.

"Sir, let us suppose that the Yankees will try to mine, and that we fail to cut their tunnel. That they explode the mine, and attack. We've nothing at all behind our first line except for the advantages of the terrain."

"Yes, yes," said Johnson. "The terrain. I was thinking of something. Using the terrain." He sat up suddenly, lit by an idea. "Yes. What were you going to suggest, Lieutenant?"

"A second line, sir, behind the first. I can't think why we haven't constructed one before."

Johnson smiled thinly. "Headquarters was afraid that if we prepared a second line, the troops might be inclined to bolt into it if the Yankees pressed too hard. They don't want to have our last line of defense on those particular hills. Too close to home, Lieutenant."

Johnson turned to the map of the lines on his wall. "I'll tell you what, though. Here's the Jerusalem Road—it runs along the ridge-top, but it's sunken in. A natural trench-line, particularly formidable to any infantry coming up the slope."

"I've seen it," said Bruce. "It's too vulnerable to artillery. We'd have to improve it to make the guns safe."

Johnson grinned. "Yes—if we want those guns to stand bombardment. But there's no need for that—we can't swap shell for shell with the Yanks anyway. No: let's suppose your Yankee mine blows up; their troops come through the breach. There's the blue chips right on the table. How do we rake them in?"

Bruce shook his head and smiled.

Johnson took it up. "We let them come on. We don't do any digging on the hilltop—nothing that might be seen. Let them come on, thinking there's nothing up there. But we'll put a couple of batteries in that road there. And we'll improve some of these little creek-beds down there—good places for reserves to get together. Let em stick their heads in, then pole-axe em, and cut it off at the neck!"

"I like that," said Bruce. "Get them to spend some of that human capital they're so well stocked with."

"While we spend mostly our inert materials—and no more of those than we can afford." Johnson rubbed his hands briskly together. "You know, we have not given sufficient thought to the *science* of warfare—I mean our ability to understand and *use* the forces of the material world. The South has been too prodigal of its spiritual and human reserves; we have not 'used the terrain,' as you suggested a moment ago. As the Russians used it against Napoleon."

"The South isn't noted for Moscow blizzards," said Bruce, with a deprecatory laugh. The man was, after all, a General, as well as a somewhat pedantic former professor of philosophy.

"Not snow, Lieutenant, not snow. But the power of our soil and of our rivers. The material force of nature, that has made the South fertile."

Bruce smiled. "I had a similar discussion with Colonel Davidson the other day. About the wastage of Southern white manhood in the war, while we husband our black resources and keep them off the board, in a manner of speaking. While the Yankees have decided to rob these resources, and turn them against us."

"I see your point." Johnson nodded. "Material versus spiritual or human forces. Something there." He paused, thinking. Then: "Actually,

I had something a lot less . . . disruptive of the social order in mind. Putting slaves in uniform smacks to me of letting the material rule the spiritual or mental. Once give a Negro a gun and uniform, and he will think himself entitled to rule. What was it that Emerson said—a thorough Yankee, but he can make a phrase—ah, yes: 'Things are in the saddle, and ride mankind.' No, we must ride the things, not the other way round. See what you think of this notion. . . ."

HEADQUARTERS JOHNSON'S DIVISION,
July 19, 1864—10 A.M.

Col. G. W. BRENT,
Assistant Adjutant-General:

COLONEL: In reply to your note of the 18th instant, suggesting for consideration the propriety of keeping one regiment of each brigade in reserve for twenty-four or forty-eight hours, instead of one regiment as at present, I have to state that I have thought it particularly desirable to adopt the former method at this time in my command and that arrangements are now made by which each brigade will to-night have about one-fourth of its strength in reserve. I would suggest that there is, however, no good cover for the reserve at a proper distance from my main line, and I would be pleased if the commanding general would direct that certain commanding grounds in rear of our lines, especially near the Jerusalem Plank Road, should be fortified and occupied by the reserves, making a system of detached works. A battery, with trenches flanking it for a regiment of infantry, should be first staked out on each commanding height. In making this proposition I do not desire to prepare a line to fall back on. I think our troops should fully understand that the present line has to be held; the system of detached works proposed will cover our reserves and bring them in a position for immediate service; it will give confidence to our men and discourage the foe; and should any part of our line be carried for a moment, it will enable us to drive the enemy back and to reoccupy that point; with formidable batteries in rear, our troops on the flanks of a breach would not be likely to abandon their positions.

If I may be permitted in this not very formal communication to introduce a very different subject, I would suggest that if the present rain continues until a flood or good rise is produced in the James River, 1,000 men with axes would, in a few days, cut from the banks of that river and float together trees enough to sweep the Yankee fleet out into the Atlantic Ocean, and leave Grant's army without pontoons, communications, or base of supplies, and without the support of gun-boats, perhaps we might drive his army into the river. The freshets in the James River are, I understand, powerful in volume of water and swiftness of current; the trees cut and floated together before a rise could be strongly united, forming almost a solid mass, and no power or Yankee ingenuity could withstand the crushing power of this raft, hurled down the stream by the accumulated torrents of the river.

I am, colonel, very respectfully, your obedient servant,

B. R. JOHNSON,
Major-General.

What an impossible fantasy, thought Bruce, when he'd read the dispatch. *I only hope they don't think he's balmy; he's an easy man to work for, receptive.* But Lord, these old planter types would sooner pray for the mountains to remove them out of their places than they would pick up the handiest weapon—even if it was a nigger—and use it.

Well, at least the suggestion of the second line had gotten into the dispatch. That was real. If that were done, he'd rest easier.

HEADQUARTERS NINTH ARMY CORPS,
July 20, 1864

General R. B. POTTER:

The general commanding desires that you will obtain from Colonel Pleasants as soon as possible and transmit to him an exact statement of the condition and progress of the mine at this time.

Very respectfully, your obedient servant,

J. L. VAN BUREN,
Major and Aide-de-Camp.

HDQS. FORTY-EIGHT PENNSYLVANIA REGIMENT,
July 20, 1864.

Brig. Gen. R. B. POTTER,
Commanding Second Division, Ninth Corps:

GENERAL: The main gallery is completed. I have excavated two other galleries, commencing at the inner extremity of the mine, and running under the enemy's work. The length of both these galleries is fifty feet (not of each). The ground is full of springs where I am now mining, but I could have made better progress if I had not stopped the work frequently to prop it securely, and in order to listen and ascertain if the enemy was mining near us.

Very respectfully, your obedient servant,

HENRY PLEASANTS,
Lieutenant-Colonel.

Indorsement
HEADQUARTERS SECOND DIVISION, NINTH ARMY CORPS,
July 20, 1846.

Respectfully forwarded for information of general commanding.

ROBERT B. POTTER,
Brigadier-General.

HEADQUARTERS NINTH ARMY CORPS,
July 20, 1864—9 A.M.

General WILLIAMS,
Assistant Adjutant-General:

I have nothing of importance to report this morning. There was more than the usual amount of both artillery and musketry last night. The enemy sounded his reveille at 3 A.M. The mine is about ready to charge now, and no attempts at countermining have been discovered. The lateral galleries can be carried farther if thought desirable and further delay in exploding the mine is decided upon.

A. E. BURNSIDE,
Major-General.

9:00 A.M. Burnside's Headquarters

"General Bartlett reporting, sir."

"Thank you, Lieutenant. Send him in." Burnside composed his face into a hospitable smile as Bartlett came limping in through the tent flap. Bartlett was the commander of the First Brigade in Ledlie's division. He had been wounded early in the campaign and was just now returning to duty. He looked awful: his body was slewed round to the left as he leaned on the stout cane they had given him; his uniform bagged on him, and his face was wasted and white. They had cut off his leg just below the knee, and the cork pegleg they'd given him seemed to stick a little bit in the ground, which was still spongy from the rain. Each time he set the leg down, pain seemed to wash over his face like a quick cloud-shadow passing across the sun. For some unaccountable reason Burnside found himself flushing with embarrassment. "Bill . . . sit down, man. Sit down." He waved aside Bartlett's salute, and the man dropped into the camp chair in front of him like a marionette when the strings are cut.

Burnside reached for the whiskey bottle, and poured them each a shot. "Here, this will take the chill off." He smiled, but felt his face stiff and false. The sight of wounded men was painful to him; he avoided it whenever possible. This made him feel guilty, as if this distaste meant he was somehow remiss in his duties (or even less than honorably courageous). He covered this embarrassment as best he could, by forcing himself to go out of his way to talk with the wounded when by chance he met them, to buck them up, make them feel better.

"It's good to be back, General," said Bartlett. "I wanted to thank you for recommending me for promotion to Brigadier. I'm glad I can do it in person."

Burnside made a deprecatory gesture, but his smile acquired some genuine warmth. "Not at all, not at all. You deserved it. I'm pleased you could rejoin the corps."

Bartlett licked his lips, and the shadow of pain licked across his face. Were his eyes feverish? Burnside couldn't decide. "Will I be commanding my old brigade again, sir?"

The fear of rejection was obvious on Bartlett's drawn features. Burnside hastened to reassure him. "Of course! Certainly! I've had General Ledlie hold the place for you. He'll be glad to see you as well. Ledlie hasn't been feeling too well himself." (*Ledlie: there were still those damned rumors about him. Sometimes officers could act like a bunch of old wives, gossiping and tittle-tattling.*) Burnside looked serious. "I'm glad you'll be here to . . . assist General Ledlie if his malaria becomes troublesome." Burnside smiled again. "Anything I can do for you . . . *General?*" (*That should buck Bartlett up! The ink on his commission still fresh.*)

"Well . . . I hate to ask it of you, if it's inconvenient"—Burnside indicated that it was all right, and he continued—"but I arrived early this morning . . . I'm a bit tired, worn out in fact . . . I'm not sure if I'm supposed to report to you first, or General Meade's headquarters."

"Not to worry," said Burnside. "I'll have Lew telegraph headquarters and inquire. I'm sure the formality can be dispensed with." A flicker of doubt crossed Burnside's mind. "You're all right, aren't you? I mean . . ."

Bartlett drew himself up, and forced a smile. "Yes, General, certainly. I feel quite fit, though the leg is a damned nuisance, I'll confess. I'm just . . . tired. Night's rest will put me right."

"Good, good. Don't worry about Meade, then; I'll take care of it. You've heard about Ferrero, I guess." Bartlett nodded. "Damned shame. A damned shame! You know, his troops were going to lead our attack. . . . Now I *know* you haven't heard of *that!* At least, I hope you haven't. . . . It's supposed to be a secret."

Bartlett grinned. "I heard about it as soon as the mail boat docked at City Point." Burnside groaned. "At least they haven't heard about it in Washington . . . not when I left anyway."

"A small blessing," said Burnside ruefully. "What are they saying about it?"

Bartlett shrugged. "Something about a big trick you're supposed to be pulling on the rebs—a mine or surprise attack. Talk is you've picked the . . . Colored troops for a night assault at the dark of the moon."

Burnside laughed. "I've heard that one! Richmond told me that the joke is, I've had them drilling for weeks to teach them not to *smile* so damn much, and give the whole attack away!"

Bartlett joined in the laugh. Then the two Generals sighed, and reached for their glasses to finish the last of their drinks. Bartlett seemed suddenly gloomy again. Pain and weariness pulled the skin of his face tight over the bones. "Well anyway, . . ." he said bleakly, "I suppose it's time somebody else took their turn getting shot up. Better them than us. Damn. Damned if I don't feel we've done enough. . . ." He shook himself. "Sorry! I really don't know what I'm saying. This whiskey . . . it's good, but it seems to have put the kibosh on me. . . ."

Burnside rose hastily. "Of course. Damned inconsiderate of me to keep you sitting around like this! Why don't you nip in and get some rest. You can go down to the brigade later."

"Thank you, General." Bartlett rose. "Thanks for everything." He saluted, and turned to walk out the door. The tip of his cork leg left small round depressions in the damp ground.

HEADQUARTERS NINTH ARMY CORPS,
July 20, 1864—1 P.M.

General HUMPHREYS:
    Have I the power to relieve Brigadier-General Ferrero from command, or must the application be made to army head-quarters?

A. E. BURNSIDE,
Major-General.

HEADQUARTERS ARMY OF THE POTOMAC,
July 20, 1864.

Major-General BURNSIDE:
    I am instructed to say that General Ferrero's application to be relieved from duty with this army should be sent to these headquarters.

S. WILLIAMS.
Assistant Adjutant-General.

Afternoon, Ferrero's Headquarters, light rain falling

He had said goodbye to Burnside that morning, when he submitted his request for relief. If he was going to Washington to fight for rein-statement, it was best he go immediately. The General was going to City Point to take up the matter with Grant and Meade; but Ferrero ex-pected nothing would come of the meeting. His clothes were all packed, and a place reserved for him on the steamer tomorrow morning.

He touched his breast pocket. There was a telegram from Lily. She would meet him in Washington. Lily. To come back to her, like this. Not in disgrace, not exactly. But in failure. In humiliation worse than any official disgrace he could imagine: because from charges there could be defense and acquittal; from this . . . neglect, dismissal . . . there was no appeal, except to . . . to beg a favor.

His aide, Captain Hicks, was standing respectfully. It was time to go and inspect the troops. He had requested this, when he told his offi-cers that he was leaving: to see the division go through its drill, and re-view it one last time.

He had the text of a farewell speech in his pocket. But Oliver had advised against his using it: the troops' morale—they would feel deserted. Perhaps Oliver was right, though some of the others thought it better to let the troops know—they'd find out anyway. Did they really understand these command arrangements? At so high a level? It was his impression that they had only the dimmest notion of army organization, a tendency to call their officers "Captain" or "Colonel" indiscriminately, as if they were back on the plantation.

It hadn't done any harm, though. They obeyed their officers well, no matter whether they could distinguish different ranks. Any white officer, Captain to Colonel, they'd follow his orders well. *My successor as well as I.*

They were good soldiers. Lord, but he would miss them!

Ferrero felt the pressure building behind his eyes.

He walked with his staff to the drill ground. More than half the division was assembled, uniforms spruced for the occasion, flags uncased —everyone not on picket or fatigue was here. Ferrero felt his head swollen with the pressure of grief, charged to bursting—nearly. The world around him seemed unreal, veiled, sounds muffled. "I've scarcely ever seen my division all in one place" he thought. But the unreality stayed, he couldn't shake it, a smothering caul that divided him from the scene.

The troops were assembled in the practice trenches and the woods. There were bugle calls, and the cries of officers. Ferrero watched the blue-black wave, flags brilliant overhead, surge out of the trenches and deploy in lines, and the long regimental fronts going forward steadily with the flash of the long rows of long bayonets, row after row. He heard the long cheer as the first troops breasted the slope of the parapet and swarmed over, the cheer spreading back through the ranks. Up on the parapet he saw the head regiments swinging right and left, the others surging up behind them, all in perfect order as if in a vision. They'd talked of it so often, he'd written out the orders himself. Here you could see the blue battalions moving true to his words, magical thing.

A dream, he thought. A dream of glory. Glory and pain. *I'm not to be allowed to see them through this. I'm not to be allowed to see my words turned into men translated into victory. A father dying before he has seen his first-born son, Moses gazing on Israel. It's bitter, bitter to swallow.*

He held himself rigid and silent throughout the exercise. When the troops filed past in review, he remarked their smiles and wondered if they would smile if they knew? He couldn't bear the answer to that: he suspected they would smile as much for anyone. They were a light-hearted race. One sergeant had said in an awestruck voice as he passed, "Lord, Gennul, ain't we pretty!" And the men around him had laughed.

Standing still, he felt their strangeness. He had never understood them. He felt his distance now, compounded by the fact of his leaving them on the morrow. Already they were a dream. He had hoped to have the vision of their drill to hold as proof of his value, when he should hear—some days from now—of their assault. But he realized that he would not have even that. It was all too much like a dream. Had he ever been a General, commanded a division? It had come and gone so easily, in a moment. It was less real in his mind at this moment than the image of his dancing school at West Point, the polished floor, the elegant figures moving to measure in the dance.

Later, as he tried to sleep on his camp bed, he realized that he had not even remembered the farewell address in his pocket. So he had not even the memory of an emotional farewell, the dream of the lingering image he would make, dying father, as he faded from the lives of his men forever.

Well, perhaps Oliver was right, and if he was, it didn't make any difference anyway.

It *didn't* make any difference.

Afternoon. 4th Division practice field

Drizzling rain soaked the ground. There were puddles in the bottom of the ''rebel'' trench and in the trenches where the men were massed.

Randolph stood in the trench. Another day, and still no pay. Damn white man use you up every time, and never pay you your money worth. Go here, do this, fetch and carry and clean the slops, and almighty *dig*. You have a word to say and they nail you in your grave box, like that poor old man back there.

Throw this over and get back to Car'lina. The cabin and the fields. Greened up good now, and the wet coming just right. Coffee, and Siah getting so big and fine. That brown woman, so tall and smell so good. Oh, that woman. Skin so soft. Breast so fine. Oh my. *Miss you, Coffee. Cassy: sound like a mourning bell inside my head. Lost Cassy. Long gone.*

He was alone inside his head. Like a man in his cabin, and the rain coming down. Nobody in the fields, nobody to come calling, nobody to go out to. They gone to come take you out of this cabin, sell your body away South? They gone leave you alone here in this cabin, nobody more around you? Man alone in his cabin, rain coming down: can't even see the fields. Ain't your fields, what you care?

Whistles and calls of the officers, and the packed mass, black-and-blue in the trench, heaved and stirred, big animal down under swamp water. They moved down the trench. Randolph felt the press of the bodies around him, moving him down the trench—a stick in the stream, bumping against rocks.

Then the smell of the packed bodies of the men came through to him, and he felt the press all around him, like he was part of a great push of water, a great push of black muscle, a flow of blood.

They were out of the trench, and they shifted into their lines, rows and rows ahead and the long rows stretching out from side to side. The rain came down, whispering, and he heard the sound of the whole division moving across the beaten-down grass and wet ground, and the multiplied whisper and shuffle of his own feet filling the air, the soft sound of four thousand big chests breathing, clicks of metal—but mostly over all that quiet long all-over mumble of the shuffling feet.

The white voices of the officers were lost in the wash of the sounds of the rain falling and the feet of the black men moving over the field,

and the single figures of the officers were dwarfed by the long mathe-
matical lines of the soldiers, their bayonetted rifles slanting forward,
moving steadily across the field with a single step, a unison of movement
and breath.

In that moment Randolph saw the division all of black men, no
white faces at all, moving by their own will and according to their own
power, across the field. They would mount the trench parapet in a black
wave, and curl over like water. But they were men, and on the other
side, they would compose their lines—he knew it so well, it was as if he
had made the plan himself, carried out his own commands—and the
doors would swing wide, and the men who marched by him in this unison
would go on through to the other side—a hill, a copse, a cabin in the
woods, a cabin that was victory victory victory. Oh Lord for that victory and the new world.

Cheering in a long drawn deep-chest roar, the first lines took the
parapet and went over, and the whole division gave their voice to it, and
in the rain-filled air, red shone out where they had stuck flags on the
parapet.

Major Rockwood turned to Major Booker, clicking his stopwatch
shut.

"Well," he said, "their morale has not suffered as much as I had
feared."

"Not yet," said Booker.

Rockwood looked up sharply. Pessimism on the score of black morale was not to be expected from Booker. "We can't keep them off *all*
fatigue indefinitely, Books. Do you doubt that they can handle it?"

Booker waved his hand dismissingly. "I didn't mean to suggest
that I did."

"No," he continued after a glance at the flag-decked parapet,
"they're set on this charge. They've taken it to heart. They won't let
go of it for anything. It could be taken away, but they'd never give
it up."

Rockwood was staring at him strangely. But Booker couldn't explain to him the source of these assertions and denials that kept bubbling
up in him. He knew too much about them, and he knew too little. That
was the trouble. He knew enough about Ki Randolph to know that this
attack was part of a kind of religious fable, tied magically to what was
most central to him: his yearning for the lost wife and for the one waiting now in his nearly lost home. What would become of Randolph's will
if he should lose that hope? if he learned that the attack was not going
to help him get the land after all?

And what would he think of the Major who had played his teacher
in the business of getting the land, and in the business of war?

If the letter Booker had received two days ago, and still held in his
pocket, were true, then Randolph's people were never going to get that
land. The letter was from an acquaintance of Booker's who was still
stationed down in Carolina—a quartermaster with whom he'd played
poker. The first part of it was chitchat, and Booker skimmed it, because

this quartermaster was not the man to write out of simple friendship. He got down to business on page two.

Rumor has it that you are "combinating" with some local people on the land sales that are coming up next month. This is a small army, Books, and nobody can keep a secret for long. I happen to have one, though, that might interest you. I'll share if you will. I've got a little capital set aside, and can get more, if you and your parties are agreeable. In exchange I'll give you my information first, because I trust you're a completely honorable gentleman and won't take advantage. If it's not good to you, value for value, forget it and nothing more need be said. It is this: I dined yestereven with the distinguished Mr. Brickhill and our commanding officer, and over brandy and cigars it emerged that Brickhill is *dead certain* that the confiscated plantations in this district will go at open auction. The talk of homestead prices, etc., is just that: talk. The auction will be held in advance of any new Congressional action, under existing statutes. Brickhill's on the ground, and he figures to scoop all competitors. Now what do you think of that? Maybe your local connections have had word of this, but it don't appear so. At least, I haven't seen any moves by anyone except the niggers who are still thinking homestead.

How about it then? Fair trade?

Booker had stood with the letter, disoriented. The facile bonhomie of the quartermaster's tone jingled along out of keeping with the hard fact it thrust forward at him.

They were defeated. Or if not yet defeated, they were likely going to lose what they had all been starving themselves to gain. They could never outbid Brickhill in an open auction.

They! It was Randolph's plantation, his and his people's. Not Judah Bookser's plantation, not to be master of and not to labor on, slave or free, either.

What would it do to Randolph's morale, to lose what he had been fighting to achieve and protect? Booker couldn't make his mind move toward an idea about that. It kept spinning around the letter. The cheap conniving mind of the man who wrote it.

Booker felt a psychic jolt, a flash of ice through the nerves. *What would Randolph think of a man to whom such a letter could be written?* The carefully built structure that bound him and Randolph together in their common cause might all unravel and come apart. *Tell Randolph.* If he trusted the black man enough to believe that he'd stay and soldier it through even in the face of defeat, he'd tell him, sure. And if he trusted Randolph's friendship for himself, he'd show him the letter and not stand here with his insides churning, wondering if the black man's eyes would glaze over hard and permanently, and envision him forever in the rank of the oppressors, along with Hewson and Sinclair and Oliver.

And would Randolph be wrong to distrust him? *Not my plantation* —yes, that was part of it. The other part was that he had found himself wishing, just as he'd finished the letter, that he hadn't learned the truth until after they'd made the attack.

HEADQUARTERS ARMY OF THE POTOMAC,
July 21, 1864—7 A.M.

Colonel RICHMOND,
Assistant Adjutant-General:
 I have found General Ferrero's application. It was with some papers that came in yesterday afternoon. The package was opened by Major Barstow and I neglected to look over his papers when searching for the application. I will send over immediately the order for General Ferrero. He can readily reach the mail boat at City Point before 10 A.M. You can send word to General Ferrero that the order is on the way to him.
S. WILLIAMS,
Assistant Adjutant-General.

HEADQUARTERS ARMY OF THE POTOMAC,
July 21, 1864.

Special Orders,
 No. 194.
1. Brigadier General E. Ferrero having reported to the commanding general that he has received official information that his appointment as a brigadier-general, volunteer service, has been revoked by the President by reason of its non-confirmation by the Senate, is at his own request relieved from duty in the Army of the Potomac. The commanding general of the Ninth Corps will assign a suitable officer to the command of the troops comprising Brigadier-General Ferrero's command.
 By command of Major-General Meade:
S. WILLIAMS,
Assistant Adjutant-General.

HEADQUARTERS FIRST BRIGADE, THIRD DIVISION,
NINTH ARMY CORPS,
Near Petersburg, Va., July 21, 1864, 7 A.M.

Capt. R. A. HUTCHINS,
Assistant Adjutant-General, Third Division,
Ninth Army Corps:
 CAPTAIN: I have the honor to report no change on my front since last evening's report. About seventy pieces of timber were put out during the night; more will be put out to-night; 400 or 500 sandbags are needed for the use of the brigade. During the late rain the earth has settled considerably, and besides many of the bags have been cut to pieces by the enemy's bul-

lets. I would suggest that sandbags instead of grain-sacks be procured. The latter cannot be used as advantageously in the pits.

I am, very respectfully, your obedient servant,
J. F. HARTRANFT,
Brigadier-General Commanding.

Respectfully forwarded with request that, if possible, 1,000 sandbags may be furnished for the First Brigade.
O. B. WILLCOX,
Brigadier-General.

7:00 A.M. *The Mine*

All along the Union lines, soldiers had turned faces up to wet them in the first rain in more than a month, standing in it bare-chested or even bare-assed. Yesterday Pleasants had watched them having their fun, and tasted sour bile at the back of his throat. The fools gave no thought at all to the future: the pleasure of new rain on dirty skin was enough to make them laugh. They gave no thought to the next day, when the trenches would be full of mud, and the sinks in the rear would overflow; and the next day's sun that would breed plagues of flies and mosquitoes out of the stink and ooze. For himself, the rain was a special curse. The ground was full of springs as it was. There was that big quicksand flow they'd had to timber up right at the start, and two smaller ones along the way. The air down at the far end of the mine was damp and chill, despite his ventilator; the men were developing sniffles and colds. They would sit around the small fire he'd had them build at the pit head, rubbing their hands tenderly together, and rubbing water-swollen knuckle joints. The rain had made it worse. The water percolated down through the sand, bringing new springs in almost anywhere, and making the existing springs flush.

Now he stood with Sergeant Rees at the head of the shaft. Already, at seven in the morning, the heat was beginning to reassert itself. Wet ground and hot sun: disease would breed furiously, they'd be lucky if the whole army didn't sicken. He motioned for Rees to follow him, and entered the tunnel, walking at the miner's habitual half-crouch.

The way ahead was flickeringly lit by the candle glued with drippings to the brim of his forage cap. It showed the floor runnelled with draining water, except where they had timbered parts of it to bridge underground springs. The walls were damp, damper than usual. In two places small spouts of water dribbled from between the ceiling timbers, and Pleasants twisted sideways to avoid having his candle put out. Icy water slashed down his back. The air was heavy with water, cold. A smell of cellars, not quite so wet and cold as the coal mines could be. Mildew.

Coming to the end of the shaft, where the two galleries branched to either side, he could hear the drip of water to puddled water, and he quickened his steps to see. *Tank tanka-tank tank tank.* Right gallery.

The candle gleamed dully on the dripping ceiling and walls, and on a puddle that spread wall to wall. Jesus! Pleasants put one hand down into the water. It was about six inches deep. The Colonel stepped gingerly into the near edge of the big puddle that covered most of the floor. He paused, decided not to step in farther. He was making some calculations. Doyle and Dorn stood aside against one timbered wall while the Colonel worked. Then Doyle pushed abruptly away from the wall and walked toward the Colonel, his feet splashing through the puddle.

"Where are you going, Private?" said the Colonel, severely. He was annoyed—the man had interrupted his calculations.

"If you don't mind, *sir*. My feet are wet, and I'm damned cold and chilled through. I'd like to stand out of the wet till you're ready to have the work begin again."

"Watch your mouth, soldier!" snapped Rees.

Doyle ignored Rees, and looked steadily into the Colonel's face. "That's all right, Sergeant," said Pleasants. "Let him by till we're through." The two squeezed against the wall. Doyle moved past, followed sheepishly by Dorn. "There's whiskey for the men when they come off shift, isn't there, Sergeant?"

"Yes, sir," said Rees patiently. "I've had the cooks heat it, and throw in a bit of sugar and lemon juice. It's a good specific. Sir."

"Where in hell did you find lemon juice, Sergeant?"

Rees's tone was inflectionless. "We found some, sir." Rees had paid a good portion of the company fund for the extra whiskey, sugar and lemon juice—to a Lieutenant in the Fourteenth New York, who had a special relationship with one of the sutlers. *A damned bloodsucker, too,* thought Rees. *I don't like boozers, but the boys had to have it, and the damn-fool army would never give it if they requisitioned for a hundred years. Generals were even stupider about getting things done and handling their men than mine owners were; and that was stupidity enough to bury the human race two times over.*

"I want the tunnel to angle back toward the left now, Sergeant. Just about enough to bring it back to perpendicular with the main shaft. Cut in at *this* kind of angle." He showed Rees the diagram he had sketched on his pad. "Same thing on the other side, only to the right."

"Aye, sir."

Pleasants started to speak again, to explain why he wanted the change-of-direction made: they were far enough behind the rebel line, and now he wanted to stay within a certain distance of it along the length of the gallery. But he stopped himself. *No need for them to know. Let them just do the work, and let me worry about the why of it. I've made the mistake of taking Rees, and the rest of them, too much into my confidence. That private's being rude. . . . You let them think their judgment matters with one thing, and soon they're arguing with orders and trying to boss you around. I've got to tighten up here. The damned regulars may not know a thing about mining, but they understand discipline. I'd better get the regiment back in line, or I'll end up looking like a damn fool.*

Doyle and Dorn squatted, leaning against the wall at a dry spot near the point where the left gallery joined the main shaft. They could make out the vague shapes of Rees and Pleasants, and hear voices distorted to meaningless syllables by the walls.

"Damn, I'm soaked through," said Dorn. His teeth chattered uncontrollably. The chills passed through him like gusts of wind. Doyle gritted his teeth when the chills shook him.

When they were working, they hadn't felt it so much. The really bad part was stepping into the frigid water, and feeling it soak through the seams of your boots. Little needles, icy cold. Then your socks would sop up the water, and the cold would grip you all around, and you'd feel it whenever you moved and the water squelched in the boots. They had worked hard on the timbering, laying big baulks across the floor, setting the verticals against them; Dorn holding while Doyle lifted the roof-piece up, and set it, and held it with his hands over his head while Dorn hastily wedged the upper and lower joints with slabs of rock and broken timber. That was the bad time: standing with your feet in the water, socks and boots like cold iron, and the feeling draining out of your arms till the fingers felt numb and dead. If you could move your upper body, wedging or lifting, it wasn't so bad. The blood would circulate, muscles flex and move, part of you anyway was warm. But standing still that way was bad. Doyle believed that when you were working, and the blood was moving, the damp couldn't get into your joints. The blood would float it off, somehow. But standing still, feeling the juice run out of your hands and into your shoulders—you could feel the cold and the damp take hold and settle in the finger joints. *Rheumatics,* thought Doyle. He could picture in his mind all the miners he'd known with swollen knuckle-joints and crippled-up legs. The hands all puffed and twisted up with the rheumatics. If it got you in the lungs, you were gone. For that reason Doyle breathed shallowly, at the top of his lungs only, whenever he stood still holding the timber. He'd only breathe deep when he could move, swinging a mallet or a pick or a shovel.

Pleasants and Rees came toward them, shadows with flickering candles in their heads. Jack-o-lanterns. They went by without a word, though Rees jerked his thumb back to the end of the shaft.

Doyle and Dorn rose stiffly. *My damn joints are full of water already,* thought Doyle. They walked to the edge of the big puddle, and stood there. The lights of their candles made orange eels in the surface of the pond, where the water still rippled from the incoming rain springs. Doyle hesitated, shifted his feet. Water squelched in his boots. His toes were stiff and cold. He sat down, and began to take them off. Dorn joined him.

"Good idea," he whispered. "Damn things are soaked through anyway."

"Oh shit," Doyle whispered. He held his boots into the candlelight for Dorn to see. The water had rotted the edges of the soles and loosened the seams, so that the sole had pulled away from the uppers. "Damn cheap boots!" Doyle threw the boots into a corner.

They rose, and stepped gingerly into the water. The water gurgled as they waded in. The icy water rose to their ankles, the bottom was slimy-slick.

Doyle set one vertical timber in place, and held it while Dorn wedged the bottom. The cold water numbed his feet, and made them feel heavy; the skin felt thick. If he didn't think about it, it felt as if he were wearing shoes.

CAMP ENGINEER TROOPS,
Blandford, July 21, 1864.

Col. W. H. STEVENS, *Chief Engineer, &c.:*

COLONEL: At Colquitt's salient the gallery was extended by the day detachment 5 feet, to a point 56 feet from the entrance: The framing was extended 53 feet; had to remove water that had dripped into the gallery, and placed four frames and accompanying sheeting. The night detachment extended this gallery 2 feet, making a total distance for the day's work of 7 feet, and a total length of the gallery of 58 feet 3 inches. This gallery has now reached a point supposed to be about 40 feet in advance of the outer slope of the parapet and nearly under or slightly in advance of our picket rifle-pits. The officer in charge of the night detachment reports that between 9 and 10 o'clock last night he heard picking; supposed at first it was pickets in the rifle-pits, clearing them out; made inquiries and found they had not used picks or shovels, and supposed the sound proceeded from the enemy's workmen in front of our works. After half an hour—our party having stopped work—the sound ceased and was not again heard; it is quite doubtful whether this sound proceeded from the enemy's miners at work on our front. The water continues to accumulate in this gallery. I have ordered its extension to be stopped, and a gallery to branch off from its end to the left, as the sound seems to be to the left of our mine. At Pegram's salient, at mine No. 1, the gallery was extended by the day detachment 5 feet 2 inches; total distance from the entrance to the back 51 feet 8 inches. The framing extended 46 feet 6 inches, extended by the night detachment 3 feet 10 inches, a total distance for the day's work of 9 feet, and a total distance of 55 feet 6 inches from the entrance. At mine No. 2 length driven by the day detachment 3 feet 3 inches, to a point 44 feet 5 inches from the entrance. Require light at each end of this gallery to work it. The night detachment extended this gallery 2 feet 7 inches, a total distance for the day's work of 5 feet 10 inches, and total length of gallery of 47 feet, 40 feet being timbered. The different detachments made a total distance for the day's work of 21 feet 10 inches. I propose for the purpose of protecting the miners from shells to bomb-proof mouths of the shafts.

HUGH THOS. DOUGLAS,
Captain, Engineer Troops, in Charge Mining, &c.

HEADQUARTERS JOHNSON'S D,
July 23, 1864.

Col. GEORGE WILLIAM BRENT,
Assistant Adjutant-General:

COLONEL: Nothing unusual has occurred along the line during the past twenty-four hours. General Gracie kept up such a brisk fire upon the enemy last night that they were unable to advance their sap-rollers. They again attempted to throw hand-grenades into his trenches, but without success. Brigade commanders report all work being pushed on. A great deal of lead, number of balls and shells of every description were collected yesterday. Private Reamey, Company B, Thirty-fourth Virginia Regiment, Wise's brigade, alone collected 1,567 minie-balls, 2 shot, and 2 shells.

The following casualties are respectfully submitted: Eli-liott's brigade, killed, 1; wounded, 11: Ransom's brigade, killed, 4 (2 carelessly); wounded, 4 (2 carelessly). Wise's brigade, wounded 4. Gracie's brigade, killed 2; wounded, 7. Total, 7 killed and 26 wounded.

I am, colonel, very respectfully, your obedient servant,
B. R. JOHNSON,
Major-General.

Noon. 22nd North Carolina

There had been the usual steady exchange of artillery and musketry fire for the past three days, while men of the Twenty-second were down in the countermine shafts; there had been intermittent periods of heavy firing. So when the mining details from the first battalion were given a day's rest from their underground labor, and relieved by elements of the second battalion, it seemed to Lieutenant Bruce that the most efficient and useful activity for the men would be gathering up spent minie balls and unexploded artillery and mortar shells. The battalion was assigned a section of ground in back of the lines where Federal overshots had landed in abundance—a section well out of effective musketry range, and out of sight of all Yankee observers but those in the signal towers and tall trees. Bruce calculated that there was not much chance that they would draw fire; if they did, there was a convenient dip in the ground between them and the lines, and a long gully off to the left where the men could dash for shelter.

It was vitally necessary, this gleaning of the fields of war (as General Johnson called it). The spent, misshapen musket balls and rifle bullets, the dud shells and solid shot half-buried in the soil, could be remolded or repaired for use by the army. It was a variation on the military maxim that one should as much as possible live upon the enemy's resources and make him bear the expense of the war. It sometimes seemed to Bruce that the entire Confederate war machine was fueled by material taken by dashing cavalry raiders from Union depots, picked up after Yankee retreats, or traded through the lines by Yankee cotton brokers while the Generals looked the other way. Or, as now, they picked up the detritus and offcasts of the Yankee war machine strewed so extravagantly over the landscape.

It was a thought that was suddenly sickening—the thought that the Confederate Army could live and fight as it had on the junk cast off by the Yankee Army as it moved about and fired its guns. He sensed, for a moment, the hugeness of a force that could feed both its enemies and itself. Morale against material, spirit against flesh, intelligence against energy, individual quality against the crushing weight of a systematic organization: Johnson's way of formulating the problem. It came to him that the General, for all his intelligence, was a romantic. The Yankees were not without intelligent leaders, however one compared Grant with General Lee; and the South would have to somehow meet the force of Yankee material with counterforce, or go under. Subterraneous torpedoes, sweeping the river clean with log rafts . . . ridiculous. Living off Yankee scrap iron, also no good. White man to white man, the Yankees outnumber us three to two, and yet we've held them off. Well, these trenches are good enough to hold them off. But beat them?

Bruce watched the soldiers going over the field with bent backs, some of them on hands and knees. When they found a half-buried ball or case shot they would pry it out with short-handled shovels. Bullets lying on the surface could be picked up and pocketed. A knife could scrape the bright splashes of lead off the face of a stone, or dig a buried ball out of the stump of a tree or fallen branch. Colonel Davidson had offered a prize of a quart of whiskey and a pass to visit the sutler's to the five men that collected the most weight of shot. It was a good idea, Bruce thought. The men were sullen and frustrated—a good outlet for their competitive instincts, something to keep them busy and not thinking about the way things were going and how hard they were being used. They reminded him of gleaners in the fields, going over the ground for stray bolls and seeds, or for fallen kernels of wheat.

Some people thought it was a good idea to offer bonuses—meat or even whiskey—for field hands, to get them to work harder. He'd never heard anything very definitive in the way of results from such experiments. Some planters held that niggers didn't care about such things, didn't have the instinct for competition but he'd never heard of a nigger who didn't have an instinct for fatback or bourbon whiskey. Bruce smiled at the thought.

You had to organize the work properly. You had to have some intelligent direction over the whole thing, some plan; and you had to have some system of rewards to keep the hands happy. And you had to have that implied presence of Force to keep them in line when their feelings got high. If you did that, there wasn't any problem about getting work out of anybody, white or black. The old superstition about man's instinct for liberty was for Fourth of July orations. The average man wanted no more liberty than he could conveniently use, and would

surrender it for bread, or protection, or even admiration for a man
with a lot of money, or a fancy suit of clothes, or a resonant voice.

The only difference between these men and a bunch of field niggers,
was that the niggers would take orders better, and they'd sing while
they picked up the lead instead of griping about it.

He was quite clear in his mind now. They would have to bring
niggers into the army, just as the Yankees were doing. They could
match the Yankees two niggers for one without straining anything. It
would be hard to get that by the politicians and the conservative planters
like Davidson there, who couldn't see very far past the gate of the Old
Plantation. Made at least as much sense as subterraneous torpedoes, or
arming the freshet of the James. It would be damned hard to get the
white troops to accept the niggers. But the whites were tired of getting
shot to pieces—they might see sense in the substitution. No other way
to win: unless they got more men, they'd have to stay in their perfect
trenches till they starved or died sick. Lee could do nothing unless they
could muster army enough to fight in the open again. And if General
Lee were behind it . . . the soldiers would go along with anything that
Lee wanted.

He would write a letter to General Lee.

"Why in hell don't they get niggers to do this kind of thing?"
complained Dixon. "If I'd wanted to plow up some damn field I'd
have stayed home and planted tobacco."

"Niggers is too valuable to waste digging up Yankee lead. You
don't take no two-thousand-dollar nigger and put him where some
thirteen-dollar-a-month Yankee can put a two-cent bullet through his
wooly head." Marriot was feeling bitter this morning. His back ached,
and he could feel the dampness still in his joints from nights down in
the shaft.

"No," said Dixon, "what you want for that is some cracker who
ain't worth two cents. Somebody shoots him, you don't even have to pay
the man. Save your money."

Marriot cocked an eye at Dixon. "Whyn't you buy yourself a nigger, Dix. Like the Colonel there. Get yourself a nigger man to fetch your
rations and tote your pack, and take care of these little details for you.
You wouldn't need no two-thousand-dollar nigger. Get yourself a pick-
aninny for half that."

"Get myself a nigger wench you mean. Damn! Now that would be
something *worth*."

"Cut it out, Dix," said Billy. *Her big butt swinging on those
strong legs against the ruffling sway of the calico dress.*

"Only problem is, you'd have to share your rations with her."

"Feed her on table scraps like the Colonel does his'n."

Marriot nodded. "Yea, only . . . last time you left any scraps was
about the last time you ate off a table. Now that's what? Two years
ago? Way I remember it, you been eating that fatback, rind and all."

"Son of a bitch!" said Dixon. "And all the while that nigger been
eaten table scraps and getting fat as a goddamn hog."

Billy sat back and mopped the sweat on his face with his kerchief.

"Seems to me like you could feed a whole regiment off the stuff that Colonel throws off to his niggers!" They looked up at him. They had never heard him speak so violently before. Billy's voice was tight, as if something half-strangled his throat. His face was red. "Seems to me like! Seems to me they starving us in this army, and other folks is living off the fat! Goddamn! And us getting all shot up and sick and run the hell off." *Tommy Woodson run to the Yankees, his teeth was all rotting out his mouth.* "Damn! Goddamn!"

Marriot looked at Billy for a moment, then spoke quietly. "Hell Billy, this army been getting plenty table scraps. We've eat our share of leftover Yankee bullybeef, and damned if we ain't filling up our ammunition boxies with leftover Yankee bullets. This here is the original table-scrap army."

Dixon continued to pick away sullenly at a flat rock on which three bullets were splashed like stars. Billy sat with a half buried cannonball between his legs, staring glumly at it.

Things is getting bad if Billy's starting to feel as mean as that Dixon there, Marriot thought.

Between them they gathered three shells, one case shot, and fourteen hundred minie balls. That wasn't quite enough for the pint of whiskey. They would have done better, except Billy was dogging it most of the afternoon. It was the first time he'd ever done anything like that at all. Marriot was worried.

Billy chewed his lower lip and his eyes seemed inward. He could not explain it. He felt himself in the grip of a compulsion stronger than the voice that spoke in his head urging his duty. Dark thoughts, half buried, rose despite his will. He felt angry, shamed, guilty; played for a sucker.

"Sam . . ." said Billy, his voice dull as if he spoke in a dream, "I figured out it's the niggers they got down there digging."

"How'd you figure that boy?" said Marriot softly. "I'd figure they had plenty miners over there. Coal miners, what-all."

"I figure it's the niggers. Wouldn't anybody else work that way. Stand it down there in the wet and dark."

"Maybe, Billy. I'd of said miners, but what's the difference?"

Billy looked down, trying to see through the ground. He could picture small men with black faces under the ground, working their way up towards him. Niggers. Coal miners with faces blacked up like minstrel niggers. What's the difference? They keep coming at you, no matter what you do. No way to keep them off. No way to keep them down. Coming to cut your throat, and you can't face them and be a Christian, can't run and be a soldier. Dixon with his talk about nigger wenches. The way that Geneva walked down the road, swaying her hips. You don't touch that, you don't think about that if you're a Christian. You ain't a man less you've had one.

I'm going to die here, and I've never had one. I never even put it to any woman ever at all. I can't stop thinking about it, and I ain't done it. So I ain't a man or a Christian, either one.

He thought about Tommy Woodson: *I should have listened, I should have helped him some. I should have held him here.*

Should have gone with him.

Oh Lord, forgive me my weakness. Help me to keep thy command-ments.

HEADQUARTERS ENGINEER TROOPS,
Blandford, July 23, 1864.

Col. W. H. STEVENS,
Chief Engineer, Army of Northern Virginia:

COLONEL: At Colquitt's salient the night detachment ex-tended the gallery a distance of 3 feet 2 inches, a total distance of 13 feet 6 inches. At 8 feet 6 inches from the entrance to this gallery turned off another gallery at right angles to it and toward the enemy's line for a mine . . . the total distance made at all mines being 22 feet.

Very respectfully, your obedient servant,
HUGH THOS. DOUGLAS,
Captain, Engineer Troops, in Charge of Mining, &c.

6:00 P.M. The Mine

The drainage channel that the miners had cut had taken off a good part of the big puddle in the right gallery. But there was still an inch of water across most of the floor, fading imperceptibly into slick-slime as it approached the walls. Water or wet mud: either one of them rotted the shoddy soles off your boots. And if you worked it barefoot, it would rot between your toes instead. Doyle had lost one pair of his boots to it, and that was enough. An hour before his shift he and Dorn shouldered shovel and pry-bar, and shuffled off down the zigzag trench of the covered way that led from the front lines to the rear of the Ninth Corps. Traffic in the trench was not especially heavy. The two soldiers easily passed the provost guards stationed at the entrance by bustling busily along, tap-ping the trench walls with shovel or pry-bar, nodding sagely, and mark-ing particular points on the wall—as if they were some sort of special maintenance detail sent to spot and shore up weak spots in the trenches. The same businesslike manner got them past the occasional officer in the covered way itself, and down to the point where a small creek cut through the trench, and was bridged by four lengths of four-foot plank-ing.

No officers were coming up the way they had come. A glance around the corner just ahead showed none coming up towards the lines. It was the work of two minutes to pry the boards off their braces and out of the mud, and then they were carrying them back down the trench, whistling. Eyes straight ahead, sweating, busy as hell. Saluting officers and passing on, till they got to the minehead.

"Where'd you get those?" asked Corporal Dolan, who was watch-ing the ventilator fire. "Sergeant Rees has been frantic for timbers since Wednesday."

"Private stock, buck-o," said Doyle, and as the last shift came blinking into the evening sunlight he and Dorn ducked under the log lintel and into the shaft, through the mildewed tube of boards and up the crusty incline of marl, to where the galleries branched off left and right. Then down into their gallery, stepping fastidiously around the wetter center of the tunnel till they reached the end.

"Now," whispered Doyle, "now we'll have a bit of comfort while we work. They hunted out some large flat rocks from the pile used for wedging the timbers, and set them at the margins of the tunnel, then laid the four boards across, side to side. There was room for Doyle to work and Dorn to stand and fill the dirt-box; or for both of them to stand dry-shod while they set and propped the log timbers.

Then they set to work digging and filling the boxes, working faster than usual to make up for the time they lost in building their platform. It was pressing their luck to have ripped up the army's own little bridge for themselves; they had better not strain things by sending out less dirt than Rees expected. They had two of them filled when they heard a shuffle down the tunnel that warned them of someone coming, and they each grabbed one box and shoved it through the slime to the pickup spot. The orange face of Rees himself floated out of the darkness, lit up by his candle like a damned Taffy jack-o-latern. Grinning. *And were they in for it now for doing that damned little bit of a bridge?*

"It's your last box of dirt, Doyle my man!"

Doyle said nothing, and Rees showed him his teeth again and whispered. "Wake up lad! We're done!"

Done! By God! Just when he'd got those planks.

"So that's it," whispered Dorn, "we've built the bloody Mine." He stuck out his hand in the darkness, missed Rees's hand, then found it, grabbed it and shook. Rees's hand flashed orange in the candlelight, and Doyle reached out suddenly and grabbed it too, and the three of them stood there grinning in an awkward three-way handshake. "Let's get out of this," said Doyle. Who gave a damn about the planks anyway? They were done.

As Doyle came down the tunnel towards the light, the box of earth dragging down his stooped-over body, he heard thin cheering that grew louder. When he came out the trench was full of the men of the regiment. They were cheering. Laughing. There were two barrels of whiskey, the tops completely off, and men dipping their cups.

Somebody slapped Doyle on the back. "Done it! Done it!"

"We're the boys for digging! Plain and fancy!"

"Damn plain! Mostly fancy!"

Rees knocked on the keg. "Keep it down! The Johnnies ain't invited, and we don't want em feeling left out!"

The men laughed hilariously.

No more digging, down under the ground all wet, waiting for the roof to come in on you.

Colonel Pleasants stood up next to the barrel. He raised his hand. "Gentlemen," he said, "a toast! To the men of the Forty-eighth Pennsylvania Veteran Volunteer Infantry, the ones with us and those we've lost—we've dug the longest mine in the history of civilized warfare, and we've done it on our own, too." There was a rumble of assent. "We showed em how," called someone, and Pleasants nodded.

"The world-beater, boys! We've dug us the world-beater Mine. I say, here's to us!"

"Amen to that!"

The men drank, and whooped. The Colonel grinned all around. His face was flushed, and his eyes flashed. "I will now go inform our esteemed colleagues of the army engineers"—someone made a flatulent noise with his lips—"that the impossible has been accomplished."

"Go tell the sons of bitches."

Now that's it, thought Doyle. *We've done with it. The biggest and the best ever, Lord, but wouldn't Corry loved to have seen it.* He lifted his glass and toasted him silently.

8:00 P.M. Meade's Headquarters

Major Duane had begged off meeting with Colonel Pleasants, so General Hunt took the duty on himself. It seemed that in spite of everything the man had managed to build his Mine. Hunt had never expected that he would have really to deal with it. Army Headquarters had washed its hands of the matter, hadn't given the miners any facilities; and yet here they were. Now the word was that the army counted heavily on the success of the Mine. One had, somehow, to act as if one had not obstructed the thing from the start.

If he had been dealing with another Regular Army man there would have been no problem. Such disagreements and misunderstandings occurred all the time. One did not make too much of them, because one knew that after the disagreeable moment passed one's opponent of the moment would remain one's colleague. Best, in such a world, to be tolerant of error, to permit things to pass as misunderstandings that were, in fact, deliberate obstruction and sabotage. The Army Way was to accept your erstwhile opponent's unstated apology, and accept him, if he wished, as copartner.

But this Colonel Pleasants was a civilian type, and Hunt could see that he was prepared to be disagreeable. He had that flushed cheek and sharp eye of a man who'd been drinking, and was looking for a bit of a shindy—he'd seen the look often enough at lonely posts in Texas and California, and it usually presaged somebody getting into a brawl, and the post commander having them up on the carpet, and then sweeping the matter *under* the carpet.

"Colonel," said Hunt, "I must congratulate you and your men on the success of your efforts."

Pleasants showed his teeth in what Hunt wished was a smile. "Yes, General. No thanks to Army Headquarters, or to yourself. Sir."

Hunt took a deep breath, held his calm demeanor intact. This would be more difficult than he expected. "I hope, Colonel, you have not been under any unfortunate misapprehensions as to our attitude. We certainly wished you every success, although, as I believe we did tell you, our own experience as military engineers had taught us that mines of such a length were impracticable. We're in your debt, sir, for the lesson." Now that was handsome!

"Misapprehension? I don't think so, no sir. We've had to beg, borrow, or steal every bit of equipment from instruments to wheelbarrows. As for the lesson . . . listen, the difference between a military engineer and an engineer is that engineers work with their instruments, and work at the profession. Military engineers put their instruments away as soon as they leave the Academy, and spend their time marching about in parades, or whatever it is they do when there isn't a war, but whatever it is isn't *engineering*. And think they know *everything*." Pleasants' eyes twitched as he spoke, he looked weary, and the angry words seemed to be jerked out of him involuntarily.

Hunt's grin froze. "Well, Colonel. Well. I imagine our conceptions of military engineering, our viewpoints, would differ considerably. But won't you give us the benefit of your insight, sir? I'd like to invite you to accompany me tomorrow on a tour of the lines. There may be other places suitable for mining. Perhaps if we pool our knowledge . . ."

Pleasants jumped to his feet. He understood very well what the General's blandishments were about. Army Headquarters was afraid that he'd stolen a march on them, got a good thing despite them. They wanted to be cut in on it. Burnside was right about them. Meade had blocked things; now he was frightened because they'd come through. It was their—it was *his* Mine! Damned if he'd cut them in!

"I'm damned if I will, General. I'm *damned* if I will. Figure it out for yourself."

He stalked out the door, carried on his anger as if on an ocean comber, lifted and flung ahead. Only in the darkness did he feel suddenly the suck of exhaustion and nervous wastage draining strength from his thighs and calves. Suddenly, in the darkness, he felt very alone. The men celebrating in the trench were far away—Rees, Doyle, the rest of them, enjoying so simply the finishing of the tunnel. And he'd gone too far with Hunt. He'd been insubordinate. . . . Lord, he was lucky not to be under arrest! *I've burned my bridges,* he thought, suddenly afraid. *If this doesn't come off, they'll crucify me.*

A cloud blew across the moon, and the air was heavy. It was going to rain. The tunnel would be soaked.

He'd have to go down there, inspect it. Make sure it didn't cave in. Keep it dry for the powder. Pray that the rebs didn't find it.

If it didn't work after what he had said tonight, it would all be over with him.

July 24. Pegram's salient

When the brigade chaplain, the Reverend Williams, came by, they brought the men up out of the shafts to hear him. It had been more than a month since the word of God had been preached to these men, they having been so long on the line. Colonel Davidson felt it was more than time, and sent the chaplain into the trenches, to meet with them in small groups, being careful of course not to draw fire.

The men hunkered in the wide space back of the battery platform, the chaplain himself sitting on a stump.

"Beloved," he said smoothly, "I am joyful to be with you this day. I have not long to be with you; I am called elsewhere, to preach the word to others such as you are: soldiers of the Lord, soldiers of the Lord. For Jesus spoke to the Centurion, in the Book of Matthew, and the Centurion said, 'I am a man under authority, having soldiers under me: and I say to this man go, and he goeth and to another come, and he cometh; and to my servant do this, and he doeth it.' And Jesus heard it, and he marveled, saying, 'Verily, verily I say unto you: I have not found so great faith no, not in Israel.

" 'Let every soul be subject unto the higher powers. For there is no power but of God: the powers that be are ordained of God. Whosoever therefore resisteth the power, resisteth the ordinance of God.' And Jesus found virtue in the Centurion, for the man was under authority, obeying as he would be obeyed. So for this reason I call you soldiers of the Lord: strong in your obedience to them that are over you, trusting in them that have the power, even now in our days of trial. That's Paul, in Romans, Chapter 13.

"But for them that lust after the corruptions of the flesh and glories of the world, the Whore of Babylon, making themselves drunk with the wine of the wrath of her fornications, for such it is said, such 'are altogether become unprofitable, there is none that doeth good, no, not one.' And these shall be judged, and cast down in that day that shall burn as an oven. The earth will swallow them, as it did the sons of Korah, that worshipped the Whore and made themselves drunk with the wine of the wrath of her fornications.'

"Boys, I want you to join me in silent prayer for forgiveness of our sin, and then we'll sing " 'Lead kindly light.' ' "

Afterwards, when they were back in the hole, Marriot hitched up his trousers where one gallus hung too long, and spat against the wall.

"Soldiers in the army of the Lord. That preaching bastard ain't been near soldiering this war, not that I seen. Fine raiment and ox meat. Shit!"

"Don't blaspheme, Sam," said Billy, quietly.

Dixon threw down his shovel angrily. "Now why don't the two of you just leave it alone, damn it! Ain't it bad enough without you going on about it?"

Marriot looked at him, with some surprise. "Ain't what bad enough, Dix? What in hell is eating you?"

Billy looked at Dixon, and said, "Leave him be, Sam," fearing Sam's mockery would shake his own faith, so strong now.

Billy and Dixon shoveled; Marriot picked away at the wall. "Preachers," he said. "They're sure enough in the army of the Lord. Stragglers, stragglers."

July 24, 2:00 P.M. Meade's Headquarters

HEADQUARTERS ARMIES OF THE UNITED STATES,
City Point, Va., July 24, 1864.

Maj. Gen G. G. MEADE,
Commanding Army of the Potomac:

GENERAL: The engineer officers who made a survey of the front from Bermuda Hundred report against the probability of success from an attack there. The chances, they think, will be better on Burnside's front. If this is attempted it will be necessary to concentrate all the force possible at the point in the enemy's line we expect to penetrate. All officers should be fully impressed with the absolute necessity of pushing entirely beyond the enemy's present line if they should succeed in penetrating it, and of getting back to their present line promptly if they should not succeed in breaking through. To the right and left of the point of assault . . .

Sanderson's first thought was, *It's not so bad.* He had expected to read the order of Meade's dismissal or transfer—rumors were thick as flies at City Point. His next thoughts were more complicated: if the attack was to be made on Burnside's front, then Grant was now a partisan of the famous Mine. And the rest of the dispatch offered specifics about the form of the proposed assault, and insisted that something must and would be done by a date certain—all signs that headquarters had broken with Meade's policy of avoiding the initiative in favor of systematic siege, and was determined to prod the Army of the Potomac into action. Army corps commanders were to be "impressed" by the necessity to take advantage of any giving away or shifting of troops by the enemy during the assault—wasn't that an implied criticism of Meade's leadership and of the willingness of Meade's Generals to take initiative in a fight? No choice for Meade but a frontal assault or a strike at the Weldon Railroad south of Petersburg, and all to be in readiness for the next Tuesday!

. . . Whether we send an expedition on the road or assault at Petersburg, Burnside's mine will be blown up.

As it is impossible to hide preparations from our own officers and men, and consequently from the enemy, it will be well to have it understood as far as possible that just the reverse of what we intend is in contemplation.

I am, general, very respectfully, &c.,
U. S. GRANT,
Lieutenant-General.

Sanderson put the dispatch down, and joined in the gloomy silence of the rest of the staff. Grant was taking things out of Meade's hands. That was clear. This plan of attack had been developed without any consultation with the commander of the principal army in the field.

With whom had it been discussed? The Grant cabal, no doubt, and probably the General's pets—Ord; Sheridan and Wilson from the Cavalry Corps; Butler might have been talked to. And that horse's ass of a Burnside had been down there a few days before, hadn't he? Well, well.

Hunt cleared his throat. "Well, General, it seems our views *will* be considered in this matter."

"But Burnside's Mine is definite! He's quite explicit on that point," said Duane.

"Yes," said Meade, leaning forward abruptly. "He gives us the choice of concentrating for a frontal assault on Burnside's front, or another sweep to the left to get at their flank or cut the railroad. If we did that, yes, then blow Burnside's Mine as a diversion."

"And have the corps commanders use their famed discretion to attack when they see an opportunity while the rebels are defending their flank and distracted by our fireworks display." Duane's tone was bitter, and Meade looked at him sharply. Duane blushed, and lapsed into silence.

Sanderson smiled. Everyone at headquarters knew how Meade felt about his commanders; but it was *not* politic to say it quite so baldly as that. Sanderson moved his right hand in a gesture, asking deferentially for attention.

"It seems a good idea, on paper, General. But—if I can interpret Major Duane's sentiments—it does not take into account the facts, as we know them here, on the ground. City Point is out of touch with us here; and we all understand that General Grant has been preoccupied with Early's raid on the Capital. First"—Sanderson gripped his index finger—"we have our experience of the attacks on the fifteenth through the eighteenth of June, when there were failures of just the sort of discretionary judgment Grant calls for in his plan of attack. Second"— he gripped his middle finger—"the attack on the rebel left on the twenty-second of June, made by the Second and Sixth Corps, was beaten back by probably inferior numbers. The troops simply would not stand any more; they'd been fought out. Third"—and he gripped his ring finger—"both attacks were made with the Sixth Corps on the scene— which has, as we know, been transferred to Washington to deal with Early."

Meade nodded. "Thank you, Captain. You are unfortunately correct. We have failed with similar plans twice before, at a time when our army was stronger by a full army corps, and a month less of covering up in trenches. The only new element is Burnside's Mine"—Duane snorted, and Meade looked at him sharply once again—"which is a . . . dubious quantity."

Meade thought again. Sanderson wondered what was going through the General's mind. He was against the attack, that was certain. Meade had little faith in the Mine, and none in his own army's ability to drive the rebels, whether in the field or from the trenches. He knew his men, and they were tired, discouraged—as he himself was, as they all were. Nobody wanted another Cold Harbor bloodbath, Grant overriding their objection to order their men up into a suicidal assault on the rebel entrenchments. And there was the personal element to consider. This was Grant's plan: how could Meade criticize it, or go against it, when his own head was so obviously on the block, ripe for hacking? Safer for Meade to acquiesce, and let Grant make his mistake . . . except that if it was another bloody massacre, and somebody had to go to the wall for it, wasn't it more likely to be the friendless—the increasingly friendless—and prickly General Meade who would go, and Lincoln's fellow-Westerner Grant who would stay? So Meade would get the axe, and probably the credit for the bloodbath as well. A nice bargain.

"Major Duane." Meade spoke crisply: he had evidently made up his mind. "I want a report from you, giving the views of *our* engineers on the condition of the rebel front, and the possibiilties of success on Burnside's line. I imagine this will differ, in some particulars, from the reports Grant has evidently received from his own people." There were understanding grins. Meade mumbled the corner of his beard, paused, then continued. "Captain Sanderson, I want you to stay and work on a dispatch with me, setting forth fully our views on these matters. For once, I intend to be a diplomat." He looked around the table to see if there were comments or questions. Then he rose. "Gentlemen, thank you for your advice. You may return to your duties."

> HEADQUARTERS ARMY OF THE POTOMAC,
> OFFICE OF CHIEF ENGINEER,
> *July 24, 1864.*

Major-General MEADE,
Commanding Army of the Potomac:
   GENERAL: In reply to your communication of this date, I have the honor to state that the line of the enemy's works in front of General Burnside is not situated on the crest of the ridge separating us from Petersburg that the enemy have undoubtedly occupied this ridge as a second line. Should General Burnside succeed in exploding his mine he would probably be able to take the enemy's first line, which is about 100 yards in advance of his approach. Beyond this I do not think he could advance until the works in front of the Fifth Corps are carried, as the Ninth Corps columns would be taken in flank by a heavy artillery fire from works in front of the center of the Fifth Corps, and in front by fire from the works on the crest near the Cemetery Hill. I do not believe that the works in front of the Fifth Corps can be carried until our lines can be extended to the left, so as to envelop the enemy's line.
   Very respectfully, your obedient servant,
> J. C. DUANE,
> *Major of Engineers.*

> HEADQUARTERS OF THE ARMY OF THE POTOMAC,
> *July 24, 1864.*

Lieut. Gen. U. S. GRANT:
   GENERAL: I have received your letter, per Lieutenant Colonel Comstock. In reply thereto I have to state I, yesterday, made

a close and careful reconnaissance of the enemy's position, and although I could not detect any positive indications of a second line, yet, from certain appearances at different points, I became satisfied a second line does exist on the crest of the ridge just in rear of the position of Burnside's mine. I have no doubt of the successful explosion of the mine and of our ability to effect a lodgment and compel the evacuation of the line at present held by the enemy, but from their redoubt on the Jerusalem plank road and from their position in front of the Hare house their artillery fire would compel either a withdrawal or an advance. The advance, of course, should be made, but its success is dependent on the question whether the enemy have or have not a second line on the crest of the ridge. If they have, with the artillery fire already referred to, which sweeps the whole slope of the ridge, I do not deem it practicable to carry the second line by assault. Now, from my examination as previously stated, together with the evident necessity for their having such a line, I am forced to believe one will be found, and I do not, therefore, deem the assault expedient. Should it be deemed necessary to take all the risks involved, and there is undobutedly room for doubt, I would like a little more time than is given in your note to place in position the maximum amount of artillery to bear upon the lines not assaulted. In regard to the assaulting force, it would be composed, so far as this army is concerned, of the Ninth and Second Corps. The Fifth Corps has no reserves of any consequence and would be required to hold their line and be prepared to resist any attempt to turn our left flank, which in case of an unsuccessful assault I should deem quite probable. Fully impressed as I am with the necessity of immediate action, and also satisfied that excepting regular approaches the assault on Burnside's front is the most practicable, I am compelled as a matter of judgment to state that the chances of success are not such as to make the attempt advisable. At the same time, I do not consider it hopeless and am prepared to make the attempt, if is deemed of importance to do so. I inclose you a report of Major Duane, which confirms my views. If Wright is soon to return and we can extend our lines to the Weldon road we could then advance against the salient on the Jerusalem plank road and make an attempt to carry these at the same time we exploded Burnside's mine. This was my idea some time ago and we have been preparing the necessary siege works for this purpose. Under your instructions, however, none of the heavy guns or material have been brought to the front; it would take perhaps two days to get them up.

Respectfully, yours,

GEO. G. MEADE,
Major-General.

HEADQUARTERS ARMIES OF THE UNITED STATES,
City Point, July 24, 1864.

Major-General MEADE,
Commanding Army of the Potomac:
GENERAL: Your note brought by Colonel Comstock is received. It will be necessary to act without expecting Wright. He is now in Washington, but it is not fully assured yet that Early has left the Valley, and if Wright was to start back no doubt the Maryland raid would be repeated. I am not willing to attempt a movement so hazardous as the one against intrenched lines against the judgment of yourself and your engineer officers, and arrived at after a more careful survey of the ground than I have given it. I will let you know, however, in the morning what determination I come to.
Very respectfully, your obedient servant,
U. S. GRANT,
Lieutenant-General.

HEADQUARTERS NINTH ARMY CORPS,
July 24, 1864—9 P.M.

General WILLIAMS,
Assistant Adjutant-General:
I have the honor to report the usual state of affairs on my line today. The enemy are constructing a new earth work in front of General Potter's right. There are evidences that the enemy are countermining. We hope they will miss us, but we may be discovered.
A. E. BURNSIDE,
Major-General.

The Mine

Pleasants was sitting in the damp darkness; orange candlelight flickered on the oozing walls of mud and wet timber. He had done everything he could. The men had prepared the chambers in the sidewalls of the galleries that would take the powder magazines. He had had them dig and redig the drainage channels to keep the Mine as dry as possible for the receipt of the powder, whenever that should be called for. He had the men at work back behind the lines building the boxes that would hold the powder, building them tight to careful specifications, sealed with pitch to keep the damp out. He had them getting sandbags together for tamping. He had laid out everything on paper, planned the shifts that would load the Mine: first the men to bring down the boxes, then the powder kegs; pack them in in relays like St. Bernard dogs carrying brandy kegs. Then the fuse. He had requisitioned wire and galvanic battery—not come yet. Of course. He could use regular fuse if need be.

There was nothing more to do or to plan. Nothing more to do to make his success happen, to stave off failure. If the rain swelled the springs, and the springs weakened or dissolved the walls, or flooded over the drainage channels, he could do nothing. It was raining now, somewhere above ground.

Or if the rebel countermine found them: an auger screw breaking through into the clear out of the mud, clay, and sand, and they'd have us.

Faint but distinctly through the walls of earth and wood he could hear the counterminers digging for him, searching for him: the muffled *clunk* of pick or shovel or dropped timber, the indistinct garble of a human voice. Was it from just overhead, where the rebels were nailing boards for their battery floor, and sentries were tramping their beat? Or was it off there in the blackness out of sight, the rebels down in their tunnels groping towards him, blindly seeking for his tunnel as a mole might drive towards the burrow of a grub, the root of a tree.

Small sounds in the blackness, scratchings, mutterings, odd thumps and rumbles. Nearer or farther off? Obscure signs, meant for him: impossible for him to read.

He shivered, and felt a kind of primitive terror of the environing earth and darkness. He felt, knowing it for unreason, that his presence might somehow protect his tunnel from the threats that surrounded it. No so. What could he do if the rains soaked down and the walls let go, or the auger screw broke through? Nothing.

Yet he sat in the dark, listening, as long as he could.

HEADQUARTERS ARMY OF THE POTOMAC,
July 26, 1864—7:45 P.M.

Major-General BURNSIDE,
Commanding Ninth Corps:

The commanding general directs me to say that 8,000 pounds of powder with fuse will be sent you immediately by General Hunt, and that Major Duane will send you 8,000 sandbags. The commanding general directs that you prepare your mine at once for explosion, but that you await further orders before springing it.

A. A. HUMPHREYS,
Major-General and Chief of Staff.

HEADQUARTERS NINTH ARMY CORPS,
July 26, 1864.

Major-General HUMPHREYS,
Chief of Staff.

GENERAL: I have the honor to acknowledge the receipt of your note of 7:45 P.M., and to say that arrangements will be made accordingly.

I have the honor to be, general, very respectfully, your obedient servant,

A. E. BURNSIDE,
Major-General, Commanding.

HEADQUARTERS ARMY OF THE POTOMAC,
July 26, 1864.

Major-General BURNSIDE:
Eight thousand pounds of powder have been ordered up. Will you have Colonel Peirce furnish a guide, as proposed, to the position of your train? Lieutenant Edie reports to me that all the fuse, 3,000 feet, has been sent to Captain Harris, your ordnance officer.

HENRY J. HUNT,
Brigadier-General.

I have seen Him in the watch fires of a hundred circling camps;
They have builded Him an altar in the evening dews and damps;
I can read His righteous sentence by the dim and flaring lamps.
His day is marching on.

Diversion
July 25–28, 1864

July 25, 9:00 A.M. *Washington, D.C.: The White House*

"General Ferrero?" said the Secretary. "The President will speak with you now."

Ferrero rose, straightened his uniform coat, tucked his hat under his arm, and stepped towards the door. He had prepared himself as best he could. Against his left breast he could feel Grant's letter of commendation and request for his continued services. It was his trump card, ace in the hole—though he had played it three times this week, to no effect. The Chairman of the Joint Committee on the Conduct of the War—Senator Chandler—had dropped the note on his desk, as much as to say: "Grant's writ won't run north of the Potomac." Seymour, his own Senator, had been polite but noncommittal. Ferrero was "nonpolitical" to be sure, which meant that in this city, in these days, he could count on neither party for friendship and support. And Ferrero suspected that the black division was his nemesis, his mark of Cain: the Democrats seemed to suspect him of being a Radical for agreeing to lead the division; while the Radicals looked at its undistinguished record, and suspected him of seeking to discredit it.

But here was Lincoln, and his last hope. The President rose from his desk, and came towards him, hand extended. Ferrero felt the man's shadow fall on him—the sunlit window was at Lincoln's back—and he felt overwhelmed by the size of the man, towering above him; and the hard grip of his hand, that made you believe all you had heard of his Railsplitter days.

"General," he said in a voice Ferrero hoped was kindly, "I have some inkling of why you're here. I've been trying to make it a policy not to interfere unnecessarily in the administration of our armies, entrusting these matters to General Grant. But I understand you carry a letter from the General. . . ."

Ferrero handed it to Lincoln, and the President indicated that Ferrero should sit down, while the President took his seat in an armchair, and stretched his long legs out in front of him.

"He speaks most highly of you, General, and of your work with the Colored division. Tell me, how are they making out?" Lincoln turned his gaze to Ferrero, dark eyes under shaggy brows. The full lower lip appeared set and slablike. This was the test: Lincoln would hear and judge. What would the correct response be?

"Mr. President, I believe the troops have done extremely well, considering their . . . opportunities, sir, and their training."

Lincoln nodded. "Yes, General Grant speaks of your drilling them while they were serving the army as train guards. I've been a great believer in learning a trade by working at it." He smiled. "You might say that's what I've been doing these last three and a half years." He shrugged. "Well, I reckon that's what pretty near everybody has been doing. You are not yourself a professional soldier? . . ."

"No, sir. I was, before the war, the proprietor of a hotel and instructor in dancing at West Point, though I did have some experience with the militia and Zouave drills."

Lincoln smiled. "It was always a compliment in my part of the country to say of someone, 'That man could keep a hotel.' "

Is he making fun of me? thought Ferrero. But he smiled, as Lincoln went on, "Certainly, General—as you say—their opportunities have been restricted. Their time in the army isn't a patch on what they've spent, waiting their chance." Lincoln leaned forward, intense. "But you know, General, there's the question not only of opportunity, but of capacity. A man might get his chances, and not have the stuff to make use of them. I've known plenty, General. Hell, I've been related to some of them," and the President smiled again.

Now he shows his teeth. I've had my chances: what use have I made of them. Have I got the stuff? Have I? "I . . . I've done my best with them, sir. They've never disappointed me." *Lame. Weak. Disappointing.*

"Yes. As far as the . . . *experiment* has gone, they've proved out all right. General, I've always loved that word, *experiment*. Politicians, historians—I guess they are just politicians who have been to college—they like to talk about the American *experiment* in democracy. It's a test, you see: will we pass it, will the thing really work? Somewhere, I guess, there's the man, God, or whatever who's working the experiment, and will judge: did it fail, did it succeed? If it fails, I guess he'll sweep the desk clean, heave out the busted equipment, and start over fresh." He leaned back, gazed now speculatively, quietly at Ferrero. "This experiment now, this matter of the Negro: so far as this life is concerned, I guess it is *we* who make the test, and judge of the results. There *is* a time of judgment coming. I wonder about what to do: if they can't . . . keep up with us, live with us—you see what I mean— what to do with them then, after." He smiled mournfully at Ferrero: "I've suggested they might want to go back to Africa, or to Nicaragua. They don't like the idea much; can't say I blame them. Looking at it from where they stand now, things look better than they have these two hundred years, but you know: they might be mistaken about their possibilities. They might not have a good idea of their chances. I wonder if you can shed some light on that for me?" He stopped, looked at Ferrero, waited for a reply.

What to say? Was he really talking about policy toward the Negroes, or indirectly getting at Ferrero's own qualities, testing him? Under the rough exterior, the President was a subtle man. You think well of yourself, he might be saying, but might not really be in a position to know. Who could speak objectively of himself? Ferrero did doubt himself, more than half the time. Maybe the doubting voice was the true one. He must try to appeal to Lincoln. But if the experiment failed, if he failed, Lincoln would sweep him off the board with a stroke.

"Mr. President, although the matter is a secret from the general public, I assume you know of the plans for an assault at Petersburg in the near future?" Lincoln neither affirmed nor denied, but his eyebrows came together. . . . "You may not know, sir, that part of General Burnside's plans for the assault on his front include a prominent role for the Colored division. In fact, sir, we are to lead the assault. Plans were drawn up . . . I drew them, I and my staff officers, brigade commanders. . . . We've been training the men for weeks in the special evolutions required in the attack. Sir, aside from all other considerations . . . I find it . . . most *painful* to be deprived of my command of the Colored division, just when our great opportunity has come. And after so much work . . ." He let his voice trail off. *That's it. I have to rest there.*

Lincoln now looked into Ferrero's face, and it did seem that the look was friendly. "General, I am extremely glad to know of this. General Grant keeps me informed as to overall policy, but there is no need for me to know of small details. It seems to me . . . I think I will be able to do something for you." He smiled. "I am not entirely without friends or influence in Washington, although it sometimes seems otherwise to me." His eyes moved to the lighted window. "I sympathize with your feelings about being snatched from command just now, like the bank foreclosing some farmer just when the corn's tasselling out, and the sow's in farrow." He chuckled. "If my managers speak truth, and things don't go any better than they have, it might be I'll know *exactly* how that feels, come November." His gaze snapped down to Ferrero's face, and its sudden fierceness was shocking, unanticipated: "If what you are going to do succeeds, I think we can begin to see the end of this, General. An end that we can all look at, and call it good, even after all this . . ." He waved his hand, and Ferrero's gaze followed automatically, taking in the massive desk and wrought metal lamp, the overstuffed velvet chairs and leather sofa, the shelves of musty books and glowing curtains.

The President rose from his chair, to tower above Ferrero, who rose after him. Again the horny palm engulfed Ferrero's hand. "I'll send a message as soon as I can. Speed, General. It's important to you, and to me as well. Leave your address with Nicolay as you go. . . ." Then he grinned. "I'll await the results of your . . . experiment . . . with great eagerness, General."

The door shut behind him. The hallway seemed somehow lighter than the President's office, though there had been ample light from the windows. Something oppressive in the atmosphere, perhaps the hangings or the furniture. Ferrero left his address, squared his hat on his head. He had done his best. Now he could only wait.

Behind him Nicolay said, "Mr. Sinclair? The President will see you now," and a fat man in a gray suit rose and entered.

HEADQUARTERS ARMIES OF THE UNITED STATES,
City Point, Va., July 25, 1864.

Maj. Gen. G. G. Meade,
Commanding Army of the Potomac:

GENERAL: Before making an expedition down the Weldon road I propose to make a demonstration on the north side of the James River, having for its real object the destruction of the railroad on that side. To execute this, the Second Army Corps, two divisions of Sheridan's cavalry (Sheridan commanding in person), will be required. Kautz's cavalry will also be ordered to report to Sheridan for the occasion. This whole force should be got, if possible, to Deep Bottom without attracting the attention of the enemy and before our own people are allowed a clue as to what is really intended. . . . It is barely possible that by a bold move this expedition may surprise the little garrison of citizen soldiery now in Richmond and get in. This cannot be done, however, by any cautious movement, developing our force, and making reconnaissances before attacking. The only way it can be done, if done at all, is to ride up to the city boldly, dismount, and go in at the first point reached. If carried in this way, the prize could be secured by hurrying up the Second Corps and sending back word here, so that other dispositions could be made. This expedition has for its object, as first stated, to destroy the railroads north of Richmond. If anything more favorable grows out of it it will be due to the officers and men composing it, and will be duly appreciated. In the absence of the Second Corps and cavalry great watchfulness will be required on the part of the other troops and readiness to take advantage of any movement of the enemy. I should like this expedition to get off tomorrow night if possible; if not then, the night following.

I am, general, very respectfully, your obedient servant.

U. S. GRANT..
Lieutenant-General.

HEADQUARTERS ARMIES OF THE UNITED STATES,
City Point, Va., July 25, 1864.

Maj. Gen. GEORGE G. MEADE:

You may direct the loading of the mine in front of the Ninth Corps. I would set no time when it should be exploded, but leave it subject to orders. The expedition ordered may cause such a weakening of the enemy at Petersburg as to make an attack there possible, in which case you would want to spring Burnside's mine. It cannot be kept a great while after the powder is put in. I would say, therefore, if it is not found necessary to blow it up earlier, I would have it during the afternoon of Wednesday.

U. S. GRANT.
Lieutenant-General.

9:00 A.M. *IX Corps Observation Post*

There were two privates and a corporal at the bottom of the tower, tying the telegraph wire through the guides. The wire dangled down from the top of the tower, where there would eventually be a man to operate a portable key; down and through guides nailed into a succession of three-foot posts set in the ground, and then it would go off into the trees and over to Burnside's headquarters. General Burnside wanted to be able to coordinate observations from all of his posts during the time his troops were on the line—that was the official word, but everyone knew it was really for the big attack.

So when one of the privates said, "Brass!" and they snapped to attention, they expected to see Burny's rosy face and luxuriant whiskers.

But it was Meade himself, the army commander, thin and nervous-moving, with his unkempt bush of beard and small bright eyes.

"Commanding officer," the corporal called up to the tower. *Hell,* he thought, *they'll figure it's Burny too.*

Meade, tailed by another General, a staff Captain and a Major of engineers, went up the ladder rapidly.

The view from the tower at that time of the morning was quite clear. It was well positioned: even Sanderson had, grudgingly, to admit that. All four officers—Meade, Hunt, Duane, and Sanderson—swept the rebel lines with their glasses.

If you had been looking for the pleasure of the view, you would have called it low country, hardly any roll to it at all. Except for the occasional gullies and woodlots, an easy ride across a slight rise toward the Jerusalem Plank Road and the Cemetery.

To men used to seeing a landscape in terms of its possibilities for concealing and deploying guns, the rise looked sharper. Even from this height the eye could not see behind the top of the ridge, where the white houses stood. That meant that troops or guns in the road were out of the line of sight, and hence the line of fire, of guns in the Union lines. If there *were* guns and troops there, Union artillery could not silence them. Advancing infantry would have a hard time trying to blanket them with musketry or take them at a charge.

The question was, Had the rebels made proper use of their advantage?

To Sanderson the answer to that question appeared obvious. Anybody who knew his business would have a line up there, and Bobby Lee certainly knew his business. Yet here they were going over the ground again, and Sanderson allowed himself a grin of near-contempt for the reasons that brought them here. Grant's dispatch had struck Meade and the rest like some premonition of fatal illness. Hancock—the best combat General in the army, and rumor's favorite choice as Meade's replacement—Hancock was to be given command of a major strike at the rebel lines north of the James, a direct thrust at Richmond. The operation had been conceived by Grant, or at his headquarters at any rate, and would be executed by Hancock independently—or so it appeared—of

Meade's authority. So all of their carefully prepared reasons for doing nothing on this front had only served to produce this diversion of their strength for a drive on another front. They had made a case for being left behind.

And what was their answer to be? What substitute operation might they offer to shift the weight of Grant's attention their way again? Why, Burnside's wonderful Mine, of course! The project that aroused their professional scorn yesterday, was today their last best hope. Eyes screwed to their lenses. they were searching the ground desperately for reasons to justify what before they had condemned.

The fields were covered with untended grass, light green washed with occasional flares of brown where the drought of June and most of July had scorched it out. But the recent rain had brought the green up a bit. So they looked for the mark of red against the green that would tell them that soldiers had been turning up the earth from deep into the subsoil clay to dig emplacements for guns and trenches for infantry. The sun was behind them, warming the backs of their necks, and shedding an even light over the fields. Up along the rebel skyline a group of horsemen moved—officers, probably, inspecting the Union lines; somebody ought to fire a couple of rounds at them.

The line of the horizon ran flat, except for the trees and the houses. There were no telltale lumps or sudden dips to mark the existence of a second line of entrenchments along the rise.

"It doesn't make sense that they wouldn't have a second line up there," said Hunt.

Meade continued to stare through his telescope. "But it is possible. From all I can tell, General, it seems that they do not. If there is a second line up there, it is not heavily fortified."

"They may have gotten careless," said Duane. "They may be overconfident in the strength of their first line."

They will talk themselves into it yet, thought Sanderson.

Meade shut his telescope. "After our experience last month I'm afraid we cannot call that overconfidence."

"They know Burnside is mining," said Sanderson. "It seems only logical to suppose they would then put in a second line." He had just committed himself to a small, but certain definition of his position.

Meade looked sharply at Sanderson, and then at Duane and Hunt in turn. "We cannot second-guess the enemy, gentlemen. Any number of things may have prevented his drawing a second line—overconfidence, lack of troops, even lack of shovels. He may have detached too heavily to Early's command . . ."

"Or sent them north of the James," said Duane spitefully. He was capable of wishing Hancock a bloody nose, cost the army what it would, so long as his own was protected.

Meade nodded, swiftly, a movement like a bird pecking. "Whatever the cause, we can deal only with the effects. It appears to me that there is no second line." Meade looked at Hunt, who nodded, then at Duane, who also nodded. "Then an assault here will be feasible, if we can have Burnside's mine off at the right time; have Hancock back for a reserve; and silence the guns in the salient on Warren's front." Again there was agreement. "Very well. We will return to headquarters, and compose a dispatch for Grant. Gentlemen. . . ." The three officers preceded Meade down the ladder.

As he descended, Sanderson made up his mind that if a liaison officer was sent to Hancock, he would be the one to go. That would confirm everyone here in the impression of his disloyalty, but things were approaching a crisis. It was necessary to choose. If Meade's best hope was Burnside's Mine, then Hancock looked like a sure winner—over Meade if not over Bobby Lee—and Sanderson meant to be with him when he won.

HEADQUARTERS ARMY OF THE POTOMAC,
July 26, 1846—12 M.

Lieut. Gen. U. S. GRANT:

More critical examinations from a new signal station would lead to the conclusion that the enemy have detached works on the ridge in front of Burnside, but they have no connected line. This fact increases the chances of a successful assault, and taken in connection with the fact that General Burnside does not now think the enemy have discovered his mine, on the contrary believes they are laying the platforms for a battery right over it, it may yet be useful in connection with further operations. I am afraid the appearance of McLaws' division, together with Wilcox's, previously reported, will prevent any chance of a surprise on the part of our people to-morrow. Yesterday's Richmond Examiner also says your strategic movements are known and preparations made to meet them, referring, I presume to Foster's operations. There was considerable shelling by the enemy yesterday afternoon all along our lines, brought on, I think, by Burnside's discovering a camp he had not before seen and ordering it shelled. No serious casualties were produced on our side, but the Fifth Corps working parties were very much annoyed and interrupted. With this exception all was quiet.

GEO G. MEADE,
Major-General.

HEADQUARTERS ARMIES OF THE UNITED STATES,
City Point, Va., July 26, 1864—12:30 P.M.

Major-General MEADE, *Army of the Potomac:*

Your dispatch of 12 M. received. I think Hancock will succeed in getting through the enemy's lines, or will force them to weaken Petersburg, so that we can break through it with the force left behind. Under these circumstances, I think it advisable that Burnside should have all the material at hand in readiness to load his mine in the shortest time. If not discovered by the enemy I would not put the powder in until we think it will be wanted.

U. S. GRANT,
Lieutenant-General.

CITY POINT, *July 26, 1864.*

Major-General BURNSIDE:
Is there any reason to suppose the enemy have found your mine?

U. S. GRANT,
Lieutenant-General.

HEADQUARTERS ARMY OF THE POTOMAC,
July 26, 1864—12 M.

Major-General BURNSIDE:
I wish you would submit in writing your project for the explosion of your mine, with the amount of powder required, that these preliminary questions may be definitely settled. You had better also look for some secure place in the woods where the powder required can be brought in wagons, and kept under guard, thus saving the time it will take to unload it from the vessels and haul it to your camp. Whenever you report as above and designate a point I will order the powder brought up.

GEO. G. MEADE,
Major-General.

They were coming to him at last, sure enough! It had always been his belief that they would. Merit didn't go long unrecognized in this country. If you built a better mousetrap the world would beat a path to your door. Mousetrap! He'd built a beauty, hadn't he? And here was Grant full of solicitude about the Mine. And here was Meade himself all ready to cooperate now, to provide whatever was needed. Burnside smiled wickedly: Meade was a bit late coming around to the proper view of things. A bit late to get the credit for this beauty. Grant knew.

What was it that had changed Meade's mind? Perhaps Burnside's personal visit to Grant's headquarters yesterday—Grant had been completely noncommittal as Burnside had laid the details of the Mine before him, but Meade had no way of knowing that. The man was trying desperately to hold on to his command of the Army of the Potomac. And now, by God, Burnside was the straw he had to clutch at! Much good might it do him!

He would have to think and prepare carefully. He must send his plan in immediately, get out his requisitions on the instant, before there could be any change of plan. There were rumors that Hancock would be replacing Meade—any changes now would only complicate things for Burnside. He groaned at the complexity of life. Yesterday he had been, in his secret heart, wishing passionately for someone, anyone, to replace Meade. Now he had almost to be a partisan of the man. Pull his damned chestnuts out of the fire.

Very well. His plan would have to be masterly, detailed, showing a complete and comprehensive grasp of the tactical picture. It must be absolutely clear to everyone that this was Burnside's show, even if Meade remained in nominal command. But the time factor . . . Ferrero had submitted a plan weeks ago! He could simply have Richmond sit down and flesh out the details with him. That would guarantee IX Corps the leading role in the attack.

And he would specify roles for the other corps as well. That was chancy—Meade was jealous of his authority. And yet . . . if the plan got by, Grant would see that there was one other General capable of conceiving and organizing a grand plan of assault. Then if Hancock's wound worsened, and he had to go on sick leave . . .

Besides, even if Meade retained the command during the assault, if Burnside laid out the plan in complete detail there would be in the record good evidence that the conception of victory had been his own. That would be something the Committee on the Conduct of the War could understand. And the papers too, if by some chance they got hold of the text. . . . Like seven-card poker: if you're holding a possible straight, possible flush, possible two pair, stay in for another card—so many ways to win the pot.

He set to work, pen racing over sheets of telegraph paper. He would reach out and take a firm grip of the powder and fuse Meade had promised him. Not until he could begin to feel those real and solid proofs of the high command's commitment to the Mine would he believe in this favorable turn of fortune.

HEADQUARTERS NINTH ARMY CORPS,
July 26, 1864.

Lieutenant Colonel COMSTOCK,
Headquarters Armies of the United States:
We need 8,000 sand-bags as soon as possible to be used in tamping the mine. Can you order them delivered to us at once? The object in having them here now is that they may be filled and in readiness to prevent delay. Please answer.
A. E. BURNSIDE,
Major-General.

HEADQUARTERS ARMY OF THE POTOMAC,
July 26, 1864.

Major-General BURNSIDE:
What length of fuse is required for the mine?
E. R. WARNER,
Lieutenant-Colonel, &c.

HEADQUARTERS NINTH ARMY CORPS,
July 26, 1864.

Lieutenant-Colonel WARNER,
Headquarters Army of the Potomac:
We require enough to make four lines of 600 feet each.
A. E. BURNSIDE,
Major-General.

HEADQUARTERS ARMY OF THE POTOMAC, ORDNANCE OFFICE,
July 26, 1864.

Lieutenant MORRIS SCHAFF,
Ordnance Officer, City Point:
Send as soon as possible to the ordnance officer of the reserve ammunition train 7,000 pounds of powder (blasting) and 3,000 feet of fuse. Some one will be sent from Colonel McGilvery's to meet and direct the train. Get wagons from General Ingalls and use every precaution in loading the powder.
JNO. R. EDIE,
Lieutenant and Chief of Ordnance,
Army of the Potomac.

HEADQUARTERS ARMY OF THE POTOMAC, ORDNANCE OFFICE,
July 26, 1864.

Lieutenant MORRIS SCHAFF,
Ordnance Officer, City Point:
Send 1,000 pounds of powder in addition to the 7,000 already ordered. Send it early in the morning.
JNO. R. EDIE,
Lieutenant and Chief of Ordnance,
Army of the Potomac

3:00–7:00 P.M. Rear Area, II Corps

Hancock's division commanders had their men on the roads by four o'clock. There were fourteen thousand of them in three divisions, each of which was followed by a medical supply wagon and twenty ambulances, and wagons to carry entrenching tools and three days' forage for the horses that pulled the wagons and that the officers rode. Behind the wagons tailed batteries of corps artillery, field pieces and their limbers hauling ammunition and spare parts.

Their route intersected the roads that ran east-west to and from City Point, where the army's base of supply was—a few regular roads, and any number of unmarked traces that peeked out of the woods where some generations of people had found a shortcut to wherever they were headed. Each of these intersections was a point of probable confusion and delay, if someone's supply train crossed the line of march while someone else's mules were feeling skittish or feisty. Staff officers galloped along the line of march, stationing themselves at the main crossroads to keep that from happening, but there were too many people and wagons on too many roads cutting in. Small eddies and whorls developed in the stream of marching men.

Captain Sanderson took some of these in as he went down the road, trotting his horse or picking it up to a canter whenever he could, heading for the pontoon bridges they had set over the Appomattox. Up ahead was the junction where a main road came in from City Point, and there was clearly trouble: Hancock's advance guard was fallen out by the roadside, wagons all across the road, a group of mounted officers was clumped in the middle of the road, arguing. They turned to look at Sanderson, noticed the staff insignia on his hat, and returned his salute.

"Captain," said the Major commanding the wagon train, "I've got orders from General Butler to bring in these wagons here this afternoon. We're having a bit of disagreement about who's to take this road here, . . ." and the man swept his hand to indicate the road north, up which the wagons were already moving, slowly, to the sound of creaking wood and the whuffing of the draft mules.

"Major, with all due respect to General Butler, I must order you to get your wagons off the road, and give these troops the right of way. We are under General Meade's and General Grant's orders to make this march as swiftly as we can. You'll have to stand aside."

The Major shrugged, indicating the line of wagons moving up the road, the head of the column already out of sight around the bend, as much as to say (thought Sanderson) that "possession was nine-tenths of the law."

Sanderson grinned, and turned to the colonel commanding the advance guard—a man he didn't remember by name, though the face was certainly familiar, probably some regimental officer just promoted to the brigade—so many general officers shot these last few months it was like a whole new army. "Colonel, you'll order your men to seize these wagons, and drive them off the road." The Major started to protest, but Sanderson stopped him, pointing his index finger at the man. "My responsibility, on orders of General Meade."

"You'll put that in writing?" said the Major, his face red with anger.

"For me, too," said the Colonel.

Sanderson reached around to flip open the top of his saddlebag, took out a pad of dispatch paper and a piece of board; rested the board across his lap, and wrote two copies of his authorization in pencil. While the Major had his men turn the wagons off to the side of the road, cursing when some became tangled in brush or tipped into gripping sand, and the Colonel got his men back on the road, Sanderson sat his horse, and scribbled a third copy of the order—for his own records, in case it ever came to a court of inquiry. After all, the wagons *were* General Butler's.

Having finished, he put his writing materials back in the saddlebag, and moved up the road again at a walk, easing his horse off into the uneven grassy strip at the side of the road to get around the first regiment of the advance guard.

On the whole, he thought, it was an efficiently managed march. That was Hancock's touch. He'd gotten his men out of their bivouacs quickly and without fuss, and he'd get them to where they were supposed to be as quickly as anyone could. From the look of things, that speed would require a night march for the men. It would take something out of them tomorrow, but that couldn't be helped. He might enjoy working for Hancock . . . and Sanderson smiled at himself: this was the first time he'd allowed himself to think at length about the possibility that had been working round in his mind for weeks. Meade looked like a loser more and more. Set aside the accumulation of things done too slowly, or half-heartedly, or badly done; set aside even the outright blunders. The man's own subordinates had lost confidence in him, and he in them. The rising crackle of temperament that would break into open quarrels revealed how far the fabric of command had deteriorated.

And now this grasping at straws, this sudden wishful reliance on Burnside's Mine, after a reconnaissance designed (it appeared) only to excuse adoption of a line of attack that was almost mathematically doomed to fail.

If this attack north of the James had anything like success, Hancock would be in the saddle. And a good thing, too. There would be no more of this internal feuding and carping, just straightforward efficiency, professionalism.

Of course, this operation might somehow become a complete fiasco, a disaster . . . that gave Sanderson pause. And there was also the matter of Hancock's health. He'd been badly wounded at Gettysburg, and the wound hadn't completely healed. Hancock had bad days when he could hardly sit his horse for the pain. If there was infection, or if the wound simply wore him down, then Hancock would probably have to leave the army. And if Sanderson had committed himself rashly and completely to him, that would leave Sanderson . . . nowhere. He would have to play his position cagily, balance between the need to make himself known to Hancock and the necessity not to burn his bridges back to Meade.

Sanderson came out of the trees and suddenly there was the Appomattox, a flat quiet stream between the woodsy banks with the pontoon bridges stretching across it—weathered boards on the boat-hulks of the pontoons. A small gunboat was anchored upstream towards the rebel lines, a wisp of blue smoke showing she had steam up; and a bigger gunboat downstream where the Appomattox entered the James. There were piles of hay along the shore. *For the cavalry?* Sanderson wondered, then realized that someone had given orders to muffle the bridge planks. A damned intelligent idea.

Sanderson dismounted and let his horse go to nibbling some of the scattered hay. His rendezvous with Hancock's headquarters was for later that evening in the bivouac laid out for Hancock's men just south of the James River crossing. He could take this time to think quietly about the important tests he'd be facing in these next days. It was as if he himself were a small army, every bit as complicated and multiplex as the great army that surounded him. He had to plan for himself as carefully as the Generals had to plan for their colossal host. Had to consider how to advance himself, without exposing himself to fatal risks. Had to guard his flanks and rear while pressing ahead. Had to keep always clearly in mind the grand goals of strategy, and the details of the tactical situation and balance of forces. Had to take key positions, central positions that could serve as the fulcrum for developing the powerful leverage needed to move the whole of his world in his own chosen direction. Smiles, gestures, looks, verbal sallies and retreats— these were his skirmishes, his reconnaissances in force to develop the strength of his enemies. These were his diversions, masking his intentions protectively, making a screen behind which he could move this way or that, choosing direction carefully before finally committing himself.

A diversion. That was what was needed. Something to cover this move closer to Hancock. Some action he might take that would bring him to Hancock's notice, without being in itself an open seeking of Hancock's favor. . . .

Evening came on. It was still light in the sky, here at midsummer. All afternoon the slow columns of infantry had wound down out of the trees, and tramped across the pontoon bridge—breaking step so as not to vibrate the bridge to pieces. The infantry marched across with a steady pace, the bridge springing and jouncing to their steps like a rope bed when children bounce on the mattress. The sound of the tramping, the squeak of leather and rattle of equipment, came across the quiet water with bell-like clarity. The dark blue uniforms blended with the shadows of the trees. Bits of metal caught the light of the falling sun and flashed it like heliographs, signalling obscurely. Whenever wagons or artillery came up to the crossing, the infantry that had yet to cross spread out on the bank to wait. The wagons took the bridge carefully, the animals plodding step-at-a-time, the teamsters holding the reins in tightly, guides walking at the heads of balky or skittish animals, while the water chuckled along below the wood.

From where he sat his horse at the bridgehead, Sanderson could see, downstream to the east, Sheridan's cavalry crossing by companies in column of twos. The jounce and jingle of the cavalry came faintly up the river. Sanderson thought how swift and keen they looked, compared to the plod of the infantry and their wagons, darting and sliding forward, guidons like lances dipping and slanting, while the infantry moved machinelike and regular. Watching the slow-moving shadows of the infantry, the swift shadows of the cavalry—it was like a sky in a stormy season, when the low near clouds glide by slow and steady, and through the rifts you see high swift clouds going over like spindrift down a rapids.

The river of men that flowed out of the forest seemed endless. There was a kind of shock to it, when all you had seen all day were clumps and broken columns of men in clearings and standing by road jams. There was no place now where you could see the army whole; yet you could feel the size of it, watching it this way: as if you'd been surprised in a field by the slow uncoiling of a snake and thought, seeing the small head and the next coil glide by, *It's a small one,* and the shock coming on you while coil after coil looped out and past, out and past.

Sanderson smiled at the image. Tomorrow the snake would strike. If the rebels were napping, they'd be snake-bit for sure.

Back at the rear of the marching column, the last wagons clumped by the crossroads where Butler's wagons still sat, covered with dust, canted over at odd angles off the road.

The Major walked down the line getting his men out from under the wagon boxes. It was time to move. From behind him, on the road to City Point, he heard the calls of wagoners, and he groaned. What now?

He stepped into the road. An officer on a horse cantered up and pulled in.

"Major," said the mounted officer, "can you hold off a bit there? I want to get these wagons by here quick as I can."

"Captain," said the Major, "I have stood here in the dust all day while half the damned army marched over me. I have an appointment with General Butler I mean to keep."

The mounted officer jerked his thumb back at the oncoming wagons. "That's a wagon train carrying four tons of blasting powder. I was hoping to get shut of it as soon as I could. But since you'd rather have all that stuff sitting here in the heat while you get your wagons out of the ditch there, I guess I'll just turn out and catch some sleep."

The major conceded with a laugh. "Take it on through. —And mind you," he said, "careful of those bumps!"

CITY POINT, *July 26, 1864—9:30* P.M.

Maj. Gen. GEORGE G. MEADE:

The enemy may show such a force between Deep Bottom and Richmond as to make our movement there more hazardous than was expected. If so, the Second Corps and the cavalry will be withdrawn tomorrow night, and by withdrawing them quietly and rapidly it may be practicable to make an assault on their return.

U. S. GRANT,
Lieutenant-General.

DEEP BOTTOM, *July 27, 1864—12:30* A.M.

Maj. Gen. G. G. MEADE,
Commanding Army of the Potomac:

GENERAL: The head of my column will be here soon. I judge the instruction contemplated no serious opposition in getting on the New Market and Malvern Hill road, but General Foster tells me that there are seven brigades of Hill and Longstreet in his front, and that they are pretty well entrenched from New Market to Chaffin's Bluff, and they are extending the line below on the Malvern Hill Road. He says the rifle pits have abatis and palisades. They will take time to take, I imagine, and the operations will lose the character of a surprise. We will not be ready before daylight, and then in view of the enemy. There is an open space in front of their works, General Foster says, about 500 yards wide. I will proceed at the earliest hour to accomplish what I can.

WINF'D S. HANCOCK,
Major-General.

Late in the evening, Sanderson had ridden out to the Broadway Landing pontoon bridge to meet with Sheridan and his commanders, and watch the last of the horse artillery being brought over. He'd had supper—and what was better, a bit of hot coffee—with some of the boys he'd known while he was on McClellan's staff—Custer was there, commanding a brigade of Michiganders now. He'd been Mac's fair-haired boy for some reason—a vain ass, but brave to recklessness. It was proof of the perversity of this democratic army that a self-promoting swaggerer like Custer should have become a General, and Sanderson—his senior in age, and at the Point, and his superior as a professional—should still be a Captain. Well, well: one had to scurry round, there was no point in complaining about Custer's success; the thing to do was take a leaf from his book and get one's *own* star.

"Big doings." said Custer nodding toward the columns that still shuffled by their bivouac. They sat near the fire, and chatted, while Custer's orderly tended Sanderson's horse. Heat and sweat brought out the slick smell of the perfumed ointment the General used on his long hair.

Sanderson nodded. "I understand General Grant has high hopes for this expedition." *Now let's see what Custer knows about it.*

"Oh yes. Infantry to hold the door open for us, so we can shake loose and tear up some railroad for him. Our pleasure. Beats sitting in a trench up to your ass in mud."

Sanderson lifted his coffee cup in a mock toast. Custer regarded him with a curious intensity. *There's something he wants to know,* thought Sanderson. *Let him stew awhile; he'll never hold it.*

"How are things at General Meade's? They feed you all right? Custer grinned, as it were ingenuously.

"Oh, all right. Not the fleshpots of City Point, but well enough."

Custer drank his coffee, and dashed the grounds into the fire. He looked at Sanderson and asked, "What do you hear?"

"What do you mean, General?"

Custer made a deprecatory gesture. "There's talk that Meade's to go north." He pursed his lips, hesitated, then said, "Think they'll bring *him* back?"

There was no need to say whom they meant.

"No way of knowing, Armstrong, is there?"

"What would you do if you were Lincoln? Bring him back? Too dangerous, wouldn't you think?"

Sanderson shrugged, Custer nodded. "I think so too." Custer rose. The firelight shone on his high boots, and the gold braid on his jacket sleeve. "Little Phil's a damn good cavalryman," he said, as if apropos of nothing.

Sanderson rose as well. "Give him my respects."

The orderly woke him at 3:00 A.M., the sky washed milky gray with the false dawn. He felt the chill of the new day, the strange hour. You never see the world this time of the day unless something is going to happen.

Barlow's division was coming across the James River bridge. The river steamed. The division appeared to be an army of ghosts, shadows, its cased colors like the skeletons of flags from which the colored flesh had fallen.

Once across the bridge the regiments formed into line, brigades forming out of the regiments as they accumulated, and the first line was going up the slope from the bank toward where there was a dark shadow of a line of trees, and behind them the second brigade was coming across the bridge and forming. The First Brigade, deployed in a long open line as skirmishers, was firing at something. Sanderson nudged his horse up closer to where Barlow, lean and rumpled, sat with his staff. The Second Brigade was formed. A rider came from the front, spatter-dash through the puddles and wet grass. Through the mist they heard the deep boom of a cannon. They stopped talking, and looked toward the front.

The second Brigade, regiments deployed in columns of companies, went forward, and Barlow turned to Sanderson.

"They've found the line of entrenchments. There's a battery, three, maybe four guns. When the rest of the division is over, we'll make a try for it."

Sanderson nodded. "I'll stay awhile. Will it be all right for me to go forward with the attack?"

Barlow shrugged. "If you want to."

Sanderson took his pistol out of the holster and checked the bullets in the revolving chamber. He loosened the sword in its scabbard. It was perhaps a bit reckless to go in with this preliminary attack. Meade would be expecting to hear from him, and the front line was not the place for a staff officer. Still, he told himself, it was important to get the feel of things. And there were no stars to be found behind the lines. Custer's career proved that.

The first action came at 5:00 A.M. The First Division was over, the Second coming up slowly, delayed for some reason. Barlow had one brigade in support, another spread to the flank, another ready to go on through. There was a patch of open swale, a belt of trees, smoke hanging low and dirty in front of it.

As Sanderson rode forward, he saw the rows of knapsacks left where the men had dropped them, glad no doubt to be rid of the load after their weary night marching up here. There was the line of attack, formed up, lying down behind a rail fence, some dips in the ground.

Whistles shrilled, and the drums began rolling the sound of rain on a tin roof. Two guns boomed from in front. The men heaved themselves up out of the dewy grass, and went forward in their lines, trotting, the officers walking their horses between the companies.

The flags were uncased, and color rippled from the staffs that dipped and pointed toward the line of trees. Sanderson's horse shied at the metal flies buzzing and biting. He kept his eyes ahead, fixed on the distant wall of smoke, and scarcely felt the hot breath when the twenty-pounder shell *whoofed* into the line down to his right. The troops began running. He stirred his horse to a trot, the jolts pounding up his body, the sword flashing out, pointing. He let the men run a bit ahead, then put his horse forward with a rush.

At a palisade of pointed stakes he couldn't keep the horse from lifting and going over, and he felt himself hang weightless in the air, sword swing loosely like some nightmare weapon brandished over his own head. There was a jolt when he hit, the horse stoppable suddenly with that jolt: he wrung back on the reins.

Men were coming by him through the broken stakes of the palisade, bundles of darkness rushing by yelling.

There were men waving flags on the parapet.

He shook his head to clear it, and dismounted.

There were four guns, big Parrotts, in the battery. Two had never fired, as far as he could tell. A half dozen men in gray and homespun sat despondent at the foot of the guns. One had a bloody rag around his arm. Another chewed tobacco, and spat against the hub of the wheel opposite him. He hit it every time.

From the east, where the right flank of the First Division lay, somewhere, came the bump of heavy guns. If there was a rebel counterblow coming in on the right, there would be bad trouble for these troops. Sanderson turned his horse, and headed toward the right. The officers supervising the carrying off of the wounded, the manning of the trenches, enviously watched him go. Staff officers could satisfy their curiosity almost any time they had a mind to. Uncertainty and doubt, the heavy weight of the line officer, was not something they had to live with.

The grassy field was full of dark boulders. Sanderson felt his horse lift, instinctively, to glide over them, even when they cried out.

HEADQUARTERS SECOND CORPS,
July 27, 1864—7:25 A.M.

Major-General MEADE,
Commanding Army of the Potomac:
The enemy have opened another battery of six guns on my extreme right. This detains me from any advance, although I am feeling my way and trying to attack that battery. My last brigade of infantry is crossing the river and the cavalry will follow immediately. Since all chances of surprise have failed it is a question now whether the cavalry shall endeavor to break through at once or wait until I advance farther up the creek. The guns captured, which I have drawn in, are four 20-pounder Parrotts.

WINF'D S. HANCOCK,
Major-General, Commanding.

4:00 P.M. *The Mine*

The orders came down to load the powder in the daylight. Some of the men of the Forty-eighth didn't like it. The enemy threw shells at every working party they saw, and it wouldn't do to be shot at while you were carrying a keg of powder. They'd waited through three nights, too, when it would have been safe.

Pleasants and Rees had gone with four companies from the regiment to take the powder up from the depot established near Burnside's headquarters. Pleasants signed the receipt for it—eight thousand pounds of black blasting powder in 320 twenty-five-pound kegs a single man could carry. "Mind smoking now," said the Captain who surrendered the stuff to Pleasants. Pleasants grinned, and Rees and the men with him laughed aloud. Things were funny today. They were nervous, felt like laughing. The perilous kegs sat squat and stolid in the wagonbeds.

They drove the wagons to the point where the covered way began zigzagging two hundred yards forward toward the front lines. Each keg had to be lifted carefully down from the wagons, and set down and rolled to where the men were rigging the slings for the kegs. The slings were to be worn over back and shoulder to keep tired arms from letting a keg go. Don't drop one hard: powder was chancy stuff, a leak of black grains from one might catch a spark somehow (never mind how) and blow the carriers and anyone nearby into fragments; maybe even start a chain of explosions that would obliterate entirely the battalion of carriers, sending skyward some weird undecipherable signal for the rebels to puzzle over. By the time they were unloading the third wagon, the first squad was on its way back for a second load, passing the second as it came down the covered way.

Up at the minehead, Rees and Lieutenant Douty were organizing the loading of the Mine. Large boxes had been prepared, and set in niches in the ends and sides of the two lateral galleries. Above each a candle was set, as above the grotto of a saint. *The powder was the offering,* Doyle thought.

Here came the first kegs around the corner and into the trench, the men warned by Rees to stay low. The rebs must not see, must not suspect. One coehorn shot into the trench now, and it would be *their* line blown skyhigh.

The men stooped low, lower, the drag of the slings crueler, numbing to back and shoulders as they shuffled down the tunnel. Crouching, doubled over, they went down into the tunnel; Doyle went, dropping to one knee as the strain told on his back, weakening him to where he had to stop. Genuflection. Stations of the Cross. Here this man labored, here that one broke his shin. The Place of the Quicksand, the Place of Marl, the Place where Corry last dug. There were muddy wet patches on the floor, patches covered with boards. The loud sound of breathing filled the tunnel—strange, to Doyle's ears, since they'd never had this many souls down the Mine before, but only two, then four men at a time working.

He turned left in the flickering light, obedient to instructions. There was a corporal in the gallery, indicating the niche to be filled, the candle over it—nobody carrying powder would wear a candle on his hat brim as they'd done when mining.

The corporal kept wiping his face with his hands. Doyle, winded from the effort, breathing hard, set his heavy keg like a big stone, *clunk,* in the box.

"Doyle, will you take my watch for me? I'm feeling sickly." The orange light made the sick corporal look hale, but Doyle, tired anyway, nodded.

He sat on a bit of rock in the corner, to wait for the next bunch. He was finding it very difficult to catch his breath. Difficult to take a full breath, it seemed, as if someone were leaning hard against his stomach, holding him from breathing. He forced a deep breath into his lungs— the muscles stiff across his front somehow; the air went in, but didn't satisfy. Dizzy feeling, nauseated, light in the head. The little panicky flutters about how hard the breathing was, how little it seemed to take up.

What is it? Too many people down in this hole breathing up the air? He snuffed it. In a mine you could smell the gas sometimes. There was a whiff of something now, a swampy-sickly smell.

Here was the next bunch. Their shuffling seemed to bong the air full of sound. He was shaky, woozy; he could feel the blood pounding in the top of his head.

"Put it in, boys, and then move out real quick. There's some bad air down here. It's got me feeling dipsy."

They seemed to swim toward daylight so slowly, so slowly. He wasn't choking, but the panicky flutter was strong, he wanted to breathe free, he wanted to breathe free.

They were out of the tunnel at last. Doyle sat with his head between his knees. *A thing to destroy ourselves, a thing to destroy ourselves,* he thought.

Like dark shapes in the sickening fog that enveloped him, the next gang floated past Doyle, the kegs of powder slung in front of their chests like nigger babies bound up against their mothers' breasts, leaving their arms free to do their work.

DEEP BOTTOM, VA., July 26, 1864—3:30 P.M.
(Received 3:50 P.M.)

Major-General HANCOCK:

In passing to the front, I left your headquarters to my left and all the infantry on the same side. Have consequently been riding for near two hours without finding you. In looking at the situation, I do not see that much is likely now to be done. If, however, you can push past the enemy's flank and double him back on Chafflin's Bluff, so as to let the cavalry out to perform their part of the expedition, do so. If you do not find this practicable, remain on the north side of the James until you receive further orders. There has been no further movement of troops from the south side of the river to interfere with you. All there is in your front is supposed to be seven brigades with a small force of cavalry. I will now return to headquarters. Please direct your dispatches to be duplicated, one going to me and one to General Meade.

U. S. GRANT,
Lieutenant-General.

HEADQUARTERS SECOND ARMY CORPS,
Deep Bottom, July 27, 1864—4 P.M.

General GRANT:

I regret not seeing you, having waited at the front where
I was told you were coming. I have two divisions feeling for the
enemy's left. It takes a great deal of time and separates my
command very much, owing to the nature of the woods in which
the operations are connected. I shall be as cautious as possible
to avoid any bad luck. When night comes I will telegraph you
whether I find the left or not. General Barlow will either assault what he supposes to be the left, or attack with a regiment,
shortly, in the way of reconnaissance. I will try and carry out
your views, but doubt whether anything can be done, though it
is possible we may frighten the enemy into abandoning his line
or re-enforcing it. The troops are very tired, having no rest
since night before last, and with no opportunity of making coffee. What is not done this afternoon cannot be done to-night. I
would have accomplished more except for the weariness of my
command this morning, consequent on the fatiguing march.

WINF'D S. HANCOCK,
(Duplicate to General Meade.)   *Major-General.*

HEADQUARTERS CAVALRY CORPS, ARMY OF THE POTOMAC
July 27, 1864—4:17 P.M.

Major-General HANCOCK,
Commanding Second Army Corps:

I have one division on the road from New Market to Long
Bridge, on the left of the enemy's line. I will get the intersec-
tion of the Central road to Richmond and this road if possible,
and immediately. I am not very far from the right of your line.

Very respectfully,

P. H. SHERIDAN,
Major-General, Commanding.

7:00 P.M. New Market Road

By evening, Captain Sanderson was convinced that Hancock's offensive was going to fail, and that all of the night's marching and day's
fighting for infantry and cavalry would amount only to a diversion—a
diversion on behalf of that monstrous Mine of Burnside's.

After going in with Barlow's infantry, Sanderson had ridden out
to the right, where the cavalry was making its sweep around the flank
to hit the railroad north of Richmond, and try to slide in behind the
rebel trenches to take the capital. He had reported to Sheridan, who received the news of Hancock's slow movement with quick nods of his
bullet-shaped head. He was a small dark man—almost Italian-looking—
a black Irishman with small eyes that were almost all pupil, like those

of a small predatory animal. He seemed hostile, but was perhaps only intense as he turned away to snap his orders. Hancock's slowness was perhaps Sheridan's chance to win the day by himself, and the word was that Sheridan was a man to like such chances. And there was Captain Sanderson, just on the spot to watch Little Phil try his luck—and of course to show the man his own quality. He'd even gone in with a charge of the Second U.S. Cavalry that Sheridan had ordered to develop the enemy on his front—Sanderson's second charge of the day, this time in the drunken atmosphere of thunder that horses hooves make when two hundred of them take a broad field in a gallop while the bugles shrill. His second charge . . .

Well, if that had impressed Phil Sheridan it didn't show. And all the charge had shown him was that even though the lines were sparsely held out here, there were still lines behind lines getting filled slowly with troops as Lee sent his mobile reserves in to reinforce the capital. Neither Custer with his gallopers nor Hancock with his plodding infantry was going to carry these works with the kind of rush Grant had called for. And so it was all up, all up, unless Hancock was ready to hit the rebel line with the full weight of a disciplined, highly motivated army corps.

Sanderson was taking Sheridan's dispatches back to Hancock. Not until he was down the road, out of sight and sound of the cavalry, did his exhaustion hit him, in a black wave rising out of his hips and the pit of his stomach, so that he almost reeled in the saddle. Two charges in one day, and he'd been riding nearly since midnight the night before. Practically without guidance, his horse paced slowly down the road southward.

When he smelled the strong burnt odor of coffee boiling, and spotted the wisp of smoke through the trees, his body rebelled, and he threw himself from the horse and clung to the saddle as he led his horse to the fireside.

There were half a dozen privates in blue, and a corporal. "Gentlemen," called Sanderson as he came up (in case they might be trigger-happy), "mind if I join you? I could use a cup of that." The corporal waved him to a seat. He sat crosslegged, and proffered his hip flask of brandy. The corporal filled his tin cup with the scalding black liquid. Sanderson burned his lips; blew on it. He drank thirstily, unable to wait for it to cool. "What outfit?" he asked.

"Sixty-third Ohio—Barlow's division. We got left behind and we're trying to catch up with them. Can't seem to find them." The others nodded vigorously.

Not trying all that hard to catch up, thought Sanderson. But it was prudent to say nothing, nod, and then, "You boys are way off your reckoning. Barlow's division is north and west of here. Nothing but cavalry where you're going." It wasn't a good sign that there were troops from Barlow's division, first over the bridge, still not reorganized.

Riding toward headquarters later, this impression was confirmed. The closer one got to headquarters the more one saw the fields and road-sides spotted with clumps of coffee boilers, troops obviously away from their regimental and brigade organizations. There were still guns coming up from the bridges, making little road jams with the empty supply wagons and ambulances drifting back from the front.

By the time he reached the campfires around Hancock's headquarters, he had a pretty fair idea of the state of the advance. It was slow work, and Hancock's men had not hit with much weight. A combination of tired-out and badly shot-up troops, and a long difficult march; nobody could have made them march or hit harder than Hancock, but it was too much to ask of the men at this point. And it wasn't ever easy, in the best of times, to catch the rebels by surprise.

He delivered the dispatches to Hancock in person. Hancock was a big man, the kind of man that flesh looked good on—his clean shirt-front was usually well filled out, and his tanned cheeks swelled sleekly around luxuriant beard and mustache. But this was not the Hancock Sanderson knew. The man was hollow-cheeked and bleary-eyed, and his clothes hung on him. The stories of his unhealed Gettysburg wound must be true then. The man was worn out. His handshake lacked force.

Sanderson, weary as he was, felt that his own reserves of strength had not yet been tapped. What a contrast to this wasted General and his fagged-out troops! He'd charged twice that day, ridden with dispatches and on scout; and he could do as much tomorrow: while Hancock grew paler, and his troops stumbled blind-tired to find the enemy, did that after too much time and trouble, then sat down to rest.

That meant that this attack of Hancock's was going to come to nothing. They might gain a few yards of ground, take an entrenched line, wear Lee's mobile reserve out with marching; but when it was over there would still be manned and fortified lines between Hancock and Richmond. Not a great failure perhaps—although they would have to watch their flanks, Lee might yet surprise Hancock's force with one of his patented maneuvers against the flank and rear. But certainly there was no hope of a great success here. And when you put that together with Hancock's pain-thinned features and air of failing health, you had to conclude that the handsome commander of II Corps would have neither the prestige nor the strength to take over from Meade.

Which put Captain Sanderson in an awkward spot! If Humphreys suspected disloyalty in his volunteering to act as liaison with Hancock, he would find it most difficult maintaining himself in good grace at headquarters. Against that he could offer . . . what? His two charges today might help him get his star under Hancock, but what would they count for with Meade if he was suspected of disloyalty?

Well, he could be the bearer of tidings that Meade and Humphreys would consider good. He could be the first to tell them authoritatively, and with convincing detail, that Meade was as safe from Hancock as . . . as Richmond was safe from Hancock, and that was safe indeed. Weary or not, he'd go tonight. Just a quick bite, and a catnap.

And after he'd delivered his news, he'd have to make sure that he did not seem to question, by word or expression, the plan that now would be the only arrow left in Meade's quiver—the wonderful Burnside Mine. He'd be as helpful about the damn thing as he could be, he'd swallow doubts shadow and all, he'd go liaison to Burnside if he had to, and play the spy. If Humphreys accepted him back on those terms, and if only they'd mention him in dispatches for those two charges today, he might get that star after all.

HEADQUARTERS SECOND ARMY CORPS,
July 27, 1864—6 P.M.

General MEADE:
    I have been engaged this P.M. in trying to find the enemy's force. As far as I went I did not find it. General Sheridan informs me he found it beyond the Charles City Road. I had not force nor time enough to develop to that point. Wherever I struck the enemy's lines I found his infantry. We also attacked the James end, but after a short contest we found the line did not end. We found him in rifle pits and in force . . . I will await your orders. . . .

WINF'D S. HANCOCK,
Major-General.

HEADQUARTERS ARMY OF THE POTOMAC,
July 27, 1864—10 P.M.

Major-General BURNSIDE:
    Hancock will probably remain across the James to-morrow, so that the mine will probably not be sprung till after to-morrow. Under the circumstances it would perhaps be better not to tamp the main gallery or so completely finish the loading as to endanger the efficacy of the mine in case of delay; at any rate there is no immediate hurry. Hancock found the enemy in considerable force in his front to-day, and has not made much progress since morning, but he is going to try it again to-morrow.

GEO G. MEADE,
Major-General.

July 27, Midnight. The Mine

Rees kept the men at work all day and into the night, mephitic vapors or no mephitic vapors. When the air in the Mine became unbearably foul, he'd take fifteen minutes break and start again. They began to fall out as strength failed them, utterly spent with hauling and scuttling through the narrow trenches and down the tunnel. They fell out by ones and twos at first, and later on by squads, by platoons. So far as Pleasants could tell, Rees had calculated their strength precisely. The last kegs went in as the last of the strength went out of the last platoon. The work of muscles completed, it was now the turn of Pleasants himself, and Rees, to set the fuses and make the final arrangements for firing the Mine.

For Pleasants, the Mine was becoming as unreal as the men had already become, abstracted into a mathematics of tremendous signification. Scarcely physical to him any longer, it had become a thing of numbers and of arguments on paper, a sacred text to be propagated and defended desperately against the fatal skepticism and downright mockery of his great enemy—the Engineering Department of the Army of the Potomac.

He wore his roll of fuse like a hair shirt, its annoyance reminding him that the engineers had made their final denial, reiterated one last time their implacable rejection of Pleasants, of the Mine. He had requested—weeks ago—the galvanic battery and wires that would permit a precise timing of the explosion. In an instant, his touch on the battery would have shot down the strands a bolt of energy, fast as thought; faster—thought could be laborious, this would be inspiration. From his brain and will to the unleashing of the Mine's power in the flash of sudden insight.

They'd denied him that.

Of course. Of course. Of course they would. They would never forgive him for being right when they were wrong. And for rubbing their faces in it.

Down the tunnel, candles flickering. The air had a slight sickly tang to it, but the ventilator was working. Pleasants forced himself to concentrate, do everything carefully: set the fuse ends into one powder keg in each magazine—two in the larger ones. Make sure the end was fixed in the coarse-grained stuff, thrust deep; fastened through the keg top and held in place so that no accidental jiggle or jerk would disconnect it. They secured the fuses against movement with hitches at regular intervals through guides fastened to the wall uprights, on into the wooden tube of linked boxes they had made to carry it past wet spots and through the walls of sandbags that tamped the tunnel—a miniature tunnel of wood, a diminutive parody of their natural tunnel carved of earth.

"Sergeant," he whispered. "You'll be down here yourself, and make sure nobody steps on the fuse, or breaks it, or pulls too hard on it, while they're stacking the sandbags, and setting the boxing in place."

Rees nodded.

Pleasants thought, *That's all right then,* and turned back to the work.

As they finished their work at the deep end of the shaft, binding the ends of the fuses from each magazine to the main, central fuse-line that would run out to the surface, they heard, faintly, the tapping sounds of the rebel counterminers, picking away in the darkness. Pleasants looked at Rees, and the two of them suddenly grinned.

July 27, Dusk. Johnson's Headquarters

The sun was gone, the sky had gone Confederate gray, and against the gray sky and dun land the Yankee bivouac fires sparkled, a scattering of orange stars. Johnson and Bruce were estimating the size of the army that stood over against them by the fires. There seemed to be as many as before. They imagined the Yankees sitting down to supper before those thousands of fires. The thought was edged by their own hunger.

"There are as many as ever," said Lieutenant Bruce, and General Johnson nodded. They both understood the threatening implication behind that perception: all day they had heard rumors and reports of a heavy Yankee blow north of the James, and still the numbers in front of them did not lessen. Yet their own reserve brigades had been swiftly sucked away by the vortex of that action to the north, and there was a sense of a great vacancy behind them where their supports should have been.

Behind them, on the road, the sixteen guns of Haskell's battery were unlimbering. Johnson had asked for troops, but there were none to be spared. Just the guns.

"An interesting experiment," said Johnson, "to see how few men it actually requires to hold a line of trenches, given sufficiently scientific fortifications and an ample quantity of artillery."

"Eventually, General," said Bruce, "we shall have resort to a fully mechanical trench line, in which some half-dozen men control the whole apparatus of guns and obstructions and infernal machines."

Johnson laughed. "Unfortunately for us, science has not carried things so far."

Colonel Haskell saluted, and stepped out of the shadows. "General, shall I entrench here?"

"No, Colonel. I want you to keep your guns in the road here, but out of line of sight behind this rising ground. No entrenchments: we don't want the Yankees to know you're here. A masked battery—except without even the mask to suggest something to be hidden."

"Yes sir," said Haskell, and he vanished back into the shadows.

"It's gathering to a head," said Bruce, staring at the distant lights.

"Yes," said Johnson. "I've instructed Goode to dig a trench across the back of Pegram's salient—that's where most of the mining sounds were heard. I've instructed the brigade commanders as to their actions should an attack be made. Troops to the right and left of any breach will hold position, barricade their trenches facing the breach, and give no ground. The reserves will form in the covered ways behind each brigade front, and move so as to contain any advance until more reserves can be brought up."

"Yes, sir."

Johnson pressed his lips together, nodded briskly. Then sighed. "Yes. We've done about all that we can do."

HEADQUARTERS ENGINEER TROOPS,
July 27, 1864.

Maj. Gen. B. R. JOHNSON:

GENERAL: One hundred and sixty-one men from your command have reported to me for duty. These men are entirely without cooking utensils, and none are to be had from the quartermaster's department in Petersburg. I have but a limited supply for the use of my own company; as soon as they are done using them they are loaned to your men. This necessarily delays them, and the consequence is that the work in the mines is often delayed. I have written to your assistant adjustant-general on this subject, and now call your attention to it in the hope that you will have your men supplied as far as is in your power. I would also call your attention to the fact that there being an insufficiency of medicines in the hands of the attending surgeons, a great many of the men are sent to the hospitals who otherwise would recover in camp.

Very respectfully, your obedient servant,
HUGH THOS. DOUGLAS,
Captain, Enginer Troops, in Charge Mining, &c.

HEADQUARTERS ENGINEER TROOPS,
Blandford, July 27, 1864.

Col. W. H. STEVENS,
Chief Engineer, Army of Northern Virginia:
COLONEL: At Pegram's salient, mine No. 1, the total length of gallery is 82 feet. At mine No. 2 the total length of gallery is 72 feet, a total distance at Pegram's of 154 feet. At Colquitt's salient the total length of galleries Nos. 1, 2, and 3 is 97 feet, gallery No. 4 7 feet, a total distance driven at Colquitt's of 104 feet. At Gracie's mine the gallery has been extended a distance of 32 feet, the total distance extended in all the mines being 290 feet.

Very respectfully, your obedient servant,
HUGH THOS. DOUGLAS,
Captain, Engineer Troops, in Charge Mining, &c.

July 28, Noon. Meade's Headquarters

It had been a wonderful day for General Burnside, and he was determined that this interview with Meade should not spoil it. Indeed, if it went as he expected, it might well be the capstone of the day's great edifice of labor and expectation. The news from Hancock was all good . . . . that is, it was all *bad*—Hancock was getting nowhere, which meant that it was all good news for Burnside and for his Mine and his attack. And he had prepared carefully for this meeting, which would probably confirm him in his expectation of a date certain, and soon, for the consummation of his plans and labors.

He had sent over his plan of attack yesterday, magnificently detailed and phrased with all the tact and subtlety he could muster. It was liberally salted with phrases making obeisance to Meade's precious authority—"may not be improper for me to say," "you must be the judge of," that sort of thing. Anything to make the plan itself palatable. Because there, *there* was the fulcrum and lever by which Burnside would move the whole army. The great attack would turn on Burnside's Mine, it would be led by Burnside's niggers and the rest of the IX Corps. Everything else, all other movement, would depend upon these two wonderful inspirations of his, these two clever devices. He read the plan over to himself, relishing its phrases. The Mine to be exploded "just before daylight in the morning," with the two brigades of the Colored division massed in advance behind the line "in columns of divisions, 'double column closed in mass,' the head of each brigade resting on the front line; and as soon as the explosion has taken place, move them forward with instructions for the division to take half-distance; and as soon as the leading regiments of the two brigades pass through the gap in the enemy's line, the leading regiment of the right brigade to come into line perpendicular to the enemy's line by the right companies 'on the right-into-line wheel,' the left companies 'on the right into lines,' " and the regiments of the other brigade doing the same things in mirror image to their left. And then the rest of the Colored brigades "to move directly towards the crest as rapidly as possible," the rest of the corps following after them "as soon as they can be thrown in."

And what more logical, more unobjectionable (that was the point when dealing with Meade) than that Burnside should remark on the necessity for the other corps to relieve his troops on the vacated lines? And to provide appropriate support? "Of the extent of this you will necessarily be the judge." That might mollify Meade, but didn't it also show the true state of affairs: that this was Burnside's show, start to finish, and Meade's contributions would be perfunctory, routine.

Well, even with his care and tact, Meade had seized an occasion already to step in, to put his damned finger in the pie. Burnside had mentioned his intention to use twelve thousand to fourteen thousand pounds of powder in the mine. A matter of technical detail on which he —as the officer responsible for the mine—might be presumed to be competent. And here Meade had fired back a note changing the charge to only eight thousand pounds. By heaven, he'd have lit a fuse under Meade for that interference—if Lew hadn't talked him out of it, got him to accept what couldn't be helped. He'd never see those extra four thousand pounds, if he prayed for a month. So Burnside had swallowed that. He was going to present Meade the very picture of a loyal subordinate. There must be no hint or suggestion of hostility or rivalry. What would happen Saturday, would happen. There would be no arguing with the facts. The Ninth Corps and General Burnside would do what had to be done. He cared nothing for what would happen after.

But if there was any justice in the world, he'd have his due reward!

Meade rose to greet him. In front of the General was a map of the lines, and a file of papers Burnside recognized as his own dispatches with the plan of attack.

"General Burnside," said Meade, "I want to be sure we understand each other as to the course this attack will follow. We can't afford any more failures of understanding."

"General," beamed Burnside, "I couldn't agree with you more."

Meade grunted. "Very well then. Hancock's expedition has drawn a very large force of the enemy north of the James—we estimate at least two full divisions, perhaps three, drawn from the reserves and perhaps from the trenches on our front. General Grant and I have decided that an attack will be made on your front, in force, following the explosion of the Mine. This Saturday, as soon as it is light. The Mine is charged?''

''Yes, General. It has been since yesterday.''

''I simply asked if it has been charged.''

Burnside flushed. ''I've said it has been.''

There was a moment's silence. Meade looked down at the papers before him. ''Your plan of attack—it is, I think, too intricate for the situation, too likely to cause delay.'' Meade looked up. ''This attack is to be something in the character of a *coup de main*. Speed is important. If we do not succeed in the first moments in carrying our objective, we will fail. All our experience with attacking entrenchments proves that. *Speed*, General.''

''I know what a *coup de main* is, General.'' *That was too sharp! Calm! Diplomacy! Oh, but the damned old maid to lecture at me like I was a plebe!*

Meade's eyes snapped. He had caught the edge in Burnside's tone. ''I wonder if you do, General. You've put the Colored troops in the lead, here. I can't allow that! Your most inexperienced, unproven troops to take the lead in an attack of this kind? I'm frankly surprised at your proposing it. A *coup de main* requires the best soldiers, veterans, to lead. It is, as you ought to know, in the character of a forlorn hope, and the troops assigned should be such as are thrown into breaches. Not the hewers of wood and drawers of water, General!''

Burnside's anger nearly throttled him. He felt his face glowing, a superheated moon. He would die of apoplexy! ''By God, General, are you questioning my judgment? I have had these men trained for the task. They've practiced maneuvers for weeks. . . .''

''I think, General, you might be more guarded in your tone of voice.''

Burnside took a deep breath, and held it, and let it out slowly. ''I'm *sorry*, General. I apologize for becoming too heated. It is warm in here. . . .''

''Yes. Well, as to the maneuvers. This splitting off to left and right, it won't be needed. I want you to form your troops in the breach as soon as possible, and rush for the crest. Better: don't take the time to form. Just get through the hole, and up that ridge before Lee can bring his reserves round. You can straighten things out once we've got the hill and the ridge. Just rush straight for the crest. Speed, General. As fast as you can go.''

Burnside's head began to pulse and spin. This was madness! His whole plan had just been torn up and thrown to the dogs. *He's done everything but order me under arrest!*

''I can't. . . . General, those plans were carefully considered and drawn up.'' He was breathing heavily. ''You'll have us just rushing up there in some damned mob! I can't see much tactics in that.''

''We can't afford tactics, General. We have tried tactics and maneuvers with this army, and we can't seem to get them straight. I'm spelling this out so simply that even a corps commander in the Army of the Potomac can comprehend it. I want things done quickly. I want the ridge taken. That's all there is to it. You're not to worry about movements to the left and right.''

''What about my flanks? What about supports?''

''That will be taken care of by these headquarters. You are to concern yourself only with matters on your own front, and with the movements necessary to establishing yourself on the Cemetery hill and ridge, and defending that point against counterattack. Do I make myself clear?''

Burnside grunted. ''If I'm not to choose my method of attack, I must insist on the right of designating the assaulting troops. My white divisions have been badly shot up these last months. . . .''

''Are you suggesting, General, that your troops are unfit to make the assault?''

Was Meade grinning? Burnside could see everything going, the whole attack taken from him.

''No,'' he said, ''no, I . . . General, I did not mean to imply that at all. I trust my troops implicitly. We have, however—as you are aware —lost quite heavily, particularly in the assault in the middle of June. We've been sniped and bombarded ever since, never a day's rest off the line—as you know. They're just . . . tired. The troops have developed the habit—it's common in siege warfare, General, as you are aware— the habit of liking entrenchments. It's second nature with them to dig in wherever the shooting starts up. My Colored troops haven't been in the line, the division is full strength and healthy, and they'll have the enthusiasm, sir. They'll go in hot and fast, I'm sure of it. All that's needed is that, and the rest of the corps will follow.''

Meade laughed. ''I guess they'd be ashamed to see the nigs get up there ahead of them.''

Burnside smiled, and sweat poured down his face. Had he carried the point?

Meade pursed his lips. His hawk eyes glittered, ''General, I can understand your thinking on this. But it may not be. We have no evidence as to the . . . reliability of these troops. How do you know they won't bolt? How do you know they'll even fight, if their service has been such as you describe?''

Now or never! Play the last card! ''I'm surprised, General Meade, to find that you share the unfortunate prejudice against these soldiers that exists in our army. . . .''

''Prejudice!'' Meade snapped. ''I have no prejudice! I said nothing prejudicial! This is a purely military question, I'll have you remember. You'll find nothing in my record even suggesting prejudice! I wonder at your own feelings, General, that you'd put these men in the position of a forlorn hope, perhaps get them butchered if the Mine doesn't go, or even if it does! I wonder about *that,* General!''

Burnside smiled: he had his man where he wanted him.

Meade looked at the papers again. ''All right, General. I want to be scrupulously fair about this matter. I'm going up to see General Grant this afternoon. Shall we let him decide the matter? Will that satisfy you?''

''Certainly,'' said Burnside confidently—although he had some qualms; there was nothing to be said once the matter went to Grant.

As he left Meade's headquarters to ride back to his own, a thought occurred to him: suppose Meade were right, and the niggers did let him down?

July 28, Afternoon. Work detail of 43rd U.S.C.T.

When was it that they'd taken them away from the training ground, and set them back to digging on the trenches, building the new covered way on the left of the IX Corps front? Almost a week. It was like the army forgot all about it, said it was all no-never-mind, and put the niggers back to being niggers. Man could bury his soul and all in as much earth as they had moved since that time. M-mm—*mm!* Huh! Randolph hummed as he jammed his shovel into the yellow soil.

They had thrown their shirts off, and left them with the packs by the wagons. They were lined up, fifty men in a row, in a hip-deep furrow that had been picked out of the ground. Their black backs glistened with sweat, except where the dirt made streaks of dullness. They swung their shovels with apparent ease, to a rhythm that held them in unison. To the white officers, watching from the shade of a bombproof built into the reverse of the slope that looked down on the furrow, there was something easy and mechanical in the movement. More than most labor, this was pleasant to watch. The officers chatted softly among themselves, and occasionally drank from a black bottle one of them passed around. The heat was oppressive, so they had unbuttoned their jackets and shirts, and taken off their hats.

Down in the trench line the men swung their shovels. The thick wood handles slicked up with sweat; the flat, heavy iron heads bit into the chopped-up earth, heave, lift, and swing. Their bodies ran sweat so that they felt themselves covered in oil, slicked and lubricated all over. Their wool trousers hung heavy on their legs, as if they'd pissed their pants, except where the sun dried them across the butt, where the salt of the sweat dried white, a powdering of ash. The heat came down hard, as they swung their shovels, the blood bonged behind their foreheads.

Randolph worked along with the rest. Thinking as he swung the shovel:

Men feeling as bad as they can feel. (Hunh!)
Damn officers sit watch us sweat. (Hunh!)
Army give you the taste of being soldier. (Hunh!)
Snatch it way fore you gets to like it. (Hunh!)
Damn white man. (Hunh!)

Up in the bombproof, Captain Shugrue was beginning to feel at his ease. He always felt embarrassed, whenever his duties brought him in contact with his colleagues in white regiments. He had been a lieutenant

in the Regular Army—not a West Point man—and he had always felt
that the West Point clique had blocked his promotions. Wasn't it proof
enough that he had never been able to get beyond lieutenant's grade,
until the chance of a commission in a black regiment had come along?
Even then, he'd only made up a single grade. There were men who had
been cadets in '61 who were commanding divisions now. Well, it was
all politics. He'd never been able, or willing, to play *that* game. It had
kept him shuffling ration returns at a succession of dismal Western
posts : but he had his pride, after all!

It was embarrassing for him to be seen with his niggers. Most of
his old bunkies didn't think they belonged in the army at all. He would
watch their eyes, to see if maybe his bunkies from the old days were
maybe thinking Bill Shugrue had lowered himself as a man just to get
bumped up a grade, when he couldn't do it in a white man's outfit.
Worse, maybe they figured him as one who picked the nigs because they
weren't likely to see any combat. What kind of soldiers could they be, the
kind of people you could just take and stick in a coffin with molasses
and flour on their face and laugh while the flies gathered on em?

But this assault, now : that would show the others. Make it easy to
meet his old comrades in arms from before the war. Proving it, he smiled,
took the bottle, and tipped back a shot.

Only : fighting with niggers could get a man . . . what had he
heard about those two officers the rebels hung down in Mississippi, Ala-
bama somewhere? Hung for leading niggers. General said it was "unfortunate" that any prisoners had been taken. All those Fort Pillow
stories : hanging, or worse. *Like fighting the goddamn Indians, save the
last shot for yourself. Ain't this supposed to be a civilized war?*

He poured the last drink in the flask, knocked it hard *spang* into
the back of his throat, and grinned. The heat of it swelled and burst in
his head and made him happy. *Ha! Saved the last shot for myself.*

The whiskey mellowed his mood, the whiskey and the murmurous
rhythmical sounds of the men working. He wished they would start
singing, he liked to hear them sing.

Down in the trench line Jethro was swinging his shovel, his head
full of pounding blood, his mind swarming with angry thoughts like a
hill full of red ants.

Hating the officers sitting there watching them work.
Hating the stupid nigger that lets himself be fooled.
Fooled to think he'd ever do more than shovel.
For some white man. For some white man.
Meaning you and me, brother. Meaning you and me.

The sky turned white at noon. The earth was crumbly and dry. The
water in the canteens tasted of metal. Salt pork and salt taste of sweat
in the mouth. Makes the mouth burn and shrink up.

Randolph spat, *ptoo!* as he rammed his shovel down. His mouth so
dry. Get it working.

"I been wor, kin."

Hunh! (Swing the dirt out to the side.)

"Sun so hot!"

Hunk! (Shovel into the broken ground.)

"I been wor, kin."

Hunh! (Swing)

"Sun so hard !" (*Hunk*)

"Tell you Je, sus."

Hunh! (The whole line grunted, swung earth together outward)

"Tell you Je, sus !" (*Hunk*)

Ah, thought Captain Shugrue, *now this is something like!* He leaned back, his legs splayed out in front of him.

Randolph sang :

"Seen ma cap, tun."

Hunh! (Swing)

"See ma cap, tun." (*Hunk*)

"Come ma time, Lawd."

Hunh! (Swing)

"Come ma time." (*Hunk*).

And Jethro, sensing that Randolph had finished saying, answered :

"Come that mo, nen,"

Hunh! (Swing)

"Come that mo, nen." (*Hunk*)

"Guide ma sword, on."

Hunh! (Swing)

"Guide ma sword." (*Hunk*)

"Now listen to that," said Captain Shugrue. "I ain't saying that running a nigger outfit is what I want to be buried doing—but ain't that pretty now ? Never hear white troops sing like that, digging."

"No," agreed his friend, "they'd curse the sun out of the sky. These is the boys for digging. Comes natural to em. They take a *shine* to it !"

"Haw !"

"Go down cap, un !"

Hunh! (Swing)

"Go down cap, un." (*Hunk*)

"Down in grave, yard."

Hunh! (Swing)

"Down de grave, yard." (*Hunk*)

"Singing something about their Captain, sounds like. Reckon that's you ?"

Shugrue pursed his lips and shrugged. "Maybe, maybe not. They mostly sing any old how, any words they think of. Make no sense anyway."

"Seed ole mass, sur"

Hunh! (Swing)

"Seed ole mass, sur." (*Hunk*)

"Down dat grave yard,"

Hunh! (Swing)

"Down de grave, yard." (*Hunk*)

The line of men swung their shovels in unison. From a distance they appeared to be a single black insect with segmented glistening carapaces and countless flailing limbs.

HEADQUARTERS ARMY OF THE POTOMAC,
July 28, 1864—1:15 P.M.

Lieutenant-General GRANT:
    I propose to pay you a visit to City Point, if you have no objection. All is at present quiet here and likely to remain so.
GEO. G. MEADE,
Major-General.

City Point: Headquarters, Armies of the United States

    Meade, Humphreys, and their staffs arrived at two-thirty. Comstock ushered them into Grant's office and shut the door. Through the paneling they could hear hushed voices, and the clatter of the telegraph. Meade and his staff were pleased to note that none of the others were there: not Butler, not Burnside or Warren, not Ord—just Grant and Meade and the staffs, the way it had been before Cold Harbor.
    "General," said Meade, "it has been too long since I've seen you."
    Grant nodded, and mumbled some polite response, nearly inaudible. He handed Humphreys a sheaf of dispatches. "You've got copies of these I imagine"—they were from Hancock. Grant turned to the map on the desk before him. Meade pulled up a chair and sat down next to him.
    "We'll bring Hancock back tonight," said Grant. *Yes,* Meade and his staff all thought, and there was a lightening of tension, a relief. Of course, it was the only logical move in view of the facts. They hadn't really doubted Grant would see it, and come back to Meade's plan, to Meade's side of the river. It was Meade's plan. They'd agreed on that. That ass Burnside had plagued them with it, but it was Meade's decision and his plan, even if Burnside had come up with it first. The only Burnside about it was the damned Mine, and if that really was a Burnside thing, chances were it wouldn't work. But then, of course, it *had* to work, now that it was Meade's plan.
    The two Generals huddled over the map. They would bring Hancock back by the same bridges he used going over—but carefully, slowly, not tipping Lee that they were pulling out, so that the troops he'd hustled over to the Richmond side would stay there.
    "When Hancock goes, it'll be up to Butler to hold Ewell."
    "Um," said Grant. "Well, he'll have Foster with him."
    The staff caught each other's eyes, and grinned. So much for Butler replacing Meade!
    "We'll have Sheridan across too—leave Kautz's division with Butler, it's his anyway. Tell them to make a lot of racket. I want Sheridan out off our left flank, to come in behind them if he can."
    Meade nodded. "That's good. But Sheridan will be slow getting

back across, and maybe worn out. They may be too tired to get around before the attack.''

Grant said nothing; then, ''Let's have him on the flank anyway.''

''Yes, General,'' said Meade.

Grant looked up. His face—sad and round, the eyes downturned and drooping at the corners—was melancholy, but unreadable. Was he being harsh? Brusque? Putting Meade in place? He said, ''If he can't go in before, maybe he can pitch in after the infantry goes through, and cut them up some.'' He chewed the butt of a dead cigar. ''With luck, Lee will look at Hancock's retreat, figure Early hit a nerve and we're pulling out. He'll come out and we'll have our innings. If he doesn't,'' Grant looked up. ''Then we blow the Mine, and go for them.''

July 28, 1864.

Col. H. L. Abbot :

Dear Colonel : The assault will take place about daylight on Saturday, 30th instant. The signal is to be the explosion of the mine. At that signal, the batteries, including the mortars, are to open so as to keep down the fire of the enemy on the assaulting column. The batteries should be put in to-night if possible. I will have it done anyhow on Warren's front, so far as he can spare the guns. Brooker's battery will hardly be in the best position. I will try and get the wood at the corner cut down, so as to let him see more to his left, and, if advisable, he might clear out Roemer's place for a couple of his guns. He will be near enough to get ammunition for them from his magazine. I have telegraphed you for the mortars, 10-inch and 8-inch. They ought all to be put in battery. I trust much to them. If, in addition, a few heavy guns can be placed in Castle Hell, so as to sweep the crest as far down as the house in front of General Warren's headquarters, burnt the other day, it will be very well. All the force you can put on, so dividing the work and ar-ranging the companies as to make the operation a success, will be well.

Truly, yours,

H. J. Hunt.

Broadway Landing, va., *July 28, 1864*

Brig. Gen. Rufus Ingalls,
Chief Quartermaster, &c., City Point :

I have received a sudden order to forward a large amount of ordnance to the lines. Please send me at once, if possible, sixty wagons and also five eight-mule teams for this duty. They will be returned to-morrow. Please acknowledge the re-ceipt of this telegram and inform me if you can send the train.

Henry L. Abbot,
Colonel First Connecticut Artillery.

CITY POINT, VA., *July 28, 1864.*

Major-General MEADE,
Commanding, &c.:
I think it will be well to stop all artillery firing except from field pieces from this time until Saturday morning and to conceal the heavy pieces. This may have an effect in convincing the enemy that we are withdrawing from Petersburg and possibly induce them to come out and see.

U. S. GRANT,
Lieutenant-General.

Burnside's headquarters

It was happening at last. Burnside fired off salvoes of orders for supplies, orders to hasten the work on the big fourteen-gun battery he'd dubbed Fort Morton. Couriers to see how things were going at the Mine. Oh it was going to be splendid, splendid! The General had come round to his way of thinking at last, and be damned to Hancock and to Old Maid Meade! It was Burnside's Mine again. Burnside's Mine forever!

Hunt had been down, poking about, deviling him about cutting down the woods in front of his line. The army engineers—always full of advice, usually too late, and none of it very good. The fool! Give the whole show away to do something like that. Nothing must be done till the last moment so as not to attract attention to this sensitive, this vital section of the front! Time enough to do that, and clear the abatis, just before the attack!

Burnside penned his evening dispatch with a full heart, and deep satisfaction.

HEADQUARTERS NINTH ARMY CORPS,
July 28, 1864—9 P.M.

General WILLIAMS:
The house spoken of by the general of the trenches as in our way has been burned by one of our batteries. The mine is completed and ready for springing. The musketry and mortar firing has been about as usual.

A. E. BURNSIDE,
Major-General.

He heard the clickering telegraph (wonderful invention!) speed the message on its way. He raised a glass of whiskey in parting salute. There was a knock at the door, and an orderly entered with a message. Hunt again!

HEADQUARTERS ARMY OF THE POTOMAC,
July 28, 1864.

Major-General BURNSIDE :
Don't forget the wood to be cleared away. I fear it can't
be certainly cut away in one night.

HENRY J. HUNT.

"Aaargh!" said General Burnside, and he crumpled the note in his
fist, and threw it against the wall. He knew his job, dammit, and would
not be bothered to death by that ass!
Come Saturday, they would all see!
He checked the telegraph again. No message from Meade about his
interview with Grant. What to make of that?
Suddenly, Burnside grinned. That jealous old maid of a Meade!
Grant had probably told him to let Burnside do as he sees fit about the
niggers. And it's eating him so he can't bear to send the message telling
me about it. Can't bear to admit defeat! Let them badger all they wanted,
now. He had what he wanted.
He turned to his camp bed, pulled up the covers, and slept peace-
fully, his dreams unremembered but leaving behind a memory of happiness and gratification.

July 28, Evening. Washington, D.C.: Carey's Theater

Dark and elegant in his uniform dress coat, tapered trousers and
glowing boots, General Ferrero guided his wife into the vestibule of the
theater. His well-shaped, curling black Van Dyke and luxuriant graying
hair shone as if oiled. His wife, short and slender, with fair skin lightly
powdered, held his arm tightly. They moved together with the graceful
purposeful unison of couples who like to dance, and to dance well together. There were small bulges colored like bruises below the General's dark eyes.
He had done all that he could, as he told himself—as Lily had told
him—and now must simply try to relax. If his appeals to Senator Chandler, and Senator Seymour, to Mr. Stanton, had fallen on deaf ears, if
he was mistaken in his impression that Mr. Lincoln had promised help—
there was nothing more he could do about it. Now he must devote himself to seeing that Lily enjoyed herself. She had tried so hard to cheer
him, spending (as he thought) her own reserves of good cheer to aid
him. He smiled at her. Going to see the minstrels tonight had been a good
idea—something utterly carefree and relaxing.
Their seats were in a box, high up on the right side of the theater,
but not so high as to impair their view of the dancers. Ferrero was of
two minds about the minstrels. As physical feats, the performances were
nothing short of extraordinary; and this troupe, Daltrey's Ethiopian
Delineators, was among the best. Still, their dances were primitive. In
his book, his *History of the Dance,* he had set forth this idea: that in the
ascent from the warlike and sensual dances of savages to the peasant

dance, quadrille, and waltz, one could trace the rise of human society from bestiality to civilization; just as in the martial arts, brutal blood-lust gave way to the decorum of chivalry, the finesse of fencing, mathe-matical science. . . . And yet he truly enjoyed the display of Ethiopian dance—its vigor and seeming lack of constraint, its sheer physicality. Thinking about this, and the analogy with fencing, Ferrero moved to-ward a further comparison: that just as this war had muscled away all the art of war . . . something to do with the war, the minstrels, some-how the idea wouldn't take form . . . so the phase of American life represented by the minstrels was sweeping aside the decorum of the dance, and the social grace and restraint it symbolized.

A saddening thought. It did not live long past the rising of the curtain. The orchestra began to "squeal and bump," as Ferrero thought of it, and here came THE ETHIOPIAN DELINEATORS, IN PA-RADE, high-kicking to the jingle of a good old plantation tune, Tambo in the lead shivering his tin and Bones at the back patter-clattering in and out of the rhythm, and solemn Interlocutor, and the Corn Meal Man dancing his dance and chanting his patter. Their blacked faces shone in the lamplight, their eyes goggled madly, and their mouths were wide and red showing big teeth. Their wool shot out of their skulls like frozen frizzled explosions, patterned in sunbursts and slats-and-patches:

> *I come to town de udder night*
> *I hear de noise and saw de fight,*
> *De watchman was a-runnin round,*
> *Crying Ole Dan Tucker's come to town So!*
> > *Get out de way, get out de way, get out de way*
>
> *Ole Dan Tucker!*
> *You're too late to come to supper,*
> *Supper's over and dinner's cookin,*
> *Ole Dan Tucker jus stan dere lookin!*

7:00 P.M. Bivouac, 43rd U.S.C.T.

Randolph's battalion came marching back into camp late, just after the rest of the regiment had finished supper. Their uniforms were stiff with sweat and dirt, and they smelled "about ripe," as their comrades in-formed them. They had spent the last two days digging, finishing up the covered way up to the front lines, where the white boys were stand-ing around and pot-shooting. Digging for them.

"What you niggers been doin' these last two days? Thought you's practicing to take Richmond," said a sergeant in C Company of the Forty-third.

Sergeant Randolph stopped, and looked sourly at the man. He was stiff with weariness, so that it took an effort to stand straight up. A small pain, a flutter of weakness at the base of the spine, made him want to slouch forward, let the shoulders slump. But he stood straight, slightly swaybacked, his powerful upper body riding the big hips and jutting buttocks like the torso of a centaur: "For a man that know nothing, you talk and talk."

"Suppose you just tell me how you plan takin Richmon'. You gone dig your way under it like a badger, I reckon."

Randolph grinned. "You want to see what it's all about? Just watch." He turned to the loose line of men behind him. "This joker here wants to see how we's gone to take Richmond. You want to show him?"

Black faces split in grins. "Haw! Yes, all right! Let's show im!"

"Right, then! Ten-*shun!*"

Randolph walked down the line, speaking in a tense, low voice. He seemed to vibrate with nervous energy. "All right! We show these country niggers how *army* soldiers do!"

"And that damn Captain too," added Jethro.

"Right!"

Randolph stepped away from his line and swept his eyes round the bivouac. There was an open field in front of them, where they stood in front of the trees. Behind the fence a hundred yards distant, Brigade Headquarters was set up in a small cluster of canvas tents. Randolph could see the white faces of the officers above the blue tunics. He grinned with his idea.

It all seemed very clear to him, simple and very beautiful like when he'd first learned to read, and the scramble of marks on the white page made sense to him. He'd studied over the training so long, living it over in his head while he'd heaved dirt like a field hand. And it was clear, he saw the sense of it.

"All right, Sergeant," he said. "You take and line your men out along that wormfence there. You the *secesh.*"

That tickled everybody.

"You jus the boys for it," said Jethro. "A trashy outfit to stand up for that buckra trash."

"You line up across there," said Randolph, "and you try and hold on and stop us. We gonna show you how we comin through that line, and over the other side. You see them tents? Well, now you pretend that's Richmond. We come through you, that's where we goin'."

The sergeant from C Company took his men out across the field, and lined them up behind the fence.

Randolph turned to his line. "All right. You remembers how we done it?" They nodded. "Now here's the way. We ain't got no whole brigade. We make three rows—Jethro take the right hand of the first row; Tobe, stand in the middle. Twenty men in the first row, the rest of us behind. We go across that field, the first row jump the fence, and you take those boys there down! You understand me?" They nodded, and grinned. "Next row coming behind, that's the corporal's squad, *Mr.* Brown, if you please"—Brown grinned back at him—"and you goin' do like the Thirty Regiment done in front of us. You splits squad, left-right, and you *hold* any fool that tries to come round and join in from the side; and you push em back to the fence, if you can do it. Right?"

"Yes, *suh!*"

"Rest of us gone take Richmond."
"Ki-yi!"

Washington: Carey's Theater

> *Get out de way, get out de way, get out de way*
> *Old Dan Tucker!*
> *Too late to come to supper!*
> *Supper over and dinner's cookin'*
> *But Ole Dan Tucker jus stan dere lookin!*

Ferrero felt his spirits begin to perk up and rise. Why did his division never sing and dance so spiritedly?

He caught himself up: he had promised himself not to give another thought to his troubles.

"Gentlemen!" called Mr. Interlocutor. And all paused. And tall Interlocutor flipped his tailcoat back and called, "Be seated!"

"Oh, Mr. Tambo?"

"Yes, Mr. Interlocutor. What kin I does fo you coureosity dis gloriferious Aunty-Meridium?"

"What dat you says bout you Aunty Miriam, Mr. Tambo?" asked Bones, rousing himself.

"I was interrogratin, brother Bones, about the matitutinal part of de day"—Bones shook his head—"de time of de risin of de fiery charity of Fear-a-Bus"—Bones shook violently from head to toe—". . . Oh Lawd! *Maw*-nin to de likes ob you, nigga, *Maw*-nin to de likes ob you!"

Bones smiled from one ear all around to the other; leaned back, eyes closing dreamily. "O-o-h!" he said. "*Maw*-nin to you too, brudder Tambo."

Ferrero laughed, almost in spite of himself. Daltrey's Delineators really were a *professional* troupe, say what you would about minstrel shows.

Now a figure entered from stage left: a woman, black as coal, her head bound and bound in layers of peacock turban, her dress a fluttering regalia of rags. Applause rose to meet her, and she bowed. "Miss Daltrey," whispered someone in the next box.

The orchestra began a jaunty, bouncing tune, and the Mammy's rags flounced in time. When she sang, her voice was light and clear, but there was surprising strength and vigor to its attack on the plantation song:

> *Oh Lemuel, my lark!*
> *Oh Lemuel, my beau!*
> *I'se gwine to gib a ball to-night*
> *I'd hab for you to know:*
>
> *But if you want to dance,*
> *Jus dance outside de door;*
> *Becayse you feet so berry large*
> *Dey'll cover all de floor!*

Laughter, and as she sang now, she lifted her skirts to show her slim ankles and danced a delicate shuffle step.

> *Oh! Lem-Lem-Lem, Lemuel I say,*
> *Go down! to de cotton field,*
> *And bring de boys away!*

And behind her the black-face chorus rose :

> *Go down! to de cot-ton field!*
> *Go down! I say!*
> *Go down and call de niggah boys all*
> *And work no more today!*

And she sang, lilting :

> *Oh Lemuel is tall! O Lemuel is fair!*
> *O Lemuel has gone today to take de mornin air!*
> *He makes de fiddle hum!*
> *He makes de banjo tum!*
> *He rattles on de ole jaw bone*
> *And beats up on de drum!*
> *O! Lem-Lem-Lem, Lemuel I say*
> *Go down! to the cotton field,*
> *And bring de boys away!*

And on cue, as the chorus finished its refrain, here came Lemuel in at stage right.

Prancing and high-stepping !

At the end of his long thin legs in bold-striped trousaloons of yellow and purple, his feets was big and long and flat, when they hit the stage they slapped flat and hard.

In the lapel of his flared coat of red velvet was a large flopping flower, tiger-orange. His wool shone with greaze and his yellow face was split by a blubber-lipped grin. His eyes, outlined in white, had the same maddened rolling look of the others—but somehow here a touch of the rakish and clever had been added.

Miss D. stepped back toward the chorus, which mimed delight in a chaos of contortions, and Lemuel stepped to the footlights to raucous cheers.

> *Oh I'se de pretties' nigga-boy*
> *You never wants to meet*
> *I has fine close upon my back,*
> *An boots up on my feet [he shook one]*
> *My lips so big an flappy*
> *I kin open dem so wide,*
> *I stretches dem each mawnin*
> *Wit one pull on eider side! Oh!*

> *Don' I look yaller*
> *Don' you look green!*
> *Ain't I de pretties nigga-boy*
> *Dat you has ever seen!*

Bivouac, 43rd U.S.C.T.

Major Booker and Colonel Hall were at Brigade Headquarters. Orders had come: the brigade was going onto the line tonight. Suddenly, there seemed to be a disturbance in the camp. They stood in front of Colonel Oliver's tent, hesitating before they entered. They looked at each other grimly. Morale was low, it wouldn't be surprising if there was a brawl in camp. The thought of having to deal with a disorder in their regiment under Oliver's scornful gaze was anguish. Others were beginning to notice; the buzz of conversation in the headquarters area stopped.

Hall started across the field but Booker held his arm. The milling about suddenly seemed to have a peculiar formality: a line of men, black posts, had taken position behind the wormfence, with their backs to the officers. Further back, in the shade of the trees, a dark cluster of black faces and blue jackets had formed.

Suddenly, the black cluster came forward with a speed that seemed an effortless swoop, and they heard a strange sound, a distant throaty "Ha-a-a-a-rh!" as the line went forward (it was a line; Booker could see that now, suddenly) and up over the fence like a comber, the black wave bowling the black standing posts down and to the side; then they heard higher shriller sounds, yells, and saw men rolling over on the ground.

Booker and Hall found themselves running across the field, toward the brawl, when suddenly a second burst of black soldiers came shouldering through, a wedge that became two lines swinging right and left like doors sweeping open, and through the opening door they saw Sergeant Randolph leading a squad of men in a column of fours, at a steady trot between the lines.

"Officers!" yelled somebody.

Faces snapped around, men down on the ground looked up, scrambled up. Sergeant Randolph's orders were lost in hubbub, but they saw his squad slow to a march, halt, and snap to attention.

"Sergeant," Hall snapped, "what is the meaning of this—brawl? Answer me, by God, or I'll have your stripes!"

Randolph looked him steadily in the face. "Sir, this just a little bit extra practice. On the drill, sir."

Hall was confused. "Drill? Drill?"

"The drill for taking the secesh fort, Colonel," said Randolph quietly. "I was just showing these boys here how we done. So they know, when the time come."

"How does it go, Sergeant?" asked Booker.

Randolph grinned. "First bunch kicks in the door. Second bunch hold it wide and watch for the dogs. Third bunch get in the smokehouse and takes the ham. That's how its done down home. What you'd say: forward columns of battalion, double-time. Left company left wheel, right company right wheel. All the rest, fix bayonets and charge. That's the army way. School of the Regiment, sir."

Booker looked at Hall, who was shaking his head. "That's right,

Sergeant. Only next time you decide to charge headquarters bivouac, give us a bit of notice.''

Randolph grinned at the retreating backs of the officers. He had it all in his head: the fiery door swinging open, the cabin on the hillside, Cassy/Coffee all together, the sky with a red sun flaring victory.

Washington: Carey's Theater

Bones: Say, Tambo!

Tambo: Yas, Mistuh Bones!

Bones: Why does de parents cry at a weddin?

Tambo: Cause they been married before and knows it ain't no laughing matter.

Interlocutor: But why is it a widow will get married so easily?

Bones: Cause dead men tell no tales.

Interlocutor: Mr. Bones, I understand you is considered a *contraband*.

Bones: Now Mr. Interlocutor, dat is a confiscated question.

Interlocutor: You means, sir, a *complicated* question.

Bones (*slaps thigh*): No *sir!* Contraband is a *confiscated* question.

Tambo: I sho is grateful to Massa Linkum for freein de slaves!

Interlocutor: Why is that, Brother Tambo?

Tambo: Well, since I is become contraband, I got free of dat Old Woman of mine.

Interlocutor: Why, Brother Tambo! I am shocked to hear you speak so! I am sure Mr. Lincoln had no such intention! The bonds of matrimony are sacred, and should not be lightly sundered.

Tambo: Well, I can't follow all dat about barns and Massa's money, but I will show you that it must be so: Is it not true that I am free contraband, duly confiscated by the government?

Interlocutor: That is so.

Tambo: And is not my wife owned by Colonel Blood-and-Bourbon, as mean a rebel as fired on Fort Sumpthin?

Interlocutor: You mean Sumpter, Tambo: but yes, you are right as to Colonel Blood-and-Bourbon.

Tambo: Well then! If I goes back to de barns of Massa's-money, den I is no longer contraband, but field hand again. And at current prices, dat is tradin wiff de enemy, and on de grand scale too! And tradin wiff de enemy is gainst the law. So, Old Woman, farewell.

Bivouac, 43rd U.S.C.T.

Remembering Randolph's ''charge,'' Booker felt a grip or twisting in the chest, like the first clutch of fear when a horse spooks and runs away with you, and you feel it leave the ground. Why feel *that*, when against all logic the blacks were still enthusiastic, still committed, when Randolph who seemed to hold the key to the spirit of the whole regiment was so clearly triumphant? When, for God's sake, they have just carried out your own wishful prophecy that they could not only carry through the plan, but take it over, make it their own. . . . *I'm afraid to see my*

*own dream come true. And it makes me wonder, where did the dream
come from? Why would a man work so hard at building a thing for himself to be afraid of?*

Randolph ought by all custom to be sullen, angry, balky, unwilling,
urged by disappointment and frustration into dragging his feet. Not
smiling and leading the charge. He ought to be resistant to me, who have
failed at every turn to protect the men, to get them respect in the army,
to get them their land.

Not smiling, grinning: and not for me. At me. That is how he was
leading the charge.

I'll show him the letter, he thought. And then: *Or maybe I'll just
tell him what it says.*

He still hadn't decided when Randolph pushed aside the flap and
stepped into the headquarters tent. "Major," he said quietly. His tone
and manner, to Booker's wrung-up attention, was subtly ambiguous—the
military title was there, but there was a hint of informality, of familiarity, for the white man to take up or let pass as he chose. *It's as close as
he ever comes to calling me friend. But if I want to deny him there's
enough literal deference to mask him, and I'd never be able to say I rebuffed him.*

It was up to Booker to reach past this barrier if he wanted to. If he
wasn't afraid to. But the letter, still folded in his pocket, radiated a chill
of anxiety through his chest, reminding him of the thousand doubts by
which he had betrayed his faith in Randolph and so acted toward him
as an oppressor. Why not show him the letter? That would show faith,
not only that Randolph would take the defeat and not give up on either
the cause or the coming battle, but also that he trusted Randolph to
have seen his own good faith, to know that whatever the writer of the
letter might say, Booker had never been in this struggle for profit, had
not been and was not part of any other group to purchase the Hewson
Plantation than the one he was in with Randolph and the rest of the
company.

His hand reached up and touched the letter, and he said, "That was
quite a show you all pulled this evening." And he grinned.

Randolph's face showed nothing. Perhaps it closed a trifle, became
more impassive. He nodded.

"It wasn't just that you knew the drill. You could lead the assault
as well as Burnside himself if you had to. And you might if enough
officers get shot."

"I was thinking that myself," said Randolph quietly, and looked
up. His face showed something now—puzzlement, he was waiting, wondering where Booker was going in this conversation.

Where am I going with it? Mentioning his own chances of getting
shot: was that to praise Randolph, or warn him, or was it an appeal for
sympathy, a reminder to the black man that Booker had something at
risk in this, too? What did he think the rebels did to white officers serving with black troops?

"That wasn't the only thing I wanted to tell you. I've had a letter
from someone I know down in New Bern. It's about the auction." Randolph stiffened perceptibly in his chair.

"It's bad news," said Randolph. His voice was even, his eyes held Booker's steadily with no wavering or hint of appeal.

"Yes, it's bad. This man tells me"—*Show him the letter,* he thought, but another thought unvoiced held him, *Be cautious, don't throw it away*—"that they're going to hold a regular auction. We'd have to outbid Brickhill dollar for dollar."

Randolph held steady. His gaze hardened, concentrated on Booker and then through Booker on something invisible behind him. "Then it's dead and gone," he said. "Even if they paid us level with white folks, we never put away more than Brick'l take out of our land and our folks, an the cotton sellin so high."

"Maybe we, . . ." said Booker, and he touched the letter again. *How can I show it now? After we've failed, after my planning has all proved out wrong.*

An inner balance adjusted itself in Randolph's eyes, his stare now focussed directly on Booker. The wrinkles of tension that marked the corners of his eyes smoothed. He shook his head, "No, Major. That's all right. We just take care of it ourselves, in our own time now."

"Perhaps if I'd thought more . . ."

Randolph's look sharpened again, suddenly. "It's not your land, Major. I believe there never was a thing to be done about it. Never make a plantation out of soldiers' pay, no way. Not white folk's pay, and sure as hell not out of nigger's pay."

Was he included in Randolph's anger now? Or in his contempt, for failing? Or was he just no longer part of the plan in the way that he had been, teacher and guide? With a pang of sorrow and of deep frustration he felt that his choices were none of them any good: in Randolph's eyes he must be either an oppressor or a failure, another Hewson or simply another white man of no use at all. Or an Oliver, offering to raise him up and inveigling him into a new kind of subjection.

What are you to yourself? It doesn't matter what Randolph thinks of you now. He's made whatever decision he's going to make. Show him the letter for your own sake. Show yourself you don't have to be his leader to have him work with you.

Booker sat, frozen.

"You meant good to us," said Randolph. "Never mind. In the day that comin, we take care of this our own way."

"What will you do?"

Randolph's face had become completely impassive. He had risen, and nodded toward Booker—in salute?—and he turned and walked to the tent flap. "You seen what we do, Major," he said, and vanished through the flap.

Washington: Carey's Theater

"Now Bones, do you have anything to say?"

"Oh yes, Mr. Interlocutor. Do you ever, sir, go to de races?"

"Oh yes, Mr. Bones. I'm particularly fond of horses."

"Well then, Mr. Interlocutor: do you know how to make a slow horse fast?"

"Why no, Mr. Bones. How do you make a slow horse fast?"

"Jess don't feed him!" (*All laugh*)

HEADQUARTERS JOHNSON'S DIVISION,
July 28, 1864.

Col. G. W. BRENT, *Assistant Adjutant-General:*

COLONEL: There is nothing of importance to report this morning. The usual amount of picket-firing and shelling was kept up along the line last night, but no change on the part of the enemy. General Gracie thinks that our mortar batteries, especially in rear of left of Ransom's brigade, did great execution yesterday. Groans were distinctly heard near the sap-rollers. Nineteen thousand minie-balls, 137 solid shot, several Hotchkiss and Parrott shells, fuses, &c., were collected yesterday.

The following is a list of casualties: Wise's brigade, wounded, 2. Elliott's brigade, wounded, 4 (1 mortally), Ransom's brigade, killed, 1; wounded, 6. Gracie's brigade, killed, 1; wounded, 3. Total, 2 killed and 15 wounded.

I am, colonel, respectfully, &c.,

B. R. JOHNSON,
Major-General.

P.S.—The scurvy has made its appearance in Gracie's brigade. Cannot vinegar, fresh meat, or vegetables be issued to the troops to prevent its further progress?

B. R. J.

Pegram's Salient

There were 280 men in the Twenty-second North Carolina, divided into six companies. Originally there had been a thousand men and a dozen companies, each recruited from a different community in Calhoun and Jefferson counties. But that was three years ago.

For the last two days Colonel Davidson had sent around extra rations of salt beef and cabbage with his compliments, a reminder that the electoral commissioners would be coming by the Twenty-second North Carolina to take their votes for governor. Most of the officers were for Vance, from whom they held their commissions, and with whom they had the kinds of understanding that grow between a Governor and the substantial citizens of a community. Most of the soldiers were for nobody or for Holden, not liking Vance or those that liked Vance; suspecting that the way out of where they had got to might lie with getting out from under the Governor that took them into the war.

There had been some Holden men in camp on the twenty-sixth. They spoke to Marriot and the Cutterstown boys, and asked them would they move around, talk to the other companies and see what they could do.

Brought stuff from him, little keg of whiskey they sneaked past the provost guards. But next morning they were gone: someone, a Vance man, had told the Colonel, and he'd arresed them and run them off. And got the whiskey.

That day, when the doctor came by on his rounds, Marriot offered to tote his kit for him, and had got round to talk with most of the boys that way. Neither Billy nor Dixon would chance going with him, so he'd gone alone. Billy wouldn't for thinking what the officers told him was true: bad thing changing government in the midst of the war. Dixon said it was foolishness either way. Marriot figured Dix for scared. He owed Davidson money. Marriot owed too. But that was one more reason for him going against the Colonel's man, Vance. Owing ain't owning.

Marriot had nothing to give the men—no whiskey, no tobacco, all the stuff that the Holden people brought was snapped up by the Colonel. Still, there were things to talk about.

"You figure Holden or Vance?"

"It'll be a close thing," said Marriot. "You just interested in backing winners?"

"Waste to do anything else."

"That's not bright. Everybody figures that way, it's no hoss race. I'd want to ask, What will the man do for me? Vance got me here, though he said he wanted to keep me home: I don't figure that for playing square."

"Reckon Holden's any different?"

"He ain't Vance."

Going round the regiment this way brought to mind how many good boys were gone. Most of the Sickletown folks were wiped out when the Yanks broke through up on the Rapidan, and those two companies were cut off in the brush. In his mind, Marriot pictured these deaths not as a man falling, shot, but: he walks in the road past a farm, the cabin is abandoned, the door swings off broken hinges, something—niggers, varmints, something—has broke through the wormfence and begun to pick over and eat out the fields, which have gone to seed anyhow. And the next farm the same. And the one after that. And no smoke rising above the trees where, back of the timber along the road, you knew there was another place, Harker's, hidden from the road. Maybe the year after, the timber'd be cut off, and the fields and woodlots swallowed up in the long slash of the cotton rows, reaching out from the white house along the river: Hewson's place, or Davidson's, or Allen's. And niggers swarming out to the labor, like ants.

Now it was 7:00 P.M. the twenty-eighth of July. Appointed time and day for the election, and here were all of the boys come together. There were two dozen men in the company going to vote. Some wouldn't bother. A whole bunch, like Billy, were too young yet to vote at all. Cal Driscoll, who'd just come up from home, wasn't fifteen yet. Lied his way in. Not that the recruiters would care to stop him. Some didn't want to cross the officers, but wouldn't go for Vance.

The bunch of men who were going in to stand up and be counted for Holden found their way into the trench where Marriot, Billy, and

Dixon sat. Dixon said "Howdy"; sat a minute, then went off, to take a piss he said, and didn't come back. He wasn't going to vote, that was pretty clear, though nobody had said anything.

Marriot smiled, and passed a twist of tobacco around. Old Clem Harding sniffed it, grinned, and passed it on. When he grinned, you could see he hadn't a tooth in his mouth, gums like a baby. He was bald and sixty, drafted that spring, and had busted his store teeth when he got pushed over at Spotsylvania, that time when the regiment got stampeded by the Yankees coming over in a wave early in the morning, rushing in out of the fog, panicking everybody. "Good shawing," he said, and the others laughed.

The twin Hubbard brothers bit their chaws off with a brusque, twisting motion, Dave gripping with the teeth on the right side of his face, Harley doing it with the left. They grinned as they chewed. Brown spittle pooled in the corners of their lips.

Micah Dorman spat a stream of brown juice between a gap in his front teeth.

I could tell who these boys was if they wore masks, just by the way they take the chaw.

He grinned all around. "It's just about time, boys."

In single file, Marriot leading, they shuffled away down the trench. Billy watched them go: a stooped-over line of lean men, gray and brown shirts, slouch hats, and Yankee pants. Dixon materialized at his shoulder.

"Waste of time," said Dixon.

"Dix," said Billy, "you dasn't vote cause you're afraid Davidson will call your notes."

"Don't sass your elders, boy!" said Dixon. Then: "He would do it, too."

Washington: Carey's Theater

Ferrero was quite forgetful of things now, as the alternation of songs-dances and the repartee of Tambo and Bones soothed him with its familiarity. After the spice of laughter, the vigor of dance, there was Miss D., in white-face now, to sing sadly, lilting:

> *We shall meet but we shall miss him!*
> *There will be one vacant chair!*
> *We shall linger to caress him!*
> *While we breathe our evening prayer.*

So sad, so moving. The thought of all those homes to which heartbreak and loss had come. A soldier's duty was hard, but it was hard also to remain behind, wasn't it? He glanced at his wife, and squeezed her hand.

And Tambo was reminded, and approached the footlights to sing of his loss, his deep voice taking the true tone of nigger melancholy:

> *O de sun shines bright in de ole Kentucky home!*
> *Tis summer, de darkies are gay!*
> *De corn top's ripe and de meadow's all in bloom*

While de birds make music all de day!
The young folks roll on the little cabin floor,
All merry, all happy, and bright!
By n by hard times comes a-knockin' at de door
Then my ole Kentucky home, good-night.

The audience seemed nearly to be singing below its breath as the chorus followed Tambo, pleading, ''Weep no more my lady, / O weep no more to-day'' and Ferrero heard in the song the same plea to the mother whose eyes were full of the vacant chair, and he wondered *why the troops in the Division never sing this way, but always of religion and death and hereafter and the rhythmic chants of work? And never a tender sentiment for the young folks, the old folks at home?*

We shall sing one song for the old Kentucky home,
For the old Kentucky home far away!

To my deer wife, Coffe,

I write in hast having just heard from our Major Booker that they will not give us our land for the good Home Stead price. But will make us bid dollar for dollar against the Man Brickhill who hold the place. Even so you must keep our money for it may not be true, but my hart tells me it is so. It is the way it always happens, that the People will go in poverty and the unrighteous in silks. It is the World, Coffe, and it gives us no thing of our own but what we can take an hold by our strength and the Lord's will. It may be I have done wrong, trusting in Man and the word of the army, when right along I know they have not done justice to us. I feels now like a man thrown in a pit, and see no way out, and lions to devour my flesh. But Coffe, there is a way out of this pit, if I must shed blood and lose blood to do it then I will. Talking to you this way I am talking to myself also, and I want to say that we must both remember that the slavery time is gone, and we never no more gone to see our blood sold off from us. And our blood gone into that ground. Our blood gone into that ground. Into that ground, and into this ground too. No matter about the paper. No matter about the dollar for dollar. When the Day come, it will be a battle, and I feel in my heart that the battle been given to my own hand.

Your loving husband,
Ezk. Randolph, Sergeant.

Mr. Interlocutor: Didn't that song touch you?
Tambo: No, but the man that wrote it did. He still owes me five!
Mr. Interlocutor: Sir! Have you no sentiment left?
Tambo: No, I just told you; I haven't a cent left.
Mr. Interlocutor: I didn't say *cent.* I said *sentiment.* Sentiment! The

tender passion of maiden's love, the maternal pang! The noble sentiment of patriotism that has led men to fight and die for their country,
without a thought of the future. Don't you care about that?

Tambo: Care? Course I cares! When they die, how they gone to pay
me my money back?

Headquarters, 22nd North Carolina

Lieutenant Bruce, who was playing cards with Penwaring, looked
up as Colonel Davidson came laughing into the bombproof and passed
back behind the blanket-door into his office. They heard him call loudly
for George, and the quiet Negro came in, and passed under the blanket.
They heard talk; then George came back out with his berry bucket, and
left the bombproof.

Penwaring looked at Bruce, and the latter shrugged. They heard
voices, and here came Allen and Hawken, laughing.

"What's up?" asked Penwaring.

Hawken motioned to the blanketed door. "The Old Man in?"

The two seated men nodded.

Hawken motioned them to gather in closer. He spoke in a low voice,
not a breathy whisper, but the quiet low voice that won't carry as a
whisper will. Bruce felt that they were like children telling secrets so
their elders wouldn't hear.

"The election commissioners were down to take the votes today.
The Old Man was nearly beside himself about the whole thing. He would
go on about mob rule and agrarianism, and damned traitors talking
peace with a war going on . . . you've heard him."

"That we have," said Penwaring.

"As Colonel, and Justice of the Peace for the county, he's the man
that has to certify the electors. So he's sitting behind the desk when
they send the men in. 'One at a time,' he says. 'The sacred right of the
franchise must be exercised in privacy.' And him sitting there with six
other fellows that butter wouldn't melt in their mouths, and every one
of them appointed by Vance."

"I can see it all," said Penwaring.

"All right. So the first man comes in, this old guy—Hardwood, I
think—and Davidson says, 'You sure you're old enough to vote,' and
the guy says, 'I'm 'thure'—he hasn't a tooth in his head. 'You're for
Vance, ain't you?' says one of the commissioners. And they get real
quiet. Davidson says, 'I know you: you're Hardwood, from Mill Landing, aren't you?' 'Yeth,' he says, and he marks down . . . *Vance!* And
Davidson calls the next one in.

"It goes on like that. Some of them tougher than some others. Couple of them say, 'Hell on Vance, I'm for Holden.' 'Can you read and
write?' asks Davidson. 'No sir.' 'Oh, well, then let me write down
Holden for you here, and you just make your mark.' "

"And he writes down *Vance,*" said Bruce. "What about the ones
that could read, and wouldn't back down?"

"I'm coming to that. Finally, this corporal—Marriot—the kingpin of the Holden mob, gets wind of what's up, and the last lot comes in all in a bunch. Davidson takes each one in turn : Are they qualified electors? When did they last pay their poll tax? He knew pretty clearly which ones had or hadn't—hell, half of the regiment owes him money, and if some sucker pays his tax before he pays Old Davidson, you know what else is to pay.

"The corporal. Marriot, says, 'We ain't been paid in three months. How you expect us to pay the tax? Take it out of what the government owes us.'

"Davidson looks at him hard. 'I'm no damned accountant, Corporal,' he says. 'What's between you and Mr. Davis's government is your own business. This here's a Carolina election.'

"Another man steps up, and lays a pile of bills on the table. 'Here's mine,' he says. 'These are just shinplasters,' says one of the commissioners, 'ain't trading at par.'

" 'Ain't Confederate currency legal tender?' says Marriot. 'But if you want Federal greenbacks, *here!*' and he throws a pile down on the table.

"Everybody's real quiet. There's enough to cover the tax. Davidson looks at the pile. Then he says, real quiet, 'Where'd you get these, soldier?' 'Won it at cards,' says Marriot. Davidson looks up. 'Trading with the enemy, I'd say. And I could have you shot for it. Till I can prove it, I'll take your word. And gambling—also against regulations.' He stacks the bills. 'This is contraband, and I'm confiscating it. I'll also confiscate those stripes. You'll not enjoy the privileges of rank, so long as you continue flouting explicit regulations.' And two of the sentries step up, and peel the stripes."

Penwaring whistled. "He is a *mean* son of a bitch, isn't he?"

Allen looked up. "I'm sure," he said, "that Colonel Davidson found this task entirely distasteful. Whose is the fault that such men have to stoop to the techniques of political brawls in order to maintain proper discipline in their regiments? We're well out of a potentially disastrous complication. Imagine if the men had voted for Holden!"

"He shouldn't have taken Marriot's stripes," said Bruce.

"Why not?" asked Penwaring.

"Because he's a good soldier," said Bruce. But he added, in thought, *And the kind of man he is, I don't know what he'll do now. If there were more like him, we'd have a hell of a time with the troops from here on.*

There was a cry from the trench, a call for the Colonel. Davidson came bustling out of his office in shirtsleeves. The officers stepped quickly to the door of the bombproof—there was a party of men coming down the trench, carrying something in a blanket.

"Colonel," said one of the carriers, "it looks like some damn Yankee has shot your nigger, George."

The Colonel's face went ashen.

The burden dropped, clump, at his feet. George had been drilled through the back of the head. Inside the red wound were white splinters of bone, and the gray slime of brain matter.

Washington: Carey's Theater

Tambo (sings):

> *I'm right from ole Virginny, wid my pocket full ob news,*
> *I'm worth twenty shillings right square in my shoes,*
> *It doesn't make a dif of bitterance, and neider you nor I,*
> *Black pig er white pig, it's*
> *Root, Hog, or Die!*
>
> *I'se de happies' darky on top of de yearth,*
> *I get fat as de possum in de time ob de dearth,*
> *Like a pig in a tater patch, dar let me lie,*
> *Way down in ole Virginny where it's*
> *Root, Hog, or Die.*

HEADQUARTERS NINTH ARMY CORPS,
July 28, 1864.

General HUMPHREYS:
Before the dispatch of the commanding general could be communicated to Colonel Pleasants the charges had all been placed, and the tamping had progressed so far that he deems it best to keep on, as the stopping at the present stage would not serve to keep the mine dry any more than if the tamping were finished, besides the air in the mine is, for some reason, becoming very bad, so much so as to make it difficult for the men to work. He, as well as the miners, say the powder will keep dry for at least a week. Shall he keep on?

A. E. BURNSIDE,
Major-General.

HEADQUARTERS NINTH ARMY CORPS,
July 28, 1864.

Colonel LORING,
Inspector General:
Let Pleasants finish the tamping, by 3 o'clock if possible.

A. E. BURNSIDE,
Major-General.

HEADQUARTERS NINTH ARMY CORPS,
July 28, 1864.

Major VAN BUREN:
There is no hurry; tell Pleasants to have it done some time to-night.

A. E. BURNSIDE,
Major-General.

The Mine

Rees walked down the rows, shaking the sleepers awake. It was time to finish up, time to tamp the Mine. Time to fill up what they had so laboriously excavated, and so complete it ready for firing.

The sandbags were ready, waiting, stacked in a sheltered spot behind the first line of trenches. Eight thousand sandbags. They'd shift them all between midnight and morning.

Rees had thought it out. There were to be five "battalions" for the labor : one to shift the bags from the stack to the trench ; one to pass the bags down the line of the trench to the minehead ; one to pass them down the tunnel to the end, where three or four men would stack them in the prearranged places ; two shifts off, resting. When the air down the Mine grew foul, and the men could do no more, he'd change shifts in the tunnel—bring the tunnel battalion out for rest, send the trench-line battalion down ; the battalion shifting from the stack to the trench would take over in the trench ; and one of the off-battalions take its place. The fifth battalion was his reserve ; he could throw it in if something about the arrangement failed to work—if the shifts had to be changed quicker in the Mine, because of the air, he might need to change things round.

This was *his* pride, his expression of power and skill. Let *Mr.* Pleasants do the drawings and take the measures ; it was a special skill, but cold and mechanical. You could do nothing unless you knew how to organize the work, and this was Rees's profession, his calling, his power. Anyone might learn to draw and cipher, but who could learn to order and command ? It was his regiment now.

He stood by the pile of sandbags and said, "All right, boys : Go !" and watched as the first bag was jerked off the pile, mastered against the downward pull of its weight, passed to the next man with a heaving, swinging motion, the two men facing as they passed, then turning backs in reciprocal motion, the one to heave another bag up, the other to pass the first bag down ; and after three bags there was a rhythm to it, the bags seemed to sweep and bob their way down the line as if under their own power, automatically. When he saw this Rees knew that the work pattern was set, and he could pass down with the bags into the trench, where the rhythm established itself, like the succession of roller-wheels in a steel rolling mill he had seen. Down the trench and into the tunnel. Here there would be a change in rhythm, a possible bottleneck : it was easier to pass the bags than to stack them. Lieutenant Douty was there to watch : when he saw things reaching that point, he was to pass the word back—"last bag for now"—and the word would pass the line of bags coming down till it reached the man on the stack, and turned him off. Then they would stand, and stretch—freed of the weight of the bags—and wait for the call to start again.

Down in the tunnel, the passing was harder, more awkward. The roof was low, the men had to stand stooped. It was easier to set them at wider intervals here and have them stumble the bags a few feet each way; and you had to keep down the numbers in the tunnel, or they'd suck the air all out, in spite of the ventilator.

After half an hour, Rees's head was swimming, and he called a halt. Cut down the number of men in the Mine still further; and change shift for them twice as often as for the boys out in the air. After that, it went more smoothly. Rees and Douty changed off, Rees watching the line of bags and ventilator fire, while Douty kept his eye on the fuse.

Down in the Mine, the pile of sandbags sealed each corridor with a column of sand ten feet long. Then the main shaft began to fill, the column of sand stretching back down the tunnel.

Each time Doyle came on shift, another section of the tunnel had been buried: the gallery where he and Dorn had worked with their feet in the wet; where they'd sweated out the counterminers. The place, at last, where they'd been working in reddish earth the day that Corry had his face blown off of him.

It was a common enough thing to dig out a mine, to take earth out to make a shaft; to stand in lines passing out earth or water, when a shaft caved or was buried, and you were after the boys down there, or their bodies. But never had he filled up the shaft as they were doing now. It was odd, backwards. When they'd dug forwards, driving ahead, it was like all his life had been, digging to get somewhere, get at something. This was like saying goodbye, like going away, like falling asleep, and dreaming yourself backwards past the places you'd been. Covering each place up as you came to it. So it was like dying.

At the end, they'd light the match and blow it all to air and dust, and that would be an end.

What a hell of a thing to do, thought Doyle, as he buried the place where Corrigan died.

Washington: Carey's Theater

Mr. Interlocutor: Tambo, do you know any riddles?
Tambo: When will water stop running downhill?
Mr. Interlocutor: Why, that will never happen.
Tambo: Yes it will: when it gits to de bottom. And what is de difference between a lucifer match and a cat?
Mr. Interlocutor: What *is* the difference between a lucifer match and a cat?
Tambo: De lucifer lights on its head, and de cat lights on his feet!
Bones: And what is it dat de more you take from it, de larger it grows.
Tambo and Mr. Interlocutor: A hole, brudder, a hole!

And now here was a new flash of fire: a rattle of Tambo, a patter of Bones! and out of the wings leaped: the Corn Meal Man, with a glosso-lalian patter and a *slap-tap-stamp*ing beat of hands and feet. Cohn Meal! he hollered, and Bones whomped his face with a puff of flour in a muff, that whitened over the blackface, layer on layer, howl on howl of laughter, as he whirled in circles and leaped highkicking:

Wheel aroun, turn aroun, and spin jes so
And ebry time I wheel around
I Jump! Jim! Crow!

I rafted down to New Orleans,
To dance wit octoroons,
I went and saw de very place
Where Butler stole de spoons.

I feel so fine in Orleans,
I git into a fight,
They put me in the Calaboze
and keep me all the night,

When I got out I hit a man,
His name I now forgot,
But dere was not'ing left of him,
Except a greasy spot.

I whip my weight in wildcats,
I eat an alligator
I drink de Mississippi up!
O I de very cratur!

I kneel to de buzzard and
I bow to de crow,
And every time I wheel around
I jump Jim Crow!

HEADQUARTERS ARMY OF THE POTOMAC,
July 26, 1864—4:15 P.M. (*Rec'd 7* P.M.)

Major-General BURNSIDE,
Commanding Ninth Corps:
The major-general commanding directs that you send a division to occupy the intrenchments formerly occupied by General Ferrero's division as soon as it is dark, in order to avoid the observation of the enemy. The commander of the pickets from your troops should have officers with him familiar with the line picketed by Ferrero.

A. A. HUMPHREYS,
Major-General and Chief of Staff.

Bivouac, 4th Division

Thomas's brigade was the only unit still in the encampment. The men sat, drying equipment over fires, swatting the clouds of flies and mosquitoes that rose from the nearby forests and marshy creeks. Others walked around shirtless in the damp heat. Except for the shocks of rifles stacked at regular intervals, the bivouac resembled nothing so much as a contraband camp, without women.

At eight o'clock the bugles called, and the slovenly camp snapped into life. Shirts went on, and boots. Fires sputtered up in smoke, and the tents fell as if before a hurricane. *Brigade moving.*

Where at?

Up on the line by the First Brigade. This the Day, man!

Naw! Can't be.

What could you do? It did not *feel* like this was the Day. There would be a different, special air to that time, a vibration through the world, a hush and a listening; not this buzz of flies, splash of mud, laughter and shouting.

But it might be the Day. *You'd best get ready.*

Pennington hailed Dobbs as the latter came trotting around a corner of the camp street.

"We're moving out to the flank," he yelled. "Picket duty. Word from headquarters."

Dobbs spat a stream of tobacco juice into the mud. "Well, long as it ain't digging."

"General White wants guides to take the troops into the lines there. Is there someone you can leave with your company?"

"My sergeant's pretty good. He can bring the boys along in back of A Company easy enough."

The two Lieutenants walked through the dissolving bivouac toward the headquarters tents. There looked to be a lot of brass up there—more horses than usual picketed by the trees and a white cavalry escort, sitting its mounts and waiting off to the right. Pennington, walking by Dobbs's side, suddenly found that Dobbs was leading them that way.

"Dobbs," he said.

"Quiet," said Dobbs, sharply, under his breath.

In front of them was the cavalry detail, the sergeant-major in command sitting his mount with his near leg, the left, in the stirrup and his right crossed across the pommel, rolling a cigarette. Dobbs walked toward him, unhurriedly. Stepped up alongside as if he was about to tap the man on the leg and ask a question. Chris recognized him just as Dobbs jumped up, grabbing both hands into the man's blouse and jerking him off the horse to the ground, and Dobbs stepped back and kicked the man hard in the face.

"You murdering son of a bitch," Dobbs said, "how come you ain't dead?"

Then there were uniforms all over the two of them, holding Dobbs, bending over the sergeant, and General White (commanding in Ferrero's place) and Colonel Thomas pushing through the circle of yelling men. "What in hell is going on here?"

"This officer attacked our sergeant."

"Right, we all saw it!"

Thomas motioned for quiet. "Lieutenant! What's the meaning of this?"

Dobbs grinned without mirth. "Damned if I can figure it, Colonel. God*damned* if I know what it means."

Pennington pushed forward. This was trouble for Dobbs. He had to do something.

"Colonel! This sergeant here . . . he killed one of our sentries, back about a month ago. Lieutenant Dobbs arrested him."

Thomas looked at the sergeant. The man blushed. "I been tried, Colonel. I paid for what I done."

"How?" said Dobbs.

Thomas gestured him angrily into silence. "What was the penalty, Sergeant?"

"Reduction in rank, suspension of pay. I had to work hard to get my stripes back, sir."

Thomas's face went white. He seemed at a loss for words. It was General White who spoke. "Lieutenant, you are under arrest until a court-martial can be convened. Striking an enlisted man without cause or justification is a serious matter, as you will find." He turned to Pennington. "Lieutenant, you will take this Lieutenant's sidearms please."

Dobbs unbuckled his sword belt and holster, and handed them to Pennington.

"Sir! Colonel!" said Pennington.

"Yes, Chris?" said Thomas.

"Sir, may I have a word with you?" They stepped aside. General White had turned and gone back to his tent. There were two officers of the provost guard standing alongside Dobbs.

"Sir," said Pennington, "don't arrest Dobbs! If you'd seen . . ."

Thomas's lips tightened. "I don't say it's just, Chris. But it's the law."

"Can't there be a delay? Sir . . . I was bringing Dobbs by to act as guide for the brigade. He's the one that knows the country over there the best."

Thomas considered. "Yes. All right. I can allow him to remain with the brigade, even while he's officially under arrest. He'll not be able to bear arms, though. No sword."

Chris grinned. "I'll tell him. And I'll tell him the officers of the brigade will stand by him!"

"To the limits of the law, Chris, the limits of the law!"

"I'll tell him!"

Out in the bivouac the men were assembling, you could feel their readiness, their energy:

> *We looks like men a-marchin on,*
> *We looks like men o'war!*

Washington: Carey's Theater

Bones: Dat music make me feel fine!

Tambo: Well, enjoy it whiles you can. You're going to be drafted into the army!

Bones: You don't say!

Tambo: I just did this minute. Are you deaf?

Bones: (Terrified) Death? Death? Oh, Lord, boss, I just got here. Dis a worrisome thing, a worrisome thing. You must tell me what to do.

Tambo: All right, I'll stand for your sergeant.

Bones: Hope you can stand for him, I know I can't.

Tambo: Now soldier, if you seed Ginral Lee and his boys a-comin, would you run or follow me?

Bones: I'd be doing both, boss; cause if de rebels comin, I be running right behind you.

Tambo: Was you ever a soldier before dis?

Bones: Yes, I was at de Battle of Bull Run. I ran, and dat's no bull!

Tambo: You ought to be in de calvary.

Bones: What for?

Tambo: Cause you're no good on earth!

Bones: Well, was you ever round where de guns was shooting?

Tambo: I was, once.

Bones: Did you run then?

Tambo: No, but I passed some folks dat was runnin.

Bones: Did you get hit in the fracas?

Tambo: The which?

Bones: In the fracas. Did you get hit in the fracas?

Tambo: No, I had that well covered.

Bones: You wasn't hit?

Tambo: No, but I heard one of them bullets whine two times.

Bones: How's dat?

Tambo: Once when it passed me, and once when I passed it.

Bones: Tambo, you is a coward. In the army, cowards is shot at dawn.

Tambo: Oh dat's all right den. I never get up till noon!

There were sherbet ices in the intermission, and time to smoke a cigar. "Crude stuff," said Ferrero with a smile, "but I have to confess I even enjoy its irreverence. It seems scandalous, with the war still . . ." His wife patted his hand. "But speaking to *them* all this week, arguing, pleading my case—I almost felt a beggar, and wished I might have had the wherewithal to *buy* what all the world knows can be bought in this city."

"Edward," said Lily softly, and he nodded.

The bell rang for the second act.

A PLAY: "THE RECRUITING OFFICE."

The Curtain rises on the Recruiting Office: a Sergeant and a Captain sit behind a table, snoring. A Whiskey Bottle before them on the table.

In staggers a drunken Irishman, red hair flaring, pitching forward somersaulting over a chair to come up, surprised on his feet! Turns around to expostulate, and goes head over heels back the other way, to wind up poised, balanced in a hand-stand, feet waving in the air, holding to a chairback!

In which posture the recruiting Sergeant, awakening, sees him. Wipes a hand over his face and declares:

"Begorrah! And Oi'll niver touch another draph in me loif!"

"Sargint, Oi wants to enlisth!"

"And do you, me bhoy? A foin thing. A Pathriotic thing!"

"Only . . . only Oi've a question or two before Oi sign."

"Anything, me bhoy!"

"Fwhat's the pay?"

"Thirteen dollars the month, me foin lad!" *To the audience:* "In greenbacks that is."

"And paid the firsth of the month, Sargint?"

"Of course, me noble laddy!" *To the audience:* "Whinever the Threasury gets round to it."

"And the food, Sargint? And dhrink!"

"Of the best, me bhoy. Beef not a year off the horse—I mean cow. And the dhrink . . . the dhrink . . . nothin but the purest of fine old Potomac."

"Potomac? Potomac? But ain't that a river, Sargint?"

"And ain't *Monongahela* a river, ye blatherskite!"

"Ah, to be sure, I'd forgot it. And one other thing. Would ye take a man that's got a mite problem with his seeing?"

"Such as?"

"Such as a glass eye?"

"No problem at all."

"And a bit of mine trouble."

"Mind trouble? A *loonathic?*"

"No, no! *Mine* trouble."

"Mine throuble? Are yez a coal miner, laddy?"

"Not that sort of mine, Sergint. There was this wallet . . ."

"Yes?"

"I said it was mine."

"Yes?"

"It was *his*. Will ye still have me, Sargint?"

"Oi'll have ye for all yer worth, me bhoy!"

"Then I'm your boy. Hic. Give me to sign."

"Here you are." *Signs.*

"Now," *says the sergeant,* "here's your thirteen dollars. Oh, minus three for clothes, and another five for the expenses of the office; and summat to square the sheriff. That leaves . . ." (*he looks at it*) "scarcely enough to bother about" (*pockets it*). "Off with you now." *The Irishman exits.*

Enter the recruit's aged Mother. Steps to the footlights and sings:

> *Our Jimmy has gone for to live in a tent,*
> *They have grafted him into the army;*
> *He finally pucker'd up courage and went,*
> *When they grafted him into the army.*
> *I told them the child was too young, alas!*
> *At the captain's fore-quarters, they said he would pass—*
> *They'd train him up well in the infantry class—*
> *So they grafted him into the army.*
> *Chorus: Oh, Jimmy farewell!*

Your brothers fell
Way down in Alabarmy;
I tho't they would spare a lone widder's heir,
But they grafted him into the army.

IX Corps Front: 14th N.Y.H.A.

It was all the fault of the damned niggers. The Johnnies had the real nose for them, knew it whenever the smokes came on the lines. And then it was bloody hell to pay—*pam! pam!* snipers by day and the pickets shooting anything that moved by night.

Neill was trapped. He'd been digging shit-holes, and the officers had his number, and Stanley had his name on the list. Another damned foul-up. His luck was shit-hole luck: nothing had gone right since they'd shot the draft-board man and he'd run for New York. Always there was some high-hat bastard like the cop O'Malley or Sergeant Stanley, and behind them some Big Shot like Oostervelt—and on bottom none other than himself. And if they couldn't do him in by catching him at it, they'd do him in by bullying and by starving, by punishment and humiliation. The'd have him shoveling nigger shit before they were done. McCarthy back in Pottsville, he'd had the word: it was the nigger over the Irishman, and they were all in it, and he was all under it.

If only they'd stop shooting: come dark, he would go on over the top. What was it that Johnny reb had told them: not Andersonville, but they'd let him just get off wherever. Well, that was all right. Get out of this suit, get to walking around. A man knows as much as I do about mining, and making out in the city, should be able to make it all right with these backwoods crackers and niggers.

Did they have mines over in the South? If they did, probably worked em with niggers. He'd find a job bossing niggers: that was work for a white man. Shouldn't be too bad if he could stand the niggers. If he couldn't, he'd walk away.

Him a gang boss in a mine would be a laugh! And the niggers had better not pull any of the fast ones, because he'd be wise to them. There wasn't any bunch of niggers in the world could know all the tricks the boys knew in the mines, and he would be miles ahead of them.

The dirty scum! He'd let em try to fool him, then turn it over on em, and watch them sweat.

He'd pay it off, he'd pay it all off. All the shit he'd had to eat.

If only the damned snipers would leave up for a little while.

Washington: Carey's Theater

Now in my provisions I see him revealed—
They have grafted him into the army;
A picket beside the contented field,
They have grafted him into the army.

He looks kinder sickish—begins to cry—
A big volunteer stading right in his eye!
Oh what if the ducky should up and die,
Now they've grafted him into the army?—

1st Minnesota, on New Market Road

They were on picket along the road, cavalry watching their flanks. Sergeant Smith didn't trust cavalry. They might just ride off, leaving them stuck out there. Get orders to withdraw or change position, and never tell the poor infantry.

Nothing was doing. They could see the rebel pickets away across the fields, too far for shooting. In the fields to either side, they heard a bugle call, and stamping, calling voices. "Captain!" yelled Smith.

"Right," said Farwell. They'd been expecting this all day. Their division was the only infantry on this road. Some damn cavalry feint or other going on; no real attack. They'd figured that come nightfall, they'd get called back.

But the damn cavalry! Those fancy-pants soldiers couldn't wait for dark to get back to hot food and warm blankets, and they were starting while the rebs could see them. That was going to mean some son-of-a-bitch reb Colonel bringing some boys out to see what's up.

A courier rode up to Farwell. "That's it," he called, "we're pulling back." Without further orders, the company got its gear together, and formed ranks, the rest of their brigade rising out of the ground around them.

"We're rearguards," said Farwell.

Smith said nothing. He was thinking, *Again. But we are just going to walk away. Nothing to do, nothing to worry about. Just walking away.*

The brigade formed column quickly, and moved back down the road. But in the distance, Smith could see a dark clot of troops on the road, scattered clots to right and left. Reb cavalry coming over for a look-see.

He felt weak and sick. Afraid to die, afraid to kill. It was going to begin again. The reb cavalry was coming at him down a long tunnel between the trees.

Just keep running away, keep going down the road. The First was halted and strung across the road in a line, and Smith kept looking back to where the rebels were coming on slowly, but faster than the retreating brigade. Where in hell was the cavalry? Always the damned infantry to do the work. *Not this time, not this time.* Ahead of him the retreating column slid down the darkening valley between the trees. He heard the sounds coming closer. Recognized them. He'd been a soldier too long not to.

"First Minnesota," called Farwell. "Load and stand ready. Widen that interval." The calls of the other battalions on their flanks could be clearly heard.

"Come here, Dan," said Farwell. The Captain was standing in the lee of a pine tree just off the road. "Stand here, will you? And keep an eye on the boys off in the woods there.'' Smith nodded. Anything not to have to stand in the road, waiting.

Farwell stepped away, back into the road. Shadows came bulking through the trees, cut across the road.

''Fire!'' said Farwell, and the line of muskets *pat-pang*ed and there were flashes out of the clots of darkness where the rebels were coming on.

Smith heard the rush back through the trees off to the right flank— *They're running*—and quick as thought he stepped out into the road, ''First squad! Over here! Goddamn flankers are running! Let's go!'' and the squad rose, and followed his gestures, lining out and going into the woods.

''There!'' he yelled, and the muskets burst in the dark woods, showing their fire now in the gathering darkness.

Wood-crack! Broken-branch sound. Someone kicked Smith in the shoulder and he fell down.

Every time he sank it was worse than dying. He could not count on dying. He could not believe that dying would only be the darkness, the *gone*. It would be dreaming, and for so long now his dreams were a more terrible place to live than his life. He fought for consciousness: *Let me not die asleep, that would be going to hell, let me not die asleep . . .*

''His eyes are open, Captain.''

''I think he's all right.''

Farwell's face. ''It's a good wound, Danny. Not bad, but bad enough. You'll be in Minnesota soon.'' Minnesota: he drifted homeward over the black earth he had turned with his plow. The earth was full of the upturned faces of those he had killed and those he had survived. He put his hand to his father's house and it flared as if to a torch, the walls seething and melting. ''You'll be home soon, Danny,'' said Farwell's voice.

If only I don't fall asleep.

Shadows carried him to the ambulance wagon.

His arm began to toll like a bell.

He cradled it like an infant against his side.

He gave birth to agony.

They put him down, and they went away. The ambulance, dark, jounced over the rutted road. He was in a coffin falling down stairs.

The last of the regiment was gone. He was alone with wounded cavalrymen. They were probably all dead, now, he the only one left.

To live his life among strangers. Among cavalrymen. No one who knew him, or spoke his language.

No one to keep him from falling asleep.

The ambulance stopped, and he smelled the damp smell of a river.

The flat fishy smell of tidal waters.

''Give me some water.''

In Minnesota the water was very clear. The water in this part of the country tasted of blood and urine. The taste of it was the last taste in his mouth.

HEADQUARTERS CAVALRY CORPS,
July 28, 1864.

Doctor PEASE,
Medical Director, Cavalry Corps, Wind-Mill Point:
DOCTOR: We have 150 killed and wounded. We'll be sent to corps hospital by boat with two surgeons. Everything is going on well. Wounded operated on; are well taken care of. Two flags captured and one gun lost. Do not try to come out. All wounded will be sent to corps headquarters.
H. A. DU BOIS,
Assistant Surgeon.

Washington: Carey's Theater

"The Recruiting Office," by pratfall and thigh-slap, was working towards its climax. The Irish private and a Dutch Captain had played the fool in their grotesque accents, "liberating" a plantation to "vree de slafes" (as the Captain would have it), and to confiscate Ole Massa's supply of bourbon whiskey. They had even turned the plantation darkies into soldiers.

Right there Ferrero had a horrible moment of recognition, as the niggers paraded in the absurd feathers and braid and mismatched finery they mistook for military pomp. He seemed to hear, almost audibly, the army slur on his division as "Ferrero's Minstrels," and for that second he himself stood for the comical Dutchman on the stage—a dago dancing master!—and heard in memory the voice out of the ranks as his division had filed by in review, *Laws, ain't we pretty!* In this light, didn't it all seem true—didn't it seem that they really were a damned minstrel show, and he the master of ceremonies, a gaudy buffoon?

And then the Corn Meal Man stepped forward, in the role of an orator, a Negro politician, looking so surpassingly foolish that Ferrero felt the weight of association that had just bound him to the stage suddenly lift and break away from him. He sat in his velvet seat, and gazed at the Corn Meal Man as the famous "Stump Speech" began, and it started him laughing again, laughing and laughing at the grotesque extravagance of it all.

"Brudderins an . . . brudderins an . . . brudderins and udder'ns! I'se a raisin befo you alls for to susplicate de mattuh of reconsterection, uh, recontsterushin, uh, raw consternation—oh, I means votes for niggers, dat's what I means.

"Brudderins an . . . brudderins an . . . brudderins an *udderins,* I stands befo you dis day to tell you, to scuss unto you, pon de nigger question. Now dis a vest, dis a vast, dis a wust—dis one *big* quest'n, becaze de one pussun never axt to twell you, to scuss unto you pon dis matter is de nigger hisself. Now I stands here, *fo* de nigger. I says unto you, dat *a horse diwided betwixt hisself cannot stan! Can't* do it! Can't stand, can't sit, can't run de scrapple chaste, can't do *nuffin!* Now de

Publicans say, dat de nigger same as de white man. Huh! I reads in de Bible where Jesus throw out de Publicans frum de Temple along of de moneychangers. Dime-at-*craps* say, do de same to dese *here* Publicans, and leave us have de House to ourselfs. Hunh! Dime-at *craps* jess wants one more shake on de dice.

"Now what is de differenshiashun? Some is for hard money, and some is for the greenback dollar. I favors de greenback. Why? If you puts a silver dollar in yo pocket, you takes it out again—silver dollar. But you put a greenback dollar in yo pocket and pull it out, it *in creases!* *Ha-ha-ha-ha-ha!*

"Mr. Greeley don't lie. Much."—(laughter)—"Now he say de nigga man is good as de white. Huh! Now ain't dat stuff! Evah see a white man dat could swaller de whole watermelon wit one bite! No! Evah see a white man dat could hoe corn and hoe down de same time! No! Evah see a white man dat could file his hair down? An make a coat out de wool? Huh! You ain't an he ain't neither. So dat equality is stuff. Comes de recstor, reconstitutor—after de war—dis darky be a Senator. Sit right next to Mistah Sumner and Old Phillips and say"— he bowed, and grinned from ear to ear—"'Move ovah dere, boss! Dis Mista *Greeley's* pet.' And dey says, 'What you got dat make you qualif- ercated to be a Senator of de United States,' an I says, 'Gemmen! A man don't have to be smart to be a Senator, an he don't have to be edder-crated, and he don't have even got to be beautiful. What he do need though, am one ting.' And dey asks, *'Whut dat?'* An I says, 'Dat am a powerfullest kind of a *appetite.* Gemmen, does you see dese lips and mouf? Does you know dat I have eat all the chicken and water- melons I have stole, and stole all they was? An do you think I can do all dat, an not be a Senator? Hell, boys: I'se as good a thief as any man in de house!'"

And the curtain descended on waves of laughter.

The audience cheered the curtain down and cheered it up again. General and Mrs. Ferrero left during the ovation, to avoid the press of people at the exit.

They strolled home to Willard's. The night air was wet and close. Their feet tapped audibly on the pavement. The Union forever, Hurrah, boys, hurrah. They were relaxed and happy. As if in response to this new mood there was a note awaiting them at the hotel.

Ferrero looked up. "Lily, . . ." he handed it to her.

THE WHITE HOUSE
July 28, 1864

General FERRERO
Willard's Hotel
GENERAL: Your reappointment confirmed at extraordinary ses- sion of Senate this day. Official confirmation will follow.

Very respectfully,

J. NICOLAY
Secretary to the President.

She looked at him. He stood confused a moment. Then : "I'll be leaving for Petersburg on the morning boat. Lily was looking at him, her eyes dim. He was going away. He felt already wrapped in vague shadowy distances, a fog of unclear plans and intentions. Back to . . . to what? His division was all confounded in his mind with the grotesque looks and manners of the minstrels. The words of the song repeated themselves inanely in his mind :

> *We shall meet but we shall miss him*
> *There will be one vacant chair.*
> *We will long to caress him!*
> *While we breathe our evening prayer.*

Night. 4th Division Bivouac.

The Brigade was ready to move. Pennington caught up with Dobbs, as the latter was checking his saddle girth, and the balance of his gear in the saddlebags thrown across the horse's withers.

"Lem!" he called.

"Chris," said Dobbs, quietly. He turned. "I'm beholden to you, Chris. For getting them to keep me with the brigade. I wouldn't want to miss the Day."

But there were questions that must be answered. "Why did you do it, Lem? There was no point : the court had its say on the matter."

Dobbs grinned without mirth. "Temporary suspension of pay and reduction in rank for murdering a soldier in cold blood. And I get my wrist slapped for arresting the son of a bitch. That's a *court*."

Chris blushed. "You're right," he stammered, "it wasn't . . . fair or just, whatever. Only . . ."

"Only?"

Chris seemed to look past or through Dobbs. "The way you went for the man. You were going to kill him."

"I was," he said.

"How can you be this way? We're—you're an officer. We're supposed to set an example of discipline to our men. If we don't stay in the law ourselves, how can we expect to be obeyed?"

Dobbs shrugged. "I don't know the answer in the way you're asking the question. I never had trouble with my men following me, and standing up to trouble. That's all I know about being an officer."

"You know," said Chris, "you act as if this war was just to settle some private grudge you've got against the world. It isn't!"

"Right there. Somebody's grudge is getting settled, but it ain't mine."

"If we act in hate . . . it will be all for *nothing!* It will all never stop, but just go on and on! You never act out of everything but hate!"

Dobbs face filled with blood, and his eyes showed heat, and something baffled. "And now we come back to 'Sweet Jesus, love your enemies.' I've said it once, and I'll say it once more, Chris : killing's too serious a kind of business to get into, unless your hate of what you got to kill is mighty strong. I make no nevermind whether that thing wears a blue coat or a gray, but I hit it where and when I can. If that don't make me a Christian, that's no surprise; though I can't see where killing what you're supposed to love makes any damn sense at all to me. Quakers, by God, is the only Christians, and I'm Goddamned if I'm one of *them*. I may not be fit to lead these niggers to Jesus, but by God I'll lead them down some goddamn se-cesh throats before I'm done. And glad for the chance!''

He stood, glaring at Chris for a moment. The look in his eyes became one of doubt for a moment, almost of pain. ''Glad for the chance, Chris,'' he said, more softly.

Chris stood, unable to speak. He hadn't meant to be angry with Dobbs. He gestured with his hand, ineffectually. He cleared his throat. ''What will you do without sidearms?'' he asked.

Dobbs grinned, and bent to pick up a hand axe lying on the ground —a heavy one, with iron head and curving ash-wood haft. ''Always preferred these anyway,'' he said. He turned, and swung up into the saddle. Turned to his troops and held the axe up, signalling them to prepare to march.

Then, with one swift motion of wrist and forearm, he waved the axe in the air, the head catching and flashing the red sunset light of the bivouac fire.

''Eee-hah!'' he shouted, and the company echoed with a roar, and from the rear rank a resonant bass voice called, ''Ho for the Wood-choppah!'' and they all began to laugh.

Pennington rubbed the velvet nose of his horse, as Dobbs and his company moved by, Dobbs sitting his horse straight-backed, holding the axe in formal pose up-and-down from right thigh to right shoulder as he would have held his sword.

As they came by him, the troops began to sing, ''We-e looks like men a-a-mar-chin on, / We'-e looks like men o war!'' and still sang as they vanished around the curve of the road and into the dark shadows under the pine trees.

Skirmish and Retreat
July 28–29, 1864

July 28, Midnight Pegram's Salient

"Sam," said Billy, "somebody shot the Colonel's nigger."

Marriot sat with his back against the trench, whittling a piece of wood with his knife. A round peg—no, he was sharpening a point—a stake, to stick something in the wall, hang up his canteen tonight.

"They say Yankees done it," said Billy, sitting down.

"But you don't think so," said Marriot.

"Small hole in back, not-so-big hole in front. I'd say it was from up closer."

"Think I done it, Billy?"

"No, Sam." Billy blushed. "You was plenty mad enough to, though."

"Not that mad." He stopped whittling and focussed on Billy's face. "If I was to shoot somebody, it wouldn't be no dumb nigger out picking blackberries for that son of a bitch."

"What you going to do, Sam?"

The knife sliced shavings from the wooden peg. "I ain't decided." The knife went *whit, whit.* "There is shit that I will not eat. Not to save my hide and hair." *And talk's cheap.*

Dixon came in and squatted on his haunches in front of the two of them. Marriot ignored him. He kept whittling, and the shavings flipped out around the broken tip of Dixon's boot.

"You boys hear about the Colonel's nigger?" He grinned. "Some Yankee potted him." He hawked, and spat. "Some damn Yankee, huh?" He grinned. "Pretty good shot for a Yankee, wouldn't you say?" His face was flushed, as if he'd had something to drink. "Teach that son of a bitch Davidson a lesson, won't it, Billy?" He looked from one to the other, like a retriever with a dead bird in his mouth.

Billy stared at him.

Sam looked up. "You yellow, sneaking, backshooting bastard. If you were worth the trouble, I'd take off your damn scalp and save it for an ass wipe."

Dixon purpled. "Marriot, you big-shot son of a bitch that used to be corporal: now's the time! Let's go to it!"

Marriot's hand shot out swiftly, catching Dixon off balance, and he landed on his ass on the trench floor. "Suck on that," he said, and got up, and walked off. When Billy looked he saw that Marriot had stuck the whittled peg right through the loose collar lapel of Dixon's shirt, pinning shirt and all to the dirt wall of the trench. Dixon sat there, sick and sweating. He looked at Billy. His eyes were dirty gray.

Everything is coming apart, thought Billy. *Since they started coming at us through the ground, everything is just coming all to pieces.* He had to do something. If he could only figure it out, and put it together in his head, maybe things could be fixed up yet.

That night, when the pickets were out, Marriot deserted, leaving behind his rifle, but taking his knife.

WAR DEPARTMENT, C.S.A.
Richmond, Va., July 29, 1864.

General R. E. LEE,
Commanding, &c.;

GENERAL: I have the honor to acknowledge your letter of the 19th instant, transmitted through the Adjutant-General, having reference to the numerous deserters from the Federal Army. It is certainly very important to encourage such desertion, but the disposition of deserters is one of the most embarrassing subjects that has come under the consideration of the Department. Whenever they have been turned loose upon parole exacted of fidelity or good behavior they have soon proved themselves disaffected or turbulent, and been productive in our cities of serious disorders and crimes. Efforts have been made at different points to arrange workshops, in which they could be employed on wages, but if near cities disorderly proceedings have resulted, and if at distant point the people of the vicinity have become seriously alarmed, and have remonstrated against the effect produced upon the slaves. In some instances in which they have been sent to the owners of mining and manufacturing establishments, the owners of slaves engaged in the same work have withdrawn them, or threatened to do so, and the people of the vicinity have insisted upon the withdrawal or confinement of the deserters. . . . I cannot, therefore, think that it would be judicious for the Government to come under any pledge to subsist and permit them to go where they please. The utmost that could be done would be an assurance that they would not be injured; that horses or equipments brought by them would be taken at fair valuation, and that when suitable opportunity offered, they would be allowed to pass the lines. . . .

Very respectfully,

JAMES A. SEDDON,
Secretary of War.

This was the way Marriot left: not waiting to go on picket, because you didn't desert when you had taken a post the boys trusted you to hold, and because it would be easy. If you were leaving, you had to do it hard, giving the boys a fair shake at stopping you. He'd left the rifle: wasn't his, and he wasn't going to shoot any of his own kind. Left his rations: he'd eat off the Yankees while he could. Them as was staying would need it. He didn't ask anyone to go with him. This was a thing you did alone. Each man would have to decide for himself. And he wouldn't tell the damn Yankees a thing they don't already know; but maybe throw in a couple stretchers so they'll lay back and not do anything bad to the boys, for a time anyway. *And that's my debt paid to all them I care about.*

He left his gear all neat. Slipped out to the sink; then, in the darkness, up around the back of the bush and down the slant of the shallow ravine that came up to the lines just off left of the trench that flanked the battery.

The trenches weren't heavily manned. Too many boys off up north to fight the Yankees near Richmond, there was only a man for every eight feet of trench, and at night the intervals were longer. This here was a twisty-turny section of trench, and if you went down, across, up and over quick, there wasn't much chance you'd be spotted. Carrying nothing in his hands, he went quickly—the soldier to the right was out of sight around a turn of the trench, the one on the left asleep, most likely: and he was over the parapets, and into the ravine that slanted towards the Yankee lines.

There was a picket post down here, where the Yankees had cut the picket's throat and snaked a couple prisoners out the month before. He gave it a wide berth, moving slowly, deer-stalking, through the brush to one side. He left the murmuring of the pickets behind and to his right.

It was so quiet—no Yank artillery tonight. Odd.

The Yankee entrenchments loomed against the rising moon.

"Psst! Hey Yank!"

He came in over the trench hunched over and hurrying, and they pushed him back against the trench side and stuck a lantern in his face. Something was wrong. It smelled wrong, there was something not right.

The faces of his captors were black, and white teeth glittered in the lamplight. *Niggers!*

They were going to cut his throat.

"What's your outfit, soldier?" A white man's voice, and he turned to it. A Major. Marriot licked his dry lips. His heart was slowing down. *Niggers. So what.*

He had nothing to be afraid of. He had done everything just right. He would tell this officer what he'd decided to tell, and that was all. Then they'd lock him up for the rest of the war, but that was all right with him.

Afterwards . . . but that didn't matter either.

HEADQUARTERS NINTH ARMY CORPS
July 29, 1864—1 A.M.

Major-General HUMPHREYS:

Two deserters have just come in. They say that the troops they belong to (B. Johnson's) man one of those intrenchments just in front of my center. They say that many troops have arrived within a day or two from the West or somewhere;

and say that they have been digging for nearly two weeks to ascertain whether we were mining them. They deserted because they were not allowed to vote yesterday. They say that in very few cases, and those depend on the character of officers, were any allowed to vote that did not vote for Vance. These men both voted for Sheriff but were not allowed to vote for Governor.

A large fire is burning now in Petersburg, and we opened artillery to prevent operations to stop it. Bells of the town have been ringing. Your letter in reference to the firing of heavy guns has been received and communicated to the proper officers.

> A. E. BURNSIDE,
> *Major-General.*

HEADQUARTERS ARMY OF THE POTOMAC,
July 29, 1864—10:30 A.M.

Lieutenant-General GRANT:
From the foregoing dispatch and other information it appears quite probable that Heth's division, Hill's corps, and Field's division, Longstreet's corps, have both left my front.

> GEO. G. MEADE,
> *Major-General.*

July 29, 11:00 A.M. Burnside's Headquarters

Burnside was just returning from his inspection of the lines. Everything seemed to be in place. He'd asked his division commanders about the morale of their troops and they had assured him it was good, good as could be expected, good. That was what he'd wanted to hear. Everything seemed to be in place and ready to go. The Mine was set: charged, tamped, fuses placed, waiting for the word. The blacks looked to be in good shape, Oliver's brigade anyway—Thomas's brigade was off on the flank, he hadn't had time to visit them, but they were probably all right, too. Hadn't been in the trenches at all, now that he thought of it—only Oliver's brigade had been on at all since late June. Oh, they'd be in fine shape!

Richmond met him at the door of his tent, a worried look on his face. "General, this came while you were out." Burnside took the telegram and unfolded it.

HEADQUARTERS ARMY OF THE POTOMAC,
July 29, 1864—10:15 A.M.

Major-General BURNSIDE,
Commanding Ninth Corps:
I am instructed to say that the major-general commanding submitted to the lieutenant-general commanding the armies your proposition to form the leading columns of assault of the

black troops, and that he, as well as the major-general commanding, does not approve the proposition, but directs that
those columns be formed of the white troops.

A. A. HUMPHREYS,
Major-General and Chief of Staff.

His brain began to bong and bong with sudden headache. What?
What did it mean? He felt like an idiot. Not approved. Grant had not
approved.

"General Meade is expected momentarily, sir. I tried to reach
you but . . ."

Not approved.

Burnside found himself inside the tent, sitting at his desk. Holding
the telegram delicately between thumb and forefinger.

He shook his head to clear it. *General Meade momentarily.*

Hadn't approved it.

It was *impossible.* There had to be some mistake.

His watch ticked loudly in his vest pocket. He took it out, looked
at the face. It meant nothing to him. Must have stopped. Went to wind
it but had to put the telegram down first.

Richmond stuck his head through the flap. "Sir, General Meade
and General Ord to see you."

Burnside nodded. How hot it was! "Richmond? What time is it?"

"Five minutes past eleven, sir."

Meade and Ord entered. Burnside rose, automatically, to greet
them. Watch and telegram still in his thick hands. Put them down.

"Hot today," he said. Heat rose up out of his collar. *Meade! Dis-
approved!*

"How are things along your lines, General?" asked Meade.

Burnside nodded affably, then blankly. "General Meade, . . ." he
said. His lips were dry. He licked them.

Meade nodded to Ord, a red-faced, choleric-looking man—Burnside
knew him slightly. "Ord's corps will be acting in reserve. He'll relieve
the division on your right tonight, when you mass for the assault, and
have two divisions to follow up and occupy your trenches when your
troops go in."

"Can't anything be done?" asked Burnside.

"What?" snapped Meade, "what are you talking about?"

Burnside's face was red as a beet. "The Colored division. Cannot
the decision be *changed?* If I speak to Grant myself, perhaps, . . .
factors not considered . . ."

"This is impertinence, General! The case has been presented to
Grant with all relevant information. Are you implying I did not present
things fairly?"

"Dammit, General!" Burnside shook his head. "Can't the decision
be reconsidered? There are things that perhaps I myself did not make
sufficiently clear . . . accuse you of nothing, General. My own fault, to
be sure. Didn't make sufficiently clear . . ."

"No, General," said Meade, softly. "It cannot be changed now.

There isn't time. It is final, and you must put in your white troops.''
Grant had agreed: not the time for experiments, with the elections com-
ing, and the Radicals in an uproar, to get the niggers in over their heads,
to mess with them at all was buying trouble—and not just for Lincoln,
but for Grant. The last thing either needed was a slaughter of black
troops.

"General Meade," said Burnside, licking his lips. He cleared his
throat. His face was purple with the heat, his eyes white against the
darkening skin, goggling like a clown's. "This will require . . . changes,
my plans. Changes. I'll have to notify . . ."

Meade and Ord rose. "You seem out of sorts. You had best inform
your division commanders." Meade looked at his watch. "Time is pressing, General."

They were gone. Burnside's heart was pulsing in his ears. Get the
division commanders here. Potter, Ledlie, Willcox, Ferrero—no, not Ferrero! White! Off on the flank somewhere.

Oh, to hell with White! And to hell with his niggers, too! Useless
useless *useless!*

Everything was ruined now.

He glanced at his watch: 11:45. Scarcely half a day until the attack.
Everything changed at the last minute. All the movements would have
to be altered.

It could all go to smash so easily, errors accumulating, troops blundering about in the trenches, confusion everywhere. The attack never
getting started at all! and Meade shrilling at him, eyes like a vulture,
hungry for my blood! The whole corps becoming unravelled, inex-
tricably tangled up. Damn Meade! Damn that bearded granny-faced
old interfering bastard Meade! He had gripped the arms of his chair
till the knuckles went white.

He took out his watch and looked at it. Nearly noon. There weren't
more than fourteen or fifteen hours until the attack.

Actually, the Plan could still work. Without the niggers the beauty
of it was lost. But it *could* work. There was still the Mine. He had an
image of kegs of powder in a cave, like little chests of treasure.

The Ninth Corps could still win the war, with Burnside's Bomb:
one heavy stroke, *boom*, right through the rebel line; take the hill, entrench, bring up the guns; supports moving up, beat off counterattack
(the rebels shrieking like women) then another lunge and we're into
Petersburg, fighting through the streets for the bridges.

Luck luck luck, his luck was out. Something to bring it back. Some
appeal to the gods to give him back his luck. Hadn't he earned it yet?
Burnside, wrapped around by plots, suddenly felt afraid.

Meade with his nasty little eyes. *Not even allowing me to organize*
my own attack. Coup de main, *don't bother to form, forget the move-*
ments left and right. Jealous because I rank him, and my people are
loyal to me! No appreciation of the loyalty it took to let him command
me, when I'm his senior by rights! Meade looks at loyalty and thinks it
is weakness.

He could feel his eyes bulging with tears of grief and rage.

Where were his precious division commanders, now that he needed them? He looked at his watch. 12:15. Only a few hours left before the attack.

HEADQUARTERS ARMIES OF THE UNITED STATES,
City Point, Va., July 29, 1864.

Maj. Gen. GEORGE G. MEADE,
Commanding Army of the Potomac:
GENERAL: I have directed General Butler to order General Ord to report to you for the attack on Petersburg. The details for the assault I leave for you to make out. I directed General Sheridan, whilst we were at Deep Bottom last evening, to move his command immediately to the left of Warren from Deep Bottom. It will be well to direct the cavalry to endeavor to get round the enemy's right flank. Whilst they will not probably succeed in turning the enemy, they will detain a large force to prevent it. I will go out this evening to see you; will be at your headquarters about 4 P.M.

Very respectfully, your obedient servant,
U. S. GRANT,
Lieutenant-General.

P.S.—If you want to be any place on the line at the hour indicated inform me by telegraph, and I will meet you wherever you may be.

U. S. G.

CITY POINT, *July 29, 1864—1:15* P.M.

General MEADE:
The enemy are evidently piling everything except a very thin line in your front, to the north side of the river. Hancock was to be careful to have his command well in hand and a strong line to fall behind, where the gun-boats can have full play along his front. I have no doubt but he has taken these precautions, but it will do no harm to caution him. I am inclined to think the enemy will wait for us to attack unless they discover that we are withdrawing.

U. S. GRANT,
Lieutenant-General.

HEADQUARTERS ARMY OF THE POTOMAC,
July 29, 1864—2:30 P.M.

Lieutenant-General GRANT:
I earnestly impressed on Hancock yesterday the necessity of occupying a strong line, intrenching it, and preparing for a heavy attack to-day, which I deemed probable when the enemy

had accumulated a heavy force. I have now sent him your telegram. Your note by Captain Hudson just received. Ord has
been with me all the morning. We have been over the line
and in conference with Burnside. I will be at my quarters
at 4 P.M., it being about as near as any part of the line.

GEO. G. MEADE,
Major-General.

Noon: IX Corps Front: 43rd U.S.C.T.

Sergeant Randolph stepped into the headquarters bombproof.
You sent for me, Major?''

"Yes," said Booker. "I wanted to tell you: orders are coming
down. The attack is going to be soon. Maybe tomorrow, maybe the day
after.''

"Praise Jesus," said Randolph. "We waited long enough.''

"We're going to have to make ladders, Sergeant. This is not the
part of the line we'll be jumping off from—it's to be the center, though
it would be best not to tell it around. We can't be sure the troops there
will dig out footholds. I want us to be ready for anything at all.''

"That's good," said Randolph. "All right. We put some together,
if we can get wood for em.''

"Take a detail back of the lines. Make em strong, Sergeant. Going
to be a lot of people going up them. Don't want to use em up too fast.''

"How many?''

"Many as we can make, I guess. Let's say . . . ten at least.''

Randolph lingered. "Major . . .''

"Yes?''

"I been wondering, looking out from the picket post. Rebel lines
as strong as this, we gonna have a time carrying through em. I remember what come of that time up Spotsylvania, when we buried them
boys that rushed the trench line.''

My God, thought Booker, *they don't know. Everybody in the whole
army must have heard by now, rumors going around. Damned if I didn't
forget. Nobody talks to these men but each other and their officers; and
officers don't tell their men all they know do they? Especially if the
officer's white and the troops black. The ones going to do the job, and
they're the only ones in the army don't know how.*

"Randolph . . . Sergeant, I owe you an apology. I ought to have
told you sooner. It's a trick we're pulling. Some miners have dug out
under the rebel fort. They're going to fill up the tunnel with gunpowder, and blow a big hole in the rebel line. Take out all the guns there,
a lot of the infantry—maybe scare off a lot of the rest,''

"Hunh," said Randolph. Taking it in. *Major: How come you never
told?* But the idea appealed to him. *Like rabbit done to the elephant.
Burn him up asleeping.* "That's smart.''

"Yes . . . if it doesn't work, though . . .''

Randolph grinned. "Oh, I get that: if it don't work, we just do it anyway. Well: that's all right, now I know. Trick don't work, there's nothing to do but whip the elephant."

Randolph's detail went back of the lines till they found the lumber dump left by the miners themselves, the extra boards and timbers they'd cut for the Mine and hadn't used. This was luck, and a good sign for sure. The detail grabbed a-hold, and carried the stuff back. In single file, the line of carriers snaked back up the covered way to the lines. In his head, Randolph pictured the line of rebel entrenchments. *Boom!* a voice whispered, and a hand like the hand of God tore the entrenchments apart and scattered them. *Charge,* he said, *through the hole, and out the other side.* The doors swing wide, left and right. Charge on up the hill to the cabin. Air full of fire and glory all over my head, and the sun of righteousness bright in the sky.

> *Do Lord, remember me,*
> *Do Lord, remember me,*
> *In that Day of fire,*
> *Do Lord remember me.*

HEADQUARTERS ARMY OF THE POTOMAC,
July 29, 1864.

ORDERS.

The following instructions are issued for the guidance of all concerned :

1. As soon as it is dark Major-General Burnside, commanding Ninth Corps, will withdraw his two brigades under General White, occupying the intrenchments between the Plank and Norfolk roads, and bring them to his front. Care will be taken not to interfere with the troops of the Eighteenth Corps moving into their position in rear of the Ninth Corps. General Burnside will form his troops for assaulting the enemy's works at daylight of the 30th, prepare his parapets and abatis for the passage of the columns, and have the pioneers equipped for work in opening passages for artillery, destroying enemy's abatis and the intrenching tools distributed for effecting lodgment, &c.

2. Major-General Warren, commanding Fifth Corps, will reduce the number of his troops holding the intrenchments on his front to the minimum, and concentrate all his available force on his right and hold them prepared to support the assault of Major-General Burnside. The preparations in respect to pioneers, intrenching tools, &c., enjoined upon the Ninth Corps will also be made by the Fifth Corps.

3. As soon as it is dark Major-General Ord, commanding Eighteenth Corps, will relieve his troops in the trenches by General Mott's division, of the Second Corps, and form his corps in rear of the Ninth Corps, and be prepared to support the assault of Major-General Burnside.

4. Every preparation will be made for moving forward the field artillery of each corps.

5. At dark Major-General Hancock, commanding Second Corps, will move from Deep Bottom to the rear of the intrenchments now held by the Eighteenth Corps, resume the command of Mott's division, and be prepared at daylight to follow up the assaulting and supporting columns, or for such other operations as may be found necessary.

6. Major-General Sheridan, commanding Cavalry Corps, will proceed at dark from the vicinity of Deep Bottom to Lee's Mill, and at daylight will move with his whole corps, including Wilson's division, against the enemy's troops defending Petersburg on their right, by the roads leading to that town from the southward and westward.

7. Major Duane, acting chief engineer, will have the pontoon trains parked at convenient points in the rear prepared to move. He will see that supplies of sand-bags, gabions, fascines, &c., are in depot near the lines ready for use. He will detail engineer officers for each corps.

8. At 3.30 in the morning of the 30th, Major-General Burnside will spring his mine, and his assaulting columns will immediately move rapidly upon the breach, seize the crest in the rear, and effect a lodgment there. He will be followed by Major-General Ord, who will support him on the right, directing his movement to the crest indicated, and by Major-General Warren, who will support him on the left. Upon the explosion of the mine, the artillery of all kinds in battery will open upon those points of the enemy's works whose fire covers the ground over which our columns must move, care being taken to avoid impeding the progress of our troops. Special instructions respecting the direction of fire will be issued through the chief of artillery.

9. Corps commanders will report to the commanding general when their preparations are complete, and will advise him of every step in the progress of the operation and of everything important that occurs.

10. Promptitude, rapidity of execution, and cordial co-operation are essential to success, and the commanding general is confident that this indication of his expectations will insure the hearty efforts of the commanders and troops.

11. Headquarters during the operation will be at the headquarters of the Ninth Corps.

By command of Major-General Meade:

S. WILLIAMS,
Assistant Adjutant-General.

ARTILLERY HDQRS., ARMY OF THE POTOMAC,
Before Petersburg, July 29, 1864.

CIRCULAR.

1. The batteries are not to open to-morrow morning until the signal is given. This signal will be the explosion of the mine under the battery in front of the advanced position of Burnside's corps.

2. Immediately on this mine being sprung the batteries will all open. The greatest possible pains will be taken to avoid interfering with the storming party, which will advance as soon as the mine is sprung, and over the ruins of the explosion. So soon as an entrance is effected here, strong bodies of troops will move to the right and left behind the enemy's line to clear out his troops, and to the front to gain the crest, and, if possible, enter the town of Petersburg. A careful watch must be kept on these movements so as to avoid the possibility of interfering with the advance.

3. The fire will in preference be turned on those batteries which command the point of assault and the ground over which our troops will move. These batteries will probably be found on the crest near the salient, or on the flank of the salient looking toward the Ninth Corps.

4. The batteries in the small redan, and the work known as Fort Hell, will not fire on the advanced point of the salient, as there is danger of such shot striking our attacking troops. They will be directed against the face of the salient, so that the shot which pass over it may strike the work on the crest above it, and after time has elapsed sufficient for an assaulting party to pass well over the crest the guns will be directed still more to the left so as not to strike the town.

5. Commanders on the lines will watch the fire closely, and take all possible precautions against injuring our own troops, whilst bringing their guns to bear on the batteries of the enemy. They will also watch for the movements of the enemy's troops toward our attacking columns, and use every effort to drive them back or retard their movements.

6. The artillery on the line of the Eighteenth Corps will open at the same time as that of the Fifth and Ninth, so as to fully employ the enemy in its front. The fire of the guns and mortars on the left of the line of the Eighteenth Corps will especially be brought to bear on such batteries in front of them as have a fire on Burnside's front.

When the enemy's fire has been silenced, the firing on his batteries will cease, and a strict watch be kept on the movements of his troops, and any attempt to reopen the fire of his batteries will be at once met.

HENRY J. HUNT,
Brigadier-General and Chief of Artillery.

Burnside's Headquarters

Meade had left . . . how long ago? Burnside looked at his watch. Twenty minutes at least. It was three o'clock now, barely twelve hours until the attack.

He looked up at his divisional commanders: Potter, Ledlie, Willcox. (Not White. He couldn't bear to be reminded. The niggers were out of this as far as he was concerned!)

They'd seen it all together—except Ledlie, of course; he was a new man. Burnside smiled automatically, so that Ledlie should not feel slighted.

The ticking of his watch seemed loud to Burnside. Seconds were passing with each series of ticks. Once each minute a bead of sweat formed in the ridges of Ledlie's forehead, and slid down to the tip of his reddish nose.

I must do something to buck them up! Burnside thought. He cleared his throat, licked his lips. Then he smiled, the genuine Burnside Beam, and rubbed his hands together, and chuckled down his throat. "Well, gentlemen!" he said heartily. "So much for all our hard work!" He looked from face to face. It was a joke! Slowly they caught the spirit of the thing—Potter's mustache moving ever so faintly as his lips tightened, Willcox grinning mirthlessly, only Ledlie giving a good frank smile, showing his mouth full of strong straight white teeth. "Seriously, gentlemen: I want to make it clear to each of you, that I repose entire confidence in your ability to join me in making the necessary new arrangements. Fortunately our orders had not been given. In a sense, we have not lost any time for moving the troops—that was to be done tonight in any case. Yes: I think we are just where we began, certainly no worse off. Do you agree?"

Willcox and Potter nodded, the latter slowly. "Yes, General," said Ledlie.

Ledlie: those rumors. The things I had to tell Meade about the low morale of their troops! Lord, if the men have heard. . . . Confidence! Restore confidence! Correct misimpressions. "I believe also, we can have confidence in our troops. They're tired out, I know—maybe a trifle prone to prefer the spade to the bayonet. But they're veterans! They know what war's all about! They'll rally, I have every confidence they'll rise to their . . . *opportunity!* They've never failed me yet!"

Potter cleared his throat. "I don't wish to seem to speak badly of the men. Still, General . . . your earlier remarks in support of using the Colored division to lead the assault . . . I must say, I concur with them. The troops have had something taken out of them these last months. I don't see it back."

"Your miners certainly didn't lack enthusiasm."

Potter shrugged. "It was their civilian work, sir, and a novelty in soldiering. And they've been promised that they'll stay with the Mine and act as provost guards during the attack." Potter blushed.

Burnside turned to Willcox. "General Willcox . . . what of your troops?" There was the faintest note of pleading in his voice.

"I'll have to say the same as Potter. They've lost fire, they've lost tone. Nothing a few weeks off the line mightn't cure. But there it is."

"General Ledlie?"

Ledlie had seemed to follow the conversation intently, his fair face flushed, his blue eyes peering intently from speaker to speaker. Yet it took him a second to realize he had been addressed.

"General Ledlie?"

"Oh, yes. I'll have to say the same for my own division. The same, yes. Decidedly."

Burnside shook his head. "I'm grateful to you gentlemen for supporting my earlier remarks to . . . the army commander. And for your frank responses here. I take it, then, that while the troops are not in the best shape, they are . . . as veterans . . . equal to the task?"

There was no disagreement.

"Then: which division shall lead? Numerically, there is nothing to choose between the three. Does any one of you believe his troops best fitted for the assault?" There was no answer. "Least fitted? Unfit? Come, come, gentlemen! I need your help here!"

Ledlie cleared his throat, and worked his tongue in his mouth as if his palate were quite dry. "My troops . . . my troops . . . were in pretty poor shape at the end of last month. You remember, General: you gave us a brief spell of relief then?"

There was silence. Burnside waited for Ledlie to finish. There must be more—what did he mean by reminding him . . . oh yes: "Thank you, General. However, I don't think that brief spell off the lines can count for anything now. They're probably in about the same shape as the rest by this time. But thank you, General, for offering them."

Burnside clapped his hands together. He was feeling better. That gesture of Ledlie's had perked up his morale. "I have an idea, gentlemen! Since you are all excellent officers, commanding divisions equal in strength and veteran accomplishment, it really matters very little which of you takes the lead. I have absolute confidence in my division commanders!" Burnside reached over and took a sheet of telegraph paper off his desk. He tore it into three strips. With his pen, he marked an *X* on one of the strips, folded the strips, and dropped them into his hat, which was perched, resting on its crown, on his camp desk. "We'll let the Fates decide! Gentlemen, draw lots!"

This was the way at last: the way of showing these men his absolute confidence in them. The way of invoking one last time the protection of Burnside's guiding genius. It was like cards: after a run of bad luck, things going against you no matter how well you played, there was always a turn, things going the other way. Genius consisted in having faith in the cards, in reading and using the turn of the cards.

He shook the big hat peremptorily, and offered it to Willcox. Willcox took a slip as he did his hole card, laying it on the table, not looking till the deal went round. Good man! Potter: a small movement of the hand, the paper taken and covered by the hand laid flat on the table.

Burnside looked into Ledlie's pale eyes and offered the hat to him. The handsome General grinned, his strong lips spreading away from the big teeth. A distinguished looking man, big jaw, big square forehead and the white-gray hair brushed straight back.

As Ledlie drew his slip, the others turned theirs open. Two blanks. Ledlie's paper had the X.

Burnside was, strangely, surprised. Troubled? No, not that. Those rumors . . . he didn't believe them at all. The man was obviously sound. Curious though, his winning. What could be meant by it?

Then Burnside read the riddle, and smiled. Of course: he had wanted to do well by the poor despised black man in this attack. He'd been prevented by bad faith. Nonetheless, here was acknowledgment that he had been right, and a promise of success: that the somewhat suspect Ledlie should replace the highly suspect niggers leading the assault.

"General Ledlie, my congratulations."

Ledlie licked his lips, and his tongue moved under his dry palate. "Thank you, sir," he said, with a frank and manly grin. "I feel just fine!" He looked at Potter, Willcox, and back to Burnside. "We won't disappoint you, sir."

"Of course you won't," said Burnside, rising. "Now, I trust you all understand what our task is—to get through the crater of the Mine as fast as may be, and move straight for the crest, without bothering to form, as we've been told. Well—you *may* form them just a little, General!" Burnside's grin was infectious. "General Ledlie, you'll be moving your troops down the trenches to your left, and form your troops for assault in the center of our line. General Potter, you'll pull back from the center, and form to the right and in rear of Ledlie, here"—pointing to the map—"alongside the covered way. General Willcox—you'll be relieved by Warren, and concentrate here, in and around the left covered way. Any questions?"

"I'll want to examine the ground there," said Potter. "It may not be entirely suitable for the purpose."

"Yes," said Burnside, "good. Are there other questions? Now's the time! Anything unclear in your minds?" There were no questions. "Good, then. Actually, it's a terribly simple operation after all. Just barge on through the hole and carry the heights!"

"Unless Bobby Lee has pulled the double bluff," said Willcox.

"Not a chance this time," said Burnside. "We've got the fox out-foxed, for once." He looked from face to face. "We understand each other, then? Very good. I'll have your written orders to you as soon as possible . . . for the record, for the record." The Generals began to leave, but Burnside bethought himself of something: "Oh! General Ledlie! It might be a good idea for you to take a look at the area of the assault from our signal tower. I'm sure you've made frequent observations before, and it's a bad time of day for making them; but best take no chances, eh? Make sure you can recognize your objectives. Any problems, don't hesitate to call on me! Gentlemen, good day!"

Good day! As if in magical confirmation there appeared, just as Burnside stepped after the generals to the door of the tent, a prophetic ghost: Ferrero!

"General?" said Ferrero—almost frightened, unsure of his reception. "You didn't receive my telegram?"

"Telegram? No. Why . . . don't tell me . . ."

"Yes. They've confirmed my appointment. Official notice should have arrived by now. But if my own telegram didn't reach . . ."

"Ed, Ed, Ed!" said Burnside, wrapping a heavy arm around the slim shoulders and guiding him into the office. "We'll get in touch with headquarters instantly, and straighten it all out. This is nothing short of a miracle! We're to attack tomorrow, did you know? . . . Of course not! How could you? By God, this is . . . this is *Providence,* by heaven! I'll get them to put you back in charge of the division or die trying!" *Have to tell him about not leading the attack—no, let that wait a while! This had to be savored! The Gods has spoken unmistakably! Royal flush, by God! He had the cards!*

"Ed, you could not possibly believe how very glad I am to see you!" He started to look at his watch—then laughed. There was plenty of time, now!

Evening. Pegram's Salient

Bruce came into the headquarters bombproof from his inspection of the lines. All was quiet. The Yankees weren't shooting tonight. Talk was they were pulling out, the blow north of the James a feint to cover their retreat. Maybe Early had hit a vital spot, somehow. Bruce doubted it. Once you looked at the size of the Yankee army, you knew it wasn't going to simply go away. More likely they would stay there as long as it took, building a little military city over against the cities of Richmond and Petersburg.

Allen was sitting at the table, writing by candlelight. He looked up. "Anything stirring?"

Bruce shook his head. "Yankees are still there, though they aren't making much noise about it. So damn many of them, sometimes I think I can hear em all breathing."

Allen laughed, a short sharp sound. He reached up to tip his spectacles back up onto the bridge of his nose. Sweat made his skin slick. The candle made twin points of light in the spectacles, giving Allen the look of a well-fed but evil-eyed tabby cat.

"They'll stay there as long as they want to," said Bruce, "unless they get sick of it; they've got folks enough out there to wait us out and use us up. And that's all there is to say about it."

Allen smiled. "Think they'd last as long as the Greeks did, waiting to take Troy?"

"Ten years?" Bruce grinned. "Well, it wouldn't take them another ten to get home: just hop the cars north, be home in a week most of them. Speed. That's the nineteenth century. Everything happens faster now."

"Ah yes," said Allen. "This idea that faster and more is better than slower and just-enough. I know you're joking, but I imagine there are plenty of people who would actually feel proud of the notion that it would take an American only five years to take Troy when it took the Greeks of the Heroic Age ten.'' He turned to look at the pages before him. ''That is why this war produces so few Achilles and Hectors, and so very *many* Agamemmnons.''

Bruce grinned. Allen was a pedant, and he patronized Bruce every chance he got. Well, he was not the only man that had been to school and read the classics. ''Yes,'' he said, ''and plenty of Thersites too.'' Allen perked up, looked quizzical. ''You remember: the 'man of interminable speech' who 'liked to quarrel with the princes.' ''

''Ah! Yes! The man who would have abandoned the siege and Helen, and piled onto the ships to go home. I'd forgotten. Ulysses put him in his place. . . .''

Bruce jerked a thumb over his shoulder toward the Yankee lines. ''Problem is, they've got Ulysses.''

Allen nodded. He smiled, more friendly than Bruce had ever seen him.

''What are you writing there?'' asked Bruce.

''Oh, this.'' Allen seemed a bit shy. He made to cover the pages, then changed his mind, decided to talk about them. ''To tell you the truth . . . it's a poem I've been writing. In fact . . . you'll have to excuse the presumption of it but . . . I'm working on an epic poem. About the siege of Richmond, the war.'' He circled his hand vaguely, indicating the earthen walls and log roof of the bombproof.

Bruce peered at Allen, trying to see through the covering glaze of light in the spectacles to the watery eyes beneath. An epic poem. Would wonders never. His impulse was to mock. But he was curious as well. After all, who knew? And they said that art was imperishable. . . .

''May I . . . is it something someone else might read?''

Allen blushed. ''Oh, it's still too rough for that. I've only been able to do parts of it, as I've found time—a scene here and there. I haven't at all been able to polish and refine. But . . . here, take a look. Let me know what you think. Seriously now.''

Now it was Bruce's turn to feel embarrassed. ''I'm no judge of poetry, but . . . if you wouldn't mind.'' He took the sheets, deciding before he began to read that he would only praise what he read.

''I was going to attempt something like the speeches of the heroes of the two armies—warrior to warrior. Using the situation of the sentries talking across the lines between bouts of battle. It didn't sound right, though. Easier when I had the officers meet under flag of truce, to arrange matters after the battle, burial of the dead. I can't catch the common speech the way Simms can.''

> *. . . these valiant dead, which strew the plain,*
> *Though stained with blood, no honor's stain . . .*

''Yes,'' said Bruce. Then: ''I like this very much.''

Allen looked at the sheet Bruce held. ''Ah, yes! The Colonel's speech, when he resigns from the Senate! He perishes, later, carrying his regimental flag into the very teeth of a Northern battery!'' And he began to speak, sing-song, from memory:

"Or e'er the kindly sky and fruitful field,
 Of our fair southland to the foeman yield,
 The soil itself, and rivers flowing wide,
 The burgeoned crops upwelling in a tide,
 Would purge the man of pelf as once before,
 A Carpenter repulsed them from the Temple's door!
 And 'gainst the pow'r of iron and of gold,
 These benisons our southern soil unfold:
 The Christianity of Jesus and of Paul,
 Against philanthropy which turns to coin
 The mis'ry of the neighboring fellow poor.
 In combat at the highest now we join,
 The charity that holds it more
 Blest to give the humble means to thrive,
 As drones do in the bee-republic's hive,
 To have their bread and not be forced to sell
 Their labor and their daughters to survive,
 Losing heaven to survive in hell!
 Bring on your armies: as the Corsican's failed,
 In Russian snows, while he 'gainst nature railed,
 So shall your powers, in fields of snow-white bolls,
 Perish and be signed in grim Death's rolls.
 The merest hinds, from cabin and from field,
 Defy you, and declare they'll never yield."

"It stops there," said Allen, shyly. "He lives in a grand house—the Colonel does. His wife holds it in his absence. Green ample fields, soft airs, and at even, the songs of the gleaners rise from the burgeoning rows. . . ."

"Sunset," said Bruce. "A lovely picture." *He probably means Davidson's place,* he thought. *Poetry.* "Good luck with this, Allen. I think it's . . splendid stuff. Though as I said, I'm no hand for poetry." He stretched and moved towards the bunkbed near the wall.

"Good night, then," nodded Allen.

"Yes," said Bruce.

"The light won't disturb you?"

"Not tonight." He turned his face to the wall and fell asleep.

HEADQUARTERS FIFTH ARMY CORPS,
July 29, 1864—4 P.M.

Major-General HUMPHREYS,
Chief of Staff:

GENERAL: I have received the programme order for operations to-morrow. I think the minimum of troops that I can depend upon including in my front line is Griffin's division, which forms a single line of battle, with one brigade of General Cutler's. This will leave me one brigade of General Cutler's and General Ayres' division, at least, to support General Burnside. If I can withdraw the most of my picket-line, and abandon the southernmost redoubt on the plank road I can also have two brigades of General Crawford to aid General Burnside. I would like special instructions on this point. In the event of success the division of Crawford would be well posted to follow up along the plank road. I am going to consult with General Burnside as to the co-operation he wishes me to give.

Respectfully.

G. K. WARREN,
Major-General.

(Indorsement.)
Abandon all south of the large redoubt; keep on the pickets.
A. A. HUMPHREYS,
Major-General and Chief of Staff.

7:30 P.M. Warren's Headquarters

It was time, and more than time, for the orders to go out. Warren had made notes of tentative plans earlier in the day, and now saw no need to change them. Yet he hesitated to begin dictating to Locke. Insensibly, at a deeper level than operations, there were new factors in the situation. Warren had been expecting Meade's removal. He still did, but he had not counted on the General's staying on through another offensive operation. There had been, after all, a month since the fiasco of the attacks on June 18, and the flanking move by Hancock that had been routed on the twenty-second. Warren had looked to Hancock as Meade's successor, unless that General's health should deteriorate— which it was doing, though more slowly than Warren had thought. Who else was there? Baldy Smith was gone, Butler impossible, Burnside . . . unlikely, unless this thing of the Mine should prove his salvation. That left Warren. Or so he had calculated.

Now what had happened? The move by Hancock to the north had failed. His troops would come back across the river tonight. Tomorrow, Burnside's Mine was to be exploded. Meade, by all accounts, was insisting heavily on his prerogatives in ordering the attack. Yet in their interview, Burnside had seemed to Warren especially sanguine. He had just been to see Grant and Meade—what secret did Burnside possess that made him so like the proverbial cat that ate the canary?

Warren had sounded Burnside, subtly he thought. Got no satisfaction. Subtlety was wasted on that pompous ass. He had had to come to the point.

"I take it then, that this is to be your attack, General?"

Burnside had nodded, and grinned. "Yes, of course! My plan of attack."

"Which, if I recall, contemplated supporting attacks from my front?"

Burnside's brow had furrowed. "Yes, the plan did call for that."

"You've seen Meade's orders to me? I'm to concentrate my corps, and hold them ready to support you. No particular time or plan of attack has been specified. . . .''

"Well, General! We'll have to see just what sort of situation arises at the time, I guess. Can't have everything all neatly anticipated—not like engineering exercises.''

Warren, an engineer himself, as Burnside well knew, bridled inwardly at the sneer, but turned it into a grin for Burnside. Given the drift of things, it might not do at all to take umbrage at any of Burnside's little quirks.

But thinking about it now, the impression Warren had had that Burnside would be in control of the assault had begun to fade a bit. The man had not actually said, in so many words, that it was *he,* not Meade, who would be calling on Warren for support. Normally, one might expect that the General on the ground, leading the assault, would be allowed to call for supports when and where he saw fit. But that was not always the case, where communications between points was as swift as the telegraph had now made it—it was not like Gettysburg, where Warren had made his name, throwing the Fifth Corps into a hole in the line on his own responsibility, Army Commander Meade being too far away to permit speedy or informed response. No, here Meade could come as close to the action, and exercise as swift control over the different corps, as any commander of a smaller body of troops could in a different situation. Would Meade give Burnside a free hand?

There were perils and pitfalls here, two "fell and incensed points" to be avoided. Meade or Burnside? He'd just have to play cautiously, take things as they came, wait and see.

HEADQUARTERS FIFTH ARMY CORPS,
July 29, 1864—10 P.M.

Major-General HUMPHREYS:
I have seen General Burnside and my division commanders. My arrangements for to-morrow were easy to make and are all completed. I have no doubt we shall be on time as expected. I will send you my circular order by a messenger.
Respectfully,

G. K. WARREN,
Major-General.

Burnside's Headquarters

It was all beginning to roll now. The whole gigantic process his genius had set in motion was bringing the force of the army to bear on this chosen point in front of his corps. Meade had usurped his plans and his attack. Meade would hold all the power he could jealously, using the letter of the law. But now things were moving Burnside's way. Now things would be happening on *his* home ground. Home ground: he must remember to disconnect the wires from the headquarters telegraph that he had been using to tap into messages from Meade to the other corps. Meade would be using these headquarters for the battle, while Burnside and Company moved their operations up to the fourteen-gun battery in Fort Morton.

Richmond came rushing it with a dispatch from Potter. Nothing wrong with the Mine? . . .

HEADQUARTERS SECOND DIVISION, NINTH ARMY CORPS,
July 29, 1864.

Lieut. Col. LEWIS RICHMOND,
Assistant Adjutant-General:

COLONEL: It will be extremely difficult, if not impossible, for me to form my division until that of General Ledlie shall have been formed. . . . If General Ledlie leaves us room enough we can form across the covered way, but I doubt if he will be able to give us the space. All the ground between the foot of the hill and the rise beyond the ravine near the mine is bad. A regiment could be formed near the mouth of the mine, but the ground is not very good, and would probably be rather near the explosion. We shall probably have merely to follow General Ledlie until we get through the enemy's line, and then move up on his right. On an examination of the ground with a view to massing troops I find there is really less space than I had supposed, and unless the dispositions are commenced early and made with celerity I fear some confusion.

Very respectfully, your obedient servant,
ROBERT B. POTTER,
Brigadier-General.

Burnside sighed, relieved. He handed the paper back to Richmond. ''Tell him it's all right, Lew. He can do as he thinks best.''

Of course there was nothing wrong with the Mine! Things had begun to break his way at last, an irreversible tidal flow. Ever since the drawing of lots and the return of Ferrero, he had sensed this drift towards himself in the current of events. All afternoon and evening dispatches had come in, the other corps commanders sending him copies of their orders. Routine of course, but there it was. An acknowledgment of the power of the General leading the attack. Then there was Warren, coming to see him. He was certain Warren had come to gauge the extent of Burnside's own power; equally certain, he had sent the man away impressed. All things coming to Burnside now.

''Lew! I want this to go out to Ord via telegraph, right away: 'General Ord: I think your division will be up in ample time. Let each commander stop at my headquarters as he passes and I think all will be right, and so you will push them past as fast as possible. A. E. Burnside, etc. etc.' '' Burnside smiled. He liked the picture of Ord's divisional commanders checking in with him. Almost, it would be like commanding the Army of the Potomac again.

Not that he coveted the position.

Still, he had always known that a return to command was within the realm of possibility. Lincoln had always been aware that the Fredericksburg setback had been caused by dissension and lack of cooperation among the McClellan malcontents, like the late unlamented Baldy Smith. For his part, Burnside had not stooped to politic for the job. But he had held himself ready (as it was his duty to do). He had always commanded his corps as he would have done a larger army, entrusting many details (most in fact) of battlefield judgment to the division and brigade commanders—content, as the commander of the army, to provide leadership, define the broad outlines and ultimate objectives. Potter's dispatch just now: that showed the efficacy of his method.

Here, now, were reporters from the *Times, Tribune,* and *Herald,* waiting and watching, hoping to see the commanding general at work. He had dressed for them, informally, in a blue-checked civilian shirt— they loved the ''Rough and Ready'' style in Generals, though Burnside on the whole liked spit and polish and gold braid himself. It would sound good: the General hard at work in his shirt sleeves. Democratic. Well, his orders had already been written. But no need to make a point of that.

He was ready to send out the orders now. Copies for the press provided, of course. Oh, yes—and a telegram for General White, to bring him back here. Have to find a place for White—let him replace Parke for a while as Chief of Staff. Ferrero can have his division when they get back together.

Poor Ferrero seemed bewildered by all the changes in so short a time. Maybe down a bit because he won't get to lead the charge? Well, he'd shape up.

HEADQUARTERS NINTH ARMY CORPS,
July 29, 1864.

CIRCULAR.

I. The mine will be exploded to-morrow morning at 3:30 by Colonel Pleasants. General Potter will issue the necessary orders to the colonel for the explosion.

II. General Ledlie will immediately upon the explosion of the mine move his division forward as directed by verbal orders this day, and if possible crown the crest at the point known as Cemetery Hill, occupying, if possible, the cemetery.

III. General Willcox will move his division forward as soon as possible after General Ledlie has passed through the first line of the enemy's works, bearing off to the left so as to effectually protect the left flank of General Ledlie's column, and make a lodgment, if possible, on the Jerusalem plank road to the left of General Ledlie's division.

IV. General Potter will move his division forward to the right of General Ledlie's division as soon as it is apparent that he will not interfere with the movements of General Willcox's division, and will as near as possible protect the right flank of

General Ledlie from any attack on that quarter and establish a line on the crest of a ravine which seems to run from the Cemetery Hill nearly at right angles to the enemy's main line directly in our front.

V. General Ferrero will move his division immediately after General Willcox's until he reaches our present advance line, where he will remain until the ground in his front is entirely cleared by the other three divisions, when he will move forward over the same ground that General Ledlie moved over; will pass through our line and, if possible, move down and occupy the village to the right.

VI. The formations and movement of all these divisions, together with their places of rendezvous, will be as near as possible in accordance with the understanding during the personal interviews with the division commanders. The headquarters of the corps during the movement will be at the fourteen-gun battery in rear of the Taylor house. If further instructions are desired by division commanders they will please ask for them at once.

By order of Major-General Burnside:

W. H. HARRIS,
Captain Ordnance, U.S. Army.

HEADQUARTERS ARMY OF THE POTOMAC,
July 29, 1864—3 P.M.

Brigadier-General WHITE,
Commanding Temporary Division, Ninth Corps:

The major-general directs that as soon as it is dark you withdraw your command from the intrenchments you are now holding and move to the position of the Ninth Corps, and report to your corps commander. You will call in your pickets upon moving. You will at once report to Major-General Burnside, and receive his instructions as to the route you will take.

Very respectfully, your obedient servant,

A. A. HUMPHREYS,
Major-General and Chief of Staff.

HEADQUARTERS NINTH ARMY CORPS,
Before Petersburg, Va., July 29, 1864.

GENERAL ORDERS,
No. 34.

Brig. Gen. Julius White is hereby assigned to duty, till further orders, as chief of staff of this corps. He will be obeyed and respected accordingly.

By command of Major-General Burnside:

LEWIS RICHMOND,
Assistant Adjutant-General.

Thomas's Brigade: Entrenchments on the Old Norfolk Road

Pennington had been anticipating the call momentarily for two days, jerking to attention with a galvanic jolt everytime a mounted courier came thumping up the pine-needled path to Colonel Thomas's tent. But they had been coming six or a dozen times a day, and finally the nerve-shock seemed to spread and become a pervasive and almost unbearable anxiety of anticipation.

To break it, Pennington closed himself in his tent like a monk returning to his cell, and set himself to writing a letter to his parents. He felt a habitual melancholy rise in him, like a seepage of tepid water, to muffle and drown his electric tension. His parents filled him with sadness and distress, even now and here. Somehow he had imagined that by following in the shadow of his great hero, Colonel Shaw, he would ennoble not only—indeed, not chiefly!—himself, but that his parents, too, would rise above their pervading fears and disappointments and approach the parents of Shaw. "We have buried him with his niggers," said the commander of rebel Fort Wagner, and the father had said he could desire no nobler place for his son to lie than with those who had fought by his side, and the mother too was glad, actually glad to have given the fruit of her womb for a sacred Cause. "Let the Hero born of woman crush the serpent with his heel! / Since God is marching on, Glory glory . . .''

But it had not been that way at all, when he had told them of his intention to enlist whether they would give him their blessing or not. His father's soft face and eyes had shown something very like fear—not the little fear with which he might face the harridan screech of some mill-girl on his missionary rounds, but something more visceral, horrible almost to see. And his mother—she who could sniff so devastatingly when speaking of her husband's parish-bound ambitions and achievements—she now spoke as if the drudgery of his scholar's room at Harvard, or even of a Methodist parish house, were superior to a calling so high that it could be sought by the Shaws, the Olivers, the Adamses, the Jameses of this world! She wept, she forbade, she invoked the ancient terrible pain by which she had given him breath in the world, that wound he had inflicted on her so long ago . . . he must hate her, she cried, to have hurt her so.

And he had stood there, tongue absolutely tied, face bursting with inexpressible feeling, able only to deny, to insist, to defy them. When what he needed to tell them was that it was not hatred or vanity that moved him, but Love. It had been Love from the very beginning, when he had gone as a small boy and a young man to hear the great preachers and philosophers of Boston speak against the great Evil, and standing with them on the platform were those fathers who had been beaten before the eyes of their sons, those mothers who had been lashed across the very nipples of their breasts for giving suck to their infants in the fields, those children orphaned by the slavemaster's will and the cruel knife of a golden dollar. Vivid as present life was his recall of these meetings, the air vibrant with song and the unleashing of overwhelming sympathy, overmastering love and grace. The smells even were vivid the faint clear lavender perfume of the young girls twisted like a thread through the saltier musk of sweat, their voices piping delicately, small pink lips and thin fluted nostrils. He had pledged himself then, given all of himself then, to a vision of himself standing before such a congregation, striking off chains with mighty blows, even with the words that flew from his tongue. That was what he had seen the day Colonel Shaw led his black soldiers out of Boston, leaving behind the eyes of the young girls, their deep and delicate perfumes, dresses like bushes of lilacs in the crowd, their voices and their odors rising for you because you were passing away from them forever, to give all for Love.

His mother had never relented, and yet he would do what he did for her as much as for anyone. But his father had . . . had *succumbed* to his passion. "Perhaps . . . perhaps it is a *manlier* Christianity that we need now, which you can give and I . . ." *Don't say that father!* he had thought silently, but said only his thanks for the letter that would obtain for him his position on Colonel Thomas's staff.

It was unfinished, that scene in the family parlor, a scene that he approached, ghostlike, each time he began to write a letter home. He had not resolved it, only left it behind in the winter mist when he had taken the train from Boston, passing in shuttered silence the profiled faces of girls waving farewell on every train platform he passed— Worcester, Hartford, New Haven, New Rochelle, New York, Trenton, Philadelphia . . . farewell to other men, their lovers, husbands, fathers, sons, friends, sad songs hanging in the cars like smoke.

> *Just before the battle, Mother,*
> *I am thinking most of you;*
> *While upon the field we are watching,*
> *With the enemy in view.*
> *Comrades brave are round me lying,*
> *Filled with thoughts of home and God;*
> *For well they know upon the morow*
> *Some will sleep beneath the sod.*
>
> *Farewell, Mother, you may never*
> *Press me to your heart again;*
> *But, oh! you'll not forget me, Mother,*
> *If I'm numbered with the slain.*

When the call finally came it came suddenly, and all at once: yet another courier had arrived.

Suddenly the air changed. The gathering darkness seemed to shift and breathe, bulking menacing somehow. His heart leaped. He looked out the flap of his tent. Thomas's big peaked tent gathered the little remaining light in its white surface, glowed softly. A black slit opened in its white surface, and the Colonel came out striding.

Pennington was outside, stepping towards Thomas before he was aware of willing motion.

"This is it, Chris," said the Colonel. Blood pounded in Chris's ears. He saw the Colonel's teeth flash wet white in his dark beard as he grinned. Felt a strong quick grip at the top of his arm. "Let's start calling the troops in."

They gathered in out of the darkness, the single pickets forming files, the files blending into companies and regiments marching four abreast out of the trees. The dark faces and dark uniforms slid out of the black bulks of the trees like parts of the formless darkness composing itself into lines, into order and purpose. Their pace was steady, almost silent on the needled paths. They moved with a silent pulse or rhythm like the movement of his blood, in time with the movement of his blood—steady, quickening.

They moved down the road, Pennington riding with Thomas at the head of the column. On an impulse, suddenly, Pennington dismounted, and dropped back. He wanted to walk. To feel the pulse of the soft pounding of the men's feet on the road. To hear, without distraction of saddle leather and horse-whuffling, the movement of his men behind him. Walking, he felt himself to be the head of the column as the skull sits on the long serried ridge of the spine, registering its shifts and vibration.

Out of the long dark column behind him the deep familiar voice rose, in slow cadence: "We-e looks lak men o mar-chin on, / We-e looks lak men o-o War!" Taken up by other voices as water takes up the movement of the tossed-in pebble, the voice spreading ahead and behind up and down the full length of the column, all the voices of the whole brigade singing in unison now, voices covering even the uniform pervasive shuffle of their thousands of feet. "We looks lak men o mar-chin on, / We-e looks lak men o war !"

Reiteration and reiteration and reiteration. The deep monotony of the words changed only by shifts in the voice, the lead singer giving the key, other singers standing forth and shifting the tone again, as if the long brigade were a single singer experimenting, varying his intention, his mood. Carrying Chris out of himself in the darkness, a blue abstraction, silent, walking his horse in the darkness.

The troops fell silent. Oh, his heart rose to meet that silence, yearning for the sound of them again, to belong there, his voice to blend in unison of that congregation, giving them his voicing of it to take up and vary and give back again, and he found himself singing.

"Mine eyes have seen the glory of the coming of the Lord"

Single-voiced, alone.

*"He is trampling out the vintage where the grapes of wrath are
    stored"*

Eyes, faces showing ahead where the staff, puzzled, turned in their saddles to see the source of the single voice, puny in midst of the dark bulks of the gathered trees.

"He has loosed the fateful lightning of his terrible swift sword!
My God is marching on!"

No sound from the black column behind, oh: a humming, a voice, seeking the melody below the unfamiliar, the too-complicated words, fumbling towards him.

And his voice went yearning now, searching, struck with a fear of being left naked alone in silence when he finally stopped.

"Glory, glory, hallelujah!"

But they were voicing now, confidently, they knew these words:

"Glory, glory, hallelujah!
Glory, glory, hallelujah!
Our God is marching on!"

And then, from the rear rank: he heard the deep voice again, heard so often before, the brigade's lead singer.

"John Brown body lies a-moldrin in de grave!
John Brown body lies a-moldrin in de grave!
John Brown body lies a-moldrin in de grave!
En we go marchin on!"

Tears poured down Chris's face in unison as the voices took the song all down the black road behind him:

"Glory, glory, hallelujah!
Glory, glory, hallelujah!
Glory, glory, hallelujah!
And we go marching on."

Wordlessly with his tears his heart flowed its thanks to the Lord hidden in the darkness, and to the voices behind them. This unison could demand anything of him, even his death. He gave himself to it wholly.

Back in the column, Private Johnson Number Five wept as well, remembering whom he sang for,

"John Brown's body lies a-moldrin in the grave
En we go marchin on!"

HEADQUARTERS SECOND CORPS,
July 29, 1864—11:20 P.M.

General MEADE:
My command is now across the bridge.
WINF'D S. HANCOCK,
Major-General, Commanding.

(Same to General Grant.)

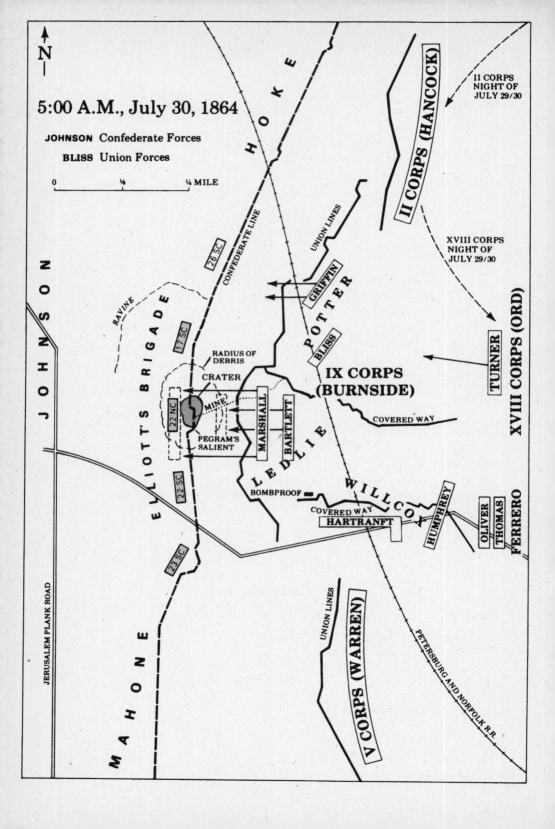

PART TWO

THE BATTLE
OF THE CRATER
JULY 30, 1864

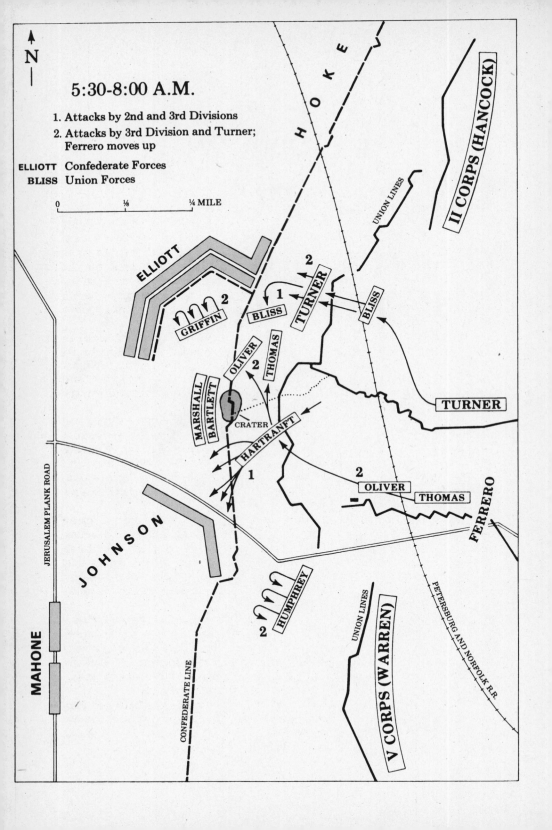

5:30-8:00 A.M.

1. Attacks by 2nd and 3rd Divisions
2. Attacks by 3rd Division and Turner;
   Ferrero moves up

ELLIOTT Confederate Forces
BLISS Union Forces

0   ⅛   ¼ MILE

N

H O K E

II CORPS (HANCOCK)

UNION LINES

ELLIOTT

2

1
BLISS   TURNER   2   BLISS
GRIFFIN

OLIVER   THOMAS
2

MARSHALL   BARTLETT   TURNER
CRATER
HARTRANFT

JERUSALEM PLANK ROAD

1

2
OLIVER   THOMAS   FERRERO

JOHNSON

MAHONE

HUMPHREY
2

UNION LINES

V CORPS (WARREN)

CONFEDERATE LINE

PETERSBURG AND NORFOLK R.R.

The Covered Way

Midnight. Washington, D.C.

The gunboat got under way slowly: an audible shift in the vibration of its engines, then a glide through the water. Behind, the city lights burned faintly. *A phosphorescence,* Lincoln thought, *like glow-rot on a swamp log.* When he'd first come to Washington back in the Forties, a new Congressman with a career a-making, he'd been excited by the place. It was never home, but a kind of eastern version of that New Orleans he'd floated down the Mississippi to discover so long ago, looming up on the horizon pregnant with the rich excitements and the terror thrill of newness, like the newness of a strange woman.

Now Washington was just a city of the dead to him: Willy gone in the fever it bred out of the rot in its veins—swamp water, filth of its sewers and packed-in humanity. Washington. By one of those lights Mary was sitting, her body knotted tight around her misery, anger, and loss. And here he was going again, on a dark ship drifting down the river, the shore a darker shadow-line in the shadow.

It was better going down to the army. Things were real there, and there was healthiness in the air for him—though he knew, rationally, that men sickened as much or more in the camps as in the city. With the army there was still that hope of new things, of the victory, the . . . grasping of whatever it was that continually eluded him. The responsive magic he had dreamed in the new city, like the dream of a new woman.

Lincoln smiled wryly in the darkness. It was a bitter sort of irony for him to run away to the army like this—a kind of deserter, abandoning the hard place of duty for the sake of his own ease. He might tell himself that he had duties as much in the one place as the other—but didn't the plowboy drafted into the army tell himself, just as he ducked out of the picket line, that the lower forty needed him as bad or worse than the army did?

Difference: the plowboy gets shot for running off, where the President has only a pair of bitter, wrung-up lips and a pair of eyes crazy with grief and rage to face up to. *I sometimes think the firing squad is the lesser of the two punishments. . . . No, there's nothing to put beside death. Death. No, I pardon as many of them as I can find occasion to, and so buy myself a little peace for my own . . . indulgence.*

But between ourselves, he thought to the darkness, *between ourselves: who was it put the plowboy where he'd be caught on the dilemma, and tempted to desert? Who is it shoots them all, but me? Oh, I pardon plenty, and the Generals don't like it. But I kill more than I spare.*

If I could, I'd make the dead live again.

If I could, I'd do it over, better. I'd make it come right, without the blood. If I had the power to do that, I would.

The encompassing blackness became a familiar place to him: he knew it from his dreams. Always the same dream came to him before a great happening, before Antietam and the victory that let him issue his proclamation freeing the slaves, before Stones River and the battle that ushered in the promulgated law of emancipation along with word of victory. The dream of himself gliding on a black ship over dark waters, and toward a dark indefinite shore—hooded shape of a new land full of strange terrors and gratifications, faces of men, faces of women. . . . Standing there on the vibrating wood of the steamer's deck the dream was real, concrete. Grant would be waiting at Fort Monroe, and he would have something to tell him. Ferrero had given him the outline of it. Perhaps it was happening even now? Perhaps it had happened already, and as he moved on the invisible water toward the hidden shore, already it was accomplished, and the victory was waiting to receive him, the word of triumph.

Give me this, he prayed to the darkness, *and what wonderful things can be accomplished in its name. The whole mass of the black and the dead, the republic saved . . .*

And afterwards I will board the train and glide over the earth heading home again: Washington and Baltimore, and Martinsburg at the mountain gap, and Pittsburgh, and across the great flat of the prairies back to Springfield.

Midnight. The Mine

There were no clouds between the scarred earth and the smooth black plate of the sky. Doyle, standing sentry duty at the minehead, looked up to the center of it, like looking into a deep well. The deep hole in the center of the sky, too cold, too far for fear. Stars like studs about it. A big emptiness drawing on him.

Who dug it?

He looked back down at the silent blue air of the trench. Behind him the open shaft of the mine seemed to breathe a damp breath. No people ever dug a hole as strange as this one, or filled such a hole up with powder to blow another place full of people into a hole in the ground.

The priests will talk about a Day of Judgment. It might be that the hole in the sky is a Mine-hole like this one, and Jesus the Judge will blow the thing sky-high.

And when it happens the dead will rise.

12:30 A.M. 14th N.Y.H.A.

The First Division began to move in single file down the winding road of the trenches. Their movement nudged the Second and Third Divisions to start, and soon there were four thousand men shifting one way, four thousand more shifting to get out of their way, and another four thousand coming in behind to take their places.

Neill was trapped in the middle of his file, held between the dark back and ass of the man in front, the heavy breathing of the man behind. The air around him was crawling with sounds—breathings, whispers, shuffling of feet, crackle of leather, brush of cloth. The sound rose out of the blackness in front and behind, and to his left; but off to the right where the enemy waited, there was a silence. No breathing, no sound. Just the occasional *bump* of a gun somewhere to remind you. Though the night was close and hot, there was a chill-numb feeling on Neill's right check, almost as if a cold breath blew from there.

He'd wanted to escape from the close ranks before, to get off in the dark, hide and run. Now the chance was gone. They were going to a big shoot-up tomorrow; there was no getting away. Now Neill wished only to bury himself in the protection of a wall of bodies, to hide in these deep trenches, with the protective breathing-shuffling sounds around him in darkness.

1:00 A.M. *4th Division Bivouac*

Thomas's brigade had arrived at the clearing in the woods, just in the rear of the covered way, shortly before midnight. The brigade had pitched camp; before it had finished, it was joined by Oliver's brigade, which had been relieved in the trenches and come back down the covered way. The soldiers were ordered to get some sleep while they could; and the slow songs slowly died toward quiet through the clearing for the next half hour. Pennington, worn out by effort and emotion, fell asleep with them, though he had intended to watch out the night. Dobbs, who had come looking for him, found him sleeping, and left him so.

A low fire was burning, and Dobbs picked out a burning twig to light his cigar. One of his boys had given it to him. Probably stole it from some staff officer. Tasted pretty good.

Dobbs had figured out what had happened without needing to be told. As soon as he'd seen the First Brigade coming back down the covered way and going into bivouac, he'd guessed. Why bring the brigade back here, if they were going to attack from the front line of trenches?

Still, there might have been some reason, some difficulty with moving them around in those narrow alleys. But now it was just about the middle of the night, everybody snoring away, and nobody getting us up there at all. And dawn is what . . . three hours off?

He grinned at the fire. Those lousy sons of bitches. They kick you in the teeth, then offer you a hand up—just so's you'll be able to fall down again when they kick you another one.

He wouldn't wake Chris. Be like telling a kid no Christmas this year. Not going to have your battle, sonny.

Somebody was moving around out in the darkness. Dobbs could see a figure, white, shapeless, a haunt—no, a man in a white duster reaching shoulder to knees.

"Lieutenant, . . ." the voice came out of the black hole between the duster and the man's hat brim.

"Shhh," said Dobbs, motioning toward Chris.

"Can you tell me how to get to the covered way? I'm Doctor Clubb, Corps chief surgeon. We've got to set up a field hospital . . ." and he gestured toward a group of shadows in his rear.

Dobbs rose. It was eerie talking to a man when you couldn't see his face. For all you could see, this doctor might be black as the ace of spades himself. "You see that bunch of fires off there? That's Division Head-quarters. Entrance is near there, somewhere. They'll show you."

"Obliged," said the doctor. His party followed him off, shadows lugging odd gear—boxes and slats of board jutting out of their shadows, swags of . . . rope was it? . . . and gurgling jars of liquid.

He looked up at the stars. Each point of light was like a needle. Yet when you looked closely, some seemed to pulse or whirl; others stared steady; others seemed to have clouds hovering around them. He'd looked at stars plenty before, needing directions in the dark. But never—or sel-dom—just looking at them this way.

I should wake Chris. Last nights like this shouldn't be. . . . No. Thinking that way, it'd be a jinx to wake him.

He stared at the sky. When he was young, he and Nancy had looked at the stars over Hackberry Creek. In winter they were sharper than now, icy. She would sing in her voice—dry and clear, like a mild win-ter—

True love has gone, to Cumberland mountain . . .
No, not Nancy. It was Mammy sung that song, back in Tennessee be-fore Pap took to driving niggers.

2:00 A.M.

Booker and Randolph sat in Booker's tent, the camp table and can-dle between them. The candlelight turned Randolph's face to a black mask, with eyes of agate.

"I had to tell you . . ."

"This time!"

"I didn't think to tell about the Mine before . . ."

"Because one of us niggers like to run off and tell ole Massa 'bout it? That's what you thought, isn't it?"

"I never thought about it. We are not supposed to . . ."

"Oh, I see. But this is different . . ."

"You had to know . . ."

" 'Cause we'd of found out tomorrow anyway, wouldn't we? When buckra do the job they give to us. They *give* to us!"

"If I'd thought you'd take it this way . . ."

"What way I take it? Do I run off the camp? You tell me they take my . . ." *My what? My time, my life, my job, my opening-up door, my attack, my battle, my first big thing.*

"We'll be in it, one way or another. Just not at the start."

"Just not the part we trained for. Like the niggers didn't get it right!"

"You got it right."

"I *knows* that!" Randolph's face burned in the candlelight. "I got that attack in here." He tapped his head. "I got that much. Damn if I don't find a way to *use* it!"

Was that a threat? thought Booker. He believed that Randolph hated him then and thought about ancient kings killing the bearers of bad news. He said, "You can tell the men, if you think best."

Randolph sat back, and looked at Booker. "What you think, Major? Think your niggers all go wild if they find out? That why no orders come around to us? Figure it break our hearts?"

"Something like that."

Randolph stood up, "I'll tell them." He turned and left the tent.

Colonel Oliver was in his tent, working on his journal by the light of an oil lamp, too nerved up to sleep tonight. If he allowed himself to sit and think about the attack tomorrow, his blood began to pound and ring in his ears so that he could scarcely string his thoughts together. Thinking about the chances of tomorrow. Oh, better that they would not be leading the assault! Better that that cup should pass from these troops of his, until they were more ready! He had not told them about it—there was time enough tomorrow, no need to have their sleep and his disturbed by wrangling and discussion. The morale of these people was, he believed, a shaky, shifting thing. Building a corps of shock troops out of such material was, indeed, building a house on shifting sand.

Perhaps, though, he judged them too much as he would himself. They would probably not—as he did—wrestle over the shiftings of chance, intellectually insatiable to find the clue of cause, effect, and final consequence—they'd probably grunt, say "Do tell!" and snore till dawn. Let them have their sleep untroubled and leave unceasing thought to those whom it suited. Uneasy lies the head that wears a crown.

He smiled a bit at himself. Oliverian egotism at its most typical. Here on the night before what was probably a major battle—perhaps the decisive conflict of the war—here he sat, scribbling away as usual.

He turned again to the notes he had made after that meeting at which Rockwood had set forth for the first time an informed vision of their great plan: the Mine, the great explosion with its concentric circles of fire and smoke and debris, and the crater that would succeed it—a vacancy of utter destruction, with *its* concentric circles of lessening destruction, from the circle of obliteration to that of mere destruction, shattered junk; and outward to a circle in which some few beings clung to life and to the shattered soil, paralyzed by the stunning exhibition of Force and by their own disrupted morale, their Fear.

Oliver had his own image of Death: that of the trench at Spotsylvania, the brigade working as gravediggers. He rode his horse toward the trench they were working on, stepping him delicately across the littered ground, the animal a-quiver with its nostrils full of the horror of death. The trench was full to the brim with the intertwined dead who died in struggle with each other. From the height of the horse the long trough of trench seemed like a can of bait-worms or a maggot-swarming carcass : and dead men, bearded or smooth, clothed or unclothed, blue or gray, dead men were the worms. Frozen in the midst of their writhing, a parody of the fierce energy of passion that carried them into the battle.

The Negroes hauled them out with blank indifferent faces, their swollen features seeming numb. For himself, there was a numbness too, a coldness, as if the deathful trench had an atmosphere or contagion of cold. This was the end of all striving, passion ; all idealism, patriotism, devotion ; all purpose, will, idea.

Suddenly the Negroes cried out, and began hauling an arm, a torso up from the complicated dead. A man hauled live out of the pit of death, his forehead bloody from the blow that had deprived him of his senses but not of life, opened his eyes and shrieked ! And his eyes went out like candles.

What an absurdity you have been led towards, Colonel, with your great idea that the battle would offer a test of your ideas about the capacity of certain kinds of leadership to stir humanity and lead it onward to a higher life, ruling the chances of history and aiming toward perfection. As if such ideas could be tested by plunging head and body, leader and led, into the self-same fire. That's leveling with a vengeance, there: the democracy of battle, in which all alike face Death in its immediacy, where it happeneth to the wise man as to the fool. The democracy—the leveling banality—of such war and death. Death itself was the proof of the test's absurdity; Death and its ally, chance. A bullet might strike me down as soon as I opened my mouth to give the one order that would bring Perfection out of Chaos; and leave some brutish black, or that anarchist Jew Booker, alive and happy in the sunshine.

Oliver yawned. Thinking and writing served him as physical labor did other natures : it relaxed and exhausted him. The animal asserted itself, hungry for its darkness, its little taste of petty death. Oliver grinned at himself. He would feed the beast, give it its little death, so that it would allow him to think and act without interference in the morning, when that which he was most—his sovereign will and reason : would meet its own test.

He snuffed the candle, darkness rushed in. He lay on his cot and fell asleep.

Tobe and Jethro were lying in their shelter tent. Flat on their backs, eyes closed. Both pretending to sleep, both waiting in the quiet dark.

Voices in the dark outside. "Hello?" *Calling. Don't answer.* "Is there anyone in there?"

Tobe and Jethro rolled toward each other, eyes opened.

Nothing to do but open.

The figure in white drapery, his black face invisible, stood silhouetted by faint starshine.

"What you want?"

"Looking for the covered way, soldier."

Jethro was silent. Tobe pointed. The white figure and the attendants moved off.

Jethro shivered. "He call you by name."

"Didn't," said Tobe.

"What that mean?"

"What it means."

They went back into the tent. Now that he knew, Tobe found it easy to relax and sleep. Jethro lay in his bed though, rigid. *It can't be, can't be, can't be.*

"Tobe," he whispered.

"Yes?"

"You show him the right way?"

"You think I'm a fool? Told him off the *wrong* way, back out of this brigade." *Ain't sending him by any our own folks.*

Tobe sighed, relaxed. Whatever comes, he knew he had done the right thing now: a sign he would do right whenever it come.

2:30 A.M.

After Randolph left, Booker sat for a time. The candle flame made small licking noises against its wick.

Something had ended here.

His friendship with Randolph? A strange friendship. Always, there had been some element of distance and mistrust. He had been Randolph's mentor, his guide into the vocation of fighter and freeman—high rhetoric, but that was what he had tried to do! There is always this . . . mistrust between teachers and those they teach. What will happen on the day when the pupil has absorbed the lesson, and stands equal with the teacher? What becomes of friendship then?

I can't bear it that he should step from under my teaching . . . selfish and foolish, but that's it.

The candle flame continued to lick round the burnt wick, a kitten cleaning itself. Staring at it made the darkness outside the circle of candlelight darker. Stranger, full of impenetrable shadows. Impenetrable. That was the look of Randolph's face. The face of one who closes a door for the last time, who casts out and rejects.

There was a painful hollow feeling in the pit of Booker's stomach. This was the truth he was seeing now: *When I was teacher, I was at home in Randolph's place and with his people; and I thought that was home. But they don't need teaching any more, if they ever did. And whatever else there is of me is a stranger to them. . . .*

Booker raised his eyes and looked outside into the darkness. A blank darkness, as if they were underground. *I shouldn't have stared so long at the candle.* He puffed, and the candle vanished, leaving a sharp tang of paraffin smoke. Goodbye. It was death, saying goodbye.

The camp was quiet, but not silent. Four thousand, three hundred–odd men lying together in a single field could never be perfectly still. Their breathing alone, if all were asleep, would make a stir in the grass, an exhalation like a morning wind.

Absurd to be so unnerved by the anger of Sergeant Randolph. Whatever was between them, he was still the commander of a battalion of troops, second in command of the regiment. He still knew how to command in a fight, how to take men into battle . . . yes, and out of it again, too. He was wolf enough to kill the wolf. Battle was a horse he had learned to ride, balky unpredictable horse but not so to him: he could call its turns and dives, and keep his seat. He could let it run, and rein it in. There were things in life he was afraid of, but war was not one of them.

2:30 A.M. *14 N.Y.H.A.*

Three times Neill had fallen asleep in his blankets sitting on the fire step in the trench. Three times he had snapped awake in panic, fear shocking all through him that it was all over, it was coming. Sleep was a safe country, close, sheltered. To wake was death. Each time he woke, he looked at the sky: it was still hard as metal, blue-black. So long as that metallic front held, he could fall asleep again, he was safe, assured, that the black night sky was holding hard, holding hard against the sun.

2:30 A.M. *4th Division Headquarters*

General Ferrero sat on his cot and stared into the lamplight. It burned steadily in the dark, a fixed point in the center of shifting, flowing shadows. He might, for all the light could tell him, still be sitting in the hotel room at Willard's, staring at the lamp; or on the steamer coming down, in his stateroom, brackish tidal waters sifting past the unseen porthole, staring at the lamp: dreaming that he was back here in his old tent with his division again, just as before.

Too many things turned on a word, a thought, a scrap of paper: *You are a General, you are nothing, you are a General; you are here, you are there, you are* where? *Here.* So many turns and changes in so few days. To give all this up, all the work, all the hope: then have it given back, *snap,* like that, at a word; and be translated, instantly, back into the tent—*Oh, but the attack gone, taken away, vanished while you were gone: so that you were* here, now, here. *Here to do what?*

Ferrero thought, *I must take hold.* He was like a child groggy from being slapped about the head by a mocking bully with fast hands, bewildered. He was in command, again. But to do what? His new orders had seemed clear when he spoke to Burnside. Hold his division in reserve, wait to be called on (if called!) to support the other divisions. All right, that was clear. And he couldn't expect to know in advance where he might be needed. That was clear. . . .

Why did these orders seem to keep dissolving, vanishing into incomprehensible vague suppositions? It had always been Burnside's method to give verbal rather than written instructions to his subordinates, to rely on their professional competence and understanding of the objectives. He had never had trouble of this kind before. Perhaps he really was incompetent, unable to turn his commander's intentions into coherent orders as a good division commander should? Better if he had never seen Lincoln! Better if he had not left Washington so hastily, he might have returned to command and the crisis over. . . .

Coward! Coward! Am I actually afraid? Not that too! I must pull myself together.

He stared at the lamp flame, concentrating his attention, bringing it clearly into focus. Where was he , really? What had he been told to do? *I have no idea really, where I should be, where go, what do. Should I stay with the division or at headquarters to receive instructions directly? My headquarters were to have been in the bombproof at the head of the left covered way—shall I still go there?*

He had no idea at all. Burnside, he was sure, had said nothing about those details. But . . . it was likely, wasn't it, that Burnside would call his division commanders in for a conference at headquarters right before the attack? Hadn't he always done so before? But Ferrero had received no notice . . . perhaps it had gone astray in the confusion. That was always happening to him, it was his peculiar destiny. It was clear now— that was what must have happened. But then, he must hurry to catch up with lost time or he would miss the council of war. At least he would be able to confer with Burnside, some help, understanding . . . and if Burnside thought him incompetent for not understanding, so be it! He must go, now.

Clear at last. He got up, buckled on his sword belt, set the cap on his head. "Hicks!" he called, and the aide materialized. "Tell Oliver and Thomas to have their brigades awake, and ready to go as soon as it's light." Anything else? He couldn't think of anything. He'd hardly spoken two words to Thomas since returning, and Oliver he had not seen at all. Well, they could handle it. He must see Burnside!

As Hicks turned to go, another thought struck Ferrero. "Oh, one more thing: get the two officers who worked on the attack plans—Major Rockwood from the Nineteenth and Booker of the Forty-third. I'll want them to come up to headquarters with me, to look the ground over again, now that things are different."

Hicks vanished. Ferrero sat down on his cot, to wait for the two Majors. His forgotten sword bumped the cot-side, twisting the belt out to the side and stopping him from completing the movement, twisting him awkwardly to the side.

He rose, shifted the sword to the front, and sat down again. The sword in its scabbard jutted out from the shadowed shape of his body at an eccentric angle.

HEADQUARTERS SECOND DIVISION, NINTH ARMY CORPS,
July 30, 1864—2:15 A.M.

Maj. Gen. A. E. BURNSIDE,
Ninth Army Corps:
GENERAL: Colonel Duncan, commanding the Second Brigade, Third Division, Eighteenth Army Corps, who reported to me at about 12 midnight to relieve my line, has just returned to

say that in the darkness he has lost all of his brigade but one regiment, which has been placed in the line, relieving two small regiments of Bliss' brigade on the right of my line. Bliss will therefore have to remain mostly on the line, as it is too late to find anything to relieve him and get it on the ground in time. I have ordered him to commence at 3 A.M. the withdrawal of the troops over the mine and within injudicious proximity to the explosion and add them to the force already relieved. General Griffin is placing his men in position and will be ready to move promptly with what support I can give him from the other brigade. Colonel Duncan will report the rest of his brigade when he finds it. I am not sure that this is much of a misfortune, as Duncan's troops were colored troops and I did not get a very favorable account of some of these troops in that corps. In case of a repulse or check this is a spot that should be well held. After 3:15 A.M., and until further report, my headquarters will be at the clump of trees near the batteries on the right of my covered way.

Your obedient servant,

ROBERT B. POTTER,
Brigadier-General.

HEADQUARTERS THIRD DIVISION,
July 30, 1864—3:00 A.M.

General BURNSIDE:
Hartranft is now being relieved. General Willcox says he will be ready at the time. General Hartranft will form in the hollow in front of the burnt house.

WM. CUTTING,
Major and Aide-de-Camp.

3:00 A.M. *The Mine*

They gathered like shadows, black, at the head of the Mine. As time passed, their faces began to appear more in the darkness: as blurred shapes, then as faces with mouths, beards, eyes.

Pleasants and Potter were there, and Rees. The regiment was under arms, awake, and formed in the trenches around the Mine. A picked squad under Rees, the best miners, stood with the officers at the mine-head. If anything went wrong . . .

Nothing could go wrong, Pleasants told himself. He had prepared everything so carefully. Yet he had been away from the Mine for a full day, talking with Potter, resting, visiting at headquarters. He was elated by Potter's appointing him to his staff for the assault—as if he had been relieved of the responsibility that had ridden him for a month. Only a day, yet it had put some sort of distance between himself and this strange cave in front of him. Somehow, in the darkness, the entrance had an unfamiliar look. He was used to seeing it as a raw, unfinished scar. In this light it had the softened air of a permanent thing, a famous place to which he and these others had been bidden on a pilgrimage.

Pleasants shook himself. *I've got nerves pretty bad,* he told himself. His whole career, his whole world rested on the point of a dream, a hollow insubstantial pattern in space. He leaned against the crumbly earth of the trench-side, for reassurance.

"Can you see the time?" asked someone.

"Three," said Potter. "We'll light it off at three-thirty or thereabouts."

Pleasants licked his lips. "Shouldn't we wait till first light?"

Potter shook his head, then said, "No. Best set it off before. In case . . ." He did not need to finish. Pleasants finished the thought for him. He shook with riffles of fear, and wished it were all over. The Mine blown, and his responsibility at an end.

3:00 A.M. Meade's Field Headquarters at Burnside's Permanent Camp

Sanderson arrived at Burnside's old headquarters just as the burly General was leaving. During the battle, Meade and Grant would use Burnside's headquarters; Burnside would set up in the fourteen-gun battery, Fort Morton. Sanderson had Meade's telegraphers with him. Some sloppy operator in Burnside's crew had messed up the wires running from Burnside's out to the main telegraph lines that connected the different corps and headquarters. Sanderson had had to supervise the splicing of the wires. He'd been running tests, sending messages to the different headquarters: to Burnside first; then to Warren; then to Ord, who wasn't at his headquarters. Hancock was supposed to receive his orders at Ord's, but Hancock wasn't there yet either. The lines to Meade's old headquarters, and to City Point, seemed to be all right.

Meade arrived, Humphreys with him. Humphreys began inspecting arrangements. When he was satisfied he said to Sanderson, "Nice work." *Welcome back.* "General Grant's people will be along soon. Grant himself won't be by until later." Sanderson looked his query. "No need for him to be. Just an observer. Meade's in charge." Humphreys grinned. "You'll be with Burnside when the attack starts."

"A watching brief?" Sanderson asked with a wry grin.

"Of course," said Humphreys. "Stay at his headquarters unless you get different orders. Take your own telegrapher with you, and use the line whenever you think we ought to know something."

"Yes, sir."

"Go as soon as you can."

Sanderson got his gear together and began the long walk up to the battery. It was still dark. He passed through Ord's encampment, the sleeping troops, into the covered way, and up the winding canyon past working parties and details. Near the main line, he felt the loom of the big battery, and wandered up.

July 30, 1864—3:15 A.M.

General JULIUS WHITE,
Chief of Staff, Ninth Army Corps:

GENERAL: I have a report from the mine; everything all right. The fuse will be ignited at 3:35 and Colonel Pleasants anticipates the explosion at 3:40 or 3:45. Could hear enemy moving up their guns this morning. Railroad trains moving all night.

Yours,

R. B. POTTER,
Brigadier-General.

P.S.—A division of some corps ought to be ready to move quickly up after Griffin if required.

3:15 A.M. *1st Division Bombproof*

Doctor Clubb and his assistants followed the twisting course of the covered way, full of black air under a sky only slightly less black, towards the front. A Third Division brigade, Humphrey's was to have been in the covered way by this time. Thank God that other people were also behind schedule this night, or they'd have had the devil's own time getting up to the front. The blacks had led him a merry dance. If they had as much trouble finding the enemy as they did knowing where their own damned covered way was, they would be a hell of a bunch of soldiers!

"Halt!"—the sentry-challenge. They were up with the First Division at last. They followed the sentry, who pulled aside a blanket, allowing a flood of light to spill out. There was a group of staff officers sitting at a heavy table, obviously looted from a house in the vicinity.

"Gentlemen!" said Dr. Clubb, "I take it this is the headquarters bombproof?"

They nodded.

"I'm the Corps Surgeon. We're going to set up our field hospital here, to handle the seriously wounded just as they come back. . . ." They looked at him blankly. "You've been notified of this, of course? It was arranged two days ago."

The senior officer, a Captain, rose. "I'm sorry, Doctor, we hadn't heard. Our orders only came down yesterday. Late."

The two groups of men stood, and looked at each other.

Doctor Clubb was impatient. He was a Major, and senior to these officers. "Well, you'll have to make way, I'm afraid. My orders are from General Burnside, personally." The staff officers looked at each other, waiting for someone to have an idea.

"Look," said Dr. Clubb. "There's no reason why we can't both use this shelter. It's plenty big enough for you to use . . . that corner over there, and the camp desk. I'll need this table here, and we'll need some crackerboxes or ammunition boxes to set our stretcher-cots on

. . . and clear out some of this space to put them in,'' and he motioned to his orderlies, who began to shift the furnishings about.

The staff officers said nothing—probably reserving protest, thought Clubb—and then he thought no more about them. A brusque and decisive manner easily reduced officers of their sort to passive obedience.

He set his field surgery up carefully. The heavy table along one wall, room to stand on both sides of it for operating; the cots, set on boxes, in a row of six up the middle of the bombproof. Space for the stretcher-bearers or carriers to walk on either side of the row. Space fore and aft of the operating table, so men could be put on one side, taken off the other and carried out for their journey back down the covered way to the ambulances.

It would be a bloody mess in that covered way, going back. Troops blundering up to the front one way, stretcher cases and walking wounded passing back the other, and the rebels likely throwing shells in every which way.

There was a small fire, and Dr. Clubb boiled his instruments—he believed in sterilization, though many colleagues did not; he read medical journals carefully, the French and German publications as well as the English. Sterilization made sense—dirt was the breeder of disease, that was obvious to anyone who cared to glance more than casually at the ruined constitutions of the urban vagrants and vagabonds, the shanty Irish, and even—he had been told—the Negroes in their hovels.

He sighed. After the first half-hour of action, he would have used up all the sterilized instruments; after that, there wouldn't be time to boil them and cool them so that he could use them on the wounded as they would be coming in, one after another after another.

He carried three sets of instruments—scalpels, scissors, bone-saws, needles, pincers, cauteries—all good quality, nothing that would break in the using—though if one did, he had replacements. Disinfectants, carbolic, morphine and laudanum—perhaps, if he could, he would try to spare the laudanum for the men leaving this hospital, counting on the insensibility of shock to aid him . . . but in all likelihood, his orderlies would dole it out as they always did.

It took an hour to set up the hospital. Clubb again became aware of the staff officers in the corner, who were playing cards on the camp desk. Somehow this offended Clubb's sense of order. Shouldn't they be working, bustling about getting ready for the attack? He'd be subtle about saying anything though: "I say, you men. We're all set up now. If there's anything you need to be doing, we'll try to stay out of your way.''

"Oh no,'' said the Captain. "That's all right.''

Clubb's face reddened. "Shouldn't you be busy about the attack?''

"Oh, that's all taken care of,'' said the Captain.

"Besides,'' said a Lieutenant, "we're volunteer staff.''

Clubb was bewildered. "I don't . . .''

"General Ledlie isn't sending the volunteer staff up with the attack. Regulars only.''

Clubb just stared.

"After all, it's their trade, isn't it?'' said the Captain.

3:20 A.M. The Covered Way

Ferrero, tailed by Rockwood and Booker, led the way up the covered way to the fourteen-gun battery. The narrow passageway was filled with troops, black bulks in the blackness of the trench, and the officers moved by fits and starts, blundering, pushing, excusing their way by the companies of Humphrey's brigade that filled the trenches from side to side. Men had fallen down and asleep on the floor of the trench, down by whole companies in some places. Finally, exasperated, Booker tapped Rockwood on the back. "Let's get up out of this. It's too damn dark for any snipers to shoot us anyway." Rockwood grabbed Ferrero by the belt. He pointed, and said "Let's go up top." Ferrero nodded. He hadn't said a word to either of them. They had no idea why he had hauled them away from their sleep.

They scrambled up out of the trench, and walked along the higher ground alongside it. From the trench the sound and smell of the sleeping brigades rose, soft, pungent-salty. The ground here was loose, with broken earth thrown out by the digging. Even so, they made better time than they had in the trench.

Lord, thought Booker, *if it took three of us all night to get through that damned alleyway, how long would it take a brigade to get down there?* When they paused to rest, he put the question to Rockwood. "Oh," said the Major, "it won't be so bad if they all keep moving. Just as long as nobody really hangs back, or a whole bunch don't fall down together. Long as nobody's going back the other way . . ."

"Wounded would be."

"Yes," said Rockwood. "It's wide enough for them to get by. Anyway, there's usually more ways back out of a fight than there are ways in. No need to take the crowded one." He grinned invisibly.

They arrived at headquarters, tired and dusty, just as the other divisional commanders were leaving.

"I'm sorry," said Ferrero, "terribly sorry. I never heard of . . ."

Burnside's face looked beet-red in the candlelight. His voice quavered a bit. *Embarrassed?* "Oh, Ed. That's all right. Think nothing of it." Burnside looked right and left, as if he had something to give Ferrero, and had misplaced it. Ferrero noticed how Burnside's eyes touched and then fled from two officers who stood by themselves in one corner. Ferrero recognized them: Sanderson, of Meade's staff, and Ludlow, of Butler's. *Here to watch?* . . . "Here, Ed. Why don't you stay with me, here, and watch the thing go off! Your troops are ready? Good! Stay then." He embraced Ferrero's shoulders, turned their backs on Ludlow and Sanderson and walked him to the large worktable.

Ferrero nodded and smiled, gratefully, vaguely. Why had he come here? He was certain Burnside had forgotten to invite him to the divisional council of war. Or had not meant to invite him. Perhaps did not consider him worthy of . . . But at least, Burnside still seemed to like him. That was something.

An aide entered, just up from the telegraph station that had been set up further back from the battery. He handed Burnside a telegraph message. Burnside read it, and his face got red again. He put the paper on the table.

HEADQUARTERS ARMY OF THE POTOMAC,
July 30, 1864—3:20 A.M.

Major-General BURNSIDE:
As it is still so dark, the commanding general says you can postpone firing the mine if you think proper.
A. A. HUMPHREYS,
Major-General and Chief of Staff.

"Send this," he said curtly but softly to the aide, with a glance at Sanderson and Ludlow: " 'Major-General Humphreys: The Mine will be fired at the time designated. My headquarters will be in the fourteen-gun battery, A. E. Burnside, Major-General.' "

Burnside picked up Humphreys' telegram and shook it. "They'd like to tell me when to sit down and take a crap today, too. If I'd let em." He slapped the telegram down on the table in front of another aide, who uncrumpled it, and filed it.

"This is one time, by God, that I'll have my orders obeyed as given." *Potter understands that he's to blow it as close to three-thirty as possible. Actually, they ought to be lighting the fuse about now!* Burnside's pulse accelerated a bit. *Everything planned to the last detail. This must be how a Napoleon would feel, knowing he'd got his enemies where he wanted them at last.* Burnside rubbed his hands. *Any minute now.*

"Let's go outside and watch," he said. The invitation did not include Meade's "spies," his look made that clear! He bounded up the stairs and out of the bombproof. The entrance was in the reverse slope of the small hill on which the battery sat. Followed by Ferrero, the two Majors, and a staff Captain, Burnside led the way to the battery. They pushed aside the woven-wood curtain that screened an embrasure designed for observation, and peered out. It was still too black to see anything. So much for the almanac.

Burnside looked at his watch.

"Three-thirty," he said, and looked grinning at Ferrero.

Behind them, one of the gunners sneezed explosively.

"There it goes," said one of the other gunners, and everybody laughed.

The air stayed black.

Nothing happened.

3:30 A.M. *4th Division Bivouac*

Reveille—staccato, reiterated—sounded between the tents. The trumpet ceased and left the air vacant. Birdsong rising after a pause came out of the fields, questions and quarrels. Their calls came from a distance beyond the camp.

Tobe rolled out of his blankets, and stuck his face out into the air. It was still dark, but there was light mixed in it, like a dribble-up of mud when you walk through a clear puddle stirring the bottom. He stepped out of the tent. His bare feet were bathed with dew. The grass felt like coarse hair.

Randolph was sitting by the campfire. There was a set to his back that told Tobe he was waiting for all of them to gather round. Randolph's face had the cold closed look it had whenever something reminded him of his wife and child sold away; or of how he killed Hewson.

One by one, the dark shapes of the men slipped from the tents, to hunker in front of Randolph. When the company had gathered, Randolph told them. "They took us out the attack." And he gestured around, to the tents, the stacked arms, the lightening sky. Of course: they all should have figured it out. Nothing more needed to be said. Each of them realized, without saying it, that he had expected something like this. Whatever you counted on or hoped for, that was the one thing sure never to come: not unless you had a power of luck. But who had such a power?

They continued to sit, in silence. Tobe no longer heard the birdcalls in the distance. It was the Day, and it wasn't the Day. What would happen now?

Randolph thought, *Maybe we's left out of the prophecy after all.* Then he shook his head. *My eyes don't lie, and what I know don't lie.* In his mind the picture of the attack was clear, a vision so clear it must be a picture of what would be fulfilled. Clear as the black face of Jesus had been.

Just then, Captain Shugrue came round the corner of the tent-row, calling, "All right, boys! Out of the . . ."

And stopped. Surprised to see them all out and dressed and sitting in a circle. Surprise, menaced—How? Why?—when their black faces turned round to him, fifty black faces and a hundred glistening eyes.

3:30 A.M. 14th N.Y.H.A.

In his hole in the ground, Neill felt the change. When he looked up, he saw that the night was going rotten, like the dark shell of a melon when the ripeness came on it: the smooth hard rind going all streaked and rayed and splotched, going pulpy-soft, going rotten.

One little kick and you'd find the hard shell wasn't more than a black skin, and your toe'd go right on through to the wetstink and rot inside it.

Oh, nothing stinks worse than a rotted melon!

His skin convulsed on him with the nausea, the disgust of it, repulsive. Shook him. Shook him again. Shook him again.

3:35 A.M. *The Mine*

At the minehead, suddenly, you could see everybody's face, the details of shape and feature, though the color was bad, pasty gray in the false dawn. "Now," said Potter.

Pleasants took his cigar from his mouth, after a deep draw. Blew on it. Pressed it deep and firm into the end of the fuse. It sputtered, caught. Sprayed firesparks out. Their faces looked warm in its light.

The sparks wriggled up the fuse like a mouse skittering a rope back into its hole, flashed between the lips of the sandbags that closed the mouth of the cave.

Vanished.

Pleasants stared into the hole, his eyes fixed, waiting.

Rees scrabbled onto the lip of the parapet, risking a sniper. He was crazy-greedy to see it go up.

Potter looked at his watch. Ten minutes for the fuse to burn.

The air lightened, perceptibly. Pleasants tore his gaze from the hole. Doyle was next to him. Pleasants could see that the corporal's chevrons on the man's sleeve were new, the nap and sizing not yet taken out of them. So much lighter.

"Ten minutes," said Potter.

Pleasants looked at his watch.

The mine had failed to explode.

3:45 A.M. *1st Division Bombproof*

Dr. Clubb and the orderlies sat along the tables and stretchers. The gaggle of staff officers sat around the camp desk at the other side. The orderlies whispered some together. It had been a warm night. The day would be hot. Dr. Clubb sat quite still, feeling the heat turn his forehead to a running fountain. *Best to wrap a handkerchief around my head when the work starts,* he thought. *Look like a damn Red Indian, but I can't have sweat running in my eyes.*

Just then, General Ledlie walked in. He was a well-set-up man, thought Clubb. A drinker—the telltale capillaries in the nose—but one of the hale-and-hearty type. Bluff-chested, strong-jawed. His aides seemed to like him. . . .

Well they might! thought Clubb. *Keeping his volunteer staff safe here while the regulars do the dirty work! Probably another of these damned political officers.*

Ledlie stepped up to Dr. Clubb, extending a large red hand. "Doctor, . . ." he said, grinning. His grip was hard and muscular. "We'll be sharing the facilities here. . . ." he gestured vaguely round him.

"Yes," said Clubb.

"Well . . . anything we can do . . ."

"Thank you." Clubb's curiosity got the better of his sense of disapproval. "Er, General . . . can you tell me when the attack will begin? I understood it was to happen at three-thirty."

Ledlie laughed heartily, though Clubb failed to see the joke. "Well, Doctor . . . military operations! Hardly go like clockwork, you know! Patience!" He turned, and walked across the bombproof to seat himself at the desk.

From the look of him, thought Clubb, you'd think the attack was scheduled for some time next week.

Ah, well! It would come soon enough!

4:15 A.M. *Fourteen-Gun Battery*

> HEADQUARTERS ARMY OF THE POTOMAC,
> *July 30, 1864—4:15* A.M.
>
> Major-General BURNSIDE:
>   Is there any difficulty in exploding the mine? It is three-quarters of an hour later than that fixed upon for exploding it.
>   A. A. HUMPHREYS,
>   *Major-General and Chief of Staff.*

"What answer shall we give them, sir?" asked Richmond.

"They can wait! It will happen any minute now." Burnside paced back and forth. He realized suddenly what he was doing. *They will think I'm unnerved,* he thought. He forced himself to sit down.

"What word from the Mine?" he asked.

Richmond shook his head. "Nothing since they said the fuse had gone, and they'd try to splice it." He paused. "How long can we wait for them, sir? Before we have to? . . ."

Send the troops without my Mine! Burnside thought. *No good! No good! A bloodbath again, and they'll lay it all on me. Or worse—maybe the fuse is still on, burning slowly down there in the damp, and then suppose the thing goes off just as our own troops. . . . Oh God!* Too frightful. The humiliation he would suffer would be annihilating, worse than Fredericksburg. . . .

He stopped himself, surprised to find that he had gotten up and begun pacing again.

> HEADQUARTERS ARMY OF THE POTOMAC,
> *July 30, 1864.*
>
> OPERATOR AT GENERAL BURNSIDE'S FIELD HEADQUARTERS:
>   Is General Burnside at his headquarters? The commanding general is anxious to learn what is the cause of delay.
>   A. A. HUMPHREYS,
>   *Major-General and Chief of Staff.*

"Sir," said Richmond, "hadn't we better answer General Meade?"

Answer him? Answer him? There was only one tolerable answer.

It must work. It must work. Soon. Now.

HEADQUARTERS ARMY OF THE POTOMAC,
July 30, 1864—4:35 A.M.

Major-General BURNSIDE:

If the mine cannot be exploded something else must be done, and at once. The commanding general is awaiting to hear from you before determining.

A. A. HUMPHREYS,
Major-General and Chief of Staff.

If only the damned telegraph would leave off chattering, and the couriers would stay away and give him some time to think!

4:35 A.M. *The Mine*

Pleasants had gone pale, and sat down. He had not moved for three quarters of an hour.

Doyle, standing in the trench nearby, his rifle in his hand, waiting to move to the front when the troops making the attack left the lines free—Doyle took it like a blow between the eyes. Between the eyes, like Corrigan. Oh the damned waste of it! The damned waste of it they've made! Oh, to use him up so, and leave nothing for it, not even get the job done right! And themselves the damned fools of the universe that thought of it themselves!

Rees's blood rose, slowly as the time ticked by, then in a burst of rage. He whirled, faced Pleasants. "The damned fuse! If you'd got the battery as you were supposed . . ."

Potter looked at the sergeant in shock and disbelief. Pleasants blushed, embarrassed in front of his commander: yet he could not disengage himself from the brunt of Rees's anger. *He had failed! He had failed after all! The army engineers would crucify him! What he had said to Hunt!*

There was a strange light in the trench. Pleasants felt he had known, prophesied whenever his childish optimism would allow him to, that this is what it would come to. It seemed to him that he had lived over these moments again and again, a terrible repetition.

"Aaah!" said Rees, and he turned to the minehead. "Give us a hand!" he called, as he hauled sandbags away from the entrance.

Someone handed him a candle. He lit it, glued it to his cap brim with drippings.

He threw a glance up towards Pleasants. He grinned like a man who had just raked in the whole pot playing poker. Stood there a moment, one hand resting on the log lintel of the mine entrance as a man might rest his hand on the flank of a favorite horse.

Then he ducked under his hand, and his boots disappeared into the dark.

The sun was nearly up now, just under the horizon. The air in the trench had turned gray-yellow.

Pleasants cleared his throat. "It's probably a defective fuse. He'll splice it, and relight . . ."

"He never took more fuse down with him . . ." said Doyle.

They stood there.

There was no sound from inside the Mine. Over the lines came the call of the rebel reveille, faintly.

Lieutenant Douty grabbed a coil of fuse. Without a word, he ducked into the mine after Rees.

HEADQUARTERS ARMY OF THE POTOMAC,
July 30, 1864—4:35 A.M.

Major-General BURNSIDE,
Commanding Ninth Corps:

The commanding general directs that if your mine has failed that you make an assault at once, opening your batteries.

A. A. HUMPHREYS,
Major-General and Chief of Staff.

4:40 A.M. *The Mine*

It was like returning to a familiar place, an old house shut up long ago. Nothing left of the past, your cot-bed, the Old Man's chair—but the ghosts and shadows of these things, memories clinging to the stains in the wallpaper.

Rees went down the shaft as quick as he could and still be careful. It was a bad splice, he told himself. Wet as it is, it would never have taken this long to blow. *And if I'm wrong, if the spark of it is fiddling along slowly up ahead, I'll take the whole dirt of the place on my back.* He moved quickly, yet without haste. The attack was nothing, time was nothing. He had simply to complete his job, as it should be done, correctly. He must splice the fuse and get out. That was the whole of his concern.

Down past the place where the quicksand sucked the props out and the walls to pieces, and they'd had to snatch off all that timber to hold the earth off. Down past the turn in the tunnel, where the gray marl had gummed the picks, and turned the points aside. The pipe-quarry. Patches of damp where springs were still coming in. Drying patches where they'd begun to stop as the rain water fell away and was sopped up by the soil.

Every several yards he stopped to look closely at the fuse, feel of it to see if it was burnt out.

He was deep in now. Deeper than he'd figured on going. Maybe a hundred feet now from the end of it, less than that from where they'd tamped the tunnel shut.

Only a blazing fool like myself would have stuck my head in the beast's mouth this way. For what? For the glory of the Forty-eighth *or* its little fine Colonel? For the bloody medal or promotion? *Be buried under the earth for that?*

His hand, groping, found the break: the cord was ashen here, there it was solid. He looked down.

Three hundred feet in, at least. *And me forgetting to bring the bloody fuse! Damned fool! Do I just walk out now and ask for the fuse, looking like a bloody ass? Or do I light the thing and run? Blow me to hell before I'd got halfway out.*

He might have done it or not, but just then he heard Douty scrabbling down the tunnel, saw the dot of jiggling light. He grinned. It would be all right now.

"Here," said Douty, whispering.

Rees took the end of the coil. With his clasp knife, he cut the fuse off well below the bad splice where the burning had gone dead. He took a bit of cord out of his kit and tied the ends of the fuse together with tight, rapid twists. Douty held it as he knotted it. Tested it.

Then Douty began to back, paying the coil of fuse out behind him. Rees hesitated a moment, breathed in the musty earth smell of the cave, then followed Douty, watching to make sure the fuse stayed clear of the wet, that there were no other defects, till he came up to where Douty was standing, holding the end. They were still in blackness, more than a hundred feet from the entrance. Rees was not sure he could see the glow of light back down the tunnel.

He took the end of the fuse from Douty. "All right," he said. "Get on out of it." The Lieutenant turned and went, scurrying, fast as he could go.

Rees gave him time to get up the tunnel. Then he took off his hat, and held the candle to the fuse end. The little orange flame licked it, lapped it around. It caught with a sizzle, tiny hot gnats of fire stinging the back of Rees's hand.

He held the flaming cord a moment before his face.

Set it, carefully, down on the floor.

He turned his back, the candle fell to the floor and sputtered out, blackness swooped in. He ran down the tunnel, skidding forward on his hands and knees down the slope where the marl was hard and slick as rock, and saw the light, and ran for it.

4:40 A.M. *Observation Post*

Booker became aware of the dull ache of tension in his hands. He relaxed his grip on the ledge of the fourteen-gun battery. Rockwood, standing with him, saw that the air was graying, lightening more and more. Bushes materialized in the shadowed ground, the dark line of the underbrush that marked where a ravine slanted across the Union lines, the contested strip, and the Confederate lines. The western sky was still a bruised purple, no longer the clear black of night in which stars could be seen. Behind them, back of the loom of the battery, the sun was rising to lip the horizon. *On the beach, maybe even back at City Point, they can probably see it already,* thought Booker.

In St. Louis, though, it would still be dark. The sun would not rise for them till it had been up a long time here. Dawning for Miriam and his son, Eli, it would send a gold finger delicately between the edge of the shade and the window frame. He remembered its movements well: how the finger would touch, seeming to warm, the twin peaks of his feet and pass across the floor to touch the little smooth curve of the boy's head where it bulged out of the blankets, to climb the opposite wall.

Booker saw his own hazy shadow fall forward out of the embrasure. He looked behind him.

Above the parapet of the blackened battery, the thin dome of the sun bulged, an eyelid-peep of fire.

He heard a *bump* like a machine starting up below the floor of a factory loft.

The ground bumped.

He turned, and looked across the field. The gray fields were flat, the long black horizontal of the rebel lines, the line of brush in the ravine.

The rebel fort bumped.

Bulged.

A black sound muscled the strata up and aside like the shoulders of a giant, *a firehead bulged out of the black,* a roar, a black wind, and he covered his head to shut out the black roaring of the air and saw behind his eyelids the firehead bulging out of the black folded earth, a head of sun, a head of fire, a birth, a death.

4:45 A.M. *Pegram's Salient*

Billy sank deep in sleep, into his old dreams. Here was his mother come to visit him in the trenches, all that way from Carolina alone. He came upon her sitting with Colonel Davidson, at the long table from the bombproof, but this time out in the trench. He came walking towards them, sustained by his friends, Sam on the right, Dixon on the left. Why had she come all the way from Carolina? The news must be terrible. His mother and the Colonel looked at him from the table, and beckoned. He reached for Dix and Sam, but they were gone. He spun around looking for them, the spinning became an uncontrollable movement of its own that he *broke* by running away down the trench, his mother and the Colonel calling after him in high terrible voices. The earth lurched, throwing, expelling him, he took flight lifting off with the speed of his running and floated uncontrollably. His stomach sucked in with terror of flight, of fall.

This is what happens when you try to get away.

He buckled over doubled over in on himself in the air, trying to hold on, trying to stop the flying, but the movement carried him higher and further into blackness, plunging down out of the sky, to the earth, to a hole in the earth. A hole full of fire.

Oh I'm sorry I ever thought to run.

Sam-Dix-Tommy, they laughed at him, their faces had turned black as the faces of devils.

Deserter! Murderer! Deserter! Fornicator! Deserter!
The fire swallowed him.

4:45 A.M. *Union Lines*

Neill shrank into himself under a sky gone all rotten with light. There was Sergeant Stanley's face coming through the gloom. The sergeant's eyes glittered and his lips twisted to speak.

The trench heaved and threw Neill to his knees. The black earth boomed down around him and he knew the earth was gone. He fainted.

Doyle and the others in the trench saw Rees come tumbling headfirst out of the Mine. Then they felt the bump of it, there was a flash of time, and they leaped for the parapet in a group, and Doyle saw the black bubble heave and rise and burst, a boiling of smoke lit inside with fire, rising and rising, mushrooming, the rising sun throwing sharp light against its black corrugated sides and catching bits of hard things tossed in the upswelling of it, and the sound hit them like a hard wind and a blow in the face.

Rees lay at the bottom of the trench, too spent to rise and see it.

Pleasants and Potter, as if a secret spell had been broken, dashed to the trench, to the headquarters for the attack up near the front line, turning their backs on the booming roll of the thunder, the skyward rise of the cloud that stood up against the sun, swelling and growing, filling the sky to darkening.

"Here it comes," yelled Rees, looking up at the sky. "Get down, you!"—and they dropped into the trench as the dug-up earth turned over and fell on them in a black buffeting dried-out choking rain. Big blocks of stuff fell *chunk* above their covered heads and all around the trench.

Burnside felt his desk jar. Dust fell from the ceiling. Richmond opened his mouth to speak and it seemed that his words nearly destroyed them, the words themselves drowned in noise as the battery overhead fired, shaking the roof. Even under the ground they could feel the earth shake and the air fill with roaring as from one end of the front to the other the artillery shot explosives flaring into the silent trenches opposite and into the black cloud that bubbled up out of the Mine.

"It's gone!" said somebody, and Humphreys turned to look. It seemed to be that a black cat was swarming up a gray wall, a hundred cats, a million cats with burning turpentine on their tails as they clawed frantically into the sky.

"Well I'm damned," whispered Duane, at his side. "It worked after all."

Pennington was standing, attentive, with Thomas outside the latter's tent. "Let the men have breakfast, if they want," said Thomas. "No telling when we'll be called on."

"Or *if*," said Chris gloomily.

"How are the men taking it?" asked Thomas.

Chris shrugged. He was angry. Angry with the way they'd been cheated of their chance to prove themselves. Angry at the men too, their docile acceptance of it. Perhaps they hadn't wanted the chance after all. Anger, disappointment in them. Oh, and with himself. Who was he to sit in judgment on others? Let him who is without sin . . . He was just like his father, after all, prim and censorious. Though he strove to be generous and open, as Emerson advised him to be.

But these clods of clay called men. Here they had been cheated of their chance to enter upon the stage of history, to prove themselves men: and they went about things as usual.

No, he thought suddenly, something is different.

He listened. From the distance, he heard a soft distinct *bump*. All the birds fell silent. He had not been aware that they were singing.

Then it came to him. That was what was odd: none of the men were singing. From the camp came only the low buzz and hum of covert, incomprehensible voices, talking among themselves. Prosaic, ordinary speech, none of the fiery poetry of their songs. The *songs* were missing.

4:50 A.M. *Observation Post*

Booker and Rockwood picked themselves up off the floor of the observation post. Booker's eyes were full of dust, and he dug at them with his handkerchief, frantically, before he was able to take hold; calm himself, dip the edge of the cloth in water tipped out of his canteen, and dab gently at the eyes.

Near him, Rockwood sneezed explosively and began giggling.

In a flash of intuition Booker knew that he was laughing at the absurd connection between the explosion of the Mine and the sneeze. That joke the gunner made . . . "God bless you!" he said. They both laughed. Gray dust continued to fall on them. It made a sifting sound, like a fall of dry rain. The explosion was over, but their ears still rang with it. Guns thundered far off to either side, but none of them could hear the silence just around them. They spoke loudly—"Wasn't that something!" "Blew em to hell and gone!"—as if calling above a continuing roar. Off to either side the batteries were firing, but in the post itself they could hear the *pat-pat* sound as Ferrero brushed the dust from his uniform. Booker almost laughed again: Ferrero slapped at himself with small, fastidious movements, as if he were strumming an invisible musical instrument.

He pulled Rockwood's sleeve. "Let's get out of this," he shouted. "They'll start firing again in a minute."

Rockwood nodded. "Idiotic place to put an observation post."

They had to pull Ferrero's sleeve hard to get his attention. He seemed dazed by the blast.

They looked around, and were shocked to see Burnside himself. He was standing on the parapet fanning his heavy arms back and forth.

Booker began to laugh, got a throat full of dust, and ended up sitting below the parapet, coughing and laughing, tears making tunnels in the dust on his face.

Around him the battery exploded once again, fourteen big guns sending shells flying westward into the hovering cloud of smoke and dust.

5:00 A.M. *14th N.Y.H.A.*

Neill could taste the grit in his mouth, and he thought the trench had caved in on him, or some lucky reb had dropped a shell into a magazine just back of them and blown the whole brigade to smithereens.

Somebody stepped on his back. He rolled, threw the man. Bodies were blundering around the narrow alley of the trench in gray-brown air full of dust. There were yells, screams, men cursing. A drum stuttered the long roll, and stopped *bang* as if someone had kicked in the drumhead or shot the drummer. "Fourteenth New York! Fourteenth New York!" someone was yelling.

"Mother of God," said Neill, "what was it?"

"The Mine, you idiot," said Beeler's voice. He turned to look. Beeler's face was blacked like a nigger's with the dust. "Jesus Joseph and Mary," said Neill, "if it ain't Brother Bones."

The drums began to go now. Drumming them up into ranks, to get up out of the trenches and go. Neill formed up, and something hit him in the back and knocked him flat.

He rolled over, cursing. The squad was milling about and brawling, Sergeant Stanley swinging his pistol butt and yelling. Some damn fools in the second line had mistook somehow, and came jumping into the trench before the first brigade was out.

"Oh Jesus," said Neill, "a bloody screw-up for sure."

"Out of this," yelled Stanley.

Oostervelt was there, his sword out. He punched one man in the back with the hilt of it, nearly jabbing a soldier behind him with the point. "Get out of the trench, you damned skulkers! You lousy bounty-jumping Irish sons of bitches! Get out of it!" Oostervelt was beside himself.

The line of men looked back and forth at the parapet, bewildered. There was no way out of the trench. No ladders, no steps cut in the trench wall, which stood eight feet high in places, five and a half at the lowest, where the rifle slits were cut in the parapet.

"Begging your pardon, sir," said Neill. "Just how are we to do it? Fucking *fly?*"

Oostervelt whirled around. Then he jerked his head right and left, looking up the trench to either side. There were no ladders anywhere.

"Here's a go!" yelled a high voice. One of the drummer-boys, a wee lad, made a run, hopped the fire step, and got an arm through a rifle slit. He hung there, drum dangling off his belt behind him, then dropped.

Sergeant Stanley stepped up, cupped a hand. The kid stepped in it, and he boosted him up. He turned, stood on the parapet, presented his sticks; and began to *drum-drum-drum* the long roll.

"Let's go, boys," yelled Stanley. Neill saw his chance, stepped to the wall first, set his rifle down. Cupped his hands and waited for the men to come up. Stanley shot him a look of understanding and pure hate.

"Wipe off the horseshit, boys. I have to eat with this, you know!"

The file stepped forward, and he and Stanley began to boost the men up.

The first one hurt Neill's hand, and he said, "Wait a minute!" whipped his bayonet out of the scabbard, and jammed it between the two logs that held the trench wall in place, holding the handle himself. "Now," he said, and the next man stepped on the blade, and stretch-jumped up to the parapet.

Dust was still sifting down. The air was still dark with it. The air was full of the throbbing sound of the heavy guns firing. But the explosions were far off, westward. No rebels shooting this way.

When the last man vanished upward, the face of Sergeant Stanley revealed itself, looking right at Neill.

"Last but not least, boy-o," said Stanley. "Up you go."

Neill hesitated. The rifle was leaning against the trench. He had his bayonet stuck in the wall. Stanley's pistol was out.

In the next second the men of the other brigade began pouring into the trench. Neill jerked the blade out of the wall. Stepped on Stanley's blade, got his elbows into the soft earth of the parapet. Heaved, wriggled, and was over. Stanley was up beside him.

He got to his feet. Stanley stood behind and to his left. Ahead of him black shapes of the company were vanishing into the gray hanging fog of dust.

Neill held his rifle across his body, and jogged forward into the hanging cloud of dust.

5:15 A.M. *Fourteen-Gun Battery*

The dust was thinning a bit up by the fourteen-gun battery. From the embrasures, the officers could see the troops going forward. Skirmishers, thought Booker. He waited for the lines to begin to form into a solid column of attack. Through rifts in the smoke, he could see only small moving clots of men.

He looked at his watch. To his surprise, he saw that it was nearly twenty minutes since the explosion of the Mine. His sense of time had been somehow numbed by the force of the blast. Perhaps that accounted for the slowness of the column as well, but it was a bad sign: the storming column ought to have been formed and ready to go. It shouldn't have taken prepared troops this long to get out and into the breach.

"There's not a single rebel gun firing!" called Rockwood. "By heaven! I think we've knocked em silly."

Burnside too, thought Booker.

Ferrero called to them, and they stepped down out of and behind the battery. "I'm going to be at the bombproof at the head of the covered way we came up to get here. It seems the best place to be . . . at least, I think so. I had thought of using it as headquarters myself before . . . well, Ledlie is there now." He paused. Then looked at them. "I'll wait for you there."

There was another pause.

Rockwood cleared his throat. "Orders for the division, sir?"

Ferrero looked sharply at him. "Ah . . . no, no specific instructions. I've ordered the brigade commanders to have the troops under arms at dawn. I expect they'll do that. I'll send word when we're ordered to advance . . . if we're ordered," and he gestured vaguely, apologetically, up to the battery, where Burnside stood. "If we go in . . . orders are to follow behind Humphrey's brigade. Right up the covered way. No chance of a mistake." He looked at his watch. "I'll meet you there. No chance of missing me."

The two Majors saluted. Ferrero turned, and walked off down the communication trench towards the head of the covered way.

Rockwood looked at Booker. Booker shrugged. "Think we can get back the way we came? Johnny doesn't seem to be shooting much."

Rockwood nodded. They slid down the slight incline, and walked along over the covered way. Below their feet and to the right was the dark trench, filled with troops of the Third Division, packed in shoulder to shoulder and back to front. Some of them had their knapsacks; others had evidently left them behind. Rockwood shook his head. That spelled confusion, officers not knowing where they were going and what they should take along.

At a turn in the trench they saw a clutch of officers, sitting on the lip of the trench. A Brigadier General, a big man—Hartranft: Rockwood recognized him.

Hartranft waved. "What's happening? We heard the big bang. Nothing's moving."

Rockwood shrugged. "Attack's getting under way, but it's slow. The explosion made a lot of dust, it's hard to see." He looked up and down the covered way. "This is a hell of a highway. It'll take you a month to move these troops through here. Why not deploy them outside? The rebels aren't shooting at all."

Hartranft put on his dignity. "I've got my orders, Major. I don't want to get caught out in the open if they start throwing shells in here. That's what the covered way was built for, if I'm not mistaken."

Rockwood saluted, and the two officers continued on down the trench. The second brigade in line was Humphrey's. Booker recognized one of his staff officers, and passed on the advice about getting the troops up out of the covered way. The man promised to suggest it to Humphrey.

"Well," said Booker. "That's something done, anyway."

"Something," Rockwood conceded.

They walked on down past the trench filled with men, filled with the smell of sweat and morning-mouth, dirty underwear and wet wool and leather and gunpowder, filled with the sounds of voices chattering, laughing, talking, kidding, muttering.

"It's a damned bloody mess," said Rockwood.

Booker's chest swelled with a big sigh, and burst. "Oh, right. Right. They should have let us do it the way we set it up."

5:15 A.M. *Pegram's Salient*

Lieutenant Bruce blinked. Blinked again. His vision began to clear. He was lying, head down, in the collapsed bombproof. A huge ceiling-beam pinned him to his bunk like the finger of a clumsy man carefully holding an insect in place. When he eased himself over, the beam's precarious balance held.

What had happened? Lying now on the floor, on a heap of debris, he saw the ruins by the light that slanted in from a crack in the roof up and to the right. He shook his head. He had gone to sleep lying with his feet towards the beam of light. . . .

He understood: the door had been towards his feet. If light was coming in from the direction his head had lain in, then he must have somehow been spun around or . . .

No: the bombproof had been shattered, blown up. The door was buried under the ruin of the roof. The beams had torn away from the wall that had backed into a solid ravine-side.

The force of it! What could it have been? They must have hit a magazine. . . .

He was awake, and himself again. The Yankees had blown their Mine. Incredible, the force of it!

He had been right! Right after all! By God, that should prove . . .

I'm still shocked, he thought. *We've been blown up and I'm congratulating myself for predicting it!* He grinned at himself. Rolled over.

Allen had been sitting at the table. Working on that damned epic poem. A big beam of the roof had come down right where the table had been. In the half-darkness, guided by the pointing finger of light, Bruce began to scrabble around in the wreckage of timber, clods of earth and rock. Digging, he touched something slick and warm, and began to brush frantically.

He cleared the debris away from Allen's face. The man had had his chest crushed by the timber. His face was blue-black, and a horrible tongue, covered with bits of soil, protruded from his stopped and strangled mouth. His eyes were full of dust: a pebble perched delicately on the dome of one pupil. Bruce, his ears ringing, picked it off, being careful not to touch the eye itself. That was extremely important.

A leather mapcase lay near Allen's ear. Bruce picked it up, tucked it into his shirtfront. He turned, and started for the light that poured through the crack in the ceiling.

Below the crack, he paused. He turned back. "Anybody alive in there?" No answer. "Twenty-second North Carolina! This is Bruce! Anybody left down in there?" There was no answer.

If the others came back last night, he thought, *they're dead under there. If they didn't.* . . . He had to get out and see.

He jumped for the break in the roof, caught a projecting splint of fractured timber. Swung his feet up lightly, caught them on the lip, dug in his heels. Pushed and heaved back against the splint, and he rolled forward onto his knees.

Out of the bunker.

All around him the face of the earth was utterly changed. Earth was broken and mounded, piled in strange clods and lumps. No sign of the ordered line of trenches, no grass or plants, a moonscape, lava-scape, dead. The air was black with falling dust. Thin cries came out of the mist. Somewhere outside the mist, shells were exploding, guns were firing.

Ride to the sound of the guns, he thought. No, walk. A good joke. He giggled, held his chest; giggled again.

He began to walk toward the sound of the batteries, thinking that he would get some help there. He could help with the guns, till he could think of what else to do. His ears were still ringing. His feet slid in the churned, loosened earth. He had no boots on. The earth was hot. *It's a hot day,* he thought.

He saw shapes coming in out of the mist. Rifles slanted, elongated, tipped with bayonets. Voices.

And then he was awake for real. And knew where he was. *Yankees coming over into the hole where they'd blown up.* He turned to run back. *Where in hell was the regiment?* He ran, slipping and sliding in the loose earth, looking for anyone he could find. Since he'd left the bunker he hadn't seen a living soul.

5:15 A.M. *1st Division Headquarters*

Down in the First Division bombproof, Dr. Clubb had felt the throb of the explosion go through the earth under and around him. Heard the batteries let go, the sound dulled by the walls of the bombproof. The yelling of the troops outside the bombproof, as they went forward, was muffled too. It sounded like children playing in the street, heard from the quiet of a study in a city apartment.

Ah, a study! To be home again. Well, there was no good dwelling on that. Dr. Clubb slapped both thighs sharply with both hands, and rose, admonishing reminiscence and nostalgia. Time to get ready for business.

He went around the area, checking the placement of his and his orderlies' tools, empty buckets and water keg, brandy and rum, laudanum and morphine, disinfectant in big stoppered bottles. Rolls of lint and bandages, shining in the dull light.

He finished, and looked over at the handsome General and his staff. They were still sitting around the desk, talking in low voices, nodding and smiling.

Outside the open door of the bombproof, a mob of soldiers yelled at each other, shoving. One man fell, cursed, pulled himself up, and cursed again.

"Quiet out there!" snapped one of the staff officers.

Well I'll be damned, thought Clubb, *isn't the man even curious to see the show? He's either a cool customer, or . . .*

He left that thought unfinished. One didn't even think such things

of a fellow officer, without . . . *provocation,* he almost said. Maybe the
man knows his job—let him do it.

5:20 A.M. *Pegram's Salient*

Billy came to himself while he was stumbling back across a field
full of smoke and roaring. *Am I alive,* he thought. *Am I dead and gone
to hell?* He could still feel the glow of the fire up one side of his face.
His right eye was full of fire, he couldn't see out of it at all, just a red
blur. But the left one showed clear.

Blowed up, he said, but heard no words. He was like a man in a
dream, speaking under water. The words made bubbling sounds that
weren't words. "Blowed up!" he yelled. *I been blowed apart, I been
blowed in half.* He felt his brains oozing out of his split skull. I must be
dead. I am walking, but will fall down and be dead.

The ground was smoking. The pit of hell was under his feet.

There was a green-sided slope in front of him, crowned with clouds
blossoming. He walked up towards the clouds, up out of the wreckage
of the valley.

He could hear nothing except a high whining sing in his head, and
thought, *Was it angels or devils?*

- Figures came running down the slope to meet him. Faces. Coming
to save him.

But his legs were weak. Devils snatched him by the knees and
hurled him down again to the horrible fiery hell at his feet even as the
figures from the cloud-crowned hill ran to clasp him.

Billy felt his lips were burnt. The whole right side of his face felt
burnt and raw. The pulse continued to bong through his head. An arm
under his back lifted him, and he felt water against his lips. Behind
him there were detonations; the ground shook, the air was bitter.

"Come up out of it, Billy-Boy! Come on." *Dixon?*

When the beating of the blood boomed in his head he knew that he
was in hell among devils, black bitter air, the volcanic bursts of fire,
burnt with the other devils, and he could feel the seared flesh up the
right side of his face and his hand. He opened his remaining eye.

"It was hell," he whispered. "Burning."

"That's right, Billy." Dixon's hand on his shoulder was shaking.
"Like all hell broke loose. Oh Lord, I don't ever want to be closer than
that . . ."

Dixon's face was the face of a devil. It was Dixon's face. He was red,
bathed in blood, blood of the nigger he'd shot. Smelled of blood and
brimstone.

The pulse continued, would not let up, but it began to slow.

"We got blowed up, Billy. The Yankees was digging a mine. They
blowed us up."

Devils digging away underneath, black hands and faces, eyes like glittering stones, laughing. Ground rotten with them. He'd broke right through into the pit of hell.

"Come on, Billy-Boy! Ain't nobody left at all but just you and me!" Dixon sobbed. "They all just got blowed away, they ain't a thing left of the whole regiment, but only us!"

5:20–5:40 A.M. *The Crater*

The rebel line was only a hundred yards away, but the explosion had made a shambles of the whole hundred. Neill trotted forward towards the Crater, over earth broken and mounded, now hard under foot, now loose as a sandpit. There were blocks of rock, boulders of clay torn up in a mass and thrown over. A shallow roll of ridge marked the place where the abatis had been smashed up and buried under the rubble.

When Neill got to the rebel side, the sun began to show pale-yellow through the drifting dust and stink of powder smoke, and threw Neill's shadow in front of him. Neill walked around junk lying all about: the broken timbers, cracked boxes, the wheel of a gun or wagon with a big bite taken out of the rim.

Over to the right, he saw something strange sticking out of the ground, and walked towards it. An oddly shaped mushroom. Closer, it was a yellowish hand, bent back and open, the fingers limp, protruding from a heap of earth. Neill stared at it, as if he expected it to move, to beckon. But it stayed, not even quivering.

Bent back on its wrist that way, the fingers softly curled: relaxed and casual, a hand reaching for something. *Pass the salt mate, the loan of your cleanin rod.* And was it soft or was it stiff? And warm yet or cold? And might the rest of the man be down there alive?

Once seen you couldn't pass it. Like in the mines, when you hear something go *crack,* and the air shakes and you must run before the earth comes in on you, and God be your help if you hear voices call from where the rocks are falling, for by all that's holy you must go back for your buddies. You must stay. You cannot go and never tell. A white hand ground between fallen coal stones, do you pull on it for the crying call you heard, or run for the air?

Neill knelt beside the hand. It beckoned him. He reached quickly into his pocket, took out a hardtack cracker, and stuck it into the hand, flat against the palm and under the curl of the fingers.

"Father Emmett," said Beeler, "and are ye givin absolution to sinners? Leave him the wafer, Your Worship, and leave us have some of the wine."

Neill, stung, turned upon Beeler. "Watch your damned dirty mouth, you." His face burned, as if he'd been caught doing a shameful thing, buying a fuck from a dirty nigger, paying a bigger man not to hurt him.

"Move up there," yelled Sergeant Stanley, and Neill tore his eyes away and went forward again, Beeler after him. *Take the bread and let me go.*

Up ahead there was a large mound of reddish earth, crumbled and heaped up across a two-hundred-yard section of the rebel trench, the broken earth spilling forward like the tip of tailings outside a mine pit. To the left of the center of this mounded ridge perched a large eccentric clay boulder, ten feet high, and just about that wide. Neill was drawn to it, irresistably, and so were a lot of the other boys. He touched the side of it, tentatively. The surface was still a bit damp from the underground, slick and oily feeling.

"Jesus," said Beeler, "would you look at the size of the thing?"

Smoke and dust still sifted down around them. Beeler and Neill walked round to the other side to see the boulder from another angle.

"It's like we're a lot of bloody damned tourists," said Neill.

"Come and see the elephant," said Beeler, and they laughed. The elephant wasn't there, thought Neill. His night-panic seemed ridiculous now, something that had happened to another man. The Johnnies must have all run off, scared to death when the thing blew. (Well, he'd almost run off himself, when it came to that!) There was a peaceful, holiday feeling about the place under this concealing mist of dust.

Beeler and Neill walked up to the edge of the Crater. Some of the other boys were going down into it, sliding on their butts and kicking up a cloud of dust, or helping each other down with linked hands.

It was a deep, steep-sided hole. From where Beeler and Neill stood, on its left side, they could see all the way across it. At its widest, it might be sixty or seventy feet across. The bottom—a broken floor of mounded heaps of earth and boulders and broken wreckage of equipment—was at least thirty feet down the sharply sloping sides. It was sheer just where they stood, and Neill felt the deep of it grab him by the belly and pull, and he stepped back a step. They could make out what looked like the far end of the Crater, off to the right about two hundred feet; but their view of the bottom was cut off by a ridge that bisected the Crater from front to back, about fifty feet from where they stood. Everything below the level of their feet on the other side of that hump of earth was hidden.

The ground still smoked.

"Let's go down for a look," said Neill. He led the way, stumbling in loose earth, along the lip of the Crater, till they reached a place where the slope was a shade more gradual—near the point where the central ridge met the back wall, just under the shadow of the big boulder. Neill held Beeler's left hand, Beeler held his own rifle in his right, and Neill extended his arm, bending, to let Beeler down as far as he could. Then Beeler let go, and stumbled the rest of the way to the bottom. Neill took his own rifle in his lap, sat down an the edge, and slid, digging his heels to brake himself.

The pebbled ground rolled under his butt as he slid, and then his foot caught a hard bit of rock, and spun him off balance, and he came rolling down the rest of the way on his side. Landed. His rifle slithered down next to him. "Son-of-a-bitching thing," he said. "Nearly killed *me*." He picked the rifle up and shook it.

Beeler sneezed. It was still dusty down at the bottom of the hole, and the ground stank of gunpowder. The walls towered up over their heads. "It'll be the devil's own work climbing out of this," said Beeler, and Neill shrugged. Leave that for when he had to think about it.

Up above him he heard Sergeant Stanley calling. There was the sergeant's face, and Oostervelt next to him.

"What's down there?" called Stanley.

"Come down and find out," Neill called back. Stanley turned his back, and they saw him start down.

The two privates began walking towards the central ridge. The earth was so badly broken up that it was difficult to walk in many places, as in deep sand.

They tipped over piles of junk with their bayonets. Under one of these they saw the back of a half-buried Johnny, and without thinking, Neill pulled back on the man's shoulder strap, and the strap came away.

"Leave him," said Beeler. Below the part you could see—the back and back of the head looking like any man's—there was nothing left at all at all. Neill's stomach heaved, and he felt dizzy.

"Hey!" called somebody from behind a heap of soil, and they plowed up over it to see some men digging at something with their hands—a pair of boots sticking up. *Oh Jesus, not another one,* thought Neill. But someone yelled, "We saw this bugger's boots moving," and in a minute they had hauled the Johnny out.

They gathered round as the man who'd found him turned him over and laid him out on his back. The man's face was covered in a mask of red-yellow dirt, except where the blood running from the ears and nose had made slick red, blackening marks.

The man licked his lips. Neill was shocked, deeply moved. It was almost like seeing the dead raised to life, to see a tongue move in that face covered with smothering earth. The man's licked lips showed bright-red, and Neill thought he looked like a minstrel-show man made up in high yaller. His hair even looked coarse and wooly and gray with the dust in it.

"Let's get him up out of here," said the man who'd found him first. They lifted him onto a blanket, but they wouldn't let Neill take a corner. "We found him," said the man. There was no arguing that. He was theirs. Neill stepped back. The others carried the man through the heaps of dirt to the wall, and set him down. They worked hard, boosting one of their number up the side of the wall. Then he let down a rope of tied-together belts and straps, and they looped it round the rebel, and hoisted him up the side of the cliff. Neill and Beeler watched. Sergeant Stanley came up next to them, and watched too. The body of the rebel reached the top, and the three men tried scrambling up after it. It took them five minutes to do it, though, and the last man needed to be boosted out by Neill and Beeler.

When they had done that, Sergeant Stanley suggested that they go up over the ridge to the other side. Wedging themselves in the corner where the ridge met the wall, they clambered up over the top.

The part of the Crater on the other side was twice as large as the one they had just left. It looked like most of the First Brigade was down in it, digging up buried rebels. One man was being boosted out of it, a leg dangling. He waved and called, "Busted it falling down a damn shaft they dug. Landed on three rebels."

"Kill any of them?"

"Naw! They was suffocated. Broke my leg!" He was jaunty, going back out of it.

The sergeant, followed by Beeler and Neill, slid down into the other side of the Crater. Oostervelt appeared above them again. He seemed to hesitate, then slid down to join them.

Beeler, tipping up a busted crackerbox, spotted the barrel of a cannon sticking up out of the dirt.

Oostervelt came bustling over, very important. "All right, all right there. Let's get busy now! Let's get to work." He lifted his voice. "I want Company C of the Fourteenth New York over here! Let's get busy now! Let's get to work." He lifted his voice. "I want Company C of the Fourteenth New York over here! Let's get this thing dug out. Quick, dammit! This is an attack, not a Sunday promenade!"

Half-a-dozen men appeared, and began digging. They hadn't brought any shovels with them, but there were some boards lying around that did for shifting the earth off.

It was damned hot though. The sun rose higher, its light lipping the back wall of the Crater. The shadow drained out of the Crater as it rose, like water out of a broken cistern. The Crater filled with heat, heavy, impacted; breathing in the air was like breathing in a furnace. Heat radiated from their bodies. Their stamping feet, as they worked, compacted the earth, and made digging harder. They picked at it with bayonets and pointed boards.

Gradually, the shape of the cannon began to emerge from the ground. They were excited by this, and in spite of the heat began to dig harder and faster, eager to finish.

"Best get some rope so we can haul it out," said Stanley.

"Right," said Oostervelt. He mopped his hatless head with his handkerchief, set his cap back on top, and hurried off.

They had got the cannon clear, and with everybody heaving on the trail or pushing the wheel rims, they horsed it over to the wall. They were drenched with sweat by now, their wool pants bagging with it, chafing the insides of their thighs. Their backs were sore.

Oostervelt and a party were waiting on the top, throwing down a coil of heavy rope. "Found it in the reb battery next to this," he yelled.

The side of the Crater here had a bit of a slope to it, but Stanley warned the men away till the heavy gun had been hauled up and over the edge, its wheels slewing in the soft curb of earth at the top.

Beeler threw his cap up and yelled, "Hurray!" and everybody cheered, and slapped his neighbor on the back.

More cheering came from the top, and they clambered up, sweating and grimy, to see what it was. Here came a party of officers, Colonel Marshall, their own brigade commander, and another one—a General with a wooden leg that kept sticking in the dirt; his orderly had to keep a shoulder under the General's draped arm to keep him from sticking.

He looks a plucky fellow though, Neill thought, and they gave him a cheer.

The General waved. "Thank you, men. But let's go forward now. Forward." He pointed across the Crater.

Neill turned. He could see the slope of a hill, with some houses on top.

As he looked a row of clouds appeared on its skyline.

But faster than any shells from the ridge could arrive, came the sound of musketry exploding left exploding right, *pat! pan! patapan! pan!* and the *whump* where a shell came chewing up the ground.

"All right, Fourteenth New York!" yelled Oostervelt, his voice cracking. "This way! Let's go!"

With a chain of explosive grunts the shells from the battery on the ridge line snouted into the ground on the other side of the Crater.

The rebels had woke up at last and were shooting back.

The fear came back to Neill all at once and in a rush.

Now it was really going to begin.

5:30 A.M.

For twenty minutes or half an hour after the explosion of the Mine not a single shot was fired against the troops on the Ninth Corps front. The Mine had blown a great hole in the center of the rebel line, destroying one regiment entire and parts of two others, destroying one battery and part of another, driving many of the defending troops away to right and left in panic and disorganization and leaving a remnant frozen to the spot unable or unwilling to move while the dark world fell around them. There was no second line of fortifications on the ridge—a few gun emplacements only, a covered way, a ravine full of scared troops, that was all.

At any time during the first hour after the explosion a disciplined rush by a single division, followed by the rest of the IX Corps, could have cleared the entire front and opened a clear road to the Cemetery Hill, and the Jerusalem Plank Road, cutting off a third of Lee's army and seizing his base of supplies. With the rough ground, and the snipers, and the fire of the few batteries that could turn their guns to bear on the ground, it might have taken a little more than an hour to have done all that. The generals had planned on an hour, but it might have taken more.

But there was no disciplined rush. The troops did not know where to go or how to get there. There were no Generals at the front to tell them, even if they knew. There were no engineers to clear away the lines of abatis, their own and the enemy's, that barred their way everywhere except where the tongue of debris from the crater overlapped and buried all other obstructions. There were no ladders or steps to allow them to leave the trenches massed for assault. And so they stumbled up to the Crater by squads and platoons and files, and stumbled into it.

Half an hour after the explosion the rebels started shooting again.

Forty-five minutes after the attack the survivors of the explosion and the panic had settled down, dug in, and decided to hold on. Resistance stiffened out beyond the Crater, and there was no mass of assault troops to cut through it.

An hour after the explosion the First Division had halted around the Crater and was firing back at rebel skirmishers. The Second Division crowded up behind, held back, began to dribble around the side of the First, not sure where it should go.

Above them to the north and west were the hill and the ridge line. They should have been up there by then. But now, perhaps it would need another hour.

Or more than that.

5:30 A.M. *Johnson's Headquarters*

The sound of the Mine explosion, rolling across the fields and up the slope, had rattled the windows of the house Johnson slept in.

He'd dashed out in his stockinged feet, to see the black ball climbing up out of the ground, the whole center of his line blown up.

The size of it, he had thought. *The size of it. Who could have imagined it would be so big?*

His servant came trotting after him with his boots, and he had sat down on a stump at the ridge line, watching the cloud billow up, seeing the heavy chunks and pieces—boulders, men, guns—rising into the air and falling out of the air.

The cloud began to drift away. From below, he could see men scattering away from the explosion, towards the rear. He ordered a staff officer to get down there, get any men who could still fight into some kind of order.

Off to his left, where the ground sloped more steeply up from the covered way to the green grass of the Cemetery Hill, he could see some battalions forming, brown clumps of men under flags faded to pink and pale blue. That would be some of Elliott's troops, rallying as they came back off the line, or pulled out of the trenches and shifted to cover the gap.

Off to the right there was apparently a battery still firing out of a grove of trees. It seemed to be finding the Yankee advance.

But the center was still a bad thing to see. With what was blown up, and what was buried by the dust that's falling, and the ones shocked out of sleep by the crack of doom and frozen with fear or running for their lives, the Yankees had wrecked or disorganized the whole of Elliott's brigade, upward of six hundred yards of trench either blown up, buried or abandoned. *No reserve infantry back here, no guns aimed this way, at the center of our own lines—except the battery I brought in and established up here on the hill. Sixteen guns and no infantry.*

What has he got over there? An army corps? Two? He could line his divisions up back to back and trot them through the hole, take the battery cheap, take the Cemetery Hill for free. And he'd be in back of half our army, closer to Petersburg than its defenders are.

Johnson looked at the hot blue metal of the sky, blank as a prison ceiling. *This is the way it ends,* he thought. The whole center section of the trenches, for five hundred yards, was swarming with bluecoats. Through the telescope, Johnson counted as many as fourteen flags waving from the rubble of the crater and the trenches around it.

What was holding the Yankees up? There must be some people in the trenches on their flanks. He couldn't tell.

Whatever was happening, it seemed clear that the Yankees were not rushing for this point. He would have the batteries open on them. They'd never imagine that the line of guns would be completely undefended by infantry.

"Taylor!" he shouted to his aide. "I'm going around to the right of the point of attack. Elliott seems to have something put together on the left . . . if he should break . . . well," he bared his teeth, "he'd best not. I'm going to try to organize something on the other flank." He swung into the saddle. "Reinforcements can form up here, behind the hill. If the Yankees haven't taken it, tell them that there's that ravine down below, about two hundred yards. It's got good cover, and it'll be better to counterattack from there." His secretary handed him a board and paper. He scribbled a note, "Lee," and the messenger took it and ran for his horse.

Johnson turned his own horse, gave it spurs, and the animal took off, lifting over a broken fence as he dashed away.

5:30 A.M. *1st Division Headquarters*

Dr. Clubb noticed a stir in the crowd outside the door of the bunker, and another General bustled into the bombproof. Ledlie rose, and extended a hand. "General Ferrero! Good to see you back, sir! Good to see you!"

The new General—a neat dark man, obviously an Italian or Spaniard from the name, thought Clubb—allowed his hand to be seized and shaken. A mild sort of chap, not what you'd expect in a combat officer. He seemed bewildered.

"General Ledlie, . . ." said Ferrero, looking about him.

"Yes?"

"I was wondering . . . this is a good place for a headquarters . . . I was wondering if I could . : ."

"Join us! by all means. Sit, man! We'll be right in the middle of things here!"

There came a series of bumping sounds, like a barrel falling downstairs. Then they heard, distinctly, the banging of a few muskets. The sound grew, a hailstorm on a tin roof, harder, faster.

Ledlie, seated at his desk, beamed in utmost friendliness at Ferrero, smiling handsomely to show his firm straight row of teeth.

Ferrero seemed more and more bewildered.

Ledlie continued to smile. He looked like a man at a party, or perhaps at a particularly friendly and celebratory dinner at his club, smiling and attentively listening to the conversation.

But nobody in the bunker was saying a word. And outside the raving of the musketry accelerated to a hysterical pitch.

5:30 A.M. *Front line, 2nd Division, IX Corps*

Potter, Pleasants, and the divisional staff had stationed themselves along their front at the important points where the troops were clambering out of the trenches and heading for the Crater. It was a mob scene, conflicting streams of traffic milling in a crowded street between the trench line and the line of abatis and obstructions set out to ward off the rebels. The officers yelled, swatted men with the flats of sword blades, trying to turn them leftward, toward the place in the center of the corps front where the explosion of the Mine had wrecked and buried the obstructions, breaking a rough road through the abatis to the Crater. What would happen beyond that, how they would form the men to make the attack on the real objectives that lay behind the Crater, they could not form any idea.

Like herding a lot of damned stupid cattle, thought Pleasants. It was a shambles, a stupid bloody shambles. By this time they were supposed to be beyond the Crater, following behind Ledlie's division in a full-scale assault on the Cemetery Hill and the ridge line of the Jerusalem Plank Road. Almost an hour since the explosion, and Ledlie's troops were still blocking the way, jammed up and clotting every foot of space between their own lines and the Crater. Some delay had been predictable, some confusion from the explosion, from the hovering cloud of dust that had blinded them. But this was more than should have happened. Every step Pleasants took showed him new failures, new blunders, terrible omissions and lapses . . . what had the high command been doing while he dug his perfect Mine? They had made no plans, the officers in charge had no idea where to send their men, and let them blunder about without direction. Instead of fifteen thousand troops storming the heights in a disciplined and formal rush, here was a mob lost and bewildered in the twisted alleys of the trenches, the littered passages between the abatis, the foul tipple of the Crater. *They've done us,* he thought. *They've done us again, and left us to stumble about alone until we destroy ourselves.*

Up ahead, Potter was yelling at someone from Ledlie's division. An hour after the explosion and still standing in line behind them. Everything ass-backwards, the support troops, Potter's, advancing faster than the shock troops of Ledlie's division. Pleasants pushed through to Potter, and felt better for being with that small, tough, competent general.

There was another man there, too, a courier from Burnside. Potter beckoned to Pleasants. "Orders from General Burnside, Henry. We are to advance immediately and take the crest." He did not indicate by any sign that the orders were absurd.

"Ledlie's troops are still in our way," Potter said calmly. "I want you to go forward, and see if you can't get our men around to the right of Ledlie's division. Cut the abatis if you have to. Let our men file around on the right, sidle past Ledlie anyway they can. And then we'll form them up on the other side. Try to find Ledlie if you can, and find out why his troops won't move. He'll probably be in or near the Crater.''

In the distance they heard the bang of cannon, and the firecracker spread of musketry.

"Get to it, Colonel,'' said Potter. Pleasants turned and began to push his way past the troops, heading for the front.

5:40 A.M. *The Crater*

Neill ran, shaking, behind Beeler. Most of his company was there, and they followed Oostervelt at a run around the rim of the Crater, and through a broken embrasure into what had been a small battery on the left side of the fort. The guns here had been overturned by the blast. Some of the troops had righted them, and turned them around. But they had a poor field of fire, blocked on the left by a stand of trees, and in front by a small roll in the ground. The roll was occupied by men in blue shirts, a line of men, firing their muskets rapidly at an unseen enemy.

"Let's go, forward at the double!'' yelled Oostervelt.

The line dashed across the flat to join the men on the small ridge. An officer—Captain Kilmer—stood there, pinwheeling his arms to direct them into position behind the roll of ground. He came up to Oostervelt, and the latter knelt down.

"No need,'' said Kilmer, "the hill gives us cover.''

"Give him absolution, Father!'' called Neill, as Oostervelt rose. *The dirty bastard.*

They could see the two officers talking. Then Oostervelt walked over to them, wobbling a little in his boots over the unequal ground. "All right!'' he said, in a hoarse voice. "On the word, we're going to charge over the top. There's a bunch of rebel skirmishers and we're going to run em off. Anybody funks, they'll get this,'' and he brandished his sword.

I'd like to make you eat that, you dirty Dutch pig. Neill's teeth began to chatter. He shook like a dog shaking off water, and it rattled the teeth in his head.

There was a piercing whistle from Captain Kilmer, and Kilmer raced past their line and over the ridge top, the troops on the top rising with him and going over; Neill and Beeler were up too, stumbling over the ridge, and Neill heard the metal zing and whirr past him, stumbling blind with fear, the musket banging his chest in his flaccid arms as he ran following the blue line in front. Somebody stumbled and fell. Neill turned a step toward the fallen man, made to jump him, tripped and sprawled, and fell forward. A shadow fell over him. "Get up, you damned slacker, or by God I'll nail you to the ground.'' Oostervelt.

Neill picked himself up, stumbling again to establish his bona fides, and scrambled forward. He nearly fell again, when the trench appeared in front of him, but recovered and jumped in. The trench was full of his friends.

Suddenly he noticed that the sun was bright and hot, and the trench full of yellow light. While he ran, it had seemed so dark he could scarcely see a foot before his nose. He looked around. They had taken a rebel trench that ran parallel to the main line, beyond the Crater. There was a dead man in the bottom of it. He wore a gray jacket. Green flies buzzed around a black hole in his throat. Neill took a deep breath, and let it out. *All right, that does it. Now let somebody else do some work.* His legs went weak, suddenly, and he sat down.

He heard a whistling sound in the air, and then the horrible grunt of a shell rooting in the ground nearby. Another came in, closer. Another.

"Where in hell is that coming from?" asked Oostervelt.

Kilmer pointed to the left. Off out of sight, behind heaves of earth and stands of brush and the cross-cutting of rebel communication trenches, somebody in one of the rebel batteries on their flank had turned a gun around and was firing at the troops that had gone beyond the Crater.

The next shell came in louder, screaming, roaring like an express train, and dirt showered down into the trench. Neill curled round his musket, making himself a ball on the floor of the trench.

"They've got this place enfiladed," said Oostervelt.

"All right," said Kilmer. "Let's move over to the right until somebody knocks that gun out."

Hurriedly, nervously, they pushed down the trench, racing the next shell. Was it in the gun? Were they pulling the lanyard? Was that the sound of it coming?

5:40 A.M.

After he had run for about fifty yards, Bruce realized he was not being pursued. *Probably the Yankees couldn't even see me in the dust.*

The air was clearer now, and Bruce could see where he was. He had run north from the Crater, up toward where they had used the dry streambed to make a covered way back to the ridge. If Johnson's plans were being followed, the reserves and the troops driven off the front line should have gone there. Maybe he'd find the rest of the regiment. If, as he suspected, Colonel Davidson was dead, buried back in the bombproof, then he was probably the commander of whoever was left. He turned and looked back, peering through the branches of the dead bush that shielded him from the Crater. It was a damned big hole they'd made. He rose, stepping carefully over the debris, and headed for the covered way.

Those Yanks were slower than molasses in January, thank God! There wasn't a soul to stop him.

"Hey there?" came a shout, "Halt! Who in hell are you?"

There was a sentry, crouched behind a makeshift barricade of boulders. "I'm Lieutenant Bruce, Twenty-second North Carolina. I got blown up."

"You sure did," said the sentry. "Come on through."

There were troops in the trench, some without officers; a few organizations mixed together. A Lieutenant Colonel of engineers was in charge. They sat there, talking quietly, waiting for something to happen. Four hundred yards away, there was a whole Yankee army corps pouring through the biggest hole that ever was blown through any fortified line in the world, and they were just sitting around.

"Colonel," called Bruce. "There's more Yankees than I ever saw in one place before coming on through the line. Haven't you got any orders to use these men here?"

The Colonel spread his hands. "I sent a man to find the Brigade Commander."

"General Johnson's standing orders were to hold the trenches on either side, if the Yankees made a breach, and hang on till the reserves came up. These men are doing no good here. There'll be plenty of troops coming this way in a few minutes. Let's get these men forward, where they can do some good."

"I . . . I'm not vetted to this brigade, I . . ."

"Colonel," said Bruce impatiently, "I've an appointment on divisional staff." He noticed the Colonel's gaze, and became aware that he had also left his uniform coat behind in the bunker. "My responsibility, sir. Acting for General Johnson."

The Colonel waved acquiescence. "You men!" called Bruce. "Attention! I am Lieutenant Bruce, Twenty-second North Carolina, if you can believe it."

"Must have been a hell of a party, Lieutenant," said a man, and raised a laugh.

"I dressed in a hurry this morning," said Bruce, joining the laugh for a moment. Then: "I want you to follow me. We're going to see what we can do to hold these Yankees up for a while. You'll stay with me till we can figure out where your regular organizations are."

He walked to the front of the line. Up ahead they heard musket firing begin to bang and roll out. "Let's go," said Bruce, and they filed up the trench toward the main line.

HEADQUARTERS SECOND DIVISION,
July 30, 1864.

General BURNSIDE:
GENERAL: General Potter has heard nothing except that General Griffin's troops are in the breach. General P. has sent two officers down and will report as soon as possible.
Respectfully,

J. L. VAN BUREN,
Major and Aide-de-Camp.

Pleasants had struggled his way to the front. The only cleared path through the Union and rebel obstructions lay in front of the Crater, and his movement took him up to it.

He could not help stepping up to the edge and looking in. The roiled earth was full of junk, and there were soldiers walking and sprawling about in it—some perhaps wounded, others just lolling about, apparently. There was no sign of a headquarters flag, no sign of General Ledlie. The pit seemed strange—deeper, much deeper than he had imagined. The steep sides emphasized the depths. Had he really done all this? Incredibly, he realized, he had expected to see his tunnel and magazines from the top, as if he had just blown the lid neatly off. Incredible. His mind had been in absolute funk since three that morning. The fuse failing like that. . . .

Pleasants wobbled a bit with vertigo. He turned from the fascination of the Crater and jogged forward. The troops were jammed in thickly here, many of them just milling about. The yatter of musketry was high, and artillery was booming at intervals. Griffin's Brigade of the Second Division was coming in over the broken edge of the parapet to the right of the Crater, in single- and double-file, picking its way through the crowds and past obstructions.

He found Griffin, and gave him Potter's instructions. "Listen, Colonel, Potter can't just send a brigade to take the crest alone. We need supports. And we've got to get some room to form back of the rebel lines here. You can't bring formed troops through that mess. And we can't storm anything unless Ledlie's division gets itself out of that damned hole." Bullets zipped, and the two officers dropped to their knees. "Tell Potter this," said Griffin. "We have to get a brigade, or a couple of decent regiments anyway, to clear those rebels out of the trenches down to the right. They'll shoot any advance in the back if we don't. Then maybe we can move up the hill."

"We had peremptory orders from General Burnside, sir. To attack immediately, and without reference to other commands."

Griffin exhaled violently. "Military science! That's the art of war. That's your tactics! White!" he called, and a Colonel came up. "Get your regiment formed up, and take them down the rebel front line to the right. Put a company in the trench itself, and keep the rest above ground. Keep going till they stop you. Give us some breathing room." White saluted, and ran back to his regiment.

Out in front of the line, Griffin was trying to get his other regiments moving forward. Their way was obstructed by clots of men from Ledlie's First Division, halted in the shelter of boulders and pieces of equipment, rising up to shoot out of rifle pits. The men in Griffin's lines kept flinching as the bullets whined overhead.

Pleasants watched them start to move forward. White's regiment, in two lines, was already trotting to the right.

The sound of musketry intensified again to the front. He walked to a wall of earth that cut off his view to the right, and peered over. He could see White's line, halted, the men kneeling behind boulders and brush, firing at a line of smoke. Some rebels in a cross-trench, hanging on and shooting it out. To the left, a group of soldiers rushed forward, heading to flank them. The sound of musketry kept on, kept on.

Pleasants felt he must do something. Something was not right here. The Mine had blown. Yet something was not right. It could still go bad. Incredible fact: it could still fall apart and leave him. . . . He hurried back toward Potter.

HEADQUARTERS SECOND DIVISION, NINTH ARMY CORPS
July 30, 1864.

General A. E. BURNSIDE,
Ninth Army Corps:

GENERAL: My division is about advancing again, but my opinion is that unless a spirited attack is made to the right we shall not accomplish anything. I understand that a part of General Willcox's division will either support the attack or participate in it, which may insure success, but my opinion that the attack should be pressed to the right is concurred in by all the officers of experience who have been on the ground. The present position of our troops has nothing to do with an attack to the right, and in no way interferes with any other troops. General Griffin is 100 yards beyond the crater and not in it. Colonel Bliss is on his right. I have no regiments in any of our old line of pits or intrenchments except an engineer regiment in the edge of the woods.

Very respectfully, your obedient servant,

ROBERT B. POTTER,
Brigadier-General

N.B.—Colonel Bliss's attack to the right was repulsed, his force being too light.

5:40 A.M. Meade's Headquarters

From Burnside's old headquarters, Meade and Humphreys could see nothing. Since the black cloud of the exploding Mine had fallen away, they had seen nothing, heard nothing until the sound of firing just a few minutes before.

"Anything from Burnside yet?" snapped Meade.

"No, sir."

"Humphreys, I'm going to have that ass court-martialed if he's fouled up again. I swear it! How many times have we telegraphed?"

"Several times, sir. Perhaps the line is down."

"Lyman!" Meade yelled. The aide materialized out of the tent. "Get down to Burnside's headquarters. Find out what in hell is going on. Get Sanderson out of whatever hole he's hiding in, and have him make some reports!" Lyman went off. "Can no one in this army do as he's ordered?"

Meade turned abruptly and walked inside, back to the bank of telegraphers. "Send this to Burnside." He looked at his watch. "Five-forty A.M., July Thirtieth, Major-General Burnside: What news from your assaulting column? Please report frequently. George G. Meade, etc."

The telegraph clacked.

After a silence—for a wonder!—it clicked again. A reply from Burnside.

BATTERY MORTON,
July 30, 1864—5:40 A.M.

General MEADE:

We have the enemy's first line and occupy the breach. I shall endeavor to push forward to the crest as rapidly as possible.

A. E. BURNSIDE,
Major-General.

P.S.—There is a large fire in Petersburg.

W. W. SANDERSON,
Captain, &c.

Meade rubbed a thin hand over the lower part of his face, smoothing his mustache down over his lips, smoothing his beard. The hand seemed to quiver and vibrate, supercharged with energy, rage, nerves. He handed the telegram abruptly to Humphreys.

"A fire in Petersburg," said Meade. "What in hell do I care if there's a fire in Petersburg? Can you tell me from this whether he has gotten anywhere near taking that damned hill, and here it is"—he looked at his watch—"an hour after that damned Mine of his blew up?" Little flecks of spit flew from his lips as he spoke.

"Courier!" yelled someone outside. Meade and Humphreys whirled and went out the tent flap. Here was somebody obviously just coming back from the front. The man had that shocked vacant look about the eyes of someone just escaped out of a close place, his mind not yet escaped along with his body. He shook his head sharply, and looked up at Meade. "Sir! I'm sorry, I . . . I seem to have mistaken . . . I . . ."

"What is it!" said Humphreys. The courier licked his lips, and his eyes moved from Humphreys to Meade, and back to Humphreys. "I was distracted, sir. Came to General Burnside's headquarters by mistake, sir, thinking . . . but he's at the battery."

Meade stepped forward, speaking sharply. "Let's have your report. We can reach General Burnside by telegraph." The courier paused. "Out with it."

The man hesitated, then something seemed to give way, he handed Meade the dispatch, and he spoke rapidly, as if throwing off a burden. "The troops are not going forward, sir. They're crowded in around the Crater. The ground is all broken up back of the lines, obstructions . . . the Crater's huge, sir. It's almost as bad an obstacle as . . ."

"This is from Colonel Loring," said Humphreys, "Burnside's staff."

"What about the rebels? What in hell is going on there?"

The man shook his head. "There wasn't much shooting till a few minutes back. Rebels ran out of the trenches around the Crater, scared off, something. They started shooting back just before I came."

Meade looked at Humphreys. His mouth twitched in involuntary rictus, a grim parody of a smile.

Humphreys spoke softly. "Let's not leap to conclusions. If they can get going now, it can easily be done. There are no rebel formations that you could see? Any second line of trenches?''

The courier shook his head.

''All right, then,'' said Meade. ''Maybe their reserves are still too far away. Let's stir Burnside up,'' and he pointed Humphreys back into the tent. ''And find out if Warren can do anything yet.''

HEADQUARTERS ARMY OF THE POTOMAC,
July 30, 1864—5:40 A.M.

Major-General BURNSIDE,
Commanding Ninth Corps:
The commanding general learns that your troops are halting at the works where the mine exploded. He directs that all your troops be pushed forward to the crest at once. Call on General Ord to move forward his troops at once.

A. A. HUMPHREYS,
Major-General and Chief of Staff.

HEADQUARTERS ARMY OF THE POTOMAC,
July 30, 1864—5:50 A.M.

Major-General WARREN,
Commanding Fifth Corps:
General Burnside is occupying the crater with some of his troops. He reports that no enemy is seen in that line. How is it in your front? Are the enemy in force there or weak? If there is apparently an opportunity to carry their works take advantage of it and push forward with your troops.

A. A. HUMPHREYS,
Major-General and Chief of Staff.

HEADQUARTERS FIFTH ARMY CORPS,
July 30, 1864—6 A.M.

Major-General HUMPHREYS:
Your dispatch just received. It is difficult to say how strong the enemy may be in my front. His batteries extend along the whole of it. I will watch for the first opportunity. I can see the whole line well where I am. The enemy has been running from his first line in front of General Burnside's right for some minutes, but there seems to be a very heavy line of troops just behind it in high breastworks. There is a battery in front of General Burnside's left, which fires towards the river, the same as it did on the 18th of June, and which our artillery fire has but very little effect on.

Respectfully,

G. K. WARREN,
Major-General.

HEADQUARTERS ARMY OF THE POTOMAC,
July 30, 1864—6 A.M.

Major-General BURNSIDE:
Prisoners taken say there is no line in their rear, and that
their men were falling back when ours advanced; that none of
their troops have returned from the James. Our chance is now;
push your men forward at all hazards (white and black), and
don't lose time in making formations, but rush for the crest.

GEO. G. MEADE,
Major-General.

Burnside's Headquarters

The harassing calls from Meade's headquarters never seemed to
cease. And there were those spies sent down here to keep an eye on him.
Burnside felt like a giant stag bayed by miserable hounds. He would
sit in the bombproof. He would go back to the telegraph station, and
listen till he could stand that no longer. Then rush outside and up to the
battery to see what was happening. But the drifting smoke of the battery, the dust and smoke that still hung in the air over the Crater, made
it impossible to make sense of anything he saw. There were dark shadows
that were his troops going from his lines to the gap in the rebel front;
there was the sound of shooting from the other side. But he could not
see what went on beyond the Crater. To stay inside the bombproof was
torture and frustration; to come outside and see nothing was worse.

Back inside again. Here was General Ord, back from the front-line
trenches.

"What's the news, General?" Burnside asked.

Ord looked hard at Burnside. "I spoke with some prisoners coming
back. There doesn't seem to be any second line back of the Crater. . . ."

Burnside pounded a fist into his palm. "By God! Then we've
got em!"

Ord's face turned scarlet. "General . . . you haven't got a
damned thing, so long as your troops don't get themselves out of that
damned big hole in the ground and *move up!*"

Sanderson, scenting blood, was drifting over from the telegraph
section. *Watch out for flank attacks,* thought Burnside.

Burnside cleared his throat, and spoke more loudly. "They may be
held up by troops we can't see, General. Perhaps if you could bring your
men forward, it might give weight to the attack, give them a push
out. . . ."

"The trenches are still full of your own men, General," said Sanderson. Burnside rounded on him, blasting him with his most terrible
stare. The staff officer's expression remained bland. "Third Division's
just getting out of the lines now," he added.

Ord let out breath, explosively. "I'm going to send a message to
General Meade, telling him that the troops are not going forward."

Burnside turned back to face him. "Don't do that, General."

Ord paused, holding his pen over the telegraph paper he had torn from a pad on the table before him.

"I'm asking you, please, not to send that to General Meade." In the quiet, the officers could hear the firing off in the distance. "By the time the message reaches him," said Burnside, "the situation will almost certainly have changed. I've ordered all divisions forward. I'm going to do that again, hurry them along." He turned to Sanderson. "Meade is too far away from things. The situation changes too rapidly for him to respond. . . ."

Sanderson turned and walked toward the door, heading for the telegraphers, Burnside treading on his shadow. "Just a moment," said the General, grabbing Richmond by the sleeve. "I want orders to go out to all division commanders, again, right now. The troops are to get out of the trenches and advance to take the crest. No forming! No sideshows! I want to see every last man in this corps charging straight up that damned hillside and take that goddamned cemetery, or by heaven I'll bury them in it myself!" As he spoke his voice quickened and rose up the scale.

6:10 A.M. *1st Division Bombproof*

The wounded had begun coming in. Dr. Clubb checked a rebel, evidently caught in the explosion of the mine—his eardrums had burst—and then ordered him taken to the rear as a prisoner. A staff officer came in, and—as Clubb thought of it—shooed General Ledlie out of the bombproof, General Ferrero tagging along after him like a lap-dog.

There was yelling and confusion outside the bombproof, where the men bringing the wounded back were running against the current of troops from the Third Division going up; the Generals should have cut another entrance or a separate trench. Generals!

Here they were at last—gunshot wounds and a couple of shrapnel. The bright blood glaring against the grayish skin of the shocked bodies. The men bringing back the wounded would lay them on the stretchers, and then stand around.

Clubb looked up from where he was probing for a bullet in a man's shoulder-muscle. "You men! Get back to your units! Don't stand around like that! Get on out of here!" Damned skulkers. Around some of the cots as many as six men had been standing. Six men to help one man with a scratch walk back here!

A man with a big chunk of metal busting in his ribs on the right side. Little bits of pink fluffy stuff there—lung tissue. Forget him. Bind it, dope him up.

Man with a bullet hole in his foot. His assistant cut the boot and peeled it off as the man writhed on the table.

The bullet hole went through the foot from top to bottom, through the arch. Dr. Clubb looked at the man's face, furious. "That's self-inflicted, dammit! Don't tell me some rebel in a goddamned balloon shot you! By God, if I had the time, I'd amputate the damned thing and teach you a lesson." He was shaking with rage. "Tie this thing up, and get the provost guard."

"No more walking wounded," he called, as the cots began to crowd up, and men were laid on the floor. "Only stretcher cases and real bad ones. Davis, stand by the door and keep the rest out of here!"

A man with his thigh laid open by a slash of shrapnel. The muscles fidgeted like worms, and there was an ivory gleam of bone in the black-red grin of the wound. The smell of blood—sharp and metallic, turning slightly bad and rotten, the smell of sliced meat standing in the heat—began to fill the atmosphere of the bunker. Dr. Clubb wrapped his head in a towel to sop up the sweat. Dizzy in the heat, he saw himself as a turbanned cannibal king gourmandizing at a feast. The bone-saw scraped and the dry smell of bone dust mixed with the blood. Small drops of sweat raced down to the point of his nose. He tried to stop them with his sleeve before they fell into the wounds he hunched over. It sometimes took all his concentration to keep from dropping his tools to catch the drops in midair.

6:15 A.M. *The Crater*

Pleasants and Potter were crouched on the Union side of the rebel parapet when Burnside's messengers found them. They had sketched out a plan of attack—Bliss's brigade to sweep to the right down the trench line, where rebel resistance was heavy, holding them within a hundred yards of the rubble-strewn radius of the explosion. Griffin was to get his troops together, and try for the crest of the hill, or at least to carry the improvised rebel line that ran through the ravines between the lines and the hill—a covered way running east-west, and a perpendicular ravine, which Griffin reported as full of rebels.

Griffin's earlier assault had come to nothing. His men were scattered around now, dug in positions from which they fired back at the rebels in the cross-trenches, fragmented and isolated by the scarred uneven ground. It would take time to get a line together. Even if they could pull the brigade into line, Potter doubted that a single brigade could carry the hill now. They needed room so that Ord could bring his troops across and lend weight to the attack.

As they had planned this, it dawned on Pleasants—though Potter said nothing—that there had been a fundamental change in the situation. Ledlie's division, which was to have swept on and carried the heights, was not moving at all from the area of the Crater. Worse, as its men took shelter in the rebel lines right and left of the Crater, they blocked the way for their supports. Potter now commanded the only organized force on the other side of the rebel lines.

That was when Colonel Loring arrived from Burnside, with peremptory orders to attack and carry the crest. And there was Meade's dispatch to back it up. No formations, no hesitations. Just go for the crest.

Potter's face looked, suddenly, old and withered. The rattle of firing rose and fell behind him, where Griffin's men were shooting it out. "Colonel," he said, and paused. "Colonel, I don't believe that General Burnside is aware of the situation. The trenches to the right are still held by the enemy. They'll take any attack on the hill in reverse, unless we can drive them out first." Pleasants thought he caught a sudden, barely perceptible sagging in Loring's face. Potter seemed to read something in it, for his voice changed, becoming all at once stiff and formal, where before it had been expressive and pleading. "It is my opinion, Colonel, that we ought to carry those trenches to the right, and attack the hill when General Ord's troops, or some other division arrives to support an attack."

"I'm sorry, General," said Loring. "These orders are peremptory. Generals Ledlie and Willcox have received the same, and will be attacking directly. The General believes that if we all push at once, we can carry the hill. The rebels will abandon the trenches as untenable once we do that."

Potter set his teeth, folding his lower lip over his upper, as if to hold back a reply. "Very well," he said. "I hope, however, you will convey my opinion to the General."

"Yes," said Loring, quietly.

Potter stared at Loring's back as the Colonel left. He turned to Pleasants. "Tell Griffin to get a line together. I'll have Bliss move up. We'll try to spread some skirmishers to cover our right and rear." He spat, and wiped sweat from his face with his sleeve. "Maybe it will work after all."

6:15 A.M. *4th Division Bivouac*

Colonels Thomas and Oliver, together with their staff officers, had gathered to hear the report of the action that Booker and Rockwood brought. There was nothing in it which told them when, or if, they would be called on to play a part. The battle was going slowly, stumblingly—perhaps it was already botched beyond repair, and the next orders they would receive would be to stand down, or to bury the dead. Whatever was happening, it went on without reference to them, muffled in distance. They sat down to breakfast together in a circle of logs and cut-off stumps, silent and depressed, listening to the distant mutter of the guns, chewing a breakfast of hardtack and salt pork washed down with tepid water. The crackers were dry and hard, like compacted sawdust; the pork had a sharp tang of salt that burned the mouth, and the greaze of it coated teeth and tongue so that water wouldn't wash it clear.

Chris Pennington held the half-chewed ball of it in his mouth, his stomach heaving in nausea and revulsion, not only for the food he had to cram down but for the deep bitter anger and disappointment that filled him. He was ready to spit it all out, curse the army, curse the smug, self-satisfied face of Colonel Oliver. He had no dignity, none, they had stripped him of every bit of it, made him weep and pray like a child for joy that the Day had come at last and then snatched it from him. Snatched it with a smug, superior smile at his grief.

Thomas leaned over with an open jar, looking for Pennington's eyes, catching them with his steady bright blue gaze. "Here, Chris," he said. "Some cucumber pickle my wife sent down to me. She put them up herself. Nothing cuts the taste of salt pork like cucumber pickle. . . ."

Pennington felt his tears bulge, the swollen horrible food bulge on his tongue—would he weep, or spit, or vomit? The face of this man, of Colonel Thomas . . . it seemed to glow with kindness. He felt a sudden intense rush of love for Thomas; he was his perfect father and his brother all at once—*a jar of pickles that my wife put up herself and sent to me from home.* "Yes," he said, "All right, I . . ."

And then the courier arrived, Thomas and then Oliver rose to meet him, Thomas still holding the jar in his hand. Orders: "This is from General Burnside. We're moving up," said Thomas, "in support of Humphrey's brigade. They'll be leaving the covered way when the rest of the Third Division goes forward. Gentlemen, you have your orders. . . ."

Pennington spat the mess of pork, cracker, and pickle off to the side. "Hurrah!" he shouted. "Thank God almighty for General Burnside!"

"You have the order of march?" snapped Oliver. "We'll take them into the covered way in double-file, I think. I'll be at the head of the column." The regimental officers hustled off to their commands, the stir spreading outward from the broken breakfast circle as the whole division began to come alive.

Randolph's men had sat around him all that bad morning, after he had told them they would not be leading the assault. As they sat there, each of them had taken the inward turn, letting the disappointment run through him like the chill-shivers of the morning, letting the shiver just take the whole body, not holding on and holding it off.

After a time, one man spoke quietly to another. They told each other it was a mighty dark morning, that the day would be hot, hotter than a two-hundred-pound bale of cotton is heavy. At the bump of the Mine going off, when the birds stopped, their voices eased. Around them they heard the birds start again, and the background noise of moving troops.

Randolph, sitting among them, felt in the quiet a stirring breath, the memory of how they had swept like a line of pickers across an open field with their rifles, felt the whole unisoned moving weight of the black brigades behind him, and he held in his brain the vision of their movement over the parapet and through the open door.

Later, in the distance they could hear the undifferentiated roar of musketry, and the punctual iteration of the batteries. That was when the air changed again. They felt the stir in the camp before they heard the words, but here were Booker and Shugrue coming through the camps, walking quickly, calling out, "All right! On your feet! Let's go! We're moving up! Let's go."

"Praise the name," said Tobe.

They rose from meeting. The roll of the drums was like thunder in answer to prayer.

The division boiled up off the ground and out of tents, forming in lines to the *rattaplan* of the drums. The sergeants went down the lines, checking cartridge boxes to make sure that each man carried his sixty rounds.

Oliver walked briskly to the head of the first regiment in line, the Thirtieth. Without checking pace or looking back, he beckoned, and the double file of black soldiers followed him into the narrow gate of the covered way. Behind them, empty circles of knapsacks marked their camping places. Then the walls of the passage, beginning at waist height, soon rose, to cover their heads as they serpentined forward.

They were stopped.

Booker, back in the lines, wondered if the Third Division was still jamming the way. He heard the sounds, whiffles of breath, groans, and knew what was coming before the first of the wounded appeared around the corner. Their faces had the odd gray pallor against which the blood shone sharply. Their lips, waxy-white, almost greenish, made them appear to be mannequins or wax automata; and the dull sheen of their eyes confirmed this. They seemed like walking dead.

Were they going to have to stand in this damned alleyway, watching this parade of horrors? There was no point in it. He'd told Oliver the covered way was too crowded. Now with the wounded coming back it would be worse. They should get out and form in the open.

But they stood there. After a time, the line shuffled forward again, the soldiers not speaking.

If the morning's news didn't finish them, thought Booker, this little display ought to do it.

The heat filled the narrow covered way like some impossible leaden fluid. Randolph and his men squatted next to the trench wall. The parade of bleeding white men went past them. Randolph looked intently into the faces as they went by, seeking the answer to a question. Tobe leaned back, eyes half-lidded and quiet, needing no more answers. Jethro, next to him, had half-turned away, toward the trench wall. He was carving his sign in a balk of timber, with a concentration that made him sweat. Corporal Brown mopped his balding head with a green kerchief. His cap, its top marked with the Ninth Corps badge—a cannon crossed with a foul anchor, in green to signify Fourth Division—sat on his knee. From time to time he adjusted its position, so that the ornate shield faced outward, toward the parade of bleeding white men.

Some of the men were complaining, soft-voiced, about the heat. Others down the line were silent, their eyes drinking the sickening sight of the blood on the white men.

Randolph could not feel sickened, or weakened or depressed by the heat, by the small jerks of movement followed by long waiting in the bake-oven trench—little teasing movements that held out the prize, and held it off. His soul had begun to suck light and energy sitting there in meeting with his men, mourning and praying without knowing it; then the brigade taking up the lifting movement of his soul, the drums carrying them into the trench, feet on the path at last. Randolph knew in his heart it would never stop now, until some things were finished. He looked in the eyes of the men returning, curious to see if he could read there the final shape of the Thing. But they were white men, and their eyes were hard to read.

The sky overhead was blue, cloudless, an unmarked slate roof. The eye of God could pierce into the most hidden fold and crevice of the earth. Everything watched. Waited.

6:20 A.M. *The Crater*

Neill, down in the bottom of the trench, could hear the high-pitched banshee shrills of the rebels. The bullets continued to zing overhead, and at intervals he could hear the snort of the shells as the gun kept looking for him.

The Colonel commanding the regiment came pushing down the trench, and grabbed Kilmer by the sleeve. Shells went overhead, in an express-train roar, heading toward the rebels.

Kilmer waved his pistol and yelled. "Get ready, we're going to charge."

"On your feet, dammit, everybody on your feet!" Oostervelt walked down the line, jerking the men up. Neill rose, stood shakily, crouching like a bear.

A whistle shrilled practically in his ear, and he felt bodies go up on either side of him, and someone pushed him from behind. He scrambled up, and over, and ran after the backs in front of him. If he kept staring at them, it felt like he was running in a tunnel, invisible to all on either side, unseen to the extent that he could not see.

Banging and shrieking burst up, loudly in the front, and past the shoulder of the man in front of him he saw a mob of blue going up over a trench parapet, and muskets swinging around, the scene frozen—

—then seemed to swoop at him as some force shoved him forward *bang* into the back of the man in front, and they fell over in front of the trench.

That bastard Oostervelt running behind me, punched me in the back, the bastard! He rolled over. Oostervelt was bent over, leaning against the hilt of the sword while he carefully and with all his force pressed the point of it forward into the ground.

He looks queer, thought Neill, as Oostervelt's point sank a bit, then flipped out and sideways as Oostervelt toppled onto his side. Neill bent over him. *Shot in the back.*

Zing! Something sang by his cheek. The ground spat. *Spat!* Neill whipped his head left, right, looking for it. "Oh Jesus!" he yelled, "they're shooting us from in back!"

He turned to scramble into the trench they had just taken, and slammed into someone charging back out of it, knocked sprawling. *Chuff!*

went an explosion, and dirt rained on them. Neill picked himself up, nearly was bowled over by another man coming back.

Ones and threes and a dozen, they were turning back, and running out of the trench.

"Come back, you cowards!" yelled Kilmer.

"Come back!" yelled Neill. "Hey for Christ's sake, don't leave me!" As he looked a man running took a bullet in the right side, spun, and fell. Neill felt the ground rock, and the hot breath of a shell on his back.

He was up, his feet spun sliding in the ground and he sobbed, *Please,* scrabbled up and ran, ran, his arms pumping. Up ahead of him he saw the scar of torn earth that marked the Crater, and he headed for that only thinking at the last second, *Jesus God don't jump off the edge you'll break your* . . . tried to slow himself, threw himself in a rolling tumble, skidding on his hands over the edge and rolling down the side, for a brief second his guts wrung with weightlessness, and he hit in soft earth. Somehow he had lost his rifle.

> HEADQUARTERS FIFTH ARMY CORPS,
> *July 30, 1864—6:20* A.M.

Major-General HUMPHREYS:

What we thought was the heavy line of the enemy behind the line occupied by General Burnside's troops proves, as the sunlight comes out and the smoke clears away, to be our own troops in the enemy's position.

Respectfully,

> G. K. WARREN,
> *Major-General.*

Pleasants worked his way forward to where Griffin had gotten a pair of regiments into line—the Forty-fifth Pennsylvania leading. That was a good sign, almost home. The men crouched, a double line of them, in the lee of some bushes and broken equipment. It wasn't a good shelter. Bullets zipping from the rebel trench in front were hitting—small *chunk*ing sounds—and men collapsed, tipped over, lay flat.

He heard the whistle shrilling from the rear. That was it. With an effort, Pleasants stood up. "Forty-fifth! Let's go!" He whirled and began running, his pistol out. The drive of muscles and the shot of nervous energy seemed to peel his weariness and discouragement like a snakeskin. He was running at last, going forward at last. The battle was in his hand, he would do it. He would turn it around. He felt this was his battle, his personally: it had been his Mine that made it possible, now he would redeem it.

Up ahead, smoke shot out of the ground in a line, and he felt the metal zip past him. Some bodies came heaving up out of the trench, running away. Smoke continued to blossom at wider intervals. Black shadows swept past him to right and left as the soldiers swooped past, outrunning him, jumping into the trench, and he followed them in.

The Forty-fifth piled into the trench, yelling and screaming. There were scuffles where some rebels were caught, and fighting. Bullets still socked into bodies, and men were falling. There were shots coming from the sides and rear, too, the men were stung to madness by all the shooting, like bulls driven mad by a storm of black-flies. Pleasants saw one rebel throw down his gun and hold his hands forward, palms out, a gesture to calm and stay, and a blue soldier, red in the face, standing in front of him with his musket raised: the Union soldier checked his swing, once, twice, then yelled in range and swung the rifle butt into the rebel's skull. It collapsed as if it were a melon.

Pleasants looked up out of the trench, tried to orient himself. Up ahead of him was the ridge line, the white house to his left; further off and to the right was the Cemetery Hill. Batteries were firing from the ridge and out of the cemetery.

A shell threw up a geyser of earth behind the trench. There must be another battery off to the right, up near the rebel main line, that nobody had knocked out. Shells rooted in the earth all round the trench, like great flesh-eating hogs. Back across the field over which they had come they could see the shells chewing up the ground where the supports were trying to come up in line, where another column was moving more directly against the ridge. Musketry was coming in from somewhere behind their right flank, where the rebels' main trench line had not been cleared. As he watched, the blue line of reinforcements frayed and fragmented. Men lay down—to fire? Dead?

Men began to climb out of the trench. Stooped, running low to the ground, carefully, not throwing away their weapons, but going back, going back without orders, their officers following, not speaking. . . . The assault troops abandoned the trench, and crept back toward the Crater.

Pleasants, leader unfollowed, abandoned, saw the whole thing fall apart, slip away, out of his grasp, lost beyond any recovery, gone gone gone, all of it, failure now and final and forever.

He thought he ought to stay and die in the trench. When he found he had not even the force of will to do that, he gave it all up entirely.

Walking erect, he shambled back toward the retreating backs of his troops.

6:30 A.M. *Confederate Lines*

Bruce had found a cross-trench that sliced back at an angle from the main line, pointing toward the covered way that ran back to the ridge. It was a good spot to defend against any troops coming to that side of the breach. He ordered a couple of men out as skirmishers, posting them prone behind some scattered boxes and bushes in front of the line.

There was no parapet—this was a communication trench—and he set some of them to work shifting dirt up.

They hadn't gotten more than a foot of dirt piled up when the pickets came back scrambling, and a Yankee line came running after them, bursting out from a tangle of unfinished abatis that the engineers had abandoned back of the lines. Without orders, his men waited till the Yankees were well up, and gave them a volley. He saw shapes spin and fall, then ducked, and heard the Yank bullets come slipping by overhead.

The firing became a spatter, as the quicker men loaded and fired faster, and the slow ones fell behind.

The Yankees were lying down, or standing behind the abatis, volleying back.

Hell, he thought, *we can do* this *all day.*

Bruce heard the musketry to his right rise to a crescendo, a hysterical yammering punctuated by blasts as shells exploded, shrieks of the rebel yell, cheers, all of it out of sight. An assault on the position he'd left, he guessed. He heard shooting start there, some yips, and exhaled with relief: the noise was from a group of their own soldiers coming back.

Colonel Davidson was leading them.

Bruce was stunned. "Colonel!" he called. "Colonel . . . I thought you were dead."

The Colonel looked angry. "I'm *not!*" he said. There was something odd, it took Bruce a minute to see it—the Colonel's face and hair were filthy, he must have dug his way out of the bunker like a damned badger—but his dress-uniform coat was spotless.

"Colonel . . . how in hell did you manage to keep your coat clean?" It was ridiculous, after all that had happened, to ask him that. *How have you escaped from the grave?*

The Colonel looked at Bruce as if he were mad. "Lieutenant Bruce? I didn't recognize you . . . out of uniform." He looked down at the coat. "I turned it inside out, of course," he said.

Off to the right, Bruce's eye caught a dark blur of movement, maybe the flank of the Yankee attack. He turned Davidson, and pointed.

"Yes," said the Colonel, and he clambered out of the trench.

"Let's go," yelled Bruce, and most of the men followed the two officers up out of the trench. The firing from the abatis nipped at them from the flank, but they dashed behind a screen of bushes, lay down, and began to fire.

A broken crowd of bluecoats was coming back, heads down, obviously retreating. The company with Bruce and Davidson began shooting steadily, taking aim carefully.

The crowd swirled and shifted back and away from the line, and shooting got difficult. Only one man, an officer, kept walking slowly across their field of fire from right to left, as if in a trance. Davidson growled and rose to his feet, pointed his pistol at arm's length and emptied it at the man.

The other troops stopped firing to watch him. Davidson threw the pistol down, pettishly. "Give me that rifle, soldier," he said. The private rolled on his back and looked up at him.

"Nah, Colonel. Let the man be. That there takes a little bit of nerve, wouldn't you say?"

"I could have you shot for insubordination," said the Colonel matter-of-factly. Then he stood, and watched the officer finish his slow walk, till he was hidden behind a dip in the earth.

6:30 A.M. *The Crater*

Sanderson followed Hartranft across the littered field and up toward the Crater. They trotted quickly, moving in the cringing posture of men under fire. A few shots from the fighting going on beyond sight, past the Crater, zipped overhead. And there was some determined musketry coming in from the left, where the rebels obviously had not left their main line.

Their route took them along the rear edge of the Crater, toward the left, and they plowed through the rubbled earth. There was a huge boulder, and a cannon perched on the edge—unaccountably pointing toward the rebels; abandoned. Sanderson followed along the lip of the big hole. Thirty feet below, he saw that the bottom of the pit was filling up with men—wounded lying while their comrades poured water in their mouths, or tended their wounds; others not wounded, wandering about, looking for officers or just malingering, it was hard to tell.

Their own way lay across a shallower section of the Crater, where the crumbled trench line merged into the crater like a dried-up streambed where a waterfall once plunged over a brink into a canyon. The ground was extremely broken and uneven, and there were spikes of the broken abatis sticking out of the ground. The regimental organizations began to break up, as the individual men sought footing.

There was a rebel battery at the top of the rubble, and a Sergeant Stanley of a Heavy Artillery regiment in Ledlie's division had got two of the guns cleaned up and turned around. At the moment there was nothing they could shoot at. The rebel rear immediately in front of them was screened by trees. Only to the right, toward the front of the Crater, did they have an open field.

The field was full of bluecoated soldiers. Drifts and currents of them, mostly—it seemed to Sanderson—winding back toward the Crater, and scrambling down into it. Every once in a while an officer would get some of these men in line and headed forward, but the magnetism of the Crater was too much. The lines dissolved, the troops drifting back like logs into a whirlpool.

A courier scrambled in from Willcox, with orders to move to the left immediately, if only with a single regiment. Hartranft was looking around frantically. His brigade seemed to have dissolved into its constituent parts in the course of wandering across the rubble-field, through the Crater and the trenches. Any regiments that had gotten into the Crater itself seemed to have simply vanished.

Hartranft was red in the face and cursing. *Not a brilliant performance,* thought Sanderson. There was going to be a charge here. For once, Sanderson told himself, he would keep out of it. He had an instinct that told him this was all waste motion.

A shellburst blossomed in front and to the right, another—mortars, looping over the trees. From the left and front, where the rebels were still in their trenches, the musketry heated up.

Hartranft got a regiment disentangled from the battery and started to deploy from it on the open ground. The Colonel of the regiment— Twenty-seventh Michigan—waved his sword, and they ran forward. Sanderson, peeping carefully through an embrasure, saw them go stumbling, saw the Colonel fall, his sword catching the light. Saw the troops halt and give a volley, and he said, ''Well, that's that.''

He turned, and looked round the battery. The heat in here was incredible, strangling. It dried the throat . . . hell, it dried the brains. Behind him Sanderson heard the muskets of the Michigan regiment rapping away. After they'd had enough, they'd be coming back.

Suddenly, Sanderson got up and walked swiftly back out of the battery the way he'd come, not even saying goodbye to Hartranft. He looked at his watch: 6:45. Three hours after the attack was supposed to have begun, two hours after the delayed explosion, Burnside's troops— so far as he could see—had not gotten more than fifty or a hundred yards past the Crater. He had to verify this, and report.

He moved quickly along the rear lip of the Crater. There were more men at the bottom now. Near a big boulder of clay perched on the lip of the Crater, he saw a hand sticking up out of the soil. Somebody had stuck a broken hardtack in, letting the stiff crumpled fingers fold back over and hold it in place against the dead palm. Some soldiers, thought Sanderson, had strange senses of humor.

He continued moving to the right. Past the boulder, he saw the rounded ridge that bisected the Crater, and on the other side, noticed a brigade flag flying from a clump of blue coats in the middle of the Crater.

''Hey,'' he called. ''What brigade's that?''

''Bartlett's,'' came the response.

The General with the cork leg. Probably got it stuck in the mud down there.

Still in a crouch, Sanderson ran along to the right of the Crater. There, troops still seemed to be coming up in some kind of order. Staff officers guided them through breaks in the lines—Potter's men; he might have guessed.

He grabbed one officer by the arm, and asked for news.

The officer, haggard looking, shrugged. ''Griffin's brigade made a charge, and were beaten off. I think there was another try a while ago, but haven't heard if anything came of it.''

Sanderson looked across the hundred yards of ground that divided him from the Union lines. The troops moving across were coming slowly, dodging shots and shells, ducking, covering themselves. Toward the center, there were plenty heading back the other way, wounded and not wounded, a steady drift.

Sanderson tucked up his sword under his arm, and began to run. He was going to get back to Meade's headquarters as fast as he could. Unless something happened very quickly, this whole assault was going to simply collapse, shot up or just given up by the troops that were supposed to be leading it.

HEADQUARTERS ARMY OF THE POTOMAC,
July 30, 1864—6:05 A.M.

Major-General BURNSIDE,
Commanding Ninth Corps:
  The commanding general wishes to know what is going on
on your left, and whether it would be an advantage for Warren's supporting force to go in at once.
                    A. A. HUMPHREYS,
                    Major-General and Chief of Staff.

6:30 A.M. *Burnside's Headquarters*

  Burnside had been holding the telegraphic dispatch for the last
twenty-five minutes. Every few seconds he would look up, to find Richmond watching his face intently. This made him uncomfortable. Why
did Richmond look so anxious? What was he afraid of? To answer such a
request as Meade's naturally required time and thought.
  But perhaps he was taking too long.
  His brain was just refusing to work. He ought to have slept more
during the night. He felt so desperately tired. He could think about anything but the dispatch.
  Hadn't the Mine worked brilliantly? If nothing else, that had
worked brilliantly. Brilliantly.
  Should he go outside to look?
  No. What was the use? You couldn't see anything from the battery.
Why didn't the divisional commanders report more frequently?
  Hadn't he done everything possible? Everything he was required
to do?
  He looked up at Richmond again, and saw his aide's eyes fixed on
his own. And looked back down at the dispatch.
  Things weren't going as planned. Not going well at all. The men
weren't advancing. Meade's fault, he should have let me send the niggers
in first, damn him! Meade's interference had wrecked the Ninth Corps,
wrecked it utterly and forever.
  Meade!
  He couldn't let Meade beat him, destroy him. Gather his forces for
another try. He looked up, met Richmond's gaze, this time holding it by
an effort of will. He must make it clear, to Richmond and his own staff
now as well as to the army, that he hadn't lost his grip on things. He'd
tell Meade to get Warren ready to move. He sat down to write a dispatch.
  "All right, Lew: send Meade this. And I want orders for Ord's
troops and Ferrero's division. We'll send them through and make another try for the hill." Get Ord and Ferrero up into the breach, send
them right through, and *bang!* he'd have it. Oh, wouldn't it be sweet
when after all—his Negroes doing at the end of the fight what Meade
feared they couldn't do at the start?

HEADQUARTERS NINTH ARMY CORPS,
July 30, 1864—6:20 A.M.

Major-General MEADE:

If General Warren's supporting force can be concentrated just now, ready to go in at the proper time, it would be well. I will designate when it ought to move. There is scarcely room for it now, in our immediate front.

A. E. BURNSIDE,
Major-General.

6:30 A.M. *Johnson's Headquarters*

General Johnson had ridden hard over to the right flank of his position. Here, to the south of the Crater, woods and broken ground masked the weakness of the force that his regimental and brigade commanders had pieced together; masked them, and gave them good positions to defend against the Yankee attackers. There was a part of the Twenty-third South Carolina which had been in the lines just to the right of the Crater—the troops had fled in panic, and been rallied in the woods. The Fifty-ninth Virginia had formed on their right, and Johnson hauled most of the Twenty-second South Carolina out of the trenches to anchor the right, forming a line at right angles to the front line of trenches. Johnson ordered two more regiments, the Twenty-sixth and Forty-sixth Virginia, up from his right, to form a reserve behind the thin line. Those lines were held by scratch companies, details, a few organized groups filing up the trenches from the right. A heavy column striking there would give them a hard time, but Johnson had no choice. He had to trust to luck and the strength of the trenches. So far the Yankees hadn't attacked them.

Through his glasses, Johnson could count ten or more Yankee flags waving from the Crater, several more in front of it. As he watched, there was a flurry of action in front of the Crater, and farther over, to the left flank of it. Flags were waving outside the Crater. It was hard to tell, but from the burst of dark-jacketed figures that tumbled into view heading for the Crater, Johnson guessed that someone had counterattacked on the north side of the Crater. There were rebel and Yankee flags waving side by side.

To his right he heard the slapping sound of mortars, looping shells over the intervening woods toward the Yankee positions near the Crater. With three regiments in line and two in reserve, Colonel Goode might hold this flank; at least he could slow any attack. Johnson was just thinking that he ought to be returning to the ridge, where he could see more clearly, when he heard horses, and turned in the saddle to see General Mahone and two staff officers riding forward, followed by an orderly with the General's guidon.

Reinforcements were coming up, Mahone's division, called from the extreme right of the line where they had been facing Warren's corps. Johnson swung his hat, his bald head gleaming in the sun. "Hey! Hurrah!'' If his boys could only hold the Yanks off a bit longer, till Mahone's brigades could come up and deploy, why . . . why he might smash em to a halt. His heart jumped, he felt the blood surge—he might even *win.* He had been a dead man at five in the morning, and by noon he might have conquered the hosts that had broken his lines and come on against him.

Mahone—*a dark-haired Celtic type,* thought Johnson—grinned in his black beard as he saluted. He gestured toward the firing, the clouds of black smoke that had begun to heap and pile up behind the trees. ''Sounds like quite a party,'' he said.

''They blew up their mine at sunrise,'' said Johnson. ''There's more than a division of them in the breach. We've managed to keep them there, so far.'' He sidled his horse up next to Mahone, and showed him his sketch-map. He pointed as he spoke. ''We've got about a brigade in here on the south of the breach, parts of another one on the north. One gun firing from this side, and a full battery close to the main line on the north. And I've got sixteen in battery up on the ridge. There are mortar batteries closer down on the left, here and here.''

Mahone glanced at his watch. ''It will take at least an hour, maybe more, for my first brigade to come up and form.'' He looked up at Johnson and waited for a response.

Johnson rubbed a hand over his mouth. It was hot. He was so thirsty all of a sudden. ''If they don't do any better than they have, we'll hold them. I haven't more than a screening force for my battery on the ridge. It's been enough so far.''

Mahone nodded. ''I'll bring my men into position near your battery, and move forward from there.'' Mahone looked off to his right, back in the direction his troops had come. ''You'd best have these men here watch their right and rear,'' he said. ''I didn't leave very many men in my lines. Just one line of infantry in the pits, plus my artillery. If the Yankees attack we might not hold them. If they get so much as a regiment through the line, they can just walk away with my artillery. I haven't got a corporal's guard for a reserve.''

The two Generals were silent under the weight of the sun. Perhaps the Yankees wouldn't attack the flank at all. Johnson looked at Mahone searchingly, and said, ''If I may make a suggestion, General. If you can march your troops further to the north than is really necessary—to the other side of the Durin house—and bring them over the crest from that point . . .''

Mahone was nodding vigorously. ''Yes: they might think we were bringing men in from our left, and leaving the troops on the right intact.'' Mahone looked at his watch.

Johnson continued, ''There's a ravine below the hill, *here,*'' and he pointed. ''It's been improved somewhat as a trench; you'll be able to form troops in there for an attack, or hold it against one.''

''One hour,'' said Mahone curtly. ''Perhaps a few minutes longer. Where will you be?''

Johnson looked back over his shoulder. His left flank brigade seemed to be handling itself well enough. Mahone would bring his force into the center. Johnson had the largest body of formed troops left in his division right here. He'd stay with it, use it any way he had to, to hold the Yankees till Mahone could get up. Attack, if need be, till he was down to his last battalion, to delay the Yankees, hold them in position, keep their heads down—anything but advancing.

"I'll be right here," he said.

Mahone saluted, turned his horse, and rode off toward the west, where the Jerusalem Road followed the line of the ridge. Far away to the south, the clouds of dust stirred by his advancing division rose and hung motionless in the stagnant air.

6:50 A.M. *Burnside's Headquarters*

At the telegraph station the keys began to chatter, and the officers drifted toward the telegraph. Richmond bent over the telegrapher, ripped the message off his pad as soon as it was completed. He turned, and Burnside was standing right there to take it.

> HEADQUARTERS ARMY OF THE POTOMAC,
> *July 30, 1864—6:50* A.M.
>
> Major-General BURNSIDE:
> Warren's force has been concentrated and ready to move since 3:30 A.M. My object in inquiring was to ascertain if you could judge of the practicability of his advancing without waiting for your column. What is the delay in your column moving? Every minute is most precious, as the enemy undoubtedly are concentrating to meet you on the crest, and if you give them time enough you cannot expect to succeed. There is no object to be gained in occupying the enemy's line; it cannot be held under their artillery fire without much labor in turning it. The great point is to secure the crest at once, and at all hazards.
> GEO. G. MEADE,
> *Major-General.*

Burnside's face began to redden, the heat-blotches merging into a single crimson tone.

"General! . . ." said Richmond apprehensively.

The telegraph clicked.

"More?" said Burnside, strangling.

"It's from Fifth Corps to Grant, not for us," said the operator.

"Take it off, damn you!" snapped Burnside.

Richmond bit his lip.

The operator looked up. "That's against orders, sir."

"By God! Can't anyone in this corps follow a simple, direct order!" Burnside glared around. The place fell silent. The telegraph clicked. The operator looked at Richmond, who silently nodded, standing out of Burnside's line of sight. The operator scribbled. Burnside bent and tore off the paper.

FIFTH ARMY CORPS,
July 30, 1864—7 A.M.

Lieutenant-General GRANT:
    Several regiments of Burnside's men are lying in front of the crater, apparently, of the mine. In their rear is to be seen a line of battle of a brigade or more, under cover, and, I think, between the enemy's line and ours. The volley firing half an hour ago was from the enemy's works in Warren's front.
C. B. COMSTOCK,
Lieutenant-Colonel.

    "Now that's done it," he said, to nobody in particular. He paced briskly back and forth two times. The eyes of the staff followed him. The operator was hunched over his key.
    Burnside came back, and stood rigid behind the operator. Then he bent at the waist, leaning over the man's shoulder, and wrote on the man's pad. "Send it," he snapped, and walked out, up to the battery.
    Richmond bent over the operator's shoulder, and read it.
    The operator looked at him. The staff officer's mouth was a tight thin line.
    "Send it," he said quietly.
    He walked to the door. Hesitated. Then followed his commander up to the battery.

HEADQUARTERS NINTH ARMY CORPS,
July 30, 1864.

General MEADE:
    I am doing all in my power to push the troops forward, and, if possible, we will carry the crest. It is hard work, but we hope to accomplish it. I am fully alive to the importance of it.
A. E. BURNSIDE,
Major-General.

7:05 A.M. *First Division Bombproof*

    Surgeon Clubb could work no more. His head was swelled to bursting with the heat. His clothes were drenched with his own sweat and the blood of the wounded; he smelled like a butcher-boy, his hands were numb. He slumped on a chair, leaning against the wall of the bombproof while his assistants worked.
    A small closet-drama was being played out near the door of the bunker. Generals Ledlie and Ferrero, and Ledlie's staff, sat around waiting for something to happen. At intervals, aides would arrive from the front. Ledlie would receive them, the friendly smile fixed on his face. Was the man mad? Or had he been struck dead by some mysterious fit, left with that curious rictus distorting his face? As nearly as Clubb could tell, he spoke to the aides without moving his lips.

A staff officer arrived. Loring?—he had been down several times now. Ferrero was behind him, and Clubb could hear them distinctly.

". . . orders to advance immediately," Loring said.

Ferrero stared at him blankly, made a vague gesture with one hand toward the packed trenches. Licked his lips. "Colonel," he said softly, "I'm afraid I cannot advance until the way is cleared."

Loring turned to Ledlie. His look was extraordinary—rage? He seemed almost helpless behind it. "General Ledlie, your troops have been ordered to advance."

Ledlie smiled. "Colonel, I've sent reiterated instructions for them to advance from the Crater." He looked about him, and his staff officers nodded.

Loring looked this way and that. He seemed like a man in a trap. He bit his lips, and turned to Ledlie again. "The General's orders are peremptory! Either get your men out of the Crater, and take the hill, or . . ." he gestured vaguely. *"Get them out of the way!"*

Ledlie nodded, his lower lip protruding, serious. "Yes, Colonel. Harrison!" he called to an aide. "I want you to go forward at once. Find General Bartlett, and have him get his men forward, at once. No delays. No formations. Straight for the crest! Got that?"

"Yes sir."

"Good boy," said Ledlie, patting his arm as he rushed out, bounced off a soldier in the trench, and disappeared.

Loring raised his hands, and dropped them again.

He turned to Ferrero, and his voice had a pleading tone.

"Can't you advance your men?"

Ferrero glanced at Ledlie, who smiled at him. Ferrero licked his lips. "Not until they've cleared the way for us. My men are in the covered way . . ." and he gestured again, that vague movement.

Loring turned, and left the bombproof. Clubb wiped his face with a towel dipped in water. The slight coolness refreshed him.

When he lifted his head, he saw Ledlie talking to his assistant, then turning to leave the bombproof.

"What did he want?" asked Clubb.

The assistant blushed. "Stimulants, sir. For malaria."

7:10 A.M. *The Crater*

Though it wasn't his brigade, Neill was glad to help set up the tent for General Bartlett. The one-legged brigadier had cracked his cork leg, landing hard on the stump, while struggling through the soft soil on the bottom of the Crater. His men rigged a shelter half as a shade, set as a lean-to against a mound of earth on the floor of the larger section of the Crater. The earth still fumed, and stank of powder. Bartlett's skin was white and bloodless, his lips pale with nausea.

Neill felt protected in the Crater, where the steep sides kept off all the rifle fire, and no shells or mortars seemed to reach. The biggest and best rifle pit he'd ever seen. There were lots of other boys from the Fourteenth down here, but somehow he'd lost Beeler—and he didn't much look out for the boys. The feeling seemed mutual. It was as if in avoiding each other they ensured their escape from death.

He also threw away his cap, with his divisional badge and regimental number. This was as good as a disguise with other officers (he was always in someone else's command). His own officer, Oostervelt, was dead. Sergeant Stanley was God knew where, and might the devil take him. Neill was feeling almost cocky.

There was a stir up above, and a courier came scrambling down, looking for General Bartlett. Neill—hungry for gossip—ambled over to listen. There were a lot of soldiers standing around the lean-to, all different regiments mixed together, even some from the Second and Third divisions.

The courier, covered with dust, saluted Bartlett, who was stretched out on the soft earth, with his stump raised on a little mound of it and his good leg stretched in front of him. Bartlett returned it. He looked sick.

"We've been trying . . . it's hard. My leg . . . I'll tell Colonel Marshall to get the men forward. Tell General Ledlie that we'll do our best to get the men forward. It's hard going. The men aren't . . ." he looked around at the faces of the soldiers that surrounded him, showing boredom, apprehension, curiosity, lassitude. "Tell the General we'll try again."

Neill, hearing that, turned to slip away—and there was Sergeant Stanley, looking him square in the face.

"Neill! You damned skulker! Get up here!" When Neill hesitated, Stanley leveled his pistol. Neill walked to the wall, and began climbing it, kicking the toes of his boots in hard to hold against the steepness and the slide of the earth.

"Threw away your musket, didn't you?" said Stanley, when Neill had scrambled up. "Well, you won't need it here." They stood in the lee of the great boulder. Off to the right, Stanley had a crew working on the cannon that they'd hauled out of the Crater. Stanley gripped Neill's sleeve with one hand, and turned to a corporal nearby. "Get over to the rebel battery we just left, with your squad. Bring back rope, handspikes." The man nodded and ran.

Bullets pinged against the clay boulder, rang off the metal of the gun. Stanley grinned, and mopped his streaming forehead. "Hot enough for you, boy-o? It'll be a lot hotter where you're headed. Best get used to it."

He pushed Neill toward the gun and said, *"Haul!"*

7:20 A.M. *First Division Bombproof*

When Clubb looked up from his work, Ferrero and Ledlie were returning to the shelter, presumably from a visit to the lines. Ledlie's face seemed redder—perhaps the heat. He blinked frequently, perhaps with the dust or the darkness inside after the bright sunlight. But his smile was still in place. If anything it seemed broader, more warm and genuine. Looking at it seemed to hearten the drooping Ferrero. Ledlie leaned over and patted him on the shoulder. Rested his hand. Patted some more, absently now.

"Buck up, General!" he said. "Here, let's sit and clear the pipes a bit." He directed Ferrero to a camp chair, on the edge of which the latter perched rigidly, sword between his knees. Ledlie sat down heavily, rocking the chair back dangerously. Grinned, looked comfortable. He poured something from his canteen into a tin cup. "Good for malaria," he said, and winked at Ferrero. Ferrero sniffed, sipped at the cup.

Dr. Clubb pressed his fists into the small of his back, where two points of pain were forming. As he watched, another staff officer came in, and stood in front of the two seated Generals.

He looked from one to the other, and said, "General Burnside orders General Ferrero to move your division forward at once, take them through and charge down to the city."

"The heights have been carried then," said Ledlie, sagely.

The staff officer ignored him. "The General wishes you to charge immediately."

Ferrero looked up. His voice seemed a bit stronger now but there was still a slight quaver. "Tell the General I cannot attack until the way has been cleared. My troops can't get out of the covered way. Tell him . . ." he glanced at Ledlie.

Ledlie made a comforting gesture to Ferrero with his right hand, *Let me handle this for you.* "It'll be plain murder, sending them up now. Plain murder. Tell the General that." And he smiled at Ferrero.

"I don't want my men slaughtered without need," said Ferrero. "They'll never be able to do anything now. Before . . . but now it's certain. Never do it. Tell General Burnside."

The officer left. Ledlie nodded approvingly at Ferrero. Ferrero remained perched uneasily on the edge of his seat. The yelling of the troops in the trenches got louder, and the musketry intensified.

7:20 A.M. Meade's Headquarters

Meade nibbled nervously at a corner of his mustache, but Humphreys was rubbing his hands together and smiling. Things seemed to be moving again. Burnside's men were in the breach, Warren ready to attack, Hancock primed to deliver the coup de grace on the far right if Burnside broke through. Perhaps that last telegram had lit the fire under Burnside. Soon, any time now, they should hear that Burnside's men had gone through and taken the hill.

Humphreys wished he could see the field. Still, it was not too difficult to visualize what was happening from the reports as they came in— the lines of troops pouring through the breach, working their way past the obstacles and debris, muscling aside the small details of formed rebels that were in their way. Slow going, but sure. A tide, rolling forward.

It was going well, one had to be pleased. But there was that annoyance, that growing annoyance with the long silences from Burnside.

The spiteful man was giving them no more than the barest necessary information—scarcely even that. Hoarding the knowledge and making them sweat.

Humphreys paced up and down the bank of telegraphers. *That fat son of a bitch. Why doesn't he use the telegraph?*

The instrument began to chatter. Humphreys read it off as it came in : ". . . am doing all in my power . . . hard work but . . . I am fully alive to the importance of it. . . ." Humphreys felt a certain amazed detachment. He knew this would be the last straw for Meade with Burnside. He realized that he had been expecting this, was almost relieved that he could see it coming.

"Give this to General Meade," he said. Then he smiled a little. "And wait for an immediate reply."

HEADQUARTERS ARMY OF THE POTOMAC,
July 30, 1864—7:30 A.M.

Major-General BURNSIDE :
What do you mean by hard work to take the crest? I understand not a man has advanced beyond the enemy's line which you occupied immediately after exploding the mine. Do you mean to say your officers and men will not obey your orders to advance? If not, what is the obstacle? I wish to know the truth, and desire an immediate answer.

GEO. G. MEADE,
Major-General.

Burnside looked up from the dispatch in a fury. "How dare you!" he shouted, and the courier, Captain Jay, recoiled a step. Richmond grabbed the General's arm. Burnside looked down at the letter. *Not Jay!* he told himself, *Meade!* The phrases—sharp, hectoring, nagging, spiteful—yammered in his brain. *What do you mean? Do you mean they won't obey you? If not, what reason? What? Immediate answer. Immediate. What do you mean, hard work?*

"By heaven, I'll answer him!" yelled Burnside, strangling.

"General, please!" said Richmond, guiding him away from the ashen-faced Captain Jay.

Burnside, a bewildered bull, let himself be led. Richmond looked around; the General had to be calmed somehow.

Here, in providential time, came Warren and Ord through the door of the bombproof. Richmond tugged Burnside's sleeve. The General rounded, glowering, saw the two Generals. Richmond felt the General's arm tense, as he composed his manner for them. It was going to be all right.

Warren had ridden over from his own headquarters, not bothering to seek concealment because the rebels hadn't been shooting much his way. All morning he had felt uneasy and out of touch with the development of events. He had no real sense of where this fight was going, or who was directing it. If anyone was. He could see so little of the fighting itself that he had already mistaken some of Burnside's men in a captured battery for the enemy. He was certain in his own mind—as he had been from the beginning—that to send his men frontally against the batteries that flanked Burnside's attack would be suicidal, another bloody Cold Harbor shambles. Unless Burnside had broken through, and could take them in reverse. . . . But if Burnside could, why hadn't he? Warren was determined to use whatever discretion he had to keep his Fifth Corps clear until he could be sure Burnside's attack had succeeded. His reasoning, he felt, was very sound: if Burnside was well into the breach, then he would not need an attack from Warren to take those batteries; but if he was not in a position to take them now, it might not be worth the risk of Warren's corps to attempt an assault to support him.

He had reached the rear of Burnside's position and made his way to the fourteen-gun battery, where he had run into General Ord.

Warren, always quicker of thought than Ord, asked the first question, thus taking command of the situation. "General, I thought your corps had been ordered forward?"

"Can't move at all," Ord growled, "Burnside's troops are jamming up the way. The damned skulkers won't move forward." He had a famous temper, Warren remembered.

"Ah," said Warren, and gestured politely for Ord to precede him into the bombproof.

There was Burnside himself, red in the face, his stupid jowls glazed with sweat, his fat eyes goggling. Warren smiled affably. He noted that Burnside held a crumpled dispatch in his left hand, and wondered what it was.

"General Burnside," said Ord, "I have to tell you that your troops have still not gone forward. I have been ordered to attack, and cannot by any means carry out the order." He clenched his fists. "*By God,* Burnside, you'd better do *something!*"

Burnside's eyes narrowed; he looked crafty. He nodded at Ord, playing the calm commander taking a report from his subordinate. Then he looked politely at Warren, waiting for him to report as well.

This was disconcerting. It was impossible to tell what the situation was. Should he ask Burnside for orders to attack, or wait for Meade? To be sure, Meade had given him discretion to attack . . . but he must know more before he exercised that perilous privilege. Things were coming to a crisis, it was very dangerous to do anything precipitately. If this attack was another bloody smashup, heads would roll.

"General," he said, "I came to find out what the state of affairs is. My wire to headquarters keeps breaking, and I find I can't see very much from where I am."

"Yes," said Burnside vigorously, "my observation post here is much better."

Warren smiled. "Yes, but still not entirely adequate. I wonder, General, if you require any support from me at this time."

"Thank you, General!" said Burnside. "Thank you." There was a pause. Burnside's beaming gaze seemed to fall apart. He looked over at

Richmond. Then back to Warren. "At the moment . . . there's no possibility of your coming in behind us. . . ." The voice tailed off, leaving Warren unsure whether it was a question or a statement of some tentative kind. There was a plaintive quality to it. "Some support—yes," said Burnside suddenly. "There's a battery on our left, if you could . . ."

Warren was shaking his head. "Our artillery can't touch it. I thought your troops in the breach might be able to take it in reverse."

Burnside's face blanched, he looked at Richmond, then flushed again. "No," he said, "the ground isn't favorable." He looked back at Warren. "Can't you make an attack on your front?"

There was a silence between them, behind which the booming of the shooting could be heard.

"I'd rather not," said Warren coolly, "without explicit orders, General." He stood, deferential, waiting.

Burnside licked his lips. His eyes moved quickly, seemed almost to vibrate in their sockets. Then he forced a smile, and put one meaty hand on Warren's shoulder. "I'll have to talk," he hesitated. "*Think* about that, I think." He swallowed. "I will consult General Meade. Will you be at your headquarters?"

"Yes, General," said Warren.

"Good," said Burnside. And he paused, heavy hand on Warren's shoulder. He looked at him, sadly. "Can't you give me some artillery support near the Crater?"

Warren shook his head. "I can try, General. But the woods on my front screen most of that area from my guns." Burnside seemed confused, and Warren glanced at Ord and added, "You remember, General, I asked that they be cut down yesterday, and you declined to do it. You didn't want to attract attention to this front."

"Woods," said Burnside. He seemed bewildered. Almost frightened. "I'll have my men cut them immediately. As soon as that's done, I'll give you all the artillery fire I can bring to bear." Warren waited for something further. Burnside removed his hand from Warren's shoulder. Warren saluted and left the bombproof.

As he trotted back toward the sheltered spot where the horses were tied, he found himself wondering what he would have done if Burnside *had* given him a direct order to attack. He would have had to choose, then. Things couldn't go on like this. Warren felt that he, Ord—all of them—were out on a limb. He had to get Meade to show his hand.

In the meantime, he'd hold his troops ready to attack, cut the woods, fire all the artillery Burnside might want—but he would not send his troops against those trenches without a direct order from Meade. If he had discretionary authority, that was how he would use it.

Nobody was going to hang this latest failure around his neck.

Burnside rounded on Colonel Loring and his aides, Van Buren and Harris. "I want the same orders issued to those scoundrels! By Gad, I'll keep ordering them to attack till midnight if that's what it takes." He scribbled an order on a sheet of paper. "Copies to Potter, Willcox, and Ferrero. In writing this time!" Harris began to copy the General's scrawl.

"And Ledlie," said Richmond quietly.

Burnside looked up. His voice was tense, strangled: "Potter. Willcox. Ferrero." Richmond stared, nodded, turned and left. Van Buren hesitated, then followed. Burnside looked at Loring. "General Ledlie has been repulsed, and must rally his troops."

Loring snatched his copy of the order, turned and left.

HEADQUARTERS NINTH ARMY CORPS,
Battery Morton, July 30, 1864.

General FERRERO:

GENERAL: The general commanding directs that you push forward at once and endeavor to gain the crest. Move forward with every available man.

Respectfully,

W. W. HARRIS,
Captain of Ordnance, U.S. Army.

7:40 A.M. *Covered Way*

Private Johnson Number Five was sickened by the procession of bleeding men. Never had he seen white folks look so sick. It must be a terrible place they were coming from. Nobody thought he ought to go there. These niggers just couldn't stand stuff like that. What were they doing here in this hole in the ground, already as narrow as a grave? He remembered the empty circles of standing knapsacks, back in the clearing behind him, and shuddered.

Lieutenant Dobbs came along the line in an interval when, by some dispensation, the procession of the maimed white men ceased.

He a banty-rooster for sure, thought Johnson, and he smiled despite the tightness of his face. Dobbs was walking with springing steps up the trench. Something projected behind him, oddly. It took Johnson a moment to recognize that he had the axe with him still, jammed into his belt with the haft sticking out behind him.

Dobbs saw his look, and grinned. He whipped the axe out, and handed it to Johnson, butt first. "Hey now! How about taking this here and giving them a couple of swings with it when we get up there? Make the chips *fly!* Hunh!"

Johnson smiled, shyly, and held his hand palm forward, pushing the axe away gently. "No thanks, Captain. I done my turn cuttin firewood. Let some these lazy niggers here do they share."

"Why, man, ain't you ever cut any Johnny-wood? Man, it's the softest cutting."

"Do tell." There was a small riffle of laughter up the line.

Dobbs grabbed the handle short, and swung in little chopping motions. "You know I'm the woodchopper, don't you, boys?"

"That's right."

"Old Abe, he's the railsplitter, but I'm the woodchopper."

"You is."

"That's right."

"I cut em fast and hard, fast and hard, fast and hard."

"Hunh!"

"And they stay cut!"

"That's right."

"When I cut em, they stay cut."

"That's right."

"What kind of wood is it?"

"Johnny-wood!"

"And it cuts so sweet and soft, sweet and soft."

"A-men."

Dobbs was almost laughing now. "Want to cut some Johnny wood, brothers?"

"A-men."

"A-men."

"A-men."

The laughter was running stronger now.

"You the woodchopper, boss," said Johnson, grinning.

Around the bend of the trench, the sounds of slow-shuffling feet could be heard again. The air overhead was full of the whispering sound of the bullets.

Oliver, up at the head of his brigade, fumed at the delay. His body, he found, was an impatient animal. His troops, even his officers, seemed content to sit here in this ditch and wait like oxen free from the goad, ruminant. Not he. He had to quiet the animal. "Wait here," he snapped to his aide, and he pushed his way forward. The wounded went by on his left. The smell of them was hideous, sickening, and his stomach nearly revolted. War was filthy business. Ledlie and Ferrero were just coming out of the bombproof when Oliver approached. Ledlie smiled his best businessman's smile. Oliver disliked the man intensely. Ferrero looked ill, but his dark eyes lit up at Oliver.

"Colonel Oliver," said Ferrero, "we've been ordered to attack."

Oliver stopped. For a moment, he was terribly afraid. "I received no orders." He barely spoke.

"No, no," said Ferrero. "I've told them it's no use to send us up." Relief washed over Oliver's frame. "Not now," muttered Ferrero. "No good to attack now."

"What's happening?" Oliver asked. His hunger to know had returned.

Ferrero glanced at Ledlie, and blushed. "There's some difficulty getting the troops forward."

Ledlie nodded affably, and ducked back into the bombproof.

Colonel Loring appeared, almost magically, and gripped Ferrero's right shoulder. "General," he said, raising his voice to be heard clearly above the tumult of troops. "General, you are to get your division forward by any means at all. Now! You are ordered to attack immediately, and without reference to any other division. Straight for the hill, and dig in there."

"I must protest this," said Ferrero, glancing at Oliver for approval.

Loring nodded, but waved the protest away. "Immediately, General!"

Ferrero turned to Oliver, and spread his hands, helplessly.

Oliver turned on his heel, slid into a moving column of wounded, and went as quickly as he could back down the covered way to the head of his brigade.

The animal had him by the throat. He had to think, but his head was filled with chatter.

Behind him, Ferrero stood by the door of the bombproof. General Ledlie stuck his head out, then stepped out himself. "Come inside," he said, "and clear your throat. This dust. When your troops go up we'll come out and watch."

Ferrero looked at him. He could think of nothing else to do now. He might as well wait inside with Ledlie. At least he would have company.

7:50 A.M. *Burnside's Headquarters*

Warren and Ord had left. Burnside stood, wavering slightly on his feet, his thick lips set, his large eyes narrowed. He had held them off, but this was it, the crisis, the end, the last ditch. Now or never. Do or die.

Never say die! That's the word. Hang on till the luck turns around. Call and raise, bluff and hang on.

A dispatch from the front:

July 30, 1864—7:40 A.M.

General BURNSIDE:
    Your orders have been delivered. I think it of great importance that the artillery on the right, which enfilades the space between our old lines and the crater, be silenced. There is a battery in the woods by the ravine on the right.
                                                                C. G. LORING
Possibly also the rebel battery by the railroad cut, opposite Ledlie's old right, can fire over here. Cannot the mortar battery be stirred up?

Mortar battery. Of course. Anything to accommodate Loring. Good man, good man. A good man.

He reread the dispatch. "Your orders have been delivered." What about *obeyed?* Anger began to rush into his head. The ungrateful sons of bitches, they were destroying him! Couldn't they obey simple instructions!

He was going out to the battery. If Ferrero's niggers didn't go forward, he'd shoot the lot of them!

"Sir," came a call. "I think Ferrero's division is going forward!"
At last! thought Burnside. It's begun to work again. He still had
that ace in the hole. Ace of Spades! Haha! Now he could answer Meade,
and he'd tell him a thing or two. Badgering, hectoring, nagging old
maid! His eyes danced quickly with new delight around the bombproof. He was playing the last card, and by God, it was a good one!
"What do you mean by hard work to. . . ." I'll answer him!

HEADQUARTERS NINTH ARMY CORPS,
Battery Morton, July 30, 1864

General MEADE:
Your dispatch by Captain Jay received. The main body of
General Potter's division is beyond the crater. I do not mean to
say that my officers and men will not obey my orders to advance. I mean to say that it is very hard to advance to the
crest. I have never in any report said anything different from
what I conceived to be the truth. Were it not insubordinate I
would say that the latter remark of your note was unofficerlike
and ungentlemanly.

A. E. BURNSIDE,
Major-General.

He tore off the sheet, handed it to Richmond and said sharply,
"Send *that!*"
Richmond glanced at it, looked up. "General, shouldn't you . . ."
"By God, Richmond, send that damn thing! Now!" Richmond
blushed.
*You've got to show these youngsters that a General has the courage
to take his chances, when the time comes.* Burnside grabbed a pair of
field glasses off the table, and headed for the door.
Anyway, he thought, as he trotted up the steps into the battery,
I said I had no intention to be insubordinate. That should cover me. The
blowing smoke obscured the battle lines. He could not see Ferrero's men
going forward. He felt, for a second, a terrible fear. He was in too far
now. His neck was on the block. If this last attack failed, Meade would
chop it off short.
Here was Richmond with another dispatch.

SIGNAL STATION,
July 30, 1864.

Major-General BURNSIDE:
GENERAL: The enemy are moving at least two brigades of
infantry from their right and our Ninth Corps front and right.
They are now passing around where the road goes toward the
town, west of those chimneys.

J. C. PAINE,
Captain and Signal Officer.

The rebels were bringing up reinforcements. A division from the northern and southern flanks of the Crater, it sounded like.

Burnside fanned the smoke. He could see nothing.

It was a foot-race now. Those niggers better not shuffle, or he was a dead man.

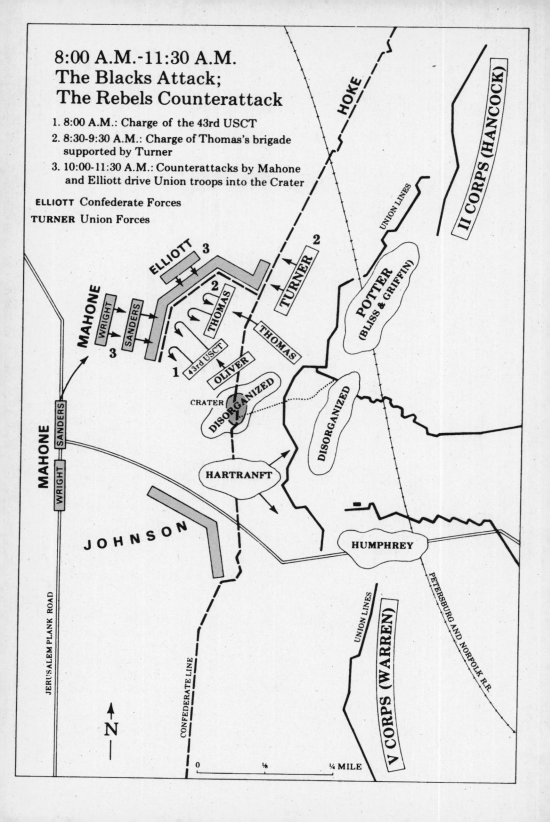

8:00 A.M.-11:30 A.M.
The Blacks Attack;
The Rebels Counterattack

1. **8:00 A.M.:** Charge of the 43rd USCT
2. **8:30-9:30 A.M.:** Charge of Thomas's brigade supported by Turner
3. **10:00-11:30 A.M.:** Counterattacks by Mahone and Elliott drive Union troops into the Crater

ELLIOTT Confederate Forces

TURNER Union Forces

HOKE

II CORPS (HANCOCK)

UNION LINES

POTTER (BLISS & GRIFFIN)

ELLIOTT

3

MAHONE

WRIGHT

SANDERS

3

2

THOMAS

2

TURNER

THOMAS

1

43rd USCT

OLIVER

DISORGANIZED

CRATER

DISORGANIZED

MAHONE

SANDERS

WRIGHT

HARTRANFT

JOHNSON

HUMPHREY

JERUSALEM PLANK ROAD

CONFEDERATE LINE

V CORPS (WARREN)

UNION LINES

PETERSBURG AND NORFOLK R.R.

N

0   ⅛   ¼ MILE

Into the Crater
8:00 A.M.–10:30 A.M.

7:55 A.M. Covered Way

Booker never heard the order to attack. He knew it had come when the regiment in front began yelling and moving swiftly down the narrow way toward the firing. He bumped one of the wounded with his shoulder and the man's cry of pain was as bright and empty as the call of a bird. The firing pulled him forward without effort or thought.

He cannoned into the back of Colonel Hall, when the Thirtieth Regiment, at the head of the brigades, stalled in the front-line trench. Slower, they waded forward, pushing, shoving. Booker remembered with a shock the ladders they'd left behind: the troops were scrambling over the trench walls by makeshift ladders of hands, backs, bayonets, rifles jammed between the logs. The surging wave of the brigade lapped forward to the side of the wall, then surged back on itself, then forward. Booker struggled, a weak swimmer in a black undertow. He got a foot on a musket barrel held by a soldier he didn't recognize, and vaulted from it to the top of the parapet.

He turned and began helping the others out. Colonel Hall first, looking whey-faced. Then Randolph, the black hand hard and surprisingly dry to his touch. More hands reached down from the parapet to haul the others out.

The grunt of a shell: he felt the wind of it on his back. The air was singing with metal, and some men were diving headfirst back into the trench. *Cowards? Wounded?* A body, arms splayed, rode the blue-black surge in the trench, buoyed up by arms that swept it backward like a log on a flood, and cast it on the rear face of the trench. A closer shot roared in his ear, and Booker saw that bodies flew in its smoke, heavily and without grace.

He stood up and turned around.

The space in front of the trenches was full of black men pushing and shoving, officers yelling them into line. Underfoot the earth was full of rubble. Booker could not see beyond the mob of men, except for the flags of the Thirtieth Regiment and the brigade guidon. Someone bumped his left arm, and he turned to see a flag corporal, Colehill, standing with the colors of the Forty-third. Colonel Hall was yelling, ''Forty-third! Forty-third! Follow me!''

It was impossible to form a line; the Thirtieth Regiment had begun stumbling off to the right. The air whined and sang, bullets bit, shells fell again and again and again, punctual as a clock; and as Booker's head cleared, he thought, *One gun, it's just one gun bearing on us here,* and he yelled, "Forty-third, let's go!" and trotted after Hall.

8:00 A.M. *The Crater*

Neill ducked behind the wheel of the gun every chance he got, every time Stanley turned his back. Three men were already laid out, dead or dying, behind the big clay boulder. Stanley, sweat glistening on his fat white back (he'd taken his shirt off) held them to it, slapped Neill in the face and threatened to shoot him when he caught him hiding.

He saw the sergeant half-turn and he started to rise, and then he saw the niggers coming across the field, a whole crazy mob of them running from right to left across the back of the Crater as he turned to watch them, and he pointed and yelled, "Holy Jesus, will you look at that!"

Stanley turned.

Neill saw his pale back against the onrushing horde of niggers, and without thinking turned, sprang for the lip of the Crater, swung his legs in and slid-fell to the bottom. His breath whoofed out, he couldn't catch it, but safety was so close that his legs somehow carried him. He sprawled out behind a broken ammunition box, covered from Stanley, hidden deep in the Crater, among crowds of men and the wreckage of equipment.

Oliver ran at the head of the brigade like a man roused from a dream, not completely convinced that he was awake and in the world. He could not remember how he had gotten from Ledlie's bombproof to the head of the brigade, or how he had gotten out of the trench. The air was alive with whinings and the buzzing of deadly horrible insects.

To the right, he kept saying to himself. *Ferrero said go to the right.*

The brigade followed him as he trotted between the lines. On his left he saw the rubble-strewn crest of the Crater. A cannon stood in front of it by a giant clay boulder, perched like some Druidical megalith in the middle of the scene. It suddenly seemed ludicrous to him: he was a schoolmaster taking his boys on a morning jog and here the whole world was coming apart and trying to kill him.

He began to angle around the right of the Crater. He dodged bulky humps and twisted shapes, some of which called and writhed, tried to trip him as he ran.

They were up to the Crater's edge. His men, their bayonetted rifles cocked at a perilous angle, rushed past him like a branched tree washed off in a flood.

Ten yards to his left, the first of them had reached the parapet of rubble, and he saw their backs turn away, saw their faces turn toward him, and he thought, *What in God's name* and *they're turning tail.* Then they dropped out of sight. He ran toward them, right up to the ridge of crumbled earth. It was higher than it looked, harder to climb, a drift of sandy earth three feet deep. The Crater opened below him.

"Not here!" he yelled, "farther to the right!" He waved and gestured. Colonel Bates of the Thirtieth turned and looked up. The floor of the Crater was a churning chaos of troops, blacks clumped and whites whirling round them. On the periphery of the black circle Oliver saw a white soldier swing his musket and hit one of the blacks, and they were yelling and swinging, one black man threw his rifle down and punched a white soldier in the back.

"Stop that!" yelled Oliver, and somebody punched him in the side and his breath was knocked right out of him. He fell, breathless, headfirst into the black-white moil of the Crater.

Randolph stood on the parapet helping the others get over. He handed Jethro up last, felt the heaviness of his reluctant body, gave an extra tug, and that was it. He turned and followed Jethro, the company strung out behind Booker.

They ran across the rubble-field, sun hot over the right shoulder, powder scratching at the eyes and throat, a big cloud of black smoke on the left hanging above the hole where the Crater was.

It wasn't at all like his vision, the row of armed people sweeping the field. He lifted and jumped over the broken bodies of dead and wounded men that were scattered across the rubble-field, some crawling back to the lines like crabs. There were bodies of men who had buried their heads in the earth, hands and arms of men like joints of strange meat. The running file bowed to the left to pass by a man who had been torn apart at the hips, a man whose looped and swollen guts had slid half out onto the broken ground.

He looked up from the back of Jethro in front of him and saw, ahead of him, the whole company again, running up to where Booker was waving his sword, and he held that in his eyes and held his head up to do it.

He saw Booker turn toward him, yelling, pointing, and he got it and yelled, "Run over right! Over right! This way!" He saw a clot of blue-black bodies—Oliver's people—sliding left toward the Crater, but he ran around their right, and the company with him.

In front of him there was a regular-looking trench parapet, harder and more shaped than the earth of the furrow at the Crater's edge, with entrances broken through it. Booker stood by one and waved them through.

It seemed quiet here, somehow, as if the parapet gave shade from the bullets and the noise of the bullets.

They worked their way forward, the company following Randolph in file as he went from shelter to shelter: leaping the open slit of a trench (white faces upturned as he jumped over), ducking behind the bulge of a roofed-over bombproof, then sliding around to the right and into the open, catching quick images of Booker, sword pointing ahead. Through the gap, on the other side, cross the slit of the trench that he jumped, the ground was tumbled and littered. Bursts of smoke rose around them, and bullets whipped through the air.

A pit with a man in it: the top of the head broken off like a chopped melon, the lower jaw intact with its small black beard, red tongue, tobacco-yellowed teeth, the top covered by maddened blow-flies in a swarm.

Behind the bulges of ground, lying against the reverse of rebel parapets, behind bushes and broken wagons, there were white soldiers lying, squatting, standing to fire ahead, slumped against each other with the heart's juice spilling out, or not spilling any more and then turning to wax.

Cries for help.

Cries for water.

Cries of ''Nigger!''

Cries of rage.

They came to the last roll of turned earth. The troops were gathering behind it, beginning to take shape as a line. Booker crouched at the right end. At the left, Colonel Hall stood up, and jumped the parapet and the trench on the other side just as Randolph came up. He turned to face the troops, raised his sword, and fell to his knees facing the morning sun, as if he was going to pray. He spat red spray from his lips. Then he fell forward on his face.

The air was full of sound. The express train sound of shells—*bump, snort, huff*—and the *whit, whit* of bullets. And the *punk punk* sound that meant men were hit. The air so full of the zip and buzz and whisper it was like the heart of a beehive.

We just getting shot to pieces here. He looked ahead. There was a black line across the ground in front of him, banked high with smoke, and red flags of the enemy waving above it like tethered kites.

Behind them were the hills. Not forested at all, but open, and the empty blue sky behind them.

That was where they were supposed to go.

Someone jumped the trench behind him—Booker—and grabbed his arm. ''Take em right! Take em right,'' he yelled. ''In line, got it?''

Randolph nodded, and whipped his head left and right to where his company was struggling up out of the trench, and he saw Captain Shugrue start to climb out, miss his grip and fall back. ''B Company this way! B Company!'' he yelled waving, and he lined them out running to the right.

8:05 A.M.

Bruce saw some of their own troops retake one of the trenches from the enemy. They all watched the gray-brown line sweep forward, the dark huddled bodies of the Yankees run back, and Bruce yelled, ''They're going! They won't hold it!'' and Davidson yelled, ''Stand up and fire, dammit!'' and they stood and shot as fast as they could, tearing up the flank of the retreating Yankees as they abandoned their trench. When Bruce looked again their own pink flags were waving over the trench.

The men in the trench were pounding each other on the back, congratulating themselves, as they followed Davidson down to where a brief run in the open took them across to the just-taken line.

There didn't seem to be any more Yankee firing, not here, though shells were landing farther away. They were too close to the Yankee advance here for the Yanks to use their artillery.

"Who's in command here?" shouted Davidson.

"You are, sir," said a Major—Christiansen, of Elliott's staff. "General Elliott's wounded. I've been commanding what I could find of the brigade . . ." and he gestured to the recaptured trench, and the flags.

"Umf," said Davidson. "Well, I'll take command then." He paused, then said quickly, "Good work, Major. We took them in the flank and routed them."

The Major swallowed and said, "Thank you, sir," throwing Bruce a look.

The Old Man will grab whatever credit is left lying about, Bruce thought.

The trench commanded the ground in front of the Crater on the left, or northwest, side. He peered through a slit in the parapet. The Yankees were mobbed down there, ten, fifteen flags waving, and nobody coming forward. There was firing coming from other places, isolated. By God, he thought, if we haven't held them.

Then he saw the flags moving on the left of the Crater, flashing through gaps in the hanging smoke. He yelled for Davidson's attention, and the troops in the trench shifted to fire at the new troops coming up through the broken entrenchments.

Something wrong.

"Niggers!" yelled one of the men.

It was true.

A horde of niggers, white officers with them, came pouring through the gaps in the trench line like ants from a broken nest. *A bad dream coming true,* thought Bruce. His letter to General Lee come to life to haunt him.

"By God! By God!" Davidson was yelling. "This is . . . this is . . . *infamous!*" He was choking with rage. "Kill all of them!" he yelled, his voice cracking. "By God, if you don't kill every last black one of them, I'll kill you myself!"

The men began to shoot, faster and faster, eager. There was a kind of shameful pleasure in it, shooting niggers. Like killing someone's horses or cattle, or burning a barn, a pure anarchic destruction. There was a criminal pleasure to it—the *way some cracker would feel,* Bruce thought, *raping some nigger wench and damn whoever is looking on.*

He aimed and shot, aimed and shot again. You could see the black bodies falling. The men in the trench gave little yips when they hit someone.

There was a line of rebels ahead of them. Booker had seen the smoke rising from a line in the earth fifty yards away when he'd crouched behind the parapet. How many rebs in it? A couple of regiments, maybe. The Forty-third had started with 350 men. If he didn't charge the line, they'd be shot to pieces right here. There wasn't room for the other regiments to deploy, as they came up through the tangle of broken trenches, bombproofs, wreckage, and the fragments of Potter's division that lay under cover and volleyed back at the rebs.

There was only one way out, and he took it; waved Randolph to spread the men rightward, sending them running in file down the line between the two fires, Potter's men and the rebels, two lines of white men shooting as black men ran between them, mad orgiastic shooting, the whole shape of sides and allegiances hopelessly mixed.

He watched his men run, his men, saw them twitch, stumble, roll, break, and fall, as the bullets from both sides punched at them, nibbled at them. His body twitched involuntarily in sympathy as the bullets made the line quiver, as if his extended arm were being struck.

The air was horribly alive with bullets, the whole earth and air was crawling with deadliness. It had bit Colonel Hall and thrown him down in the dirt; Bates was stuck in the Crater; and Oliver was swallowed up somewhere. Other troops were coming up, but so far as he could tell, he was the only field officer at the head of the brigade. Booker swung on the balance-point of his fear, an acrobat perched on the point of spear. As sure as he knew himself, there was death for him here, his body splitting open and darkness washing his brain, all of it gone—Miriam, Eli, Wolf's Brother, the Crow woman, Randolph, father, mother, memory of grandfather, St. Louis, Berlin, the high mountain pass where the air came up out of the valley and he saw the village the first time.

His heart pulsed hard, and he threw all that away, and gave it to death, beckoning it with a wave of his arm; Randolph came running toward him, and he looked behind him.

Let us see, is it real, this life we are living.

And saw that the line was in place, turned to the fire and waiting, blackfaced, menacing, ready to go.

Tobe stood next to Jethro. Tobe was very quiet. He'd been named, but hadn't been called as yet. Till the call came there was a charm laid on him.

Jethro's face was panicky, and Tobe said (you couldn't hear him for the noise, but his lips moved and the meaning was clear to Jethro), "It ain't yet. It ain't no use to hide when it come." Jethro, in agony, twisted his face to the front, and stood.

Booker waved, and Randolph ran to him. The two stood flanking the color-bearer's red-striped banner in the stark sunlight. Booker's sword flashed in the light and they ran forward, all in a line, some falling, some lying down, but most running, running on together across the field, their black shadows running ahead of them. Their bayonetted rifles cut shadows that looked like long black spears.

Hurrrrraaaaaah!

Lost in the shooting, Bruce hadn't noticed that the niggers never stopped shifting to his left, always to his left. The movement seemed natural, like the running of a deer or rabbit across a field. He never tried to interpret it, but suddenly—the moving line of niggers stopped, and stood.

Then it started to come forward.

Bruce felt his blood leap into his chest and throat, his muscles rigid with tension.

The rebels paused in shooting, then started again. The pitch was high, frantic, ragged, and Bruce saw the black-face line sweeping forward onto the flank, and knew that his men were letting go, were going to break and fall apart and run, run for their lives with a horde of maddened niggers baying down their trail.

The flag-bearer fell away at Randolph's left hand, and he and Booker ran a footrace and neck-and-neck for the line of smoke and fire ahead.

Through the banked smoke Randolph saw the shape of the distant hill, and he yelled in triumph—he was invulnerable. His legs gathered and surged him past Booker, and he saw the red flags waving at the center of the smoke, coming closer. He knew that the door was right there. The smoke engulfed him. His finger pointed and jerked the pistol trigger in reflex at the shapes in the smoke.

There was a roar in his right ear, fire scorched his face, a shape, he pointed the pistol and shot again, his arm jolting with the shock. The ground fell away, and he tumbled into the trench, bumped, fallen-on.

He pushed something off his back and saw the sunlight on the pale face of a white man—boy—sandy hair, blue eyes, a mole on his chin. His hand pointed his pistol and the boy's face exploded.

In the next instant the trench was full of people, yelling, crying, shooting rifles. Someone was clubbing a shape on the ground. A white hand—Shugrue—where the hell was he before?—snatched the man away. The trench was dark with black men in blue uniforms, pushing, pressing. There were white men lying on the floor, and black men too; white man rolling around with his hands over his face while Jethro stuck him in the belly with his long bayonet. The man's white hands grabbed the rifle barrel, and he turned slowly against the stabbing iron.

"Don't kill the prisoners!"

It was Booker's voice. Randolph got up. He held a rebel battle flag in his hand, and yelled, "Praise Jesus, and look here! Never mind that trash, look here!" The flag jerked as bullets tugged and pulled at it.

Booker's face was close to his, grinning, yelling something he couldn't understand. Happy! Pounding him on the back. The troops surged back and forth in the trenches.

The sound of firing was less. The rebels who had escaped were firing, but there weren't too many. There were lots of prisoners in the trench. Some stood where a low place in the trench made it safe. Some sat on the ground, heads between their knees, like they were sick to death.

More white men kept coming down the trench, down the gauntlet of black men yelling and laughing and pushing. Their faces seemed very pale and white. "Hands up!" someone was yelling. Some of the white men had put their hands on their heads; others held them up shoulder-high, hands dangling limp; one man had them stiff and high in an excess of zealous compliance. A man with a bloody shoulder held his other hand high.

"Got to take this buckra trash back to the lines," said Randolph.

Tobe smiled quietly and said, "Maybe we try and sell em South, or down Cuba," and everybody laughed.

They kept milling around, laughing, high and nervous, jittering. Couldn't believe the taste of victory. The dull faces of the buckra prisoners—they had caught the whole damn pateroll this time. *"Whoo-ee!"* said Randolph. "I have a thirst." He opened his canteen, and took a sip. There was a white man next to him, a big cut along the right side of his face. Blood kept oozing into the man's right eye, stiffening there. He moistened a finger with spit to wipe it clear.

Randolph took the edge of his neckerchief, and tipped some water from the canteen onto it. He reached over, and dabbed softly at the corner of the eye.

"Obliged," said the man, hoarsely.

"You be all right," said Randolph, and the man nodded.

Tobe took a swig out of his canteen, and passed it to a prisoner. The man took it, sipped, and handed it back. Tobe corked it.

Four big shells boomed up a wall of dirt and rained it into the trench. The distant hill was topped with smoke, and jets of black smoke spurted out of the intervening ground where the rebels they had run off had taken cover. Randolph's heart felt like it had begun to churn and glow inside him. His legs felt sore from the charge, felt like they had begun to go cold and stiff on him. All around him his men were sitting down, hunkering down away from the shells and bullets or just feeling they had run the strings of their legs all loose. "Get up there!" he snapped, "Get off your butt their! Ain't but halfway there. *Crouch* down, dammit! Don't *lie* down. Nobody takin a nap!" *Why didn't they get on going?* His legs wanted him to just give out, but he wouldn't give in till he had done what was set before him. *Damn those shiftless, white . . . just let us get on up there before the day gone.*

Down at the far end of the trench he saw Booker poking his head up, craning around. Except for Shugrue, who was sitting spraddle-legged on the floor of the trench, he was the only white officer in sight. Behind their trench the other regiments of their brigade seemed to be coming forward slowly over the disordered ground, lines of men, clumps, sometimes a platoon in column. Behind them, closer to the first line of rebel trenches they had come through, other troops were shifting past them and to the right of their advance. Some of the white troops whose remnants they had passed through got up to join the advancing black companies. Most didn't. Nobody seemed to be ordering or directing these shifts and rushes of men. They seemed to move or stay still or dodge sideways according to their own impulses and the chances of the ground.

SIGNAL STATION
July 30, 1864—8:30 A.M.

General BURNSIDE:
Troops are being concentrated in rear of the works blown up. The colored regiments have gained the same position. I can see ten regimental flags on the destroyed work, others to the

right and left. The rebels still hold their rifle-works on our left, but will soon have to evacuate or be taken prisoners. The position looks very encouraging, if they but push along. There is but one line of rifle-pits in our immediate front, and that does not extend more than 200 yards. The main work has been taken, which was the blown-up fort.

J. C. PAINE,
Captain and Signal Officer.

8:30 A.M.

Even after they had been ordered to attack, it had taken Colonel Thomas and Lieutenant Pennington an eternity to get their men up and over the parapet on the improvised bayonet-ladders. Oliver's brigade had gone on ahead of them, and as they hurried along across the front of the Crater they could see the rearmost regiment of that brigade huddling up against the reverse of the rebel parapets and the hump of earth at the Crater's lip, covering up while they waited their chance to go forward through the jam-up. They heard the shooting burst up suddenly, and cheers, and Pennington wondered if some part of Oliver's brigade might actually be going into action that very minute, and he almost involuntarily jerked his stride out longer, racing to catch up, nearly passing Colonel Thomas in his eagerness. Behind them the brigade, a disorderly file grouped by companies, tailed along the front of the parapet of the main rebel line. Thomas gestured. "Get ahead," he panted. "Find gap through parapet. Look for big smoke bank. We must be to right of it." He shook his head. "Too crowded otherwise. Understand?"

Chris nodded and ran ahead. There was a low place where a shell, probably, had chewed off a bit from the top of the parapet. Chris scrambled over and through it. He looked and saw the smoke bank to his left. Something snatched his hat, plucked at his sleeve.

Bullet, he thought.

Froze. A second. Paralysis.

Then dropped. He got sand on his lips and tongue, and spat, spat to clear it. He'd almost tasted the darkness then. Stupid! Stupid thing!

He turned, dropped back outside. Waved to Thomas. Looking back, he could see the brigade coming on, framed in dirt-brown blasts that had in an instant the shape of brown autumn trees, maples without color full of black clumps—seedpods, bodies—before they dropped away.

Thomas's face was close to his. The bright blue eyes had deep wrinkles in the corners, the pink smooth cheeks were flushed. He gripped Chris's biceps sharply, tenderly. Making sure of him.

Then he pointed, and the two of them went first through the gap in the parapet. They scrambled through, leaped a trench. The field in front of them was littered and cut and full of smoke and men. Thomas paused, and pointed. At the tip of his finger there was a small clear point, a place where there seemed to be a patch of smooth ground, and no men or bulky humps or cuts or bursts of smoke. There. That was the place. A clear lit space at the end of the terrible corridor. They were going there.

8:30 A.M. *1st Division Bombproof*

Ferrero, standing in the front line of trenches, peering through a slit in the parapet, unconsciously wrung his hands, and craned his neck to see. Below him and to his left he could sense the presence of General Ledlie. Such a friendly man, he had seemed, when Ferrero had come to him earlier in the morning, feeling cast adrift: a warm handshake, good smile, hospitality. But he was growing to loathe and fear the man's presence, that blank stare and continual grin. Ledlie seemed to dog him. Perversely, it seemed that Ledlie—who had been his own comforter in those hours of horrid vagueness and detachment this morning—now sought his company, his comfort. Ferrero's loathing for the man now filled him with guilt: Ledlie must be feeling something like what he had felt, shame and the disapproval of his superiors. The First Division had done badly, despite Ledlie's orders.

Yet there was something wrong, something wrong with the man. Something horrible.

The last of Thomas's brigade was climbing out of the trenches to go forward. He wanted to follow them. Ledlie had said, "Don't go up with the troops. Better to stay here, where the staff officers can find you easily." That made sense. It was a General's responsibility to command, a luxury to lead the charge. Burnside had tried to teach him that. . . .

Oh, but to throw it all away, and go in with the men! And leave this horrible Ledlie behind!

He hesitated. The last of his troops passed out of sight through a gap in the parapet.

He turned, looked down at Ledlie. "I'm going up," he said suddenly, on impulse.

"No!" said Ledlie. "That's not a good idea!" The words were banal: but the intensity and the sudden intensification of the staring eyes! Ferrero was torn, pulled by them, disoriented. He wrenched himself away, turned to the slit in the parapet.

It was blank. Filled with smoke.

For a moment Ferrero wobbled, disoriented, off balance. *Which way? Which way did they go?*

Then he grabbed the sides of the slit with both hands, and thrust with his feet hauled with his arms to push himself through.

He stood outside. *They must have gone to the right.* Captain Hicks came up behind him. The two began to trot after the brigade to the right. Drifting smoke and the whine of bullets filled the air. An invisible, palpable barrier, a fog more than a fog of smoke and noise, seemed to hang between Ferrero and the vanishing tail of the brigade.

It began to seem pointless to keep running, stumbling after. Ferrero felt he looked ridiculous, thumping clumsily along like this, as if he were a dull schoolboy chasing futilely after swifter, keener children who ignored him and ran off. He halted, and Hicks did too, looking up perplexedly.

The division was gone, taken from him finally and forever. He'd never really understood it. They'd never really given it to him in one piece for him to command. Wasn't it only yesterday he'd been in Washington, seeing the minstrels, the division a dream? His fingers were the vague fingers of a dreamer, turning to mud as they reached to grasp a nameless wish. The face of Ledlie was more present and real than his chimerical division. Ledlie: a friendly face, concerned, sympathetic. *Warned me it was useless to come out here.* Perhaps Ledlie was right, a General's place was at headquarters, not out here in the smoke and confusion. If he were needed, they would know where to find him. If he were needed.

He turned to Hicks. "Go forward and find Colonel Thomas," said Ferrero, scribbling a message in his notebook, tearing the sheet loose. "Tell him he must continue the advance, until we have carried the hill."

"Yes, sir," said Hicks, taking the paper; and then he vanished, and Ferrero was alone with the smoke, the thundering detonations of the guns, the shadowy hulks of squads of men—not his men, no concern of his—that hurried forward and hurried to the rear.

Ferrero dropped back into the trench, and a bunch of hurrying men bumped him hard and pushed him against the front wall. He was out of reckoning—had come back in somewhere up the line from where the division had debouched, an anonymous section of trench cut off by turns either way he looked. He began working his way through it, fighting the surging, mindless pulses of troops in the narrow trench that seemed always blocking his way. It did not occur to him to climb out of the trench now that he had found a road that was so clearly bounded and marked.

8:30 A.M.

Randolph had kept himself wrung up tight, ready to go, still ready, ready while the sun climbed and grew stronger and began to load the heat more heavily on their backs. But his flesh weakened in spite of his strong will, and he leaned and let the earth of the trench take a little more and a little more of his weight, a little more of that juice that keeps the muscles supple on the bones and ready to go.

Then he heard Booker's voice, calling him, and he had to gather it back all of a sudden, pull himself out of the ground to rise and answer.

Booker's face was gray. "Sergeant-Major, I want you to take these captured flags and the prisoners back to headquarters. Captain Shugrue will go with you, and the rest of our walking wounded."

His weakness controlled him, made him cry out, "No! I won't!" with misery in his voice instead of power—and Randolph's anger flashed against Booker but also against himself.

"It's an order, Sergeant-Major," Booker repeated his title.

"We ain't taken the hill yet." Randolph heard his voice as half-strangled. He wanted to defy this man that was ruining them, but he'd let the misery show and his tangled feelings made the words come out plaintively.

Booker stared intently at Randolph, searching his eyes. "We can't take the hill . . ."

"Damn fool white man!" Randolph exploded. "Can't you just let me *go?*"

"Take them back to headquarters," Booker pleaded. "Show them these prisoners, the flags we took—you took—the regiment took. Show them."

"Show them! We show them that hill when we take it!" Randolph glared Booker eye for eye. The white man looked sick, and that made him wonder. "What you doin', Booker? You just want me out of the way?"

Booker waved his hands around at the troops milling in the trenches, the men crowding up through the broken ground behind, the fragments of Potter's division. "This lot isn't going up any hill. Not soon. Not unless somebody gets up here and pulls the rest of these troops together, and gets us some support. Tell them: show them the flags and the prisoners, and then tell them."

Randolph grinned, without mirth. "And they'll say, 'Thank you, nigger,' and do as I say."

Booker's dirty face reddened. "You're going, Sergeant," said Booker. "It's an order."

Randolph hesitated. Something said to him that this was necessary, an obscure prophecy working its way to the light. He would not say his "No!" to Booker here and now. The time had not come round for that.

"Yes, sir."

There were fifteen men in the party Shugrue led back from the captured rebel trench, guarding the prisoners—almost two hundred—and carrying two rebel flags and one recaptured Union flag. They were cheered as they came back through the ranks of the other regiments of the First Brigade, which were still struggling up toward the front through the tangle of trenches and the fragmented lines of the white troops who had charged before them.

Back further, they passed places where the advance had clogged and stopped, the black troops mixed with companies and squads of whites, the two groups sitting uneasily side-by-side in silence—till the detail came by with the prisoners, and then the blacks cheered, and the whites watched with interest.

Still farther back, where the old rebel front line ran, the big trench was full of white soldiers who watched, silently, as Shugrue led the file across.

Randolph walked at the rear. The bullets still whispered overhead, none of them speaking for him. After they had passed through the gap in the main line, a runner from Shugrue summoned him to the point.

The line of prisoners and guards knelt in the shelter of the rebel parapet. For a second, Randolph saw a vivid picture of the scene on the landing at City Point: the gray warehouse, dead-fish smell, hot sun, white soldiers sitting in the shade, his own men in the sunlight guarding them. Recruits, *huh!*

Shugrue was talking to him, asking him the best way to get back across the rubble-field to their own lines. His eyes narrowed, and he watched the field carefully. The tag end of the Second Brigade was still moving up, shifting in front of them and moving toward their left as they looked back toward their own lines. Shells were landing there, chewing up the ground. The bursts blossomed in the crowd, picking up men and tossing them in the air. It hadn't been this bad where they started out.

He leaned across Shugrue and pointed to their right. "Go 'long the side this trench here, and back across the back of the Hole. Cut back to the line further over there. By the big rock standing there, maybe."

Shugrue licked his lips and nodded. He didn't speak. He gestured, jerkily, for Randolph to take the lead. When Randolph grinned at him, the nigger's face reminded him of the face of a crocodile.

Randolph whistled, and waved his arm, and began running along the parapet at a crouch. Shugrue followed. Behind him he heard the rest of the detail, the prisoners, coming on.

Moving by fits and starts, Randolph led the way across the back of the Crater. The high drift of crumbled earth was a kind of parapet. Better, nobody seemed to be shooting at them: aiming for the Big Hole, for the lines of troops moving up the opposite way; for a gun that some white soldiers had got set up right near the big boulder.

Randolph dashed forward, crouched over, till he judged the file behind him was all protected by the earth mound of the Crater. He looked ahead to the left. At intervals, a shell-boom blossomed in the field. No bunches. Like one man shooting one shell at a time. Canister: you could hear the *whizz*. He had it now. Watch for the canister gun to go *bang*. It does, then you send em rushing across, one man and a dozen or so Johnny prisoners with him.

He turned and looked at Shugrue. The white man had the face of a sick dog. *White man.*

"Go long up past that gun there: bout a hundred long steps. Lie down en wait." No damn *Captn* for this trash.

Randolph moved back along the line of crouching men. "Follow the man up to where he stop. Give a wait—two-three-four breaths, then follow. Like quail covey." He looked at the buckra prisoners and laughed. "You de chicks, these the old black hens here. Follow good you don't get hurt." Repeating it, varying it, down the line.

Shugrue must have started, for he felt the third group rush away behind him as he moved patiently down the line. *Damn white man in a hurry.*

On the other side of the abandoned cannon, Randolph ran the length of the line of prisoners and men, to where Shugrue lay, half-leaning against the drifted earth at the lip of the Crater. Ahead and to his left, Randolph marked the burst of the canister shell, and saw a group of men tumble and fall as the musket balls in the shell came scything across the field.

Shugrue held his right hand on the ankle of his right boot.

"Sprained it," he said, with an exaggerated wince. "You'd best take them across." Randolph stared at him. "I'll follow if I can."

Without saying anything, Randolph turned. He watched the field. The canister shell burst in the middle of his field of vision. "Now!" he yelled, and the first group started across, sprinting, running low, and he watched carefully as they went, dodging round things, across the field.

"Get ready!" he said. "Head a bit to the left." The canister went *bang,* in the rear of the first group as they came up to the lines. "Go!" he said to the next group.

When Randolph left, running with the last group, Shugrue let them get halfway across. Then, satisfied he had done his duty, he turned, crawled over the lip of broken earth and slid down into the Crater.

July 30, 1864—8:30 A.M.

General BURNSIDE:
Humphrey succeeded in forcing the rebel pits to the left of the crater. Is now working still farther to the left . . . with the left portion of his brigade. I supposed Warren would attack, but of course without authority for thinking so. Hartranft is in same pits with Fourth Division.

O. B. WILLCOX,
Brigadier-General.

The rebel gunners picked up Thomas's brigade as it swept around to the right of the Union advance, and came forward through the wreckage of Potter's division, files like schools of fish blindly fixed on the purposeful advance of their flags. The commander of the rebel battery north of the Crater did not know the names or the character of the units in front of him, but he knew his business. He called to his men to shift their aim to punish this new forward lunge of the enemy, to break up these new troops before they could organize for a rush. He had been doing this successfully all day, first pounding the vanguard of Potter's division as it had come on to the north of the Crater, till its fragments had halted, taken shelter, exchanged the attack for a sluggish and sullen returning of fire. Then there had been the sudden surge up closer to the Crater's edge, where Oliver's brigade had come forward, and the battery commander had elevated his guns to harass, slow, halt that attack, keeping it from sweeping the open ground between the Crater and the hill. The Yankees had gained some ground, but it didn't look as if they had sufficient mass and momentum to go farther.

And now these new troops: lower the elevation, lead them a bit, hit the forward elements—that's where the commanders will be. There was no trouble left in Potter's troops below his position; there was no trouble by the humped-up earth of the Crater—confused masses of dark-clad men surged backward and forward there, where the elements of Ledlie's men who had gone beyond the Crater clashed with the troops trying to get forward to the attack.

Far off beyond the Crater to the south, the battery commander could see nothing—only a thick rise of smoke that marked the place where Willcox's division had been halted in its advance, and where Johnson's reserves were mounting a counterattack.

It might well be that the Yankees would keep sending men forward like this, packing them in so that dead or alive the ground would not contain them, and they would burst the thin line of infantry, and come up here and capture or wreck his gun. But it was his business to keep shooting at whatever looked most threatening, as long as his orders and his ammunition held out—and he had plenty of ammunition, and the orders hadn't changed. He watched the effect of his fire on the new troops, saw them duck and tumble, files burst apart and vanish, and those that remained still coming on behind their flags. *Even shooting well,* he thought, *you never can kill them all.*

8:45 A.M.

Pennington ducked behind the dome of a rebel bombproof and sprawled flat. *"Drink!"* whispered a hoarse voice, and his heart banged. Chris hadn't seen him. The man's uniform was so covered with dirt as to be unrecognizable. His left eye hung by a string down onto his face, and it jiggled as he talked. Chris stared at him. "Drink," said the man.

"No!" Chris cried out, and raised his hand in reflexive denial of the horror.

He felt a strong hand on his shoulder, and turned. Colonel Thomas. "Yes?" he said. His voice seemed to come from another place than his own throat. His own throat was full of dust.

"We have orders to attack from General Burnside. Ross's regiment is up and in line."

Chris nodded. The Colonel's blue eyes were strange; they seemed to glow.

"Stay with me." Thomas spoke with a peculiar earnestness, and the phrase kept repeating in Chris's head.

They ran forward, at a crouch, and jumped into a small communication trench that cut across the front here. The black bodies of the Thirty-first Regiment were packed in to left and right, but Chris could not smell their familiar black smell, only the prickle-smell of the powder smoke.

"When I give the order," said the Colonel in a loud voice, "we're going to charge."

The blacks jerked their heads up, looking at each other, at the trench. This was it. They were going to make their charge. They were in the clear space they had been seeking. So long getting here. The blowing smoke was all that stood between them and what they sought. Chris felt his chest swell and fill with fire. Now at last, now at last it was going to happen. It was going to burst out.

Thomas blew his whistle, a piercing shriek.

It shot like a flash of electricity into Chris's head. The air was full of sound. Black faces rose out of the ground, yelling. The air was singing. The commander of the 31st leapt onto the parapet and yelled. Then he turned, and twisted slowly in a contortion that was strange for its twistedness, the slowness showing the care of a man sitting carefully down in a bad place. Chris scrambled over the parapet with the mob. Someone bumped into him and he fell by the lip of the trench. Colonel Thomas leaned over him. The heavy weight of his chest pressed on Chris's side, and he gripped Chris's chin hard in his smooth hand, and turned Chris's face to his own. The pink lips in the smooth brown beard were very close. He could smell the tobacco on the Colonel's breath, sour-sweet.

"Stay with me!" the Colonel yelled.

Then he rolled away, and Chris saw him scramble back to the trench. *Oh no,* something cried in his head, *don't go back now!*

A great black bubble of rage and despair rose in his chest and strangled in his throat. His hand fell on a staff. The brigade guidon. Corporal Smith's dead black hand with its peculiar pink nails held it limply.

All of these things were exactly as they should be. The strangling hand on Chris's throat let go, breath surged in and out, his mind was full of a terrible rapture, the bullets were singing to him and plucking him by the sleeve, impatient. His left hand grabbed the staff. His right hand found the hilt of his sword. His legs gathered under him, and shot his body straight up in the air almost in a leap. And he cried:

"Charge! Charge! Thirty-first Colored! Charge! Charge! Charge!"

Thomas, lying at the bottom of the trench, heard the boy's voice crying for the charge. He had told Chris to follow, he had been certain that Chris was right behind him, close as his own shadow. "NO!" he cried. "No! No!"

"Look!" yelled a black voice.

Pennington was running along in front of the trench, the brigade guidon fluttering from the broken staff in his left hand, the sword in his right hand flashing in circles as he ran along the face of the line. Behind him, a shadow trying to follow the fleeting body, black figures bulged up out of the trenches.

Thomas saw the bullets pluck at Chris's sleeve, annoy, pluck, pinch, sting, begin to bite; he heard the crack like a tree limb breaking and saw Chris's head vibrate on the thin pale neck like a child's jump-up toy knocked over and snapping up; and the bloom of blood. "NO!" he cried. "No! No! No!" Chris was dancing in the air. The bullets would not let him fall down, plucking, biting, biting; he danced in the air, twirling round incredibly round and round and round.

Thomas had buried his face in the soft earth of the trench side. Not all the thickness of that earth could keep the vision away.

Time passed.

Someone pulled him by the sleeve—Hicks, Ferrero's aide, with a note: "Colonels Oliver and Thomas: If you have not already done so, you will immediately proceed to take the crest in your front. Edw. Ferrero, Brig. Gen. Commanding Fourth Division."

Thomas looked at Hicks. He looked at Major Van Buren. He felt very calm, but he found that he was weeping, his face flooded with tears. They made everything waver and shimmer.

A courier rode up to General Johnson, who sat on his horse in the shade of the small grove of trees. In front of him the General could observe three lines of his men, brown uniforms blending with the brown soil. Smoke rose from the farthest line; the other two waited quietly. When he raised his field glasses, he could distinguish the men in the first line clearly. Their limbs jerked spasmodically as they rammed cartridges into musket barrels. Raising the glasses, he could see the line of smoke that marked the line of the Yankee advance to the Confederate right of the Crater. Occasionally through the smoke he could see bluecoats running this way and that. The direction was impossible to establish. The Yankees were disorganized, yes, but just when it seemed that their spastic lunges and heaves were beginning to loosen and drift backward, here would come formed troops, attacking furiously until halted by the artillery fire, or troops in the confused maze of trenches.

He raised the glasses, and swung them to his left. The ridge line danced into view. Clouds marked the line of the sixteen-gun battery, firing down toward the Crater.

He could not see Mahone's flags, but he knew they must be near the battery by now. That was what this courier was coming to tell him. That Mahone's men would soon be forming behind the crest, and moving down into the ravine below, ready to fall upon the Yankee right.

"Colonel," said General Johnson, "I'll ask you to move your troops forward directly. You'll take the two left regiments of the first line, and one from reserve—Twenty-third South Carolina, Fifty-ninth Virginia, Twenty-sixth Virginia. Leave the Twenty-second South Carolina to hold your first line, and the Forty-sixth Virginia behind your front as a reserve." He intoned the names of the regiments with a certain portentousness. Each consisted of only two or three companies. He pointed, and the Colonel turned to look. "You'll move forward at an oblique angle to the right, and drive those advanced troops back toward the Crater. I judge they're about ready to be driven." The courier from Mahone rode up and jerked his horse to a halt, but Johnson held up a hand for silence. "I've sent a courier to whatever officer commands that skirmish line across the front of the Crater. Perhaps your left can connect with his right. In any case, if he's gotten my orders, he'll move up on your flank when you go in. Questions?"

"No, sir."

"Thank you, Colonel."

"Sir," said the courier, "General Mahone sends . . ."

"Yes," said Johnson absent-mindedly, "I know."

Below the two men, the Colonel had reached the first and most distant of the three lines. The puffs of smoke ceased to burst from this line. Johnson raised his glasses. As if at that signal, the first two lines rose out of the ground, and began to rush forward. The sound of their yelling drifted back, strangely disembodied and disconnected to Johnson's ears. As he looked at them through the field glasses, they seemed to vanish in absolute silence down a long black tunnel to a circle full of fire and smoke.

9:00 A.M.

Randolph herded his prisoners into the covered way, and around to the reverse of the fourteen-gun battery, where he recognized the head-quarters flag.

"Holy Jesus," cursed a white staff officer, as Randolph marched up to the door.

"Look at this," called a voice from inside, "look what this nigger caught!"

White faces appeared at the door. Randolph walked up, and stood facing them.

They saw a short black man, a real blue-gum nigger, with short legs and an ass like a shelf: standing there, weirdly, like a monster dropped from the moon, with his yellow eyes glittering.

He saw their pale faces and sprouts of dark beard, the quivering jowls of red-faced Burnside towering in the back.

"Come in," somebody said, and they stepped back, and Randolph walked in, followed by the two soldiers carrying the rebel flags and the recaptured Union flag. Outside, some white provost guards began march-ing the prisoners off to the rear.

Randolph stood at rigid attention. "Sir, Sergeant-Major Randolph, Forty-third Regiment, United States Colored Troops, reporting. With two hundred rebel prisoners of war, and two colors captured. Also a flag of our own, recaptured. And reporting we captured a rebel trench, out to the right of the Crater. Hundred, hundred-fifty yards, the Major told me to say." He handed Booker's dispatch to the General.

His vision was clearing, he could see them all now. Burnside was rubbing his thick hands together, the way Masr Hewson used to do after his dinner. And looking off away just so, just the way Hewson used to look so as not to have to see the niggers fetching his brandy and cleaning up his leavings. His big red face looked happy, looked fat; but then again there was a boiled look to it, like the General was angry about something, getting ready to climb up on his anger and start thrashing down all around him. "Thank you very much, Sergeant-Major," said Burnside, looking everywhere but at Randolph, "you can turn your prisoners over to the provost and . . . get some refreshment. Go on now, go on. Wait outside there," and he brushed Randolph away with back-handed movements of his thick hands.

"Sanderson!" called the voice of General Burnside. "Why don't you wire *that* to General Meade, eh? Don't want to be the bearer of good tidings? Why don't you just ask him, what does he think of my niggers *now?*"

"I've already telegraphed . . ." replied a voice, and Randolph could hear the muttering rise and fall as the white men bickered behind him. Outside the sun was strong. Back here behind the battery you didn't hear the shooting so clearly. There were gangs of men going back down the covered way or drifting over the open ground all the time. His men looked up at him. He shrugged and sat down outside the door of the bombproof. There was nothing anywhere to tell him what to do, no orders, no sign. He was thirsty, so he sent a detail to fill all of the canteens they could find.

A white officer came out of the bombproof, hurrying stiff-legged. Randolph gathered his weary legs, reflexively rising to stand and salute the man, but the officer stalked by him with only a sharp dismissive glance, and as he did Randolph recognized the face of the Captain who had sneered at his men that day when they picked up the bounty-jumpers down by the docks.

Damn hot sun must be making me stupid, thought Randolph. What was he doing, waiting outside the door like a lazy house nigger hoping the bell wouldn't ring? Was that what Booker had had in mind for him? Well, he'd seen and done all he needed to back here. Maybe they'd send up supports, and maybe they'd go on out and take charge, like Booker had asked for them to do. But these Generals looked like the kind to stay indoors with cotton to make. Anyway, none of these Generals was going to listen to any nigger sergeant tell them what to do. There was a call to him from the place where his people were fighting, getting killed, killing Johnny. That was the place to be.

The men with the canteens returned. Behind him, where the battle was, he could hear things heating up. He threw a glance at the bombproof and said, "Let's git."

The men sloshed as they walked carrying eight–ten canteens apiece. They followed him round the left of the battery, heading back toward where his old-time acquaintance, the one canister-shooting gun, was marking the time. He'd get across that field the same way he done before. Just as they turned the corner and dropped into the trench he caught a glimpse of the ground he'd have to cross: the rubble-field was full of white faces coming back from the Crater, coming back by tens and dozens, running in little jerks or just walking back with their faces calm and set. "Look like buckra through working this day. Git along, children, it's a long time till supper."

9:00 A.M. *Meade's Headquarters*

The tension at headquarters was piling up like the heat, a weight oppressing breath and movement. The staff was silent. The distant monotonous thunder of the artillery promised no break at all. The brief electric flash of anger when Burnside's insubordinate dispatch came in was a transitory relief. They listened avidly to the telegraph, unconsciously hoping for another such release, remembering the outburst almost with longing. But the flies buzzed persistently around the lips of the standing horses, and the telegraph chirped on mindlessly, like a cricket.

Meade and Humphreys sat in the shade of the headquarters marquee, the pile of dispatches in front of them periodically increasing.

Grant sat at the other end of the table, looking over copies of the dispatches, whittling carefully on a piece of pine.

"Warren wants you to come forward and take charge," said Humphreys.

"I've already told *him* why I can't," snapped Meade. They could not help taking a quick look over at Grant. "Warren has sufficient orders for the case—if he sees an opening he is to attack." He went on *sotto voce*. "If he can't use that much initiative, what sort of excuse does he have for wanting to command the army?"

New dispatches dropped on the pile with a pat.

Humphreys's face screwed up with careful thought, he had something to say but was reluctant.

Grant's voiceless presence, his detachment, seemed to imply his leaving matters to them. But he was always there, an audience to which Humphreys and Meade found themsleves playing. Their conversation had a stilted, histrionic quality; they did not so much confer with each other as speak stage whispers, listening anxiously all the while to the audience, which might or might not be attending, might or might not be finding fault. And it was hard enough to talk to Meade alone these days, with his temper primed for firing at anything that moved. "Perhaps . . . if you went forward, you might . . ."

"You? You too? Another damn nervous old woman like our precious General Warren?" Meade gripped a sheaf of telegrams in a talon and shook them at Humphreys. "I have enough *here* to know that things are not going well for General Burnside. Because he's been lying to me, and he's been trying to hide behind a lot of dust about army politics—and that's what Burnside does when he's in trouble. And when Warren's having trouble he won't do anything. As far as I can tell, the Ninth Corps *still* hasn't gone forward. . . ."

"What time is it?" asked Grant quietly, and the two generals realized with a start that they had missed the whispering sound of his whittling for some minutes now. Had he been listening closely? Meade gnawed a bit of his mustache, and Humphreys answered, brushing dust from his freshly sponged coat with small fastidious gestures. "Five past nine o'clock, General. Four hours since the Mine went off." Though his pulses were still thick with the jolt of surprise he had felt, Humphreys actually felt a peculiar relief. Grant had spoken at last. He was no longer sitting at the other end of the table, hunched over himself like a malevolent Buddha listening and judging. Now the audience would join the players on the stage.

Meade spoke. "The attack has probably failed, if Burnside has gotten no further than his last dispatch indicates." Meade was trying very hard not to look over at Grant, to keep his eyes on the papers before him, the maps and dispatches. Humphreys wondered, *Did he hide his eyes from Grant so that the General would not see how much Meade wished to have the burden of this decision taken from his shoulders, the decision of calling off the attack as a failure? And yet, how Meade would hate the relinquishment of command that would come with Grant's intervention and judgment! He would be hating Grant now, resenting Grant's aversion of his eyes but fearing the steady stare that would force Meade to drop his gaze, to answer questions, to acknowledge superior power.*

The pull was too strong. Meade looked at Grant. "It's still barely possible, of course, that he will succeed. . . ."

"I'll need copies of those dispatches for my files," said Grant. He shifted the dead cigar from left to right in his mouth without touching it. His small square hands were laid on the table before him, as still as those of a dead man. "You might want to go forward and take a look for yourself," he said.

Meade's eyes flicked rapidly round the headquarters tent, touching Humphreys, the couriers, the cavalry escort, the banks of telegraphers. *A bankrupt farmer whose goods were up for auction*, thought Humphreys. *Grant was the banker*. Was that an order Grant had given? A suggestion? Or just an inquiry to which no real importance was attached? Meade cleared his throat and said crisply, "No, General, I think it's best I stay here. It will cause too much confusion if I shift now. All the corps commanders have been told to report to me here." He paused. "Unless, sir, you wish to order me forward."

There was a quiet moment, in which the distant shooting could be heard, and the chatter and laughter of the escort.

Grant shrugged, and picked up his knife and stick. "As you prefer, General."

Meade looked at Humphreys, his eyes glittering. Grant had not taken the battle away from him. It seemed to fill Meade with energy. "As I see it, then, the attack has probably failed. If Burnside has wrecked it, it's better for us to call it off now and get the men back to the lines. You do more harm persisting in these attacks after the first rush has failed than if you give them up before the enemy recover their wits. Keep it up and you only pad the butcher's bill. Don't you agree, General?" There was a twinkle of sprightly malice in Meade's eye: they all knew he was referring to Grant's error in persisting in the assault at Cold Harbor after the failure of his first surprise attack.

Grant nodded and said, "Yes. That's a good idea."

Meade leaned back, relieved of some of his load of spite and anger, feeling the least bit Olympian. "We'll wait a little longer and be sure."

Once the word "failure" had been uttered, the fact itself did not seem so horrible. They had suffered reverses before. This would not be as costly as some others Meade could think of. And it was not a failure that could fairly be laid at his door. Too bad about wasting the Mine, but still they might try something further on the left, swing Hancock's troops around behind Sheridan's cavalry and go for the Weldon Railroad again. Meade was framing a suggestion to offer Grant should the right moment appear, when an orderly handed him a message:

HEAQUARTERS NINTH ARMY CORPS,
July 30, 1864—8:45 A.M.

General MEADE:

One gun has just been taken out of the mine and is now being put in position. Have not heard anything from the attack made to the left of mine. One set of colors just sent in, captured by the negroes.

W. W. SANDERSON,
Captain and Commissary of Musters

Meade felt the blood drawn from his face, and handed the note to Grant. He felt the tension return, springing out of his bones like a hidden animal, a latent fever. He had suffered his agony already, accepting the idea of a repulse. And now it was all to do over again. The Negroes! The Negroes had captured some colors. This was a terrible, malicious joke. There was a conspiracy to humiliate him, to make him hop back and forth, up and down like a stiff, jerky marionette.

Grant passed the message to Humphreys.

"Message for General Warren," snapped Meade. He looked at his watch: 9:15. " 'Your dispatch is received. The Major General commanding directs that you go in with Burnside, taking the two-gun battery. The movement on the left need not be carried farther than a reconnaissance to see what forces the enemy has holding his right. The cavalry are ordered to move up on your left and to keep up connections.' That's all. Let Humphreys sign it."

He looked up at Grant. "General, we may be on the verge of success now." His voice, in his own ears, lacked substance or conviction. The clear picture of the map of the front that he had held in mind was gone, somehow he had dropped it and let it go. If life was playing some vile trick on him he could do nothing now but fall in with it. He had no idea, really, of where Burnside's troops had gotten to or what shape they were in. The Negroes had taken some colors. Well.

He sat at the table, with his arms resting on it, and watched Grant whittle on his stick.

9:15 A.M.

Sanderson had left Burnside's headquarters shortly after the Colored sergeant had delivered his flags and his prisoners. He had to see for himself, or find someone who had seen and whose word he could trust. Potter's division was the best the Ninth Corps had, and Sanderson had seen that it had been disorganized coming through the lines, and then stopped, cold, by the rebel rearguard in that maze of trenches beyond their main line. Now here was this story about the niggers going on through and doing something big, taking colors and prisoners. Burnside had nearly capered with joy; his fat beaming face showed the glee of a liar who had just—against all hope or logic—*proved* his lie. It shouldn't, couldn't be true. Sanderson had gone out briskly, turned west, and dashed across the open ground and up to the Union first line.

The trench, once he got into it, was crowded, jammed with soldiers pushing and shoving and yelling: wounded men, stragglers, men lost and looking for their outfits, surging in mindless pulses left and right, backward and forward.

In the press, Sanderson slammed right into General Ferrero, coming back the other way. The General looked vague and confused. He was covered with dust. "I was standing on the parapet," he said, responding to a question Sanderson had never asked.

"Where is your division?" asked Sanderson.

Ferrero gestured jerkily over his right shoulder. "I was up with them on the rebel line. Then I came back here." He looked at Sanderson with sudden intensity. "I was standing on the parapet!" he said. "It's terribly confused. I had to be where my officers could . . ."

Sanderson made a wiping-away gesture. What was Ferrero talking about? "What is your division doing? Have they carried the hill? Are they advancing?"

Ferrero flushed. "I gave them orders to advance. They have their orders! There can be no mistake about their orders!"

"General, in God's name! Are they advancing? Will they carry the hill?"

"They're doing as well as can be expected. . . ." Ferrero suddenly noticed Sanderson was shaking with rage, and started like a man wakened from sleep. "Captain! . . . No, I . . . no. I don't believe they will be able to advance and carry the hill."

"Hah!" said Sanderson. "Thank you"—and he turned and began to bull and push his way down the trench back the way he had come.

"Wait!" cried Ferrero, hurrying after him, bucking the crowd of troops and losing Sanderson. "Wait! I never thought they could do it. Not today, I mean! Not today, not when they ordered us to attack. If they'd kept their word, yes, I always said . . . we planned it . . . but I protested. Captain! I never thought they could do it!"

But Sanderson ignored him, and hurried as fast as he could, sidling and slipping through the crowds, he could see it clearly now, he knew all he needed to know. He had seen Willcox's men stopped on the left. Now the attack on the right would fail. The blacks would never get anywhere. The attack was a bust-up, and he had to get Burnside to call it off and bring the men back before the rebels recovered. Meade's orders were clear: don't prolong the fighting once the attack has failed. We don't want to fatten the butcher's bill.

Burnside was still buried in his dimly-lit bombproof, his thick-lipped mouth set stubbornly in the heavy cheeks and jaw. Sanderson was having a hard time regaining his breath in the terrible heat; his voice sounded impotent and thin to himself, no match for the General's heavy anger.

"I don't believe it," said Burnside. Richmond, standing to one side, looked positively ill.

"I spoke with General Ferrero himself. You can see the men coming back. . . ."

"Ferrero!" Burnside spat. "Where in hell was he? Why wasn't he up with his division?" His face turned deep red and his cheeks shook. He looked like a rabid boar.

Sanderson, still dizzy, was thrown back by the question. He couldn't answer. Why hadn't Ferrero been with his division? It took an effort to remind himself that that was not an important detail—not yet. It was important that the assault had failed. "General, I spoke with Ferrero. I saw the men coming back. The white troops have been whipped. There has been a repulse. . . ."

"Willcox's division has been stopped," said Richmond. Burnside seemed not to hear him.

"White troops? Well, what about the niggers? Didn't you see that . . . Richmond! Get that nigger sergeant back in here, and we'll just see what in hell is really going on out there!"

"No sign of him out here," called the sentry at the door.

The color that had swollen Burnside's cheeks now faded suddenly, and the General seemed to freeze, staring at the empty door of the bombproof. Richmond laid his hand on Burnside's sleeve.

Burnside shook himself. "My men still hold the Crater. If we can put Ord's men . . ."

"Ord's men are coming back with Potter's," said Sanderson. He felt stronger, suddenly. Burnside had reached for his ace in the hole, his ace of spades—and it wasn't there.

"And Warren. Warren must make that diversion. Why in hell he hasn't already done so is beyond me!" Burnside glowered at Sanderson. "I'd look into that if I were you!"

"What do you intend doing, General?"

"Orderly!" yelled Burnside. "I want this dispatch run down to the telegraphers immediately: 'General Meade: Many of the Ninth and Eighteenth Corps are retiring before the enemy. I think now is the time to put in the Fifth Corps.'" He paused. "'Promptly,'" he added. "Sign it. Will that satisfy you, Captain?"

Sanderson shrugged. "I've already sent a telegraph report to General Meade."

Burnside grinned. "I suspected you might. My dispatch will take precedence with the operators, however."

Sanderson shrugged. He'd sent another copy by runner in any case. It shouldn't arrive too long after Burnside's telegraph message. Then Meade would have to decide whether to put Warren in or not. Sanderson was glad the decision was not his.

An orderly ran in, and handed Burnside a dispatch. Sanderson read the copy after Burnside had let it fall drifting to the tabletop.

SIGNAL STATION,
July 30, 1864.

Major-General BURNSIDE:

GENERAL: The columns I reported a few moments since are still moving and at double-quick. I judge them to be, in all that have thus far crossed the road, full a division and a half. Their right has been very much weakened.

J. C. PAINE,
Captain and Signal Officer.

If that didn't do it, nothing would. A division and a half coming up to attack Ferrero's Minstrel Show. There would be one bad stampede over there before long. If Burnside didn't pull the men out now, he was beyond rescuing.

Burnside left the bombproof and walked up to the battery. Sanderson, following after, saw him there, peering through an embrasure, fanning the smoke with his hands.

9:20 A.M. *Warren's Headquarters*

The orders from Meade had been on Warren's desk since 9:15. "The major-general commanding directs that you go in with Burnside, taking the two-gun battery. . . ."

Well, that might seem definitive enough to someone outside the army. But in itself, Warren found it insufficient to require him to commit the Fifth Corps to a bloody frontal assault. Corps commanders on the line of battle were expected to exercise discretion. He had made his reputation not by following orders unquestioningly, but by interpreting both the orders and the situation intelligently, refusing to attack when he saw no point in it. Meade had told him earlier that he might attack at discretion. Surely that understanding continued—the order was not precisely a peremptory attack order.

Warren lifted his field glasses to focus on the battery to the left of the Crater. He had been wrong in an earlier observation that the enemy controlled that battery. There had been a flurry of firing just now, and the smoke was clearing. Gazing through the glasses, behind the wavering heat-dazzle that rose from the ground and the drifts of smoke from cannons and rifles, he could see flags waving—dark-shadowed, sometimes the colors showing clear. Quite distinctly, it seemed to him, Warren caught the flash of rebel colors over the battery. Were the other flags national colors? He couldn't tell. He could not read the flags over the Crater itself.

It seemed to him possible . . . no, *likely,* that the battery to the left of the Crater had been retaken by the enemy. From this it followed logically that Burnside's attack was doomed. He must word his dispatch to Meade carefully—stick to the observable facts, and suggest no more than the testy Meade would bear hearing.

Should he go and see Burnside?

Warren shook his head, ending the internal debate. No, Burnside would only try to talk him out of it. Facts were facts, and one ought to face them, not try to talk one's way past them. No, he'd spare himself the ordeal of telling Burnside that Warren would not be lending the Fifth Corps to pull his chestnuts from the fire.

HEADQUARTERS FIFTH ARMY CORPS,
GENERAL BURNSIDE'S TELEGRAPH STATION,
July 30, 1864.

Major-General HUMPHREYS:

Just before receiving your dispatch to assault the battery on the left of the crater occupied by General Burnside, the enemy drove his troops out of the place and I think now hold it. I can find no one who knows for certainty, or seems willing to admit it, but I think I saw a rebel battle flag in it just now, and shots coming from it this way. I am, therefore (if this is true), no more able to take that battery now than I was this time yesterday. All our advantages are lost. I await further instructions and am trying to get at the true condition of affairs for certainty.

G. K. WARREN,
Major-General.

HEADQUARTERS NINTH ARMY CORPS,
(*Rec'd 9:20* A.M.)

General MEADE:

The attack made on the right of the mine has been repulsed. A great many men are coming to the rear.

W. W. SANDERSON,
Captain, &c.

HEADQUARTERS ARMY OF THE POTOMAC,
July 30, 1864—9:25 A.M.

Major-General WARREN:

The attack ordered on the two-gun battery is suspended.

GEO. G. MEADE,
Major-General Commanding.

9:30 A.M.

Booker and Colonel Thomas were huddled together behind a sheltering hump of bombproof. So far as Booker knew, he was the senior surviving field officer of the First Brigade.

"Colonel Oliver is wounded, Hall was shot as we came over the parapet. Colonel Bates was shot in the face—*Shot in the face? What did it mean?*—mounting the crest of the crater to get the troops out—I don't know if he's live." *With his face destroyed.*

Thomas seemed to have trouble focussing his eyes. Whenever he blinked, Chris would rise up and run across the front, whirling and jerking in his spastic dance as the bullets tore his thin body apart.

"You don't know," he said faintly, "where the other regimental commanders are?"

Booker shook his head. "I have about half of the Forty-third here, and the Twenty-seventh—Colonel Wright is wounded, he can't move around but is staying with his men. The others are jammed up behind—in the Crater, or back on the line. There isn't room enough to move them forward, unless we move these white troops out. Or take some more ground." Booker found himself shivering uncontrollably.

"We have to attack," said Thomas faintly, as a wave of nausea shook him. "We have positive orders to attack."

"Well, we'll attack," said Booker. His ears were ringing; he did not believe a word he was saying.

Off to the left they heard faintly the sound of rebel yells and the musketry became feverish. Counterattack. It did not concern them at all.

Booker's stomach was precarious, he might heave his insides out if he moved. It was terrible that they would have to move. If they could stay here! Even the sounds of the shells and bullets were becoming comfortable as they hunkered here in shelter.

Thomas looked into Booker's eyes. They shared the identical malady. How beautiful and important each man's face seemed to the other. "Give me ten minutes to get the Thirty-first Regiment out of the way, and bring the rest forward. The Thirty-first is . . . it can't do any more. Watch for me to start. Then you come too."

"I will," said Booker. And Thomas moved off, crouching, running.

SIGNAL STATION,
July 30, 1864

Major-General BURNSIDE:
GENERAL: The enemy are moving at least two brigades of infantry from their right and our Ninth Corps front and right. They are now passing around where the road goes toward the town west of the chimneys.

J. C. PAINE,
Captain and Signal Officer.

9:30 A.M.

Dobbs and the rest of the Nineteenth Regiment were last in the line of Thomas's brigade. They were to have been first in leading the assault according to the original plan: the last regiment of the Second Brigade would have been in the center of the assaulting line if they had formed up in the front-line trench as they had planned doing. But with the division dashing forward hastily, without forming, the Nineteenth had had to rush along in the wake of the brigade. Now they were waiting in the shelter of the rebel front-line parapet while the leading regiments picked their way forward through ground so packed with broken troops, ground so cut up by trenches and wreckage, that the column jammed, trod on its own heels, backed up at the breaches in the parapet where the rearmost elements were forced to halt and wait. Dobbs was fuming, bouncing on his toes with angry impatience at the traffic jam when the ground on the other side of the parapet burst and exploded, and a wall of dust leaped out of the earth dotted with bodies where two shells had bitten meat. The shell-bursts cut the brigade into pieces, cut the Nineteenth off from the regiment just ahead, split the regiment in two. Men surged, a group bulged backward out of the gap in the trenches through which most of the brigade had gone as the regiment recoiled upon itself. More rounds came in, and there were bullets coming too from God knew where—rebels off on the flank whose fire swept the breaks in their parapet.

Off beyond the sheltering wall, Dobbs could hear sudden rises in shooting and yelling that suggested movement in the hidden battle. Overhead he could hear the sound of the bullets. The regiments shifted slowly forward. Dobbs leaned out from the wall and looked to the right, saw an officer leap on the parapet, wave his sword, then dive backwards into the mob of troops below him.

Major Rockwood, his round face purple with the heat, came pushing down the line. Dobbs grabbed his arm and pointed to the left, back the way they had come. "Maybe we can get em over back that way," he shouted. Rockwood nodded and waved them to follow, and Dobbs sang out for A Company to come on and fell in behind the Major without a glance back. Rockwood stopped and pointed up to a spot where the parapet appeared to have been partly beaten down. It was still too high to climb. Dobbs took the axe from his belt and began swinging it, chopping at the parapet, chopping footholds. Private Johnson, following right behind Dobbs, began jabbing his bayonet into the wall.

"I'll take em over!" yelled Rockwood. "Get one platoon to boost the next one up." Rockwood stepped up to Dobbs's footholds, set his boot in the bottom and his right hand on Dobbs's shoulder. He paused on the first step, Dobbs taking his weight—he was porky for a little man—as Rockwood pushed down on Dobbs's shoulder. Dobbs heard his hands scrabble at the top of the parapet, heard the earth grate on the wool cloth of his shirt, and Rockwood was up.

"Hurrah!" he said. "Come on, men!"

Then they heard a socking sound, the sound of a boot kicking in a rotten board. Rockwood fell headfirst off the wall and landed at Dobbs's feet. As Dobbs bent to see, the six black men who had climbed at Rockwood's side fell or slithered back down, shot.

Rockwood had been shot through the back of the head, through the spine, and through the right elbow. There was a black crater where his right eye should have been.

Dobbs hefted his axe and chopped it into the wall in grief and frustration. The battle was just the other side of the wall and there was no way he could get in, locked out like a snot-nosed kid starving for fruit and he can't get over the garden wall. Lemuel D. Dobbs and his blue-gum niggers, shuffling along at the ass end of the parade, waiting at the back door for table scraps. *Ain't that the goddamn story of my life?*

Shit! He was through following after and doing what he was told. *This ain't my farm, brother: Lemuel Dobbs is moving on.* He took Rockwood's pistol and jammed it in his belt. Then he jerked the axe out of the ground and flourished it.

"Right with you, Chopper," said Johnson Number Five, and Dobbs looked at him in sudden surprise: in his rage he had nearly forgotten the company, had almost been ready to go stalking off alone with his axe to look for a way into the battle. The black man gave him a grin like a wolf's, and Dobbs grinned back.

"Hey, Company A!" yelled Dobbs. He threw a glance along the line of the regiment: there wasn't a field officer in sight. "Let's get out of here!" He slapped Johnson Number Five on the shoulder and ran, crouching, back down the length of his line. The men rocked forward in his wake, rising to follow him. Dobbs led them back southward along the reverse of the parapet toward the Crater. At a spot where the force of the blast had flattened the parapet and half-filled the trenches with dirt, he turned to his right and led his men single-file through the breached trenches. Off to his left the mounded lip of the Crater rose, with a dozen flags black in silhouette jammed along the front rim.

Slanting out from the side of the Crater, the line of the rebel trench had been shoveled out. It was full of white soldiers, and some blacks from the First Brigade. Dobbs jumped the trench at its narrowest point, the men in it looking up as he and then his black troops went over. Ahead of him smoke-gusts shot abruptly out of patches of ground, hung blackly in the breathless air.

Off to the right was the confused maze of trenches and bombproofs in which his own brigade and a whole bunch of white troops were crowded in too tight to move or do any fighting. But ahead and to the left, things had cleared out a little. There seemed to be a line of their own troops, firing out of a trench that ran across the rear of the Crater. Thirty yards farther away there was a rebel line, and it looked like a battery back of that.

"Come on!" called Dobbs, and he jerked his arm straight up to signal. Without looking back he began to run at a crouch, dodging across the field, heading for the trench.

As he went he heard the bullets start to zip, spit up ground, and hum past him, and he knew that he was getting there now.

"Hey! Ninth Corps, move over there!" he yelled, and then he tumbled into the trench. It was full of white troops. They backed away as the blacks piled in after Dobbs; it looked like he had fifty of them now. Damned if he hadn't picked up a couple when he'd passed by the Crater.

"Got any officers?" he asked, and a white Captain came pushing forward—a tallish man, brown-haired, with drooping mustaches. He looked briefly, surprised, at the blacks crowding in. Then at Dobbs. "Come on in," he said, "there's plenty room."

"Thank you kindly," said Dobbs with a grin, "don't mind if we do."

"I'm Gregg," said the Captain. "This is the Forty-fifth Pennsylvania here. What there is of it."

"We're the Nineteenth Ni . . . Negroes, and some others come along for the fun." He couldn't break himself of the habit. "Niggers" they were to him, no matter what Chris might think was proper. Nineteenth United States Niggers, that was his outfit. "What's doing here?" he asked Gregg. "We-all got stopped out to the right. Too many snouts going for the one tit."

"We were supposed to take that battery," said Gregg, gesturing to the front. "Couldn't find anybody else that wanted to go along with us. After a while we got tired of playing alone, and came back here." His tone was bitter. "Most of us, that is."

"We'll keep you company awhile," said Dobbs. "If you want to make another try for it, we might just tag along."

Gregg looked at Dobbs, then over Dobbs's shoulder. Dobbs saw it working on Gregg—the doubts, the fears about the niggers, would they fight, were they any good, did you want to have them around even? He watched Gregg handle it. "Thanks," said Gregg. "We might just give it another try at that. If those suckers on the left will give us a little . . ."

"Captain, look!" yelled a white soldier, and Gregg turned and looked over the top of the trench.

"I think they're working themselves up to charge," he said.

Dobbs leaned forward and looked. He could see the rebel flags wigwagging frantically over the smoke bank that marked their trench line. They had stopped firing. He stepped aside, and pulled up Private Johnson Number Five. "Take a look," he said. Johnson peered out. Dobbs leaned into the opening; their sides were pressed together, their faces close. He pointed. "They'll come up out of there. Don't shoot any of them till they get about level with the busted wagon wheel." Johnson nodded. The white man was awful close. "Git down the line," said Dobbs, "and tell the rest of the boys. Tell em shoot low, shoot for the knees. Then come back here. Git now."

The troops stepped up to the front of the trench, took position along the whole length of it. Johnson went along the line. "Chopper say let em come up till the wagon wheel there. Chopper say shoot low for the knees"—all the way down the line. Then he turned and ran back. "They comin!" yelled Private Duckworth as he came up to Dobbs, and Johnson stepped up to look out.

Across the littered rubble-field he saw the heads bob up in a line; the sun caught the bayonets and a sudden flash went from one end of the line to the other. Unconsciously, Johnson Number Five jammed his right hand deep in the soft crumbled earth of the parapet, drying the sweat, and wiped it on his trouser leg. He gripped the stock and trigger of the musket. The brown hand and the dark brown wood made nearly one color.

He looked up again. The Johnnies seemed not to have moved, frozen till he had done those necessary things: dried his hand and cleaned it, and looked at it how it looked against the musket stock. Then they slid forward suddenly as a unit, no visible effort of arms and legs, like a gator sliding into a slough.

He heard Dobbs and the other white Captain calling, "Steady!" "Hold on there!" "Not yet!" calmly, like overseers toting up the bags of cotton—One, Two, Three, Four.

Saw them come level with the wagon wheel, and he looked down the long barrel into the moving brown of the wave and his finger moved by itself, and the gun slammed him hard in the shoulder, the smoke blinded his eyes, and behind the smoke the whitefaces were screeching like owls. He felt his voice rising out of his chest, big and loud, "Eeeeeyahhhhh!" and he jumped right up out of the trench. His head came out of the smoke. The whitefaces were still coming on. "Goddamn!" he heard Dobbs yell. "Let's go!" and he heard the little white man scrambling up behind him, and his own people coming up on his right. He yelled again, the yell as deep and powerful and complete as any song he'd ever sung, calling all the people up out of the ground, and he ran toward the whitefaces. Out of the wave a single face emerged, black eyebrows, and Johnson swatted the man's bayonet aside with his own; stuck it in him, drove him to the ground, leaned on the hard length of the musket.

Something exploded near his ear. Dobbs's pistol. He looked, saw another white man falling down where Dobbs was pointing. *Chopper!*

There was yelling. Two men were writhing about on the ground, and for a minute a picture flashed in Johnson's head, of that girl back in the contraband camp twisting underneath while the Yankee soldier that paid her was screwing her hard, and then he saw it was that other Captain wrestling with a reb Captain. He stepped over. The reb Captain was on top. He rammed his iron-shod musket butt down onto the back of the man's neck. And that was that.

Dobbs ran up to him. His face was red, and he was laughing and fairly jumping around. "By God! By God! If you ain't the smartest nigger there ever was! Oh by God, if you ain't the best! By God!" He slammed Johnson on the back. "Now that's taking it *to* em! That's *soldier! God*damn*!*" He whirled. "You beautiful black sons of bitches. give yourselves a yell! Nineteenth United States Niggers, by *God!*"

"Eeeehah!" yelled Johnson, and the others took it up, but the earth bumped, and the dirty breath of a shell woke them up.

"Back into the trench!" yelled Gregg.

Off to the left they heard the firing going higher and higher, and they heard the screechowling again, the screeching rising and the musketry rising. They were hurrying back, jumping into the trench, and they heard it: the screeching, the shooting. Then more screeching than shooting.

A cry came down from the left: "We're flanked!"

The white soldiers in the trench seemed to take a deep breath, like tired laborers will do when they've sat down and rested a spell, before they rise and work again. Then they began climbing out of the trench, and going back toward the Crater.

"Can't you stop em?" yelled Dobbs.

Gregg shrugged. He gestured toward the left, where the firing was coming on again, but you could still hear the rebels shrieking. "What's the point? They've got us flanked out of this line, unless those troops back in the Crater come out and push them out of here." He spat.

"Which from what I've seen, they ain't likely to do." Gregg looked at the black troops waiting behind Dobbs. "Why don't you and your men come along? You seem like handy boys to have around."

Dobbs jerked his head toward the rear, and the men behind him began slowly to scramble out. Johnson waited by Dobbs to hear the rest.

"All right," he said. "Shame to break up the concern, when we started out so good. As the one trapper said to the other, before their canoe went over the falls."

Under the sullen booming of the rebel guns, the remnants of Gregg's and Dobbs's men picked their way back toward the rim of the Crater. Johnson felt tired, but he felt good. He remembered how it had felt: how the cry came up, and his body had come up; how perfect it felt running; and killing perfect, too—he dreamed it as he trotted after Dobbs, and in his dream his roaring face was not restrained by the rigid length of the bayonet and gun, but swept forward right into the white man's face, meeting and killing him eye to eye, and teeth to teeth.

9:40 A.M.

Rees and Doyle were with their company, manning the first line of rifle pits as provost guards, when the troops that had gone up to the attack with the rest of the Second Division began coming back. Just the wounded first, and they came shambling and stumbling, holding their hurts, or helped along by friends; Rees passed them through without a word, and Doyle pointed them up the covered way to where the hospital was. They found niches for the worst cases to lie down a bit before moving on. Poured water on lips parched and bitten.

The roar of the fighting was as meaningless as the sound of a waterfall, its rising and fallings scarcely marked after a time—taken for a trick of the ear. The noise was out there, behind the line of the abatis and the rebel trenches. That was all they needed to know. Yet Doyle and Rees found each other pricking up their ears at intervals, when they remembered that the roaring was the echo of the great roar they themselves had made, the child and increase of it, the validation.

The heat was stultifying, deadly. Doyle felt the veins and fluids of his head swelling, dipped his neckerchief in water and wrapped it round to take the swelling down. Rees's Welsh face was red as scarlet flannel.

Then more men were coming back, a lot of them now not wounded at all. Just coming back. Walking stooped behind the shelter of the abatis. Then, later, they came running, hurrying—there were shells falling in front of the abatis; in it, in behind it. Hurrying. More of them now, and the officers trailing after.

Rees looked at Doyle. Their faces looked boiled. "Let's stop this now," said Rees, and Doyle called the company up closer. Bayonets fixed.

They were lined out at intervals in front of the trench parapet, and they winced when shells striking in the abatis kicked broken branches and earth their way.

The troops were coming back by companies now, Second Division men and Ord's men, the privates in front, some officers shambling after, some of them yelling and waving, some walking along. Rees stepped in front of the line, and grabbed the shirt of the first man in a group of a dozen. "That's as far as you go, mate," he said. "Where's your officer?"

The man reached up calmly, and pulled Rees's hand off his shirt. His companions kept shuffling by.

"Pre-sent!" shouted Rees, and Doyle and the rest snapped their bayonetted muskets to the front. The group of stragglers was three feet in front of the line.

They paused, the fraction of a second, and bunched a little closer. As if this closeness gave them energy, courage, they stepped forward again.

Doyle waited for Rees to call "Fire!"

His heart bolted, banged. His arms legs neck head were frozen rigid. Thought stopped.

The first man stepped level with the tip of his bayonet and delicately, with a kind of courtesy, edged it to one side. The stragglers slipped through the line.

Doyle looked at Rees, his muscles still locked in the strain of that horrible suspense. He hadn't ordered them to fire. Would he order them to fire? What was going to happen?

The stragglers continued to come up, and walk through the line, pausing as they came, as if performing some formal ceremony of re-entrance.

We can't shoot our own, can we! We mustn't shoot our own!

"You bloody cowards!" yelled Rees, "Get on back there."

The stragglers, coming back, seemed too tired, too exhausted, to take this personally. They looked up at the loud voice, perhaps even looked about to see to whom it was addressed. They were coming from a far place, a very far and foreign place.

Rees shut up. Doyle looked at him. The sergeant was standing straight as a statue. Doyle followed the line of his eyes. That was when they saw Pleasants coming back, with the tired spent look, walking slowly.

"You miserable bastard," said Rees under his breath. "You high-and-mighty kiss-my-ass stupid bastard."

The rage, the anguish, the effort of mining, of digging the mine, Corrigan, Rees, the stragglers, the losing of it all, being ready to shoot his own people for stragglers and not shooting them, throbbed in Doyle's head, and gathered around the ashen face of the Colonel as he came back. *You sold us out, you pig; you used us to death and sold us, you bastard.*

Pleasants walked through the line, not seeming to recognize them. He muttered something as he went by Rees.

"What did he say?" asked Doyle as the Colonel vanished into the trench.

"He said 'Carry on, Sergeant,'" answered Rees, his mouth wrung up to one side with the strain of his held-back anger. "That was what the man said."

9:45 A.M. *Burnside's Headquarters*

HEADQUARTERS ARMY OF THE POTOMAC,
July 30, 1864—9:30 A.M.

Major-General BURNSIDE,
Commanding Ninth Corps:
    The major-general commanding has heard that the result of your attack has been a repulse, and directs that, if in your judgment nothing further can be effected, you withdraw to your own line, taking every precaution to get the men back safely.

A. A. HUMPHREYS,
Major-General and Chief of Staff.

General Ord will do the same.

Burnside took in the sense of Meade's dispatch, though the precise wording would not stay in memory. He sat, very calmly and quietly. He himself was amazed at the rocklike calm with which he took the dispatch. He was a great rock. The dispatch washed over him like a dark ocean wave. He wasn't shaken by it. He read it once; and then, after an interval of calm thought—so calm that words scarcely formed themselves in his mind—read it again. The repeated breaking of the waves.

HEADQUARTERS ARMY OF THE POTOMAC,
July 30, 1864—9:45 A.M.

Major-General BURNSIDE,
Commanding Ninth Corps:
    The major-general commanding directs that you withdraw to your own intrenchments.

A. A. HUMPHREYS,
Major-General and Chief of Staff.

He noted the time with surprise. A fifteen-minute interval, at Meade's end. About the same here. He'd been sitting, thinking, for fifteen minutes. He looked at his watch. Yes, it took about fifteen or twenty minutes for the dispatches to be transmitted and run up to his headquarters here. It was now—he looked deliberately at his watch, a study in calmness for his fidgeting staff—it was now nearly ten. Yes: fifteen or twenty minutes. Fifteen in this case. Fifteen.
    Yes, fifteen.
    The sounds of the fighting were a dim thundering heard from down here in the bombproof. Fifteen minutes. It would take him scarcely longer than that to ride to Meade in person. To explain.
    Richmond cleared his throat. "There's a message from General White."
    "Ah yes. . . ." Yes. "Yes!" said Burnside. "He is still on the line?" Richmond nodded and passed him the dispatch. Burnside looked

wistfully at Richmond, and said, "He's right up near the front line, isn't he? If he says we can still take the hill, that would settle the matter. Don't you think?"

Richmond opened his mouth to speak, then shrugged. Burnside had no other recourse but to read the message. Almost absentmindedly, he began reading it aloud. " 'Major-General Burnside,' " he read, slowly and softly, " 'I respectfully recommend that our troops be directed to intrench and hold what we have, connecting on the right and left with our old line. J. White, Brigadier-General and Chief of Staff.' " Burnside looked up.

Every eye in the bunker was on him. The silence was as thick as the heat. The battle seemed very distant. Every softly uttered word had been distinctly heard.

"He does not say," said Burnside, "that it is impossible to advance farther."

Richmond rolled his eyes, and his voice sounded half-strangled. "It is the implication, sir. He says we can hold, entrench. To advance . . . he says nothing about advancing. . . ."

Burnside looked at his watch. "I must go and speak with General Meade, directly." He looked round at his aides. "It will be best not to commit ourselves to any definitive movement until I return. You will inform General White that he is to await a message on my return."

"And in the meantime . . ."

"My orders remain the same." Advance. Advance, and carry the crest.

9:45 A.M. The Crater

Booker lay flat against the sloping side of the trench wall. The ground shook from shells coming in. The air was alive with the whining, greazy slide of bullets. He could smell his own sweat—sharp, tangy, souring slightly. The wool collar of his jacket chafed the back of his neck. The sun leaned heavily on his back. *Mistake to have sent Randolph away! What kind of idea did I have anyway, protecting him? There's no protection from anything. I need him here.*

Tobe and Jethro crouched in the trench next to each other. From time to time they looked at each other. There was nothing more for either to say. They had come here to die, they had been called to it. They could wait, patiently or impatiently, for the call to come. Not when they left the lines, or when they charged the white troops and whipped them out of their trench! That wasn't the time. That was a taste of victory, but it wasn't the victory itself. Jesus was going to give them the victory, they had the peace in their souls proving it. Even Jethro could feel it, and wasn't impatient any more. He passed Tobe a drink from his canteen.

They watched Booker.

Thomas jerked his head left to right, checking the bunched troops in the trench, his smoke-irritated eyes tearing. *Advance and take the crest.* He listened for the sound of firing to the left. Something to tell him that the supporting attack he'd asked for was being made.

He looked at his watch: 9:45. Time. He reached out with his left hand and gripped the top of the parapet. He took his whistle in his right hand, put it quickly to his lips, and blew.

The dark bodies sailed upward, bursting out of the trench. Thomas pushed with his legs, hauled with his left arm, and came scrambling over the top. The air was alive, swarming, hysterical with noise.

The shell-bursts came in a row, right down the line, *Chuff! Chuff! Chuff! Chuff! Chuff!* The ground shook as they snouted it up and tossed it, gored men flipped and fell, the air bit them and tore at their clothes. The hot breath of a shell knocked Thomas flat, his orderly fell over him with the side of his head shot away.

He looked up from the ground, and the shadows of his men tumbled and fell, down forward, twisting back. Lay humped, fidgeting when the bullets touched and prodded and pried. Thomas began to crawl backward, still facing up toward where the bullets were coming out of the smoke. His feet passed over empty space, and he thrust with his arms, and fell back into the trench.

Tobe and Jethro heard the whistle and they jumped up together, and scrambled out. The air was full of the crazy insects, plague of locusts, and the shells came pouring in after them, but Tobe and Jethro ran forward with the other men stretched in a line to their right. Up ahead the smoke shifted and they saw the clear space on the top of the hill where they were going at last, a line of them—called out of all the rest—sweeping into the fire like a harrow going across a field. Tobe felt his heart shout glory as three shells chewed the string of men from end to end, and the wall of smoke lit with fire cut Tobe and Jethro off behind a wall of cloud, fire and smoke to right and left, and they ran on between the pillars, shouting *Hurrrraaaah!*

Up on the hill, off to the right of the battery on the Jerusalem Plank Road, Billy leaned against Dixon's hip. Dixon stared down the field.

"Oh Jesus," cried Dixon, "black niggers! Billy, it's the black niggers again!"

Coming for him again. Billy rolled on his side, and got up. Dixon's musket was lying on the ground, he picked it up.

Black devils came dashing and darting across a field full of smoke and flame. They fell into pits and were swallowed in eruptions, but they came on, darting singly and in rows. This was a vision for him, for Billy. Dixon's cries were like the scratchings of an insect, void of meaning. This was for him.

He watched as God permitted the devils to come on, to come on. Fire and smoke took them group by group. A row of figures in gray and brown crouched in a line in the ravine ahead of them. Smoke poured from them, but a row of devils continued, passing them by on the right as Billy looked.

The devils disappeared in an eruption of yellow smoke.

"They're gone!" yelled Dixon, and Billy laughed at him.

The devil leaped right out at him from the midst of the cloud of yellow smoke. Cannon fire shook the ground, and men were shooting, little spouts of earth went up around the devil, but he grinned and came on, his sharp teeth white in his black face, his jaws dripping human blood, his eyes rolling like an animal's.

He came closer. He kept coming on. Dixon fell down flat on the ground.

Billy could deny the devil no longer. He was full of witness. He stepped forward to meet him.

As he did, the devil stumbled, his leg buckled. He fell, curled, seemed almost to be kneeling before Billy.

The power of it surged in Billy, and he ran down toward the devil, and he was full, brimful of the Lord at last, given to struggle with his devil.

The devil raised his head and showed his bloody teeth and eyes, his nigger face his nigger face, and Billy *swung, whammed* his rifle butt into the middle of the face. And felt that the devil had a face, and the devil's face had broken under his blow.

He straddled the devil, and raised his musket, and pounded the butt down at the broken face of the devil, again, did it again, did it again, till he felt the face break open and fall apart.

Then he stepped back. He pointed his rifle at the devil's cock, at the devil's balls: and fired.

Then he fell on his knees.

The sun was bright and hot.

He looked behind him. The gunners, standing next to their pieces, stared at him. They were scarcely ten feet away.

As he stood, watching, men appeared between the guns, more and more of them. Clean uniforms, flags in the front. They slipped through the battery, formed columns, and began to sweep quietly down the hill.

10:00 A.M.

Bruce and Davidson and the survivors of their patchwork command had taken shelter in the ravine that ran north to south midway between the Crater and the ridge. Davidson had lost his sword in their flight, and now sat sulkily by himself, while Bruce hustled about the line.

Bruce saw Mahone's columns coming down the slope at a run. Some long-range Yankee artillery found them, and shell-bursts bloomed brown around them, bit the edge of a column and tossed the pieces. Even as he watched them coming on still, the first elements of the new division were tumbling into the trenches at the far end of the ravine, and sweeping leftward to the part of the line that the remnants of Elliott's brigade still held.

"Colonel!" said Bruce, gripping and shaking Davidson's arm. "Come on, Colonel. Here's reinforcements. We'll attack again if we can form the men up." Davidson's eyes were still dull, his face sagging and stupid, but he got to his feet.

"Was it your idea to make me run from that pack of niggers?" he demanded.

"Colonel, we must prepare to charge," said Bruce. And he walked away to get the men ready. There were drums and bugles sounding already as the oncoming troops built up in the ravine like water in an earth-dam, ready to bust loose and go. Bruce looked, and he saw them surge suddenly out and over the top, weathered red flags topping the line, and he heard the yell, and started to yell charge, but the troops had already started climbing out. So he ran back down the trench to where Davidson was standing, and he shook his shoulder and said, "If you want another sword, let's go," and the two men climbed out of the trench and followed their men into the attack.

Thomas picked himself up from the floor of the trench. He had scarcely fifty men around him. One officer, his face black with powder. The brigade flag was lost, lost with Chris.

He looked wildly over the parapet. The vague humped forms in front were unrecognizable. With all the blood and dirt you couldn't tell black from white.

As he looked to the left, he saw a figure with a flag, running up over a hump of ground and he almost thought it was Chris, but then he saw the others coming, more white men in blue uniforms running up over the hump of ground, some falling. The color-bearer hurdled the trench, heading for the rear, and the men behind him tried it too. Thomas saw some of them miss and fall into the trench. Another one jumped across, a second jumped, and bumped tangling with a black man crawling up out of the trench. And then he felt them move, felt them let go and move—climbing out the rear of the trench. Bullets kept whining and picking at them, but the shells stopped.

Thomas climbed out the rear of the trench. "Stop!" he shouted. "Halt! Second Brigade!" He waved his sword.

He looked back. Across the field on the other side of the trench he saw the rebel line coming on, a line under flags, saw some few men rise and scatter back there, rabbits scared out of covert by the beaters, some falling some falling, and he heard the rebel shriek, and he began stumbling after his men, crying *halt*.

Back across the lines of cross-trenches and traverses, around the humped bombproofs, wreckage of equipment, through the maze of trenches and lanes and bushes, jumping dead and wounded. Back, going back. Going back to the lines.

Booker's hands let go of the parapet, and he slid to the bottom of the trench. He looked down the trench. Half-a-dozen men stared at him, crouched like him below the parapet. The wall of the parapet heaved suddenly and vomited earth, and the rocking of the ground threw them over.

When Booker looked up, two or three men were buried under the knocked-in trench wall. The rest picked themselves up, and clambered over the rear parapet, and disappeared.

Booker looked at the trench. It was empty. He had lost them all, every last one of them.

No point in staying now. His head rang like a bell. I've killed them all. Tobe, Jethro, Brown, Colehill, all of them. It seemed clear that this was why he'd sent Randolph off: so he could kill all their men, and go back. He clambered over the wall, and followed the men who had left before him. Ducking and running from shelter to shelter, he worked his way back.

He came to the edge of the Crater. Looked down into the bottom, which was swarming with men. He put his feet over the edge, and slid down to the bottom.

A black man approached him. "Major," the black man said. "Major, I brung this off." The man was holding the regimental flag, its staff shorted a third of the way, broken off jagged.

"I'm sorry, sorry, . . ." said Booker.

"Major," said the black man. "I brung the flag."

He reached out, and touched the man's cheek, then rested a hand on his shoulder. It was Colehill, the flag corporal. He was real. They weren't all dead.

Booker licked his lips. "Can you climb up there?" he asked, pointing to the crest of the Crater, twenty feet above them.

The black man nodded.

"Stick the flagstaff in the parapet up there. So our people will know where to come back to."

"Right, Major." The man turned, and scrabbled up to the top. Bracing himself, he rocked his body back, and rammed the staff down into the soft earth at the crest of the Crater. It hung limp in the breathless heat. Occasionally it twitched, as bullets plucked at it.

The black men gathered under the flag. Ten, maybe fifteen. The sun, burning in behind them, threw them in black relief on the red-yellow wall, multiplying them.

And Booker felt, then, looking at the shadows, how very many many of his men were not there. How many he had lost: seen clearly in the clear light showing those here who had been saved, who had saved themselves.

10:00 A.M.

Neill found Beeler. Just after, the niggers had started coming into the Crater, and someone said they were making an attack.

"Fine attack," said Neill. He watched as a group of blacks came poking around through the wreckage on the Crater floor. "Who are they attacking? Us, I'll bet."

Beeler laughed, harsh barking sound. He had managed to hang onto his own musket, and he kept looking strangely at Neill's empty hands, but not saying anything.

Neill remembered how the Crater had looked to him the first time he'd peered down into it: a pond of loose dust mounded in heaving waves, wreckage floating here and there in it, smoke and dust rising off it like a fog. Nobody in it, nobody alive and moving around: just the mounds of dust, and the wreckage, and the low morning sun slanting so the bottom was in shadow, and seemed cooler than up on top. Now the sun was down into it, pouring the heat in hard, and the bottom seemed to have spawned soldiers the way a carcass spawns maggots—black and white.

"Got any water?" he asked Beeler, and Beeler shook his head. They began to poke around, looking for canteens. There was a pile of them over near the central ridge, where some of the wounded were laid out. If any of them died, you might be able to pick up the canteen of water.

"Where's the rest of the boys?" asked Beeler.

Neill shrugged. He didn't know. People could blame him for that, if they were minded to, but there wasn't a thing he could help about it: he didn't know.

Beeler's eyes wandered around the floor of the Crater. The men, milling about, stirred the fine powdery dust, and made thirst worse. The sounds of fighting came as if from a far distance, as if down here out of the level of the earth they were truly detached from the war. Safe.

"I bet the niggers have full canteens," said Beeler. "Maybe they'll trade."

"Catch a disease if you drink from something their lips got on," said Neill.

Randolph took his patrol across the trenches. An inrushing gang of whites nearly bumped him backwards into the trench, but he rolled aside and they picked their way forward. Randolph watched the movements of the clumps of whites running back, calculating the drift of their movements the way a farmer calculates the shifting and sliding of rain clouds sweeping across a big level plain. Watched the big drifts, and waited for the canister gun to fire. Then he'd up and go, and the men after him, ten yards at a time, slanting away from the big bunches that the gun would surely be shooting for, using the ground and the junk for cover, using the white soldiers for cover, using the timing of the gunshots for cover.

They came up to the rim of the Crater, and crouched behind the curb of broken earth that rimmed it. On all fours, they scrabbled sideways, up to the big clay boulder. They stopped there. The sun lit up the side of the boulder, radiating heat down on them. Alongside it, they could see the cannon, poking its blunt finger toward the uncaptured heights, stupidly insistent, bodies around it. They hadn't had much luck with that gun.

Randolph eased himself up toward the top of the rim. Near the top, he nudged the earth with his hands, making a small dip in it so he could look over without raising his head too much.

His hand touched cold skin. Smooth, and cold. Little bit of cloth round it. Dead man. He shivered.

He eased himself higher. The sun threw a blot of shadow down. His eyes, sensing it, looked up. There was a hand thrust up out of the earth. The skin of the arm was ivory-white, the color of fresh wet bone. The muscles held the stiff fingers in a terrible twisting posture, as if the arm squeezed and wrung something with its complete force. Yet there was no motion, and the fingers held—delicately, carefully—a broken-edged piece of hardtack bread.

For Randolph, the noise of the battle stopped. He reached up and touched the hand and the hardtack. The skin of the hand, in all that heat, was cold and smooth. The surface of the hardtack was roughened, crumbly. Randolph gripped the edge of the bread, thumb and forefinger; lifted slowly, and cracked off a piece.

Spit moistened his mouth. He put the hardtack in, softening it with the juices of his mouth. Then he crumbled it with his teeth. Chewed and swallowed.

The cloudless sky burned blue with the heat. Randolph felt power flowing into his body out of the earth, cool and dead and steady, bread out of the earth in a dead hand. Bread in the wilderness, and life in the dry bones. That was a promise, made now to him. He closed his eyes.

When he raised them, he saw Colehill jamming the color-staff of the regiment into the opposite rim of the Crater. The coincidence did not seem strange. It was inevitable, as perfect as the finding of the bread.

White faces and black faces turned upward as he called to his men, and slid feet-first to the bottom of the Crater. His men, their canteens sloshing musically, came down after him, one after another.

The soldiers in the Crater began to gather to the water, like wolves coming up to a scent, and Randolph was up quickly moving efficiently, ignoring them, taking his men past the crowds that rose up out of the holes and hummocks of the Crater floor and came toward them, like bodies out of the grave: taking the water back to his own people, over by the flag.

"Come along, lambs," he said quietly.

Picking their way in single file, around groups of men and bits of wreckage, they worked their way across the Crater.

10:00 A.M. *Meade's Headquarters*

HEADQUARTERS ARMY OF THE POTOMAC,
July 30, 1864—10 A.M.

Major-General BURNSIDE:

You can exercise your discretion in withdrawing your troops now or at a later period, say to-night. It is not intended to hold the enemy's line which you now occupy any longer than is required to withdraw safely your men.

GEO. G. MEADE,
Major-General.

(Same to General Ord.)

Unexpected by anyone, without any warning, General Burnside appeared outside the headquarters tent, General Ord trailing after him—red face, thick lips set in a bitter angry line. Burnside slapped hard at his uniform, and the dust puffed away. His large round face framed by the thick brown scallops of his whiskers was bathed in sweat, and the dust had clung to the runnels of sweat.

Burnside's face was set in an unnatural calm. He seemed to believe that by staring stolidly and speaking in a voice of suppressed tension he concealed his feelings: but his face looked boiled, and it wasn't just the heat of the sun.

Burnside and Ord came in under the marquee where Meade and Grant were sitting. Meade did not even look at Burnside. He looked directly at Ord, and spoke to him. "General Ord: you've come to discuss the withdrawal?"

"Yes," said Ord, "there are difficulties. . . ."

Burnside interjected, harshly: "Since General Ord's troops have all left the scene of the action, there's no trouble about his men withdrawing! None whatever!"

Ord rounded on Burnside, red-faced. "By *heaven*, Burnside!"

"Do you deny that the only troops which remain in the breach are the Ninth Corps?"

"Gentlemen," said Grant, and they stopped and turned to him. "Sit down."

They hesitated. Then sat down.

Burnside shot a glance at Ord, and spoke. "General," he said—he glanced uncertaintly from Meade to Grant—"General, I have come to protest, in person, the order for withdrawal." Ord breathed out loudly through his nostrils, and Burnside's eyes flickered toward him, and he began to speak more rapidly, as if to forestall interruption. "My men now hold a considerable portion of the rebel lines. We can use the point as a salient, flanking the batteries to right and left." He looked at Ord, and seemed to be answering an objection made much earlier, made again and again, to judge from the annoyance in his voice. "Yes, if they're on our flanks, it's equally the case that we're on theirs. We haven't fought long enough today. It's barely ten. Not long enough by half. If we'll only persist a bit. I've always believed . . . I've always been taught: persistence. If you don't keep at it, if you give up . . . nowhere. You get nowhere."

"My orders were peremptory," snapped Meade, and Burnside went off, hair-trigger.

"Yes! Dammit! And you don't even know the situation. They can enfilade the area between the lines, we'll just be shot up if we bring them back now. . . ."

"By heaven," said Ord, "don't you even listen to *yourself?* You've just been talking about using the salient, and now you can't even bring the men back because of enfilading . . . God!" Ord choked on his anger.

"I take it," said Grant, "that you disagree with General Burnside?"

Ord turned to the voice, and seemed to take hold of his anger. "Yes, General. The men have been repulsed . . . dammit, they've been whipped good, those that had the courage to even try to go forward, and the rest of them are damned slackers from the start!" He swallowed and took hold of his temper. "Yes, I disagree with General Burnside. You couldn't hold Gibraltar with the men that are in there. Let alone a place that you can't get even small parties over to without artillery hell breaking loose.''

Meade cleared his throat, interrupting, drawing Ord's eyes away from Grant's face. "I don't suppose you gentlemen received my last dispatch, modifying the order to withdraw?''

That held their attention. Meade saw Burnside's fat bovine eyes nearly roll in his head with surprise. Humphreys beckoned the secretary over, and passed his copy of the dispatch around. "It is still an order to withdraw. But you may use discretion in the matter. If what you say is true, nightfall might be the best time.''

Ord looked up. "I'd rather it were now," he said. He looked at Grant.

Burnside looked at Grant also. "I don't wish to withdraw at all. I don't want to . . . *compromise* here. I believe . . . I believe it is possible, it is still possible. If you'd only given . . . if you'd give the order for General Warren's troops to make a diversion in our favor. The troops in the Crater are rallying. I believe we can carry the crest.'' He looked wildly from Meade to Ord to Grant. "By nightfall, we could carry it. Or the pits at the bottom, at the very least. . . .''

They all looked at Grant. The General's eyes were absolutely void of expression. "No," he said. "There are to be no further attempts to take the crest. The orders must stand as written.''

Burnside opened his mouth, as if he would have cried out. His eyes seemed to swell and charge with fluid. "Well, I have discretion then as to the manner and time of withdrawal.'' His voice was a harsh whisper.

"Yes, General," said Meade. "So long as you *withdraw* them.''

"I understand the orders," said Burnside.

The two men glared at each other. In the silence, each man played out in his head the intense imaginary dialogue that would have carried them to blows and court-martial if they had uttered it.

Then Burnside rose, and turned back to his horse. Ord slapped the table with both hands disgustedly, and rose to follow him. They walked out of the marquee. Burnside mounted and rode off. Ord, taking his time, ignored Burnside's departure, following a little after. At a walking pace, the two parties proceeded up the road, separately, back toward the rising smoke of the battle.

Under the marquee, Meade looked at Grant, and Grant looked at his watch. "I'm going to return to City Point," said Grant. "You'll notify me as soon as the troops have been withdrawn.''

"Of course," said Meade. "Will we be making the sweep against the Weldon road?''

"Let's think about that." Grant paused. "Let's see what things are like after the men have been withdrawn and are back in our lines. Where will you be?''

Meade looked at Humphreys, then back to Grant, and shrugged. "I'll return to my old headquarters as soon as we can close up shop here." Grant nodded, and Meade turned to give orders.

Outside the marquee the staff officers began packing up their camp equipment, books, and papers. Over the horizon the guns still muttered, distantly now. It was someone else's battle.

"Not a very brilliant occasion," said Humphreys.

Meade snorted. "Burnside," he said.

"There will have to be an inquiry. . . ."

"Yes," said Meade. "There will be that."

Grant finished his dispatch and handed it to an orderly. His staff had everything ready to go. He nodded to Meade, swung into the saddle, and trotted off. Meade and Humphreys watched them go. The bustle of breaking camp stirred up the dust, and they each took a drink from the water butt. "We'll pass by Sheridan's headquarters," said Meade, "and see if the cavalry is fit for service yet. Tomorrow . . ."

"The cavalry, plus Hancock, against the Weldon road?" asked Humphreys.

Meade nodded.

"The Battle of the Crater," said Meade, contemptuously.

"It could have been much worse," said Humphreys. "As it is, we've probably killed more of them than they have of us, and ripped up a good deal of their fortifications."

Meade brushed his hands together, clearing them of dust. "Let's get back to headquarters. Let Burnside clean up the rest of this mess." Humphreys looked round the littered campsite—scraps of papers blowing about, piles of horseshit from the cavalry escort, scraps of food.

CITY POINT, VA.,
July 30, 1864—10 A.M.

Maj. Gen. H. W. HALLECK,
Chief of Staff:

Finding that my efforts to surprise the enemy by sending an army corps and three divisions of cavalry to the north bank of the James River, under cover of night, for the purpose of getting on to the railroads north of Richmond, drew all his forces from Petersburg except three divisions, I determined to attack and try to carry the latter place. The enemy's earthworks are as strong as they can be made, and the ground is very broken and favorable for defense. Having a mine prepared running for a distance of eighty feet along the enemy's parapet, and about twenty-two feet below the surface of the ground, ready loaded, and covered ways made near to his line, I was strongly in hopes, by means of opening the way, the assault would prove successful. The mine was sprung a few minutes before 5 o'clock this morning, throwing up four guns of the enemy and burying most of a North Carolina regiment. Our men immediately took possession of the crater made by the explosion, and a considerable distance of the parapet to the right of it, as well as a short work in front, and still hold them. The effort to carry the ridge beyond, which would give us Petersburg and the south bank of the Appomattox, failed. As the line held by the enemy would be a very bad one for us, being on a side hill, the crest on the side of the enemy, and not being willing to take the chances of a slaughter sure to occur if another assault was made, I have directed the withdrawal of our troops to our old lines. Although just from the front, I have little idea of the casualties. I think, however, our loss will be but a few hundred, unless it occurs on withdrawing, which it may not be practicable to do before night. I saw about 200 prisoners taken from the enemy. Hancock and Sheridan returned from the north side of the river during the night, and are now here.

U. S. GRANT,
Lieutenant-General.

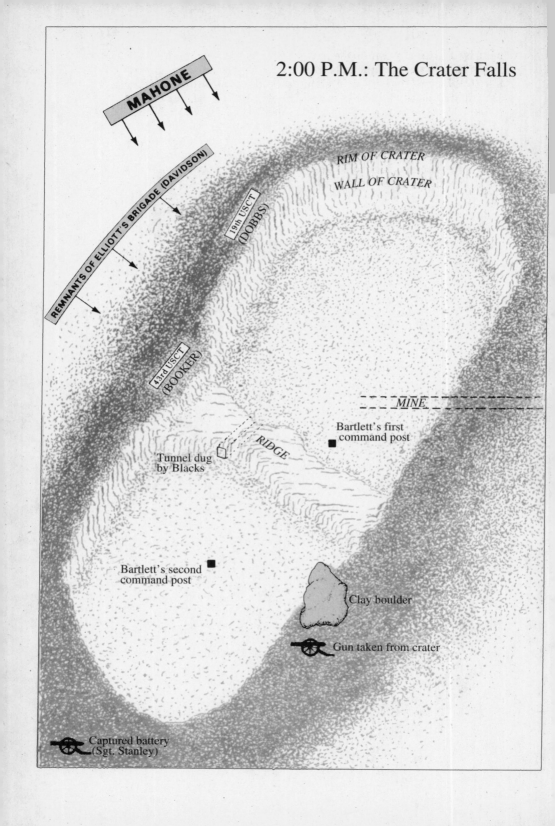

2:00 P.M.: The Crater Falls

MAHONE

REMNANTS OF ELLIOTT'S BRIGADE (DAVIDSON)

19th USCT (DOBBS)

43rd USCT (BOOKER)

RIM OF CRATER

WALL OF CRATER

MINE

Bartlett's first command post

Tunnel dug by Blacks

RIDGE

Bartlett's second command post

Clay boulder

Gun taken from crater

Captured battery (Sgt. Stanley)

The Battle in the Crater
10:30 A.M.–Midnight

Down in the Crater, Randolph led his patrol toward the place on the front wall below the flag of the Forty-third Regiment. There were crowds of soldiers all around, sitting or lying on the mounded earth. Some were wounded. Some sat and talked in low voices. He recognized Booker, and saw that he had some kind of handkerchief round his head. Wounded? No blood showing. The battle muttered outside and overhead. You could not see out of the Crater from the bottom. All you could see was the blue sky, blue as metal, and the sun, burning white as it mounted to the peak.

As he came closer, he saw Booker's skin was purplish, and he thought, *Heat got him,* and he saw Booker's face go changed: sickly-dead looking, and suddenly a twist in the lines of it, and the eyes sharpening up, and he knew he'd seen him. Booker rose to meet him.

"Ki," he said. His voice was a harsh-edged whisper.

Randolph halted. His eyes held Booker's eyes tightly. "I come back," he said. And then his heart bumped inside his chest, and he said sharply, "Did you think I wasn't goin' to?"

"I should have figured . . ."

"Well, now here I is." His eyes never left Booker's, but he had seen how few men there were round the white man. "Where is the rest?"

"They're gone," said Booker in that strange whisper. "I'm sorry I . . . they're gone. Lost em all. Lost em."

"Tobe?" asked Randolph. Booker shrugged.

"Now damn you to hell . . ." Randolph started to say, and he felt a grip on his arm. It was the thin private, the singer from the other brigade. "The man have a touch of sun," he said in a deep voice. "Bes leave him be."

Ki looked at him. "The man threw my people away."

Private Johnson Number Five shook his head. "Nobody throw nobody away. The brigade got whupped good. But we whupped some too."

"I was wrong to send you off," said Booker, as if something were becoming clear.

"Nothing no one man could do," said another voice. A runty white man with an axe.

Booker shook his head. "That isn't it. It was wrong anyhow. The wrong thing to do."

Ki looked around. A strange white officer, a Captain, was staring at Booker in disbelief. The runty white man was on his feet, standing next to Johnson. Booker looked up at the white man and said, "We should have stayed in Kansas, Lem."

Dobbs grinned down at Booker. "Hell, Books, if we hang around here long enough it might come to Kansas quarters yet." He extended his hand to Booker to help him up. "Listen," said Dobbs. "This ain't the time to bury the dead. Have to dig em up anyway, and make room for more. We're in a hole here. *The* hole."

They looked around. The high walls of the Crater cut off vision, except upward to the sky. Up along the steep rim, some men had kicked footholds into the earth. Elbows propped in the soft earth mounded at the upper lip of the Crater, they waited, watched the ground in front. There were about twenty of them now—more than half of them black. Dobbs's men, and some of Booker's, and Gregg's.

Gregg stood up, batting dust from his pants. "Let's see if we can't get the troops organized. Is anybody in command down here?"

Dobbs spat. "Ferrero's my division commander, and he's gone home. Thomas had the brigade, and he might be in hell right now. Or heaven."

"Oliver's wounded," said Booker.

"My regiment's Second Division," said Gregg. "First Division was supposed to go in first. So it's Ledlie: or Bartlett or Marshall."

"There's a brigade guidon over there," said Randolph, and he pointed back toward the ridge that divided the Crater. "One-leg General there," he added.

"That's Bartlett," said Gregg. He seemed pleased. "I'll go talk with him."

"How are we going to defend this place?" said Booker. "Those men can barely hang on, let alone fire and load."

Dobbs hefted his axe. He took a short run at the wall, and scrabbled up to the top. Holding the shaft short, he swung the axe in short chopping movements, cutting a foothold into the sliding soil of the steeply pitched Crater-side. He turned the blade, and tried packing it hard. Then kicked his boot into it. Shifted and moved down.

"Anybody have shovels?" asked Randolph. "They's wells all over the place. Figure the Johnnies was digging for water?"

Booker shook his head. Why would they dig for water in the front lines? He let Randolph lead him to the head of one of the wells: deep enough so the climbing sun didn't touch its bottom yet. Deep enough so a cool breath came from it.

Water or not, might be some shovels down there.

Booker looked over at Randolph, but Randolph was already moving around, shifting piles of junk, looking. He threw a short length of rope over near Booker's feet. Booker waved and whistled, and Private Johnson came over, and started the other men looking for rope.

They didn't find much of it: two pieces, maybe ten feet altogether. They joined the pieces, Randolph cinching the knot hard, and clinched them to a chain of doubled belts and straps, some of them found, some taken from their own pants and packs. The rope of belts and cord was about twenty feet long. Randolph knotted one end through his belt;

Booker grabbed the other, and did the same. They did not speak to each other until Randolph was ready to go. "Hold on to the side all you can to ease the weight," said Booker. "I'll let the curb take the most of it, but I don't want it rubbing too hard."

"Give me a bayonet," said Randolph. "I'll stick this in the wall as I go down."

Booker nodded. Randolph stepped to the side of the pit, and lowered himself over it, like a man easing into cold water. The cord creaked as it took the strain: creaked and stiffened. Three men were holding it, and Booker near the lip paying it out slowly as Randolph went down out of sight, and they heard his knife chunking into the wall, and the patter of falling dirt.

Booker took the strain across his back. His muscles stiffened and corded to hold Randolph, immeasurably heavy as he sank slowly to the bottom of the shaft. Sinking into the darkness, held by the cord at his belt looping his waist and looped also around his left arm, Randolph felt himself hang on the point of a slip-sliding fall, delicate and precise point of balance. His feet scrabbled and slipped, vague and incompetent as an infant's random movement. His left arm numbed with the strangling grip of the rope. His free right arm skillfully jabbed the knife into the wall at just the angle to give him his hold, stab and go, stab and go, swiftly down to the bottom.

His feet touched bottom, and he yelled. The earth was soft and powdery down here, must have tumbled in when the blowup came. He sank in it to the shins as he walked. There was no direct light, but enough filtered down through the dusty air to let him see what he was doing.

He touched a cold rod: arm of a dead man? He gripped it, firmly. His hand went round: wood. He twisted, rocked it, pulling, working it out of the soil. A pick. He yelled again: dropped the pick through a loop on the end of the cord, jerked it twice, and the pick rose toward heaven.

He felt around some more. Touched a cold hand. Cold and wet, a hand under the soil. A dim charge of electricity shot through him. He remembered the hardtack in the dead hand thrust out of the earth. This was no evil: a touch out of the world of the dead, an offering of bread. He moved his hands around, and the dead man gave him a shovel. The empty rope was down again, and he looped the shovel through, jerked twice, and sent it up toward the sky and the heat of the sun.

It was cool down here. Almost as if there might be water; but if there had been, the dead would have offered him some. The rope came again. He looped it around his waist, and took an easier turn about his left arm. He gripped the knife carefully. He'd try to help with that all he could.

It might be death if the rope broke. But these dead did not call for him, and he wasn't really afraid.

He jerked three times, and felt them begin to haul. The rope stiffened, gripping him hard, and he began helping with his free swinging arm and knife, digging his feet into the wall.

Booker felt him coming out before he saw him: felt it as an intensification of the strain and vibration of the rope, as if the higher Randolph came the nearer he was to death, not life.

Randolph's head broke past the lip of the well. His black arm flashed out and drove its blade into the hard-packed earth behind the wooden curb. His other arm, shoulders and chest were out, and Booker held the rope taut while the others ran and grabbed him, taking the weight so suddenly that Booker dropped ass-flat with the relief. He rose, and Randolph rose, batting the dust from themselves. Booker grinned and Randolph grinned and spat dirt out of his mouth. Someone handed Randolph a canteen and he drank and passed it to Booker who tipped it back and drank without wiping from the wet mouth of the canteen. Then they untied the cord from around their waists. Randolph shook his left arm, restoring circulation.

"I'm glad that's over," said Booker. His head was so full of blood and heat he could scarcely think. The shape of fear and guilt in his mind—the shapes of Randolph's men, the men he'd taken from Randolph by sending him away, falling down into death—they were there, but fainter now. He had held Randolph; he had drawn him back up out of that pit, not letting go for an instant. He had held him. Whatever he had done before, and why ever he had done it, he had paid it off somehow.

Then Death spoke again, a blast of raw noise and a brown ghost-shape that shot its head out of the ground behind Booker and yards away, and its bitter breath knocked them down and made their lungs burn. "MORTAR!" yelled somebody, and dirt-balls, wood and clods of meat fell around them.

And another one.

And another one, and Booker, peering back, saw a torn arm floating on a bubble of brown dirt and a face with eyes.

Instinctively, the men near the pithead had jumped or fallen toward each other.

Another blast covered them with dirt.

The rebel mortars had found the range.

10:45 A.M.

Bartlett's staff had moved their lean-to up against the rear wall of the Crater, the wall closest to the Union lines. There had been shade there earlier in the day, but now that the sun mounted toward noon there wasn't shade anywhere, the sun stared hotly down into every crevice and depression of the Crater floor, filling them with merciless, impersonal light and heat. The General was bathed in sweat, a sweat of the heat alternating with cold sweats that seemed to swell out of his insides, leaving him as weak and sick as he had felt in the hospital when they had cut off his leg. He had cracked the wooden leg off short. As the morning wore on, he began jabbing the broken end of it into the earth, unconsciously, while he gave orders and saw how things were going.

Saw how things were going! It was impossible. He was stuck here, legless and weak, in a big damn hole in the ground, his vision cut off by the high walls of the Crater. He might as well be in a bombproof back of the lines.

Captain Gregg appeared, saluted, introduced himself. Bartlett motioned for him to squat down.

A young man, Gregg. Captain commanding a regiment. That was the way things were getting to be in this army. Wastage and weakness. He wanted to organize the defenses, dig pits in front of the Crater, a connecting tunnel through the central ridge to connect the two parts of the Crater. . . .

Bartlett was hearing him from a great distance. The sickness in his body rose up like a curtain of heat-waves out of the earth, setting a barrier of distortion between him and all around him.

"These men are no damn good," said Bartlett. "They're a damned rabble. A mob."

Gregg's manner became studiedly patient. As if he had to cajole a recalcitrant child into doing something distasteful: not like an officer talking to a commanding officer. "I believe my men are still fit for action, sir. And there are two battalions of Negroes formed on the parapet, and ready to fight."

Bartlett felt his annoyance rising. Petulance and weakness, they went together. He'd been a shamefully bad patient. He took hold, and apologized to Gregg. "I intended no slur on your men, Captain."

"Isn't there an engineer company with your brigade? We have no entrenching tools. . . ."

Bartlett made an abrupt gesture. "You'll have to find them somewhere. I haven't seen any engineer company." He looked around him. He could see the blacks up on the parapet opposite him, like black lizards on a mud wall. "Get the niggers to dig your trenches, Captain. That's what they're for, isn't it?"

That was when the first mortar shell hit. Then the second, and another hit, and they ducked down, and another hit, and Gregg went dodging back across the Crater to where his men lined the parapet.

General Johnson sat with his sketch-map on a board between his legs. He spun his compass, figuring the arc of fire for his mortars and his battery of field artillery. He took a bearing on the grove of trees that was his most prominent landmark. If his men shifted their fire a few degrees to the left, and extended the elevation so as to get more range, they ought to hit the Crater with some consistency. The battery was another matter. Less useful for the present. To move it where it could fire most effectively would expose it to Yankee musketry and artillery. Best wait until it was most needed, making all preparations to move it up.

It was wonderful how this army, a great animal, could respond so efficiently when attacked: how each change in conditions required, and by requiring evoked, the exact quality of adjustment and response, the officers directing the soldiers as the brain directs the muscles. Too bad that such perfection of response could not be cultivated into a perfection of anticipation! The army, like most human institutions, could engage its powers only when attacked. Never had the South and the institution of slavery been so precious to him, never had he appreciated their place in the overarching order as much as when both were threatened. He supposed that much the same feeling actuated the other side: never had they loved the Union so much as when Sumter was bombarded. How else explain their three years' loyalty to the shambling corrupt ape in the White House? Their toleration of the excesses of the Abolition fanatics? Perhaps this war, this battle, was the crucible in which a new perfection of order might be forged: a social machine capable of responding to the crises of peace and workaday reality as the army responded to war. If only the memory would not fade. The soft, sentimental South! Tried in the fire, would she have the strength to bear the burning scar, and gird herself against the future need in a regime of iron?

"Captain Montgomery!" he called. "I should like for you to shift your mortar-fire. . . ."

11:00 A.M.

Neill and Beeler had learned the terrain of the Crater floor as quickly and thoroughly as they could have sized up and mastered a new neighborhood: there were the bad districts under the eye of the cops, the places where you took your life in your hands just walking upright, the safe districts where you wouldn't be seen or bothered. There were charmed circles where the brigade headquarters were, and where certain groups of officers gathered to talk about rallying the men. There were other bunches of officers who were, like themselves, concerned not to be seen. An especially good spot, close enough to the field hospital so as to make their being wounded or sunstruck plausible; not so close that the wound-dressers would spot them and check them out.

The first mortar shell looped right into the middle of the Crater, not twenty yards from where they sat. Then the other shells started coming in. The sun glared straight down, and the mortar shells seemed to fall out of the sun, as if the steady heat had built so high it could come in bursts, and they needed shade.

"The Wall!" yelled Neill, and Beeler nodded. They had to get to the front wall, where the shells wouldn't reach so easily. They rose, crouching, and began to run for the point on the wall where the central ridge joined the front wall. Neill thought he heard the sky whistle overhead, and he stopped, grabbing Beeler to pull him down, and somebody ran right up his back, and all three went down together. Debris from the explosion of the mortar shell rained down from overhead.

When it stopped Neill rolled around, and saw that there was a Captain on them. The Law had materialized out of the shell-burst. They were caught.

"All right," snapped the Captain, "get forward. Keep going. Where in hell's your musket, soldier?" he said to Neill. "Never mind: you can load em for the men that's firing. Get on up there now!"

They were right up to the wall. Another shell made them cringe.

"Get on up there, you damned slacker," said the Captain. Neill and

Beeler looked up. A row of grinning niggers looked down, like a row of nigger-dolls in a sideshow waiting for you to bowl them off and win a goddamn prize. Neill stood at the base of the wall, and the sliding dirt drizzled around his boot tops as Beeler went up.

"You'll stand down here with these others, and load muskets. And you'll come up when there's room. And if you run, I'll shoot you like a dog." The Captain turned to a black corporal. "Watch this . . . *coffee boiler,* soldier," and then he climbed up the wall.

Neill stood next to his jailer, the nigger with the corporal's stripes, and watched the Captain climb. Maybe a reb sniper would pick the bastard off. Then he'd handle the nigger.

He saw Beeler's feet kicking footholds in the sliding gritty earth; he was holding on by elbows and belly friction.

The sun blazed down. Mortar shells landed in the middle of the Crater. Smoke and torn earth burst up where they fell, and bits of wreckage, meat, screams, and cries.

In the battery, to the left of the Crater, Hartranft's infantry had stuck a captured rebel flag in the parapet. "The damned thing nearly scared me to death," said Stanley—bare-chested and sweating, the dead-white skin glazed with sweat and dulled with washes of gray where dust had stuck in it. "I look up at it from hauling on that damned gun, and I think, 'I'm dead,' standing right in front of the goddamned embrasure hauling on that pig of a gun."

"Maybe we should take it down," said the staff officer.

"Leave the flag," said Hartranft. "What about the gun?"

Stanley shrugged. "Ground's too broken up, earth's too deep and soft. It keeps bogging down. And every time we get it started the rebs drop a shell in near us, and everybody leaves hauling and lies down." Stanley tried to work up some spit, and couldn't. He reached round his canteen, swirled the water with a thin sound, and drank. The canteen was empty when he corked it and put it back.

"So we can't use it," said Hartranft.

"I left it, loaded and turned to fire across the top of the Crater if we ever need to do that." He looked inquiringly at Hartranft. The air above the battery was full of the hum of bullets, and the punctual blast of artillery sounded off in front of and behind them.

"Humphrey's brigade tried to go in on our left, and got whipped back to the lines, . . ." Hartranft started to say.

"Run back like a bunch of fucking rabbits," said the staff officer, and Hartranft glared at him.

"We've got two guns here," said Hartranft, "both firing down to our left. I want one of them trained to fire to the right front. A good sweep of the front of the Crater." Stanley nodded.

The three men stood for a moment in the glaring sun. Their faces looked dull and blunted, like the faces of statues worn and worn by water or gritty wind.

Hartranft's orders had a very simple meaning. They meant that the brigade would no longer attempt to attack. The guns would be pointed to defend the Crater. The ground in front was still held by a sketchy line of skirmishers left from the three—no, four—divisions that had attacked. From this line men still came running back toward the Crater, by individuals and groups and even formed lines of troops. These men were right in the sights of the gun that Stanley slewed around and set pointing rightward. But soon, Hartranft was figuring, the drift would turn gray-brown, like river water cutting through a bank of lighter sand and changing color.

I better get some protection here, thought Stanley. The gun, pointed out the back of the rebel battery, was not protected by a full parapet from troops advancing against it. There wasn't but one shovel among the men in the battery, and it was going to be the devil's own time getting any kind of barricade thrown up. Boxes and barrels, thought Stanley, and pile the dirt on top.

He hadn't more than started on it when they heard the bugles go, and the musketry went hush for a minute, and someone said, "Oh Jesus, here they come," and Stanley jumped in behind his knee-high embrasure and yelled, "All right! Ready to fire!" And behind him he heard the shriek starting and their own muskets stop for that second with the shock of it as they always did, and only one stupid rebel gun off to the left still banging away as if nothing were happening.

11:15 A.M.

"Here they come," said Dobbs. Private Johnson Number Five heard him in the sudden lapse of sound in the firing, and he noticed that the smoke in front where the rebels' trench was, wasn't thickening any more. He had just reloaded his musket, while his heels dug in against the steeply sloping side of the Crater, trying to hold with his skin to the skidding clay. He had bit the cartridge, tasting the powder grit between his teeth. Rammed it home with the thin flexing ramrod while he held the butt steady against his foot. Stuck the rammer in the soft earth to keep it handier, and rolled back to look through the little slit he'd cut himself in the earth that curbed the Crater.

He was glad he had loaded up. He didn't want to be hanging there by his ribs when Johnny came for him.

At the other side of the peeled and littered swale he saw it again: the line of heads bob up in a long row, and rise higher, and he caught the sudden flash from one end of the line to the other as the sun caught the edges of the rising bayonets and went left to right like a gleam on the ripple of a running wave. Johnson jammed his right hand into the earth to dry it in the dust, then wiped it on his trouser leg. He looked at it. Everything just as before, brown skin against the brown gunstock. The veins in his hand stood out like cords.

He looked out and the enemy line flashed again and swooped forward, red flags overhead like attendant vultures. He could see their white faces and hear their screeching.

"FIRE!" yelled Dobbs, and Johnson squeezed the trigger and smoke exploded, a wall shielding him in a moment from the wave. *How in hell can I reload?* He clung with his skin to the sliding earth, bit cartridge, dropped it in the barrel. Rammer, a springy twig. The sun burned. Through the earth he seemed to hear the rumble of the white-face wave flashing and rolling in the vibration of its coming, even seem-ing to jiggle the earth loose around him. Then the smooth gunstock was against his cheek and the brown wave was closer, and the screeching, and the red birds, and he squeezed the trigger: the stock kicked hard, smoke-burst, and then smoke-burst again, bigger and louder right in front. *A cannon*, fired at the rebels from the left. The drifting smoke hid the sight of it from him, but he could hear them screaming.

Randolph heard the yell, and led the sprint for the wall, Booker on his heels, some of the men scrambling up after. To their right the bigger half of the Crater stirred and swarmed like an ant's nest. To their left, the same scene appeared on a smaller scale. For some reason, no mortar shells were falling on the smaller part of the Crater.

They lined out left and right. White troops to either side slid over, making room; there was a gesture of avoidance in it. Randolph kicked his boots into the side of the Crater for foothold. Down below, he saw Gregg, chasing a couple of white skulkers. One of them, a white man with the face of a drunk, came climbing up to the top. The other, a man with hair like fire, stayed at the bottom. Gregg scrambled up as well, and as he reached the top and slipped in on Randolph's right they heard the rebel yell, and Randolph knew they were coming.

The lie of the ground brought the rebel attack against the right half of the Crater. The troops toward the left had to fire obliquely at the oncoming rebel line. They could see the whole thing, and know them-selves safe by some strange margin, in that they were not directly at-tacked. They began to fire, quickly. Gregg leaned across the parapet, right arm braced in earth, and pointed his Colt's pistol. Randolph did the same. He wished he had a rifle, one of those repeaters.

He saw the rebels coming on, and he saw them start to tumble, and then he saw the dim black flash of something that swept left to right from the far left end of the Crater, and knew what it was when the smoke went *bang!* in the middle of the rebels and he saw them go down like string-cut puppets, and said to himself, *Canister!* Now there were rebs close enough to kill with his pistol: brace against the parapet, aim and point very steadily. He was learning to shoot very well with the pistol.

While he aimed and shot, he was aware of other things: the sound of firing all along the lip of the Crater; the bang of their own canister gun; the shape of the rebel attack, like a cloud breaking up in a big wind. Suddenly there were gray and brown-clothed white men throwing guns down, and ducking in with their hands out, huddling up under the raised lip of the Crater yelling "Don't shoot!" just to get away from the canister gun that kept banging away, one shell, another shell, and the rifles firing from the lip.

Randolph saw the cloud break and slide back faster than it came on, and he yelled, and slapped Gregg between the shoulders, and Gregg was yelling, and he rolled around, and shook Randolph's hand hard, smiling.

A shell landed in front of them and to the right, and they felt hunks of metal whizz by. The man Gregg had chased up to the top had just leaned forward to help a rebel prisoner in over the parapet, and they heard the metal go *chunk* when it hit.

The man twisted and fell back in, one leg grotesquely bent, the other caught by a piece of broken timber that pierced the trouser-cloth. He hung head down over the edge of the Crater, face to the dirt. The shell fragment had torn his throat out, and blood was pouring out of the hole like wine out of a busted skin. Blood and blood and blood till it seemed he would never be empty.

Neill looked up, and Beeler hung down. The nigger faces watched the blood running out of Beeler, and Neill saw them lick their black lips and their yellow teeth. The blood kept running out of Beeler, like a man was just a bag of blood, he kept expecting him to go all flat. The blood ran down the side of the Crater, and Beeler hung like a butchered steer, and the blood shone slickly on the dirt of the Crater wall, and Neill thought of all the times he and the boys had dammed up rain runnels with twigs and green turf when they were young. At the bottom of the Crater, where the clay earth had been pounded flat and hard by feet, the blood sat on the surface in a pool. Neill thought it would fill the Crater to the brim. "Man, I'm thirsty," said a nigger voice, and Neill waited for him to bend and drink from the pool of his friend's blood.

Somebody gave Beeler a shove, and he slid down with his face against the gritty wall. It was so steep that he began to tumble, his ass and legs rolling forward, till he landed with one hand in the pool of his blood. Neill looked up. A nigger had slid into the spot on the skyline Beeler had fallen out of.

11:30 A.M.

Over on the Confederate left, where the Federal Second and Fourth divisions had attacked and been repulsed, Mahone's counterattack had started the Yankees moving backward. Davidson and Bruce, leading a scratch force of the survivors of their own brigade, kept moving on the left flank of the counterattack. Out of sight to their right, they heard the attack against the Crater itself going forward, and they heard it break and go back. But here Mahone's men were coming in with them, they were moving forward as the Yankees and niggers went back.

Things were going very nicely indeed. An eight-gun battery off on their left kept breaking up organized Yankee lines. Davidson had even picked up a sword. They were up on the main line, and working down it toward the Crater. The Yankees fired, and pulled back; or just started going back. Bullets zipped around them, but they weren't taking many losses.

Bruce grinned at Davidson. "I guess we're still in business," he said.

There was a surge of firing, and some of their men went by them in a rush. Bruce looked and saw the Yankees flush from cover and head back, except for some that stood and held their hands up. Prisoners.

Here were some more troops coming in with prisoners on the right, and one raggedy private was waving. "Colonel!"

The raggedy private came toward them, and Bruce recognized Dixon. A figure shambled after him, a face peeled raw on one side, the flesh blackened and burned. A horrible face, a demonic face. *Right sort of friend for Dixon,* thought Bruce, but the inward joke died without comforting him. The face was too horrible.

"It's me and Billy," said Dixon, looking eagerly from Bruce's face to the Colonel's. "I thought we was the only ones left."

Bruce looked away from the face, and saw his troops waving from the captured barricade. Dixon reminded him: they hadn't seen any of their own men all day.

"I thought we was the only ones left," said Dixon again, and Bruce said, "We are."

Off to their right they heard bugles, drums, and officers yelling for the troops to keep in formation. The four survivors stood in the burning sun. Four out of near a thousand out of Jefferson County and Kinston and New Bern.

Billy turned first, and crouching low, began to work his way forward again.

11:40 A.M. *Burnside's Headquarters*

All of the division commanders were there. Potter and Willcox sat side by side, faces black with dirt and powder-grit, eyes hollow and weary. Ferrero sat to one side, slim and dark, looking anxiously round the room and from face to face, seeking the answer to some question he had not asked. Ledlie sat apart. No one looked at him or spoke to him, the orderlies politely avoiding contact with him. He sat erect in his chair, red-faced, his blue eyes looking attentively and intelligently ahead —but unwaveringly ahead; the only object they could have held in view would have been the blank wall of the bombproof. He smelled of medicine, a smell of camphor and cloves.

"Can we not push the men forward, and carry the crest?" said Burnside. He sat at his table, one fat hand resting on it. His reddened face streamed with sweat, his whiskers were glossy and moist.

"It's impossible," said Potter flatly. "I've been on the line myself."

"I have too," interjected Willcox, and Potter glanced at him.

Ferrero cleared his throat, but did not speak. *Why can't I say, "I've been on the line too"?* He thought of Hamlet's uncle in the play, and why he could not say amen.

"The troops would not go forward before," said Potter.

"They're a lot of damned cowards," said Burnside, and he slapped the table.

"They've seen hard service," said Willcox.

"And some of em are badly led," said Potter, and the room fell silent.

Burnside passed a hand over his face. "All right, all right. Gentlemen. For God's sake, let's not begin backbiting and fighting among ourselves. We must give each other mutual support now. We must hold together.''

''We've got to get the men out as soon as possible,'' said Potter. ''We've been ordered to retreat. There's no point in staying.''

Burnside set his jaw. ''White tells me the troops in the Crater have just beaten off a counterattack.''

''Yes,'' said Ledlie, ''that is right.'' They ignored him.

''Perhaps the place can be held till nightfall,'' said Ferrero helpfully. ''If we can . . .''

Burnside looked at him and nodded, even smiled. ''Yes, if it can be held, perhaps it will turn out that we want it after all.'' Potter snorted. ''In any case, it will be safer to pull the men out in darkness.''

Potter spread his hands helplessly. ''What is the state of affairs in the Crater? Has anyone here been in it? Or near it in the last hour or two?''

''White has been!'' said Burnside. ''And he advises that we hold it!''

Potter picked up the dispatch that held Burnside's instructions and White's endorsement to the division commanders. ''Let's circulate this to the brigade commanders in the rebel lines for their opinions. In writing. They're the only ones who can see for themselves what can and can't be done.''

The others nodded slightly, made small gestures of agreement. Ledlie nodded vigorously, sitting by himself.

A staff officer took the dispatch, got his orders, and stalked out. Burnside rose. ''Gentlemen,'' he said, ''you had best return to your commands to await my further orders.'' Potter rose, and Willcox. Ledlie remained seated. Ferrero rose, against a strange heavy drag that seemed to grip his thighs and his shoulders, making his strength feel watery. He had, in that moment, absolutely no idea in the world of where to go after he walked through the door of the bunker. His brain simply would not work. It was enough, for the moment, that he was able to rise and walk through the bombproof door. That was more than Ledlie had been able to do.

11:45 A.M.

Wright's brigade of Mahone's division had advanced straight against the Crater and the sections of trench to its right and left. The ground between them and the Crater there was relatively clear, but the Yankees in the rifle pits and trenches and in the Crater, and the Yankee gunner firing canister out of the battery on the south side of the Crater, had cut them up, and shot the legs out from under the brigade, and they'd wavered and stopped, the first line ripped apart, some going down, some going back, some crawling up under the Yankee parapet yelling surrender, anyone who hesitated getting shot where he stood—and then the brigade had poured back into the recaptured trench that cut across behind the salient.

Mahone was watching from the ravine at the base of the slope, where his second brigade, Sanders, was mustering. He sent another staff officer to pull the remnant of Elliott's brigade of Johnson's division out from his left, and bring them over to cover his right and center. He'd want his strongest and freshest troops sweeping in from the left, where the oblique line of fire—obstructed by the lie of the trenches—would partially block Yankee fire coming from the Crater and the battery, and shield his men from the gunners on the Yankee main line. He sent his orders out just as soon as his first wave of attackers had finished running back from the Crater and had settled down.

He had thought of asking General Johnson, over at his right, to alter the targets of the mortars and artillery over there. But it seemed, from the view of shell-bursts he could see out of the ravine, that Johnson had anticipated him. So he gave it no further thought. He wrote: "General Lee: I am preparing to retake the Crater. Will assault at two P.M. Mahone, *Major-General.*"

Noon

Bartlett had gotten one of his staff officers to bring some of the blacks down off the wall, and get them to dig a tunnel connecting the two parts of the Crater under the central ridge. The mortar shells began looping in again as soon as the infantry attack stopped, and shell-fire was coming in too: not from high enough to drop into the Crater, but shells chewed into the parapet wall, and ricochets bounced over it. Wherever they struck, they struck meat.

The shells fell around Bartlett and his staff while they waited for the niggers to dig them through. Then his aides gripped Bartlett under the arms, and hustled him to it, and through it scrabbling on hands and knees. As he went, he looked back, and he heard the screaming of the men who had been chewed up by the mortar shells, and saw the floor of the Crater writhe with men moving and crawling about on the hummocks of broken earth.

In the smaller part of the Crater things were better. There were wounded men and skulkers on the floor here too, but fewer shells seemed to drop in. Hartranft was down from his headquarters in the captured battery. The two Generals looked at each other. "They've driven most of Griffin's men out of the trenches on our right," said Bartlett. "Next time anybody tries to take this place, they'll do it."

"You ought to get out," said Hartranft.

Bartlett shrugged, and moved his leg-stump. He could never make it. It was a relief not to have to even think about it. He was certain that he'd be dead or a prisoner before supper.

Hartranft looked around. "When they get our dispatch, they ought to send water."

"Who'll bring it?" asked Bartlett, and Captain Gregg materialized at his shoulder.

"I've asked for volunteers," said Gregg. "None of the white troops will go. Some of the blacks are willing to try."

Bartlett grinned sarcastically. "I'll bet. They're brave enough for trying to go back, I suppose. What odds that they'll come back if they find the water?"

"I think you mistake their temper, sir," Gregg said.

"Do I?" said Bartlett.

"Gentlemen, let's not bicker among ourselves," said Hartranft. On the other side of the ridge a man had begun screaming, a high piercing female shriek that unnerved everybody in an instant. Mortar shells continued to throw dirt into the air.

"Let the niggers give it a try," said Bartlett. "They're supposed to be drawers of water, aren't they? And let's get some of em digging a covered way back to the lines. One from here, one from the other side." He licked his lips. His mouth tasted of bile. He was nauseated, sick to death. "This rabble isn't even brave enough to run for its life in the open."

The middle of the Crater was death. If you wanted to live, you stayed by the high walls. Mortar shells kept dropping out of the sun, and they chewed up the bodies of the living and the bodies of the dead, worrying and playing with the pieces like an animal. The heat fell out of the white sky, and sank into the ground. The clay baked like brick, the ground held pools of new blood deep enough to splash when you stepped in. The wounded crawled like crabs while the ground boiled and threw up, and the sun poured down.

Neill held his arms over his shuddering head and shaken body, curled into a cusp of the earth that rocked and spat and fumed and stank, and saw with his eyes closed bodies bursting like balloons full of blood. The niggers rimmed the bowl of his prison, with yellow eyes and sharp teeth. Starving and hungry, animals, they'd drink his blood and slice the flesh from him living if the sun set on him.

Someone kicked him and he fell over. "Get up, you damned skulker." He looked up, and an officer stood above him, but the officer looked away and yelled up at the niggers on their perch. "Hey you! Get down here! Get your black asses down here now!"

"Our officer said for us to wait on him," said a deep voice, the nigger sergeant.

"Where in hell is he?"

"Gettin the rest of the regiment together, suh."

"We'll never mind about that! General Bartlett needs some digging done and some boys to go fetch water. Now get down here, and no more sass."

The sergeant looked down, not moving. (This man was not his officer.)

The officer cocked his pistol and pointed it.

Neill rolled and ducked, and slipped off along the wall as the officer stared at the sergeant, and Neill never heard the niggers coming down but he didn't hear a shot, either. There was a broken crate off a bit to the right, and Neill ducked behind it.

Randolph and his detail followed the staff officer to the tunnel through the ridge, through the tunnel, and to the rear of the smaller half of the Crater. They picked their way among the bodies of the wounded and the worn-out. The Crater stank of blood and explosives— and shit, too, where men had begun to relieve themselves here and there. All of it baking under the sun.

"I've got one party digging on the other side," said the officer. "You and your men will dig from here. Slant the trench out at an angle, left of here till you're about twenty feet past the edge of the Crater. Then straight back toward the lines unless I tell you different."

Randolph stood impassively.

"You can *understand* that much, can't you?" said the officer disgustedly.

Randolph stood.

"Well move your black butt then, and don't stand gaping."

The detail turned to, and began hacking at the wall with a spade, pick, some old planks, bayonets.

"I want some volunteers to go for water," said the officer. Randolph turned and looked at him. "I know a good way to get across," he said. "I'll bet you do," said the officer. "Just do as you're told, boy, and there won't be any trouble. I want you *here*, understand? And I want you *digging!*"

Four black men volunteered. While Randolph and his detail, clinging halfway up the side of the Crater, hacked and picked at the start of the trench that would take them back to their lines, the officer had the volunteers load up with all the canteens they could carry. They climbed to the top, their backs humped like the backs of buffalo. "Wait on the canister gun," yelled Randolph, but couldn't tell if they'd heard him.

They went over the top, and began scrabbling forward, except for one that was shot in the back of the head and fell with his feet quivering projecting over the side of the Crater. The other three were shot going across.

12:30 P.M.

They swung picks, boards, and shovels. The jolt of striking the ground shivered up their bones, muscles too stiff and tired to take the shock soft. Shirts off, backs running sweat. The air was hard and hot, swathing swaddling them in cumbersome heat. The sun blazed down from overhead and dazzied off the ground, beating them, back of the head and front of the head.

Time going by. Swing the pick. Water poured out of their skin. They drank from the canteens. After a time the canteens were down, the little bit of water rattled in them like seeds in a dry pod.

Randolph felt a hand on his back. He turned and looked. It was the other white Captain, Gregg.

"How do?" said the Captain.

"This is stupid," said Randolph. "We never scratch our way across in a week. Get out much farther, they gonna drop shells on us like dropping pebbles down a well."

Gregg nodded. "I'm going to take a dispatch over, have them make an attack and get us out of here. Get them to send us some water. Most of the men have no more bullets, either.''

Randolph looked at Gregg. ''Listen, Captain. You want to make it across there, you go slow, crawling out maybe twenty feet. Then you wait on that canister gun to fire, and you watch for a bunch running off to start going too, if you's lucky enough to get em. That happens, you make your run, countin . . . maybe twenty while you go, and then you go down again. See? Till the canister gun fire.''

''All right,'' said Gregg. ''Thanks.'' He hesitated, at a loss. Then he wiped his hand on his shirt, and shook Randolph's hand. Then he shook the hands of the other three diggers. They were in a little five-foot bay that the four had scraped in the rear of the Crater wall, under the shadow of the giant clay boulder. They heard the canister gun fire, and then Gregg went over the top.

''If he bring water,'' said one of the men, ''I hope he remember to come back this way.''

''Um-hum,'' said Randolph. He was thinking about Gregg running back across the field. The way *he* would go, the way he would take his people, if so be he had to get them out of here in a hurry. He swung his pick.

IN THE CRATER, *12:40.*

Generals GRIFFIN AND HARTRANFT:

It will be impossible to withdraw these men, who are a rabble without officers, before dark, and not even then in good order. Please let me know what your plans are.

W. F. BARTLETT,
Brigadier-General of Volunteers

I think the best way to withdraw is by making attack from our pits and batteries, bearing on our right and left— the men here are a rabble—and then let them withdraw immediately, whenever you approve the plan. They are suffering very much from [want of] water, and the troops cannot well be organized.

J. F. HARTRANFT,
Brigadier-General of Volunteers.

I concur in the above.

S. G. GRIFFIN,
Brigadier-General.

1:20 P.M.

After the attack had been beaten off, Booker had slipped down from the wall, leaving Sergeant Randolph in charge, and had gone back to the right of the Crater to get the surviving men of the Forty-third. He had an idea of keeping his troops together, so he could use them better: organize their fire, rotate men on the wall, hold out a reserve in an attack for . . . for whatever came up. He wasn't thinking too clearly, he couldn't really plan ahead. He just decided to get his men together, and went after them.

He picked his way along the wall to the place where the regimental flag hung on its pole. Up under the wall there was a cluster of black soldiers, a small space around them where the whites drew their line of avoidance. Men lying at the base of the wall, others hunched over, tending them, holding them, feeding them water from nearly dry canteens. One man held another, wounded man in a tight embrace, chest to chest. The wounded man's stiff arms and limp-necked head lolled and looped as the man who held him rocked slowly forward and backward, a crooning sound bubbling from his lips.

A white officer sat nearby with a platoon of troops apparently still under orders. "I'm taking some of these troops over to the left," said Booker. "You can put your men up there." The officer looked up stupidly, a million miles away. "Listen, Captain," said Booker, "That's no suggestion, that's an order."

The Captain looked at his men to see if they could help him. When nobody moved, he slowly got up, cringing as another shell looped in and burst halfway down the Crater.

"Git them niggers to clean up after theirselves before we go. This place is a shit-hole," said one of the men.

The men of the Forty-third—twenty of them, some wounded—were gathering. The first of the white soldiers moved toward the wall and bumped a wounded man with his shoulder, and suddenly there was shoving and muskets came up, and Booker stepped up and pushed into the middle. Pushed them apart, and got his own troops moving off.

"Better get them niggers out of here before the Johnnies come back. They'll sell all they don't cut, and you too, you nigger-loving son of a bitch."

The group of black soldiers convoyed the wounded carefully over the broken ground, jostling against crowds of whites. There was yelling, and Booker saw fists swinging up at the head of the line as he rushed forward, knocked sideways into his own line when a mortar shell burst off to his left and the air of it caught him. It was a nightmare, the air dark with dust and thick with heat and shrieking, and these eruptions of men blocking his path, grabbing, pushing, beating at his soldiers. He stumbled up to the front, and moved along the wall.

Up above his head Dobbs and the survivors of the Nineteenth Regiment were lining the wall and firing carefully and slowly, to keep the rebels from plunging right in here into the midst of this nightmare with them. It was crazy. They were enemies, why keep them out of the worst place in the whole world?

The only way Booker got his men back to the place on the wall by the central ridge was by forming the strongest ones and leading a rush right against the mob of white slackers who yelled *niggerniggernigger* and shook their fists. Maybe one of them even took a shot, but they ducked back into the earth when Booker rushed them, and he pulled his men together under the wall. Somehow he'd lost five more. And started them up to relieve the men on the wall.

He climbed up to the spine of the ridge, to his place on the wall. The soldier with the broken flagstaff, Colehill, had stuck it in the earth of the parapet. He looked at Booker, grinned, and said, ''Man, we safer up here than down there.''

Booker looked back into the Crater. The boiling dirt of mortar shells tore up the heart of the Crater, while the mobbed gangs of broken troops huddled toward the walls, fought each other bitterly for place.

It was like a vision of the pit of hell, and here he was with his cheerful black volunteers manning the perimeter to keep another bunch of devils away from the bunch they had already. Fall forward or fall back, and you're meat either way.

''Take the flag down,'' he said to Colehill. ''It's just drawing fire.'' Colehill looked glum, but complied.   .

Where was Randolph? The regiment gone, the attack gone to hell. Booker reached out abruptly, and tore the flag from the staff with two sharp jerks. He held it out to the color guard. ''Here,'' he said, ''put this inside your shirt.'' He rolled over and looked through the fire slit. The rebels were shooting, and behind the smoke bank he thought he saw shadowy bulks shifting around—troops moving up, building up for another charge. ''If we have to get out of here fast,'' said Booker, ''I want you to get the flag out. Whatever happens, I don't want *them* to get it.''

That was what there was left to do. To deny the enemy the flag. Not to give them the last bit of satisfaction.

From his perch on the wall of the Crater, just below the rim, Booker could see down into most of the churned and tumbled floor of the pit. But the high curb of churned earth that rimmed the Crater cut off all view of the world outside it, making a distinct horizon line backed with the blank slate of the blue sky. A little world. Like the cities of bugs you uncover when you overturn a big flat stone, swarming. Black men and white men, soldiers and officers and orderlies all jumbled together, cried out or shrieked, begged for water, called names of people, cursed, called on gods, bent hunched over another giving water, stealing water. A piece of a world. Gone mad. Gone to hell.

A world without a single woman. It hit Booker at that moment: the strangeness of it, never somehow realized before in the bustle of the camp, the march, the trench line. As if all the women in the world were gone, vanished or turned at one stroke into men. . . . *No—you left her behind. To save her, you said, from the wolves. These others too—they left women behind them. How many like yourself were driven to this world of war because what was home was more fearful still: love and tender feeling that told you how easy it was to lose yourself in love and then to lose what you loved, so that loving made you so afraid of the wolves you couldn't stay put?*

Wasn't it better, wasn't it better in every way to meet them far from home? Not at your own door?

You'd think so. But write this down, Booker thought, *make a note of*

this. Man is wolf to man, yes: but not all men are wolves to all men. Un-
less they come to your door for you, how can you be sure? How can
you be sure that you aren't the wolf yourself? Was it better to stay at
home and wait for the wolves then? Oh, by then they might be so strong
that you'd have no chance against them at all.

But at least you'd be sure.

Private Johnson lay on his back. He'd borrowed Chopper's axe
and cut himself good solid footholds, and a knee-rest in the side of the
Crater. He'd opened his shirt to the belly. The hot sun was killing folks
down in the bottom of the hole. He kept his cap tilted forward to cover
his eyes.

Dobbs was next to him, lying on his belly. He'd put his pistol aside
and gotten a rifle from the bottom of the Crater. Axe by his left hand.
He figured to take one, maybe two, long shots when they came again.
Then do the rest of it with the pistol up close. Then the axe. The sun
made his ears ring, and he'd cool his head by rubbing his forehead into
the sand.

"Man," said Johnson, "you a clay eater?"

Dobbs looked up. "What in hell's a clay eater?"

Johnson uncorked his canteen and passed it over to Dobbs. "There's
folks down home eats clay. Women mostly does it. There's some say it's
a power in it. But it don't seem to work for everybody. Leastaways,
there's only few of em got the taste for it."

Dobbs sipped gingerly, as if his dried lips were pained by the
touch of the metal.

"I've eat all the clay I want to for now. I'd admire a good strong
pull of water, and a bucket of it for my head."

Johnson looked at Dobbs's face, the cracked lips and reddened eyes,
and the flush that white folks got when the sun was on them bad. "Go
ahead," he said. He meant, *Use the water on your head.*

Dobbs dropped his eyes, then raised them again to meet Johnson's.
The black man's eyes were brown water-pebbles set in yellow glaze; the
white man's blue-white china crazed with red lines. "Thanks, but we'd
best save it."

"Woodchopper," said Johnson Number Five, "I think I'll take
that corporal job, if you still wants."

2:00 P.M.

Randolph was still swinging his pick, a steady rhythmic chopping
that used his muscles and was easy on them. The steady swing-chop,
pull loose; swing-chop, pull loose—it was a movement his body did without need to spend his mind or spirit on it. As he worked he listened: the
steady roar of the musketry firing and the punctuating blasts of the
artillery became familiar to him. He perked up and paid attention when
the sound shifted, going higher or dropping down. He could sense it
building slowly, like a stream beginning to build when it's rained way
up on the other side of the hills. He listened and thought, running over

in his mind the shape of the Crater, and where his people were on the opposite side, lined out where the central ridge ran across like a bridge over the tunnel they'd dug. There were two things to think about. One was easy: when the attack came, he was going back to where his people were, and he was going right across that bridge. Nobody who went down into that hole full of men was going to be able to move more than ten feet.

The second thing wasn't easy. If they stopped this attack like they did the last, that was good. If they didn't . . . if they didn't, he wasn't going to let any of his people fall into the hands of those white men. He wasn't leaving any of his kind ever again to the lash, and the branding iron, and the cutting blade in the white man's hand.

"Think Tobe dead, Ki?"

Randolph shook his head. Tobe's face appeared when he closed his eyes. The skin was smooth brown, the features smooth too: like pebbles on the shore. But he had no image of the eyes. Could not say if there were eyes or there were not eyes in the face. The lips lay together and did not move.

Randolph turned and looked out of the bay. There was the bridge, the black soldiers on the wall, and beyond them, the smoke from the shooting was banking up. Banking higher and higher.

He looked down, calculating the height of the jump. Captain Shugrue appeared, was given to his eyes as a kind of sign. The Captain was crouched, listening to the rising sound of the firing. He looked up and his eyes met Randolph's.

Shugrue snatched his cap off his head. With the point of a clasp knife he ripped at the stitching that held the green shield of the insignia onto his cap: the cannon crossed with the anchor for the Ninth Corps; green for Fourth Division. For the Nigger Division. Then Shugrue ripped the regimental number from his collar tabs.

And that was the sign. *They coming now. They going to take this place right now.* The musketry was roaring louder.

Louder on the right than on the left.

Smoke banking higher on the right than on the left.

He grabbed his men, one at a time, shook them by the right shoulder. "Listen! I'm going back up for the rest of our people. When we come back cross this bridge here, when you see me coming, you get out this hole, and up behind the dirt on top, and give us some cover fire. You hear me? You hear what I tell you?" They nodded. They could hear how the gunfire was raving now themselves. "Anybody try to stop us, I don't care if they Yankee blue: you hit them!"

"Yes, Ki."

He turned. Shugrue had vanished, hidden in some nook of wreckage. A mortar shell, and another one, tossed dirt and a body into the air. He heard the screaming rising out of the Crater. He slid and scrambled to the ridge. He began running, the single figure moving across the welter of the Crater from back to front, running along across the bridge of earth with the boiling halves of the Crater on either side full of blood and smoke and the cries of the wounded and dying.

2:15 P.M.

They had no real organizational entity: a regimental-strength agglomeration of men from Elliott's brigade, Davidson commanding. Mahone's orders pulled most of them out of the traverse they had recaptured, leaving skirmishers behind until Mahone's Second Brigade could move up. They picked their way back, hopping from traverse to bombproof to ravine. The ground was littered with bodies. Sometimes a bluecoat moved, and Davidson would point his pistol and finish the man off. There were niggers around in there too, and the men walked past them without getting too close. Except Dixon. He went over to one, and cut off his ear with his clasp knife. He caught up with Billy and pulled his sleeve. He held the ear in his hand, like a withered black fruit—dried apricot or prune, with its tail of blooded gristle. Dixon couldn't look in Billy's torn face, the horrible burnt-out eye was like a Judgment eye. But he showed him the ear, and tried to put it in his hand, as you would try to force a coin on a man too proud to beg.

Davidson led them to the left now, into a trench that cut across the base of the salient. In front of them there was another trench, and they could see some of their own men—hanging on there after they got whipped in the first attack.

Pretty soon they'd go up there with them and charge again. Up from behind they were bringing more troops in, you could feel it building like water in a mill-race. Dixon was afraid. He looked up at Billy, but he was on the wrong side, and the red mask on the face and the bloodied blind eye made Dixon shudder, and then he figured it: of all the enlisted men in the regiment, just the two of them survived. They'd come through the fire, and bathed in the blood, and the marks was on them. They was marked with the blood, and was safe. Dixon felt the fear lift off him, and when Davidson gave the order he leaped out of the trench lightly, and ran up to the forward line without even hearing the bullets that whined overhead and picked at the ground around his feet.

They hit the new trench, Bruce piling in behind Davidson. Davidson stood erect in the trench to peer out at the Yankees, and Bruce pulled him down. The Colonel's senses seemed to have been jarred loose by the mine blast, the niggers attacking, everything. He seemed to act purely on impulse, firing at the enemy like a private, killing the wounded with his pistol when the idea occurred to him. His eyes the eyes of a very busy man, details coming in so quickly there was barely time to respond to all of them.

The Colonel looked at Bruce furiously. Bruce knew, somehow, that the Colonel had been about to order the charge immediately. "For God's sake, Colonel! The orders were to wait until we heard the other brigade begin its attack!"

Davidson clenched his teeth and glared. "Nobody tells me how to handle my niggers," he said.

What in hell was Davidson talking about? Did he want to get a bullet in the back from one of these crackers? "They're not ours yet,

Colonel,'' he said. ''We'll get em soon, though.''

Davidson blinked. Bruce handed him a canteen, and he drank. He shook his heavy head again, as if to clear it. ''I never liked you at all,'' he said. ''But you've been helpful to me. Maybe I misjudged you.'' When he looked at Bruce he seemed very calm. ''When you have a chance, later, come and see me. You've never owned your own plantation, have you?'' Bruce shook his head. ''Pity,'' he said, ''but it's never too late to learn, if you've got any brains. And a feeling for handling men. Never too late.''

Bruce wondered where the Colonel thought he was. Was he proposing to take him on as a partner in his plantation? *Or ere the fruitful fields* . . . Allen's crazy pastoral-epic poem—he thought Davidson was Jesus Christ, and his plantation the Garden of Eden. What in the name of reason did any of it have to do with this trench, and getting ready to go in there and start killing Yankees and niggers one more time and for good and all? The poem was tucked away in the dispatch case he'd taken from Allen's body. By God, if he lived he'd make Davidson read that damn thing to him. The Colonel was crazy enough to be able to make the connection, and explain it all to him.

They heard the sound of firing begin to swell, begin to expand off to the left. They heard it rise and begin to fill the air, and their own men caught the frenzy, and began to fire faster.

Davidson stood up. Took a grip on his sword. He didn't seem to pay any attention to the soldiers rising on his left and right. ''Fix bayonets!'' yelled Bruce, and he heard the knives clack against some gun barrels, and the gunfire came louder and louder on the left and they heard the long-drawn cry of Mahone's brigade beginning to charge. Davidson yelled, ''Spare the white man and kill the nigger!'' and they were climbing out of the trench.

Dobbs, Johnson and Private Duckworth heard the pitch change, the yell rising on their right. Johnson rolled back onto his belly, and felt the sand grit on his bare wet chest. His musket was loaded, ramrod stuck in the ground, cartridges handy. He took the time to do everything necessary. To stick his right hand in the earth, drying it. To look at his brown hand gripping the brown gunstock before putting the piece up and sighting. This time, he did another thing: looked to his left, and saw Dobbs chunk the axe blade into the earth, handy by his right hand. Pistol loose in the holster, while he started to poke the musket through and do his squint for aiming. Their eyes touched one time: black in amber, blue in pink. *Woodchopper*. Beyond Dobbs, Duckworth had taken his rest, squinting against his gunsight. They swung front, and he saw the brown uniforms bob up out of the line of black smoke, and the flags move, and the sun catch the points of the knife blades stuck on the rifle ends.

Booker heard the rush of feet back of him, turned and saw Randolph coming in, and then Randolph was sliding in next to him. ''You got em together Booker! That's *good!*'' Randolph's face was shining with a kind of crazy joy.

"They comin," said Colehill. Booker looked down the line to his right. The flag corporal rolled onto his belly, the flag under him now. The black man just past him stuck the cork back into a canteen and flipped it, turning through space, till it popped in the hand of a man down below. Beyond him Booker saw the rest of his own men in line, and a half-company of white troops next to it. Somehow the last black soldier on the end of his line, and the first one on the left of the white troops, had switched places, as if the two lines of troops were coupled and inter-locked magically at that point.

He turned and looked the other way, past the far left end of the Crater. He could just make out a humping bulge of new earth that showed where the Third Division troops had improved the rear of the captured rebel battery. Booker saw heads bobbing up like corks and he thought, *They ought to keep down*. Randolph was breathing heavily, leaning on his right shoulder. Booker turned his head, and looked at him. Up close he could see the large pores in the black skin that looked so smooth from a distance; and the brittle lines and pouching of skin around the eyes that spoke of Randolph's age, and his tiredness. The eyes were bright and dark brown in ivory whites. The wide mouth was grinning, and the grin made the face move and live. It was all right be-ing up here. Down below them in the Crater, men were unstrung with fear and heat, or torn up by metal, hurt and dying.

"Booker," said Randolph, " this place ain't gone to hold."

Booker was silent. Randolph saw something like a fog drift in to cover the pale eyes, and tiny muscles lapsed letting the corners of the eyes and mouth droop. Booker was taking in the truth, and it was sad. "There's a way to get the people out."

The musketry fevered and fevered and suddenly went wild off to the right and someone was yelling, "Here come! Here come!" and Randolph yelled, "Watch me when the time come," and they rolled their heads back to look out, and saw the humped-over shapes coming out of the powder-smoke low and fast.

Booker rested his elbow in the soft crumbling earth. Pointed the pistol carefully. He clutched his right wrist with his left hand for steadiness. Squeezed a shot and the black gun barked and he saw it bite a man and the man twist and drop. Shift right, point: squeeze-*bark;* squeeze-*bark,* and a second man dropped. It was easier than the first one because the man was closer.

A black line flashed from left to right and the canister shell burst white. Booker put his face into the ground as the stray shot whizzed by him, and when he looked up there were humps of rags all over the field, and shots coming from behind some of them.

The firing on the right was going higher and higher.

The canister shell had wrecked the first charge of Davidson's troops. A ball had cut across Davidson's thigh, dropping him; another one tore Bruce's borrowed jacket across the back and sent him sprawling. As he fell he saw Dixon grab Billy and throw him down, and he was crawling over toward them almost before the canister-shot stopped whizzing. He dragged on Dixon's arm, and got them to look over to the right. From where they lay, they were looking right down the embrasure of the reconstructed battery from which the Federals were firing. Dixon rolled, rested his musket on a body that lay to his right, rested it across the small of its back. Bruce grabbed a musket and rolled up next to Dixon. In the slit of the embrasure they could see the gunners working, blue coats and one man with his shirt off. Dixon shot; and Bruce shot; then Dixon. Other men were shooting. He saw a blue coat tumble. In the flash before the gun fired again and filled the hole with black smoke he saw the white back of the shirtless gunner slashed with ribbons of red as if the man had been lashed with a whip.

When the shell-blast and the whizz of shrapnel stopped, they were still alive. There was no movement around the gun.

From behind them and to the left they could hear the roar of the shooting and the loud piercing call of their own troops charging on the north end of the Crater, and it sounded like the time. Bruce saw Davidson struggling to his feet, and he got to his knees and yelled, ''Ready,'' but somebody punched him in the front of his right shoulder and knocked the breath out of him.

He couldn't move.

He began to feel very cold.

He felt a warm liquid pulsing in his right shoulder.

The troops were still lying around him, bunching themselves up, ready to spring and go. There was a rhythmic pulsing in the air, a chanting harsh and rhythmic, the words fuzzy and out of synchronization. Then he heard distinctly Billy's young clear voice chanting, *''Spare the white man kill the nigger, spare the white man kill the nigger,''* and as the rhythm accelerated the men seemed to uncoil and spring and leap out of sight as Bruce fell out of consciousness.

Dobbs heard it coming, *Spare the white man kill the nigger,* on the right like the bleat and thunder of cattle. He saw that the rebs were coming in obliquely from the right, and you could just know from the sound of it that this was the finish, this was the wave that oversweeps the sandcastle and melts it back to nothing.

Kill the nigger spare the white man kill the—

He put his pistol down and picked up the axe.

Looking over he saw Johnson lying on his back with his musket between his legs and up along his belly and chest, ramming the bayonet onto the end of the musket, and Dobbs grinned and laughed to find they'd thought of it together. *Nigger spare the—*

2:30 P.M.

—white man kill the nigger.

Randolph had it clear in his head now, even as he aimed and shot through the firing slit. Big sound coming on the right, cannon still clearing them in front of us here and over to the left.

When the screechowl sound come in big on the right, that's the time. When it come close, I get them ready. When it come over right up to the edge, then we go. He saw in his mind, without words, a very clear picture of the enemy coming in over on the right, their eyes and guns held by the men in front of them and in the pits, just a few of them up on the edge like there was few of us now: and that was the time to run the bridge to the other side of the Crater, where his rearguards were waiting. And then back the old way he'd come, where only the one canister gun was firing: while the enemy was busy eating up the boys in the hole.

The yammer of the shooting on the right climbed along with the screeching of the enemy mouths as they charged in, climbing to a crazy pitch. Randolph noticed that their own gun wasn't firing no more on the left, and he heard the words: *Spare the white man kill the nigger.* The screaming reached the point of wildness he wanted, and he grabbed Booker's shoulder and said, "Get ready to go when I tell you! Back across the bridge, right side of the boulder I got men waiting to cover. Tell em!" Booker's eyes held on Randolph, and then he gave it up to him and said, "Yes," and the word went left from Booker, right from Randolph, "Get ready to drop this and follow Ki," and then the *white man kill the nigger spare the white man kill*—"NOW!" yelled Randolph, and scrambled back and got his feet onto the bridge. He felt the rest coming on behind him, shot a glance to the left and saw the dark shapes leaping down the yellow well of the Crater and the hunched smoking shapes of the enemy at the brim and coming over.

In the smoking pit of the Crater Neill heard death coming for him, roaring like a beast. Even his prayers became a hideous yammering in his skull. *No way to escape, nowhere to run, no absolution, no pardon.* He saw the rebels at the rim of the Crater and his panicked mind raced to find a way to appease them, to earn their mercy. Their chant came to him like a revelation—*Spare the white man kill the nigger*—there was a nigger coming down the wall right over his head! He sprang out of the ground and grabbed the man's boot and flung himself back, dragging the nigger down, shrieking, "I got one!" *Kill the nigger.*

Dobbs felt the sudden absence of the black man's presence on his right. He looked down and saw a red-haired white man grabbing the barrel of the musket while Johnson twisted on the ground. Dobbs jumped down too, boots jarring hard, and he kicked the red man sprawling backwards. He sensed someone coming in on his right, and he swung the axe blindly. The iron wedge bit into the face of a white man in a blue shirt who had been going after Johnson where he lay on the ground. Now the redhead was getting up, reaching again for Johnson's musket, and Dobbs rushed toward him. Someone grabbed for his axe and a bullet seared his ribs. He staggered against the side of the Crater and his breath went out of him. As Dobbs fell he saw a bayonet swung by the redhead ram into Johnson's belly.

His axe was gone, but his right hand got the pistol butt as he hit the ground. There were men in brown and gray screaming and shooting. Men in blue were waving their arms and yelling *stop* and *surrender.*

Dobbs saw the red-haired man spin away as a devil-masked man with his face half blood caught him on the point of his bayonet and tipped him off like a man pitchforking hay. The devil grinned and smashed the butt of his musket into Johnson's head. Dobbs pointed the pistol and shot the devil in the face just before the shooting from the Crater's rim began to lessen as the rebels swarmed down, yelling in triumph.

Booker helped a dozen men onto the ridge. There were more behind them but it was too late, and they began to run. The dirt of the ridge was skidding under his feet, bullets were grabbing at his ankles. A bullet kicked the black man in front of Booker screaming into the smaller pit on the right and he saw the white hands reach up to grab him, and Booker ran.

There was a bay in the wall in front of him, and Ki in it with his hand out, and Booker jumped, gripped, and the sergeant pulled him up. Up above their heads guns spoke where Randolph had lined out his rearguards. Back on the wall there were smoke puffs, rebels creeping round the outer abandoned parapet to fire over but held down by Randolph's rearguards.

"Where's Colehill?" he asked. Colehill was the man with the flag. Then he realized Colehill was the man in front of him shot off the ridge and into the pit, where the enemy had captured the flag. The enemy. Every white man, blue or gray, had become the enemy.

"You'll take them back?" he asked Randolph.

"Starting now!" A canister shell burst behind them. Across the field between the Crater and the lines, drifts and single soldiers were running, stumbling and falling, as the bullets sang out of the air and the canister pellets scythed across the field. "Down when I down!" and Randolph got up and began running.

That was very good, thought Booker. *He will carry them safe across if it can be done, and get them free of this.*

He turned back to the Crater, and looking back across the ridge his eyes fogged over with the vision he had seen in crossing, the white soldiers killing their comrades in black skin, the white enemies crying *spare the white man kill the nigger,* all mixed in a blind wolfpack wrestle of destruction and murder, the final uprising of madness and death.

He darted to the side, to where the abandoned cannon poked across a depression in the earth curb of the Crater's front. Bullets rang off the metal. Booker guessed that the gun was sighted to clear the opposite parapet, on which the enemy now perched, leaning over to fire into the Crater, like shooting fish in a barrel. Perhaps the gun had been left loaded as well?

He gripped the lanyard. There was no cure for the Crater but this. He remembered the blooming rise of the firehead out of the earth when the Mine went and he had felt it touch the central fire as if the whole earth would go with it.

Booker stood up, jerked the lanyard. As he did so, a bullet shattered his left bicep and he went down. The gun roared and recoiled, smoke belched, the shell flew across the Crater and burst out past it where some of the Confederate wounded were beginning to gather their strength and crawl back toward the rear. The shell tore them to bits.

Bartlett was lying in the bottom of the hole with his throbbing stump and the weight of the heat and despair leaning on him. He saw dark figures running across the central ridge and he yelled, "Get those deserters!" and heard some men potting up from the tumbled ground around him. He rolled his head to the left, and saw rebels trying to poke their heads over the parapet, jerking them back—somebody was firing from the opposite face of the Crater, and a cannon flashed up on the top and the shell went over.

Then the rebels were back, rats popping through dips in the parapet, holding rifles pointed down and firing. Bartlett yelled "Surrender! Goddamn! Goddamn! Surrender!" Someone was waving a cloth, an undershirt behind him. The rebels couldn't hear or see, kept blazing into the smoke, and he shouted *surrender* like he was summoning the enemy, and finally the shooting dropped off to occasional pops of fire.

There was shouting, scuffling. Some of his men were fighting among themselves. That was all part of it. Cowards and slackers. Damn em to hell.

A reb Colonel materialized out of the smoke like a wraith.

The Colonel wore a dress-uniform coat sodden with sweat and soiled with powder smoke, but the braid on the sleeve was shiny. There was a tear in one trouser leg, and a bandage round the thigh. "My name is Davidson, Colonel of the Twenty-second North Carolina Infantry," said the figure, and saluted.

Bartlett stiffened and sat up straight. "I am General Bartlett, commanding the First Brigade, First Division, Ninth Army Corps." He tried to raise himself but couldn't, and fumbled for his sword. Single shots still sounded in the smoky humped bottom of the Crater, and there were still cries and screams.

"You're hurt, General," said the Colonel softly.

"Not this time," said Bartlett, his face twisting in a grin. He indicated his missing leg. The rebels were pushing up around to see and listen, herding their prisoners up. "You boys," said Davidson, "give your General some assistance." Two black men reached for his arms, and Bartlett's body twisted away, revulsing.

"No niggers, dammit. Isn't there a white man in the pack of you to give me a hand up?"

"Sholy," said a reb, and bent to offer his hand, and one of Bartlett's officers came up and gripped him under the arm on the other side. Davidson said, "I'll have these men carry you back to the field hospital, General. I hope to converse with you at a later time," and four men linked hands and wrists under his rear and across his back, and began to carry Bartlett across the floor of the Crater. There were men waiting to hand him up the side of the wall, into the trench and the fallen battery. They set him down next to a dead man, whose bare white torso was slashed with blackening bullet trails.

Davidson watched the Yankee General rising up and out of the Crater. He saluted the man. Courtesy was the quality that separated the murderous brawls of savages from civilized warfare. Davidson walked toward the tunnel that cut through to the larger half of the Crater. A dead nigger lay across the entrance, and he rolled him over with his boot tip. He aimed his pistol directly at the tip of the man's nose. He jerked his head and the soldier next to him kicked the nigger in the side of the head. No shamming, it was dead.

A strange bit of colored cloth stuck out of a rip in the shirt.

The soldier bent and ripped open the shirt. The nigger had wrapped a flag of some kind around its middle. A bullet had gone through it— two bullets—and broken the heart and soaked the flag with blood. The soldier started to unwrap it, but Davidson said sharply, "Don't touch it!" He toed the man back over onto his face, stepped across him and ducked through the tunnel.

Doyle and Rees, waiting in the front line of trenches, heard the sound and saw the smoke building over the Crater, and they thought, *Will they hold it, will they hold it?* The attack had failed. *Oh,* thought Rees, *hold on to it or what's the use of it all?* His head throbbed from the terrible heat, and he remembered the cool underground of the tunnel, and crawling down the mouth of it to where the fuse lay. *Why ever did I do it if they don't hold the Crater?* And Doyle was thinking the same thing—*otherwise why was Corrigan dead, and all that sweat and blood into the ground?*

The men were still running back from the Crater, one at a time and by squads, some of them shot on the lip of the lines, others crawling in with their holes running blood, and a man with a ripped belly dragging a loop of his guts out in the air for the world to see.

Here came a big burst of men, a flood of shapes out of the Crater. The screeching told them that the enemy had it, and there were men pouring across—and tumbling into the trench. A black sergeant started to push his way through the trench full of milling, yelling men, followed by his own men all keeping together in a tight, quiet bunch.

Dobbs couldn't move at first. It felt as if someone had driven a spike into his side.

Johnson lay on the ground, mumbling through his broken face. Blood pooled on his belly where the knife had gone in. The muscles writhed and fidgeted around the hole, and Johnson cried when they writhed. *I must help him,* said Dobbs, then realized he hadn't spoken. It was hard to breathe, hard to catch his breath, the spike in his side had driven it out of him. *Woodchopper,* he called me. *Chopper.* "Chopper," he thought someone said by his side. He looked. It was Duckworth, one of the other boys from his company. Duckworth reached under Dobbs's shirt, pressed a wad of some kind of cloth there. Took off his own belt, and bound it around.

Officers and men, they were all shoved against the front wall of the Crater, the Johnnies standing guard in front of them. *Just like that time on the docks with those damned bounty-jumpers and now it's our turn.* In the blaze of the sun it was hard to see what the other Johnnies were doing: wandering around among the humps of mounded earth and broken equipment, and you'd hear shots here and there.

There was a Johnny bending over another one. When the head of the one lying down lolled, Dobbs saw it was the devil-faced man that he'd shot, and he grinned. He was beginning to feel better. Duckworth cinched the belt, and he said, "Not so tight," because something stuck him, and he guessed a rib was broke as well as he was shot.

A reb Colonel, white hair and no hat, came limping along the line. He had a bandage wrapped around his thigh, and his pants hung where whatever had cut him had torn the cloth. His eyes were bright blue, and they moved about with a certain vivacity. He seemed to be praising the soldiers, muttering words that made some of them smile and bob their heads. The reb officers he'd stop and shake by the hand. He carried a pistol in his left hand.

He came along the line.

Dobbs heard him ask a prisoner, an officer, what regiment he was. "Help me up," he said, and Duckworth lifted, and he braced his back against the heated wall of the Crater.

The reb Colonel came up to a Captain that Dobbs recognized. "Sugar"-something was his name. He belonged to the division. Booker's outfit. "What's your regiment?" asked the Colonel.

"Fifty-first Massachusetts," said the Captain.

Dobbs grinned. So *that* was how it was going to be.

Johnson mumbled and groaned, and the Colonel turned around, looked down, and shot him with the pistol. Dobbs heard quite distinctly the crack of the skull as the bullet broke it, and thought he heard the sound of the bullet breaking through into the earth. Johnson's body quivered.

"What regiment?"

The next officer was one of theirs also, but he'd thrown away his insignia, and he said, "Forty-fifth Pennsylvania," and then the reb crouching on the ground by the devil-face got up and stepped up to Duckworth.

"Chopper," said Duckworth faintly, and Dobbs turned slowly, and the reb pressed the musket into Duckworth's solar plexus and pulled the trigger.

Dobbs closed his eyes, and heard Duckworth slide down the wall.

He opened his eyes, and there was the Colonel. He heard the sound of scattered shots behind him. "What regiment?" asked the Colonel. Dobbs grinned at him. "You Johnnies is just like Comanches with prisoners and wounded, ain't you? But if Ben Butler finds out, you'll have to pay the devil."

The Colonel's right hand shot out, and Dobbs felt the slap, and tasted blood.

"What regiment?" said the Colonel, in a calm and temperate voice.

What a stupid way to get caught, at last! Dobbs laughed at it, laughed right in the face of the Colonel, and said:

"I am Lieutenant Lemuel Dobbs, Nineteenth United States Niggers, by God."

DUNN'S HILL, *July 30, 1864—3:25* P.M.

Hon. JAMES A. SEDDON,
Secretary of War:
At 5 A.M. the enemy sprung a mine under one of the salients on
General B. R. Johnson's front and opened his batteries upon
our lines and the city of Petersburg. In the confusion caused by
the explosion of the mine he got possession of the salient. We
have retaken the salient and driven the enemy back to his lines
with loss.

R. E. LEE.

HEADQUARTERS SECOND DIVISION, NINTH ARMY CORPS
July 30, 1864

Lieut. Col. LEWIS RICHMOND,
Assistant Adjustant-General, Ninth Army Corps:
COLONEL: The troops have been driven from their advanced
position back into the old line. The Ninth and Eleventh New
Hampshire, Seventeenth Vermont, and Thirty-first and Thirty-
second Maine are reported to be captured almost entire; also,
the Fifty-eighth Massachusetts and Second New York Mounted
Rifles, and the Second Maryland Volunteers are almost entirely
captured, besides several hundred of killed and wounded left
upon the field. The line from which we advanced this morning
is so weak that it is in great danger. I beg leave to call the
attention of the commanding general to the fact that my division is reported as nearly annihilated, and cannot therefore possibly occupy the position from which it advanced this morning.
Very respectfully, your obedient servant,
ROBERT B. POTTER,
Brigadier-General.

P.S. General Griffin sends me word that General Bartlett
fell into the enemy's hands. My brigade commanders report
that a very small proportion of the wounded were removed
from the field.

3:30 P.M.

Colonel Thomas had returned to the divisional bivouac. He had
about two hundred men with him. The bivouac was quiet. The sounds of
fighting came from a long way off. They hadn't even heard the Mine go
off very clearly, Thomas remembered. Yes, they were a long way off.
There were probably things that had to be done. Thomas sat down to
try and think what they were.
Circles of knapsacks stood in the trampled grass of the meadow.
From the surrounding woods you could hear the blackbirds, shrieking

like disturbed spirits; occasionally one would flit and perch on a knap-sack.

Gradually, the circles and rows began to fill out with people. Men returned, singly and by squads. They came to their circle of knapsacks. They slumped wearily by them. Took out hardtacks and munched them.

The cooks and other noncombatants were walking among the circles carrying buckets of water. They would dip drinks for the black men covered in dust and blood. Thomas could imagine with perfect clarity the tinny taste of the dipper, the flat taste of the tepid water, the feel of the water running over the dry tongue and parched throat, clearing the dust, cutting the dryness.

They had sat there just that morning. Cutting the taste of the salt-pork fat, the greaze, with the sharpness of the pickle.

He remembered Chris sitting there at breakfast in the morning, and suddenly the horror of it was all real to him, and he felt he was going to cry, he was going to start barking like a dog, and the only way he could save himself was to make a noise, any kind of noise, a long-drawn *aaaaaah*, hard and intense and just below yelling out loud. Every time he felt it breaking out in him, he would call out that way, half-strangling with the muscular contraction of his neck. After a time he was able to stop.

The men were still returning. Nearly half the places were filled in some of the circles and rows. Perhaps it was not so bad after all.

The sun was beginning to drop into the west. Half of the knapsacks were still standing alone in most of the companies. Some circles stood completely abandoned. One of these, in the First Brigade's area, stood so for a long time. Eventually a sergeant and half a dozen men entered the circle and sat in it. Thomas watched them. No more came, and the circle remained empty.

There should have been a pause, a cessation then, when it was really over. The ear waited, the mind waited to receive it: listening. A pause of utter silence, after which the cries and supplications of the men who were hurt and lying in the field that the bullets still whined over, or stumbling blind into the trenches and just then beginning to feel where they had been torn—the cries would have come into air cleared for them, and they would have filled the air with screech and yatter and sob, each sound distinctly heard.

But the guns never stopped at all, and the screams and cries rose through the blanket of whining metal and detonation.

But the cheering had stopped. No one any longer attacked or de-fended in front of the Crater. Because of that, the only human sounds beside the sound of the guns that were still firing were the sounds the wounded made, where they lay in the chewed-up ground between the lines, and in the trenches around the Crater, and the fields behind it; where they lay in the field hospitals and the surgeons were preparing for them.

Booker was awake. The sudden sharpness with which he felt awake told him how far down in dark he had gone, not knowing, never even struggling against it, and his nerves twisted with panic. He had expected death, and to sink twisting in struggle when it came; and the struggle would mean it couldn't have him yet, the dark couldn't have him yet. But he had been gone.

He had been gone.

What was he doing here? Where had he come from?

Bullets were ringing off the metal of the gun.

A snake had bitten his left shoulder and arm. He felt the blood throbbing. He tried to cry out. If only he could force out his breath, it would be all right. His soul, rising like smoke, would escape at least. "Get me, out."

He could feel the dryness of his mouth and throat when he spoke.

His voice seemed to break a spell of the heat. Cries and screams rose out of the earth all around, all across the broken field that lay to one side, a red field bathed in yellow sunlight like an oil. He could hear them clearly. They cried for water. For pain to end. For death to come, and to stay away. For mother. For girls' names.

He began to weep. The salt taste of the tears that ran into the corner of his mouth was sharp but clean, not like the salty metallic taste of the blood.

His arm was a strange thing, it wrung him over and over with pain, and he clenched and writhed the muscles of his back and legs. Feeling them.

He felt a deep cold coming on, out of the darkening sky, and out of the Crater. The sun was going. The terrible sun. Now he wanted it.

He saw, quite clearly, Miriam playing with Eli, in a golden air that darkened and cooled. He must stop it cooling: he could not. She played with the child like a strange maned lioness with a cub, fierce and tender, bats of a paw and little bites of the muscular mouth, a playing of hurting and tenderness, her strange eyes lit up, the eyes of a lover and fierce predator. There was not a language in the world to speak and tell her what these images meant and where they came from. But the darkness lurched up to take him, and he spoke them anyway, and called her.

"Hey Yank? Yank?" a voice called from the other side of the earth wall. "You still there, Yank?"

"Unhh."

"You must be hurt bad, Yank. Just hang on. I can't reach over and get you cause your friends won't let. I'll toss a canteen." A shape arched in the air, and plopped sloshing.

"Hear that sound, Yank?" said the voice.

"I'm cold," said Booker.

"Yeah, well that noise is me. Digging through this old wall right for ya. If the sun don't go down first, I'll haul you in that way. Okay, Yank? You okay, Yank?"

"Anh."

"Don't die now."

Booker lay and heard the hands of the enemy man behind the earth wall scrabbling in the ground, digging through the ground toward him. His right hand reached for the canteen, but the movement made him too dizzy. So he lay, and waited for the hand that would reach up out of the earth and touch him, to see if he was still alive.

HEADQUARTERS,
Near Petersburg. July 30, 1864—6:30 P.M.

Hon. JAMES A. SEDDON, *Secretary of War:*
General A. P. Hill reports that General Mahone in retaking the salient possessed by the enemy this morning, recovered the four guns with which it was armed, captured 12 stand of colors, 74 officers, including Brigadier-General Bartlett and staff, and 855 enlisted men. Upward of 500 of the enemy's dead are lying unburied in the trenches. His loss slight.
R. E. LEE

HEADQUARTERS ARMY OF THE POTOMAC,
July 30, 1864—7:30 P.M.

General ORD:
Can you not get your wounded off after dark tonight? The last time we had wounded left on the field, Beauregard, on my application, refused to have a flag of truce to take off the wounded. It would, therefore, be useless to try again.
GEO. G. MEADE,
Major-General

HEADQUARTERS EIGHTEENTH ARMY CORPS,
July 30, 1864.

General MEADE:
The enemy have a terrible cross-fire at short range on the ground. It would be impossible. They have many wounded and dead there, and our trenches rake the place so that an offer might be mutually acceptable.
E. O. C. ORD,
Major-General

HEADQUARTERS ARMY OF THE POTOMAC,
July 30, 1864—7:40 P.M.

Major-General BURNSIDE,
Commanding Ninth Corps:
The major-general commanding desires to know whether you still hold the crater, and, if so, whether you will be able to withdraw your troops from it safely to-night, and also to bring off the wounded. The commanding general wishes to know how many wounded are probably lying there. It will be recollected that on a former occasion General Beauregard declined to enter into any arrangement for the succor of the wounded and the burial of the dead lying under both fires, hence the necessity of immediate and active efforts for their removal in the present case.
A. A. HUMPHREYS,
Major-General and Chief of Staff.

HEADQUARTERS ARMY OF THE POTOMAC,
July 30, 1864—10:35 P.M.

Major-General BURNSIDE,
Commanding Ninth Corps:

The major-general commanding desires to know whether you have any wounded left on the field, and directs me to say that he is awaiting your reply to the dispatch of 7:40 P.M.

A. A. HUMPHREYS,
Major-General and Chief of Staff.

Midnight

It was never quiet, never. As the sun dropped down behind the enemy lines and the dark began to rise from the east, the gunfire slackened, and the cries that came out of the broken field came clearer, but it never stopped. There would still be spots of gunfire: single potshots, cannon-bang; then a rattle, *patapatpan,* and it might pick up and rise again so that for a second your heart would stop, thinking it was starting again.

So with the cries. Sometimes you would hear one voice calling over and over again its hackneyed invocation. You'd identify it clearly, like birdsong: the man crying for his mother, the one who wanted help, the one who wanted a man to come and finish shooting him, the one who wanted water and made your mouth dry so you wanted a drink from your canteen, but how could you? So you'd run your hand into the loose dust and hold off drinking till he stopped.

It wasn't like the shooting at all. With the shooting, it was when the single shots began to connect and merge and rise toward sheer noise that the fear came rising like the darkness in the east. With the cries, it was better when you lost the particular in the general: when it seemed to you that one great swarming buzz of crying rose undifferentiated out of all the holes and crevices in the earth in one massive prolonged exhalation, and you did not have to attend to any part of it.

The moon slid across the field like a blue spotlight. Peeping through the fire slit, you could see the field turn blue, and though the heat was there still, you thought of ice. In that light, white faces took on the blue glare of death, and lips or wounds turned purple, as did the faces of the dead that had begun to decay.

PART THREE

REPORT OF CASUALTIES IN THE ACTION OF JULY 30, 1864, IN FRONT OF PETERSBURG, VIRGINIA

Flag of Truce
July 31–August 1, 1864

HEADQUARTERS ARMY OF THE POTOMAC,
July 31, 1864—8:10 A.M.

Major-General BURNSIDE,
Commanding Ninth Corps:
 The major-general commanding directs me to call your attention to the fact that you have made no report to him upon the condition of affairs in your front since he left your head-quarters yesterday, and that you have made no reply to the two special communications upon the subject sent you last night at 7:40 and at 10:35. I am also directed to inquire as to the cause of these omissions.

A. A. HUMPHREYS,
Major-General and Chief of Staff.

HEADQUARTERS NINTH ARMY CORPS,
July 31, 1864—9 A.M.

General WILLIAMS,
Assistant Adjutant-General:
 I have the honor to report that all was quiet on my line. There was comparatively little firing. The remainder of General Ord's troops will be relieved during the day, if possible; certainly to-night. Everything that could be relieved by me was done last night. Nearly 100 wounded are lying between the lines in our front, which possibly could be brought in by a flag of truce.

A. E. BURNSIDE,
Major-General.

CITY POINT, *July 31, 1864.*

General MEADE,
Headquarters Army of the Potomac:
 I have been on Burnside's front to-day, and am told that among the large number of our men now lying around the crater some are still alive. As General Grant is now absent at

Fort Monroe, I am unable to report the fact to him without delay.

C. B. COMSTOCK,
Lieutenant-Colonel and Aide-de-camp.

HEADQUARTERS NINTH ARMY CORPS,
Before Petersburg, Va., July 31, 1864

Major-General MEADE,
Commanding Army of the Potomac:
GENERAL: I have the honor to request that a flag of truce be sent out for the purpose of making arrangements for assisting the wounded and burying the dead left on the field of battle. The number of the wounded left between the lines and beyond the first lines of the enemy has been exaggerated by rumor. They are not believed to amount to over 100 in all. Of these there are but few between the lines, the greater part being beyond the first line of the enemy's works.

I have the honor to be, general, very respectfully, your obedient servant,

A. E. BURNSIDE,
Major-General, Commanding.

HEADQUARTERS ARMY OF THE POTOMAC,
July 31, 1864.

Major-General BURNSIDE:
Your communication of this date, respecting the wounded and dead left on the field in the engagement of yesterday, has been received and laid before the commanding general, and I have the honor herewith to transmit a letter addressed to General R. E. Lee, commanding Army of Northern Virginia, asking for a cessation of hostilities sufficiently long to enable us to bring off our wounded and dead, which you are to send to the enemy's lines, and you are authorized to instruct the officer who takes the flag to say to the officer who receives it that the object of the letter is simply to effect the removal of the dead and wounded, and that if an informal arrangement for this purpose can be entered into it will not be necessary to forward the communications to General Lee.

Very respectfully, &c.,

S. WILLIAMS,
Assistant Adjutant-General

July 31

The night had partly emptied the field of wounded. The earth had taken some of them, drunk up the last of their bleeding. Some had shot themselves: you'd hear a shot, muffled and closer than it should be.

Some had crawled towards the lines—the nearest parapet looming in the dark, enemy or friend, and come on whispering the password, "Don't shoot. Wounded coming in. Don't shoot. Wounded and coming in. Don't shoot." Some mistook the brushy ravine to the north of the rubble-field, or the broken-off grove of trees on the south, for the lines, and crawled in there. A man might get lost in the tangles, roots, and rough ground, wear out and die there, and no one to find him till he was bones and rags the next spring, when the war was over and the rebels abandoned their lines. Or a man might be caught out in the center of the field, start crawling across to where he figured his own lines to be, and be worn out before he made it. Or a sniper might see the moving hump of shadow and get itchy.

It was proverbial that after a battle there would be rain. It was not necessary to believe in the magic of human sacrifice to explain this; the jarring of the cannon, the irritating smoke filling the sky, these might be sufficient cause. But it did not rain on the thirty-first. The only water that the wounded got was passed out from hand to hand from the trenches, when Burnside's officers got a three-hour truce: nobody came out of the lines, but you could stick your head up to pass canteens out. Water and whiskey, the canteens went bobbing hand to hand. You couldn't tell if they all got a taste, or even see where they all were.

Did a lot of them die in the night? Or was it the weight of the sun that throttled the crying out, and dulled it, so that to the men in the trenches it seemed less?

The sun blazed as it had the day before. The sun did not want to give up fighting the battle of the Crater. But the people had had enough. So the sun killed as many of the wounded as it could, and passed over.

HEADQUARTERS NINTH ARMY CORPS,
July 31, 1864.

Major-General HUMPHREYS,
Chief of Staff:
    The telegraph operators at my headquarters were arrested this morning, and I understand that the cause of their arrest was the taking off of messages and delivering them to me. Whatever they have done in that way was by my direction and for what I conceived to be for the good of the public service. No cipher messages have ever been taken off. I am entirely responsible for this and am to blame if anyone is. They have been active and efficient during the campaign, and should not be made to suffer for what they could not help doing.
                                          A. E. BURNSIDE,
                                          Major-General.

HEADQUARTERS ARMY OF THE POTOMAC,
July 31, 1864—3:30 P.M.

Maj. Gen. A. E. BURNSIDE,
Commanding Ninth Corps:
Your dispatch relative to the arrest of the telegraph operators at your headquarters has been submitted to the major-general commanding, who directs me to say that he is surprised to learn that you had given them such orders after the conversation he had with you upon the subject, in which he declined to authorize your doing so. The commanding general further directs me to say that the operators were expressly prohibited from taking off any messages except those directed to the commanders with whom they were serving, and must therefore be tried for the offense.
A. A. HUMPHREYS,
Major-General and Chief of Staff.

HEADQUARTERS ARMY OF THE POTOMAC,
July 31, 1864—3:30 P.M.

Maj Gen. A. E. BURNSIDE:
The commanding general desires to be informed whether you have communicated with the enemy with a flag of truce, and whether any proposition for an informal arrangement for bringing off our wounded and dead was acceded to. If not, was the letter addressed to General Lee preserved and forwarded to him? The commanding general desires to be informed what is the condition of affairs in your front at this time.
S. WILLIAMS,
Assistant Adjutant-General

HEADQUARTERS NINTH ARMY CORPS,
July 31, 1864—6 P.M.

General WILLIAMS:
I sent one of my staff to endeavor to make the informal arrangement in regard to relieving the wounded, and if not made to forward the communication to General Lee. He was unable to effect any arrangement beyond supplying water and whisky to the wounded between the lines, and passing whisky into our wounded in their lines. They declined to receive the communication until their general officer could be consulted. Pending the answer a cessation of hostilities on our front took place for about three hours, when the enemy insisted on resuming firing and the flag ceased. There are not more than twenty wounded between the lines. The enemy are to inform

us when they have permission to renew the flag and receive the communication.

A. E. BURNSIDE,
Major-General.

HEADQUARTERS ARMY OF THE POTOMAC,
July 31, 1864.

Lieutenant-Colonel COMSTOCK,
City Point:
The above is the latest report from General Burnside. Show it to Lieutenant-General Grant on his arrival.

GEO. G. MEADE,
Major-General.

HEADQUARTERS NINTH ARMY CORPS,
July 31, 1864—6:38 P.M.

Major-General HUMPHREYS:
The enemy informed us of their willingness to receive the communication, which was accordingly delivered to one of their company officers, the highest officer seen was Major Lydig, who had charge of the flag. They said it would be impossible to say when an answer would be given us. The flag still continues.

A. E. BURNSIDE,
Major-General.

HEADQUARTERS NINTH ARMY CORPS,
July 31, 1864—6:40 P.M.

Major-General HUMPHREYS:
The loss in this corps, in the engagement of yesterday, amounts to about 4,500, the great proportion of which was made after the brigade commanders in the crater were made aware of the order to withdraw.

A. E. BURNSIDE,
Major-General.

HEADQUARTERS ARMY OF THE POTOMAC,
July 31, 1864—7 P.M.

General BURNSIDE:
The commanding general directs that you at once withdraw the flag of truce. When the answer to the communication addressed to General Lee is ready it can then be received under a flag. The commanding general did not anticipate that the flag would be kept out longer than might be necessary to effect an arrangement for the recovery of the wounded or to deliver the letter to General Lee to the officer sent to receive it.

S. WILLIAMS,
Assistant Adjutant-General.

HEADQUARTERS ARMY OF THE POTOMAC,
July 31, 1864—7:20 P.M.

Major-General BURNSIDE,
Commanding Ninth Corps:

Your dispatch relative to the loss in your corps yesterday is received. The commanding general requests that you will explain the meaning of the latter part of the dispatch, and again reminds you that he has received no report whatever from you of what occurred after 11 A.M. yesterday.

A. A. HUMPHREYS,
Major-General and Chief of Staff.

HEADQUARTERS NINTH ARMY CORPS,
July 31, 1864. (Received 9:10 P.M.)

Major-General HUMPHREYS,
Chief of Staff:

Your dispatch of 7:20 P.M. received. Just before the order for withdrawal was sent in to the brigade commanders in the crater the enemy made an attack upon our forces there and were repulsed with very severe loss to the assaulting column. The order for withdrawal, leaving the time and manner of the execution thereof to the brigade commanders on the spot, was then sent in, and while they were making arrangements to carry out the order the enemy advanced another column of attack. The officers, knowing they were not to be supported by other troops, and that a withdrawal was determined, ordered the men to retire at once to our old line. It was in this withdrawal and consequent upon it that our chief loss was made. In view of the want of confidence in their situation, and the certainty of no support consequent upon the receipt of such an order, of whose moral effects the general commanding cannot be ignorant, I am at a loss to know why the latter part of my dispatch requires explanation.

A. E. BURNSIDE,
Major-General.

HEADQUARTERS ARMY OF THE POTOMAC,
July 31, 1864—9:30 P.M.

Major-General BURNSIDE,
Commanding Ninth Corps:

Your dispatch explanatory of that in relation to the loss in your corps yesterday is received. The major-general commanding directs me to say that the order for withdrawal did not authorize or justify its being done in the manner in which, judging from your brief report, it appears to have been executed, and that the matter should be inquired into by a court.

The major-general commanding notices that the time and manner of withdrawal was left to the brigade commanders on the spot. He desires to know why there was not a division commander present where several brigades were engaged, and by whom the direction of the withdrawal could have been conducted.

A. A. HUMPHREYS,
Major-General and Chief of Staff.

HEADQUARTERS ARMY OF THE POTOMAC,
July 31, 1864.

General R. E. LEE,
Commanding Army of Northern Virginia:
I have the honor to request a cessation of hostilities at such time as you may indicate, sufficiently long to enable me to recover our wounded and dead in the engagement of yesterday, now lying between the lines of the two armies. I make this application that the sufferings of our wounded may be relieved, and that the dead may be buried.
Very respectfully,

GEO. G. MEADE,
Major-General, Commanding.

HDQRS. DEPT. OF N. CAROLINA AND SOUTHERN VA.,
July 31, 1864

Maj. Gen. GEORGE G. MEADE,
Commanding Army of the Potomac:
GENERAL: Your letter to General R. E. Lee, asking a cessation of hostilities to enable you to remove your wounded and bury your dead between the lines has been received. Your proposition is acceded to, and hostilities will be suspended for the purpose to-morrow morning at 6 o'clock. The cessation will continue for four hours.
I am, very respectfully, your obedient servant,

G. T. BEAUREGARD,
General.

August 1—6:00 A.M.

It was quiet. Nobody was shooting from either side. Sanderson looked at his watch. An hour had gone by since his orderly had raised the flag. Thomas wasn't here yet. He'd give him another minute or so. Sanderson turned to Dr. Clubb. "Are you and your assistants ready?"

"Of course," said Dr. Clubb. Yesterday the backwash of the battle had overwhelmed him. Working on the last of the wounded back from the Crater, straining against the electric nervous impulses that shot through his arms and hands, urgent with speed to be done with it—he'd had to force himself to stay in the bombproof. It had been bad, very bad: like drowning in a cesspool.

Later he'd washed himself carefully, top to toe. Taking a long time. Holding off the desire to sleep till he'd done that, then throwing himself on a clean cot in an excess of luxurious surrender.

He'd woken up twelve hours later and was himself again: alert, precise in observation and movement, inquisitive, humorous—he'd found himself musing annoyedly that he'd been so busy with the flood of casualties that he'd utterly forgotten to observe the differing responses of the black and the white wounded—if in fact they had differed, since the question was still scientifically moot. Then he'd nearly laughed at his own annoyance.

Actually he remembered nothing of the black wounded, only how brilliantly dark the blood seemed and how white the bone showing through sliced-open black skin. But the muscle—inside it was all the same red purple meat and purple and yellow guts, there wasn't a damn bit of difference in the world.

And maybe that *was* the scientific truth of it.

There was a bustle in the trench behind and Colonel Thomas arrived with a detail from Ferrero's division. He'd drawn men from each of the regiments to go out and bury their comrades. Thomas's face was pale, and his eyes had the curious intentness of the very ill or the very drunk. They seemed preternaturally alert to Clubb; yet they did not focus on the faces of the other officers, but fluttered away to look out towards the field.

Sanderson saluted Thomas. The man looked scared, he thought. Well, that's as it should be. After a fiasco like that of the thirtieth, any brigade commander whose troops had got run off had plenty to worry about—especially if he was Regular Army, as Thomas was, and had a career yet to make. There were long memories in the service: they still talked about what Grant had said when drunk on a certain Sunday at some godforsaken post in California. Sanderson snapped his watch shut. "Gentlemen, shall we go?"

Nobody demurring, he turned, mounted to the top of the parapet by a stepladder—there had been a whole pile of them back of the covered way. When Burnside's men had needed them there hadn't been one for love or money; then—when you didn't need but one—there was a whole pile. Well, that was the army!

Sanderson led them across the rubbled field. The bright and hot sun at their backs threw their shadows ahead of them into the field. Behind, they heard the rustle as details from the other divisions came out of the trenches to look for their dead, name them, record them, haul them off and bury them.

The field stank horribly. Two days in the yellow heat of Virginia sun cooked the corpses and swelled them up till they all looked like fat nigger minstrels, with their bulging sides and eyes. Blowflies rose out of the ground in iridescent clouds. The air was still, and the stench floated in it like mud dissolved in water: shit and worse-than-shit, shit of disease, the smell of rot, of muscle starting to liquify, to cheese.

This was duty for slackers and for niggers, gravedigging. And they deserved it. If they wouldn't take their chance of death with the soldiers, they must have their taste of it this way. Discipline and law, no army could run without it.

Thomas walked at the head of his chosen men. He'd called for volunteers, and he remembered the look of each one who stepped forward to accept his call. This was the last office of love. The best of the men came to do it: the ones who could fight, but who had hearts to feel as well. He remembered how it had been when he'd buried his son: it was the end of life for himself and Elizabeth both, he'd known it then. He'd tried to comfort her, to still the horrible wailing that seemed to rise out of some deep cave within her. He'd felt that, too. Yet for him the despair had not been perfect. She'd spun the child out of her own substance and nursed him out of her own body, but he had the father's relation, morally close but physically estranged. So it was now, with these who came with him seeking the dead.

He was aware of them, of the cries of finding. He walked away from them, looking from face to bloated face with reluctance and intensity. Oh, but it was hard to keep looking for him. Hard because he knew he must see what had become of him. At least there had been, with his son, the mercy of his going into the ground before flesh began to rot. There hadn't been that mercy for Chris. Yet imploringly, wishing for the strength to truly want to find the boy's body, he moved on: to bury the dead, and lay all to rest.

A group of Confederates under the white flag marched forward to meet Sanderson. The officer in charge had one arm in a sling—evidently one of the wounded himself. As he got closer Sanderson recognized him—Bruce, he'd known him at the Academy. Should he greet the man? It was hard to know. Sometimes there was a kind of special courtesy, an affection almost superior to that one felt for one's own comrades, between classmates meeting across the lines. Probably the petty conflicts and jealousies that divided one's fellows from oneself didn't enter into that kind of meeting; just memories of the old times, and an evocation of what was best about the new—the war, the actual warring itself, and not the damned paperwork and politics.

Bruce seemed cold at first. Sanderson decided not to risk a rebuff, then he saw Bruce's face take on a friendly, if tentative, expression, and he realized that Bruce had just then recognized him—sun at his back probably blinded the man.

"Sandy?" he asked.

"Right," said Sanderson. "It's Brew, isn't it? You haven't changed much."

Bruce grinned. "I didn't recognize you with—" and he swept his good hand across his lower face, suggestive of the mustache Sanderson wore.

"You seem to have gotten hit. Nothing too bad?"

Bruce shook his head. "Just a ball through the meat of the

shoulder. Made me miss the last act.'' He looked at Sanderson. ''Funny thing was, the men who picked me up and were taking me to the **rear** were killed or badly wounded, all of them, by a canister shell. Never touched me.''

''A charmed life.''

They walked together along the front of the earth-curb or parapet that edged the Crater. To their right the field swarmed with men looking and bending over, lifting bodies up on blankets, crying in disgust and anger; or grunting with work as they turned earth over what wouldn't bear moving or touching. Just as in the bottom of the Crater, many of the men wandered about, shocked and aimless, like lost souls in hell, while around them the dead lay frozen and other living men twisted their muscles in labor.

''The fact is,'' said Sanderson, ''it was a damned fiasco. Complete.''

''Many of the men fought well. Some of the officers were superb.'' He remembered the officer who had walked slowly back under their flanking fire, and the private who wouldn't lend Davidson a rifle so he could kill him.

Sanderson nodded, acknowledging the courtesy. ''Oh, it's clear that we haven't the human material, in point of quality, for a first-rate army. Haven't had since the beginning. And some of the men who get to be officers, . . .'' and he shrugged with disgust.

''Your army had a better tone earlier in the war. Ours too, I daresay.''

''The truth is, the army's gone to pot since McClellan was relieved.'' And he looked intently at Bruce.

Bruce nodded. ''I've felt that too'' *though I wouldn't have said so till you did.*

''You've still got Lee, and the others . . .''

''Yes,'' said Bruce. ''The top is good as ever, though the war has thinned them. But our troops aren't what they were. We've had to scrape the bottom of the—'' and he stopped.

They had come to the body of a dead black soldier. It seemed to throttle conversation. There was a palpable withdrawing of each from the other as they looked.

The dead man was black. He was naked. Somebody had broken the face with a rifle butt; it was a twisted lumpish mask whose one eye and broken teeth were facelike enough to disgust you. Somebody had taken his knife and sliced off the cock and the balls and cut up the belly so that the swelling guts protruded in livid parody of the thing that was missing.

There was a curious mark on the chest—a scar shaped like a spread-out letter *D. For ''deserter?''* Sanderson wondered. *But we don't brand em on the chest, we do it on the hip. And the scar's too old to—*

It took all his moral courage for him to raise his eyes and look at Bruce. Sanderson felt that he'd offered the man some unforgivable discourtesy or insult, the kind that dishonors the man who gives it as well as the one who receives it. He looked at Bruce, and saw in his eyes the same embarrassment. In a flash of intuition Sanderson saw it all: he was ashamed because his own people had scraped so low in the bottom of the barrel as to bring up this nigger, which even in mortal extremity the rebel had never contemplated. But Bruce was not at all angered by this; nor did he even seem to be pitying, which Sanderson had feared almost more than censure. No, Bruce was embarrassed too, probably about the way the corpse had been mistreated.

Looking into each other's eyes, the two officers sensed the source of each other's embarrassment, and smiled. The fellow-feeling was so strong, it was nearly a tie of kin. Each man had an impulse to seize the other's hand and shake it, or even to embrace. Each seemed to sense this, and it increased their embarrassment but changed its key and meaning, so that they smiled at each other.

Someone came up and joggled Bruce's good arm, and he turned in real annoyance at the breaking of the mood. "What is it?"

"Sir," said the sergeant—and he *too* seemed embarrassed about something. "Sir, that Yankee Colonel who came out with the . . . the others. Well he, he come too far over to the lines—looking for someone he said, someone who got killed, a friend I guess, but he come too far." The sergeant's eyes flicked to Sanderson. Like all enlisted men, he figured that when something went wrong enough to make life complicated for the officers, like as not the enlisted man would have to pay for it some way. To Sanderson's amused thought, that was not a bad assumption for him to make. "Anyway, sir," said the sergeant, "he been arrested."

"Oh Jesus," said Bruce, and he looked at Sanderson and spread his good arm out from his body in a gesture of helplessness and apology.

"Don't worry about it. We'll arrange an exchange to clear it up."

"It's too bad, but I'm sure he must have gone well beyond the designated line or he'd not have been bothered."

"I'm sure that's true."

"He come plumb into our lines," said the sergeant incredulously. "Said he was looking for a friend!" and he grinned.

Bruce turned to the sergeant and snapped, "Get about your business," and the sergeant wiped off his grin, and went.

The poignant sense of kinship and nostalgia they had felt before had been fatally interrupted—no recalling it now, but it was there as a good memory. Strange how the dead nigger had torn them apart, and brought them together! Sanderson thought for a second that he might try to bring that moment back, by telling Bruce that Thomas was the commander of one of the nigger brigades. But he thought better of it. Best not thrust the fact that Sanderson's people were using niggers continually under Bruce's nose. And it might not do Thomas any good.

So Sanderson said nothing, but offered Bruce some tobacco. And when the wounded man couldn't stuff his pipe, Sanderson kindly took it and did it for him.

Then they sat down, put their backs to the front wall of the Crater, and smoked, talking occasionally in a reminiscent vein, the sun warming their faces as it rose over the field of men who wandered about in the rubble, or poked and dug in it, or hauled things away.

HEADQUARTERS,
Near Petersburg, August 1, 1864.

Hon J. A. SEDDON, *Secretary of War:*

There was a cessation of hostilities this morning from 6 to 10 A.M. at the request of the enemy for the purpose of caring for the dead and wounded. Seven hundred of the enemy's dead were buried or turned over to him for burial; 20 stands of colors instead of 12, as reported, were captured on the 30th.

R. E. LEE

CITY POINT, VA., *August 1, 1864*

Major-General HALLECK,
Washington, D.C.:

The loss in the disaster of Saturday last foots up to about 4,500, of whom 450 men were killed and 3,000 wounded. It was the saddest affair I have witnessed in the war. Such opportunity for carrying fortifications I have never seen and do not expect again to have. . . . I am constrained to believe that had instructions been promptly obeyed, Petersburg would have been carried with all the artillery and a large number of prisoners without a loss of 300 men. It was in getting back to our lines that the loss was sustained. The enemy attempted to charge and retake the line captured from them and were repulsed with heavy loss by our artillery; their loss in killed must be greater than ours, whilst our loss in wounded and captured is four times that of the enemy.

U. S. GRANT,
Lieutenant-General.

Court of Inquiry
From August 1, 1864

Major-General HALLECK,
Chief of Staff:

I have the honor to request that the President may direct a court of inquiry, to assemble without delay at such place as the presiding officer may appoint, to examine into and report upon the facts and circumstances attending the unsuccessful assault on the enemy's position in front of Petersburg on the morning of July 30, 1864, and also to report whether, in their judgment, any officer or officers are censurable for the failure of the troops to carry into successful execution the orders issued for the occasion, and I would suggest the following detail: Maj. Gen. W. S. Hancock, Brig. Gen. R. B. Ayres, Brig. Gen. N. A. Miles, Volunteer service; Col. E. Schriver, Inspector-General and recorder.

U. S. GRANT,
Lieutenant-General.

From The New York Times, *August 2, 1864*

THE PETERSBURG LINES
The Assault by Our Troops on Saturday.
Desperate Attempt to Carry the Enemy's Position.
FAILURE OF THE ATTEMPT
The Colored Troops Charged with the Failure
The Loss on Both Sides Between Four and Five Thousand.
A Detailed Sketch of the Whole Matter
From Our Special Correspondent

HEADQUARTERS, IN FRONT ARMY OF THE POTOMAC,
Saturday Evening, July 30, 1864.

I am called to the fulfillment of an ungracious task tonight. Instead of success and victory which the morning fairly promised, I have to write of disaster and defeat. To-day's aborted history affords another striking proof of the uncertain issue of battle, showing how the shrewdest and most elaborate strategic planning may be completely thwarted by an error or an accident in action. To-day's disaster finds solution in the old story that "some one has blundered," in a manner "worse than any crime," but precisely who the blunderer is I do not know, and if I did it would not devolve on me at present to tell. A military tribunal must decide that point. Happily, however, the blunder is not irreparable . . . the result does not dishearten the Army of the Potomac, and it should not depress the people. The soldiers who fought on Saturday have received the baptism of blood on other fields, and know how to bear reverses manfully as they bear successes modestly. They bate not a jot of heart or hope, and they only ask the lesson to the country from today's mishap, that their thinned ranks may be promptly reinforced. The army is still unfaltering in its faith, and will try and try again until the day of decisive victory. . . .

But just here the first misfortune of the day occurred. Upon Col. Pleasanton's attempting to fire the mine, the fuse or slow match failed, and another was tried, I am told, with similar result. The third fuse was successful to its mission, but the hour's delay had made it broad daylight, . . . and we were robbed of the advantage of surprise.

This was a great misfortune. The army felt it to be such as they stood in suspense and silent impatience in the cold gray of the morning, crouching on their arms . . .

The noise of the explosion was a dull, rumbling thud, preceded, I am told, by a few seconds swaying and quaking of the ground in the immediate vicinity. The earth was rent along the entire course of the excavation, heaving slowly and majestically into the air, and folding sideways to exhibit a deep and yawning chasm, comparable, as much as anything else, to a river gorged with ice, and breaking up under the influence of a freshet. But there was a grander effect than this observable also. Where the charge in the burrow was heaviest, directly under the rebel work, an immense mass of dull red earth was thrown high in the air, in three broad columns, diverging from a single base, and, to my mind, assuming the shape of a Prince of Wales feather, of colossal proportions . . .

The awful instant of the explosion was scarcely passed when the dull morning air was made stagnant by the thunder of our artillery . . .

The Fourteenth New York Heavy Artillery were the first to enter the breach made by the explosion. They bounded forward at the word, in the midst of the shock of the artillery, and clambering over the debris, found themselves violently pushed down into the yawning crater. The sight that met them there must have been appalling. Bodies of dead rebels crushed and mangled out of all semblance to humanity, writhing forms partly buried, arms protruding here and legs struggling there —a very hell of horror and torture. . . . But the time was not favorable to the play of humane emotions. . . . The assaulting column was reformed, and at the word of command dashed forward once more to storm the crest of the hill. It was a task too great. They gallantly essayed it, and nearly gained the summit, subject all the time to a withering fire, which increased in fierceness at every step, until they became the center of an increasing storm of shot and shell. . . .

The colored troops, upon hearing of this repulse, were ordered to charge, and they moved out gallantly. A hundred yards gained and they wavered. Then the Thirty-ninth Maryland regiment, which led, became panic-stricken and broke through to the rear, spreading demoralization swiftly. Their officers urged and entreated them, threatened them, but failed to rally them, and the mass, broken and shattered, swept back like a torrent into the crater which was already choked with white troops. The confusion incident to this wholesale crowding and crushing of the Negro soldiers into the ranks of the white troops, very nearly caused the panic to spread . . . but at the moment the rebel fire, which had been murderously directed upon the place, mercifully slackened, and the white soldiers recovered their stamina. . . .

HEADQUARTERS ARMY OF THE POTOMAC,
August 3, 1864.

General Orders,
No. 32.

The commanding general takes great pleasure in acknowledging the valuable services rendered by Lieut. Col. Henry Pleasants, Forty-eighth Regiment Pennsylvania Veteran Volunteers, and the officers and men of his command, in the excavation of the mine which was successfully exploded on the morning of the 30th ultimo under one of the enemy's batteries in front of the Second Division of the Ninth Army Corps.

The skill displayed in the laying out of and construction of the mine reflects great credit upon Lieutenant-Colonel Pleasants, the officer in charge, and the willing endurance by the officers and men of the regiment of the extraordinary labor and fatigue involved in the prosecution of the work is worthy of the highest praise.

By command of Major-General Meade:
S. WILLIAMS,
Assistant Adjutant-General.

Indorsement.
Lt. Col. Pleasants has gone on sick leave.

WAR DEPT., ADJT. GENERAL'S OFFICE,
Washington, D.C., August 3, 1864.

Special Orders,
No. 258.

43. By direction of the President, a Court of Inquiry will convene in front of Petersburg at 10 A.M. on the 5th instant, or as soon thereafter as practicable, to examine into and report upon the facts and circumstances attending the unsuccessful assault on the enemy's position on the 30th of July, 1864. The Court will report their opinion whether any officer or officers are answerable for the want of success of said assault, and, if so, the name or names of such officer or officers. . . .

By order of the Secretary of War:

E. D. TOWNSEND,
Assistant Adjutant-General.

Extract from the New York Herald, *August 4, 1864*

But it is not only the incompetency of two generals that we are to blame for the failure. . . . We must blame also the President and his whole Cabinet, with its nigger-worshipping policy. They who have insisted against all opposition that niggers should enter the army are even more to blame than all the others. Niggers are not fit for soldiers. They can dig, and drive mules; they cannot fight, and will not fight. . . .

August 8, 1864

Maj. Gen. G. G. MEADE, U.S. Volunteers, being duly sworn, says:

I propose, in the statement that I shall make to the Court (I presume the Court wants me to make a statement of facts in connection with this case), to give a slight preliminary history of certain events and operations which culminated in the assault on July 30, and which, in my judgment, are necessary to show the Court that I had a full appreciation of the difficulties that were to be encountered, and that I had endeavored, so far as my capacity and judgment would enable me, not only to anticipate but to take measures to overcome those difficulties.

The mine constructed in front of General Burnside was commenced by that officer soon after the occupation of our present lines, upon the intercession of Lieutenant-Colonel Pleasants, I think, of a Pennsylvania regiment, without any reference to or sanction from the general headquarters of the Army of the Potomac. . . .

I informed him of my disapproval, which was based upon the ground not that I had any reason to doubt, or any desire to doubt, the good qualities of the colored troops, but that I desired to impress upon Major-General Burnside (which I did do in conversations, of which I have plenty of witnesses to evidence, and in every way I could) that this operation was to be a *coup de main.* . . .

. . . and as I consider that my conduct is here the subject of investigation, as much as that of any other officer or man engaged in this enterprise, I wish to repudiate distinctly any responsibility resting upon me for the manner of the withdrawal. . . .

August 9, 1864

Maj. Gen. A. E. BURNSIDE, U.S. Volunteers, duly sworn, says:

I, in a considerable conversation, urged upon General Meade the necessity for placing General Ferrero's division in the advance. . . . I will here present to the Court some of the reasons for forming this opinion, which reasons were presented to General Meade. Take an intermediate date, say the 20th of July, and there were for duty 9,023 muskets in the three old divisions of the Ninth Corps, which occupied the line. From the 20th of June, which was the day after the fight at this place, these divisions lost as follows: killed, 12 officers, 231 men; wounded, 44 officers, 851 men; missing, 12 men; making a total of 1,150, which is over 12 per cent of the command, without a single assault of the enemy or of our own troops. . . . The Ninth Corps also lost in the fight of the 17th and 18th of June 2,903 men . . .

Although this narrative is very disconnected, I believe I have stated in it all the material points. I do not know of a single order of mine that was not carried out by my division commanders. I do not know of any lack of energy on their part in carrying out my views and the views of the commanding general, except, possibly, in the case of General Ledlie, who was quite sick on that day, and who I thought afterwards should have gone to the crater the moment his men were in, but I understood he was very sick and could hardly have walked that far under the oppressive heat. He was within 120 yards of his brigades, I should say.

August 29, 1864

Maj. J. C. DUANE, Engineer Corps, sworn, says
(questions by the Judge-Advocate):

Question: Could the troops have gone forward by division front?

Answer: I think they could if proper working parties had been sent to remove the abatis.

Question: Were there any working parties with them?

Answer: I do not know. I was directed not to interfere with

General Burnside in his operations. I had no control over the operations in that part of the line. . . .

Maj. Gen. G. K. WARREN, U.S. Volunteers, sworn, says (questions by the Judge Advocate):

Question: Will you please state what in your opinion were some of the chief causes of that failure?

Answer: To mention them all at once, I never saw sufficient good reasons why it should succeed. I never had confidence in its success. The position was taken in reverse by batteries, and we must, as a matter of course, have expected a heavy fire of artillery when we gained the crest, though we did not get near enough to develop what that would be. I never should have planned it, I think.

August 31, 1864

Brig. Gen. EDWARD FERRERO, U.S. Volunteers, being duly sworn, says (questions by Judge-Advocate):

Question: State to the Court how the Fourth Division (colored troops), your own command, conducted themselves on the occasion.

Answer: I would state that the troops went in in the most gallant manner; that they went in without hesitation, moved right straight forward, passed through the crater that was filled with troops, and all but one regiment of my division passed beyond the crater. The leading brigade engaged the enemy at a short distance in rear of the crater, where they captured some 200-odd prisoners and a stand of colors, and recaptured a stand of colors belonging to a white regiment of our corps. Here, after they had taken those prisoners, the troops became somewhat disorganized, and it was some little time before they could get them organized again to make a second attempt to charge the crest of the hill. About half an hour after that they made the attempt and were repulsed by a very severe and galling fire, and, I must say, they retreated in great disorder and confusion back to our first line of troops, where they were rallied, and where they remained during the rest of the day and behaved very well. I would add that my troops are raw, new troops, and never had been drilled two weeks from the day they entered the service till that day.

Question: If your division had been the leading one in the assault would they have succeeded in taking Cemetery Hill?

Answer: I have not the slightest doubt from the manner in which they went in, under very heavy fire, that had they gone in in the first instance, when the fire was comparatively light, but that they would have carried the crest of Cemetery Hill beyond a doubt.

August 31, 1864

Col. H. G. THOMAS, Nineteenth U.S. Colored Troops, being duly sworn, says (questions by Judge-Advocate) :

Question: Were you at the assault on the 30th of July, and what was your command?

Answer: I was at the assault on the 30th of July, and commanded the Second Brigade, Fourth Division, Ninth Corps (colored troops).

Question: How did your particular command retire from the front?

Answer: In confusion.

Question: Driven?

Answer: Driven back by a charge of the enemy.

Question: And not by any orders?

Answer: No, Sir; they received no orders. . . . I sent word to Colonel Oliver's brigade, that I was about to charge, that we should go over with a yell, and that I hoped to be supported. I went over with two regiments and part of a third, but I was driven back. The moment they came back the white troops in the pits all left and they after them. I was not supported at all in my charge.

Question: How did the colored troops behave?

Answer: They went up as well as I ever saw troops go up— well closed, perfectly enthusiastic. They came back very badly. They came back on a run, every man for himself. It is but justice to the line officers to say that more than two-thirds of them were shot, and to the colored troops that the white troops were running back just ahead of them.

Surg. H. E. CLUBB, Ninth Corps, being duly sworn, says (questions by Judge-Advocate) :

Question: Were you at the assault on the 30th of July, and in what capacity?

Answer: I was in charge of the surgeons on the field of the Ninth Corps, to see that the wounded were attended to and taken to the rear. . . .

Question: General Ferrero was present?

Answer: Yes, sir.

Question: Any other generals?

Answer: General Ledlie was present. Those were the only generals I saw.

Question: Did General Ferrero leave that place and accompany his troops to the front when they left?

Answer: He did. General Ledlie, I think, left the bomb-proof for a very short time. That was about the time of the stampede of the darkeys. Then, I think, both General Ledlie and General Ferrero returned about that time. I am not positive, however, for I was busy seeing that the wounded were being attended to. General Ledlie asked me for stimulants, and said he had the malaria and was struck by a spent ball.

Question: You say that during the stampede Generals Ferrero and Ledlie returned to the bomb-proof. How long did they remain there?

Answer: General Ferrero remained a very short time. He was exhausted. I think he came in for the purpose of getting some stimulants, too, and I think he went out immediately after I gave him the stimulants. General Ledlie remained some time longer, probably half an hour, I should judge.

Question: You mention stimulants. What were they, hartshorn, materia medica, or what?

Answer: It was rum, I think. I had rum and whiskey there, and I think I gave them rum.

Question: How often did you administer stimulants to those two officers during that day?

Answer: I think that once was the only time. I was not in the bomb-proof all the time while they were there. It was perfectly safe in there, but it might not have been outside. I had to go out to look after the wounded.

OPINION

. . . It remains to report that the following-named officers engaged therein appear from the evidence to be "answerable for the want of success" which should have resulted:

I. Maj Gen. A. E. Burnside, U.S. Volunteers, he having failed to obey the orders of the commanding general.

1. In not giving such formation to his assaulting column as to insure reasonable prospect of success.

2. In not preparing his parapets and abatis for the passage of the columns of assault.

3. In not employing engineer officers, who reported to him, to lead the assaulting columns with working parties, and not causing to be provided proper materials necessary for crowning the crest when the assaulting columns should arrive there.

4. In neglecting to execute Major-General Meade's orders respecting the prompt advance of General Ledlie's troops from the crater to the crest; or, in default of accomplishing that, not causing those troops to fall back and give place to other troops more willing and equal to the task, instead of delaying until the opportunity passed away, thus affording time for the enemy to recover from his surprise, concentrate his fire, and bring his troops to operate against the Union troops assembled uselessly in the crater.

Notwithstanding the failure to comply with orders and to apply proper military principles ascribed to General Burnside, the Court is satisfied he believed that the measures taken by him would insure success.

II. Brig. Gen. J. H. Ledlie, U.S. Volunteers, he having failed to push forward his division promptly according to orders and thereby blocking up the avenue which was designed for the passage of troops ordered to follow and support his in the assault. It is in evidence that no commander reported to General Burnside that his troops could not be got forward, which the Court regards as a neglect of duty on the part of General Ledlie, inasmuch as a timely report of the misbehavior might have enabled General Burnside, commanding the assault, to have made other arrangements for prosecuting it before it became too late. Instead of being with his division during this difficulty in the crater, and by his personal efforts endeavoring to lead his troops forward, he was most of the time in a bombproof ten rods in rear of the main line of the Ninth Corps works, where it was impossible for him to see anything of the movement of troops that was going on.

III. Brig. Gen. Edward Ferrero, U.S. Volunteers.

1. For not having all his troops formed ready for the attack at the prescribed time.

2. Not going forward with them to the attack.

3. Being in a bombproof habitually, where he could not see the operation of his troops, showing by his own order issued while there that he did not know the position of two brigades of his division or whether they had taken Cemetery Hill or not. . . .

Without intending to convey the impression that there was any disinclination on the part of the commanders of the supports to heartily co-operate in the attack on the 30th of July, the Court express their opinion that explicit orders should have have been given assigning one officer to the command of all the troops intended to engage in the assault when the commanding general was not present in person to witness the operations.

WINF'D S. HANCOCK,
Major-General, U.S. Volunteers, President of Court
ED. SCHRIVER,
Inspector-General U.S. Army, Judge-Advocate.

On February 6, 1865, the Congressonal Committee on the Conduct of the War completed its own investigation of the assault on July 30, 1864. It took testimony from all of the principals examined by the Army Court of Inquiry, and from others not examined by that Court. It produced a statement from General Grant to the effect that he believed after all that the Colored troops might have done better if allowed to lead the advance.

In its final report, the Committee declared that:

the cause of the disastrous result of the 30th of July last is mainly attributable to the fact, that the plans and suggestions of the general who had devoted his attention for so long a time to the subject, who had carried out to so successful completion the project of mining the enemy's works, and who had carefully selected and drilled his troops, for the purpose of securing whatever advantages might be attainable from the explosion of the mine, should have been so entirely disregarded by a general who had evinced no faith in the successful prosecution of the work, had aided it by no countenance or open approval, and had assumed the entire direction and control only when it was completed, and the time had come for reaping the advantage that might be derived from it.

Burial of the Dead
1864–1877

Report of Casualties, 19th Regiment United States Colored Troops
. . . Major Theodore D. Rockwood, killed in action, July 30, 1864
. . . First Lieutenant Christopher Pennington, killed in action,
body not recovered . . .
Lieutenant Lemuel D. Dobbs, killed in the Crater.
Private James Johnson #5, killed in the Crater.
Private John Duckworth, killed in the Crater.
Private Harison James, missing . . .

43rd Regiment United States Colored Troops
. . . Private Tobe Young, missing supposed killed.
Private Jethro Cousins, missing presumed killed.
Corporal T. Brown, killed in action.
Color Guard Matthew Colehill, killed in action.
Private Demian Joseph, killed in action.
Captain Thomas B. Shugrue, taken prisoner in the Crater . . .

Thomas B. Shugrue
Taken prisoner in the Crater. Confined in Libby Prison, Richmond,
until the city fell in April 1865. Promoted to Captain, Regular Army,
for wartime service, 1866. Stationed in various posts, Arizona Terr.,
Dakota Terr., California, Texas. Reprimanded by court-martial for
drunkenness. Retired as Captain of Infantry, 1886. Died Phoenix, Arizona Terr., 1892.

Sergeant Wesley Stanley, 14th New York Heavy Artillery
Killed July 30, 1864. Awarded a Congressional Medal of Honor
for his handling of the captured artillery during the battle.

Private Robert Emmett Neill, 14th New York Heavy Artillery
Wounded in action on July 30. May have died in Libby Prison,
Richmond, Va., but destruction of records makes this uncertain. He
was not among those liberated when Richmond fell, April 3, 1865.

Sergeant Henry Rees, 48th Pennsylvania Veteran Volunteer Infantry
Promoted Second Lieutenant, October 30, 1864. Mustered out with
his regiment, May 1865. Died shortly after the war, in Pottsville, of a
lung complaint.

Private Samuel Marriot, 22nd North Carolina Infantry
Held in prisoner of war camp at Point Lookout, Md., until the end
of the war—except for an interval when, with other prisoners, he was

put to work under fire on General Butler's Dutch Gap Canal project: this in retaliation for the Confederates' using captured Negro soldiers from the Fourth Division to dig entrenchments under fire. Both sides then desisted, although they refused to negotiate the question directly.

Paroled April 14, 1865 at Point Lookout. May have gone to Wyoming Territory.

Private Thomas Woodrow Dixon, 22nd North Carolina Infantry

Mustered out on September 1, 1864, his regiment having ceased to exist. Returned to Kinston, North Carolina, as sergeant to assist Colonel Davidson in recruiting. Paroled at Goldsboro, N.C., April 16, 1865.

Leader in New Bern region Ku Klux Klan, 1869–73. Arrested and tried for murder of a Negro schoolteacher; acquitted. Arrested and convicted of Klan terrorism during election in 1874.

Sheriff of New Bern County, 1874–77.

Shot and killed by a Negro farmer during an attempt to evict "squatters" from the old Hewson plantation.

Abraham Lincoln

Reelected to the presidency of the United States, November 8, 1864, defeating General McClellan, the Democratic candidate. At his second inaugural he called for the completion of this war "with malice toward none, with charity for all," and he noted, with characteristic ambivalence, that it was not inconsistent with his or anyone's notion of a just God to suppose that He would have the war go on till every drop of blood drawn by the lash had been paid off with another drawn by the sword.

He might have reconciled these contradictions, and the others, given time. It is an article of faith with us to believe this might have been so.

We know that he dreamed the last night of a ship carrying him towards a dark, indefinite shore and that he was assassinated, Friday, April 14, 1865.

He lay all night with the black blood swelling in his bullet-tunneled brain like a thought unspeakable, and when you could feel the morning begin he opened his mouth and breathed a breath. They took his giant corpse in a black catafalque with black plumes and sable velvet back home on the train, via Baltimore, Philadelphia, New York, Buffalo, Pittsburgh, Cleveland, Columbus, Indianapolis, Chicago, home over the prairies to Springfield.

Lieutenant General Ulysses S. Grant

Promoted in time to General, and twice elected President.

His story, like Lincoln's, a fable of the times—for he had risen not merely from obscurity, but from failure and disgace. And unlike Lincoln he lived to live the fable through, proving that the only thing left to do once you have transformed failure to supreme success in war and peace is to transform Success back to the original, the essential Failure. Botched his Presidency, ran through two pension funds, his stock brokerage firm went bankrupt and only the fact that his partner had skinned him prevented his acquiring the odium of swindler himself, wrote his memoirs, cashing in on his popularity one last time, and died of a cancer in his throat.

Major General George Gordon Meade

Retained in command of the Army of the Potomac to the end of the war, though the major strokes at Lee's flanks were commanded by Hancock first, and after Hancock's invaliding-out, by Sheridan.

Commanded several Military Divisions, Districts and Departments after the war, but never rose to command the Armies or to lead the active campaigns in the West. If he had any political ambitions they were disappointed.

Died in Philadelphia, in 1872.

Major General Gouverneur K. Warren

Was never criticized, let alone censured, by any of the groups that investigated the Crater disaster, despite evidence that had he made a supporting attack on Burnside's left it might well have gone through the spot vacated by Mahone's brigades.

Peremptorily relieved of command of V Corps by Sheridan on the field of Five Forks, April 1, 1865, for tardy and faulty execution of an attack, though Sheridan eventually won the fight.

For the rest of the war he commanded the garrison in captured Petersburg, and held brief command in occupied Mississippi, before returning to the Engineers as a Major to do river and harbor work from the coast to the Mississippi.

He never ceased asking for a Court of Inquiry on Five Forks (but Sheridan was slated for, and then became, General of the Army). After Sheridan died, in 1879, a Court met and vindicated Warren's reputation, publication of that finding being delayed until three months after Warren's death.

Major General Ambrose Everett Burnside

Was retained in his commission, at Lincoln's personal insistence, till the end of the war; vindicated in part by the Report of the Committee on the Conduct of the War, which blamed the cold-blooded engineer Meade and praised the warm-hearted Burnside.

After the war his personal fortunes prospered, he was President or Vice-President of several railroads. (It turned out that two of these appointments had been taken on while he still commanded IX Corps in 1864 and 1865, one of these being the presidency of the Illinois Central Railroad, which he had served before the war as subordinate to General McClellan).

Governor of Rhode Island, 1866–68; went to Europe on railroad business in 1870–71, and acted as a go-between in the peace negotiations of the Franco-Prussian War (such a frank and forthcoming gentleman, both sides trusted him implicitly); U.S. Senator from Rhode Island, 1874–81, dying in office, the only way that his many dear friends in Rhode Island would have consented to his retirement.

Brigadier General Edward Ferrero

Was retained in command of the Fourth Division, despite the finding of the Court of Inquiry (they probably expected him to resign, but he didn't) and was vindicated by the Committee on the Conduct of War, whose report found that he had not been "habitually in a bomb-proof," had not taken "stimulants" to the point of drunkenness, and was not a coward.

After the war he owned and operated several ballrooms in New York City, including the one which housed the Tammany Society, New York's Democratic leadership, but he himself took no part in politics, and died in 1899.

He was the author of a *History of the Dance,* published in 1858.

Brigadier General James H. Ledlie

Was never charged or tried by court martial, but was forced by Grant and Meade to resign his commission to avoid a scandal for the Army. Resigned January 23, 1865. Grant, in his *Personal Memoirs,* said he was not only "inefficient" but "proved also to possess disqualification less common among soldiers," by which he meant: the man was a coward.

After the war he returned to engineering. He took the entire contract for construction of all bridges, trestles, and snowsheds for the Union Pacific half of the Transcontinental Railroad (there was a scandal about the financing of those contracts that rocked the world of international banking, the Crédit Mobilier affair that forewarned of the great crash of '73, and there were claims that construction was shoddy and the contracts underperformed, but Ledlie was never charged), built the breakwater in Chicago harbor, became chief engineer and then president of a railroad, and was considered a wealthy, respected, and useful citizen when he died in 1882.

Major General Bushrod R. Johnson, C.S.A.

Returned to Tennessee after the War as Chancellor of the University of Nashville, and worked to build a major educational institution in his state; but the University went bankrupt in the panic and depression of 1873, and Johnson, broken in health, retired to a farm in Illinois, where he died in 1880.

Major General William Mahone

The Hero of the Crater. Fought to the end of the war at Appomattox. After the war, he got into the railroad business (like everyone else, it seems), and was president of the Norfolk and Tennessee.

Exponent of a "New South," leader of the "Readjustor" faction in Virginia, friendly to certain measures of Reconstruction, relatively liberal on matters affecting civil rights, for both ex-slaves and poor-whites, for which he was branded a scalawag, and referred to contemptuously as "Billy" Mahone, as if he were a declassed Irish *bhoy* and not the Hero of the Crater.

Defeated for Governor of Virginia in 1878; U.S. Senator from 1880 to 1887, when his faction was at last definitely defeated, the work of "Redemption" completed, and blacks and poor-whites substantially disenfranchised.

Died in 1895.

Lieutenant Colonel Henry Pleasants, 48th Pennsylvania Veteran Volunteer Infantry

Went on sick leave immediately after the Crater, resigned from the army shortly thereafter, not fooled by Meade's letter of congratulations.

He knew the Army would never forgive him, and his health was never the same.

His good friend, Benjamin Franklin Gowen, took over the Reading Railroad and with it control of a virtual monopoly of the Pennsylvania coal fields; Pleasants couldn't go back to engineering, no more tunnels and mines for him, but Gowen made him chief of the Coal and Iron Police, to keep discipline in the coal fields, run out union agitators, infiltrate and disrupt unions in the fields.

The Irish in the coal fields were seething, for the work was bad and deadly, the pay meager, and the company town a prison.

The Long Strikes of 1874 and 1875 were like wars in the coal fields, and who better to command than an ex-Colonel, an army man? The strike was broken, and Pleasants and Gowen brought in Pinkertons, and Pinkertons uncovered the Molly Maguires and used them to hang the union.

July 21, 1877. Philadelphia, Pennsylvania

The courtroom was packed for the sentencing. The first batch got the noose. The rest got long prison terms. Doyle got twenty years for accessory to murder, and the blowing up of the pumphouse.

The Judge in his black robes intoned the sentences, dwelling repeatedly and for each man on the "hang by the neck until you are dead, dead, dead," and Doyle muttered to his buddy, "They can't hang you but the once, no matter what he says," and the man said, "They can do any damn thing they please."

Then the spokesman for them all, Kelly, threw the lie in the Judge's teeth, and said they were being legally murdered for union men, there was devil a word of truth in the stories of Molly Maguire. Then the Judge made a speech. There was criminal anarchy loose in the land, and here was the original plague spot to be cauterized. Everyone, even the prisoners in the dock, knew what he was talking about. The railroad men had struck against the wage rollback, the militia had joined them in some places, there was shooting in others. It must be stopped.

The prisoners, chained at wrist and ankle, shuffled out clanking in single file. Pleasants, the vest badge of the Coal and Iron Police peeping from behind his lapel, stood by the door.

He stopped the line, and stepped up next to Doyle.

"It's a shame to see you in this, Doyle. I remember you as a good soldier."

"And still am, but not in your army," said Doyle.

Pleasants flushed. "I'd have thought the army would have taught you better than to play with anarchy and murder."

The cop prodded Doyle in the kidneys with his stick, and the line stepped along. The chain that linked them arm to arm and leg to leg, swayed rhythmically to their movements down the long corridor.

Sergeant Major Cato Ezekiel Randolph, 43rd United States Colored Troops

Stayed with the regiment for the rest of the war, went with it when all the blacks in the army were gathered together into XXV Corps, marched with the first elements that entered Richmond in April 1865, with the Confederate remnants fleeing to the west, and bells pealing behind the smoke of the burning streets. Cheered Lincoln through the Richmond streets on the President's flying visit to the enemy capital; mourned the President dead in the day of victory. They didn't want the whole Nigger Corps in the Grand Review, so they shipped most of them to Texas to try and scare the French out of Mexico; and after a time they shipped those that were left back home, via New Orleans, then steamboat and train back to North Carolina—

—to find that the Hewson place had been sold in a regular auction to Mr. Brickhill, the progressive Yankee entrepreneur who knew how to make the South a paying proposition, and who could bid three dollars made out of wartime cotton profits against every dollar the former slaves could bid out of money saved from market gardening and wages from digging trenches at New Bern and washing laundry for the soldiers and from the company fund of the Forty-third Regiment.

Challenged the sale in the military and civilian courts of the District: "Cato Ezekiel Randolph, *et. al.* petition for voiding the sale of the land denominated as. . . ." And in the meantime he held the place, not only with his own people but with a committee of poor-white squatters from land back in the piney woods that Hewson hadn't gotten round to driving them off of before the war: they had squirrel guns and army guns, some of them marked *C.S.A.* and some of them marked *U.S.A.* Brickhill brought some soldiers up from town on a gunboat, and Ki and the rest were there on the landing with their guns; and it turned out that the soldiers with the army officer on the gunboat were black, too. And the officer looked around, and smoked a cigar. Had a cup of coffee and some bread. Then went back. Ki and the others held the land.

Cato Ezekiel Randolph: elected Sheriff of Craven County three times, and Captain in the State Militia during Reconstruction. On a dark night in 1870 he and his son Josiah were ambushed by six Ku Klux Klansmen on the road between Hewson's and New Bern. The Klux figured Ki for two pistols, but they never figured the boy (who was sixteen), and between the two of them they hit six and killed one, running their horses right up to them yelling on that narrow road, and the Klux horses rearing and twisting away when they come at them, yelling.

Till the government disbanded the black militia, and gave the state back to its "Redeemers," and Ki went back to the cabin on the river, with the woods between him and the town, and thought about things. The river went by slowly and steadily. There was no way at all, now, to keep Brickhill and his paper off the land, with the gun taken out of their hand. When they went into New Bern or to Raleigh they saw Brickhill and Colonel Davidson, whose place was just up the river, walking and talking together. The seasons turned bad, the cotton rotted from the early wet; the waste fields were full of gulls in from the coast, scavenging.

July 20, 1877. Hewson's Plantation, Craven County, North Carolina.

Two things happened that morning. First, the final decree came down. The last petition had been denied, and the land formerly known as Hewson's Plantation, specified by individual allotments as set forth under the interim action of the Court, and including the outlying timber lots and clearings that white squatters had come back onto during the war—all of that was now finally the property of the Neuse River Railroad and Land Development Company.

The second thing that happened was that Siah came back from Kansas. There was his Pappy sitting in the cabin, the army gun set handy by the door, the pistol from being a sergeant strapped around his waist. Young Tobe and Little Ki, the brothers that was from Coffee, not out of his own Momma—they ran to the door calling his name.

Ki smiled at Siah. "You's back," he said.

He sat down at the table, and grinned. Coffee came in, and bent and put her cheek to his; her hand rested lightly on his shoulder—touching but lightly, out of respect for Siah's Momma being gone.

"It's all right," said Siah. "I got the papers all filed. Land being surveyed. We got out this spring, we'll need tents till we can get cabins built. Timber ain't plenty. They uses sod."

"Kansas," said Coffee.

"John Brown was from Kansas," said Ki. "That's all right."

Coffee began to put supper on the table, a stone crock of buttermilk. Ki stepped to the door and hesitated. Nothing moved in the bushes. He stepped out.

The sun was going down, orange. Its light fell in familiar patterns through the trees and bushes. It touched on the white boards where the baby was buried, and Old Tobe, and where the stone was for Young Tobe that was never found, but they knew him dead. He had wanted to put a stone for Cassy, but he didn't know her for dead. Coffee wouldn't say yes or no, though it wasn't hard to see what she thought. But she would not say what she believed. *No, it ain't right to put a stone.* Because she didn't know her for dead. So he said no himself. But he still thought about it.

He'd gone looking for her, when the war was over. Found Hewson's boy's plantation, but there wasn't anything left; just burnt-out house and cabins, and the wild vines crawling everywhere. No word, no sign, no record she ever been there.

He'd thought about her living out there, lost in a strange country. There was no place on earth he knew her to be. She never wrote or sent word.

But he didn't know her dead.

A rabbit darted from the woodpile to the brush.

A jay scrawed from a branch.

Rabbits don't go to die in some strange country where their kin never were. Only people dies where they wasn't born, where none of their kind was ever born, off away somewheres. And nobody from home ever knows how or where, or finds the body, or knows if there is a body to be found.

"Come on in, Ki," she called, and for a moment he didn't know whether it was Coffee or Cassy.

He looked around one more time. The air over the graves darkened to gray. On each mound stood a cracked vase or bowl, dried flowers, crisp and red-brown, set in them. One twig lifted a delicate shape like the bones of a baby's hand, picked bare and weathered brown. He remembered—hardtack in the empty hand. The Crater. All the ones he'd left behind there, Young Tobe and Jethro and Colehill and all of them. And Booker. *Booker: that followed me back across the bridge, but then he turned back. Crater held to him, like Sodom held to the wife of Lot that looked back one more time. Watched us go, and then turned back, and he kept it—whatever it was in that Crater—from following us, and kept it off our trail.*

He crouched by the grave and slipped his finger into the brittle grip of the twig. Plenty of white folks would try to stop them from leaving. Pick off the leaders if they could, maybe even mob up and come after them all. His anger rose to the idea: he had his pistol, and his carbine, the cabins here and the woods and swamps all around. Maybe Booker's way was the way for him now. He could write red fire and judgment across the trail of their leaving for a sign to the Egyptians. *Go into the ground here, and in this place, pull the ground up over my head like a blanket. Show my people the way to where they can have their bread: and feed these damn Colonels and Ku-Klux like I fed Hewson. On Judgment. Feed em on Judgment. Earth rest easy on my head like my Daddy's hand, and us going down to the fields. . . .*

His rage seemed to pass off into the ground like the fire of a lightning stroke. He sighed, and stood up. He felt no call in himself to die: not yet, and not for this place. Why had he been spared out of the Crater, and all the rest died there, if it wasn't so he should know that his calling was to keep the remnant together, and carry them off to safety? He'd tasted what it was to lose the most thing you could ever hope or dream on— whatever it was they would have won if the promise had been fulfilled and they had gained the victory. *He would come upon her in her cabin, and they would weep for all their pain, and her words would make the crooked path straight and no more confusion, or dissatisfaction. Cassy, Coffee: but just all of us gather in together, just as it ought to have been.*

What was losing the Hewson place next to that?

And there was work to do, gathering in all the people and their kin that were coming, and they'd have to keep everybody protected till they could leave for the railroad, and then going to the train, and after that when they got to Kansas. . . .

Kansas. He saw in his mind exactly how it would be. They'd load the wagons, they'd be ready to go even before the dispossess came. The men would sit on the wagonbox, women and children ride. They'd have their army guns, squirrel guns, handguns, shotguns right out where you could see. March em up the road, single-file, to the depot outside New Bern. Tickets all bought and paid. Kansas. Think about the white folks, watching all these niggers going some place together. Nobody to work that Hewson land, this time. And look: not a one stay behind, but every one of them go along.

Other folks had done it. Even been stuff written in the white-man newspaper, about how bad it was, folks leaving the land, "mean lazy black folks." Oh, but that was families and small bunches. Here goes a whole plantation town of them, marching off. And that bad nigger Ki Randolph ahead of the bunch.

He smiled. It was very clear. The railroad to Kansas was a thin metal bridge, carrying them all together to a place where they could live.

Judah ben-Levi Booker, or Bookser, Major, 43rd U.S.C.T.

Wounded and taken prisoner in the action of July 30, 1864.

Exchanged on August 2 for a wounded Confederate major, and brought out by Colonel H. G. Thomas. It is believed that the Confederates were not aware of his commission as a Major of Colored troops, as their policy was to deny all such exchanges, which implied an equality of honor between commanders of white and of Negro troops. His wound did not necessitate amputation, but left his left arm crippled. He was invalided out of the service and returned to St. Louis to recuperate in the bosom of his family.

After the war he was unable to obtain work in his trade of iron-molder, because of his wound. Worked as a journalist for the *Labor Herald* in St Louis and, after 1868, for the *Labor Tribune* in Pittsburgh. In addition to articles of current interest, he published stories drawn from his pre-War wanderings and wartime adventures. His major source of income, however, came from translating works of political economy from the German for his newspaper and for other socialist organs in the city. During the railroad strikes of 1877, he—

July 21, 1877. Pittsburgh, Pennsylvania

When the door creaked, Elijah Bookser kept as still under the covers as he could. His mother cracked the door and peeped in. He breathed softly and slowly. She closed the door. He eased his position somewhat, ready for the second visit, his father opening the door to look in and see if he was still sleeping. After that, he let out a breath and lay still, eyes open, listening to the two of them downstairs, smelling coffee, bread, sizzling eggs. His stomach turned over. He was hungry as anything, but he waited.

His mother said, "Do you think there will be trouble?"

A mumble, sounds like "yes." All right! At fifteen he knew that his parents thought all sorts of things were "trouble" that were actually better than the usual things that happened all the time. Going to be a *war* in Pittsburgh today, and of course they'd try to keep him away, except it wasn't going to work this time. The two of them were going off to see it. Why shouldn't he?

The thought made the hairs on his belly prickle.

He heard the downstairs door open, another voice. His aunt was there, she was supposed to watch him and keep him at home today. He smiled. He made his features grim and determined, and silently, with deep scorn, said, *Ha!*

He heard his mother and father talking, outside the house now, their heels clicking on the stone steps as they went out. Gave them a chance to get far away. Footsteps on the stairs. Auntie comes to take her look: still asleep, the little dear.

When she closed the door again and went downstairs he got out of bed in his underwear, drew on his pants dead silent, shirt over that, slung his shoes over his shoulder with the laces tied together. Out the window, onto the woodshed, off the edge in absolute silence, and then across the yard, bare feet splashing dew off the grass, hurting when he got onto the pebbles but he didn't stop to put the shoes on till he was hidden behind a fence.

And here, right on time, was everybody else, the rest of the gang. "Let's get down to the yards right away."

"Hey, can't we eat something? I'm starved."

Jerry, who who always prepared for everything, said, "Here," and passed over a cloth bag full of stuff he'd hooked from home, couple of apples, cold cooked potatoes, even an end-cut of a big smoked ham. Eli had water in his father's old army canteen. The bunch of them ate as they marched, hardtack and salt pork, the soldier's hardy fare, they would have sung as they marched if it weren't something that would make them look silly, so they slouched along in a bunch, sometimes falling into step, humming or whistling each to himself, *Rally round the flag, Wore a yellow ribbon, Johnny fill up the bowl.*

Jerry said, "There's gonna be killing for sure." He was making a promise, a wish. Frightened and eager.

"Think so, Jerry?"

"For sure. My dad says they're bringin in niggers and nigger soldiers and there ain't anyone will stand for that a minute. Going to move them niggers right in and kick out the engineers off the trains and everybody. Move em right into your house, and you feed em or go to jail!"

Jerry was so self-important. What the hell did he know? It made Eli angry sometimes the way he took over and bossed everything. And he hated that word, that *nigger.* What the hell did he know about *nigger?*

"Hey Jerry! What do you know about it? My dad says. . . ."

"Well what does he know? . . ."

They stopped and gathered around in a circle. Eli at the focus of their eyes, maybe a little scared, but what the hell: he was good as Jerry any day. These guys could take it from him as easy as they did from Jerry. He knew what was what anyway. "Listen: my dad's been down to the Phoenix House every night for the paper, hasn't he?" The Phoenix House was where the striking unions and the city's other labor organizations met nightly to confer on plans to resist the militia the railroads had called for. "They ain't bringing in no such thing, except just the regular Philadelphia militia. White militia."

Jerry was stubborn. "My dad says niggers, and there'll be shooting if it's niggers."

"If it's white militia, maybe there won't be no shooting," said one of the others, and Jerry turned on him.

"Yeah, and I bet that's just what you're hoping for, ain't it? That *nothing* will happen."

The eyes swung toward the one who had, seemingly, wished away their war, speaking the fear they had, but hid.

"Wait a minute," said Eli. "What are you picking on him for? I'm the one says different, ain't I?" And they were back to him.

"All right," he said, "why don't we stop jawing about it, and go on and see something real for a change?" They turned on his word, and his blood soared up so high he nearly broke into march-step—he was what Jerry used to be and wasn't, their leader.

The sweat on his shirt made him smell like his father smelled, he felt his father's knowledge and strength were absolutely his own, and now by God if he wasn't Major Bookser commanding his soldiers. Major Elijah J. Bookser! Who else had learned all about war from someone who commanded troops all over the war from Kansas to Richmond? Who had got his arm crippled but still fought his way out and back home? *And* was an officer? Jerry talking about *niggers*. Negroes. His Daddy had commanded a whole brigade of Negroes, he'd freed all of them from their chains like Moses and Israel, and led them into battle, wonderful soldiers, they would have followed him into the jaws of hell at a word. Eli could tell them about Negroes, too, if they wanted to know.

They followed, single-file, their secret path along the riverbank and up the drainage culvert. Up ahead in the railroad yards they could hear the rumble of the crowd, a different sound from the roar and clang of steam and machinery when they'd sneak into the yards on workdays to swipe coal or bags of wheat or sugar off the cars. Following Eli and Jerry, they slipped between the freight cars on the sidings, a row of cars with baled hay, three oil cars, toward the center of the yards. Between them and the louder rumble was a row of open-topped coal-cars, and there were men and boys behind the cars and up on top of them. "Let's get up top," said Jerry, with a glare at Eli, and they followed him up a vibrating metal ladder to the heaped coal, fitting into the narrow empty space Jerry had spotted.

The section of the yard in which they sat was slightly higher than the center, where the roundhouse and switch-house stood. The shallow bowl before them was filled with people, milling, shouting, calling out, waving banners and signs. Beyond them they could see, from their slight elevation, the soldiers in their blue-and-brass, with bright flags overhead, and their muskets tipped out with bayonets that caught the light like splinters of broken glass. There were some contraptions on wheels —cannons maybe, but they looked funny—at the rear of the column of troops.

"White!" said Eli, and grinned at Jerry.

Behind the crowd and the soldiers rose the mass of the great ridge, a brown sheer of sliced rock and then a green-sided wall, people clinging to it like flies. That was where they used to picnic, and watch the trains switching around in the yards. His parents were probably up there right now, looking down.

Eli grinned and shivered. Oh! would they be absolutely *crazy* if they knew he was down here!

Brigadier General John Hartranft

Became Governor of Pennsylvania after the war, and spoke frequently on the conflict between labor and capital; he thought such conflicts foolish in the extreme, believed government should act in the public interest to reconcile the parties, using military force only in the last resort.

And called out the militia and federal troops more often and in greater numbers than any state governor before his time, in the Long Strike of the coal districts, and the Molly Maguire disturbances, and the Great Strike of 1877, when the railroad workers struck against a ten percent wage rollback in the midst of a depression, and touched a nerve that shot violence approaching revolution down the metal tracks and telegraph wires, and the crowds came out from New York to San Francisco. In Pittsburgh they burned the railroad yards when the militia fired on a crowd and killed men, and women, and children.

There was one perfect vantage point from which to view the struggle in the railroad yards, and Judah and Miriam went to it without consultation: the park that sat on the great monolithic ridge that divided Pittsburgh. From the spine of it, any night in the year, you could stand there and watch the city. Streetlights and houselights were pinpricks of fire, dimmed and drowned in the boil of black smoke. But the factories and workshops glowed like coals in fierce outbreaks of light and fire, and the railroad yards at the foot of the ridge flashed and glared. The city seemed like a boiling pot on the rise. It brought Bookser back to the day of the Crater, when the earth shook him and the great firehead bubble of the explosion bulged and burst upward out of the split earth.

Miriam was next to him, the pressure of her body pressing his dead left arm against his side. She reached her hand behind his back, and twisted two fingers into the leather strap that bound the arm to his side, resting her hand there.

Looking down into the yards Bookser saw in one instant that there was going to be trouble. There were many more people in the shallow bowl of the yards than any Trainmen's Union could muster, crowds and crowds of them, men and boys from the streets and playing hooky from school, and not more than one in five—one in eight—under the discipline of the Union. The Union men were up front, he could see their signs and hats and armbands, but the great bulk of the crowd buzzed and muttered and pressed up behind them, filling the yards and bulking up the sides of the great ridge and the higher end of the yards, like water in a bowl. The side of the hill rose sheer or nearly so out of the yards, and people kept pouring down like trickles of water into a quarry pit, and Bookser felt the pull of it, and remembered how the troops had been drawn into the great hollow hole of the Crater, bewitched by its depths and its smooth sides.

Who could have imagined there would be so many to be drawn here, and so full of rage? Down in the pit, he saw, the militia from Philadelphia had arrived. The Pittsburgh companies were all up on the hillside, mixing with the crowds there, the picnic crowds, mixing with his own people and their placards and basket lunches. Pittsburgh was a labor town, and the militia wouldn't kill its own, that was what they all said, and so the railroad managers had brought up the Philadelphians.

Down below, at the hub of the yards, the Philadelphians in their blue uniforms trotted out into ranks. The ranks shifted, crystalized rapidly in a new pattern.

"Look at that," said Bookser, "they're forming a hollow square."

The Philadelphians had bayonets on the ends of their rifles, and these had been polished. They caught the clear sunlight, and flashed. In front of them the trainmen formed a line, under banners and placards the way troops in the war had rallied to company guidons. It was going to be bad.

He felt the weight of Miriam's hand in the strap. *I'm not a soldier any more,* he told himself. *I'm here to observe, to explain, to describe, to watch.*

"Miriam . . ."—what to say, he wanted her to get away to be safe, it was going to happen.

Right here.

The blue-and-brass regiments stepped forward. Their bayonetted muskets pointed at the chest of the crowd.

"It's coming."

There was a magic line between the crowd and the soldiers. The soldiers kept moving up to the line. Then, when they reached it, you would see: they would stop and refuse to go forward.

Or they would not stop.

"They ain't gonna stop!"

"Who says they ain't?" said Jerry. "It's your damned white militia, ain't it? From Philadelphia, ain't it? If it was niggers maybe they'd . . ."

"What the hell do you know about . . ."

"Oh Jesus. Look!"

The line of bayonets like a row of harrow-teeth held up in the air swept past the magic line. You could see men fighting to escape. They heard the screaming start, thin piping cries like infants at that distance.

"The sons of bitches! The sons of bitches! They're killing our own people!"

"No!" yelled Jerry. "They can't!"

Eli was looking, he saw the smoke spurt up out of the crowd. "They're shooting!"

"No," yelled Jerry, his face dissolving, "they wouldn't." Not Philadelphia Militia. "Sonsabitches." He grabbed a piece of coal and threw it. Eli grabbed and threw. The lousy Philadelphia traitors were trying to murder everybody and he'd give them *that* to chew on. His rage was like a big wind. He threw and threw toward the center of the yards, where the crowd was trampling itself to death to get away from its murderers.

Bookser saw the smoke before he heard the sound, but even so he took too long to recognize it. It was like a sound in memory, he was confused, they were all out in the open on the hillside like people at a picnic, there was a loud crack like the breaking of a tree branch, and ten feet away a little girl's head broke open.

"Get down! Down!" and he threw himself toward the earth, dragging Miriam after him, her hand twisted in the leather strap dragging her down with a cry of pain.

Overhead the air hissed and whispered—*whit whit whit*—alive with sound.

He looked up. A man was crouched over the body of the child. He howled like a dog over his meat, and Bookser in his fever had the crazy idea he had killed the child in his madness, but no: he was her father, her father. The man stood and pulled a pistol from his belt and began to blaze it into the pit of the yards below. *Too far too far he'll never hit anything*—and he looked into the hole where the geometric ranks of the soldiers were contracting round the Gatling guns, were wavering, were beginning to lose their shape and slither back toward the round house. The Gatlings began to crank out their load of bullets, a maddening incessant yammering of concussions like a whole brigade gone berserk, and when he turned again the man had vanished pistol and all, leaving the broken child behind, and he felt Miriam's hand bound to his back, heard her sobbing.

Colonel William W. Sanderson

Promoted to Colonel for his gallant efforts during the battles of Deep Bottom and the Crater; served out the war on Meade's staff, later went to Texas with Sheridan's expedition, reverted to Captain in the Regular Army and held several staff positions in Washington and New York.

Resigned to become Chief Engineer, Pennsylvania Railroad, 1870–71.

Vice-President of the Railroad and later a Receiver when the line went into bankruptcy in 1874.

In 1877 he led a regiment of Philadelphia militiamen into stormy Pittsburgh. It was his own regiment and he had drilled it very carefully, and they formed a hollow square and fired on the crowd, killing strikers, bystanders, Pittsburgh militia, women, children. The troops were besieged in the roundhouse while the maddened strikers burned the Yards around them. For his actions, Colonel Sanderson received an honorary sword, gift of the Pennsylvania Legislature.

Returned to the colors as a Brigadier General of Volunteers in 1898, but saw no action during the Spanish-American War.

Appointed Military Governor of Sambar, Philippine Territory, and entrusted with suppressing the Insurrection, doing so with a severity that seemed about to provoke a Court of Inquiry when he died in 1901, of heart failure.

July 21–22, 1877. Night

The roundhouse sat in the center of the railroad valley, under the sheer looming wall of the hillside. Shots spattered from it. The Gatlings yammered and raved and kept the tracks clear on one side. Some of the Pittsburgh militia had taken off their uniforms and run their cannon up to fire it at the roundhouse, but the riflemen kept picking them off, and they never fired it.

Militia is still the same, Bookser thought.

He had gotten his army jacket and put it on, with the left sleeve pinned to his side. Out in the yard some of the other men had gathered with their guns, those that were veterans wearing their jackets. The boy, his home, the rest of the city was safe. They had the war and the wolves caught in a pit here.

He and Miriam were together, hidden behind a row of cars. Bullets pinged and zipped through the yards. He grinned at her, and she said, "Is this how you did things in the army?"

"No. If this was the army, we'd have a General here, and he'd tell us to fix bayonets and rush the roundhouse, and never mind the Gatlings."

The man next to them spat. "Lucky for us, they got all the Generals in there."

"I heard we shot one of them. One of the bhoys, Pat I think his name was. . . ."

"Pat would have to be his name, wouldn't it?"

"Pat, I said. Swore to get himself a General, and by God if he didn't pot one with a rifle."

There were crazy men enough around, sniping at anything in uniform, anyone from Philadelphia, crazy with rage. His own men he held well in hand. The others were torching everything, burning and wrecking as if fire was whiskey, and a free barrel of it just found. Like the good old Jayhawking days in Kansas and Missouri.

This fight didn't make sense, any more than the war had made sense. However you figured it, you were killing your own kind. The white men in the Crater killing the blacks up on the wall wasn't any crazier than both of them killing the poor crackers that came on screaming. Wasn't any crazier than Philadelphians killing Pittsburghers.

"What can we do?" Miriam asked. "How can we get them out of there?"

Before he could answer, he heard a laugh, and suddenly he recognized it. *That laugh belongs at home, not here.* Eli came walking toward them, grinning and laughing, carrying a torch. He saw them: and his face dropped its laughter, there was a look of wanting to hide.

Then the grin came back. His parents, both of them here together, shooting at the damned Philadelphia Militia, he might have known it!

Well, he was a soldier, too. "Here," he said, and handed the torch to his father. He was pleased: of course the Old Man would be in the thick of it!

"What were you going to do with this?"

Asking me! said Eli to himself. *"Watch!"* and he flipped the torch into the boxcar full of hay behind which they crouched, jumped to the ladder and clanged to the top, throwing his weight against the brake-wheel till it squealed and gave. "Push!" he yelled, as he scrambled down.

Bookser, Miriam, the rest of the crowd got behind the boxcar and pushed, and they felt the dead weight of the car begin to move, begin to roll down the track, begin to take up the push itself and roll away from them, fire shooting out between the slats, the breeze of movement fanning the flames. The burning car slid down the smoothly graded incline toward the dark blank of the roundhouse where pinpricks of fire darted out of the central mass of shadow, gliding irresistibly on its rails to the center.

"It's the *Mine*," chirped Eli. "Don't you remember? You told me. I remembered."

The yards were full of cars, boxcars and coal cars, cars full of oil and kerosene, and all the tracks ran down a slope to the center. You could hear the cheering as other hands got the idea, and other cars began to flare and move, while the first one still slid down the path of rails, fire gleaming on the rails to make a bridge of light in the darkness.

"Did you remember," Bookser asked, "did you remember that I also told you that we lost? That we fought as hard and well as we could, that we had the best cause and the best of people with us, and still we lost?"

Eli shook his head, and swung his hand: an affirmation of memory and a wiping away. "We'll win," he yelled. "This time, we'll win!"

July 30, 1877. Petersburg, Virginia

General Thomas was standing by the window of the hotel room, fully dressed. His wife had seen him there when she herself awoke, just as the windows had gone gray. Saying nothing, she had washed, made her toilet, begun to dress, rung for breakfast. An old Colored man with skin of polished mahogany and white wooly hair brought it on a silver tray with ornate handles. The china was not matched, however, and the service pewter, not silver. A prewar tray, she thought, and Reconstruction service. Was the Colored man prewar or Reconstruction? Prewar, she guessed: he was deferential without that suggestion of either sloppy unconcern or sly defiance which, her Southern acquaintances had told her, characterized the emancipated race in these days.

General Thomas looked down at the street. In the gray light the red brick of Petersburg's buildings had a dingy wartime look. Yet the street was quiet. The sun rose, warm and yellow, and the street took on warmer colors, the bricks warmed and reddened, painted sashes making neat outlines of the windows, the cobbles went yellow. A Colored man drove a water wagon down the street, laying the dust. For a moment, lost in reverie, he was back in Petersburg in '64, in the room they'd brought him to after he'd wandered past the rebel lines while the flag of truce was out. Looking for Chris's body.

I never found it.

That was, somehow, the worst of it. Not to have found the body, to speak words over it, to bury it with honor. It would have been a thing to carry with me back to Boston, to his parents, a thing to give them along with the bare cold word of it. I walked into the room—they already knew of course—yet must hear of it from me. I had prepared the words so carefully, the grief of it given dignity and height, given honor. And saw his mother's face, her eyes—her eyes broke the speech in pieces. I could say nothing intelligible, though I focussed on the father's face thinking I could better bear to look on his eyes seeing the loss: but I knew she was there, and her wailing told me that there was nothing I could give them in repayment for the loss.

They must have thrown him like so much meat into the undifferentiated mass of a common grave. *I knew what the bullets did to the body, so thick they flew.* Picked him to pieces. They probably couldn't identify even the uniform. . . .

I should never have come back here, he thought. There's a kind of impiety in it, a making-up to his killers. To the men who killed Chris, and the men who did what they did to our prisoners. They tried to conceal it, but I heard things when I visited the prisoners. And could see: that they were keeping the officers from the Colored regiments, some of them, separate from the rest. Someone told me they marched them into Petersburg with their black troops, not with the other officers, and that the citizens egged them through the street. What a people, that could do that! And conceive that it was shaming our officers by marching them with their own troops, while they stood by with their slaves!

They shot the wounded, and those who tried to surrender. And mutilated the dead. *This I come to memorialize and celebrate.*

They breakfasted, speaking in quiet voices. What was to be the day's program? A carriage ride out to the Crater, where they would all meet. Then dinner and speeches at a nearby inn. *Why have I come?* To celebrates my losses, my defeat? Well, these battlefield reunions, these reconciliations of blue and gray—someone had to be defeated each time, and unless that were accepted, how was reconciliation possible?

The day was hot, but not so fierce as he remembered. They trotted down the white-dust roads he remembered well. Here and there the land was still scarred with marks of fire and of spade. The closer they got to the Crater, the more of this they saw.

The old entrenchments were there, as if waiting for the armies to return and fill them again. Only the air was different, smelling of grass and manure instead of gunpowder, human shit, and blood. Only the ground was different, the mounds and hummocks of the trenches and battlefields grassed over, a soft green fur on the hide of a sleeping—no, a dead—beast.

There was the Crater itself.

They got out of the carriage, and walked up the worn path that led from the road over the ridge and down through the fields to the Crater. They were up on the ridge, the Cemetery Hill on their left. They would see it all, as the rebels had seen it. Thomas gripped his wife's elbow suddenly, and guided her toward the cemetery. She went, somewhat reluctantly. They stopped, and stood amid the tombstones and unkempt grass.

From here, the Crater was a black hole in the middle of the green field. The sun made the grass fragrant, and it was easy to dream, easy to awake with a shock that the armies had disappeared, annihilated somehow. . . .

"What is it?" she asked. . . ."

"I was just thinking," he said. "So far as I know, I am the only man of the division to stand on this hill as a free man. Our prisoners may have passed over it, and I was near it when they sent me back through the lines. But I was a prisoner myself then." He had brought out a Major he knew from Oliver's brigade, Booker—he'd found him, badly hurt, among the wounded officers, evidently they hadn't figured out that he was with the Fourth Division. Thomas had bargained for him, worked out an immediate exchange for a rebel Major they'd taken when the Mine went. . . . It was something to bring back, something to save out of all that wreck, even if it wasn't Chris.

"I almost wish we hadn't come," she said, and he nodded. "You felt we had to, though."

He smiled. "I'm gathering material for my article," he said. *The Century* had asked him to contribute a piece on the battle for their series of articles on the war. He'd be in the company of Grant and McClellan, Longstreet and Sherman, . . . he'd have a chance to vindicate the reputation of his men. He owed it to them to do that. Just as he owed it to them to come up here and stand in the cemetery at last.

They walked down the hill. The others were gathered by the Crater, a small group. Again, Thomas found himself shocked by the change in the land. Even the Crater had mellowed, its humped-up lips of broken earth covered in a light sprinkling of grass, not thick—the red earth showed through. In the bottom, puddles of stagnant reddish rainwater stood, where he expected the pools of stagnant blood. Weather had softened and rounded the humps and clods—the great boulder had been whittled away by tourists and some wags had tipped it into the bottom of the hole. The ground was less grassy down there—the light was less, and he guessed the ground was poisoned by the gunpowder.

The sides were as he remembered them, but gullied by rain. Too sheer, for the most part, for grass to grow: although when he looked closer he saw that tufts of the stuff had taken root in the wrinkles and crevices and bays that marred the sides.

The group of men waiting for him was weathered too. Oliver was there—still the face of an aged baby, but perhaps a bit drier and more wrinkled, and the hair fringing the bald scalp was quite white. He extended a hand, and smiled his little smile as Thomas and his wife came up, and Thomas saw that he held his left shoulder oddly.

"Ah, General, and Mrs. Thomas! It's splendid to see you. You seem not to have changed a bit! Permit me to introduce"—he turned to two gentlemen in dove-gray coats—"Colonel Davidson and Colonel Bruce, formerly of the Twenty-second Regiment, North Carolina Infantry." Davidson was large, fair and florid, Bruce small, neat, and dark. *Davidson . . . oh yes, candidate for Governor. Or was it the Senate? Bruce is his man of work, I imagine. Yes.*

They talked, and all the while Thomas felt the breath of the big hole on his left. No one seemed to look into it, though. And it seemed impolite to stare away from the conversation.

He got only one glance before they were called away to the carriages: the sun was pouring into the hole, an intense illumination, as if focussed by a burning glass.

"Davidson's an extraordinary man," Oliver was saying. "Bruce and I had the devil's own time convincing him to come. This to-do's all on account of Mahone, you know. He's running for Governor of Virginia. Davidson considers him a damn crook and scalawag—begging your pardon, Mrs. Thomas. Billy Mahone's in very deep with the Radical gang that ran Reconstruction here. Things have gone much better in Carolina, and Davidson's sure to be elected. End of Reconstruction, of Radicalism, and of Rabble-rousing, if I may quote our friend Bruce, who manages the campaign—and very nicely."

"I had no idea you were interested in politics," said Thomas, and Oliver blushed. "I am, I confess it. My father was Governor of the state, it comes with the family portrait." The blush deepened. "I'm to be named Chief Justice of the State Supreme Court next month. Open secret."

"Congratulations," said Thomas. His wife echoed him, adding, "How very proud you must be."

Oliver made a deprecatory gesture. "Oh, my concern with our nation's politics is not primarily personal. The writing of history remains my passion, if it has been unfortunately only an avocation." He grinned. "Actually, it was that which brought Davidson and me together. A mutual distaste for the doctrines and administration of President Jefferson. I had thought the Southern aristocracy worshipped Jefferson as a god, having let all virtue and good sense go to rot when the Whig Party died. Not at all the case. Davidson was touring the North then, giving lectures to various clubs and societies about the gorgeous time before the war." Oliver laughed. "He was quite a spellbinder: could make you smell the honeysuckle, and taste the hoecake and ham, and smell the sun on the ripening fields . . . well, the whole picture, he could make it breathe. Then a toss of that manly head, and the ladies would be at his feet!"

Oliver paused, and seemed to think. "Actually," he went on, "he hadn't a penny. Plantation confiscated or taken for debt, he was earning his bread as an entertainer. Told me later that losing the plantation killed his first wife. It was I that put him in touch with Brickhill . . . did you know him? The one practical philanthropist of the age. Brickhill, Bruce, and Davidson put their heads together and remade the state: put a railroad together, land development company to reclaim plantations that had gone to seed or to squatters, eventually got strong enough to throw the rascals and demagogues out of the State Legislature . . . oh yes, quite a man!''

"But he can't abide Mahone?'' asked Mrs. Thomas.

Oliver shook his head, and smiled. "We'll be luckly to avoid an explosion. It was necessary, though, that Davidson be here. Otherwise Mahone would have had it all to himself. It's not his sort that we want to see at the head of this phase of national reconciliation. No, the fanatics and the crooks should be kept well out of it. Well out of it. Only the best of North and South should meet on the old field, to shake hands. . . .''

They arrived at the carriages, and mounted. Thomas glanced back toward the Crater, a shadow in the midst of green fields. What was the sun doing there now? No telling.

"Oliver,'' said Thomas, "does he know we commanded blacks against him?'' Thomas was surprised at the edge in his voice.

Oliver looked amused. "He does, most assuredly. Holds no grudge at all. His lieutenant, Colonel Bruce, actually wrote to Lee urging that the Confederacy recruit among the slaves! Something of a public embarrassment to him now, but there it is! In a curious way, it's a bond between us. Davidson's commanded them himself, all his life in a manner of speaking,'' said Oliver, and laughed at his own wit. "I felt quite uneasy about it the first time we spoke, and told him—by way of mollifying or explaining, I don't know how—told him that it was probably blacks who carried me out of the Crater and back to our lines, through shot and shell, while I lay unconscious from my wound.'' He reached up, and rubbed his left shoulder. "An *ex post facto* justification, I even realized it at the time. But he was quite urbane about it, laughed and said that he knew the race well, and that loyalty to their . . . leaders was their supreme moral quality.''

Oliver mused: "He also loved their singing while they worked. Really, quite the affectionate patriarch. I told him of the song our soldiers made up to sing before the battle—but never could recall it. I've no memory for music. . . .'' He looked inquisitively to Thomas.

"It's been such a long time,'' Thomas said vaguely, looking to his wife as if for . . . help or comfort. "They never sang it again—after.''

The restaurant had been entirely taken over by the celebrants. Burnside had declined to come—no surprise there. Others of the chief commanders were dead, or absent on military duty, or at their diplomatic posts, distant places of business. Mahone was there, very much in evidence, a wiry man in a big black beard, smiling and shaking hands. The Hero of the Crater. Davidson was sitting at another table, looking sullen. Oliver, chipper as a bird, went about greeting people. The bullet seemed to have let some sociability into the man, thought Thomas grumpily. Then he felt ashamed of the thought. He remembered Oliver on the surgeon's mat, out of his mind with pain, writhing under the probing of the knife while his blacks held him down, and murmured some soft nonsense for comfort.

Thomas felt his excitement begin to rise. He could not eat. Anxiety built and built in his stomach, a fierce muscular tension. He kept reaching into his breast pocket and feeling the crinkle of the papers that were his speech, pressing them against his heart. He could barely pay attention to the speeches, Mahone obviously campaigning for governor, Davidson—mellifluous sound came through, quotations from poetry about fruitful fields and something else, not familiar, *I was never one for poetry*.

The speeches were momentarily interrupted by Colonel Bruce, who asked leave to read a report which had just come in over the telegraph: Governor Hartranft, at the head of a brigade of militia and Regulars, had reoccupied Pittsburgh. The rioters' term of pillage and anarchy had been terminated, and the national colors now flew again over the burnt-out railroad yards and the rebellious city. Blue and gray applauded together this aversion of a new rebellion "more dangerous and sinister than any we have hitherto known," and Davidson proposed a toast to General Hartranft—"Once our chivalrous opponent, now our gallant and virtuous fellow-countryman." *Hear-hear!*

Then Oliver rose for his turn to speak. Thomas was next. He tried to gather himself, to pay attention to his surroundings. But some force seemed to draw his attention inward, to the vacant place inside which was filled with mourning for his losses, for all his losses, and against that pull Oliver's voice was weak, only fragments came through.

"Moralists and philanthropists of the armchair sort may seek to reshape the destiny of man according to a plan of comfort, and evenly distributed riches. But for those who have known the battle the great truth is not that of ease and comfort, but of struggle and triumph. Combat and pain are still the portion of man." Oliver's face glowed red in the lamplight. What a strange, cherubic face he has. Demonic light, cherubic face, a wizened baby. "For my part I believe that the struggle for life is the dynamic principle of the world, and of all human progress, as Darwin tells us it is of all animal development. From the onset of Time, war has been for our people, the children of the German forests and the British seas. Beowulf, Milton, Dürer, Rembrandt, Schopenhauer, Turner, Tennyson sang from the first the warsong of our race, or set its image before us, for a model. Who here does not glory in the name of gentleman? And what are the marks of the gentleman, the man of parts and powers and cultivation—what are these but the characteristic traits of the soldier: courage, honor, fidelity unto death. High and dangerous action teaches us to believe as right, things which the skepticism of our age would otherwise undermine and weaken. It fits us for headship and command as nothing else. And if in the winnowing of the battlefield there are many of the best slain with the worst, we know that on those that survive a trebled measure descends, so that they carry themselves the valor and quality of their fellows who have fallen. . . ."

The applause was thunderous, it seemed to obliterate the last shred of Thomas's composure. He rose, and felt that he held himself together by main strength, anger bulged in him ready to burst. He found, to his amazement and shock, that he hated with all his heart his comrade-in-arms Colonel Oliver, Mr. Justice Oliver, and all that Oliver had said. There was truer speech in his mouth that evening when he lay on the surgeon's table, nailed to the board with the agony of his wound, and held from tearing himself on the surgeon's knife by the hard gentle hands of the black soldiers who had brought him out of the Crater. There was better philosophy in their mumbling songs and soothing sounds and controlling hands. Weak insults came to mind. Challenging Oliver, challenging Davidson to a duel. Walking out of the room. But he had only his speech. There was nothing else he could trust himself to say. His rage made the scene shake and dissolve, threaten to explode. What a scandal he had the power to make!

But what right had he to make it? He could not bring himself to take that power on himself. The ceremony must be gone through.

He began to read his text. It seemed to him paltry and anecdotal. Yet he could not edit or omit one single detail, the homely touch about the pickles—God, he writhed in embarrassment now. He had dreamed, he had anticipated how pleasured Elizabeth's face would seem when he read of that, heard him remembering her gift and showing what it meant. He could not look at her now, but went on. Ahead of him was the part about Chris, and his throat constricted against it. What words could ever—

He paused, and looked up. Her eyes were shining. To her he spoke it, not reading now, these words were his by heart.

"With his sword uplifted in his right hand and the banner in his left, he sought to call out the men along the whole line of the parapet. In a moment, a musketry fire was focussed upon him individually, whirling him round and round several times before he fell. Of commanding figure, his bravery was so conspicuous that according to Colonel Weld's testimony, a number of his men were shot because, spellbound, they forgot their own shelter in watching this"—he swallowed—"superb boy, who was an only child of an old Massachusetts clergyman, and to me"—her eyes—"as Jonathan was to David." He paused. Her face was the center of the whole room. "Two days later, on a flag of truce, I searched for his body in vain. He was doubtless shot literally to pieces, for the leaden hail poured for a long time almost incessantly about that spot, killing the wounded and mutilating the dead."

He looked out now, and could see the faces through a mist. It was out of him now, and he had spoken the words for the dead he had come to speak. The wound, the grave, was closed. And so he added, "He probably sleeps among the unknown whom we buried in the long deep trench we dug that day."

And sat down.

NOTE

THE CRATER is a work of fiction based on history. I have attempted to make the narrative follow as closely as possible the historical sequence of events, and the historical record as it concerns those events and the individuals who figured prominently in them. Most of the dispatches in the text are taken verbatim from the *Official Records of the War of the Rebellion*. However, several have been either invented or significantly altered; and in some cases I have altered or interpolated words, dates, or names of fictional characters for the sake of clarification or of narrative consistency. The most significant single alteration is the substitution of the Twenty-second North Carolina for the Eighteenth South Carolina as the regiment blown up in the Crater—a choice necessitated by novelistic concerns, and not intended to deprive the Eighteenth of credit for its sufferings and accomplishments, which are hereby acknowledged. Nor should my Twenty-second North Carolina be confused with an actual regiment of that name, which served elsewhere in the same army. Otherwise, the units mentioned in the battle are those which actually participated.

Interpretations of character and motive are, of course, my own, even where historical personages are involved.

I want to acknowledge my debt to the historical studies of slavery and Afro-American culture by Herbert Gutman, Willie Lee Rose, Lawrence Levine, and Eugene Genovese; the Civil War histories of Bruce Catton and Shelby Foote; and the studies of labor struggles in the 1860s and 1870s by Wayne Broehl, Herbert Gutman, and Robert V. Bruce.

I want also to thank my agent, Carl D. Brandt, for his faith in this project, and my editor, Thomas A. Stewart, for whose critical good sense I am very grateful. And finally, I want to thank my wife, Iris, for the insight and the encouragement she has given me.

Richard Slotkin

Richard Slotkin was born in Brooklyn, New York, and educated in New York City public schools. He received his B.A. from Brooklyn College (1963) and Ph.D. in American Civilization from Brown University (1967). His first book, *Regeneration through Violence: The Mythology of the American Frontier, 1600–1860* was awarded the American Historical Association's Albert J. Beveridge Prize as the best book on American history in 1973, and was nominated for a National Book Award. He has also published an anthology of writings about King Philip's War called *So Dreadfull a Judgment* (1978), and numerous articles. *The Crater* is his first novel.

Since 1966 he has taught at Wesleyan University in Middletown, Connecticut. He lives there with his wife and their son.